# THE AXE OF WANDSBEK

# ARNOLD ZWEIG

*has also written*

# THE AXE OF WANDSBEK

## A Novel

*by*

ARNOLD ZWEIG

*Translated from the German by*
ERIC SUTTON

1948
Hutchinson International Authors
Limited
LONDON   NEW YORK   MELBOURNE   SYDNEY   CAPE TOWN

*Oct 1956*
*ell*

*Made and Printed in Great Britain by*
GREYCAINES
*(Taylor Garnett Evans & Co. Ltd.)*
*Watford, Herts.*

# CONTENTS

## PART ONE

# PART TWO

*Part I*

*BOOK ONE*

# A FRAIL VESSEL

## CHAPTER ONE

MEN DO THEIR BEST FOR THEMSELVES

EVENTS, AS THEY are here to pass in sequence, culminating in the four-fold swing of an axe, a revolver-shot, and the tightening of a soaped noose, often have their origin in some trivial act. In this case it consisted of an energetic thrust of a pen into an inkpot, by the powerful hand of Albert Teetjen, a handsome fair-haired man of forty-two, with a curved moustache above a pair of attractive lips, and vague broad-lidded eyes, the blue-grey steady eyes of a North German.

He sat with rolled-up shirt sleeves, at the oval table in his living-room, which his wife had hurriedly rubbed dry after the evening meal, using a large newspaper as a blotting pad—a copy of the *Hamburger Fremdenblatt* of Friday, August 27th, 1937. An expanse of transparent greenish-blue firmament hung above the tall brick walls of the houses, on the ground-floor of which was situated Teetjen's shop and dwelling; but he did not look up, he noticed nothing. Stine Teetjen, on the other hand, stood motionless, her uplifted face bent backwards, her sandy hair caught in the dip of her neck and shoulders, at the open window. Still holding the dish-cloth clasped behind her back, her large grey eyes ranged over the sky with an expression of shy ecstasy, as she thirstily inhaled the evening air. From the floor above her to the left, and from opposite across the yard, came the melodious strains of two wireless-sets, both revelling in the same chamber-music, which the Hamburg transmitter, together with all Germany, picked up from the Koenigswusterhausen station. Stine did not know what kind of music she was listening to —Mozart's clarinet quintet in fact—which the Petersens on the entrace floor, and the Lawerenzens in the side-wing opposite, simultaneously enjoyed. But the sounds that streamed into her consciousness, wafted in with the turquoise light, thrilled her with delight. Blue-green music, she thought to herself—forget-me-not and larkspur and heather on the Borstel heath. How grand it was to sit there on the warm herbage and lie back, and oh, how good it smelt! And yonder was

Albert poking his stick into rabbit-holes and mole-hills and an abandoned fox-hole; not another human creature in sight, only an aeroplane buzzing across to Gothland—and she could pull up her skirt to prevent it from getting creased. And Albert stopped wondering about the riddles of the earth's interior, which was his favourite hobby all the time, and told her what pretty legs she had and—— At that moment the presence of her handsome husband came full into her consciousness once more, and she recalled that he had been racking his brain the whole afternoon in the composition of that damned letter. The till was as good as empty, and the rent to be paid on the first of next month, not only for the shop and flat, but also for the refrigerator, the slicing-machine, and the scales, which in these days had to be a polished, white-enamelled article, an essential equipment to a butcher's shop, if the butcher was to keep his customers. She turned round, noticed that he had not yet switched on the light, drew the ceiling lamp, which hung from a large and rather clumsy hook, lower down over the table, clicked the switch, and said in a bantering tone: "I'm glad you haven't put anything on paper yet, you'd ruin your eyes if you did."

He did not catch the point of the words. Gloomily he glared at the flimsy, yellow penholder, flecked with dark brown stains, which he held in his hairy, ruddy fingers, scrubbed clean after the day's work. "I can't put the thing together. It's like trying to climb up a sand dune and always slipping back. Look here, you'd better dictate yours to me." So saying, he reached up to the shelf above the red plush sofa on which he was sitting, and took down a cigar-box, opened it, and sniffed greedily at the contents; it contained some discoloured, rather scorbutic cheroots, of which he selected one, put the box back, and as Stine took a black cloth-bound Bible from a drawer, he drew out his great clasp-knife to cut off the top. Then he inhaled the fragrant smoke, and said, while she took her scribbled notes from somewhere between the pages of the Old Testament: "Yes, it fairly gets me down, when I sit alone and worry over the damned dough, as though there wasn't the city of Hamburg all around, with one and a half million people in it, and all safes well filled with cash."

"No one is alone," said Stine, poring with her great expressive eyes over a few lines of the Prophet Hosea. "Shall I begin?"

"All right, begin," he said, rammed the penholder through the neck of the bottle into the coarse bluish ink, and wrote with a by no means awkward hand, in clear German script, sentence by sentence, as the words fell slow and incisive from his wife's rather pallid lips, in her Hamburg dialect and schoolgirl voice:

*"Hamburg—Wandsbek: Wagnerstrasse 17. 27.8.37.*

*"Dear Volksgenosse and comrade in arms. It is a long time since you have heard anything from me, not since we floated down the river Niemen together on that raft, and sold the brass shell-cases and oil-drums in Memel. I often think of those gay and carefree times, and how you used to enjoy my concertina. Well, I have long since given up the sailor's piano. After my old man's death I had to take over the butcher's shop, which was the*

*trade I had learnt. But everything seems to be going wrong with me these days. The competition is killing me now that the branches of the big Stores in the Wandsbek Chaussée sell meat and sausages as well. The housewives from our neighbourhood can get there in ten minutes by tram. They say there is more choice, and they can save the fare on the lower price. Can't you use your influence on the City Council and get an order passed forbidding those Trusts to open shops in the residential districts? My Storm-leader Preester doesn't agree with me, but I am quite sure that the Führer means to help the small man to get his living. Dear Comrade Footh, I should be very grateful if I might come and see you soon, as I have never approached or bothered you before. A message to Otto Lehmke's beer-shop, Wandsbek 8494, will always find me. In true Party comradeship: Heil Hitler! Cordially yours, Albert Teetjen, Master-butcher."*

Teetjen gazed at his signature, to which he had imparted an energetic upward flourish, dried his pen on the newspaper, re-read the letter, and observed with admiration: "Well, you have got the trick of it, Stine. It's just as I might talk myself, only better."

Stine laughed. "Yes, you silly old boy," she exclaimed, ruffling his immaculately parted hair. "Our school at Blankenese certainly made something out of me. And why have you been worrying yourself into such a fluster ever since our trip to Farmsen last Sunday, about nothing more than the writing of a letter and doing it my way?"

"Because it is no joke begging from a rich shipowner like Footh. That's what it's come to by now. And no big fellow in the Third Reich likes to part with his cash."

Stine wrinkled her auburn eyebrows into a frown. "Don't call it begging," said she indignantly. "One man helps another. And you got him out of a hole three or four times during the war. You always forget that."

"Oh yes," said Albert, folding up the letter. "But that was a long while ago. There's been a lot of things happened since those days. When we met, of course, he was always the polite and friendly Party Comrade. But who can say what he feels like nowadays? Climbing mightily upwards, our Mr. Footh, looks for and finds useful contacts. Why, he's one of those big business men. He already owns a tanker fleet of five ships. They are often pointed out to me in the harbour, and when I say we were in the same regiment in White Russia, and did all sorts of jobs together, they congratulate me, and say: 'Well, you're all right then, Albert. Come along, old chap, it's on you.' And then I have to stand a round of schnapps or brandy, if we're in the Free Port. He's done nothing but cost me money up till now, has Comrade Footh."

"Never mind," said Stine, sitting down beside him on the sofa. "This time he'll bring us luck, will Comrade Footh. Here's his address."

And she handed him a grey cream-laid envelope on which was written the address in a neat feminine hand:

> '*Herrn Hans P. Footh,*
> *Hamburg-Roterbaum; Harvestehuderweg.*'

"It's his private address," she said; "so that it shan't get overlooked among his business mail."

"Bless me," exclaimed Albert, "what a clever little girl is our Else."

"Stine," said she, correcting him, knowing better than he did that the words came from an old Grimm fairy tale. He flung his arm round her, shook her and kissed her, which so excited him that he pushed her before him into the bedroom, where in the falling dusk the two beds seemed to dominate the quadrangular room. The summer air hung heavy between the bright distempered walls. It was much too hot to lie under the eiderdowns, at any rate with any clothes on.

"The light's still on over the table," urged Frau Stine mockingly, as she slipped down her skirt and pulled her vest over her head.

"Never mind," cried Albert hoarsely, but he dashed back and turned the switch. The music of Mozart had long since died away.

"There always used to be great doings at the Nathansohns—while they were still here—a Garden Party and a drawing-room concert in celebration of the Day."

The girl who made this remark on the following afternoon, lay in a deck-chair with her arms crossed behind her ash-blonde hair. From the terrace on which it stood the view opened out over the villas and housetops, in the foreground, to the basin of the Outer Alster, which was here several kilometres broad.

Hans Peter Footh, his heavy hands dangling between his knees, fixed his little piercing eyes in surprise on his lovely brown-and-golden friend's pale lips. In long white silk trousers, with nothing on her body but a scarf striped red, white and blue like the Dutch flag, she lay there, and talked in riddles. But that was just what he adored in her: in his own winning way he was sure enough of where he stood in all important matters to allow himself a few vulnerable spots. Annette Koldewey, the daughter of a prominent Government official, the Governor of Fuhlsbüttel prison, was known as a well-educated young woman. She had been familiar with the Society of Republican Hamburg: and nobody need have been ashamed of knowing less about facts than she did.

"Celebration of the Day?" he asked. "Why, whatever happened on August 28th?"

Annette smiled faintly: her brown Slav eyes, set deep between high cheekbones and an imperious forehead, surveyed in friendly fashion a man in blue-grey yachting trousers, with a hundred and fifty workers at his bidding, to whom she had given herself—while she pleased, and for the present. She deliberately avoided the expression—'love', to describe what linked her to Footh. He had divorced his wife years before, and was ready to marry again any day, if Annette had shown the least inclination in that direction.

"It's Goethe's birthday," she informed him. "The Nathansohns always used to celebrate it. Indeed, in the days of the Republic it was an anniversary for many people. And now the Nathansohns are over yonder in Stockholm, waiting until they can come back."

"Won't that be rather a long time?" laughed Hans Footh.

"We saw them last spring," she retorted. "Consul Nathansohn is an astute fellow. I give your Führer another year or two, he said, then he'll commit some appalling folly and set the world ablaze; after that we shall come back. His extraordinary notions of England and America will break his neck."

"A very astute fellow," said Hans Footh mockingly. "Your father lets you keep some very strange company."

Annette smiled, conscious that she chose it for herself. Then she frowned, her expression clouded, and she was about to reply, but instead she raised the glass of tea to her lips, and inhaled the fragrance of the blend of Darjeeling and Orange Pekoe that she had herself compounded, and drank with slow enjoyment. They had spent the first hours of the afternoon on Herr Footh's sailing-boat, and had not long been back. As the week-end began on Saturday midday, the water grew more populous every hour, which was an inducement to many to drink their tea at home. Too much singing and shouting, and too many gramophones.

"Poor Papa," she sighed.

In the bedroom at the back of the terrace, which was indeed a projection of it into the open air, the telephone buzzed. Herr Footh rose heavily out of his steel-tubed chair, backed and seated with bright-coloured webbing in the latest fashion, and went in. Annette noticed the rolling gait that he had picked up from the Captains of his tankers. His braces ought really to have been hanging down and dangling against his legs, like Jannings's in the film, she thought with an angry smile. And she found herself hoping he would one day show as much under-standing of his daughter's ways as her father had done of hers. Her father was worried. The illness of this man Denke—of Oldenburg, at first only a trifling upset in official routine, had been causing him the acutest anxiety for the last few days. Annette, his eldest daughter, who since her mother's death had been accustomed to share with him all his cares and joys, turned over in her chair with a movement of bafflement. Her gaze ranged over the blue summer sky, as though seeking counsel; then she reached for a cigarette. Who could help anyone else in this world?

Herr Footh came back with a letter in his hand, which had been sent up to him in the dinner-lift. "Do you know the handwriting?" he asked Annette before he slit the envelope.

"Yes," said she; "that's Käte Neumeier's writing. She has settled down in Wandsbek, hasn't she? What does she want?"

While she was speaking Herr Footh had read the letter, folded it up, and put it back in his pocket. With a half-annoyed, half-amused expression, he stared into vacancy. "Your lady friends ought to be rather more careful with my private address," he observed. "The letter comes from somebody quite different, though the envelope comes from her. A comrade in the last War, who wants help. Would you like to read it?"

Annette let the thick grey envelope drop on to the wooden planking.

"I'm not interested in strangers while Papa is as worried as he is at present."

Herr Footh knew what she meant. Hours ago, Annette, while lying outstretched on the deck of the yacht *Goldauge*, looking like a brown naiad, had told him that the Senate had urgently warned her father that he must at last carry out the execution of the four men long since condemned to death, and free their cells. The Führer himself intended to visit Hamburg for the planning of the great suspension bridge over the Elbe, which he himself had projected. But all outstanding matters must be first cleared up, and the case against Timme and Co. got out of the way. The Ministry of Justice had been getting restive. But Herr Denke, the executioner from Oldenburg, was still ill in bed. Her father was now being urged to find a substitute.

"If your old man keeps these lodgers of his much longer he will get the reputation of being a Communist himself," Herr Footh had observed with a laugh, and dived into the water. while Annette held the sheet, and threw him a rope: for *Goldauge* would soon have skimmed out of reach before the light breeze.

Now, abruptly, he got up from his chair, walked to the veranda-rail, came back, poured himself out a cognac from a stocky bottle labelled 'Martell', and said: "I can do something for the man: for both men —for your father, too. Read it, please."

And he handed her the opened letter with a hand that faintly quivered. "A birthday present from the late Herr Goethe," he said.

She glanced at what was written, and looked up at him with a puzzled expression.

"A friend of war-days," she repeated. "Quite. Albert Teetjen. And what has that got to do with my father?"

"Silly girl," he exclaimed, and underlined the signature with a movement of his forefinger. "Albert Teetjen: Master-Butcher," he said meaningly.

Annette dropped the hand that held the letter, and the paper fell on to the planking. The wind blew it a few feet across the veranda, and it now lay beside the grey envelope. Then she looked at him, wide-eyed and impassive.

"Don't let the precious address fly away," cried Footh, and he set his yachting-shoe on the two fragments of the morning's post, picked them up and slipped them both into his side-pocket.

"How much, did you say, would Herr Denke's professional services have brought him in for this job?"

Annette's lips were slightly parted. She laid her brown hand on her chin, above which the firm, delicately curved, almost heart-shaped cheeks, looked distinctively Slav.

"Two thousand marks, I believe," she answered in an undertone, as though the shadow of a fear had come upon her.

He did not understand what was stirring in her mind.

"What'll you bet that it comes off?" he exclaimed. "What do I get if I can help your father to enjoy his glass of wine again?"

A happy smile curved her lips, and as she stretched both arms out towards him, and lifted her shoulders up to him, she heard—she knew not why, a voice within her speak Gretchen's two famous lines: '*I have already done so much for thee, there's nothing else that's left for me to do.*' But she did not utter them, as he would certainly have asked her where they came from. And no one, she least of all, would have had the heart to reproach so kindly, helpful, and sincere a man with the lapses in his education, which belonged almost to his type; and a good, new, solid type it was.

It's getting on towards autumn, thought Herr Koldewey, as he prepared to shave: pearl-grey morning light and a breeze from the sea, the tops of the rowans yellowing already, and the berries crimson, like Mexican opals. People like me, he reflected, couldn't get through life without September. Indeed a man in his sixties may be said to live in September. He would have liked to grow whiskers or a beard, in the best Hamburg tradition for an elderly gentleman. But his sense of physiognomy and propriety forbade. His head with its high forehead, long upper lip and long chin, and lips always slightly parted—all, in fact, rather tending towards length—would have looked absurdly Hamburgian with a beard. At any rate, his daughter Annette used to say so, whenever he hinted at any such intention, and he deferred to Annette for more reasons than one. There were secret backgrounds to the relations of families and human beings, out of which acts and feelings grew, and which friends could only observe from the outside, thought Herr Koldewey, as he slid the gilded safety razor over his cheeks. The razor had been given him by an American friend and professional colleague, and nothing seemed to Herr Koldewey more symbolic of modern society than this golden implement—expressive of a positively imperial luxury, and yet which, solely as material, hardly represented the value of a halfpenny. With its ornamented shaft, and polished head, this little gleaming product of skilled workers in a famous razor factory, had, by the labours of advertisement, been glorified into a choice and expensive bit of merchandise, a worthy gift from a Governor of a gaol in New Jersey, to a Hamburg colleague, who had had to tolerate a concentration camp within the sphere of his authority. The world beyond, so his thoughts continued, was curiously comparable to his shaving-bowl, considered in the abstract. From the little table on which it stood, it curved invariably outwards, and thus seen it was convex. But to him it curved invariably inwards, and from his view-point, it was concave. So it was with the inter-relations of human beings. They were dominated by quite distinct systems of co-ordination, according as they were viewed from without or within. It was part of the duty of an educated man neither to aspire to know everything, nor to let anyone else look into his cards. The endemic fear of the sergeant-major, the tax-collector, or the pastor—this was Protestant ethics, Luther's bestowal on the Princes. Pray turn your inside outside so that we can see that you are nothing but dough. Such was the demand of the Party to-day. Very well, gentleman, *habeant sibi*. When the Kaiser was still in power, he—Koldewey—had been a Bismarck man; during the Republic a conservative Hamburger: was he now to capitulate to the human rubbish to which the country had been sold by the great Industrials? His line of life was his, and his alone. No, gentlemen, you have been able to impose on us a gangster for a *Gauleiter*, who had conferred the Iron Cross, First Class, upon himself, like Herr Hitler, though he had never been near the front like Herr Goebbels, and adorned himself with the Flying Cross and a wound stripe. To this chief and his Block-Warden I am of course accountable, even in the early morning— he thought ironically. Then Herr Koldewey dried his face, rubbed it with fragrant essence, and cleaned the gilded apparatus, to which was attached an equally elegant case. And then he waited eagerly for his daughter Annette. Whenever the hum of a motor reached his ears, he bent out of the window, but it was nearly always an aeroplane, flying to the airport at Fuhlsbüttel, or taking off from it: cross-shaped dragon-flies buzzing across the wide sky. He must begin early who wants to distinguish a Horch from a Daimler, he reflected with a smile: that is, by the sound of the engine. Thyra and Ingebottel could, not to mention Annette. They had indeed begun early, the little baggages. The two first names indicated his younger daughters, being the nicknames they were known by in the family—strapping, slit-eyed girls, who had already breakfasted with their father, and then gone off. Like most young women of decent family nowadays, they both had jobs, and on weekdays were tied down to their desks, one in a merchant's office, and the other in the State Administration, but on Sunday they dashed off into the country, where, on the Harksheide or the Tangstedt Forest they pursued a wholesomely pagan physical existence—in so far as those areas were not barred off by the more recent needs of the Army and the Party. Koldeway, then, had company to his coffee, but at eight he was alone: at nine, after her breakfast and a swim, came Annette. If a man was wise he lay down on his bed again with a volume of Nietzsche and smoked a cigar. No telephone, no messages, no visitors. These were the advantages of the official residence, the red-tiled villa outside the red walls, and indeed a good distance away from town, although close by the highly developed traffic system which was a legacy of the Republic; and excellent walks over to Ohlsdorf, where there was bathing in a lake, after a little not unpleasing philosophic contemplation in the proximity of the dead in the Central Cemetery. The dead were innocuous. Only the living caused trouble. Yonder was the concentration camp, beyond his influence and access—and there it was, not to be shaken off.

Not until Annette awakened him with a kiss did he realize that he had gone to sleep, with his cigar lying neatly across the ash tray, and his hand holding *The Twilight of the Idols* on the coverlet of the double-bed, which he, although so many years a widower, had never got rid of.

"My dear," he exclaimed, "did you fly in through the window. What sort of time have you had? Fine—I can see that."

She sat down on the edge of the bed, and powdered her nose, which was slightly flushed from the drive in the sports car, and anyhow was rather freckled.

"I've brought something for you," she said.

'Yourself', he thought, with a touch of jealousy against her friend, of whose part in her life he was very well aware: a disciple of Nietzsche must not deceive himself.

"Wait a moment," he said, "or I shall forget the place I was meditating over when I must have dropped off to sleep. 'Is a man responsible for the shadows that he casts, a poet or writer for the misunderstandings which he causes, that may indeed bring him to his end?' Tell me that."

"This is the great question of the morning," she smiled, contracting her pretty eyebrows: "Is your old friend Nietzsche responsible for blond beasts, and so on?"

"Certainly the fundamental problem of our day," he agreed, and went on reading. " 'How little makes for happiness.' The skirl of a bagpipe, perhaps; and indeed without music life would be a mistake. The German conceives of God as singing songs.' Thus the moustached Friedrich. Listen, he is here alluding to the couplet:

> *From far the German voice comes ringing*
> *And God in Heaven singing—singing.*

He seems clearly to follow the popular tradition here, and presents God as active and in the nominative, instead of—as the intention was—passive and in the dative. Indeed he nowhere suggests the opposite. Am I not right?"

And he held out the book to her. But Annette took it and shut it up. She had represented her mother long enough to permit herself any liberties: besides, she longed to unburden herself of her joy, and tell him the news.

"Herr Footh," she said, "sends his respects; he is on the track of a deputy for Herr Denke, and hopes to have something definite tomorrow evening. So on the strength of it I've invited him to a crab supper. I thought you wouldn't mind."

Herr Koldewey slowly raised himself in bed, thrust his underlip over his clipped moustache, laid his two hands on his daughter's shoulders, and said: "Tell me more, Annette."

And with the lids drawn back from his rather prominent eyes, he listened.

"Ha," he observed at length. "You know that I've been rather more passive over this whole affair than is consistent with my character. Why?"

"Because you regard those four condemned men as innocent?" she asked.

"Clever girl," he nodded. "In any case not so guilty as the verdict pronounced them to be. If a shooting affray between two bands of excited young men is to be brought in as premeditated murder, that is their affair—the affair of Prussian lawyers in Altona. Now listen to me. Do you remember *The Fisherman and his Wife?*"

"A Grimm fairy tale, which is always printed in Low German?" she smiled. "I should love to read it again."

"Now the point of that story is that there could only be any hope for the married pair, which here stands for humanity, if the female member of it tried to be contented. But she didn't: she kept on tormenting her good-natured husband by always wanting more and more. It is a Malay story, so I have heard, a tale of magic brought back by sailors, and for that reason told always in Low German. Well, in the matter of those four people, I have been behaving a little like that patient magic fish, the enchanted Prince, only the other way round. I procrastinate. I find no one. I provide our State, our Hamburg, the Reich, our Social System, with one more chance. Petitions for reprieves for all four have been put in, and at the very same time Executioner Denke falls ill and takes to his bed. So you see—something may happen. And now here come you and your Herr Footh and start everything up again."

"And I meant so well," lamented Annette.

"I know," he said affectionately, and kissed the corner of her mouth. "You are only an instrument, and so is your friend Footh, and I, and all of us. Something fulfils itself in this our world, and we have the honour to lend our help."

"But it isn't yet certain that anything will come of the affair," she said, by way of comforting herself.

"No," he said slowly, and got up. "It is not yet certain. A week or two ago I read that modern physicists no longer believe in mechanical determination. Even among molecules certain decisions lie upon the knees of the Gods, so says James Jeans. Oh yes, there is certainly hope. The chances stand at fifty-fifty. If the four are saved, the cross will pass us by. Let Herr Hitler plunge into war, and the whole nightmare will be engulfed in a welter of blood. If they perish, the Third Reich will remain in power and poison our nation—or the earth, I would rather say, without possibility of hope. For it will not collapse from within. That's how I look at the whole damnable business."

"How desperate it all seems," she said softly. "And a year ago I thought the dice had fallen. Wise old parent." She kissed him, not in any girlish fashion, but as a grown-up person kisses another. A year ago her fiancé, Hans Wieck and her cousin Manfred Koldewey had been shot down by a Russian fighter, while flying in Spain in the same bomber, after they had laid the Basque cities in ruins. But for that event, which the papers had had to describe as a tragic accident, Hans Footh would most certainly not have found acceptance. Father and daughter both thought of that steep-set curve. Then he said: "Would you care to come out with me a bit? About twelve I should like to be at Hagendoerps. They're playing Brahms. 'The tragic melancholy of impotence,' says Nietzsche about our beloved Johannes. I wonder what he meant exactly."

The multifarious clamour of the harbour on a Monday morning was at the moment overborne by the deep bass of a steamer-siren hooting persistently as she drew in to her moorings. "Yasukuni Maru," said

Herr Footh as he reached across the table and laid a hand on Captain Carstanjen's shoulder, thrusting him back into his chair. Captain Carstanjen, broad and bald and very smooth of speech like so many sailors, observed politely that Herr Footh obviously knew all about everything that went on in the harbour anywhere near to his office.

"It would be a scandal if I didn't," laughed Footh: "these days when every street-boy can tell by the sound of the engine the difference between a Dornier and a Junker. These Japanese are good ships, so they tell me."

The Captain agreed. "Very good. Up-to-date motor ships, they cross a rough sea like an iron crosses a board."

With their black hulls and yellow funnels, the Maru's of the Nippon-Yusen-Kaisha were to be encountered now and again in Naples or Marseilles: but he had never yet seen one in Hamburg. He sat listening uneasily to the sounds without, where, beyond the broad window on the fifth storey of the office building, lay beneath the swirling smoke and haze the crisped surface of the harbour—or rather of a small part of it, amid swooping seagulls, creaking cranes, and barges and tugs plying to and fro: and beyond it all, the tall upstanding tower of St. Michael's Church, dominating the inner city of Hamburg, a labyrinth of clustered houses like an insect city. Captain Carstanjen's *Neunauge* sailed on the Mediterranean route, and had just arrived from Haifa with her tanks full of precious oil. He was anxious to find out whether his next voyage was only to be to Constanza, or through the Black Sea as far as Batum. He would be fifty in the middle of October, and wanted to spend that anniversary at home in the company of his son and son-in-law: and as one of them had a job with the *Lufthansa* and the other on the railways, it was high time to make the arrangements.

"Don't you worry, Cap'n," said Footh. "It doesn't altogether depend on me. By the middle of October you'll certainly be back home, but perhaps we'll be getting lubricating oil from Tampico, and then everything will be different. We'll know for certain the day after tomorrow."

He enquired on the telephone whether Fräulein Petersen had yet found out where the Distribution Office had sent the oil from the *Neunauge* for storage: out of reach of the boring operations for the Elbe suspension bridge, above or beneath the earth, where there was still space for petrol.

"It will be wonderful to see a great structure like that spanning our Lower Elbe at Finkenwärder or wherever it may be. A challenge and a symbol of the new Reich," observed Herr Footh gravely, turning again towards his visitor. "Unfortunately, there's going to be trouble with the subsoil, so the geologists say. Well, the Führer will bring it off."

A large wall-map behind his head displayed North-West Germany, air-ports, motor-roads, and tank-installations, with a number of yellow circles in the neighbourhood of railways and canals. These latter indicated the huge subterranean reservoirs, under the control of the Army Command. On the left and smaller wall, and half-obscured by

Captain Carstanjen's massive blue form, hung a more schematized map of the world on a lesser scale, on which the petroleum ports were indicated by red shaft-towers: while miniature flags, numbered one to five, marked the points at which Herr Footh's fleet then lay.

"As far as I can see, you're still at Haifa," laughed Herr Footh, pressed a bell, and requested Fräulein Krüger, as she entered, to transfer flag 3 from Cadiz to Hamburg. In Spain, Franco had conquered. Neville Chamberlain's Englishmen did not dare to protest when "un-identified U-Boats" sank or fired on British Merchantmen: and the Russian aircraft sent in aid to the Republicans proved worthless. The authoritarian principle had won the day on all sides, when it openly appeared, and still more decisively behind the scenes.

"I'm curious to hear the reports that Captain Meinke will bring us from Rio. Latin America is going ahead magnificently. In the U.S.A. the Republicans have chosen Wendell Wilkie, a man of German origin as their leader, and at the elections in a year's time—no, they're due in two years, of course—Mr. Roosevelt will disappear, and the old lion, Great Britain, knows very well that his teeth are getting loose. What's the outlook for him and his Jews in Palestine? Revolts all over the country. Fill another pipe, Captain."

Carstanjen knew that his accounts were being checked in the mean-time, and that he would have to sit here for a good quarter-of-an-hour longer. He filled and puffed at his pipe, and told his tale. All over the country mines exploded under lorries carrying British troops to specially threatened points. During his presence at Haifa a portfolio with a bomb inside it had exploded in the business quarter, and wounded an Arab bicyclist in the leg. In the port the Italians were very much in evidence with the ships of the Lloyd-Triestino and the aeroplanes of the Ala Littoria: the besotted British just looked on and did nothing. The Captain's trick of splitting his S-p's and S-t's gave a homely flavour to his discourse, as he went on to say that the German colony at Haifa knew more of the secrets of the rebellion than the Intelligence Service, though less than the Italian Consulate. He had himself been present at a particularly pleasing incident at Shuk. An enormous table had been set out with a display of butchers' knives from Solingen, which a member of the N.S.B.O. on the *Neunauge* had brought with him from Party stocks for re-sale by the Arabs: long, straight blades, so suitable for secret usage, as the Arabs understood it. They had auctioned the table-full with all the appropriate patter: unfortunately little had been bought— for the time being, because the Japanese had spoilt the market with their own "Solingen" stuff. But a brave Jewish lady, who passed on a shopping expedition, had to lean up against the wall, and then hurry back home. Perhaps she had second sight, like so many people in a seaport, and saw visions of more blades thrust into her own people's backs.

"Butchers' knives?" repeated Herr Footh smiling. "That reminds me of something. Excuse me, Cap'n," and he picked up a receiver and asked Fräulein Blüthe to put him through to Wandsbek 8494, and call his old army comrade Albert Teetjen to the telephone. The answer would come from Otto Lehmke's beer-house. Then he asked casually what the Haifa dockers would be likely to say if they saw the Swastika flag hoisted in the harbour. And he looked suitably complacent when the Captain assured him that they would not cause any trouble at all. Indeed, on occasions the new Reich flag was hung across the street in the German colony; and when distinguished German tourists arrived at the Windsor Hotel, such as Major von Hindenburg or Herr von Papen, the new German colours were also displayed.

"Very right and proper," grinned Herr Footh, and he told the Captain, who had only heard it briefly on the wireless while at sea, how much the English King had enjoyed himself at Salzburg the year before, and how warmly he had been greeted by the Austrian Party Comrades, as he went about making purchases in white leather breeches and Nazi stockings. Edward VIII had in the meantime abdicated. But in England's history Kings had been throned and dethroned before, at the behest of some powerful King-maker, such as would be, for example, the future victor in the German-Russian War. The Captain leaned forward in his chair: did Herr Footh believe in a war? The English fleet, in Alexandria for example, was in no sense a rotten nut. The battleship *Hood* and the cruiser *Repulse* had lately left their visiting cards at Haifa: they were certainly not show-pieces, with their gigantic guns.

"Our Führer will secure everything without a war. We can drink on that." And Footh telephoned for some kümmel and two glasses.

They were brought by Fräulein Blüthe, who with a modest smile set a tray upon the table. Then, as the gentlemen clinked glasses, she asked what she should do. Herr Teetjen was at the Central Slaughterhouse and could not come to the telephone, but his wife was there—could she do anything? Herr Footh replaced his glass on the polished nickel tray, and let his eyes dwell meditatively on the young woman's pretty face. "Listen: this is important. Will Herr Teetjen lunch with me to-morrow at Cölln, at midday punctually. That will do his credit good—at least at Otto Lehmke's pub," he added with a chuckle, and as he spoke he noticed how prettily the girl had done her hair, and how particularly she had wanted him to notice it. Alas, and now he had to say something that would depress her. "Then ring up Fuhlsbüttel and say that there wouldn't be much point in my coming out to-day. Ask whether we could eat that crab on Tuesday instead."

"Certainly, Herr Footh," and with a flash of her forget-me-not eyes Anneliese Blüthe hurried to her telephone, where the black receiver still lay on the table.

The Lehmkes were among the Teetjen's best customers; they gave large orders for loin of pork, tripe and sausages. Herr Lehmke sat at one of his own tables, sorting out a number of packs of cards which Preester's S.S. men had left all mixed up from the previous evening, thrust a stick of chewing tobacco, commonly known as Priem, into his mouth, and said to his wife—who stood rinsing glasses behind the bar:

"Now you see, old girl. Teetjen is a fine man. Only fine folks have fine friends."

Frau Lehmke, who came from Kiel, a corpulent dame with a bun of grey plaits tightly drawn across her skull, and small sharp eyes, nodded, but not with the good nature that is usually ascribed to women of her build.

"Yes," she replied. "Albert looks smart all right in his uniform. But if anyone asks you whether Stine Teetjen dyes her hair, you just say that your wife says she does."

"What's it got to do with you?"

"Right you are, but I like to say what I think."

As an old married pair the Lehmkes understood each other beyond what was actually uttered. Frau Fiete Lehmke had not failed to notice the lively look which her husband had thrown after Stine as her tall, slim figure had hurried through the door, in fear lest the rice might have caught on the stove at home.

"And I thought their friendship with Footh was over long ago." She put down the damp cloth, took a dry one out of a cupboard, and started polishing the glasses.

"Why," he replied. "The S.S. is Adolf's *élite*. Damned useful to be one of them."

"I always thought Albert just good enough for the S.A. S.S.—a bit too much for him."

"And now it pays. Wonder whether the rich shipowner, Footh, would telephone a simple S.A.-man Teetjen."

"And invite him to Cölln. There's plenty of duff there—I'll bet he's got Trade Union—I mean Labour Front—money in his business."

"You shut your trap. Never heard anybody say anything like that here."

"Right, right! Inviting him to Cölln! Lehmke's pub's not good enough!"

"Quieten down, old girl. Footh's also an S.S. man. Comes to us too and has a drink with Albert."

"Yes, and making a pass at Stine, if Albert isn't careful."

"I don't think so," he said as he rose, and went to the cupboard to lock up the cards, proverbially known as Devil's prayer-book. "He wouldn't want to get across Albert. A butcher, who isn't fond of children; otherwise they are always so good natured."

"If he wants a bit of cash again, what shall I do?"

"Give it him: he has always paid us back. And now all the more."


Stine Geisow, whose married name was Teetjen, was well worth looking at, as she hurried along, slim-hipped and bare-legged beneath her short skirt, striding sturdily down the street on her way back to the shop. She held her hands against her breast, for in those late summer days she liked to go about clad as lightly as was decent, in a flimsy cotton dress, bright coloured with white spots, as dictated by fashion and the big stores: its olive-green ground went well with her maize-coloured hair. She was well aware of Otto Lehmke's admiration, but compared with Albert, Lehmke did not come into question—such a bull of a man. Tavern-keepers always sat around pouring beer into their bellies, which expanded accordingly. The Lehmke woman could set her mind at rest, and stop looking at her so venomously.

Stine had to hurry. She had a Hamburg cake in the oven, an imposing mass of dough stuffed with almonds and currants, and skilfully flavoured with lemon, to celebrate Albert's success: moreover there was the rice on the gas, turned low, with an asbestos plate between saucepan and flame. None the less, rice was tricky, and if you weren't very careful, it caught. And to-day there would be rice with small sausages, which had not been sold and had to be used up before they were turned off for dogs' food. Fortunately this hour of the morning, from half-past nine to half-past ten, could be regarded as very suitable for telephoning. The housewives who had got up early had already come for their stewing meat; and the others who wanted something that could be quickly grilled, because they don't make up their minds till the last moment—pork cutlets, veal cutlets or mutton chops—did not come before half-past eleven. In the meantime Dörte Lehmke sat at the counter, snipping off the ends of a garlic sausage and serving customers. She did so with much satisfaction, a fat, puffy little girl, who took after her father; she aspired to become a saleswoman on the top-floor of the Tietz shop, where smart young people came to eat sandwiches and drink a glass of Malaga in the luncheon-room. They knew their way about, they enjoyed their lives, and left a bit for other people. Dörte, her name was really Dorothea—had not long left the Hitler Young Folks to become a member of the German Girls League, and cherished the usual sentimental admiration for Baldur von Schirach, poet and patrician, since she had first set eyes upon him at the inauguration of a Horst-Wessel street fountain. She was still more eager to see Hermann Göring, who from his photographs looked most like her father of all the leaders of the Reich. But he no longer came to Hamburg. He was establishing the *Luftwaffe*, for the crushing of the Red Communists in Russia, who had enslaved and plundered the unhappy Ukraine. Dörte hated the Communists, for her father hated them; they had destroyed his business in the years before 1933.

"Yes, Frau Teetjen, I *have* sold something," cried Dörte triumphantly, as Stine dashed in with a feverish tinkle of the door-bell. "Herr Lawerenz had an unexpected visitor, and came for a quarter of pickled tongue. And I should like it for lunch, too."

"God bless me, Dörte," laughed Stine. "You talk as if your mother starved you."

"Oh no," retorted the little creature, and snatched eagerly at an overweight slice from the frozen tongue she had slipped into the white enamelled frigidaire, which filled half the back wall of the shop opposite the broad street window.

"Hm-m," she murmured as she chewed. "It isn't bad. But it could be nicer still between two bits of bread and butter."

Frau Stine in the meantime had re-emerged from the kitchen, where she had been just in time to shake up the rice to prevent it sticking to the bottom of the saucepan and spoiling the whole dish.   The marrow-bone, which Albert had chopped up small before he went out, was cooking busily, and emitting an agreeable odour of soup, pot-herbs and parsley, as she lifted the saucepan-lid and replaced it.   In so doing, she felt somehow as though she were back again in the job of cook which she had filled so long with the Plaut family.   Plaut the chemist in the Rothenbaumchaussée, and Dörte Lehmke took the place of fat little Marga Plaut of those days, who had long since had a daughter of her own in Bloemfontein in South Africa; and she found herself saying: "Goose-fat, of course, child: butter isn't to be had."

"Guns instead of butter," exclaimed Dörte gleefully, and dashed off home, using the kitchen door into the yard, so that the shop-bell should not ring needlessly.

But Stine, light and lissom, slipped into the bedroom, took her clothes off, peered into the little mirror over the wash-stand, and noticed the reddish hair in her left armpit, and laughed happily.   Her handsome Albert was still in love with her, after nearly ten years of marriage. That was something.   They had married in the winter of '27, when the year of mourning was up after her beloved parents' death, who had fallen victims to the great spring-tide of '26, in their home at one of the Hallig, near the Danish coast.   At that time the Hindenburg Dam, which was being built by the Republic from the mainland to the island of Sylt, was swept away in the grey waters of the North Sea, and the old Geisows, together with many other inhabitants of the Hallig's, were swept off their low-lying island.   With the little property she had inherited from them, they had modernized Albert's shop, which had been a costly business. But now it looked as though the hard times were over.   Perhaps she could now think of buying the lovely brown sports-shoes on which her eyes lingered so longingly whenever she passed the Lehmann's shoe window in the Wandsbeker Chaussée.   It was indeed very late in the year for brown shoes, but by the middle of September they would be reduced in price, and she did not mind about the time of year.   Brown shoes always looked cheerful about the house, and the street mud of winter knew no difference between brown box-calf and black.   In any case she would now get her outdoor shoes soled.   Something would surely come of that date to-morrow at twelve o'clock at Cölln, and of course she would not let herself in for any definite expenditure until the result of it was known.   It was indeed doubtful whether Herr Footh was in a position to exert any influence upon a great multiple concern.   But perhaps Albert could make a contract to supply fresh meat for his five tankers, to be stowed away in their ice-chests when they started out on a voyage.   Regular receipts—that was what was needed: to set against their regular expenses.   At this point she had tidied her hair again, put on a blue kitchen apron instead of her frock, and drawn the kitchen-chair into a position from which she could at the same time keep an eye on the shop and her kitchen fire.   She had brought in a bag of early apples, as green as the rat-poison which Herr Plaut used to weigh out for the shipping companies in his delicate scales, for sprinkling on the floors of their warehouses and cellars.  They were really autumn fruit and rather maggotty; so she mashed them into pulp to make the *compôte* to which Albert was very partial, and so was she.  If only it didn't use up so much sugar!  When they were peeled, and the innards taken out, as Frau Plaut used to call the cores, there were only the little quarters left to plump into the water in the enamel saucepan.  No matter: there were no larger ones to be had.

To-morrow at twelve o'clock in Cölln, Albert must positively have a little cash to put in his pockets.  Rich people were often mean, and accidents might happen.

## CHAPTER TWO

### TEMPTATION

"MOST GREAT CITIES," observed Herr Footh, as he squeezed a little lemon-juice on a piece of toast spread with sturgeon-roe, commonly known as caviar, "most great cities owe their aspect to the interplay of water and fire.  All of them have been thoroughly burnt out some time, as though of set purpose."

Albert Teetjen continued to chew.  He didn't care much for caviar, and had taken only two or three modest spoonfuls out of the barrel-shaped porcelain jar, labelled *Beluga*.

"What God does," he observed in due course, "is well done, both for the builders and the real estate owners."

Herr Cölln—there had not been a Cölln for a long time—had opened his restaurant to help and establish the sale of the brewage of West and East-Phalia, in deliberate competition with the South German beer.  As a consequence, a hundred years after its foundation, his guests could then drink beer from Dortmund and Eimbeck, which nowhere reached the table in better condition.  The timber of these tables, unstained and merely waxed, yellowish-green with age, appeared in all its natural and original beauty, for there were no table-cloths at Cölln's, and the guests all sat on broad brown chairs and benches, without cushions and yet in perfect comfort.  A staircase led down into an underground room, from the ceiling of which hung elaborately finished models of old schooners and frigates; the room was cool and full of grateful odours, for Cölln's served only the very best of everything, and

held to the old tradition in matters of food: solid, plentiful, and super-
lative in quality.   The two men in S.S. uniform had been able to choose
their table—for the luncheon hour was late in Hamburg, indeed before
half-past twelve the kitchen was hardly in a position to serve the dishes
announced on the menu.   However, that did not matter; they had thus
been able to esconce themselves in a corner, behind a heavy tapestry
curtain, half-drawn, and get a little talk undisturbed.   A long brown
dachshund, called Ebert, had accompanied Herr Footh out of the light-
grey Mercedes, and now lay curled up beneath his chair awaiting the
offerings that would fall to him from the upper world in the shape of
bits of meat and bones.   No other table stood near enough for anyone
to overhear the conversation which Albert Teetjen so eagerly expected.
But he had learnt to master his feelings and preserve an impassive
countenance.   It seemed to him already a good omen that Herr Footh
had from the outset used the Hamburg dialect, when they met at the
top of the entrance staircase.

Hence it did not sound in any way strange to be addressed as "My
son," though they were of an equal age.   Moreover, the Low German
speech, like Dutch or Yiddish, carries with it a kind of familiar
charm when spoken by those accustomed to use it from their earliest
youth.

"Yes, my son, what you have in your mind just can't be done, of
course.   We of the Transport branch can't interfere in Distribution
arrangements.   You belong to the Prepared Food branch.   But the
Senate and the Council are keeping their eyes on the consumers, as
indeed they must do.   Before the Führer tightened up the rearmament
drive, we were in the thick of a consumer crisis, and the machines
were delivering much more than people could pay for, in spite of their
needs.   You people, dependent as you are on a low monthly pay system,
are still feeling the draught.   Well, here's your health:" and they both
drank.

Where was this going to lead?—Teetjen wondered, and spoke up in
defence of the suggestion he had made in his letter.   His business could
show a decent average profit if the public came to his shop as before.
But it was going down because the women clung to the displays in the
windows of the great stores, like flies to glue-paper, and it would be
slowly strangled by its fixed outgoings.   There had been no change in
the population of Wandsbek since it had been included in the Hamburg
area this year.   The inhabitants of the district were mostly employés
of the great industrial works, both officials and workers, together with a
number of teachers, labourers, and small property owners.   People must
use sparingly what they had.   If they didn't win something in the lottery,
they wouldn't get fat.

Herr Footh nodded his rather florid countenance, smoothed his
moustache, and summoned the waiter.

"What would you like to eat?" he said to his guest.   And for the
next course they both chose Hamburg steak—ribs of beef grilled
on slabs of toast, with an agreeably acid accompaniment of gherkins,
onions and mushrooms.   The small white barrel was removed and

replaced by two large tankards of English porter, a drink which was well suited to the Hamburg climate and went down very well. For a time the electric light shone on the polished surface of the empty table.

"Supposing," said Herr Footh, "Supposing you were offered the opportunity of earning a certain little sum, which would help you over the immediate future? It takes time to get proposals put before the Council and the Senate. You realize that, don't you? And I know of such an opportunity, which is at the same time more or less in your line of business."

"Good enough," said Albert, and asked for further information.

But at that moment the waiter appeared with a large, oval tray, knives and forks and dishes, and the pair set about their lunch. They both looked like officers, in the black uniforms of a Corps which, in the days of their comradeship in arms had not existed, and as they ate they talked of old days in Lithuania and on the River Niemen.

"Those were the times, my boy! Do you remember that crazy old tale of the Schaulen Forest?"

Albert Teetjen did not remember it, and Herr Footh, after ordering Westphalian black bread, Emmenthaler cheese, Pomeranian *schnapps* (curaçao), and selecting two almost black Brazilian cigars, assisted his memory. Had there not been a certain Sergeant Ruckstuhl, who had fallen in with a Jew driving along a forest path in a farm-cart full of firewood which he had cut, this being plain theft of what was the property of the occupying authorities? Ruckstuhl had promptly condemned him to death, pulled him off the cart, made him kneel down on the frozen ground, and beheaded him then and there with his own axe. There was fearful ado when the next carts came along and found old Itzig lying beside the timber-track, with his pony sniffing at him, and his grey-bearded head beside him, as though he just dropped it. And it would have gone ill for Ruckstuhl, had not a certain Captain Kissenbaum, whose job was to act as court martial advocate, taken a special interest in the case, which seemed incompatible with the honour of the uniform he wore. Herr Kissenbaum was able to show that Ruckstuhl had been blind drunk on the Sunday morning between ten and twelve, and moreover that he displayed symptoms of defective reasoning power, in the form of epileptic attacks during which he might commit any act without knowing what he had done.

Herr Kissenbaum was of Jewish extraction, and a Social Democrat, but he thereby acquired so much merit in the eyes of the Prussian Conservatives, that he still drew his pension to-day, though domiciled in Palestine of course.

Albert sat leaning back in his broad wooden chair, sipping his liqueur savouring the sweetish flavour of the schnapps combined with that of the Swiss cheese, and fingered the rough outer leaf of the fresh Braziliar cigar. In the meantime almost every seat in Herr Cölln's cellar, restaurant had been filled, as indeed was apparent from the subdued clatter and the buzz of talk.

"Ah yes," laughed Albert, who had in the meantime clearly

remembered that lunatic young man: "That fellow Ruckstuhl was lucky to get out of it like that. Fairly got above himself he did—though in these days it would have been passed over, I daresay, as an act of the master-race, eh? If, instead of Kissenbaum, he had got into the hands of the Catholic advocate Dachert, the Centre Party fellow, and Erzberger's friend, he would have been promptly put up for murder, instead of manslaughter with extenuating circumstances, which was how Herr Kissenbaum managed to cook up the case."

Yes, that was how it had happened. It all came back to Albert now. He had been sitting around in the station canteen at Schaulen, when the fellows from the *Kommandantur* had been waiting for the Berlin express, to take Ruckstuhl for observation of his mental condition by Professor Willbrandt. He, Teetjen, had just come off leave; Ruckstuhl and the N.C.O.'s had a compartment to themselves, and they gave him a seat in it, telling him he could get an excellent night's rest in the luggage-rack. He remembered, to this very day, how he had laughed to think that Ruckstuhl, who was the cause of this benefaction, had to content himself with the floor of the compartment, where the jolts of the badly-sprung rolling-stock could most be felt. But, said his guardians, he mustn't mind that, he had thoroughly deserved such a punishment, as he must himself admit.

"Excellent," exclaimed Herr Footh, with an approving laugh. "I didn't know that. The train episode was new to me. I do admire our people's indefeasible sense of justice. And what would you say if I had a similar sort of proposal to make to you? Ruckstuhl was indeed an amateur—you are a professional. Strike four times, and two thousand four hundred marks are yours."

And in his genial, humorous Hamburg speech, he explained how he could earn the favour of the Senate and the Reichsstatthalter. Now and again a new arrival would pass the curtain, peer in, apologize and withdraw. The great clock in the Petri tower struck one, high above all their heads. Teetjen emitted wafts of blue smoke, and stared in front of him with bated breath at the shipowner, Standard-Führer in the N.S.K.K. and old comrade in the war, who sat there and proposed that he should deputize for the Oldenburg executioner. He had filled him with good things, he had been lavish of beer and schnapps, and duly brought the business up, incidentally as it were; but there were snags and objections. Something within him had immediately exclaimed "Yes!":—two thousand four hundred marks, who would turn down such a sum! And yet, obstacles and difficulties there certainly were. And they were—Stine, and the neighbours. The office of executioner was of a special character, sinister and abhorrent. By reason of the graves it filled, it stood in some dark fellowship with the secret places of the earth, the mysterious soil beneath. In middle-class society the killing of people was a ticklish matter. He must make this clear to Herr Footh, who had tried to make the matter appear so innocent and even honourable.

"No, I don't really see myself doing this executioner's job. First, because of my wife: and secondly, because of this uniform."

Herr Footh raised his eyebrows. On the first point he could say nothing, that was friend Albert's affair. On the second, there was of course a way round—by means of an overcoat and mask. In a black, or indeed a white, mask, your own father wouldn't know you. That, indeed, was perhaps an exaggeration. Fathers always recognized you. But would neighbours and householders do so—or comrades of the S.S.? Not a chance. It was true that these performances took place in public, but the spectators had to be invited. Not even Press representatives were admitted. Herr Denke had sent his deputy from Oldenburg. *Basta.* And now they would take another cup of coffee among the trees in the Uhlenhorster Fährhaus. Herr Footh still had half an hour free, Albert could have until then to make up his mind. "Come along, Herr Ebert," he said to his dog; "we must make a move."

In a crowded district of narrow streets, even small cars find it difficult to make a way through the throng in the middle of the day. Herr Footh had, of course, paid the bill, and sent his guest out first, as was proper. Now he was driving slowly down to the Alster, and Albert beside him, doing his best to hide the satisfaction with which he leaned back against the grey leather of the cabriolet. Marvellous weather. A faint haze hung between the walls of the houses, veiling the sunlight and the clear blue sky. God!—how glorious it was to belong to such a world, to sit in a grand car, and be carried from one restaurant to another. Under the late chestnut trees stood tables set with brightly-coloured cloths: sometimes a leaf floated down and ruffled the surface of the water, deluding the swans, who promptly paddled up to it.

"Silly creatures," said Footh; "they might have noticed long ago that they were fooling themselves."

The dachshund barked at them, and they hissed at him, with outthrust necks, until he was called to heel. Half an hour went by almost unobserved. The two men in their comfortable chairs smoked their cigars to the end—with the help of the white spills at their side—enjoyed their coffee, the fine weather, and eyed each other genially. Teetjen stirred his coffee with his spoon: when was the ceremony to take place. He couldn't take on the job without a certain amount of training. (As a good Hamburger the English word slipped naturally off his tongue.) Footh laid his lower lip against his moustache: the game was won. He had almost let out how great the service was which Albert had undertaken, and told him that everything depended on his action. Instead of which he asked how much time a man so experienced in the use of an axe would need for practice. Surely ten days would be enough?

"A week," said Albert Teetjen. But an overcoat and a mask, supposing he agreed, would have to be supplied to him. Otherwise the expenses would be too high for a fee of two thousand marks. There were places, replied Herr Footh, where all that sort of thing could be hired. The cost of it would be met. And if Albert had made up his mind, he would drive him home; the car would buzz along the Wandsbeker Chaussée in a few minutes, in spite of all the pipes and wires, like the veins and sinews of a body, which the Municipal Road Office was always so busily laying bare beneath the asphalt. He had almost said: of a beheaded Jew's neck, thinking of Ruckstuhl. But he stopped himself in time, on account of Albert's hesitations. "Agreed?" he asked as he pushed back his chair.

"Yes."

"Once and for all?"

"Well, I'd like to sleep on it."

"So you shall. It's barely half-past one, you can be at home in ten minutes."

What a pity that Stine couldn't see him roll up, thought Teetjen, when the grey Mercedes stopped outside the butcher's shop; she did so enjoy a bit of display. Then, lightly, as the whole interview had been conducted, Footh proposed that he should give him a definite answer that evening at nine o'clock at Fuhlsbüttel. The number was under Z —Central Prison—in the Official Section. "Just ask for Commercial-Counsellor Footh."

"Commercial-Counsellor?" he gasped. "Since when, my dear fellow?"

But Footh laughed complacently, waved a familiar hand, Albert Teetjen raised his arm, and the grey car slid away. "Like a cat," observed Frau Stine, who at that moment stepped into the shop door-way, and gazed with wondering eyes at the car as it gathered speed. "Come along in, Albert, and tell me all about it. I'll give you a good cup of coffee. You've pulled it off, that's as plain as your face. Now I shall be able to get the box-calf shoes."

And hitching up the shop-bell they went through into the living-room. Albert promptly went on into the bedroom, to make himself more comfortable. While Stine set one side of the oval table with coffee-cups and yesterday's cake, which gave it quite a festive appearance, Albert, seated on the edge of his bed, let his high boots rattle on to the floor, extricated himself from his black tunic and his stuffy riding-breeches, and proceeded to wash himself in the large earthenware basin adorned with sprays of green water-roses. Drying himself with deliberation, he stood in the doorway:

"What's all that for, old lady? Counsellor Footh didn't let me starve."

- "Nor pay either," said she. "Fetch the asters out of the shop window, and then we shall be all set."

Lilac asters, and the old-fashioned gilt porcelain vase, which Frau Plaut, the chemist's wife, had given to her faithful Stine on her wedding, lent a well-deserved air of celebration to the most noteworthy hours of this last day in August. Again Albert enthroned himself upon the red plush sofa, she on the narrow side this time, to the right of him, so that she could see the shop, and bit into the cake with a satisfaction that surprised him.

"Did you get an advance?" she asked sagely.

"Advance on what?" he asked, rather taken aback.

"Well, you've fixed up something," she laughed. "And the

instalments are due to-morrow. Even if we should find casual work that won't help us much at the end of the month."

"You had better go to the landlord's office to-morrow, and tell them that all arrears will be paid up by the fifteenth of the month, including those standing over from the previous year. The day after to-morrow I'll let them have a line in confirmation of this from Commercial-Counsellor Footh."

"Commercial-Counsellor Footh?" said she. "That sounds pretty good! He hasn't been that very long, I daresay; well, I'm all for the Labour Front! And just what have you fixed up?"

Albert's face assumed rather a worried look: "You mustn't ask, and I mustn't tell you."

"You know I'm not inquisitive," she said good-humouredly. "You'll tell me when you can."

"That's my sensible Stine," he said approvingly. "And, by the way, you can use a few more coffee-beans now. The coffee in the Uhlenhorst Fährhaus was better than this."

"Do you think you're going to make enough out of this business to take me out now and again? To Stellingen, perhaps, to Hagenbeck's Zoo. I'm longing to see the little gazelles and foxes and bears. And then I want a little dog or cat of my own, like that one over there." And she pointed with her thumb at a framed postcard which hung on the wall near the shop-door, displaying a picture in bright colours of two goggle-eyed kittens with ribbons round their necks and a large bunch of violets between them.

"Of course you shall have one," he said. "Anything you like after the fifteenth."

And then he went on to explain that any measures against the great Stores, even with the best favour of the Party, would take time, but in the meantime he had found a temporary expedient, about which he could not speak.

"I'm quite satisfied," she said. "Only on one condition. All must be done legally. My Albert must not let himself be used against the State and the Party. There's no salvation to be found in that."

He eyed her in amazement, holding out his hand with the empty cup in it. "Footh the shipowner? Against State and Party? Why, Stine, how do you suppose he got where he is?"

"I've no idea," she said doggedly. "But there are so many ordinances out nowadays. Guns instead of butter, and all that sort of thing, you know. When a fellow is always steering into foreign ports, he easily drops into doing what he shouldn't."

"What I'm going to do for him is strictly within my own job. And what could a butcher do against the law?"

"He could smuggle mouldy pork off the other fellow's ships, or on board for the crews," she said, trying to make a jest of her apprehensions.

"Nonsense," he retorted with a frown. "You've still got the Russian film in your head, about the Red cruiser and its maggotty meat. No,

Stine, that's not it. Only first-class meat gets aboard German ships.
And now I must lie down for a bit, beer makes a chap sleepy; wake me
at four." So saying he adjusted himself to the familiar curves of the
plush sofa, yawned and closed his eyes. Root out that Red rabble.
How would Stine stand it? He had already behaved to her as though
everything would go smoothly now. He had only to consent. And
while she went to and fro, busy clearing away and washing up, he had
a strange vision of a Russian country road, frozen and deep in snow,
and on each side of it an unbroken rampart of tall trees, like the grey
houses of the Wandsbeker Chaussée. In the middle of it was a bearded
Jew, his anguished face and long neck outstretched, walking in front
of a man in shirt-sleeves, brandishing an axe. On and on walked the
Jew. "Besides," he muttered to himself, "it was war then, and now it's
peace? Let Stine go on dreaming of the cruiser *Potemkin* and what she
contained." Albert was in fact trying to establish a distinction between
himself and Ruckstuhl of the M.P., attached to the Forest Section
at Schaulen. He had acted like a lunatic, he struck on his own account.
But Albert would do everything in the manner of the Führer himself;
all strictly legal. With God for King and Fatherland, the words were
engraved on the clasp of his belt of polished brass. *"The sun brought
it to the light of day"*—so ran the old song.

In the evening Stine learned what Albert had forgotten to tell her
all along, that it was a matter of two thousand marks: a sum that used
to be worth a hundred English pounds, and was now worth a hundred
and seventy-five; cash on the table, which opened up all sorts of prospects.
But for just that reason no one must know anything about it, and least
of all the Comrades of the Preester Storm-platoon. If they got but an
inkling of it they would want to squander it or drink it. And that would
be beyond all bearing. While talking thus they were walking down the
Wagnerstrasse about half-past eight in the evening; the warm blue
dusk hovered above the deep cleft of the street, and the reddish-yellow
panes of the dwelling-houses and shop-windows lent a friendly glow to
the city highway, where the day's work was at an end. Albert had
to telephone, but this time he preferred the automatic telephone in the
post office.
"We've said as much as we need to keep up our credit. Anything
more could only do harm."
No one, not even Stine, must know that he was calling up the Central
Prison. People were so inquisitive and malicious; a dirty lot, in fact.
A man was a fool to let them get any hold over him. And Stine, as a girl,
had been an Adventist. A Mennonite, who kept Saturday sacred instead
of Sunday, and studied her Bible. For that reason she had in days
gone by taken the job with Plaut the Jew, that law-abiding compounder
of poisons, and kept it for so long. She would have preferred to convert
Albert to vegetarianism, and feed him solely on green-stuff. Well,
she hadn't succeeded, and in the end she had married him, and still
loved him, a fellow who lived by killing innocent beasts. Contradiction

upon contradiction. But such was man. If Stine got to know anything too soon, her imagination was in flames at once; she would have been out of hand in no time, and made no end of heavy weather. But confront her with a fact, and like all decently sensible people, she could come to terms with it. And a man was no man who could not keep such a matter to himself for a fortnight, and do what needed to be done. This time he was not to operate on harmless cattle, but on sub-men, convicted criminals, enemies of the people, who shouted 'Heil' to their destroyers in outbursts of community shouting. Sleep, little Stine, sleep—your Albert is no sheep, he hummed gaily, as he told her to sit down in the blue twilight outside the door of the post office, and himself slipped into a cushioned cell, to search the telephone-book for the telephone number of the Central Prison at Fuhlsbüttel. The fat volume hung from a chain—exactly as in a gaol, he thought to himself with a grin.

As they were walking home after an hour's stroll in the public gardens of the former Wandsbek City Park, where sat pairs of lovers on all the benches, themselves an older pair of lovers, the waning moon rose over the outspread country and the cloudless black horizon. In the Wagner-strasse, there were many windows still open, and from the loud-speakers of the more well-to-do came the faintly oiled voices of the announcers, describing in the evening news what gigantic preparations were being made by the City of Nuremberg to celebrate the Party Day. They took occasion to enumerate, in undertones of triumph, the foreign diplomats and representatives of foreign Governments received by the Führer, despite the campaign of hatred conducted by the emigrants and all the organizations connected with the Jews. Two years before, Albert had had the joy of attending such a ceremony; the journey through the green land of Franconia, after a night of sleep through central Germany, had brought back great memories of the war, all those peregrinations from Altona to Flanders, from Flanders to the Argonne, from the Argonne to Alsace, from Alsace to Rumania, and finally up to *Oberost*. He had always kept in mind a sentence from a Field newspaper: 'The German does not in general travel much, but when he does, he goes with his rifle slung across his shoulders and gets himself respected.' Those words had been written by a man with a French name, and so it was : in those days 'Strength through Joy' had not yet been heard of. It was grand to see the world, and stare out of the compartment window, as though the cows and the railway stations, the sunflowers and the roofs of town looked quite different from what they did between Altona and Berlin. 'Strength through Joy' was a great show. That was another of the Führer's hits. It was a fact that envious members of the S.P.D. who had been converted to National Socialism, maintained that the old Party had in its day organized holiday trips of this kind. If they had, no one had ever heard or talked about them, and they might as well not have existed.

When at home Albert discovered a fine thirst for a bottle of cool beer. "Showing off—eh, my girl!" he said to Stine, who had taken off her hat, and let her plaits ripple down into a magnificent horse's-tail. "These sausages must be got rid of. Bring me the remains of the supper and the mustard." Stine had opened the kitchen window, and was listening up into the sky. From somewhere near the roof came the faint notes of music. The outer front of the house had a sloping roof with a steep tiled coping like the whole street. But the side wings towards the yards were built much higher, topped with zinc and corrugated iron, and more or less flat. Up above, exactly opposite the Teetjen domicile, a small figure was gliding to and fro, scarcely discernible in the grey enveloping darkness, playing the concertina. Only its head could be seen moving beneath the stars.

Stine clapped her hand to her forehead. "Bless me, I've just remembered! I must take three pairs up to Barfey. I borrowed her wash-house on Friday, and I still owe her for the last time." So saying she picked up three of the five pairs of sausages, and was about to run out. But Albert held her fast by her auburn horse-tail, and walked with her to the window, still chewing. "That's my bellows-piano," said he, leaned out of the window listening, and nodded approvingly. "Tom's a great hand at that. I had thought I should have to take it away from him and sell it. Better let him be. You see, one can't blame him for detesting our revolution and the New Reich. He has been like a man condemned to prison, ever since, poor devil."

Stine sighed. "Do you think I can go out with my hair like this?"

"No one is going to make a pass at you on the stairs."

"I'll put a scarf on," said she, put the three pairs of sausages into a blue enamel saucepan, and was just about to slip through the kitchen door to the opposite back-entrance. But Albert still held her fast.

"Two pairs are enough, keep the third for yourself."

Stine, freeing herself, said she had no appetite, and wanted to keep her figure.

"We'll see about that—one of these days," said Albert, sliding his hand over her body. "And now, off with you, my girl."

Geesche Barfey, the laundry-woman, with her son Tom, lived in a room in the gable-front of the house, which really ought not to have been let at all. It was only accessible over the roof of the side-wing, since the clearance which was to secure the upper stories of the house against air incendiary attacks. Although it was a time of profound peace, and war was confined to East Asia and Spain, and Adolf Hitler, as an old front-line soldier, declared his horror of war, the Government of the Reich had in its parental care and foresight caused the accumulations of lumber to be removed from the garrets. But the occupation of these parts of the house was tolerated. The widow of Sergeant Barfey, of the 76th Regiment of Infantry, now a laundry-woman, and her son, born in the Spring of 1919, still dwelt in these upper parts ever since that time. They belonged there. The arrival of the boy Tom into the world, a cripple, with puny, shrivelled legs, had been ascribed by some to the young war-widow's trouble, by the others to the fact that until the very last day of her pregnancy she had been leaning against the wash-tub over the dirty linen of the entire neighbourhood. It was a marvel that he had survived the perilous first year of his life, and afterwards, when during the inflation the price of milk, vegetables, and fruit had soared to unimaginable heights. But Geesche fought for her Tom with all the resources of a strong young woman, and the child in the little basket was grateful to her. His little brown eyes were clear and bright, and followed every movement, every fly in the room. As other children learn to stand, he had learned to sit, and his arms grew into muscular organs of support. Fortunately his youth fell in that period of the Weimar Republic, which, without venturing upon actual socialization, was accessible to all social and humane movements, and provided the non-possessing classes with all the aid and assistance from municipal and national resources, which the well-to-do could furnish from their own. Since Hamburg with its Socialist majority on the City Council was in the fore-front of good example, the Prussian neighbour and sister cities such as Altona, Harburg, and Wandsbek could not well be left behind. So Tom Barfey got ray treatment, vitamins, and curative exercises like a grown-up panel-patient, swinging himself down the stairway by his arms, and when he was six, propelled himself to school, like a little cripple of the Great War—to one of those Hamburg municipal schools in which the teachers, in their modern attitude to life, knew how to restrain the innate brutality of the other children, and arouse their natural sympathy for their schoolfellow, the son of one who had died for his country. All the inhabitants of this quarter knew little Tom, and beamed when on two occasions he brought home prizes for general knowledge. It was then that the headmaster urged the mother to apply for a free place at the Hamburg High School. For this purpose her widow's pension had to be increased, as she would otherwise have benefited by her boy's earnings as a copyist, as soon as he had passed the school age. This was in the Spring of '33, on the occasion of the seizure of power by the National Socialist German Workers' Party, the Reichstag fire being the prelude to the upheaval. Young Tom, however, did receive an excellent leaving certificate. At first the school teacher, the Welfare Officer Dr. Käte Neumeier, and the other childrens' parents, succeeded in surrounding Tom with something of the old atmosphere of goodwill and guardianship, when he, a little crippled invalid, propelled himself through the streets on a platform which he had constructed for himself out of some roller skates someone had given him, with hand-grips of his own contriving. But since the boycott of Jews in the year 1933 a cleavage had appeared even between the non-political sections of the population, and the Reich Government had, through its Propaganda Minister, proclaimed the cult of youth, beauty, and health, and flatly declared war on any coddling of the sick, the streets grew more and more uncomfortable for Tom Barfey, and it soon became impossible for him to be about in them. Thanks to his preternaturally strong arms and his skill in stone-throwing he usually came off victorious; but against grown-up S.A. lads, it did not matter if he waited until midnight before trundling down the Wagnerstrasse and the Wandsbeker Chaussée.  And when they began these attacks on Republicans, Jews, and Socialists in the early dusk, it became more and more ill-advised to encounter these heroes and volksgenoffen.  But Tom Barfey did not give up.  He discovered the world of roofs—flat as well as sloping.  With the disappearance of the Republic and its government, its Socialist and Jewish-Democratic officials, its humanitarian and democratic organizations, he had been robbed of his youthful world—indeed of life itself.  He was young, his eyes were keen and clear; as he could not use his legs, he used his brains.  Albert Teetjen was right enough when he guessed that Tom Barfey was no friend of the Third Reich.  But the nature and extent of his enmity to so widely popular a political phenomenon, was known only to himself and his mother Geesche.  She brought him work by which he earned his keep; writing addresses, copying and duplicating business prospectuses, advertisements and notices for posting up in the streets.  Since the German Christians had taken possession of the Church, it was he, too, that duplicated the parish announcements of his Pastor and erstwhile patron, Stavenhagen, who kept his faith, until that stout-hearted man had to atone for his courage and Christianity in a concentration camp on the Lüneburg Heath.  His conduct had not, of course, succeeded in weaning Tom from his refusal to believe in a good, wise, and just God, who managed His business from an upper storey.  Tom had read with eagerness and care dozens of Kosmos volumes from the school library, which described the origin of the world, the earth, life and humanity, in a fashion that seemed to him more natural and attractive than the obscure and complicated fairy-tale world of the Bible Stories.  But the fact that people should let themselves be hewn in pieces for it, as for Karl Marx's 'Communist Manifesto', did make an impression on his young heart.  What happened to people who had nothing to sell but their power of work, he saw in his mother's person every day; and also what the promises of a ruling class were worth, for which his father had allowed himself first to be maimed and then shot dead.  But there was worse than this.  He had been sitting at his little floor-desk damping address-labels with a little sponge and sticking them on, while Frau Dr. Neumeier had explained to his mother what sort of application and to what authority she should make, in case any question should arise of castrating her Tom, in order that the crippled life might not be perpetuated; she must urge that his crippled condition was due to her own overwork and not to any sort of degeneracy, and that if his manhood were taken away, the vital substance of a brave soldier of the Great War, and a perfectly healthy man, who had been killed in action, would be destroyed.  That would do the trick, said Dr. Neumeier with confidence, and in case of need she was ready to take Tom before certain Hamburg authorities.  But the crass Prussians and Bavarians must not be allowed to meddle with this affair.  Käte Neumeier had in all sincerity gone over from the Social-Democrats, who let their programme remain a programme, to the National Socialists, as far back as 1931, when no doubt was left that the Weimar Republic could not fail to be diverted into a cause of reaction.  Behind the so-called Nazis stood, as it seemed to

her, the revolutionized and youthful masses of the German people who
would repair the errors of 1918, and break up the great estates into land
for State settlement, the moment they got into power.  Now she believed
it all no more. . . .  Within her circle all that she could do was to heal,
or at least to mitigate, the consequences of the disaster that she had
helped to bring upon Germany.  She had scarcely realized how distraught
she had herself been on that afternoon of a spring Sunday, when she
had warned Geesche Barfey.  And she had shuddered when she heard
a sound from the floor—the sound of the grinding of clenched teeth.

"Castrate me, eh?" said the cripple, in an unnaturally smooth voice.
"I know an attic hereabouts, where there are some hand-grenades
stored from the old Spartacus days.  I dare say they'll still be in working
order, when the Reichsstatthalter happens to drive along the Wagnerstrasse or the Wandsbeker Chaussée.  Or when a Commissioner comes
along to take me away."

Frau Dr. Neumeier, a woman with prematurely grey hair, and an
energetic furrow between her eyebrows, ran her fingers through his
hair and tousled it, and said:

"Do you want to endanger your mother and behave like a fool?
You'd like to throw hand-grenades at anyone who laid a hand on
mother's little flower and comfort, eh?  Common sense and the regulations are too tiresome and unexciting, I suppose?  You are a silly little
boy, Tom."

As a matter of fact nothing of this kind had happened up to date,
but Tom's deadly hatred found expression in the way he followed every
motion of the new State, in the Reich, in Prussia, in Hamburg—everywhere.  Anyone who associated himself with this State, or held himself
at its disposal, was in his eyes damned.  On the day of reckoning he
must be removed.  The fact that this same State was burdened with a
bad conscience could be seen in a hundred small symptoms.  Why, for
instance, were there four men who had been condemned to death still
in Fuhlsbüttel gaol?  Had not their case dragged on long enough, and
had not all four of them, or at any rate three, been proved to belong to
the outlawed Reds, the K.P.D.?  And yet nothing was done about them;
nor would be.  Condemned to death, certainly; but executed?  Things
took a long time to happen in Hamburg.


Before Stine set about climbing the iron ladder that led from the
topmost storey of the side-building to the roof, she knocked three times
with her little saucepan on one of the steps.  The metallic rattle of it
stopped the dance-music up above at once, and the sound of little wheels
was heard rolling towards the trap-door which opened above her head,
so that she did not need to have to raise it with her shoulder.  She was
promptly greeted with a kiss, against which she could not defend herself,
as her body was still only half out of the aperture, and she was holding
out the little saucepan in her right hand.

"Ah," laughed Tom.  "This is where I score by being a little fellow.
I say, what a lovely mop of hair," and he buried his face in it.  The

scarf had long since fallen off her head. She dextrously slipped out of his grasp, sat down on the attic-boards with her legs still set on the ladder, and pushed him back by the shoulders.

"My dear," said she, in a whisper, "you're very saucy to-day. I'm not little Lawerenz or the Petersens' Olga. You'll make me all untidy."

"Stine," he implored her, "do come up into my room, and let me look at you—your dear eyes, and forehead."

"Indeed I won't," she laughed. "I'm going off to sleep, but not with you."

"Stine," he exclaimed, "you're so unkind to me, and yet there's nothing I wouldn't do for you. When I was big enough to put my arms round your knees I began to love you, and I love you still, more and more."

"Yes," said she, and set the saucepan down beside him. "And you'll have to carry your love into the grave. And yet I might have been quite fond of you, if you hadn't been so impudent a lad."

"Stine!" he exclaimed, "I've kissed you—and no one can take that away from me. Tear my ears off, if you like, but I know how your lips taste."

She tapped him lightly with her fingers on the back of his mouth. "You've got a little moustache already, dear; if the room wasn't so dark, I could almost see it. Now be sure and cook those sausages to-night. Albert won't guarantee them for to-morrow. And tell your mother that she begins at our place on Friday at seven in the morning. And if she wants to come earlier, tell her to slip a note under the door. Then I'll have everything ready; I'll put the stuff in soak in the wash-house on Wednesday evening, and bring the key up to you here."

"Do bring it," he pleaded with eyes and voice. "I've known you so many years now, and you haven't changed a bit, except that you've grown more beautiful. And no children."

"No, no children," she said, turning to descend; "no; not into a world like this."

He pushed himself close up to the opening. "Don't say anything against it, Stine; the world isn't up to much, but life is glorious."

Again he managed to get his arms round her shoulders, and pressed his lips passionately to hers. Her eyes glittered angrily, but his shone with such ecstasy, that she had not the heart to push him away.

Lightly, but cautiously, she stepped down the ladder, and her head vanished through the trap-door.

"Do bring me another book from the library, Stine," he cried after her. "*You and Nature*, or *You and Life*."

"You'd better get your grandmother to do that for you," she called up unresponsively to the trap-door.

# CHAPTER THREE

### DRESSED CRAB

HERR FOOTH NEVER failed to be delighted with the clever ideas that were always occurring to his charming Slav, Annette. Had she not made that jacket he was so fond of, out of pieces left over from a summer evening frock, a gay little garment, cut low at the shoulders, with a sea-blue, white and red criss-cross check design that recalled the tricolours of many countries, with all of which we now lived in peace, but with which we had once been at war: France, England, Russia, America, Czecho-Slovakia. How lithe and gay and graceful were her movements, whether in a clinging silk dress or in sports clothes. The display of a red dish of crab on a red tablecloth and with red napkins had a practical purpose—so that the stains shouldn't show: but who else than Annette would have thought of lighting the table by means of a dozen white candles set in red Californian apples. Only Californian apples, which were to be had any day in an import city like Hamburg, exhibited that deep, uniform red, from which all other shades of the colour that dominated the evening took on a brighter sheen. And as a good housewife, Annette had already arranged that they should be washed next day or the day after and made into a purée. Ice-cold Rhine wine in cut-glass decanters, and table decorations of ivy-leaves and wild wine, which she had herself picked in the garden an hour before. Yes, Hamburg was familiar with the elegancies of life. The six diners at the long narrow table, set with high-backed chairs like those in a refectory, had delighted in the dish of crab and its rather penetrating odour: and Annette by way of a humorous table decoration had produced her father's office calendar, which indicated in gigantic letters "AUGUST 31" the last day of a month without an "R!" On that day the crab season was interred: not until the first of May could the admirable dish again be brought to table.

Black and white, like a pair of solemn woodpeckers, sat Dr. Koldewey and Footh opposite each other on the narrow sides of the table; on Father's right the lady doctor, Käte Neumeier, with short grey hair, in an evening dress of the same colour; and on Herr Footh's right, Annette, inwardly delighted that everything was going so well that day. The only odd thing was that Herr Footh had not been rung up, as he had assured her he would be. She had kept the little party lingering at the table, so that the call should not come while they were walking in the garden and might not hear it; she had turned down the wireless, on which chamber-music was being played; and she had maintained the conversation in a way that interested everybody, even her sisters Ingeborg and Thyra. As a matter of fact both the girls, hardly recognizable in their large-patterned, flowered frocks, were waiting to be called for and taken off to the Club where, by a fortunate coincidence, there was a dance that evening, a preliminary celebration for the Party Day.

Though indeed young people needed no such pretext for a dance, and both girls were inclined to fly from a house which they regarded as too highbrow. But this time Annette had proved an astute hostess; and the evening was an admirable farewell to the crab-season.

Dr. Koldewey turned his long, benignant countenance from his table-companion to his children and back again. As the two younger ones were present, he said little, and preferred to listen. They were hardly of an age to appreciate his heresies, which they might have repeated in Party circles, and that—although Dr. Koldewey was afraid of no man—was better avoided. He had sent for the report of the trial, in which were set forth at tedious length all the proceedings against his four lodgers in the condemned cells, and spent a contemplative day over them; they had recalled all manner of notable instances and memories, which he would have been glad to express in words. But his two younger girls had no understanding of the vicissitudes of human careers, that snatch people out of the ways of order and deposit them in gaol, and then take them out again. They called the Central Prison the central rubbish-dump, since, to Dr. Koldewey's no small dissatisfaction, its hospitality was extended to political prisoners, and merely expressed the opinion of their circle, in which everyone eagerly drank in the pæans of *Gauleiters* and Ministers on life ascendant, the flaming youth of Germany, the renascence and renewal of the German nation through its preparedness for war and death.

"All these people in Papa's charge," they would say, "belong to the rubbish-dump. They are human refuse from the dust-bin of society."

"And I have heard *Standartenfüehrer* Riechow say," added Ingebottel, a name bestowed upon her as result of some unexplained dealings in her babyhood with her milk- or pap-bottle, "that he would undertake to liquidate our entire establishment with one machine-gun post, while the inmates were exercising in the yards. Then they would only need to be buried."

"Or thrown into the Elbe as food for eels."

"But as the crabs would soon join the eels, our inmates would very soon appear on our tables, and you wouldn't like that," observed Dr. Koldeway, by way of enticing his girls on to slippery ice. And indeed it was promptly clear that he knew them well—little social savages, he used to describe them to Annette.

"Really, Papa, you don't want us to be sick on the spot, do you?"

And Frau Dr. Neumeier, the energetic furrow still prominent between her brows, even when she was amusing herself with such innocent speculations as this, supported the girls, pointing out that human flesh was only permitted to be eaten for religious purposes, even among cannibals, but that otherwise it very properly arouses invincible disgust.

"Long pig, the South Sea islanders called it, while they were allowed to eat it and combine piety with *gourmandize.*"

And Annette, to switch the conversation round, interjected: "Isn't *gourmandize* wrong—oughtn't we speak of them as *gourmets?*"

In the meantime the cheese stage had been reached, followed by bitter chocolate and sweet *Mokka*. But the absence of a telephone message still troubled the background of her mind.

Then they all went into the garden to join the two gentlemen, whose white collars could be seen glimmering from the foot of the steps. Thyra and Inge, hurried after them, clattering neatly down the steps with lightness of youth, despite the high heels of their dancing shoes. They caught up with their father while he was still on the terrace, flung their arms round him and kissed him good-bye. Herr Koldewey felt the dance fervour thrilling in the two young bodies, as they pressed against his creaking shirt-front. As he held in each hand one of the outstretched bare arms, he said:

"What sort of dance is it likely to be, now that jazz is forbidden?"

"There's foxtrots and slow foxtrots, tangos from Rio, rumbas from Mexico," they cried as they dashed towards a little door in the wall, from outside which came the expected hoot of a motor-horn.

"Don't forget your cloaks, you silly children," cried Annette to the hurrying pair, as she bent over the railings. She would have liked to go with them, for she was very fond of dancing.

The two men were strolling up and down under the mountain-ash and poplars, which with various kinds of bushes completely masked the high wall surrounding Dr. Koldewey's red-tiled official residence: and winding paths led across the lawns from the snow-ball bushes to a bank of long since faded jasmine. The smoke of their cigars kept off the mosquitoes, offspring of departing summer, which still flitted about pursued by bats; but in any event they were now too weak for their stings to penetrate human skin.

"Is it a fact that the former Chairman of the Stock Exchange, Kley, has been given the hint to emigrate?"

"Obstinate old Hebrew," rejoined Herr Footh, with a shrug of his shoulders.

"But without his donations the University of Hamburg would not have developed so quickly into a centre of biological research. And now his son isn't allowed to stay as a private tutor."

"Well, he might be worse off," observed Herr Footh. "And what sort of acknowledgment this fellow Kley—by the way, isn't the family name really Alkaley?—will be expected to make before he's allowed to pass the frontier, we need not now enquire."

"Yes," said Herr Koldewey. "It was the young one who wrote that elaborate thesis on the growth of cancer cells from normal tissues. He used to dance with Thyra at Frau Röthlich's place. Well, I must try to see the old boy again before he goes."

"He ought to have forbidden his eldest son to revive the old name, and join the Spanish War on the side of the bandit Government in Madrid and Barcelona. All these fools didn't know that anyone who takes up with that stale old rubbish called Democracy is backing the wrong horse and bound to lose the game."

"Isn't it rather too early to generalize?" said Koldewey, cautiously. "In Italy, and here, they certainly collapsed without a fight, so much is true. And our contemporary Frenchmen are indeed behaving very oddly. They contract for aeroplanes and get their money, and then don't deliver them."

"And the noble League of Nations leaves one member, Abyssinia, in the lurch, after having already commended another, China, to the sole care of the Almighty," observed Herr Footh, with a booming laugh. "And what about Great Britain, content to look on while her merchant ships are sunk in Spanish waters, and heavy batteries installed round Gibraltar. Could you ever have conceived it possible? No, Herr Doctor, Democracy is as dead as mutton. And what's to be done with it, is a matter on which we should enquire of our Annette. It's a kitchen problem, solely."

Herr Koldewey, who seemed rather upset by Herr Footh's familiar reference to 'our Annette', gazed up at the stars gleaming dimly through the night-haze. But, after all, hadn't Herr Footh the right to speak so? Wasn't he at all times ready to enter the family as a respected son-in-law? He who wants to eat a chicken oughtn't to shrink from killing and plucking it.

"What has happened about your telephone call, Herr Footh," he asked after a pause, by way of slightly embarrassing his guest.

"I can't imagine," replied Herr Footh. "It ought to have come through long ago. I suppose you've told your office to put it through?"

"God bless my soul!" exclaimed Herr Koldewey, letting his cigar-ash drop on to his black trousers. "I completely forgot."

So saying, he got up from the bench on which they had sat down a few minutes before, to wait for the ladies.

"Don't bother," said Herr Footh, and held him back. "I shouldn't be surprised if Annette hadn't seen to that. She is so sensible, and thinks of most things."

"We'll have a glass of cognac in the house later on," said Herr Koldewey, sitting down again in prompt acquiescence.

"Anyway," said Herr Footh, leaning back and resting his patent-shoed foot on his left knee: "Anyway, we now know why the four forgotten men are to be disposed of so urgently. The Führer is angry with Hamburg. The Lower Elbe suspension bridge is held up for some reason; and he doesn't give a damn for the geologists' report. In his view, it's the workmen who won't do the job. Their bathing beach at Finkenwärder means more to them than the expressed wish of Adolf Hitler, Artist and Leader. A suspension bridge, like the one over the Golden Gate, as a symbol of the Strength and Glory of the new German Reich. But that sort of thing doesn't appeal to our lads. It's all one to them if visitors from all over the world have to duck their heads a bit when they go under a bridge. They think only of themselves. So they're going to get a sharp reminder. Here are these four brethren of theirs, even though Labour Front men can't be regarded in the same light as these. But proletarians stick together. It will give them occupation for six months, and bring them to reason, if heads fall here in Fuhlsbüttel. Adolf Hitler—he knows them."

Dr. Koldewey noted the suppressed rage with which Herr Footh expressed himself.

"But surely, my dear sir, you must agree that the geologists' opinions count for something? The estuary of our old Eridanus has been slime and clay since the dawn of history. A lung of the sea was what Pythias of Marseilles called it, when he discovered it for the ancient world four hundred years before Christ. In those days, so the historians say, there were huge deposits of amber here, just as good as the Baltic stuff. But without a foundation of rock the Elbe bridge can scarcely be transformed from a beautiful drawing into a reality, in spite of cast steel and rivets, and all the efforts of Blohm and Voss."

"There's concrete," rejoined Herr Footh, "which can be sunk in blocks. The Third Reich can deal even with weak foundations."

"In politics, certainly," agreed Herr Koldewey. "We have seen that for ourselves. And here comes Annette. Slow but sure, eh?"

And indeed Annette was running across the lawn, with a silver shawl over her shoulders.

"It's Papa's fault," she cried. "Your man did ring up. Isn't that splendid? Aren't you glad?" So saying she laid a hand on her father's shoulder, and the other she reached out to Herr Footh; and she looked entrancingly attractive in her happy excitement. "And now let us go indoors. The Frau Doctor is waiting for her glass of cognac. The wireless is playing the most delicious tangos—you must both dance with me."


They had seen their guests off, Herr Footh having offered to drive Frau Dr. Neumeier back into town, and were walking slowly up the steps. The moon was shining through the eastern window, and the house and garden lay still and silent.

"Can you spare me a few minutes?" asked Herr Koldewey.

"Always," said Annette.

He led the way up to the top storey, took a key off a hook, and opened the door which led into the attic. It smelt of warm timber, and long-enclosed air. In the summer it was little used: it was stacked with all sorts of lumber, trunks, and ladders propped against the walls. The slope of the roof lent a sort of tent-like appearance to the long room. Herr Koldewey opened the round window, rather like a port-hole on a ship. Through the night-air, as though from the roofs of the buildings outstretched below them, came a cry, a rhythmic shriek, muffled and yet quite distinct, like the howl of a starving wolf caught in a trap.

"That's a baby being born in the Women's prison," observed Herr Koldewey. And Annette, her slanting brows meditatively raised— "It's strange," she said: "how the little creatures mostly choose the night in which to take their first look at the world. At least, that's what Käte once told me, and I'm sure I can take her word."

Father and daughter both knew what other meaning might be attached to this half-human, half-animal cry, since the day when a concentration camp had been housed in one of the wings of the Central

Prison. But they did not speak of it. Be careful not to let your thoughts dwell on the inevitable, as do the common herd, says Nietzsche somewhere, and that was Herr Koldewey's view. One must learn to look the other way. But races are distinguished by the amount and kind of things that they do not deign to notice.

"It was from here that your mother saw the melancholy spectacle that took place once only in the days of the Empire. Since then our guillotine has been housed in the Museum. In the days of our poor Republic it was not used. Nor is it now," he added after a short pause. "Herr Goering prefers the axe, the pride of the ancient Germans. Between those two facts, many things—lie buried."

"Käte Neumeier has already sent in her name," replied Annette.

"As a doctor it was probably her privilege."

Above the tree-tops, which flickered in the moonlight, father and daughter saw at the end of their field of vision a sharp-angled yard, between the huge wings of the Central Prison. Like most modern establishments of this kind it was built on the plan of a diagonal cross, so that from a central inner hall, like the well of a staircase, a watch could be kept on the long galleries edged with cells.

"If you use my eighteen-power field-glass, you will in a manner of speaking, be present at the scene without needing to hear anything. The impact of the eye, as an organ of observation, is much less vivid than that of the ear, conceived as gradations in the reality-value of our senses, as friend Nietzsche would put it."

So saying, he laid his arm round his daughter's shoulders, and turned her towards the door.

"We'd better shut the window," said Annette. "It might rain to-morrow." Then she switched on the light, peered about her in housewifely fashion, and nodded: "Yes, Frau Brose kept the place clean—scarcely a cobweb, and floor-boards looking as though they had been waxed." She shut the door behind her, and hung the key up in its place, while her father stood beside her. Then she followed him down the staircase, her delicate brows wrinkled, and a puzzled, almost tormented look in her deep-set eyes, as she gazed down on his shoulders. Not another word was spoken until they had reached the study, a small square room, where he lit a cigar, and offered her a small round American cigarette, which she preferred at night.

"And I thought I had done something to please you," she said in a tone almost of lamentation.

"So you have, little one," he replied. "I told you some while ago, surely you haven't forgotten, darling? I regard it as a signal."

"Of what?" she asked.

"That remains to be seen. At present, it's as though a major-domo with his staff came before the curtain and announced that the play was about to begin. What it will be, neither the audience nor the players know. That was the ancient custom."

"You frighten me, Papa."

"Don't say that, darling."

He sat down in the opposite corner of the leather sofa, laid his right leg across his left, looked up at the ceiling, and went on in hesitant tones.

"In these last days I have been thinking a great deal about the course of human life, as you must have noticed. For opportunities such as ours, our friend Nietzsche would probably have given all the meagre earnings that his immortal works brought him in his lifetime. Since the Renascence there have never been the like—not among us. Do you know who Van der Lubbe was?"

"But Papa, every child knows that; the man who set fire to the Reichstag."

"Yes," said Herr Koldewey. "Every child does know that. And it is true that he was found in the Reichstag, and that he shouted and danced for joy. And he said what he was meant to say, like a well-behaved child: and was no doubt very much astonished when matters became serious and his friends had him beheaded. A young man out of work, utterly off the rails, a refugee and reject from a society to which he never had belonged, and abused by those who had picked him up by the wayside. A certain Dr. Bell, if I am not mistaken, got hold of Van der Lubbe, and was killed later on somewhere in Tirol, by Röhm's orders. And Röhm himself is gone—does that surprise you? What about the pair who did set fire to the Reichstag, Ernst and Heines? Both gone. All of which sounds very astonishing, but isn't."

Annette gazed fascinated at her father's face, and unconsciously flicked her cigarette ash into the room, which she never did, and always reproved her sisters for doing.

"Have you become pious, Papa? Do you see the finger of God?"

Herr Koldewey lifted and dropped his long eyelids.

"Piety, my child, faith—in your sense of the word—seem to me an inadequate attempt to cope with the riddles of life, and discover the laws of its structure. For there are such laws. No, my meditations have been setting in another direction. We have among us another such refugee and outcast from Society, another such instrument, who has been, and will be, thrust up and upwards. The fact that he has named himself Führer is part of the farce, or the play, of which, as you know, we are spectators. What it means, I do not know. But look at those curves. One outcast sends another to the scaffold. One helps another to imperial omnipotence. A whole nation falls on its knees, one half under compulsion by the other half, shouts Hallelujah, and enthusiastically renounces the highest happiness within the compass of humanity. What shall be the end of it all? How long will the dance or the play go on? I am no longer young enough to be afraid of what may happen. Such careers usually last for half a generation. And what will come afterwards? What will become of you—the children, I had almost said; and of yourself. I would gladly see you in safety, Annette. And I would gladly help you to reach safety. That is why I look at all these things with some apprehension."

"Good old Koldewey," said Annette; sat herself down affectionately on his knee, and kissed him on the ear. "And I was such a little fool as to be disappointed because you weren't so pleased as I had hoped."

"Pleased!" repeated Herr Koldewey, as he clasped his hands round the girl's body. "Supposing this thing comes upon us too. Supposing, in some way, our help is needed, before the signal is given, and the staff clashes on to the floor. There is very likely some governing principle running through all this. With the execution of the innocent it began, and with the execution of the innocent it may end."

"You regard these men as innocent in spite of the trial and the law?"

"Consider, my child," said Herr Koldewey. "Life isn't made of marzipan-dough; we see its elements more clearly than other people— but in France, too, and Russia, and all over the world, there's living substance being moulded now. What did Abyssinia cost? Who was responsible for non-intervention in the Spanish Civil War? Only a few days ago, a gentleman in San Domingo, by the name of Trusillo, consigned twelve thousand unwelcome immigrants to the sharks. Thus a negro to his fellows. And that sort of thing is always happening somewhere on the earth—among the Asiatics, Indians, Russians or Jews. This time it has spread to us Germans. A hundred thousand people in the concentration camps, a hundred thousand expelled from their homes and bundled over the frontiers into alien lands. No doubt the philosophers may regard it as a profitable transplantation, for which the world from Paraguay to Persia will one day be thankful. We are the pelican of the legend, we feed ourselves on the blood of our own breasts. What will be the effect of it on our way of life? Ask Ernst Barlach if he can give you any answer."

He lifted his long slender hand from Annette's waist and laid it on the head of a peasant woman carved out of a trunk of oak, a primitive Wendish type, a strangely impressive crouching figure in her scarf and shawl. The death of the sculptor in a Mecklenburg hospital had only recently been made known: the Third Reich had let him starve to death as a degenerate.

"What must he have suffered?" whispered Annette.

"As he was a poet, too, I daresay he saw the meaning of it all. Our culture is decaying from within. It still stands as an imposing façade of technique, organization, routine and tradition. But who knows how long it will endure? If the fools bring on a war, the rest of it will soon disintegrate; then the wooden Hindenburg or Adolf will come down with a crash, and after that, when the dust has cleared away, we shall collect the debris and begin again. Such are, and have been, the avocations of men and ants and angels. But if the others get their way, it may last for ten years yet. And I shouldn't like to go through that, you see. For which reason I wonder what that telephone message was which Herr Brose never put through to us. There's trouble coming, my little Annette."

"They can't be innocent, Papa."

"Would you like to read the records of the trial, my dear? Germans fire on Germans. Call it self-defence, civil war, manslaughter, or murder. When civilization is so shaken, as in our case, these distinctions are perhaps too fine. They're a wild lot, these Nazis, who have taken possession of us, just us. The herd within was plainly waiting for the horde; for the exuberant vitality of our luckless Fritz, the victorious type of him, the blond beast. We have them on us now, God knows. And now go to sleep, child. You have to be out early to-morrow."

Annette slipped from his knees, she really felt quite depressed, surprisingly so, after so delightfully successful an evening.

"I wonder where the children are," she said, as she put up her hand and yawned. "And when do you think to stage the tragedy, as you call it?"

"In a fortnight," said he. "To-day is the first of September—on the fifteenth, then. After that, Herr Hitler proposes to honour us Hanseatics with his visit."


H. P. Footh, his car, and his dachshund were all of a picture. Käte Neumeier knew that. She had smiled good-humouredly when Herr Footh had to whistle several times between the house-door and the outer gate before Herr Ebert deigned to join them, with perked-up ears and wagging tail, emerging from the bushes or the main buildings.

"Confound the little brown beetroot," said Herr Footh in a tone of affectionate annoyance. "Always want to get in first, do you? Excuse him, Frau Doctor, he has no manners. He usually waits till he hears the starter."

In the meantime, the good-byes had been said to the Koldeweys; Annette had waved her farewells—indeed her gestures could have been taken to mean many things, and had vanished with her father behind the iron gate.

"How charming Annette always looks," said the Doctor, as she pulled up her coat collar, and crouched down behind the wind-screen. Herr Footh let the car go full out. He drove thunderously up to the City Park, and at first replied only in belated monosyllables. "Do not talk to the driver", was the inscription to be seen all over Europe. This driver was possibly out of temper. He would certainly have preferred to take the charming Annette back to his nest, instead of dropping Dr. Käte on the Wandsbek Chaussée. Why on earth didn't he marry her? Koldewey was a shocking egotist.

Herr Footh, too, was at that moment thinking of his future father-in-law. The man had a few unpleasant qualities, to which he would have to accustom himself; one was that he didn't allow dogs into the house, and wasn't particularly pleased when they nosed about the garden after hedgehogs or mice. However, he ought to have thanked Footh for the fact that Teetjen had telephoned. The provision of an amateur executioner isn't a thing that can be arranged every day. But these high officials took as a matter of course everything that a non-academic person might do for them, kept their noses in the air, and were not at all forthcoming. Yes, and they did just what they liked. Look at this fellow Koldewey, who had the face to display that horrible Russian peasant-woman statue beside his smoking-room sofa, a sort of degraded wooden Hindenburg in female shape. Everyone assumed that he merely did it to shock or amuse his guests. For on the wall behind it hung a beautiful morning landscape of Ruegen by a certain C. D. Friedrich, a painter widely esteemed. Well, it didn't matter whether the old man thanked him or not, Annette did so, and would again prove her gratitude—indeed she would have done so that day, if he had not had to turn up at the Club. It was *Skat* evening, the tenth, twentieth, and the last of every month. Something always came out of these occasions. Information, business, and last but not least, winnings, although he was often told he was lucky in love. Then he had to slow down, they were nearing the City, red and green bulbs began to glitter against the dark sky, towards which he had to steer. This Käte Neumeier was a fine woman, with a good figure and young eyes, who could still make a fellow in his best years very happy. Had she not, by the way, a nephew in the S.A., Bert Boje, draughtsman in a firm of hydraulic engineers, who was keen on Annette? He must preserve that fact in some recess of his brain. Every fact proved useful at the right time. . . . What an excellent thing was this control of traffic, and the city lighting system. Passengers stuck to the pavement . . . though we had to look out for tram-lines.

"Lübeckerstrasse or Wandsbeker Chaussée?" he asked, as they neared the district in which, as he knew, the Doctor lived.

"Wandsbeker 2," she answered. "Just by the corner." He braked the car, he handed her out, she thanked him and said good-bye, and as the street-door closed behind her, and he was just about to start the car, an inspiration came into his mind. This was the street he had driven down that day at twelve o'clock with Teetjen, already sure of his game. Well, but he must not now let the man out of his grasp, he must look after him. After all, it was easy enough to say 'Yes,' and pocket two thousand marks; but some good work would have to be put up in the meantime. All these people were inclined to take things too easy, let themselves go, and believe the good God would stand by them when the moment was at hand. That's where he would be wrong. H. P. Footh had taken this job on, and it would have to be done in first-class fashion. Koldewey didn't worry whether his deputy was any good or not—so much the worse for him. Fortunately, he had shown foresight in the choice of his daughters. And so there could be no slacking on the part of the worthy Albert, who would be kept down to it until the job was done. His training must begin as from next day. And Herr Footh knew how. Carstanjen was taking on supplies of fresh meat, and to-morrow the *Einäuglein* was due from Tampico, and was to put to sea again almost at once for Constanza in the Black Sea. Something was up, the Air Ministry was energetically filling all its underground reservoirs. A butcher should be swinging the axe to stock the cooks' galleys with beef and veal and pork. Albert must be there, to loosen his muscles and joints, and not disgrace his old friend Footh.

He had a note-book in the car, and a pencil; and in the light of the street lamp he wrote, leaning against the warm bonnet of the car: "Ring me up at the office to-day at 10.0. Foot." He would see to the delivery of this message himself. The car would be quicker than the post. Slipped under the shop-door, it would be found early in the morning; the wife didn't look as if she lay abed. Morning hours are hours of gold.

# CHAPTER FOUR

## TRAINING

THE IDEA THAT old comrades of a war know all about each other is often merely a delusion. At least, Albert Teetjen would have good reason to bring that fact up against Herr Footh, had he guessed from the terms of the message the disparaging reflections that had passed through the mind of its author. Early next morning he was kneeling before a cupboard, from which he took out Stine's store of spare linen, carefully piling up the sheets and bedspreads on the floor. Right at the bottom of the great cupboard, having lurked there unseen for some while, lay an object swathed in oilcloth, not unlike a musical instrument so long as it was not removed from its yellowed wrappings. This he did not do, until he had put the linen back in its place, and closed the heavy cupboard without much effort. The musical instrument revealed itself as an axe—an axe with a broad blade and slightly curved edge, which he had seen in use by his father, but which originated with his grandfather, Teetjen the cooper from Winterhude. It was made of the best steel, manufactured in Sheffield, but had not seemed handy enough for his father's daily work, who had, however, held it in high honour. English steel! When that axe was imported, Solingen was not yet Solingen, and Essen was not yet Krupp. And the English enjoyed a monopoly, as they did later of armour-plate. But much had altered in the interval, and German industry, after the inscription "Made in Germany" had so long been a term of contempt, like "Made in Japan" to-day, had made vast progress; and Solingen was entering into brisk competition with Sheffield. None the less, it remained what it was, English manufacture, good and expensive. And Albert, grasping the haft in his left hand, tapped the pale grey blade with the knuckle of his right forefinger; it rang. The faint sound, delicate and clear, delighted his musical ear, and he spent a few minutes making it ring by tapping various objects against it—a key, a kitchen ladle, and the pocket-knife he carried in a leather sheath. It rang far best against the ladle. Grandfather had not been stingy. Then he swung it from the wrist, his elbow, and his shoulder. Indeed he was sadly out of practice. He would certainly need a great deal of training to fit himself for the job, and justify the confidence placed in him.

He put the axe away again, and began to pace up and down the room. Foolish people naturally thought that a master-butcher of to-day did nothing else but cut off heads. The trade had in fact developed and split into various branches, like every other. He, Albert Teetjen, had for a long while had nothing to do with killing animals. The Union of Slaughterers, and the staff of the Central Slaughter-house managed all that side of the business. Of course as assistant and apprentice to his father he had learned every detail of the profession: he had strapped the masks on to the steers, cocked and handed to the assistants the long-barrelled pistols which shoot a steel bolt into their victims' brains; then, too, he had learned the trade of the butcher proper: how to slit the animal's throat, drain it of blood, skin and eviscerate it, and cut it up. Well, that was long ago, a quarter of a century ago. The axe was used in these days merely to cut up the dead body, cleave marrow-bones, and sever the larger limbs. In his father's day, half a calf or a pig would be hung lengthwise from the hooks, adorning the walls of the shop as near as possible to the door, to tempt the housewives inside. Hence the many stories, highly awe-inspiring to children, and to the son of the master-butcher, lord of life and death, spun by cooks to the young visitors to the kitchen, hair-raising to hear and the cause of much amusement among those who knew: stories of little boys and little girls who fell into the sausage-machine or were metamorphosed into salted pork.

It was just as well to pay due heed to a man who thus wielded axe and knife. In such circumstances it was a matter of ease for the son to take over his father's business. Stepping into the paternal footprints, he would have nothing to do with ill-conditioned persons who neglected to behave with due accommodation and politeness, or broke their undertakings. Grandfather's axe should receive its meed of honour.

As he paced with long strides up and down the shop and living-room, waiting until it was time to ring up Footh, he saw in memory's vision his father presiding behind the counter, dissecting joints, veal cutlets, and legs of mutton, with deft strokes of the axe. Yes, he had been a virtuoso on such apparently clumsy implements as axe and block. There was no one better than Butcher Teetjen at extracting a calf's brain from the skull without damaging the thin containing membrane. And what an artist he was with knives! He loved them, too, kept them impeccably sharp and clean, and boxed the ears of his son and the apprentices, and spoke pretty sharply to mother, if they weren't treated with proper care. The fact that a butcher's knife was not a kitchen-knife, to be used to cut wood and paper, had led to many an explosion until mother at last understood and gave way. True, she came of an obstinate family. She had been the daughter of a shepherd and bee-keeper at

Buxtehude, Anna Posthorn, then she had gone as waitress and laundry-maid to the 'Jug' at Winterhude, and finally married Philipp Teetjen. With her came song into the butcher's shop—for a post-horn must surely be sounded, she often laughed—and a passion for washing. He would never forget that constant fetching of water, and emptying of buckets into the copper. Indeed the child of four and five had greatly overstrained his strength in trying to do his bit and help his mother. When the blood-stained smocks and aprons disappeared into the cauldrons, and then after due boiling were taken out to be rubbed and squeezed and rinsed, and then, snow-white and heavy with moisture, spread on the grass to bleach, his mother, a crown of fair hair above her clear deep eyes, had taught her little son that after blood comes bleaching, and after guilt atonement. And grandmother Posthorn was equally alive still in Albert's mind, when she came on a visit, or later on came to stay with her son-in-law to help her daughter in her manifold avocations as housewife, butcher's wife, and mother of three children. Grandmother Posthorn used to say in her soft, clear Schleswig dialect, her snow-white hair neatly parted over her brown, wrinkled face, when Albert, Theodore, or little Anna were disobedient, had to be punished, and then would not say they were sorry: "You mustn't be more obstinate than the murderers in prison, who take their punishment like men. They insist on it, indeed. Better lose your head in honour, than be chased away unpunished, like gypsies." Yes, she had no love for gypsies and Jews, had grandmother. A roving crew, who could neither sow nor settle. Yes, washing was a fine occupation, and so was killing pigs. Though you had to stop your ears, the beasts squealed so when you started in to stick them.

He grinned, filled a morning pipe, laid the axe ready to hand on the chest of drawers, and went out to sell the Petersens' maid a mixture of beef and pork, which could be eaten raw as *Beef-steak Tartare*, and also fried into German Beef-steak or Mock-ham; and to the widow Paradeis from across the way, half a pound of the best liver, and some split bones for soup. Then, as Stine had not come back, he got ready to go out and telephone from Lehmke's. In earlier days, shop-keepers could scarcely have allowed themselves to be absent from business in the morning. But those were earlier days, when Hamburg was still the gateway of a vast export and import trade, and the Republic put borrowed money into the pockets of the people. . . . He sighed, spat into the rinsing-bowl, and broke off his meditations. At that time, between ten and eleven, all his women customers had thronged into his bright, gaily-tiled shop, deposited their market baskets or string-bags on the counter, taken a cut of red roasting beef, pale pork or white bacon, wrapped in clean grease-paper, paid for it in good silver money, to the accompaniment of a little gossip, and a new joke or so, while all the time assuring him that they hadn't a minute to spare. And now, how hard they were to please, and how few of them there were. . . .

From a drawer in the counter he took out a placard, with a red border and yellowed by exposure to the sun, inscribed: "Back in ten minutes." This, hung against the door from inside, often induced casual customers to wait, or to do another errand in the meantime. He used to hang it outside against the shop window, but the infernal children used to mess it about, and scribble over it: "Yes, I don't think", and so on. So that he was forced to hang it inside from an india-rubber cap. It wasn't so nice, but he couldn't help that. He walked up to the window and laid his forehead and nose against it. The street belonged to the children—at least, such an unfrequented street as the Wagnerstrasse did so. They played ball there, or tops, or hoops, according to the season of the year; they had chosen the spot just outside his shop to chalk the broad paving-stones into a rhythmic succession of sections, the game being to hop from one into the next, calling them Heaven and Hell; they had chosen the gutter outside his very door in which to fix little dams when it rained, and float their little ships: bits of wood, scraps of straw, and boats made of elaborately folded paper; or played round games and sang their counting songs, getting in the way of the customers as they came in and out. And it was no good cursing them— on the contrary it made matters worse. These customs were subject to unwritten laws, more unalterable than any written ones. This part of the Wagnerstrasse was a childrens' playground—and so it remained. And if Herr Teetjen didn't like it he could move elsewhere. Above all, since the youngest generation had been embodied in the Hitler Youth as Young Folks, they had power at their disposal.

Albert Teetjen, emerging from the shop, closing the door and stepping out, found himself sardonically longing to be a boy again, a boy as he once had been, who played Indians, and made himself a spear and tomahawk out of laths and old boxes. He would perhaps have joined this band, as Chingachgook, the mighty serpent, Chief of the Delawares, with a crown of feathers in his hair, and a scalping-knife in his belt; he would have had his way with them, none could have stood up against him. Instead of merely reading Cooper, Gerstecker, and Karl May, he would have led them about and around, as we used to do in those days, in the Winterhude, before the city of Hamburg had spread so far. Yes, in those days he had at least had Teddy and Anna. But now Anna was married in Oldenburg, and Teddy had not returned from his last voyage as mate on U-36. It was a pity about the lad. But it couldn't be helped. The English were set against the Germans in those days, and they got their way, confound them. In 1914 we had no Führer who will bring us what Tirpitz had promised —world-power for Germany, but without war. He—god-sent, the greatest genius for centuries.

People who go about a great deal on foot allege that the way back is quite different from the way there. It is the lay-out of the environment that makes the difference. Albert Teetjen, who was used to walking, and often made excursions with Stine into the outer suburbs, could have confirmed this observation; but, in regard to the Wagnerstrasse, he made it for the first time. He had indeed traversed the way from the shop to Lehmke's a thousand times, in all lights and seasons and moods. But never had he before emerged from Lehmke's tavern so plunged in meditation, and tramped home, peering round him as he went. What on earth had come over Footh? He had spoken to him as to a paid servant. So many heads of cattle and pork had arrived at the cattle-quay, to be slaughtered and cut up at once, and taken over to the cold-storage chambers in the oil-quay. He, Albert Teetjen, was to report to the Customs-Inspector at Halle Four, bringing with him the tools he thought he would need. Who would pay him? No one, my dear fellow. This was the necessary training for the grand occasion. What did it all mean? Not a hint of the old geniality in his voice. Nicking off four heads was no great matter. "Well," came the reply, "just so that you won't bring any discredit on me, Teetjen." On whom! On the mighty Herr Footh.

Had the houses hereabouts really always looked so sooty, the tiles so blackened, and the alleys so narrow? Surely it was time that plumber Drohm had his place cleaned up a bit, and renewed his shabby old lamps, and cake-racks, and baking moulds. Hadn't the street urchins adorned Graef the midwife's brass-plate with a crude drawing of a little angel with outstretched wings, by way of indicating that she was respon- sible for many angels. Did the neighbourhood always smell so of cabbages if one didn't walk in the middle of the street, but—as a respect- able man should—on the right-hand pavement. Ah well, Comrade Footh was right, training was necessary, and he must not be surprised. The times were past when he could merely have joined his fellow- professionals who had business at the slaughter-house. As matters stood at present, he—an S.S. man and over forty, would have been greeted with something like an outcry, and done his credit no good. He owed the Cattle-distributing Centre at the Central Purchasing Associa- tion a tidy little sum—indeed but for Footh he would have had to apply to Lehmke or the Storm-leader, and asked him or the Storm Squadron to stand surety for his liability. But that would have got about, and would have done him no good. He would have got a respite, certainly, but would he have done better that way? Certainly, many things had improved in Hitler's Germany. The labourer and working-man enjoyed more respect, and above all, outside Germany, beyond the frontiers, we began to be feared once more. As was right and proper. On the re-occupation of the Rhineland last March, the French had not dared to lift a finger. And indeed it had come out later on, after the triumphant victory at the plebiscite, that the generals had opposed the move, and the Staffs had already received their orders to retreat. Our Adolf— the man from the people. When he appeared bareheaded and in his modest overcoat among all those captains of industry, and notabilities, and all the glittering uniforms, orders, and marks of rank, to go over a new dock, or made his way under the gigantic cranes at Blohm and Voss, or the Vulkan Works, to inspect one of his many great new warships lying side by side under construction, everyone remarked that he was a man like yourself. He understands you, he shares your troubles, he thinks and toils for you and for your children's sake. Stine had as yet borne no children, she had had one miscarriage after another. Dr. Neumeier had to put him off with promises. And indeed it was just as well that they were alone. So long as the watchword held good: "Guns instead of butter"; so long as meals were limited to one course, and rich dishes were banned, many such desires must be foregone. To be perfectly honest, this particular sacrifice did not bear upon him very heavily. Others must take their own ways. Yes, indeed. . . . There had once been an unalterable programme established: the trusts were to disappear in favour of the small man, small holdings were to be arranged, and the great estates broken up. How they had discussed all these things! Now he no longer went to those debates. He could abuse the Jews well enough in his own home. And the Hamburg Jews—they didn't amount to much these days. Everything had been transferred into Aryan hands. But had things improved at all on that account, had life become at all easier? His Stine, who had been a servant for so many years in the house of Plaut the chemist and taken no harm from it, had always pulled him up when he launched out against the Jews. Oh, stop it, she used to say. The Jews are best let alone. God has kept that sort of thing for Himself, and He can do it much better. Anyone who attacks them meddles with God's handiwork, and has to stand the consequences. "Vengeance is Mine", says the Lord. Was it, in fact, the Jews, who had destroyed his business, or was it re-armament? Had wages been brought down too far? He, Albert Teetjen, an independent Master-butcher, stood in two distinct relations to the workers. When their women came to buy bacon, pork offal, stewing-steak, he was delighted. A well-paid working-class formed the backbone of trade and commerce. But when they combined to exact higher wages, and started this Trades Union racket and the Class War, got their representatives into the Reichstag and organized strikes—then Albert Teetjen banged his fist on the table, and fairly burst into a fury. This was mere insubordination and sedition. They had no natural sense nor loyalty to the Reich. Moscow was always round the corner. This sort of thing must be dealt with—and it would be, by means of the Axe.

By the time he had shut the shop door behind him, all was clear: he must go over to the harbour, dressed up like a slaughterer, and behave like one. He had plainly pledged his freedom for the next few days. He would get the axe ground, but not till later on. For the present it would do if he whetted it. To-day was the first of September. He couldn't leave the shop unattended. The people had received their pay, they would not wait until Sunday, they would want their stewed steak or cutlets on the table to-day. The sooner he changed his clothes, the better. In the meantime Stine, too, returned. There were still a hundred and twenty-three marks in the Post Office Savings Bank account. He would indeed have felt a rope round his throat if he had to write a cheque for the rent of his flat and shop without prospect of the subvention he would earn by his honourable labours on the 15th. Yes—life and death; in the words of the old proverb—"What's an owl to one, is a nightingale to another".

And as he emerged from the door of his shop, the loose threshold
plank creaked under his foot, and an idea came into his mind. He was
above the average height, indeed he always regarded himself as a fine
upstanding man, overtopping the passers-by in the street. This he was
particularly aware of in the doorway, though he did not touch the
upper beam with his carefully brushed head. But:—the haft of the axe
seemed too short, even with his arm outstretched. In Störtebecker's
time criminals had been beheaded with a long sword. But the corpulent
Göring was all for the axe, in accordance with the ancient Saxon and
Frankish usage. Well and good; but no one liked to get bespattered
with blood; and that was scarcely to be avoided with an eighteen-inch
handle. At least another foot would be needed. That would do the
job much more handily, and—moreover—lend greater weight to the
stroke, and give the striker a chance to get out of the way of the spurting
blood. But an eighteen-inch handle weighed less than one a foot longer.
If he went into training now he must get the thing done first, and call
in at Wachsmuth & Co. on his way. Canadian or Russian ash, whatever they had in stock. Hamburg was a strange city where English
tool-steel could be fitted to the appropriate woods from beyond the sea,
the Atlantic or the Baltic. He must fix a new haft to grandfather's axe
before it did its new business: and he was still grinning at the thought,
when the shop-door tinkled as Stine came in.

A green white-spotted dress over a rosy skin, flashing eyes and ruddy
hair make their impression even on a husband, to which it was all so
familiar. The weather had plainly improved, the lowering clouds had
cleared. The sun shone behind Stine through the shop-window. In
the crook of her arm she held a great bunch of violet-coloured asters,
which she bought very cheap off an itinerant barrow belonging to the
Wandsbek municipal gardens. Albert chucked her genially under the
chin.

"Well, old Footh came up to scratch," said he.

"I've had a time, I can tell you," she cried in with girlish gaiety.
"First the old bitch wouldn't open up; she must ask Herr Piepenbrink
to telephone to the Registrar's office. Kept me standing for ten minutes,
though they ought to know that's not good for any woman. There was
an advertisement of the Society for the Prevention of Cruelty to Animals
hung between the windows, but they don't bother about cruelty to
humans. I would have taken a chair, but there was a grey straw hat
on one and a walking-stick on the other. But when she came back, she
was all sugar and smiles. She even cleared a chair for me herself, and
remarked 'Stick and hat, and that's that, but only for one.' 'Well,'
said I, 'Have you gone yellow? Isn't the labourer worthy of his hire?'
The lady laughed: 'You may well say so, since the Party came in. But
we deal in pennies saved.' However, all's well now, and I thought I
would buy you some chrysanthemums."

"They're asters," he corrected her, as he fingered the heavy blossoms,
"and not quite fresh."

"So I said to the gardener, but he insisted they were chrysanthemums, and assured me that if they were put into water at once, they would last a week. Can you cut off the stem-ends while I'm changing my clothes? Just a tap with the chopper."

"I must get along," he rejoined. "I have only been waiting for you. Business for Footh on the cattle-quay and in the slaughter-house."

It was already done. Stine was not surprised. Her man, she was thankful to know, loved all growing things as she did, all that drove its roots into the earth, and from slender stalks and stems so magically produced crowns of leaves and blossoms. And indeed it was little less than magic, that a seed no bigger than a fingernail or a hazelnut or acorn should increase and produce a growth that often outlasted the man who planted it. Strange things went on in the brown earth. . . .

"Oh, dear," said she, "am I to eat my pork and beans and fritters all alone?"

"I've got a job to do, Stine," he said, in a consoling tone, as he slipped into his leather jacket. "From nothing nothing comes."

"Stop a moment," she cried; picked up the hair brush, neatly parted his moustache and brushed up the ends. "I want people to see what sort of fellow has come to work with them. And you'll be back at five. I'll be waiting for you with the coffee."

He nodded, clapped the parcel containing the implement under his arm like a guitar, smacked his lips boyishly, with a sound like a plucked violin string, and stepped out into the street. What a delicious little morsel his Stine still was—such shoulders, and such a neck. No, they were not a bad-looking pair when they went about together. In a fortnight all would be over, and then she should know. How he should tell her, he would not yet contemplate, nor indeed how she would take it. He would wait till the time came. At the moment here he was making his way alone to the electric trams, master of the event. Among the day's news, as he was waiting at Lehmke's for the telephone and turning over the pages of his *Hamburger Fremdenblatt*, he had come upon an announcement that the execution of the four Communists condemned to death had been fixed for the middle of this month. The technical difficulties which had delayed it for so long had now been removed. And as he left the telephone-box, Dörte had switched on the radio which was broadcasting a recorded speech by little Goebbels delivered the day before in the Sports Palace to an audience of God knows how many devoted Nazis. The Party Day month had begun, and the astute Doctor expressed himself as infinitely proud of the progress that had been made in the last few years, thanks to Hitler's genius and prophetic gift, in the extirpation of the Communist world-pestilence. In '33 they could still dare to set fire to the Reichstag; to-day the Komintern snake no longer ventured to show any of its heads where the Swastika banner waved. Perhaps the future party should be called the Party of Unity and Freedom. Albert Teetjen, as he patiently waited searched his memory for a snake with several heads, which had, however, been cut off by some one person—he could not remember by whom. Yonder, anyhow, in Fuhlsbüttel were lurking four such heads, and here came one who would deal with them—one behind whom stood the will of the Führer and of all Germany. In point of fact Stine could be proud that her very Albert had been chosen for the deed—proud as she was of his Iron Cross. It could not indeed be made known just yet— so few were able to get over their ancient prejudices. But later on . . . and here came the tram to carry him into his new career. Up, and away!

# BOOK TWO

# THE REICHSWEHR REMEMBERS

## CHAPTER ONE

### THE NEWS

THE HAMBURGERS ARE a critical race. They enjoy expressing their spleen when past generations can be made responsible for deeds ill done, the consequences of which survive to influence the future. In this way, the failure, in planning the city, to appreciate the Alstertal with its undulating landscape; the offence of establishing prisons on Fuhlsbüttel instead of an artists' colony; and the incapacity to foresee the development of greater Hamburg—all these were themes that brought much applause to speakers in the Municipal Council, the Hamburg Parliament, and even in the Senate. They would proceed to enlarge on the scandals of speculation in real estate—though they were not wholly serious: for it is characteristic of the German to talk very large about his grievances, but to be equally averse to drawing the practical consequences of his remarks. (It was very noteworthy that there had been no more such speeches since a concentration camp had been housed in the Fuhlsbüttel Municipal Prison, although it did not in any way add to the amenities of the neighbourhood.) And so, for three generations past, in the middle of a most attractive landscape, had stood three gigantic buildings each with several wings, surrounded by high red walls, and together with the offices of the administration and services, the quarters for the State officials and the Governor's villa, formed a self-sufficient little town, of most unpleasing architecture, and only made endurable by the interplay of market-gardens, meadows, foliage, and the open sky, with the swiftly-flowing river Alster, hastening southwards into the Elbe, at the point where in ancient days Karl the Great with his Frankish falcon-eyes had recognized the possibilities for a city— Hammaburg. The fact that since the dawn of history Slavonic fishermen, akin to the Wends and the Obotrites, had erected their clay huts in that very spot, does not diminish the achievement of that mighty founder of cities and civilizing genius.

It is the duty of telephone girls to hold their tongues. But it is difficult to conceive how they can contain themselves when, for example, they are friendly with a man who may be immediately concerned by what has passed through their ears. It may, indeed, have been the case that the altered expression with which, on the morning of September 1st, Warder Bilski unlocked the cells in which the four condemned men had been confined for months past, was purely accidental. But no sooner had the announcement appeared in the *Hamburger Tageblatt* that it had at last proved possible to find a deputy for Executioner Denke, who would carry out sentence of death on the four Communist traitors, Friedrich Timme, Albin Merzenich, Willi Schröder and Walter Benjamin Mengers, that the rumour spread like wildfire through all the buildings. News can be tapped through the pipes of the central-heating system and carried almost as effectively as along an electric wire; at exercise, a few random words can be whispered and muttered to convey a meaning, even when speaking is forbidden; and in the office buildings, the kitchens, the common cells, the working parties on the beet fields, and the workshops, there are plenty of opportunities for the prisoners to "pass something on." And there was much wagging of heads over this present business. Hadn't the Nazis started by manufacturing the Reeperbahn case out of a shooting and stabbing affray in St. Pauli, waited years for the witnesses for the prosecution, who had disappeared somewhere in Persia, then kept the trial going until it produced four death sentences, and finally invented the illness of the executioner, to lengthen out the fight that raged behind the scenes, because there were still just judges left in Hamburg? Well, well; they were all living in a perilous jungle world, call it Hamburg or call it Germany. And you, my lad, may well be glad you're in for burglary, incest, or forgery, which can't be worked up by ambitious statesmen into a case of high treason. And now they pretend to have discovered a fellow willing to kill four innocent Comrades. The question to which of the Nazi organizations the fellow belonged provoked a dispute in the carpenter's shop. To the S.A.? Nonsense; an S.A. man wouldn't condescend to any such business. You would have to apply to the Voluntary Labour-Service, or the S.S., my son. The S.A. of to-day are no longer those of '33, you can be sure of that. Besides, every rat's-tail in St. Pauli knew that the Reichswehr was behind it all. They were after Friedrich Timme, and they had meant to get him, ever since '18. Under the Republic, my lad, that sort of thing couldn't be done. But when Hitler had set fire to the Reichstag, that gave the signal. From then on the epauletted gentry could do what they pleased, even to the taking of a general's life, on that 30th June more than three years ago. All sorts of absurd mischances had helped to bring about this state of affairs. However, who really rules in Germany?—tell me that, my dear boy. The answer to this question would have led to open strife had not the warders shouted 'Silence!' Some maintained that the actual masters of the country were the Generals; others, the Banks; the third section voted for Industry; and a fourth, rather diffident body of opinion declared for the National-Socialist German Workers' Party, the Nazis. But they would have been the first to be suppressed: they had the fewest supporters among the convicts employed in the carpenter's shop.

The first person upon whom our news exercised a certain effect, more far-reaching, perhaps, than most of the events in her life, was the prostitute, Lene Prestow, chief witness for the defence, and first victim of the Reeperbahn affair. She lay in the infirmary of the woman's prison, in a room of many beds rather above the ground level, that enabled the patients as they lay in bed to catch a glimpse of green tree-tops, now beginning to turn russet, and of delicately blue sky. The stab in the lung inflicted on her by the seventeen-year-old Anton Brässe at a street corner in St. Pauli, had taken a bad turn and the tubercle-bacillus had attacked the damaged and weakened organ; the doctors knew that she could not survive the first of the five years imprisonment to which she had been sentenced for her offences. (Having had a good deal of rum, and no dinner, she had savagely denounced the homosexual excesses that had become the fashion among the ruling classes under the Nazi régime, with the result that she and her sisters were subjected to unfair competition from members of the Hitler Youth such as Anton Brässe— though they paid taxes and served society, just like soldiers, with their bodies: except that soldiers did so with their heads, and she and her colleagues, with other parts of their persons.)

This same Lene Prestow, a pale-eyed, freckled, blonde, with an unattractive little snub nose in an otherwise haggard face, slowly lifted her heavy eyelids, as the female warder reported this new turn of the machinery, to which she had herself already fallen a victim. Young Dr. Laberdan who, since Dr. Israelski's departure, had looked after the health of the three non-political establishments, which lay side by side in Fuhlsbüttel, the women's prison, the men's prison, and the convict prison, this youthful and exuberant Nazi doctor had diagnosed Lene Prestow's disquieting symptoms accompanied by a high fever as "apathy." In those few minutes Lene Prestow became once more the girl Helene Prestow who had just left school, daughter and eldest child of Ferdinand Prestow, the mechanic, called up for the *Landwehr*; who had had to toil to help her mother through the starvation winter of 1917-18, and get themselves and the two children through it. Her father had been christened Ferdinand by his parents in honour of Lassalle who had founded the German Workers Union, and helped the German proletariat to organize. Yes, Lene Prestow came from an environment inimical to the State, as the State Prosecutor had observed: and when her father had come back from the war, in the spring of 1918, with about half a left hand, and was out of work and remained out of work, Lene, with her pretty face and light-hearted temperament had made many men friends. Twice she might have married, it was said.

When she heard that the heads of the four were to fall on the fifteenth of the month—Sister Adelheid realized that she had said too much and bit her lower lip; for the date in question was only known in official circles and had not appeared in the paper—she gazed at the ceiling, blinked at the gleaming white clouds sailing across the airport, and said "Freddy Timme! And that smart lad Mengers. Well, I'll be up above first and announce them to old St. Peter. I want to see my father, Sister Adelheid. Please put in an application for me . . . Freddy Timme!

They'd have liked to make him into a Horst Wessel, wouldn't they? But that wouldn't work. He was a pal, and a fine fellow. And so the fun's over now; do you think they'll allow it, Sister?"

And then she drifted away again, and left all the rest to Sister Adelheid.

When Dr. Laberdan was asked by the chief inspector how matters stood with the Prestow, as she had asked to speak to her father once more, he growled out: "Spitting blood, can't last long." It had indeed been of no service to test, as he had done soon after taking over the post, all the rooms of the infirmary with a divining-rod, so as to arrange the beds as favourably as possibe. It was his professional duty as a doctor to withdraw them from the malignant rays emanating from sub-teranean water-courses, the existence of which he had suspected since being transferred here. Moreover, the prospect of a four-fold execution filled him with disquiet—he hadn't the least idea what attitude to adopt to it. Should he display the Party spirit, and be present, or take the leave that was in fact due to him this August? On the Lake of Garda, or the Mendel—above the cloud-level one could lie out in the sun in October, and even in November.

There were people who died in the early morning, at the end of sleep and of the night, in order to escape awakening once and for always. And others, who were troubled by death because they had to leave behind them some earthly matter unresolved, some charge to near relations or intimate friends. So, on the following morning, or the following noon, to be more exact, sat the one-time foreman and engine-room mechanic, Ferdinand Prestow, at the bedside of his Lene, a man of five-and-fifty; he had been taken on again by Blohm and Voss to manage a crane, for which in general only the right hand is needed. His short grey beard gave him a respectable air, and his carefully shaven cheeks and a neat suit did the rest. But when he looked at his daughter, lying so helpless in her bed, sharp lines running from her nostrils to her mouth, the tears welled up in his eyes.

"Lene," said he softly. "My little darling."

Her hand almost disappeared in the gnarled fist, so frail had it become.

"Yes, Father," she said, speaking in the Hamburg dialect, commonly known as Missingish or Messingish; "your Lene won't dance on your seventieth birthday. You might keep an eye on Anton Brässe, who did me in."

"That's the fellow," replied her father, as he wiped his eyes with a red-edged handkerchiet, "who took his oath he did it in self-defence, isn't it? The one who acted the smart Corporal of the Forty-Seventh at the main trial, and then when he was discharged to the Reserve, got a job at our place in the Steel Foundry? He's dead. Fell off a crane one night in June during the black-out practice, and broke his skull. So I can't do anything about him, can I?"

A faint smile lit up Lene's mouth and eyes. "That's good," said she. "Now St. Peter knows I'm coming. Father, are you still being nice to Mother, and bringing back the pay-envelope unopened? Ah well, a bit of a drink now and again don't matter much. But you must stand up straight on your legs when the time comes to trample on the Hitler rag and hoist the Hammer and Sickle."

"You shouldn't be talking so much, dear," said her father, one of those fundamentally gentle characters who had been attracted to Socialism by the principle of mutual aid, and clung to it. But she shook her head, and shrugged her shoulders impatiently. "You go and see Patroness Neumeier, Father—the inspector will have her address. Tell her that your Lene stuck to everything she said until she died. They wouldn't let me take the oath, but that's better than an oath. There," she said, and stretched herself, "that's the truth. Someone must know it and pass it on. The truth isn't a doormat, as Goebbels and his crew want to make it. And they'll find that out one day. The truth will bring them down. I always thought I should be there. A spot of truth is stronger than any Party boss. Yes, we had no Lenin. Give my registration book to Walter Mengers as a keepsake—tell him to put it by and show it to his grandchildren one day, so they'll know what went on in Hamburg at that time." (The dying woman had quite forgotten that the young man would not survive her by more than a fortnight.) "And a kiss to Mother and the girls." From the sitting position to which she had pulled herself up, she bent over her father's hand, but a fit of coughing seized her, and then came a rush of blood: she tore open her night-dress and pressed her fingers against the scar of the knife, and then collapsed forwards, drenching the sheets with blood.

"Sister, sister," cried foreman Prestow in a panic. But Sister Adelheid could not work miracles.

All the public service institutions of Hamburg enjoyed the warm support of the women of that city, a fact which was fully represented in the legislative development of the Hansa Republic. The orphanages, hospitals, and prisons were placed under the supervision of so-called patrons, who provided a closer contact between the real needs of the inmates and the resources at the disposal of the administration. Originally a privilege of the ladies of the patriciate, in the course of the previous century this honourable office had been laid open to the women of the third and even of the fourth estate, and indeed it was those latter, whose time was already so heavily burdened, that did so much excellent work in the service of those handicapped and weak. Käte Neumeier had been one of the patronesses of the women's prison at Fuhlsbüttel before the "Seizure of Power", and was one still. She had always been an energetic person, and towards the end of her studies at Rostock and Kiel, she had left the Union of Free Students and joined the Socialist League of Youth, and after the fall of the Imperial régime she had for the first time voted Social-Democrat; but the election of Marshal Hindenburg as successor to President Ebert she had regarded as disastrous and ill-omened, and from it she had drawn conclusions that must alienate her from her former friends. If the German people loved their army, and looked on the soldiers' profession as providing the proper rulers for the

State, the great organized parties must take account of these tendencies. After all, if the Germans were militaristically inclined, it was illogical not to recognize that fact. In these days a form of Socialism was coming into existence, different from what had been hitherto understood by the term, just as England, Italy and Russia had developed their own types of Socialism. Any attempt at a lasting and permanent social improvement could not ignore the structural principles of the German attitude of mind. Our development led directly towards rearmament. A nation's reputation depended on its war flag. As a Hamburg woman she loved the great ships. When the Social Democrats in the year twenty-nine first voted against a new armoured cruiser, and then soon afterwards approved it, she thought this a foolish performance. At that time the National Socialists were right in their struggle for the majority, and Käte Neumeier went over to them. Since then, a great deal had happened and in herself as well. . . . Every fortnight she visited the prison and her protegées, among whom she took special note of Lene Prestow. She had, in fact, hoped to combine her last August visit with the crab-party at the Koldeweys. But that had proved impossible; a case of fish poisoning in her immediate neighbourhood, which threatened to decimate a whole family, had kept her fully employed at that time and during the succeeding days. And several days had passed before she could include in her time-table the long journey to Fuhlsbüttel. Thus it was that foreman Prestow met her in the office when he came to enquire where he could find his Lene's grave in the Ohlsdorf cemetery, and to fetch the belongings she had brought with her when she had started to serve her sentence: a few jewels, clothes and underclothes, and especially a valuable watch, a present from a sailor who had fought in the Spanish Civil War, and pocketed some loot, on General Franco's side, of course. That Lene Prestow was one of those who would be gathered in the autumn harvest, was quite obvious to Käte Neumeier: she had tried to effect some improvement in the lung by arranging for special diet, mainly of chopped up raw vegetables, such as turnips and carrots, and fruit—particularly apples. She knew quite well that it wouldn't do much good: concentrated juice from these products and a complete prohibition of cooking salt might have achieved something. But, as was frequently pointed out, a prison was not a sanatorium, and thus it was that Käte Neumeier, who had no medical standing in the place, had but succeeded in getting this interesting and vital young woman at least over the winter. It was in this sense that she spoke to the father, from whom Lene had plainly inherited her fine and distinctive character, and probably regarded this interview in the prison office as very unpleasant. But Lene had no cell now, nor even a bed in the infirmary with its barred windows, and it was hardly worth while to go to the visitors' room for so brief an interview. There were, indeed, only two matters to be settled: the first being that Lene had bequeathed her registration book to Mengers, one of the condemned men in the Reeperbahn case: but this was in the possession of the police. However, he should be informed that Lene had wanted to leave him a small memento. The second was a message from Lene to the Frau Doctor—that she stood by every point of her statement, even on her deathbed, just as though she had made it under oath. These matters disposed of, there was nothing more for him to do there, and he took his leave, after thanking her for all her kindness to Lene. But after all, they belonged to different camps, and it was not right that his Lene should have been punished so much beyond what she had done. So saying, he put his cap on his shaggy grey head, pocketed a note of the lay-out of the Ohlsdorf Cemetery, hitched his parcel under his right arm, cast a meaning glance round the bureaucratic room, exclaimed "Heil Hitler", and disappeared. Käte Neumeier, during the course of these formalities, stood for a few minutes pondering on Herr Prestow, who had once been Comrade Prestow, but was not a Party Comrade, struck by the reference to the Reeperbahn case, and searched her memory for the statement of which the truth had been so gravely called in question, but which Lene affirmed on her very deathbed. All that lay so far back. The excitement, interest and significance of the affair had long since faded—only someone who had been intimately concerned in an event could think that what she then had said must still be remembered. When she had finished her round, which she that day performed more superficially than usual, she asked to be put through on the telephone to Annette Koldewey and her father. Annette was paying a call in the town, but Herr Koldewey would be delighted to offer Frau Doctor Neumeier a cup of tea and to answer her questions. So she went across. It was about six o'clock, and the falling dusk had drawn a light mist over the tree-tops and the expanse of sky.

A tea-trolley constructed of glass, brass and ebony beside the study sofa, struck a slightly exotic but not displeasing note. Herr Koldewey, rather tired by the change in the weather and the day's work, now three parts over, was enjoying the golden beverage, gathered on the estates of the great Chinese importer, Mathieson, and sold by the pound to his customers. He was, moreover, refreshed by the visit of Annette's friend, whom he liked best of all her circle. And he wanted to talk to her about his daughter. Indeed?—was Lene Prestow dead? Ah, yes; he had noted it in the report. What was the statement she had made, by way of exculpating Timme and the rest? He could not now remember. But it would not be difficult to trace it. He had a memorandum on the whole case, drawn up by the judicial authorities in Altona, for the information of the Senate, and clearly by a capable hand. She could borrow it, if it would be any use to her: it was not a confidential document, but had better not be left lying about in her waiting-room, but as a responsible private person she could certainly keep it for a few days. So saying he opened the lower doors of the bookcase, and took out of a broad, flat drawer, obviously intended for maps and atlases, a number of documents carefully filed in folders, and labelled with a summary of the contents. "Reeperbahn Case", he read out; "1934 to 1937"; turned over the typewritten pages clipped together in the cover, and smiled to himself as he slipped it into a large folded envelope: "I had two annexes put in with it, which make it all the more serious to let such a document out of one's hands. The Gestapo won't do anything to me if they find it in my possession—indeed I myself am, in a manner of speaking, the Gestapo. But I mustn't be caught lending it. So I herewith deliver myself into your hands. What says Goebbels? Let us live dangerously."

Käte Neumeier burst out laughing: it sounded so ridiculous for a man of Koldewey's calibre to be quoting Goebbels, who could scarcely be regarded as an intellectual light.

"I'll return it to you the day after to-morrow. I hope I shall catch Annette, as I missed her to-day. Please ask her to telephone and pick me up if she can. It's almost a day's journey by the old elevated railway. Well, this time I've got something to read."

It often happens that people make their way into a new epoch of their whole existence when they believe themselves to be merely returning home. Käte Neumeier sat in the middle of an empty compartment beneath the light and plunged into the Reeperbahn case; and it gradually came over her that she was losing herself in her own past, and drifting back into the last decade, a part of her life that had long since been done with, put away and buried. She had almost forgotten to change at Eppendorf; and when she finally got out, she did not, as usual, hurry along the familiar streets with her energetic strides, she hailed a taxi, so that she could resume her reading as soon as possible. Friedrich Timme! The phrase—Reeperbahn Case—served, in the newspapers, to cover up all the facts that revealed living people, and life as it was really lived. In the year '34, when all this began, she had indeed been in a turmoil of her own, madly in love with the man of her life, and thus more inclined to forget than to remember, to live in the present rather than in any kind of past. Yes, she had lived an intense and vehement life in those days; she had seen disillusion and despair come upon her, when Karl August left Hamburg and got himself posted to Buenos Aires, in the wake of a pretty young South American secretary; she had plunged for consolation into work, and taken but a fleeting interest in the affairs of the day. Reeperbahn Case? Why, of course—the Reeperbahn was the main thoroughfare in St. Pauli. It ran parallel to the landing-piers, and then on to Altona. It was frequented by prostitutes and sailors, populous with night-houses, and was the scene of much brawling and disorder—nothing unusual in Hamburg. There were such districts in every great city, to which the police patrols paid particular attention. In the summer of '34, round about June 30th, high treason was in the air, another upheaval in the form of an attack by the S.A. against the Money-power and the Aristocracy. The searchlights of the world were then directed upon Munich, where the Führer himself re-established order, as it was called. Moreover, the *Reichswehr* had also come into view in those days, embodied in a certain Major Walter Buch, whom she, Käte Neumeier, thought she remembered from her student days in that city. But the world's gaze was also directed towards Berlin— what went on in Hamburg was scarcely noticed. And that she now sat in her study by a lamp carefully adjusted to spare her eyes, with both elbows on the table and both hands buried in her hair, and read. And yet she would not have rightly viewed or understood the course of events, if the astute Herr Koldewey had not had two annexes clipped in with the Memorandum. An illustrated supplement of the *Hamburger Fremdenblatt* reproducing two photographs which had already appeared in its issue of November, 1918, and an article on yellowish paper printed in Latin type, and clearly cut out of an *Emigrant's Magazine*, issued in conjunction with a certain Berlin weekly which Käte Neumeier had read regularly in the days of the "System," and to which indeed she had subscribed. Later on she had cancelled her subscription and given the bound volumes away. At last she went to bed, and switched off the light. But she lay long awake, pondering and sorting out what she had read, digesting it and clarifying it, as though it had been a demonstration in physics, or a difficult medical case.

It began with an abusive outburst by Lene Prestow, who had been drunk, against highly-placed S.A. leaders, and the young men reputed to be their favourites. But in that district, and in those haunts, there had always been clashes and brawls between members of the old Republican Schutzbund with the supporters of the Nationalists. In those days the German people, distracted by unemployment, inflation, and profiteering by the Trusts, lived on the very verge of civil war, a fact which was violently demonstrated on that very night. Both parties summoned reinforcements, shots were fired, and some persons fell. When the police patrols had broken up the rabble of brawlers by the aid of clubs and rubber truncheons, and arrested them, the officers swore that the mechanic, Friedrich Timme, had been seen with a weapon in his hand, and two of the Nazis maintained that he had shot their friends. The statement of the bookseller's assistant, Mengers, who had blood on his hands, that he had merely pulled one of the injured men out of the way in order to bandage his wounds, was not believed. The docker, Merzenich, and the mechanic, Willi Schröder, were denounced by others as having used a club and a revolver. All of them had, up to the year '32, belonged to combatant organizations of the Left—the *Reichsbanner* (Black-Red-Gold) and the Communist Red Front. Several others unknown had no doubt taken to their heels, as it was between eleven and twelve o'clock at night and they knew the neighbourhood well. Seven wounded persons were taken to the hospital, and three corpses to the mortuary. Thus had it begun. Merzenich, Schröder, Mengers, and Timme remained in custody.

Nor did they ever regain their freedom. After the preliminary interrogations, the authorities issued warrants against them and transferred them to the great modern penal establishment on the Holsten glacis, to await their trial. It was very soon made clear that they would in due course be indicted for activities endangering the State, and for plotting high treason. Their membership of the Republican Defence troops now proved very damaging, and indeed paralysed the efforts of their counsel, who had been chosen by the families of the accused men from among the old-established legal circles of the city, men of various views—Left, German-National, or Conservative—but all possessed of courage and ready to do their best, even for Communists. An orderly administration of justice was the pride of Hamburg, and a centuries'-old

tradition stiffened their backbone. They took every advantage of the fact
that after the first few months the two chief witnesses for the prosecution
were not to be discovered. It was said that they had gone abroad,
which, in a seaport like Hamburg, was not surprising, except that the
men in question, Piessling and Brandt, had disappeared for longer
than two years; proceedings were nevertheless not revoked. . . . .
There must, however, have been quarters in which something was
known of the two men's whereabouts, and where news was received
of them from time to time—quarters where influence enough prevailed to affect the course of events. In the extract from the above-
mentioned Foreign Supplement it was clearly stated that the pair were
actively engaged in the employment of the N.S.D.A.P. in the Middle
East, as agents for stirring up unrest among the Arabs in Syria and
Palestine by the lavish distribution of money, and indeed had extended
their activities to the Bedouins of the Desert and the Persians of Iran;
it was therefore clear that they could not be summoned home for a
tiresome little case of this kind. They did, in the end, get back for the
main trial. But that, too, went on long enough. In it were at stake the
lives of four young men, who defended themselves vigorously against
the charge of having plotted to overthrow the new form of State Government in Hamburg, and insisted that they had merely fired in self-defence
and with the weapons they had seized from the Nazis. But that did not
help them; anyone suspected of Communist leanings, or who had to
admit that he had formerly belonged to organizations of the K.P.D.,
had thereby committed a crime for which, in the Third Reich, there
was only one penalty.

Friedrich Timme—in those days he was called Friedel. Käte herself
was still a young thing, who had just outgrown the *Wandervogel*; they
had got to know each other on excursions into the country, only to
engage in the most violent disputes. Both were firmly based on the
Social Democratic outlook, he, as a lad—inclined to the proletariat of
the Left; Käte, coming from a more solid social status, was more disposed to the Right elements in the Party. His handsome rebellious lips
had been laid on hers, and his arms had embraced her, but only in
dance. Then, at the age of barely seventeen, he had gone to the War,
against the Tsars, the Russian slave régime. When she saw him again
at the end of 1918, he had won a passing fame as ringleader of those
military revolts which took place even in Hamburg on that tenth of
November.

Corporal Timme, revolver in hand, had compelled the bewildered
officers to pay proper heed to the Soldier's Councils which the authorities
had then ordered to be established, to allow the regimental accounts
to be audited, and to assign him a place at the office table opposite the
adjutant as representative of the rank and file, and hasten the return
from the front. Moreover, during the time when the army was being
demobilized, he had represented the other ranks in combined meetings
with the Hamburg Workers' Councils, and supervised the distribution
of good new outfits, boots, and great-coats to men on their discharge;
and he had been a supporter of Karl Liebknecht, whom he had visited

E

in Berlin at the expense of the regiment, to invite him to Hamburg. If only he had come at that time, and stayed in Hamburg. The murder patrols from the Eden Hotel would never have been able to lay hands on him and Rosa Luxemburg. Thus had he sworn at a meeting with Comrade Käte, he at that time on the way to the Spartakus League and the Communist Party, while she was of opinion that Friedrich Ebert's way was the right one, and indeed the only way open to a beaten Germany. "Well, good-bye then, Käte," he had said. "It's a pity—you're a grand girl. You will never understand the proletariat; one day you will discover where all this is leading you." Well, it had led her to Karl August Lintze, who was then studying for the Consular Service in the Overseas Institute of Hamburg University, with a view to a post in that land of promise, South America; and in those days his framed photograph stood on her night-table, a face with bright, compelling eyes, and rather too compressed lips. Now it reposed in a drawer. He had carried her away with his enthusiasm for everything German, his pride in the country's history, the Nordic race, its contribution to world culture. They had shared a profound admiration for the *Ura-Linda Chronicle*, and refused to consider the suggestion that it might be a forgery. "That is just pitiable jealousy on the part of our Jewish fellow-citizens," K. A. had said contemptuously; and he had taken occasion to observe of Friedel Timme that it was only by accident and quite unjustly that he had escaped the firing-squad. Well, his eldest brother, Otto Lintze, had done good service as Senior Lieutenant and Intelligence Officer in the 76th, the Hanseatic Infantry regiment, taken over by the Reichswehr; while his sister, Paula, who ought really to have been called Ingeborg or Thusnelda, had married the State Prosecutor, Russendorf. Proud of their kind, nationally self-conscious, deeply patriotic; the Aryan in very essence.

Next morning she awoke later than usual, with a shock at the heart, and a strange sensation of obsession by a dream, a vision that had risen before her with the particularity of an old Dutch picture. She saw all its figures with extraordinary clarity, brightly coloured, sharply defined little forms, and among them herself. But it was the funeral of Lene Prestow in the Ohlsdorf cemetery which she had thus dreamed, against a white background as though snow were covering the landscape. Inmates of the three prisons, in a procession four abreast, followed the coffin, which was carried by—the four occupants of the condemned cells. They would not be deprived of their right to form a ceremonial escort to the final resting-place of one who had fallen in the class war, and they marched along with averted faces in their dun-coloured jackets and shapeless trousers, fettered by their hands and feet. To the right and left of each file marched a warder with rifle at the ready, while immediately behind the coffin walked the Prestow family. The mother and two sisters had adorned their hats with black crape, while Herr Prestow played Lene's favourite songs as marches on a concertina. *Annchen von Tharau* and *The Lindenbaum*. Of course, said the dreamer to herself in her dream, no one could play *The International*; that was a song to be sung with heads up and level eyes. It was immediately obvious that all these marching people were possessed by a subversive thought, which (in her dream) seemed to pour out of their heads in a sort of schoolboy script: "We are holding on, and in five years it will all be over." Out of the window leaned the lanky form of Dr. Laberdan, with a microscope beside him on the window-ledge, in which he had been investigating the activities of the tubercles in destroying the black, white, and red corpuscles in the Nazi flag. "Koldewey is far too tolerant," he shouted to her. "Red—red, everywhere. *Hyperæmia socialis*, blood-letting is needed, heads must roll." At these words the dead Lene Prestow sat up in her coffin, the lid of which had suddenly sprung open, shook her fists and cried: "Mercy!" while the warders clapped their rifles to their shoulders and halted the procession at a heap of sand beside an open grave. Mercy! This word had awakened Käte Neumeier. There was still time. The condemned men must certainly have put in petitions for a reprieve. She must make sure. Koldewey must know.

As she stood under the shower, sluicing luke-warm and then cold water over her lightly tanned skin, she abandoned her intention to ring up Annette at once; she would try to include a hurried visit to Fuhlsbüttel in her programme for that day. She must be careful not to make herself ridiculous, and must, above all, keep a clear head. Thus meditating, she unthinkingly took off her india-rubber cap, which protected her cropped grey hair, and luxuriated in the sensation of the water rippling over the skin of her head. (She made a mental note to turn on the hot air at breakfast.) What would Annette be thinking, and Herr Koldewey, a man of much intelligence? And what did she, Käte Neumeier, herself think? She soaped herself, scrubbed herself with a loofah, and then rubbed herself dry with the rough bath-towel—the latter in her bedroom, where the polished parquet floor seemed to merge imperceptibly into walls of a similar greenish brown. The tall mirror presented the picture of a muscular woman in her prime, skilfully flicking the last drops of moisture from her person with a face-towel, by a half-open window in the mild September sunshine. Pity that men were so foolish, she thought, and always went in pursuit of crude young creatures. They would be much better off with someone like herself. Who was the Frenchman who had discovered the *femme de trente ans*? Was it Maupassant, or someone earlier? She must ask Koldewey. In any case, it was about time that the *femme de quarante ans* came into her own. Would she find a place in the literature of to-day? Probably not. The contemporary theme was heroism, the larger life, the classically idealized form; though what had hitherto emerged was scarcely up to that mark —prizes of honour bestowed on Lehar and Rudolf Herzog for mere sergeant-major's stuff. Yes, it was a long while since she had lain skin to skin with any man. Throw it in with the rest. If she had been as far forward then as later, or as now, Friedel Timme would never have escaped her. But in those days she had understood so little about herself, or indeed anyone else. She had let herself be put off by her fellow-students who dinned into her ears the pronouncement of the Professor at Vienna, that confounded old Jew, now so bitterly attacked. 'Woman actively seeks a passive sexual aim.' Indeed no one else could have written such a sentence. She really ought to have abjured him after the burning of his works by the students on the Operaplatz. But that was to go too far. The old Hedwigskirche must have been surprised to observe how efficiently these non-Christians conducted an *auto-da-fé*. No, my dear good friends, we had much better leave science to the scientists. And now to ring up Koldewey. Whereupon, having put on straw-slippers, porous underclothes, and a wadded dressing-gown, she went across to her living- and waiting-room, in which the faithful Marie had already laid out coffee, eggs, and fresh Hamburg rolls beside the morning paper and the morning's letters. An air-mail letter with the Argentine post-mark. Thanks to our Zeppelin, which crossed the Atlantic much more reliably than any aeroplane could ever do.

She sat and read and drank her coffee, bit into her roll and read on. The Spanish-speaking lady had indeed proved herself a butterfly, as Käte had summed her up from the beginning; but the letter brimmed with enthusiasm for the skill with which the greatness of the Third Reich and its liberating mission had been presented to the A.B.C. states, despite the emigré Press, which was continually scattering the poison of Paris and Amsterdam, and latterly of Moscow. In South America there was little or no hostility to Adolf Hitler. The main battle for him must be fought in New York, and the ambitious writer of the letter obviously intended to get there one day. Had K. N. kept up her excellent knowledge of English? A strange question; which would formerly have sent the blood coursing through her veins. At the moment the thought of it brought little pleasure to Käte Neumeier. Times had changed. To leave the Third Reich, in which so many able Jewish doctors were no longer allowed to practice, would be folly from a personal point of view, and grossly neglectful of the public need. Now was the moment to telephone. With the newly-arrived letter in her hand, she could quite well ring up Paula Russendorf, and then ask for her husband to come to the telephone. A patroness of Fuhlsbüttel could always produce reasons or pretexts. No. She decided to ask Koldewey to clear the position before proceeding further, by making enquiries of the State Prosecutor. It would be highly injudicious to rush into the foreground. In the Third Reich the motto was: Shoot from under cover—and don't miss.

# CHAPTER TWO

### PETITIONS

WHEN HEINRICH KOLDEWEY's nephew, Manfred, was allowed at eight years to pay his first visit to his uncle at Fuhlsbüttel—not at the villa, but within the walls—he later on confessed his disappointment which did all honour to that bright lad. A prison governor's office had to be situated in an airy glass tower, equipped with steel shafts and electric bells, and providing the occupant of this cage of the four winds with a kind of omnipotence and omniscience, which was essential to him in case of need, as the tamer of such dangerous beasts. "You must regard me as kind of dear Lord, Manfred," Herr Koldewey had said jokingly, and received from the boy—fair-haired, smooth-headed, and with bright clear eyes—an answer that left him open-mouthed and with the long face longer still. "Your Lord is no more than a prison-governor, either. But don't tell Papa." And now, for many months past, this same Manfred had been lying in his grave in the Basque country, fore-runner of those countless young Germans who were not to survive the epoch of Herr Hitler; his boyhood days were effaced, except that Herr Koldewey's office in the side-wing of the prison was still known as the bird-cage. It was in fact a dignified brown-panelled room, whose chief ornament was a larger framed picture representing the sea-battle off Heligoland, where in 1400 the Hamburg fleet defeated Klaus Stoerte-becker and his merry men. These Levellers, as they called themselves, Communists of the Middle Ages, since the Hamburgers were never inclined to any sort of jest on such a point, had to be exterminated root and branch. Once more Herr Koldewey entertained his visitor, Käte Neumeier, with the often repeated anecdote, how at their execution a Senator had sympathetically asked the headsman—who by this time was up to his ankles in blood—whether he was strong enough to finish off the exhausting work. *Och*, the man had answered, he felt quite strong enough to behead the whole honourable Senate if need were. But this light-hearted bit of *lèse majesté* brought the headsman himself to the block. "Which goes to show that one should never fall into familiar colloquy with executioners: it may involve the loss of a head, even that of the executioner himself." Käte Neumeier smiled, refreshed by a cigarette in the comfortable armchair, and waited until Koldewey, the philosopher, should feel disposed to apply himself once more to the present. Yes, he had again got into touch with the State Prosecutor's office. Herr Russendorf, whom Dr. Käte of course knew, was a very unapproachable gentleman even on official business. Petitions for a reprieve had been sent in, though not by all those concerned: they would not be likely to carry much weight. The chief culprits and the ring-leaders, Herr Timme and Herr Mengers too, had not deigned to do so, which would, of course, not be likely to benefit the cause of the two others; in any case, Russendorf had said with a laugh, now that Koldewey had found a deputy for that sad invalid, Herr Denke, he could have four coffins made. In any event, Herr Denke's experienced assistants would be available, and there would be no objection on the part of the State Prosecutor's office to the use of a mask by the amateur. Certainly not! His brother-in-law, Lintze, had already offered to dispose of the tiresome matter by means of a volley from a squad of the 76th. "So you see," Herr Koldewey had said, in a meaning undertone, nodding his long head solemnly, "the gentleman domiciled abroad, whose memorandum I had not inappropriately attached to our file, knew what he was talking about. The only way to achieve anything definite would be through Herr Lintze—or Lieut.-Col. Lintze, as he has in the meantime contrived to become. What was formerly called the Ninth Army Corps now appear as the Tenth Defence Group; but otherwise everything is as it was before. The work of Herr von Seeckt, who was given a State funeral last year."

"I feel inclined to go and see him, if that is so," returned Käte Neumeier impulsively, flicking the ash of her cigarette over the floor; "and I would like to speak to Timme and Mengers first."

"That is easily arranged; but since when, Frau Doctor," said he, lifting the lids from his prominent Hanseatic eyes, "have you been so interested in delinquents?"

Käte Neumeier looked up, and fixed him with calm eyes. "I have been thinking about them a great deal. After all, they are fellow-countrymen, and Timme indeed was an acquaintance of my youth, when we were still handsome, green, and voted Social-Democratic. He was not an ordinary man, Friedel Timme."

"Mengers, the Israelite, is not an ordinary man either," observed Koldewey. "The books he asked for from the prison library were not in it, and no one had ever asked for them before. Friedländer's *History of Roman Civilization!* Bachofen's *Matriarchy!* Delbrück's *History of the Art of War!* What did the man think of us?" And Herr Koldewey uttered a sort of bleat, and gave a tug to his long goatee beard.

"However, I was rather pleased to have those three books applied for, and I ordered them, putting them in the library budget as new acquisitions, and thus became possessed of three excellent authors; so Herr Mengers got his books. But the Delbrück was confoundedly expensive, and we could only run to the first volume. It's time there was a popular edition."

"Then I'll get along at once;" so saying, Frau Käte got up.

"Gently, gently with the young horse," he said, to restrain her eagerness. "In daylight men understand how to use time, that niggardly allowance of time that constitutes their lives, to the advantage of their many schemes. Moreover, you, as patroness of the prison, being allowed into the cells, can at the same time secure them the privilege of having their lights on a little longer, if you go across there after dark. Personally, I shall be curious to know whether you produce any effect. Don't you find it absurd, and indeed significant of our epoch, that anyone should have positively to ask our prisoners to petition for a reprieve?"

"Good Lord," said Käte Neumeier, flicking a spot of ash from her dark blue autumn suit, "the whole affair is out of the ordinary. Your case, the time it has taken, and this executioner of yours—why shouldn't it be so for the accused as well?"

"*My* case!" exclaimed Koldewey. "Really, I must ask you! I am not to be identified with it, neither with its beginning, nor its conclusion, which indeed is not yet a fact. You are pleased to regard me not as the director of a play, but of a stage. And that is Annette ringing up," he added, pointing to the telephone beside his chair, which buzzed at that moment. "Mengers at half-past six, and Timme at seven."

The days were past, thought Käte Neumeier, when warders clanked on their rounds with gigantic bunches of keys, and their children held out crusts of bread to the prisoners. Except that our 'constables' have retained their character from the days of the good old Republic, and still hurry through these long corridors as though the place were a beehive of social betterment; though the new masters of the State promptly did away with the principle of gradations in the fulfilment of a sentence, wasn't it grossly imprudent so expressly to abolish such an element of humanity? What if they themselves should one day come under judgment?

The prisoner, Mengers, got up as the warder and the lady came in, closed his book, said good evening, and offered her his stool. He himself stood leaning against the wall, a tall, rather emaciated man with a long lean neck on which was not ungracefully poised an intelligent head with near-set Jewish eyes. Käte Neumeier was angry with herself for noticing the neck of a man condemned to death, but found it excusable in a doctor, and indeed justified. The bed, which was folded against the wall in accordance with the regulations, could not yet be pulled out. Mengers, with apologies, sat down on a small table. Käte Neumeier looked at the window high up in the wall as she carried out Lene Prestow's dying request. Mengers had already heard that Lene had died and was buried. "She wished to leave you her registration-book."

"No doubt because I'm a bookseller," smiled the man with the melancholy eyes. "But that is the property of the police and must go back to them. From dust thou camest, and to dust shalt thou return—in saying which I am not referring to Lene. She had character, and she was loyal. It is very improbable that I shall forget her, even without this memento."

Käte Neumeier objected to the word—dust—as a designation for an organ of government in the mouth of this Jewish bookseller's assistant, but she suppressed her impulse to retort—as, for instance, that Herr Mengers would not have enjoyed the possession of this memento for long. Those thin, bony hands of his must have packed up many a book for her in the Mönkebergstrasse. However, she did ask him whether he intended the observation in an ironical sense.

"Because I have only ten days or a fortnight to live? That's exactly what I can't believe. I believe neither in Herr Denke of Oldenburg who is ill, nor in his deputy from Hamburg. I don't know whether you know anything about our absurd case, Frau Doctor? If you do, then you must also know that no death sentence can be based on such evidence, from witnesses that had to be fetched from the other side of Europe. Perhaps among thieves of the S.A. and S.S. type, and in a drunken row. But even they would be ashamed of such a judicial murder when they had sobered up again. Our farce has lasted for three years. We haven't been so badly off all the time—the old régime still continues, the same officials in the Glasmoor prison, the same daily round, pleasant work in the fields, and a good bit of freedom by and large. 'No one is such a fool as to try to escape from Glasmoor prison' was the invisible inscription over the great gateway. And now—a bloody ending to it all? No. It wouldn't be Prussian, nor Hansa, nor even German."

To Käte Neumeier the man seemed suddenly very young, very ingenuous, and very remote from any world but that of books. Was it his voice, with its pleasantly husky intonation, or was it the movements of his hands?

"But that shouldn't have prevented you from putting in a petition for a reprieve," she exclaimed in an almost imperious tone, and tapping her fist lightly on the table.

"Do you really think there would have been any sense in interfering in the struggle between the old and the new powers? In Hamburg as it was, we should simply have been brought before a magistrate. And I should have protested against that, for I merely tried to drag Krischan Haas, who had been badly wounded, out of the way of the S.A. men's jack-boots. As sure as you are sitting thère I saw two fellows, who had fired revolvers, climb over a wall and disappear. At the police-post the constables maintained that this wall wasn't visible from the place where I said I was, and from then on they nailed the thing on to me through that statement of mine. They would not admit that I might have confused the sides of the street in the half-light of early morning, and mentioned the wrong corner, I was too intelligent for that. No, Frau Doctor, it is very nice of you to want to put heart into me, but in this struggle of two contending areas of force for the upper hand, a petition for a reprieve from such an insignificant person, signed W. O. Mengers, would have no weight at all."

Käte Neumeier looked at her wrist-watch. Her real visit was to Friedel Timme. She was impatient, and anxious to get to him. In other circumstances she would have enjoyed this interview with the man who sent for and read such solid books.

"My dear Herr Mengers," she replied, "I must point out to you that no positive area of force is so certain of its power that it does not readily attract every electron that may intensify its strength. According to your view, the conservative, sustaining powers embodied in the administration are fighting against the mass attack of the Party, the S.A. Would it not be better counsel to give a handle to our Hamburg tradition by way of a petition to the Senate for a reprieve?"

"Yes, if that Senate had not bent its back to this buffoon of a so-called *Reichsstatthalter*, who now bestrides it like the Old Man of the Sea did

Sindbad the Sailor. We Mengers came to Hamburg from Bremen, where you can find our tombs since the days of Henry the Lion; the younger branch migrated here in the times of Moses Mendelsohn. When Lessing was here publishing his *Hamburg Dramaturgy*, and Matthias Claudius his *Wandsbek Messenger*, my ancestor, Benjamin Mengers, had already shown so much feeling for literature as to collect the parts and bind them into volumes; in the great fire of a hundred years ago they vanished as ashes into the Alster Basin. Ask the gentlemen, whom I am to petition for mercy, what they then signified for Hamburg, or Hamburg for them?"

"I like the Spaniard proud," quoted the Doctor, and made as though to get up. But Mengers reached out a hand:

"Don't misunderstand me, dear lady. I know how kind your intentions are to us. If you really want me to, I will put in a petition for reprieve to-morrow. And the point of it is, of course—to be able to breathe in Germany. To establish the fact that, though Germans may be tortured and murdered by Nazi beasts, there is still something that survives in the orderly procedure of the Law, something known as justice. How?—well, that makes no matter. We know that in this Republic we waded waist-up in injustice. Everyone against the workers, so soon as they dared to raise their heads. We fought against it, we strove for a better Republic, and that we could have had. But if *Justitia* is now to turn her back on us, then all is up. Let the officials, the banks, and the Stock Exchange, play their little games *ad libitum*. But somehow I don't believe we are at the end of all things. In the face of such a disaster, the earth would split asunder, the houses collapse, and the gas mains burst. Flames would pour out of the pavements; in times of flood, the Elbe would stand three yards high in the streets. The people would have to use rafts and gondolas. Has all this happened? It has not. The mud does indeed stand pretty well up to our hips. But there is firm cement underneath it. The house of Germany will be cleansed again one day. The Soviet Union will pull us out of the mess—the Russians won't leave us in the lurch. I should indeed be lying if I pretended I understood everything that has happened there since '35, but . . ."

Käte Neumeier got up: "Are you, or are you not, proposing to submit a petition for a reprieve, Herr Mengers?"

She's connected with the Senate party, was the thought that sped through Mengers' head, or she's got a brother on the Bench.

"Yes," he said, "I am." He would ask for some foolscap paper next day, and address a formal communication to the prison authorities for transmission.

Käte Neumeier, bewildered by his want of appreciation of his own position, said with a sigh that she hoped it might be successful. But this strange personage now demanded a favour in return. He revealed himself, among his other pursuits, as an author. He had written the script of a film, on the life of Karl Marx—not fearsomely realistic, but expressionistic. His Marx was represented as dying in London, and lying in Euston cemetery, his enemy Bismarck surviving

him.  But this Bismarck was surely a reincarnation of Paul of Westphalia,
the brother of Karl's beloved Jenny.  But what happened in Euston
cemetery was the resurrection of Karl Marx in the guise of another
emigrant, a little Russian lawyer, Vladimir Ilyitsch Lenin, who visited
his grave to lay a few flowers on it.  The shadow that he then threw
on the churchyard wall was damnably like that of a bearded old gentleman of eighty in a slouch hat.  If, therefore, anything really happened to
him, Mengers, he asked Frau Dr. Neumeier to enquire for his papers
at Glasmoor.  Here at Fuhlsbüttel he had no more than the materials
for a biography of the late Paul Levi—the Berlin lawyer and Deputy,
whose fate had meant the closing of so many doors in the Republic,
when, in delirium after influenza, he threw himself out of a window.
He would, he concluded, ask for several quires of foolscap paper and
sketch out the scheme of such a biography.  So saying, he thanked the
good genius of Lene Prestow for sending the Frau Doctor to him, and
he promised to draw a plan of the place where his Karl Marx manuscript was hidden at Glasmoor.  With that he said good-bye, and
as Käte Neumeier opened the door, he dismissed her with a bow
that ill accorded with his prison garb, and tilting his head slightly
to the left looked at her with a genial and grateful expression in his
eyes.

The warder, formerly known as the turnkey, came to meet her from
the end of the corridor.  He raised his hand, which might have indicated
a greeting, or that he had a message for her.  The patroness stepped
towards him, excited by her success, but now impatiently intent on the
real encounter of the afternoon.  He informed her that Nos. 317 and 320
were already awaiting the Frau Doctor in the visitors' room.  So saying,
he opened the door of a lift, and they sank to the central hall, its somewhat characterless architecture of steel and concrete looking almost
rhythmical in construction; and he ushered Käte towards the visitors'
room.

"I shan't be more than ten minutes," she said.  "Please don't go
away.  We will keep the lift down here.  I shall go up again immediately
afterwards."

"Ah yes, to No. 319," replied the officer, in a high, cackling voice.
He was glad not to be sent away, and pass the time in the boredom of
waiting; indeed he looked forward to being present at an interview at
which something human might be expected to happen.  Nor was he
disappointed: the Doctor spoke in very friendly fashion to the two dock-
hands, sturdy young men of about four-and-twenty, both with fair,
neatly parted hair, and clear untroubled gaze.  The visit was a surprise
to them, but they had heard of the lady, and the interest she had taken
in Lene Prestow, besides being patroness of the Women's Barrack.
With a shrug of the shoulders they accepted her commendation for not
making matters worse by being too proud to send in their petitions for a
reprieve, for the success of which the odds were about even.  They were
too polite to betray their amusement.

"Yes, ma'am," said Merzenich; "we're liable for army service. If Hitler starts his war in the East and strikes at Danzig, then we're for it, anyhow. Whether a bomb drops on our onions, or the executioner hacks them off, don't seem to matter much."

"It would be quite nice—we should get another reprieve," said Schröder, by way of supporting the companion of his fate; it was, in fact, he went on, more especially his parents and the lawyer who had pestered him into signing the petition. This sort of scepticism made it easy for the visitor to break off the interview and withdraw.

"Well, Mr. Warder," she said, "take me back to the upper world," and took her leave with a nod that was rather chillier than she intended. Merzenich's impertinent whisper to his friend: "There goes the *Kaiserin*," may have escaped her, but perhaps it did not.

When she was still outside the door, in the corridor, a man could be heard pacing up and down his cell, the soles of his shoes creaking rhythmically as he walked. When Käte Neumeier entered, the prisoner stood still, then, with his back to the door, marched up to the window, swung round and said: "Well now?"

Later, on the return journey, and at night when with Annette, Käte Neumeier fell to pondering why she had been conscious of such an inward shock when she set eyes so suddenly on the prisoner, Timme, in his cell, in the stark and merciless light of an unshaded prison bulb. She had, in fact, expected to see once more the Friedel Timme of old days, a well-set up, broad-shouldered youth of middle height, with fair hair parted in the middle. But the intervening years had done their work; face and form had sagged a little, and grown heavier, his hair had thinned, and was already greying round the temples. Had he given way to alcohol at all? The eyes of a Hamburg workers' doctor were trained to notice just such details. These observations restored to her the sense of superiority which, as she now felt, she had lost in the excitement of seeing the man again.

"Yes, Friedel," she said. "here I am. Never in my life did I think to see you among the accused in the Reeperbahn Case. Why, the very name of Reeperbahn suggests a band and a garden and green poplar-trees, and lads and lasses dancing—out at St. Pauli; not this kind of thing. I probably wouldn't have been here to-day but for Lene Prestow. She kept on insisting, let me tell you, that what she said in Court was true."

"Thank you very much," he nodded, with hands behind his back. "They did her in, too. 'Prestow the Prostitute' ought to have been written on her grave: 'a pillar of society, broken in the class war.' "

Käte Neumeier jerked her head involuntarily, as though to shake off a buzzing fly—a reminder of her dream, which she had in the meantime nearly forgotten. She did not like to think that she had conceived the very thoughts that he had now uttered: so she said in an anxious voice: "Haven't you looked a little too often into a glass these last few years, Friedel?"

"Yes," he replied, with a shrug of his shoulders; "When one has to look on and see the working classes comitting suicide and wrecking every

chance they've got, and can't do a thing against the powers that be—
why—now and again a fellow needs something to ease things up a bit.
It hasn't done me any harm, anyway; the new executioner will cut off
a perfectly healthy cranium."

"Yes," she interjected hurriedly, "that's why I'm here. Do you
think, as your friend Mengers does, that it won't come to that extremity?
Is that why you haven't sent in any petition for a reprieve?"

Again she sat down upon a stool, and again the man leaned against
a bed hinged up to the wall.

"Poor Thomas," he said in a mocking tone; "unbelieving to the
end. . Genuine S.A.P.—never can make up their minds. No, my
former comrade, I sent in no petition because I know it wouldn't make
any difference. I feel the jaws of the *Reichswehr* at my throat. That
is a bulldog that never lets go."

Käte Neumeier was on the point of an outburst, but she controlled
herself. "My lad," she exclaimed, stretching out a clenched fist towards
him, "would you let a possible chance go—out of a petty desire to be in
the right and know best?"

He looked at her, dropped his eyes meditatively to the table, and
then again met hers. "Yes," he answered gravely, "that always was
our disability. We overvalue the prerogative of being in the right and
maintaining it. But that was so—it is so no longer. When I recognized
those two ruffians in the witness-box—Piessling and Brandt—I knew
what was coming. The old reckoning would be squared now."

This was the effect of drink, she thought. "Do you truly believe
in all that stale old trash?"

"My dear old friend Käte," said he, sitting down, as he spoke, upon
the table. "Have you been about at all in the neighbourhood of
Hamburg? Have you seen the new aerodromes, the training-grounds,
the countless barracks, K.Z.'s and labour camps? You go about
Germany a bit and count them up. There were a few people at Glasmoor who knew what was coming. The *Reichswehr* is arming for
revenge. That is the whole purpose of this Nazi beastliness, as we have
always said. All disturbing elements had first to be put out of the way.
So a beginning was made with Liebknecht and Luxemburg, Erzberger
and Rathenau. Then the S.P.D. and the Centre had to be stamped
flat, and the Jews got rid of, and the intellectuals. The populace
reduced to a sort of corpse-like obedience—nothing but Heil for whatever
they were told: War and Death and Germany's greatness. That is why
we had to be put out. And if a few innocent people went with us—
well, millions went out in war. And would do so again. Doesn't that
make sense?"

Käte felt cold in this cell. She had been sitting in cells for nearly
an hour: the central heating didn't begin until October 15th. "And for
such fancies as these a man will risk his head," she murmured, as though
to herself. "Well, it can't be helped, I suppose."

"I have a wife, and two small children, whom I should like to have
brought up. For our cause—for a better Germany," he replied; passed
the back of his hand across his eyes, and wiped his hand on his jacket.

"I could have left the country in the spring of '30, and gone to live in the Soviet Union. But I didn't want to. That was the mistake. When it comes to the point, I thought, the comrades will see how the wind is blowing. Stand together as in the Kapp *putsch*, and put a stopper on it all. Better than they did in '24. In '33 we could have defended ourselves, held Hamburg, and the whole lower Elbe. The Nazis wouldn't have got the upper hand here. You can take poison on that. But we waited for the signal from Berlin, and it didn't come. And that's why we sit here in gaol, waiting for the end."

"Timme," cried Käte, and shook him by the shoulders. "That is all absolute stuff and nonsense—and I'll prove it to you. Now you write your petition, and I will myself take it to your old regiment; I know the commanding officer, Lieut.-Col. Lintze. Write that you were twice wounded, and how you escaped from the Russian prison camp, and got home with those Austrian doctors through Persia: everything that you told me at the time. Then we shall see."

He looked at her, shook his head, and smiled. "Haven't you heard, Comrade Käte, how they treat men in the concentration camps—men who wore the gold wound-chevron and were four or five times wounded? —they thrash them with steel rods. My dear, you are still not living in the present—in the Empire of the Sun-God Adolf. Perhaps you may get the other three let off, with the help of your man Lintze—wasn't he going to become your brother-in-law—so I seem to remember? There is one way," he went on, lowering his voice and coming close to her. "A good steel file, five hundred-mark notes—what we used to call blue rags, and at the appointed hour a motor-cycle, filled with petrol, left by the entrance gate, against the wall and ready to start. We are out for exercise from two to three; for a hundred marks each five warders would shoot to miss. I should merely risk my head: it need never be known who had helped me; it would be put down just simply to the Party or the Russians. Well, Käte? What about it?"

Käte Neumeier looked at him with horror in her eyes, and rose slowly from her stool. "You shouldn't ask me to do such a thing," she whispered, "and I can't do it." She made her way with faltering steps to the door, and heard his short laugh as she clicked it to behind her. Cell doors clicked so neatly into place, she knew from many visits—so she thought, as she stood in the brightly-lit corridor. Gladly would she have flown home on the wings of desire and gone to bed instead of sitting at Annette's supper-table and talking about Herr Footh. But the astute Herr Koldewey would cheer her up again, and perhaps there would be some music on the wireless.

# CHAPTER THREE

### MASTER OF HIS HOUSE AGAIN

WHEN KATE NEUMEIER replaced the telephone receiver—it was early on the following morning, and she had slept a deep and dreamless sleep —she said to herself, "Well, that's almost uncanny; enough to make me superstitious." For it had appeared that on that very day Lieut.-Col. Lintze had some business about noon in her neighbourhood, in connection with the training-grounds, and he could easily call for her. A little walk under the yellowing trees would be just the thing for an office soldier who was beginning to put on weight, and do no harm to her either, though he was convinced that she was as fit as ever she was when the Lintze family had the pleasure of seeing her oftener. At a quarter to two, if that would suit her—2 Wandsbeker Chaussée, wasn't it? He would think of two o'clock, and that would keep the number in his mind. Good-bye, then, till later. Charming fellow—charming, if a little too suave. Hadn't he pretended to know her address? But unfortunately Käte Neumeier had sharp ears; and the sound of pages being hurriedly turned over in a note-book was only too recognizable. Well, she wasn't born yesterday either, and had her plan ready to hand.

The field-grey service car of the 76th pulled up punctually at the street door, where Käte Neumeier was standing with just the same exactitude, a few steps above the street and looking down it. The Colonel himself jumped out, and helped her into the car, delighted, as he said, to have made so quick a contact with earlier days. He and his wife had been genuinely sorry that with Karl August's departure they had somehow lost touch with each other. He put her down in the gardens, and then drove back to the former Hussar-barracks, in which he had barely ten minutes' business, and could then enjoy her company for a half-hour at least. Here were walnut and lime trees, and comfortable benches, a matter to which the Republic had paid so much attention —and the less time he spent here talking now the sooner he would be back again, and he was most curious to know what she wanted him to do. For, after all, everybody wanted something from everybody else.

"I don't," laughed Käte Neumeier. "I'm bringing you something."

The Colonel thanked her in advance, kissed her hand, laid his to his cap, and disappeared. Käte Neumeier leaned back in the white-painted latticed chair, so comfortably shaped to the human person, and decided not to think of what she now had to say, and on what so much depended. Alertness, intuition, a sense of what was in the adversary's mind—that was what mattered: nothing was more ill-advised than to advertise beforehand what one was going to say and how one meant to parry the attack. Much better watch the crows manœuvring in vast flights just below the clouds; they circled through the air like black tattered veils, as though in imitation of the glistening threads of gossamers now wafted across the avenue. And in speculating whether they could really be crows which were leaving the heath, or swarms of starlings preparing for their winter journey, she passed the time of waiting almost without noticing it. A verse of the poet, Gottfried Benn, ran through her head the while—a lovely couplet:

> 'And as the gulls in winter fly
> To the sweet waters—to the harbours of their home.'

"In half-an-hour, Ehlers," said the Colonel, as the huge car slid to a standstill almost without a sound, sat down beside Käte, offered her a cigarette, clicked his lighter—several times in vain—and then said abruptly, "Well, fire away."

He had a fresh-coloured, ruddy face, a notably small mouth topped by the clipped moustache then in fashion, and looked like a dimmed and diminished version of his brother, who always produced a much more masculine effect. He would never have permitted himself such a direct attack upon a lady.

Käte Neumeier blew a puff of smoke slowly out between her lips. "I am one of the so-called Patronesses of Fuhlsbüttel. Some petitions for reprieves are to be sent in from there in connection with the Reeper-bahn case, and Herr Koldewey advised me to approach you. How you can really be concerned with the affair I can't imagine except, perhaps, in so far as one of the accused men served under you, and was, I believe, twice wounded. A man by the name of Timme."

"You little Communist," said the Colonel genially. "Is this a relapse into old days?"

"If you like," she retorted. "What else could I have in mind? But I'm serious. Do you really come into this business at all? Is there any sense in telling the condemned man, Mengers, to put any hope in a petition for a reprieve? I wouldn't like to arouse expectations which can only prove deceptive. Mengers was a well-educated bookseller's assistant, who often recommended me a book, and scarcely ever a bad one. I want to help him, not to torture him."

"Then keep your charming fingers out of it, Käte. You rightly said—this man Mengers *was*. The fact that the final scene has been so long postponed is certainly a scandal, but now, at the twelfth hour, it has been possible to fix it all up."

Käte Neumeier nodded agreement. The astute Herr Koldewey knew his way about.

"Yes, Koldewey leaves a better impression," said the Colonel, "than a Major of Landwehr usually does. His eyes remind me of the elephants in Stellingen. They're thick-skinned, like we are. We waited fifteen years until we made them again understand who was really master in this house. But now the very hippopotami and the Hamburgers have realized it at last."

He laughed shortly and tapped a switch—which he had broken off a tree—against his immaculately polished top-boots.

Käte Neumeier wagged her head, grey-haired but still youthful and fresh.

"What in the world can all that have to do with the Reeperbahn case?"

"Käte," said Lintze, "you are a sensible woman, and you nearly married into the family. The fact that you didn't, we regard as much to the disfavour of Karl August, whether you believe it or not. The affair was nothing to do with Mengers, nor with the other two—Merzenich and Schröder. We have turned their petitions over and over again until we decided to ask the competent authorities to refuse. It was a case for the good old proverb: 'Caught in hanging company is as good as hanged.' Now the man Timme threatened his officers with a revolver in '18. He embodied the spirit of upheaval and revolt, he went through the cash-box and books of his regiment, put in claims against the Supply Department, and took part in the crime of November. Since then he has been accepted as a sort of symbol by the Hamburg workers, and in him was embodied their spirit of popular revolt. Though his importance was purely local, he was a personage of importance here. Your Mengers is of no account compared with Timme."

"But that is not just," retorted Käte Neumeier, filled with a strange feeling of triumph that she had kept her adversary so completely unsuspicious of her true aim, and of despair at the crass assurance of the military mind. "Neither just nor wise. For you are plainly underestimating the sense of justice and injustice in our workers. If you believe that that is going to stimulate the labour needed for the armaments drive——"

The Colonel raised his eyebrows. "Possibly not; that would be an undesirable secondary consequence, which we might have to consider later on. One more reason for inviting the Führer's personal intervention. His intention is, anyhow, to keep an eye on justice in Hamburg, and get his Elbe bridge forward, which isn't very popular here. But if that is so, he has only to come and talk with that spell-binding tongue of his, and he'll have the little man at his feet. The main point is: Woe to him who lifts a weapon against his superiors. The rebel is due for the wall or the block—sooner or later. A few months ago a friend of mine brought me a story from Berlin, from the War Ministry, which may perhaps throw light on the point. A true story which unfortunately can't be told, publicly I mean, to the workers. As between us two it doesn't matter. It will go to show that we are in the middle of a war, and that ideas of peace must necessarily produce a misleading picture. False scales must distort any topographical observations—but that isn't the fault of the ground surveyed, which is mostly quite normal in its lay-out."

"H'm," said she. "That's a point to be dealt with later on. In the middle of a war, you said just now? Have other countries been informed of the fact? What would your brother say if the *New York Times* or the Columbia Radio drew conclusions of this kind from these Hamburg sentences, and their execution by means of an axe. Does your brother already know the answer that he should give? The

American journalists in our country—haven't they shown themselves extremely astute fellows who fully understand our circumstances? You may turn one of them out, but his successor will be just as intelligent. He will merely express himself with rather more caution. That's all. The leader-writer on the other side will be all the more explicit—and no Jews, Colonel."

It was at this point that Colonel Lintze began to take this interview seriously. His underjaw protruded slightly, which altered the expression of his face unfavourably, and the menacing look with which he stared into the distance was, she felt, really intended for his companion.

"Was this the present that you had in mind, dear lady?"

"Certainly," replied Käte Neumeier; "And as it seems, you are not disposed to thank me for it."

"Not at all," he replied with disingenuous politeness. "As the lad has obviously written to you to say that he is trying to get to New York, and you want to spare him trouble, I venture the conclusion that all is not yet over between you, and that you are after all not disinclined to become Frau Vice-consul Lintze. In that case, this is to be regarded as a family discussion, which—so I am told—sometimes becomes a trifle exacerbated."

And he took a fresh cigarette out of his silver case. Käte Neumeier also helped herself to another. She was again conscious of the triumphant sensation of a few minutes before, with which a dangerous wild animal is seen departing on a false trail; but in general she felt no nearer to success. It seemed to her the better plan to wait and leave him the first word.

"America," he observed meditatively, "is uncommonly well off. She has ten per cent. more oil than she needs, and consumes more of it than two-thirds of the rest of the world. As our reservoirs are not yet full, we must avoid any cause of quarrel. Moreover, we need her helium for our airships, our sole link with her southern sister-continent. So we shall do well to keep this execution dark."

"But how, then, will you achieve your aim with the Hamburg workers?" she asked softly. "You mustn't misunderstand me, my dear Otto. We are pulling at the same string, but I'm only afraid you are taking it up too short."

The Colonel broke his switch and flung the fragments over his shoulder into a plantation, by the iron railings of which they were sitting. "Our Führer is a great artist," he then said; "he plays on two pianos, a loud one and a soft one. In reality he only performs on the loud one. We manage the soft one for him. You hear the sort of abuse that is poured out against the Soviets in Nuremberg these days. But our soft one gets in its piece and the Russians hear and understand. It's all part of the game. And the programme is the same for America and England. The wise man chooses wool, as the advertisements used to say. We are still surrounded by a common front. But Adolf knows its weak places; and he will astutely insert his crowbar just at the right

F

spot, as he did in the case of the German Republic—indeed, he himself—though he may not know it—is our crowbar. We are slowly drawing on our great war-boots, like Napoleon in the old song of the Ems Fountain. 'When Napolium heard this, he called for the great boots his uncle used to wear,'" he murmured to himself, and recovered his good humour. "In the meantime the Anglo-Saxons are shuffling around in carpet slippers because we have pointed out to them that our iron footwear will save them putting on their boots: indeed there will be no need for them to set foot to ground in the unpleasant European weather now threatening in the East—we are there for that: As I said, a piano duet. The theme a little difficult, but anyone with ears can hear it."

Käte Neumeier grew cold. "Do we really mean war?" she said. "But we haven't doctors enough."

"True," he agreed. "You are thinking of your Jewish colleagues. But we'll provide ourselves with substitutes, first from Austria—and besides, it won't really come to war. Our war will be waged in peace. Adolf backs himself to bring back everything we want without firing a shot. But the pre-condition remains, of course, that we should be in a position to shoot, should need arise. I quote another old shopkeeper: *si vis pacem, para bellum*. Well, we've got the parabellum pistols all right. What we still lack is the heavy stuff, the indispensable small cash in the shape of tanks, and a few thousands more of those bumbles overhead," and he pointed his thumb up to the sky, where an aeroplane was circling high above them over towards the Fuhlsbüttel airport. "Our friend Göring has done marvels. And the way he has managed to wrap up his English colleagues in silver paper—well, I kiss his fat hands for it."

Two o'clock struck from several clock-towers, the chimes blending harmoniously with the organ-note of the propeller.

"Have I rightly understood?" said Käte Neumeier. "Is it the intention to attack Austria when the time comes?"

"There will be no attack, Käte," he replied. "Adolf and his people will repeat the Rhineland re-occupation performance with a different caste. Herr Schuschnigg will accept his fate, and the join-up with Austria will be completed before anyone can utter, and the Anglo-Saxon's sense of justice will once more be satisfied, always pre-supposing that it costs nothing. That's how it will happen, mark my words. Then we'll take a look over the Brenner, and get a few ships afloat in Trieste, and Uncle Benito will soon realize on which side his bread is buttered. He does already suspect who really plays the first fiddle here —the captains of Industry, or we. Never mind whether we are rearming so that the chimney may smoke again, or vice versa—because we mean to fight the last round of Autumn, 1918, all over again, after the short breathing space, that our friend Seeckt signified as necessary. The name now is no longer Seeckt, it is Fritsch, but names don't alter facts. And then comes my excellent Ehlers. 'Herr Count, sixty horses there are saddled.'"

They got up, and walked along the carefully-rolled path to the car, where it waited in the cement road that cut across the gardens at right-angles.

"So the petition had better stay in its drawer?" she asked, resignedly, as she put on her light felt hat.

"Yes, indeed," he replied. "The two petitions ready to hand will serve for the other gentlemen, at least for one more. I am, of course, not so stupid, nor so sure of my case, that I shall not pass on your suggestion to higher quarters. What is the use of telephones, and why have we heads above our epaulettes? He who gets more pay has more understanding or better connections, and gets to know what's what. The pull between the Party and the higher chiefs produces that constant state of flux, about which the ancient Greek was so oracular. Yes," he went on, as they settled themselves comfortably into the cushions and the car slid noiselessly away, "I owe you a little story. It does bear on the matter in hand, because it also happens to concern four people, one of whom pointed a revolver at a superior officer. He didn't know him for a superior officer—which was all the worse for him." And as the car glided through the streets, where the passers-by were enjoying the already weaker autumn sunlight of midday, hooted as it crossed tramlines, and meticulously observed the red and green signs of the traffic lights, Käte Neumeier listened to her companion, more and more depressed at the thought of the gulf that yawned between the world of Hamburg everyday life and that wild-west world to which Germany's destiny had consigned her; and indeed perhaps a like destiny awaited the whole of European civilization. It was common knowledge that on 30th June, 1934, General von Schleicher and his wife had been shot by S.S. men. At that time, explained Lintze, there was clearly no one to guide the course of events: victims fell to left and right within our sphere. But when normal conditions returned, and there was time to survey the wreckage, there were headaches in high places. The old power, the seat of authority—*we*, in fact—he spoke the word with emphasis—did not address themselves to a policy of reprisals. A statement was drawn up on the Schleicher 'blunder', for which the entire Third Regiment of Footguards had sworn vengeance. General von Fritsch encouraged the survivors to bring an action against the *Reich* for damages—after all, Schleicher had not merely been Minister for Defence, he was a General Staff and Guards officer, with thirty years of service behind him. The leader-class were naturally greatly incensed that anyone should get away with this sort of thing. Most who were shot had to be accounted for as having fallen into disfavour, a condition which is blacker than ink, and more adhesive than pitch. Hands off," observed Lintze genially, with his customary clarity of speech. "Well, the said papers were at the War Ministry in the drawer of a Major von X's table, and a certain Herr Himmler, also a personage, wanted to get them into his possession. The S.S., for whom he was effectively responsible, did not come well out of the affair: the *Reich* would have to pay, and payments ought solely to find their way into the Party chest, not out of it. So one morning four S.S. men in beautifully polished uniforms called on Major von X and demanded the surrender of the

Schleicher papers. And when Major von X displayed some difficulty in understanding what it was they wanted, one of them committed an error that was to cost them their lives; he produced a small pistol and held it under Major von X's nose. No doubt he thought he was dealing with a bank official or a Jewish lawyer. Von X laughed. He sat behind his writing-table as though it had been a sort of castle, and was, oddly enough, not in the least afraid. But the S.S. men did not know that: they had no inkling of the fact that the raising of a weapon against a Prussian officer is an act of war, and war obeys its own laws. Von X bent—apparently—towards a drawer, but in fact towards a bell. Those below on the ground floor would know what the ring of the bell meant, and where it came from. In the meantime Von X handed his courageous gentlemen the wrong papers in order to give the guard time to get up the stairs—there are a great many stairs in the Bendlerstrasse, are there not? When the intelligent emissary had discovered the Major's mistake, and Von X had apologized, and the genuine documents concerning the murder of General Kurt von Schleicher were being fingered by the gentlemen in black tunics, the door flew open, the *Reichswehr* appeared on the scene, and the room was filled with steel helmets and rifles. 'Take them away,' was all that Major von X said. Whether the four young gentlemen grew pale or not, I don't know; in any case, they soon found themselves in the cellar, where they were shot out of hand, passed on to the crematorium, their ashes consigned to four tin boxes and this returned to Herr Himmler, who would, it was hoped, realize whose whiskers he had been pulling. You see, Kate," he concluded, in a high polite voice, as the car stopped obediently outside No. 2 Wandsbeker Chaussée, "no American will ever hear or tell that story. And yet it would be very informative, and would contribute to the proper understanding of many things, on this side and on that. In civil war four people fall here or there, perhaps at the hands of the Party, perhaps against the Party, by a bullet or by the headsman's axe. He who stands, and stands steady, behind all this, is master in the house, and on him you can rely. Business first, and that goes for the Yankees above all. And now, when will you come and drink a cup of coffee with us?"

"Whenever your wife cares to ring me up," replied Käte, still rather overcome, as Ehlers opened the door for her. "And when, may I too ask, shall I know whether any of the petitions have been granted, and for which of the four?"

"It all depends on the official machine; no one can say how long that will take to revolve. The latest and surest respite is on the morning of the execution. When the passing bell is tolling, and the executioner is sharpening his axe, the State prosecutor can still announce that the petition for mercy has been granted, and the penalty mitigated into so and so many years' imprisonment. I am myself curious to know what the decision will be, whether with heads or without."

Käte Neumeier stood for a moment on the pavement outside her flat and stared after the car which disappeared into the Lübeckstrasse, and did not notice that she had been shaking her head for several seconds, and must have looked strange to the passers-by. For some years past people had got used to overlooking such trifling oddities on the streets. A grey car was disappearing into the haze and mist of the Lübeckstrasse, which was an ordinary event of every day. But Käte had the feeling that the ground beneath it had become transparent, the asphalt with all its pipes and cables, and that in following the car with her eyes, she was looking into the entrails of German everyday life. Among these pipes and cables would, among other matters, be decided the fate of Friedrich Timme, Mengers, the bookseller's assistant, and the two dockers Schröder and Merzenich, with all their satellites— some twenty heads in all. One single axe threatened them all, and Käte Neumeier would see it fall. And as she mounted the stairs to her flat, a rather dark and narrow wooden stairway, faultlessly waxed, and edged with polished brass, she marvelled at the change that had taken place in her since she had asked Herr Koldewey to be allowed to witness the event in his company. From an independent doctor she had in the meantime changed into a far from independent person, though she did not know what kind of person she had actually become. That two conversations with prisoners could only produce such far-reaching reactions, if there were hollow spaces in the individual's soul responsive to such echoes, she admitted with a heavy heart. What on earth was going on inside her head? Was the astute Lintze right? Was the past stirring within, and not the past of yesterday but of a while ago? "The wood is working," her Marie used to say, when, with much creaking, fissures appeared in the kitchen table. Dead wood was not really dead, life remained life. The same sort of process obviously occurred in people. She had almost an hour's free time before her first patient. She would rest, but only for twenty minutes; then she would read one of the articles on psychology in certain yellow periodicals that still appeared in Vienna, though the Party was against them. They made many matters clear, even as regards the human personality. It was odd that all these publications appeared in yellow covers. It was as if these yellow periodicals exclaimed defiantly: "Look out, we come from Jews! You will use us at your peril." Well, Käte Neumeier was not afraid of them. No; as she lay down, and covered herself with a plaid rug, smoothed its fringes away from her chin, closed her eyes, and nodded to herself; it wouldn't be at all a bad thing if something survived in her of the former youthful Käte Neumeier, that bold and energetic girl of twenty years ago, and waited, for its appointed day. It was a good work to have put the Lintzes off the trail. Friedel Timme would be pleased with her. As she dropped asleep she smiled at a youthful Käte Neumeier, a *wandervogel* with two thick fair plaits and a tousled head of hair. When her consulting hours began, the faithful Marie had to awaken her, help her hurriedly into her white smock, and sluice hot water over her hands from the red-lacquered tap.

The transition period from summer to autumn claims its victims, as all doctors know. As the equalization of day and night draws near, powers of resistance that have been rather deceptively maintained through the summer, tend to become exhausted. In Dr. Käte Neumeier's card-index figured a woman with cancer, a child with tuberculous bones, and a very old woman, who absolutely refused to leave the earth in which she had pursued her course for ninety years. These three cases took up all her time and attention, and all her skill. When the wives of Russendorf the State Prosecutor, and of Colonel Lintze, rang her up in the course of the following week, to remind her of her promised visit, it was with a good deal of reluctance that she accepted both invitations, and solely in the hope that she might incidentally learn something about the petitions for reprieve, which would be decided in the realm of cables and pipes. But the ladies knew nothing, and their husbands, both of whom appeared at the coffee-table, smoked cigars and made themselves very affable, said nothing. On her way home from the Russendorfs, Käte saw the young, waxing moon suspended above her street, a pallid sickle

> "*Little moon, little moon*
> *Will there be news of my four soon?*"

she hummed to herself, with a touch of shame at her foolishness and relapse into the days of the Leagues of Youth and fairy-tales. Of course the moon couldn't answer, intent as she was upon amplifying her outline. She was quicker about it than was poor Fräulein Holz-müller, whose pregnancy she had been asked to interrupt. The girl had returned from a labour camp, and had old-fashioned people for parents. It would be a fortnight—perhaps a little longer until the moon was full, and the hope that Nature, assisted by encouraging injections, would, of her own accord, start her courses again, had finally vanished. Käte had that much time to consider whether she meant to help Holzmüller, the post office clerk; little Liese herself hardly came into question from the point of view of morality; she would let herself be done by just as was thought best. Yes, but what about those four men in their cells? They, too, would not be consulted; they would be dealt with as a higher power might dispose, and indeed they had an even shorter thread of life than the little growing fœtus in Lieschen's slim body, and the waxing moon. When she reached the full-moon circle, at which in deceptive glory she dominated the night and this time marked the equinox, she must thereupon go down once more into the pit, like Eurydice evading the grasp of Orpheus. For the moon was Luna, a Goddess, and would indulge herself, *en passant*, in the act of death. But Friedel Timme had no one who would fetch him back; if he went, down he went for good. And she caught herself wishing that an accident might happen to the substitute executioner, whom Herr Footh had pro-cured, as it had to the witness, Bräse, who had fallen off the crane at A.R.P. practice, probably not without assistance from his neighbour, and had broken his neck. Oh dear, she had still not visited Lene Prestow's grave, and as she opened the flat door with the Yale key, she made up her mind to ask Annette to drive through Ohlsdorf next time she fetched her

to Fuhlsbüttel.    Just as she was opening the flat door she heard the
telephone ring.    The faithful Marie would not be far away, but it was
always better to answer the telephone oneself.    Still in her hat and coat,
she gladly answered Koldewey's enquiry: the appointed day still held
good, it was the fourteenth, a Tuesday, and Annette wanted Frau Käte
to dine with them on the thirteenth, and stay the night, for the ceremony
was to take place at half-past five next morning.

# CHAPTER FOUR

## THROUGH A ROUND WINDOW

FORTUNATELY KATE NEUMEIER carried Herr Koldewey's valuable
binoculars attached to a strap round her neck, though in spite of their
sixteenfold magnifying power they weighed very light.    For when she
had seen the Wandsbek axe, the origin of which she did not know,
flash for the fourth time, and for the fourth time heard the dull faint
thud—familiar from the slaughter-house—with which the blade sheared
through flesh and bone on to the block—when the Doctor had endured
this four times, her strength deserted her.    She clutched with both
hands at the round window-frame, felt her knees give way, and sat down
on the floor, leaning her back against the sloping gabled roof.    Annette
Koldewey had long since been crouching on the floor, her hands pressed
against her ears and her eyes tightly closed.    She had in fact only used
the binoculars for eight or ten seconds, just time enough to make out
her father, Herr Footh, the executioner with his mask and elegantly
waxed moustache, the axe, the block, the low scaffold which had been
set up in the western and most secluded yard of the establishment, the
twelve or twenty persons standing as spectators in a close-packed group;
then the little bell of the prison chapel had begun to clang in a vehement
and most unwonted fashion—indeed the clamour sounded like an
agonized cry for help.    Then the first prisoner, Mengers, was led out
into the yard, or rather escorted by the chaplain and two warders, who,
however, had no need to support him.    He walked with an easy stride,
his head tilted a little sideways on his thin neck, and his eyes—those
brown, sad Jewish eyes of his—fixed at first upon the ground.    Then,
in frightening fashion, they encountered those of Annette, when the man,
in the face of his hopeless situation, looked up at all about him, far and
near, knowing that there was no God, and indeed nobody at all, to
bring him help.    A sixteen-power binocular sees objects at nine hundred

yards as though they were only fifty yards away; Annette felt those
eyes of horror upon her, shrieked aloud in consciousness of complicity,
tottered and fell, first on to a chest, and then on to the floor where she
lay, faintly sobbing.  Only her hair still quivered as she drew her brown
fur coat close round her pyjamas and buried her bloodless face in its
folds and thick collar.  She ought never to have come up here, was her
sole thought, her father should have warned her; a Governor's house
should not overlook the walls of a prison; lead us not into temptation,
but deliver us from evil.  If only there had been a coverlet up there
under which she could crawl.

Käte Neumeier, on the other hand, did hold out until the end.  She
was witness of the killing of Mengers, the bookseller's assistant, who
with bent back, swinging arms, and head slightly tilted on one side, but
in control of himself, mounted the two steps of the scaffold.  The two
dockers, Schröder and Merzenich, one of whom burst into shouts of
horrifying and semi-imbecile laughter, when the State Prosecutor
delivered his brief allocution in resounding tones; while Merzenich, in
the same situation seven minutes later, broke out into a savage roar,
tried to assault the two warders, and still yelling that he had been
'betrayed', had to be forcibly held down over the block by the executioner's assistants.  This was really too much for Käte Neumeier's nerves.
However, she endured, in the absurd hope that three might be enough,
that the fourth would be spared.  But Friedel Timme was not spared.
Indeed he was kept, as the real object of this performance, to the last.
But Käte's memory was haunted by visions of last-minute reprieves,
accounts of shootings that had not taken place, although the squad had
already been drawn up before the victim, his eyes bandaged, the order
"prepare to fire" given; but a little pause always occurred before the
utterance of the final word "Fire", and had been followed by the final
order "Ground Arms".  Thus had it happened to many, whose guilt
had been no greater than that of Friedel Timme; and one of them,
Dostoievski, had described such a scene.  But this time—Friedel had held
his head high, looked the substitute executioner squarely and steadily
in the face, and uttered a few words before he dropped on his knees before
the block.  What he said did not reach her ears, in spite of the soundless
stillness in which the performance took place.  A savage and impotent
indignation shook her before she collapsed on to the floor.  "The brutes,"
it cried inside her; "the filthy, murderous brutes!"  If her wishes could
have prevailed, all these spectators would have been struck dead on the
spot, especially the murderer-in-chief, the executioner, who had voluntarily accepted the office of headsman, and Footh, Annette's Footh, who
had produced him.  Then she would gladly have fainted.  But that was
not to be; there was too much strength in her, and well that it was so.
Somebody had to be there to avenge Friedel Timme on that moustached
blackguard who had so deftly handled the axe.  That moustache, that
mouth, that out-thrust chin—she had seen them all before, she did not
know when and where, but she would remember.  She sat on the floor
in her black fur cloak, her heart fluttering in her breast, and God or
the Devil alone knew how she was going to get the strength before

twelve o'clock to deal with her time-table of patients for that date, and make the arrangements for the curetting of little Holzmüller. Her lower jaw quivered against her upper teeth. Her skin broke out into a cold sweat; she would in fact surmount the crisis by the aid of certain tablets, but she must find the lavatory at once.

Man can stand more than he thinks, especially when he is hardened by medical studies and lives in an epoch of political corruption. An hour in bed does wonders, so does a bath and a cold shower; he can then even deal with a second breakfast and recruit his strength with eggs, ham, coffee, and cream. Herr Koldewey took his place at the breakfast-table, his face longer than usual, his cheeks looking as though they had fallen in, and dark shadows under his eyes. He said little about what had taken place, and confined himself to a few quiet words of appreciation of all those who had taken part: Russendorf the State Prosecutor, who had had to grip his stick to keep himself steady; Colonel Lintze; the substitute executioner, who had been quite equal to his heavy office. When the rising sun burst through the reddish golden clouds, though the pale golden disc of the moon still hung in the west, all was over. The last words of Timme, the mechanic, he had heard distinctly, and indeed had written them down with the idea of including them in the file, which Käte Neumeier knew as Annexe No. 3. "You will soon see, all of you, what you will get out of this business, and especially you—you poor stupid brute"—this to the executioner: "You must all drown in my blood, and then we shall return."

"A strange world," said Herr Koldewey, "which the last war left behind it. So must Noah and his sons have felt, when the waters had fallen and receded, and partly dried, and they went out of the Ark, and set their feet once more on dry land. Was it old or new, changed or the same? The air, in any case, that filled their lungs, did them good—it was fresh and vigorous on the uplands of Armenian Ararat. And yet in all the valleys there must be vast deposits of putrefaction, myriads of drowned creatures would soon be revealed, and the vultures, ravens, and jackals which had been rescued in the Ark would have much to occupy them for a long while. And yet nothing is recorded of all this; the earth grew green once more, the whole business continued, and humanity did not condescend to make any lamentations or take any precautions for the future. We are a strange race, Heaven help us. I should truly like to know whether any generation will succeed in abolishing all this bad old business, and, if so, when and how!"

Yes—when—thought Käte Neumeier, as Annette drove her home. The city of Hamburg was intent upon its daily affairs, no one suspected that anything unusual had happened, no one could have any such suspicion. Yet she felt as though she must cry out, seize people by the shoulders and shake them awake, strip them of their self-possession, their laughter, and their damned hide-bound indifference. There echoed strangely in her recollection some words spoken by the actress Else Lehmann as Frau John in Gerhart Hauptmann's *Rats*: 'Bruno, you're on the wrong track.' No one, not even herself, could have imagined why this reply had so stuck in her mind and now haunted her at this very moment. Man is a strange animal, she thought, as she took leave of Annette, thanked her for her hospitality, and was already mentally picking out the small white pills that she would swallow with a little water, in order to carry on with her work.

When she lay in bed after the day's work was done, she expected not to be able to go to sleep at once, and indeed was quite content not to do so. A human creature must possess some sort of place into which he can withdraw, to ponder on the impressions of the day, and the species can be sub-divided in those who favour for this purpose the time when they are lying in bed or in a bath, sitting in a café, or on a country walk. Käte Neumeier was a lier in bed. But never in her life had she felt so shattered, and at the same time so worked up as she had done that day. Unless she recovered herself she realized that she would not be able to get to sleep without the aid of a narcotic. It may be mentioned that she was of those doctors who, in the conflict of opinion as to which was the more harmful, a sleepless night or a little dose of a morphia derivative, gave her verdict against the latter. Her faith in the healing qualities of Nature endowed her with an exaggerated fear of poisons that her patients had often reason to be thankful for, and a passionate delight in any sort of hardening treatment. She had in fact intended to listen to a talk on the wireless by a colleague on Swedish medical science, and the use of the divining-rod; but she really hadn't felt up to it. The excellent Laberdan would excuse her.

So there she lay, dog-tired but with her mind at full stretch, on an elastic mattress under a light but warm coverlet, more comfortable than, in her view, she ought to have been. For the four men with whose fate she had—too late—begun to concern herself—where, and in what condition they might be at that moment, she did not care to picture to herself. She knew the anatomy rooms that waited for them, the horde of students who would be instructed on their bodies, the abominable jokes that passed current at the dissecting table. The next generation must learn, and they must laugh a little in the process. And yet, had she ever reflected who they were that sold their bodies to the anæsthetist, or what were the human destinies that came to a close under the scalpel? Now she knew four of them, and accounted herself fortunate that she had contributed nothing to this result. The fact that she had nearly become connected with the Lintze family she reckoned almost to her discredit.

The room around her, familiar and quiet, lay in almost complete darkness; only through the window came an occasional electric flicker from the street. More disturbing was some music, which broke in upon her from a gramophone or wireless on the first floor below, or from the house next door. As she had never gone to bed before nine o'clock, she had not hitherto had the opportunity of hearing these expressions of life on the part of her fellow-townsmen; it was their perfect right to divert themselves, no one could object even if it inflicted positive torment on a woman who wanted nothing more than to be escorted into sleep by an ordered succession of reflections. But a human mind, in which an inner tribulation is astir, can be so tormented by Weber's *Freischutz* with its choruses and arias that its sensibility is positively blunted. Käte Neumeier took from her writing-desk some packets of cotton-wool impregnated with wax, such as Odysseus used against the Sirens, and closed her ears with them; the acoustic world without was thereby expelled from her consciousness. But unfortunately the inner voices then spoke much more loudly than before. It was stupidity on the part of Nature or of God not to provide the human race with ear-lids. Or was there some purpose in that omission? Was it that Man was too prone to jump on to the running-board and flee? Must the gift of sleep only be enjoyed in incompletion?—must the sleeper always be listening suspiciously into the darkness, peering out for enemies that may devour him, if his soul is not bemused by the delights of dream? Those airy pictures, illusive counterparts of life, which had been regarded as the stock-in-trade of poets, gypsies, dream-books, until, thirty years ago, a certain Herr Freud in Vienna. . . . She saw before her a photograph, a deliberately distorting presentment of him peering out from beneath his hat with a foxy, sidelong glance. Käte Neumeier had seen the great man; in the house of his Hamburg relatives, one of the oldest Spanish families in the city, whose youngest daughter he had married pretty nearly sixty years before. The little fair-haired Käte had grown very friendly with one of her great-nieces, and there in the drawing-room with the portraits of famous professors and Rabbis on the walls she had that afternoon been introduced to a black-bearded gentleman with flashing yet friendly eyes and an attractive Austrian voice, and between his fingers, on one of which was an antique seal ring, a large and handsome cigar, who nodded encouragingly at her, when he learned that she intended to become a doctor later on. So she could appreciate the malice and stupidity, with which that false presentment had been made. The work of the Party was often entrusted to incompetent hands, but still. . . . However, she must not allow herself to plunge too deeply into the ramifications of her own soul, caution was the mother of wisdom, so much was true. Then strangely it transformed itself into the face of her sage friend, Herr Koldewey, who had delivered himself so oracularly on the subject of Noah and the Flood—he, too, had been powerless against this beheading, of which he so heartily disapproved. But then his daughter had that fellow Footh round her neck, who was indeed at the bottom of the whole disaster, having produced that revolting operator with his mask, whose axe had disposed of the petitions for reprieve. Ought not she to be grateful to the two poor young men, Merzenich and Schröder, because they had kept up their courage, put in their petitions and believed in the Führer. In earlier days she had really been one of those ingenuous persons who were convinced of his goodwill, if only he could always and everywhere determine for himself on what was right! Now, as she lay here in bed, this seemed to her by no means certain any more; though what tormented her more at the moment was her betrayal of the two young men, rather than the indefeasible fact that Mengers and Friedel Timme were much more valuable people, and much nearer to her mentally. It was not to be denied that Friedel Timme, too, assumed for a moment the face and form of those

young men of five-and-twenty. He had not believed that a petition
for mercy would help, and maintain the just cause. The jaws of the
*Reichswehr* were set with steel, they bit with blades. Dear me, those
last words had the alliterative ring of an old German poem. And the
German had always been versed in the give-and-take of blows. Otto
Lintze's narrow lips and his voice appeared before her consciousness,
the bench among the autumn trees, the flights of crows and the webs of
gossamer. Where was it? When was it? Before the Flood, before
Friedel Timme's blood had gushed out, black in the morning light, and
engulfed her world.

This was getting beyond a joke. She didn't want to, but she must.
So she switched on the light, went into the consulting room next door,
and surveyed the preparations supplied to doctors by the highly-organized
chemical industry. To-morrow was also a day; she must take care to
keep efficient, and be able to do what was needed. She chose a brown
tabloid in which the sedative bromide is blended with luminal, which
affects the large outer membrane of the brain. Then she lay down again,
picked up a book, turned over the pages—it was not Bachofen's
*Matriarchy* nor Friedlander's *History of Roman Civilization*, but an
animal story written by a distinguished Canadian author, which had
hitherto always held her attention whatever mood she might be in.
But to-day it seemed to her trivial. Since men slaughtered and devoured
each other, what better could be expected from the beasts, on land, in
the waters, and in the air. The fact that one destroyed another, and
then a third destroyed the first, until in the end the two survivors
perished, because they proved themselves ill adapted to altered circumstances—all this was exemplified from the animal world, but was
hardly a great achievement. Show the human animal that: *hic Rhodos
hic salta*. Still, it was no bad thing to be a wild cat and bite through the
backbone of a terrier dog, used only to house-cats, who had been
taken for the first time by his master for a summer holiday in the
Canadian forests. Perhaps she was acting unwisely, unjustly, feebly
even, in allowing herself to be thus carried away by loathing of the
executioner's appearance—his moustache and mouth and jutting
chin. Perhaps it was merely some illusion of memory—what is known
as a *fausse reconnaissance*, her belief that she had seen that segment of a
face before, and more than once, she felt convinced. A patient? One
of her sick-club visitors, to whom she devoted so much care? No matter;
he had taken on the job and been paid for it, which should not be forgotten. Hamburg was not the world, a man could not get lost in it.
She would begin by sounding Annette as to how Footh had got hold of
the man. Yes, that was the line to take. Lene Prestow had shown
character, and had enjoyed Friedel Timme's approval and esteem.
One of these days she would put a pot of asters, in his name, on her
grave, and stick a taper on it on All Souls' Day, in the Catholic fashion.
It would burn like a candle flickering in a room unobserved, but rejoicing
the heart of some unlooked-for visitor who opens the door and enters.
Such a light she saw, like a long stump of a taper, burning on Friedel's
table in his Fuhlsbüttel cell. It stood empty, with the door open, a

gust of air blew in through the window, the tallow oozed down its sides, but it was not extinguished. God knew whence this light could be renewed, thought Käte, this light which in Germany had already sunk so low. It flickered, dipped, and dwindled to a glimmer, it—but no, it did not go out. God knew how it kept alive. But perhaps even God did not know, and she must ask Herr Koldewey, who sat upon Mount Ararat, with puppet strings in both his hands which he pulled to make the puppets dance. He shed his showman's guise and was revealed as Uncle Peerenboom, whom Theodor Storm has described, or was it Claus Groth. Pole Popenspäler, Jantje Claas, the eternal Punch whom the South Germans call Kasperl. And then the light burned very low, dusk fell upon the cell, its inmate had departed, and in the coffin it was very dark indeed. An absurd jingle began to run through her head: "We'll stand by you thin and thick—Friedel, Schröder, and Merzenich." And while she was trying to find a rhyme for Mengers, she fell asleep.

/

# CHAPTER FIVE

## AMONG FLOWERS

ANNETTE TOOK CARE that Käte Neumeier should not forget the hewer-off of heads. She rang up next day, full of remorse for the deplorable impression made on both of them the day before. It must be replaced as soon as possible by a pleasanter one. On the day after to-morrow a large Autumn flower-show was to be opened for the benefit of the crippled survivors of the last war, in which we had been involved as a result of President Wilson's astute campaign of Notes—so the *Hamburger Nachrichten* informed its readers. "Then it was Wilson, now it is Rosenfeld—Roosevelt", was the line taken by its leader-writers; however, the Autumn flower show would be a very fine affair. As her two sisters were acting as honorary saleswomen, she—Annette—had a free admission to the display which was not yet ready nor opened. She would call for Käte in the middle of the day, and drive her home again. If the sun was shining, it would be pleasant to sit beside the lake. For ten pfennigs they could buy from a disabled ex-soldier a bag of small fish, to be picked up by their tails and hurled at the seagulls which caught them in the air, thus combining entertainment, sport, and kindness to the birds. And after all there is still a feeling for flowers and birds, even in official Germany.

"At half-past twelve, then—I'll bring a little lunch with me—of the sandwich kind."

Once more Käte Neumeier caught herself shaking her head, though only for a second or two, as she hung up the receiver. What on earth had come over her? Did she catch a double meaning in Annette's friendly chatter—something like irony, and accusation? Or was her soul also soaked in bitterness, and was her ambiguity intended? The Third Reich had never been ashamed of its severity to the holders of false creeds, indeed it had taken credit for its attitude; but its express policy had always been to protect Nature and the animal world, as though that could not possibly be misinterpreted. Moreover, Käte Neumeier had never hitherto objected to such contradictions. "I am a man with a man's inconsistencies"—surely that was a quotation from C. F. Meyer's *Hutten*. Times of upheaval involved much harsh dealing of many kinds; but to the self-subsistent and enduring world of plants and animals, man must always behave with humanity. That had seemed quite sensible until the day before yesterday. But now an echo of some horrible merriment seemed to accompany those unexceptionable attitudes.

Towards the end of the morning something happened which nearly upset the arrangement. As Holzmüller, the post-office clerk, was going out, after making certain arrangements with the Frau Doctor, he met her nephew in the passage, one Boje by name, an engineer's draughtsman, son of a schoolmaster who had been killed in the war; and had married Grete Neumeier and lived a happy life with her until it was cut short by the agency of Wilhelm II. Bert Boje stood well with his aunt, who put her books at his disposal, and would have paid for a course of study for him, no matter what it cost; an offer which young Bert had with a gay laugh declined. Life had become a revolution, but Käte—he mostly called her familiarly by her Christian name—had not heard the echo of it yet. Universities! Even the curtailed curricula carried people out of contact with real life, the real nation and what it stood for. Moreover, all academic professions were overcrowded in Germany and elsewhere. No one in his senses to-day should enter on any long-term course of study, when technical knowledge was making such prodigious advances every day. An American engineer, whose name, by the way, was Moses, had invented an extraordinary system of motor-roads whereby the overcrowded city of New York could be shortly and painlessly relieved of its Sunday motorists and business men who wanted to get home in their own cars after the week's work. Such exit-roads, over the roofs or under the houses, would soon be adopted in the frontier cities of Germany, in the Ruhr, in the Hamburg district, in central Germany, and in Berlin. The Hamburg solution would be particularly exciting. Bert had got the morning off, as a difficulty had arisen out in Finkenwärder in connection with the Elbe bridge project, an objection by the *Reichswehr* against the fulfilment of certain plans, which might well have been made known three weeks before. They insisted that there must be no interference with the exits and entrances to the great subterranean petrol reservoirs in that area which belonged to the 9th

Army Corps, as the General in Command had indicated by a Frederickian *marginalium* on the plan submitted, and, moreover, this plan did not contain the complete truth, which was that the full extent of the scheme would have brought these tanks into the foundation works of the new bridge and necessitated their removal farther towards Cuxhaven. Supposing these gentlemen had to do without these tanks for one or two years, if it had been only possible to carry out the plan at this point and no other, just see how they jibbed at the slightest interference with their approach roads, the . . . ! Thus far Käte Neumeier let the impetuous young man run on—he had come to ask to spend his free morning with her, in such lovely weather, either in the restaurant of one of the great Stores, or on a long walk by the Alster Basin. At this point Herr Holzmüller intervened; he had been searching in the dark passage for almost as dark a glove, and without success. The young gentlemen in their brown tunics had—he said in his quavery, husky voice—every reason to be careful what they said, when the Army was concerned. That was a matter of discipline and order. In the Army camps and barracks scarcely one young man had come to any harm, though the Social Democrats were always shouting that many of them had. But anyone to-day who looked deeper into the matter, and into the needs of youth, realized this with even more conviction, and he would like in all modesty to deprecate such criticism of the best element in the Fatherland. So saying, with a venomous glance at the young S.A. man, and an old-fashioned bow to the Doctor, he took his departure. Bert Boje watched him with a laugh, though he was a little taken aback. "When these fellows are sitting behind their office window, they're full of courage, they keep the public waiting and generally do the heavy Wilhelm," he observed; "but it's odd that he should dare to behave that way in open country, unprotected, as though there were something personal about it."

"Let him be, Bert," rejoined Käte, as she got ready to go out. "Everyone has some sort of a parcel to carry; all isn't gold that glitters. I'm so glad you've got some free time—I've arranged to go to the flower-show with Annette Koldewey, a sort of pre-view, and she'll gladly take you in with us."

Bert Boje lifted his eyebrows. "Can't be done, unfortunately. I've just remembered that I must return some books I borrowed from the Public Library at Altona before one o'clock. Another time, with pleasure; and I'll bring them here. It's on my way."

Käte Neumeier remarked, but did not say so, as they went downstairs, that it was not on his way, but that Bert seemed to avoid any contact with Annette, though he certainly did not dislike her, as Käte thought she had noticed. Quite the contrary. But he possibly knew she was in firm hands, as the young people used to say in former days . . . and perhaps that rather upset him.

"Just when you can manage it, dear," said she, by way of closing that part of the interview. "We must keep ourselves free without fail for next Sunday, you and I." And on the way she got him to tell her more about the great opportunity which this project of the Führer's was regarded as offering to the young practitioners in the hydraulic-engineering world. Would Adolf Hitler manage to get his way as usual? He would no doubt impose his will on Hamburg landed interests, as he did upon his German people, and all Europe—and indeed upon all the forces of the age. Nothing must or could stand in the way of a genius.

The name Koldewey served as a password when they tapped at the closed glass doors, behind which could be heard much busy coming and going, the shifting of tables, and the unloading of crates. Annette, looking very attractive in her admirably cut coat and skirt of light grey tweed, and a stylish little felt hat fitting close over her cropped hair, greeted the official who was walking about with lists and pages in his hand, nodded to the under-gardener and proved herself an observant guide. Asters and dahlias would be the high lights of the display. What the growers had achieved in the way of colour, variety, and form, for the development of so commonplace a bloom, bordered on the miraculous. The haughty dahlias were rather thrust into the background, only the chrysanthemums maintained their royal dominance, and, indeed the chrysanthemum section was the most nearly ready. "Let us look at those," said Käte Neumeier, who felt uneasy among a half-finished display. Her eye caught an array of yellow and violet asters in pots, secured to tall sticks, on each side of the gangway. Here was a rich choice for a certain grave.

"Do you think you could very kindly get one of those pots for me to take away—if they're not beyond my means," she said, casually—"to Ohlsdorf, for Lene Prestow. You know what I mean."

"Certainly," nodded Annette. "Thyra gets a reduction. It won't cost the earth." As she spoke, she caught her lower lip with her neat young teeth: she should not have chosen just that word.

The display of chrysanthemums was indeed worthy of celebration by a poet, as the representative of the Berlin Ministry of Propaganda exclaimed on the opening day. On their tall firm stems, backed by their grey-green fringed and feathered foliage, ranged in admirably gradated hues, stood the magnificent great blooms: the white ones with petals rolled into heads of unbelievable size evoked all too early visions of snow and winter, the smaller ones, lilac and violet, seemed reluctant to part from summer; their petals, when rubbed, exhaled a minty fragrance. Among the yellow, almost honey-coloured flowers, Annette would gladly have lingered for a while had there been any sort of bench to sit on. They seemed to accord so sweetly with the years that she herself embodied, those unwearied years that lead from youth into maturity. Käte Neumeier, on the other hand, confessed a preference for the twin-coloured flowers, topped with striped fur caps of russet and amber, which looked for all the world like the busbies of fantastic grenadiers: they gave out a faint odour of camomile from close at hand. They stood, as she expressed it, betwixt and between, as lovely as women's breasts, firm and full.

"It's a sort of symphony on the theme of autumn colours, red and yellow," exclaimed Annette in wonderment. "Just the ones you hardly notice when you walk on fallen leaves."

"Yes," said Käte; "but for flowers, lilac and yellow are reckoned autumn colours, because they can still get most of their effect from the fading light. 'Economy, Horatio, economy'."

At this Annette indignantly protested; she agreed with the Chinese, who devised enchanting tales of love affairs between students and the Dryads or Fairies who inhabited such flowers. "Except that they introduce the peony into these legends. Now peonies are stupid and have no souls."

"I agree," said Käte Neumeier. "But what about the Chinese variety?"

"Lotie Garchow was born in China. We might ask her," suggested Annette. Then she burst into a ripple of laughter. "But she has come back aged seven years old, and doesn't remember anything she saw. She has turned into a peony herself."

Through the glass walls—Annette reminded herself to tell Ingebottel to get them polished before the opening day—through the high glass walls shone the autumn noon, smoothly and delicately blue; nearby the air was clear, but the distance was veiled in haze. The two women, one young indeed and one still young, walked up and down between the arrays of pots, bent over the blossoms, and called each other's attention to this or that specimen: but the attraction of this display of the gardener's art soon began to pall.

"My wise father, who sent his best regards to you——"

"Thank you," said Käte Neumeier.

"——discovered, he says, the observation in a Swiss newspaper that the Weimar Republic will later be compared with an autumn flower-garden, where everything is for the last time gathered in a brief burst of glorious colour, before winter puts an end to all that blooms. In conclusion the writer quoted some stanzas from Stefan George's poem 'The Years of the Soul'."

"How short-sighted," cried Käte Neumeier, "to compare the Third Reich to winter. Though—perhaps not: winter must come forth to announce the spring." And then she had suddenly to stop herself shaking her head as she wondered which Käte Neumeier had said that? She of to-day? Or she of the day before yesterday?

Fortunately Annette was not then looking at her: from the next room, among the dahlias and asters, something of a dispute began to reach their ears.

"Let's go outside and eat our sandwiches and get a cup of chocolate, and sit in the sun like two city dames on an outing," she suggested. Then—"What on earth is the matter with those excited gentlemen next door?"

Someone had discovered at the last moment that the rows of flowers in the main hall—blackish-red chrysanthemums, purple dahlias, yellow asters, arrayed in broad strips, presented the colours of a certain, now outlawed, but once popular *Reich* flag, the Black-Red-and-Mustard of a previous régime. It transpired that this arrangement had been thought-

G

lessly adopted from the last flower show, which had taken place almost
five years ago in the same hall.   It would have promptly consigned all
those responsible to a concentration camp.   Orders were given for all
the hundreds of pots to be interchanged, the yellow asters replaced by
white, and the red dahlias to be set in the foremost and lower rows of
shelves.   It would mean two hours labour, but the *Reich* colours,
Black-White-Red would be restored.

The two ladies sat—though they did not know it—on the very bench
where Herr Footh had concluded that momentous luncheon with Albert
Teetjen: but, as though the great chestnut tree, a witness of that day,
were radiating influences down upon them, they were talking about
Albert.   Swans glided across the broad waters of the Alster, attracted
by the sight of people eating.

"How could we have been so foolish," said Käte Neumeier, as
though speaking to herself, "as to go to see that horrible performance?"

"You yourself proposed it," replied Annette softly.   "A doctor should
not shrink from anything."

"So I did," admitted the other; "and I bitterly regret it.   The
vision of it still haunts me."   And she took a bite of sandwich.   "But
how did your friend, Footh, find that horrible fellow?   It can't have
been easy to have got hold of such a museum piece—such a positive
throw-out from the age of paganism?"

Annette smiled at the odd expression.   "To please me, and with
your assistance."

Käte Neumeier's sandwich almost dropped from her hand.   "I beg
your pardon?" she said softly, but in a tone of such intensity that Annette
almost trembled.

"It's true," she persisted.   "He wrote a letter containing all sorts
of suggestions—asking for the protection of the Municipality or the
Senate.   But the envelope was addressed in your hand."

Käte Neumeier sat speechless, her wide-open eyes fixed on Annette's
face.   "Is there no mistake?" she said, breathing heavily.   "I do
sometimes give to people who want work, and deserve help, the addresses
of personal friends who are likely to be of use to them—and more
attention would be paid to a letter addressed to you in my handwriting.
But I can't remember. . . . Did I give one to you?   When was it?"

She fell silent, staring at the opposite bank; but her vision was so
clouded that she could scarcely distinguish what she saw.   It just
couldn't be so.

"One of Footh's characteristics is that he keeps letters in their
envelopes.   Whether for the stamps, or as being tidier, I couldn't say.
But I'll ring him up.   And you shall have the proof in your own
hand."

Käte Neumeier felt as though the earth was trembling beneath her.
The sight of the envelope might remind her for whom she had written
it at the time.   She could not endure to think she had had any share
in this act of shame.

"Yes," she said.   "Please let me have it.   As a *memento mori*, so
that I may give up the practice.   I'll never do so again—if that is

how it happened. What can be set in motion by such a scrap of writing —one simply does not realize."

My Friedel!—said a voice within her. "Could you drive me home now? It was a good idea of yours to come."

"Say it with flowers," said Annette, quoting a placard then much affected by flower-shops. "May I take you to Ohlsdorf on Sunday? Thyra will have brought your asters to us by then."

"That's very kind of you. And Herr Footh's envelope?"

"You shall have it by to-morrow's post."

.  .  .  .  .  .  .  .

Anneliese Blüthe followed and approved her chief's meticulous habit of keeping private letters in their envelopes. Not only was she enough of a stamp-collector to feel a sacred reverence for the idea of the stamped envelope, she had also read of the remarkable dispositions of destiny such envelopes sometimes brought about. She had merely hesitated whether she should lay it silently on her chief's writing-table when he telephoned for it about three o'clock, or whether she should take the document in to him herself; finally deciding on the former alternative. If she wanted to achieve a purpose not yet clearly envisaged, she had better keep out of the way, and be strictly impersonal.

And so, about half-past three, Herr Footh found Teetjen's appeal, in its envelope, under a letter weight which was the sole memento of the world war that he had carried with him into his new existence; a sort of Roman sword, hammered out of the copper nose-ring of a heavy shell, a rough and rather unfinished article, as the cuts impressed on the metal by the barrel boring at the moment of discharge could still be seen. "Albert Teetjen, Master-Butcher"—well, the old boy had done his job well, and brought no discredit on Herr Footh or his own profession. His tail-coat had given him a rather awkward appearance, but there had been nothing awkward about his operations. In return for the 7 marks 70 which Herr Footh had invested in him up-to-date he had certainly done manful service. His training had been of much benefit to the store-rooms on the tankers *Einäuglein* and *Rotauge*, but the execution of his duties must have duly impressed the *Reichsstatthalter*. It was now for Herr Footh to announce the favours that he expected in return. He—Footh, of course—not Teetjen. A great deal of money was being made in Germany at the time. New blocks of shares were being issued or pushed on to new owners. Economic resources were accumulating in quarters which, before Hitler's rise, could only have dreamed of such prosperity. The Party harvest was in full ear.

Herr Footh stood up before his writing-table, and with his hands in his pockets walked across to the great window from which he enjoyed a wide view of a pale-blue, misty expanse of harbour, where his ships, too, had their home. From every side came a din of hooting, buzzing, whistling and hammering: At the moment none were lying below in the black, gleaming waters over which the little green ferry-steamers were darting to and fro.   Nor did he see much of the buildings, piers, tank installations, or pumps.   He looked into the grey clouds driving in from the open sea, from the North Sea, a good eighty kilometres away to the North West.   And he looked into his future.   Two alternatives lay before him: he could either negotiate for himself and his fleet to be advantageously absorbed in the *Reich* Transport Company, which was taking an ever-increasing share in his supply of fuel to the State, or he could establish himself as the nucleus of a Transport Company, which he would develop into an important concern before negotiating, on suitable terms, an association with a larger undertaking.   The Jewish Shipping Company "Thetis" had been compelled to cease operations.   Its tankers would be swallowed up by the *Reich* navy, unless disposed of otherwise.   Three handsome vessels.   Should Herr Footh suggest to the *Reichsstatthalter* that it would be to the interest of the crews, who were Party Comrades, to leave them in private employ—*i.e.* in Herr Footh's employ?   The *Reich* could be compensated by suitable sums from the funds of the Labour Front.   Concentration of interests was much in the air.   When the suppression of Trusts was plastered up as an irre-fragable item in the Party programme, the N.S.D.A.P., was, as the phrase goes, still in nursery shoes.   No sensible person thought the worse of the Party for that.   Only if it had stuck to such a project, and taken no account of the realities of life, would there have been any ground for protest.   Man must be rational, adapt himself to facts, and take care to warm himself at the little fire he had so dexterously kindled.

Herr Footh would have liked to discuss his dilemma with someone. But Annette was no good for questions of this sort.   Her sphere lay on the other side of business in the agreeable domain which—God knows—he supposed must be called reality too.   But to enjoy this second reality, a man must meet the claims of the first.   And to deal with it, a man must carry his nose as high as did the priests of the land of culture, such as Annette, her haughty papa, or this Neumeier woman, who wanted her envelope back—God knows why.   It would be only polite to write a few lines with it.   He telephoned for Fräulein Blüthe.

Anneliese tripped in with a gay, swinging gait, which she had tried in vain to subdue.   Her pretty nose, her bright eyes, her mop of fair hair, aroused agreeable sensations in Herr Footh.   The girl was certainly no fool.   Why shouldn't he consult her on the question that was now burdening his mind ?

"A couple of lines to Frau Doctor Neumeier, Wandsbeker Chausée, 2."

He eyed with approval the quick, deft movements with which she slipped a sheet of his smaller notepaper, and the flimsy for the copy, into the machine, and produced the covering letter as quickly as he could dictate it.   He hastened—so the letter ran—to send back the envelope which had performed so valuable a service to the State, and to thank her for it.   "Yours sincerely."   Then she typed the address on a business envelope, put letter and envelope into the folder for signature, as her custom was, and laid it open before his chair.   In the meantime the telephone bell rang; enquiries as to when the lubricating oil might be expected to arrive, and information about the capacity of a new subterranean reservoir on the Lower Elbe, the completion of which would be wholly unaffected by the projected Elbe suspension bridge. What neat, slim hips the girl had. Footh replaced the receiver, signed his letter, and asked Fräulein Blüthe to sit down for a minute. So saying, he pointed to a corner of the writing-table, on which she sat herself without a trace of embarrassment. Her short skirt exposed an expressive knee, on which she laid her clasped hands. She had been long enough in the business, said Herr Footh, to have formed a just estimate of its prospects. He for his part wanted to get a clear view on a certain question, and he thought she could help him. She would use what brains she had, she promised him, with a swift flick of her long eyelashes. Oil, he said—as she must know—was not merely the basis of industry, but also of modern warfare.

"I know that quite well," she answered. "My brother is serving in the Ninth tanks."

"Indeed," said he. "What exalted connections! I was merely a plain infantryman, a foot-slogger."

She laughed. "That's why you're now an oil Admiral, Herr Footh," she rejoined; "and fly the flag of the N.S.K.K."

"You put it very nicely," said he with a smile; got out of his chair, and sat on, or rather leaned his thigh against, the corner of the writing-table next to her, resting the weight of his body on the other leg.

"Do you think our business is capable of expansion, or had it better be amalgamated with a larger group? That is the dilemma I am facing now."

She looked at him so intently that the pupils of her light grey eyes widened until the eyes seemed almost black. She made as though to jump down from the writing-table.

"Herr Footh, how can anyone advise you without investigating our plant and resources, our credit, and the secret reserves. True," she went on, thinking aloud, "the three Thetis ships are to be had. Perhaps a chance in a life-time."

He nodded genially, took her hands by their slender wrists and held them in his left hand, while with his right he stroked her knee. "You are right," he said in a husky voice. "We must talk it all over. Would you have time to take a cup of tea with me, Anneliese?"

"If I may telephone home," she replied, without moving.

· · · · · · · ·

And so Käte Neumeier got her envelope by the morning's post. She held it in her hand, her finger tips recognized the letter paper, the sheets of which she had used up in bulky letters to Karl August Lintze, so that a number of envelopes were left over. She had used them for recommendations and appeals. But to whom had this one gone? She ought to form the habit of entering anything she gave away in a book.

She was much too casual about such matters.   Now everything depended on her being able to remember such details.   She sat down in her breakfast chair, relaxed, closed her eyes, and tried to summon up forgotten trivialities.   Sundry details of her recent activities passed through her mind—the chrysanthemums of yesterday, the asters, Lene Prestow; a sandy hill in Ohlsdorf cemetery, which she had never yet seen. Then Tom Barfey came into her thoughts, the crippled youth with his little wheeled trolley, which he could now scarcely use in the street. Yes, that was it.   Gesche Barfey had wanted to get Herr Footh's washing to do, and she had written the envelope for her accordingly, so that the handwriting might serve as a hint to Annette to employ the stout-hearted little laundrywoman.   She drew a deep breath, looked into the room, and into the future.   The journey of this messenger of death could now be followed up . . . "which had performed so valuable a service to the State" . . .

# BOOK THREE

# WITH THE STREAM

## CHAPTER ONE

### BRAVE STINE

A MAN WHO has money in his pocket, walks quite differently through the streets of his native city from what he does with a pack of debts upon his back.  He treats himself and his wife to a bottle of port wine, he tells her she can get herself the brown shoes, which have now dropped in price as winter is at hand, and have her black ones soled, and not to be surprised if he brings home a new box of cigars, not another discoloured parcel of rejects, but genuine Brazilians, and two pfennigs a piece dearer than the former lot of *Vorstenlanders*.  She had had to clean a tail-coat before it went back to the hire department, but that was hardly a matter for surprise in the case of a slaughterer, and bloodstains are easily removed.  He would have liked to display himself to Stine in this guise.  But Herr Footh had prevented this: he had him fetched from home, made him change his clothes in the attic in Footh's house, drove him to Fuhlsbüttel, and brought him home in uniform once more.  Except for the days of training the whole affair had only meant a few hours departure from Albert's daily life—a sort of dream, no more.  Not a pleasant dream—there was no denying that. . . .  But two thousand four hundred marks for an hour's work in the early morning, that was something that could be seen and heard, felt and admired.  These hundred-mark notes were no witch's money, they did not change into watercress leaves when they were brought home and locked into a drawer.  They remained beautiful bright banknotes from Dr. Schacht's magic workshop, and that was that.

Albert Teetjen's immediate neighbours did not, during the first few days, see any alteration in the conditions of his life.  He was astute enough not to make any display of his improved circumstances.  He knew that when a man pays his debts, the fact gets talked about, and if he gives no explanations the creditor's satisfaction at being paid is combined with astonishment at the favour vouchsafed by destiny, and evokes a feeling of respect.  Moreover, Teetjen had no notion of paying any dues to his comrades of the S.S. Prester Sturm out of what he had earned on September 15th.  The job hadn't been so pleasant, though the men from Oldenburg had got the victims very expeditiously into

place on the block—"Now then, Sir, neatly through the vertebræ!"
But in Hamburg they did not deign to obey instructions that applied
to Prussians, even though they came from Hermann Göring himself.
An amateur can't learn the art in a fortnight, as the *Reichsjägermeister*
would expect it to be practised, and slit the victims' throats.  Hamburg
was a city of tradition, and what was good enough for Klaus Stortebekker
and his Merry Men must also suffice for the actors in the Reeperbahn
case.  Even so, the proceeding had been quite enough for Albert
Teetjen's nerves.  It would be time to talk about his performance
later on, when the papers were allowed to report it.  Then, in a month
or two, as opportunity offered, he could produce a newspaper cutting
from his pocket and show it to his comrades: "That was I who settled
those Red dogs' business for them."  For the present he would content
himself with drinking his glass of beer at Lehmke's in the quiet hours of
the morning between nine and ten, and reading his *Hamburger Tageblatt*
more carefully than was his wont.  But hitherto it had contained nothing
about the incident, not so much as a line.  To some extent Albert
Teetjen was glad about this, but on the whole he was annoyed.  On the
one hand, the reporters had probably tried to discover the identity of
the executioner, if newspaper men had been admitted to the ceremony,
and the probably ensuing prejudice might have caused him a certain
amount of trouble.  On the other hand a man liked to figure in the
paper—honour to whom honour is due: if no one could know about it,
what was the use of so emphatic an example of the fulfilment of a public
duty.  Well, Teetjen must sacrifice that satisfaction for the moment.  In
any case, there were those in the know who could bear testimony in case
of need, as for example, and in particular, his old friend Footh.
   The greatest temptation against which he had to contend arose
from his heightened sense of self-importance.  Should he not at last
engage an assistant who would relieve him of the coarser labours of his
calling?  So far as they had not been performed by the slaughter-house
employé's, Albert Teetjen carried them out himself in the former wash-
house which he had rented from the landlord, as immediately adjoining
his shop, only a few steps across the yard.  (A well-lit and convenient
room—a former carriage-house, in fact—had been set aside for the
housewives who did their own washing.)  For the space of a few days
it now seemed to Albert undignified that he should himself stand there
in a blood-bespattered apron dissecting half a pig or half a sheep, after
he had performed his duty as it were upon a stage.  But a brief calculation
with a pencil on the back of an order-form warned him against prematurely launching out.  True, he could now put capital into his business.
Winter was coming on, people would need more meat even under the
one-dish-a-meal order, which gave housewives a weekly opportunity
of doing their duty by using up scraps.  The farmers would kill their
pigs, the Martinmass goose was the proper fare for Luther's birthday,
as could be observed from notices in the newspapers.  Advertising cost
money, but earned it too.  However, a shop window adorned with
flowers was very useful, and this was a job that Stine understood; the
Autumn Show in the Alster Pavilion would, when it was over, provide

a cheap supply of asters and chrysanthemums, and pots of such blooms on the right and left of a cardboard pig's head, with a cardboard lemon in a cardboard spoon stuck in its snout—such a display of garden flowers lasted a long time, and did tempt customers to enter his shop. It was this sort of decoration that lured people into the provision department of the accursed Stores; God punish them! In the World War there had been people who had made their letters and accounts more impressive by the aid of a rubber-stamp inscribed with the battle-cry: "God punish England". Albert in those days reflected whether he should but suggest to the Butcher's Association the creation of a stamp inscribed: "Avoid the Stores". With due respect to the worthy Footh's misgivings, now that he had a little money in his pocket, why not make a firm appeal to the Senate and Municipality, and show them how and where they were neglecting their duty? God had bestowed many glorious gifts on the Führer, and the whole nation gave thanks to him for what he had done; indeed elderly ladies, so it was reported, did so on their knees. But the great man had paid dearly for it all, in Albert Teetjen's view. He understood nothing about women nor about roast meat. In the matter of continence and the monkish life there was no cause for argument, every man must settle that for himself, though Albert Teetjen could scarcely have got through the week's work without his Stine. What the Pastor called married bliss, and what in the Army was called by various other names, had to exist. But the fact that vegetarianism was lunacy could be scientifically proved. Man, said the doctors, in their talks on the wireless, was constructed intestinally just like the pig, with due respect to humanity; and like that useful domestic animal he was adapted to eat anything. A Führer who not merely played the vegetarian but— alas—was a most rigid and convinced devourer of spinach—such a Führer was an awkward sort of hero for the butchers' fraternity. Not a back of bacon, a leg of veal, nor even a succulent lamb cutlet would find favour in his eyes. How could the people, the mob that followed in his footsteps, be expected to take the right views about food? If the fat and genial Göring, patron saint of airmen, had not done his bit to help the butchers and the hewers-off of heads, where would they have been? Well, however this might be—he must advertise. The urge to buy must be stimulated. Under rearmament the German citizens' earnings were, generally speaking, irregular, but he did earn. And despite the rise in the cost of living, every man had some part of his wages to take to the butcher, and it would be very wrong if he didn't.

"I suppose you're well in with Footh, Albert?" So saying, landlord Lehmke sat down confidentially beside his neighbour, who had just put down eighty marks on the table, part of which had been owing for nearly a year; and he put two schnapps' glasses and a bottle of crystal-clear Kümmel on a small tray, in order to celebrate the event with due propriety. "Anyone can make debts," he observed philosophically, as they clinked glasses; "but when it comes to paying them—that calls for more character and decency than the average man possesses." And after they had savoured the sweet, acrid taste of the liqueur on their tongue and gums, with a sort of humorous indignation he told the story of a Düsseldorf publican's son, a typical, plausible *Rhinelander,* to whom he—Lehmke —had been crazy enough, at the outset of his career, to lend the sum of two hundred marks because the banks were shut. The young man had vanished never to be seen again; but five years ago had turned up in Haifa, in Palestine, where he had opened a café in the harbour quarter, and had astutely evaded the activities of the Consular authorities who had tried to get Herr Lehmke his rights. Albert listened with much amusement. Lehmke used the most violently expressive words, contracted his wrinkled skin upon his forehead, and rolled his little eyes beneath their reddened lids, in imitation of the Rhinelander, thus indicating how well he understood the distinction between that gentleman and the reliable Albert.

"Footh?—Oh yes," said Teetjen, gladly accepting a second glass. "Haven't I told you how he would never have come to anything without my help. He has often enough admitted as much to me, and I'm not boasting when I say so. But it's nice to remember how a man began, and see him make a success of it." And he went on to tell how Footh and himself, in the year '17, when all scrap metal began to be scarce, had belonged to the same search unit, which had scoured the great forests by the Lithuanian rivers for any such material. Russian prisoners were detailed for the service, and with their help they discovered in a broad sandy clearing a veritable treasure of brass shell-cases and grease tins, and metal from the wheels of guns, timbers, and lorries. It was clear that, somewhere about 1915 probably, a Russian artillery park had been destroyed, lock, stock, and barrel, by bombs and a forest fire; but the brass fitments were undamaged, and the vast heaps of empty shell-cases proved that the batteries, each of eight guns, had well deserved the attentions of the airmen. So Sergeant Footh, and Corporal Teetjen, spent a whole summer and autumn extracting the brass scrap, and making the prisoners carry it in long procession down to the Niemen, which they did in high good humour. For, as could be imagined, there were many more unpleasant tasks that prisoners could be set to do. Then the winter hid the hillock of brass under a covering of snow, and its situation was known only to Footh and Teetjen, who had reported their hoard—as it was called by the authorities at *Ober-Ost*—for removal, as their duty was. But nothing happened. The wheels of the official machine did not rotate. And from the end of '17, the network of railways had to transport a number of divisions to the west, a gigantic fighting army, complete with its equipment of guns, field-kitchens, stores, and ammunition. The mound of brass remained where it was, and in the meantime German housewives were urged to bring their mortars, door-handles, even oven-doors, and lay them on the altar of the Fatherland. When the end came, which fell out so differently from what had been expected, the mound of brass still stood, now partly covered with verdigris, at the top of the steeply escarped bank of the Niemen. "Then the great idea came to Footh. He got into touch with the raftsmen who inhabit those parts, helped them to build rafts from the trees felled by the Forest Section, loaded the whole dump, with the aid of the prisoners under my supervision, on to the rafts, promised the *Flessaki* the sale-price of the timber, which they could sell in Memel, as pay for their part of the job, and so set off with me and the whole outfit downstream. I had my concertina with me, and it was a jolly journey home, as you can imagine. Well, at that season of the year timber had never been shipped down the Niemen, and we had covered up the brass with old army tarpaulins, which also fetched a very nice price in Memel; you can imagine me on top of them with my old squeaker, trolling out: 'Home again, home again, that's the place for me.' And those rafts on the Niemen were the beginning of the Footh Shipping Co., as you see it flourishing to-day. A thing like that brings fellows together and keeps them together."

"It's a good story," grinned Otto Lehmke. "Warms the heart, and it shows you what a man who really takes hold can do for himself. Yes, those were the times. What was the use of the bit of loot that came our way when the Party seized power? Even a wily fellow like Footh would have been hard put to it to get started on such a business with the help of a few sticks of furniture and books. Well, it's worth another kümmel. And what have you been up to this time? Good health, Albert!"

Teetjen knew, in fact, that in those January days Lehmke's stock of house-linen had doubled.

"That's the sort of question people ask, Otto, and it's also the sort that can't be answered. But no offence meant, of course. This kümmel is prime. And so—here's your health!"

It was thus that he meant to evade the questions that might have been put to him by his S.S. comrades, if Lehmke had not kept his mouth shut. It was better that no one should know that he now had ready money in his pocket. As the papers did not mention his heroic deed, this could be managed without any trouble, particularly as in the last few weeks the attention of the public had been diverted from internal matters. The Party Day had been celebrated in a spirit of violent hostility to the Bolsheviks and the Komintern; Communism had been classed with all that Russia stood for, hatred of civilization and plans for world conquest, and the diplomats present had had the crusade against World Enemy No. I dinned into their ears. But, at the same time, in well-informed circles, to which the Preester *Sturm* belonged, thanks to the fact that the editor of the *Hamburg Economic Review* was among its members, another rally-cry was to be heard. And this was—bauxite, magnesite, light metals generally, and related to large deposits of these substances in little Austria, which could not utilize them, while they were indispensable for putting the German aircraft-industry on to a war footing. For that reason the people must be prepared for the *Anschluss* with Austria to be realized within the next few months. All too long had the comrades beyond the frontier groaned under Chancellor Schusschnigg's Catholic yoke. Much would have to be made good to the Austrian Nazis, the original and traditional Leaders of that name. The Ambassador, Herr von Papen, the Führer's astutest agent, had done his best to sell the pass. Mussolini had been induced to abandon his watch upon the Brenner. The main problem was to convince the Western Powers, those accursed Democracies, of the injustice inflicted on the German people when, by the terms of the Versailles and St. Germain's treaties, the ardently desired union had been blocked and prohibited. The Poles must be stirred up to fall upon the Czechs, those besotted and hereditary enemies of Germany, and the world at large warned of the horrors that would be involved in the invasion by the Red Army of the European castle of the Grail, whose bulwark was National Socialism. That was to be proclaimed as the mission of the Führer and his faithful followers, among whom the Comrades of the S.S. were the most prominent. Their social evenings were taken up with discussions of this kind. In comparison with all these matters, the changes of command in the highest places of the *Reichswehr* was of little importance. Anyone fortunate enough to lead against the enemy, under Hitler's eye, the new popular army he had created, whether Fritsch or Blomberg, Keitel or Brauchitsch, was a matter that left a real National-Socialist cold. These gentlemen had learned their profession, and woe to them if they did not practise it to Adolf Hitler's satisfaction. The 'Black Corps' had already called an aristocrat War Minister to account. The lion's spoor was terrifying. When such observations fell from Comrade Editor Vierkant, in Lehmke's back room, Albert Teetjen stroked his moustache, and flashed his fine, blue eyes round the little assemblage. Nobody knew that he had been one of the first to do his part in the struggle against Bolshevism, had proved his loyalty, and fulfilled his duty. A man must know when to be silent and trust to the fact that in a well-ordered State founded upon justice, no good service ever passed unrecognized.

He had even said nothing to Stine. To her credit it must be added that she had made no difficulties for him in the matter. A woman has many means of indicating to a man that she wants to share his secrets, or of extracting them from him, as for instance in his Sunday hot bath, or, using her last trump, in bed. But Stine had made no efforts of the kind. Completely unchanged, and unburdened by any curiosity, she let those weeks pass by. And it was very proper behaviour for a man in his position, in a city where the harbour with its tanks and industrial installations, and all its wharves and quays and docks in the time of the re-armament-drive was brimming with all manner of activities that must not be mentioned. She could, indeed, have made a fuss and pestered him, and taken offence because he could not trust her discretion; but she did nothing of the kind. Even when the whole affair was at an end, and a handsome little bundle of blue bank-notes was slipped into an envelope and locked into the top drawer of the cupboard, even then she refrained from any comment that went beyond an understandable joy and relief. A grand girl, his Stine. On the other hand, this state of affairs must end, and end soon. She would carry his notes to the post-office, pay them in at the Savings' Bank counter, for to keep such a fortune in the house was a mere invitation to a burglar. Not but what the Third Reich had pretty well got rid of such personages. No one could deny the sharp drop in the curve that depicted, for statistical purposes, the frequency of burglaries and robberies with violence. "Everything among us is conducted in a highly legal fashion," Editor Vierkant of the *Economic News*, who was something of a humorist, had once observed: "Even the forcible acquisition of wealth." But it would be really cruel for a man to compel his wife to put eighteen hundred mark notes into her handbag, and pay them across the counter of the Wandsbek Branch Post Office, without telling her whence this blessing had come. And cruelty was not a quality of Albert Teetjen. A butcher is not cruel, he does his job, and is justly indignant when the children are afraid of him, or dance and sing outside his shop, to prove that they are not in the least afraid of him—such as "Little Mary sat on a stone, and then came brother Charles, and stabbed Little Mary through the heart".

And so it came about that she learned the secret on an ordinary week-day, in the morning, while Albert was slipping selected bits of beef and pork into the sausage machine, to produce a very popular kind of mixture known as mash. . . . Meanwhile, Stine was polishing the brass trays and weights of an old-fashioned scales, which stood on the counter beside the modern weighing-machine with its figured dial and indicator, and descended from Albert's father, Master-Butcher Hermann Teetjen, still remembered by dozens of customers in Wandsbek. Albert made sure that she was thus busily employed; a man should not spring surprises on a woman when she is in her periods. The recurrence of these periods, which are often the subject of comment and conversation among married people, provided the Teetjens', too, with occasions of the sort. Stine wanted children, Albert did not. She would have gladly carried her offspring on her arm, and fed them at her breast. But Albert demonstrated with his pencil after closing-time that during the inflation of 1923 the blessing of children would have been for both of them a leak in the boat which his butcher's shop could have done nothing to plug. When the Party came into power, with an unalterable programme promising support and help of every kind for those engaged in trade, Stine believed that her harvest would come to fullness, and her body would be suffered to carry the compact little blooms of womanhood; but the monthly accounts still demonstrated the contrary. And, strangely enough, as if Albert had been absorbed into her very fibres, her body did refuse to conceive; and this though in her light-hearted fashion— for she did indeed want to know herself fruitful—she in no way assisted his precautionary measures, and very reluctantly took any steps if anything went wrong. She was unwell every twenty-six days, with a regularity that the wife of an official might have envied. Her doctor, Frau Käte Neumeier, who had read a great deal and was full of ideas, one night as she lay in bed unable to sleep, came upon a possible explanation of this fact. The probability was that Stine Teetjen shared this barrenness with certain aunts and great-aunts of the Geisow line, who laid an addled egg every month. By Mendelian law such exceptions always recurred. But it might well also be that something in Stine Teetjen herself revolted against her husband's trade. She had once laughingly told her doctor how odd it was for her to have married a butcher. She came of a sect of Mennonites, or Adventists. Käte

Neumeier was incapable of distinguishing between these strange enthusiasts. Stine's grandmother had refused to recognize Sunday, and had
instilled into her granddaughter that the Lord, the preacher of the
Sermon on the Mount, beside the Lake of Genezaret, had kept the
Sabbath only as a day of rest, but that Sunday was for work. She had
also taken care that Stine took a position as maid in a pious Jewish
house, and also imparted to her a distaste of eating meat. "And then
I go and fall in love with a butcher," Stine had said, "which was by no
means a small matter, as it turned out. I also thought that I should
feel much more strongly about it than I did, when Albert was hanging
round me. But, Frau Doctor, I didn't mind at all. No one knows how
love is going to take you, and Albert was such a handsome lover.
And indeed I have had nothing to regret, God knows. And as for the
sectarian disputes and 'serious searching of the Bible', and all that—
why, I just dropped it." Dr. Neumeier, outstretched in her bed, had—as
she pondered over all that Stine had told her—applied a question-mark
to that last statement, and made up her mind to discuss it with a colleague
sometime, perhaps with young Laberdan at Fuhlsbüttel. Was it delving
too far to ascribe to the grand-maternal influence this failure to conceive
with a master-butcher in the father's rôle? However that might be,
she had soon forgotten her purpose. Stine herself was, of course, very
far from such speculations. . . . At that precise moment, she was
crouching on her little stool, with one bowl of the scales in her lap and
polishing the other with an old woollen stocking, with a faintly roguish
and significant smile on her face, at being able to exchange one secret
for another; for the day before yesterday should have been her Day.
It would have been a happy coincidence, when, now that her circumstances had improved and her little ship of life seemed to have ceased
to be a 'leaky boat', if a little fair-haired Teetjen had announced its
arrival, boy or girl, no matter which. However, she wasn't going to let
it out to Teetjen straight away, especially as he had been so very far
from frank with her of late.

"If you've quite finished with father's scales, young Stine, put this
little packet of duff in your pocket, as we used to say among the Prussians,
when the pay-master came round, like a revolving searchlight, every
ten days. And don't let anyone pinch it before you get to the shop.
Besides, the money was too hardly earned for that."

Stine was immediately conscious that she ought to have asked him
then and there to tell her how he had in fact earned it. But she wouldn't
so far gratify him, and replied instead:

"Anyone who did get hold of them would soon find himself in
trouble. I took the numbers of all the notes at once, as Frau Plaut
taught me to do."

Albert Teetjen looked up from a slab of pinkish dough that he was
kneading, and shook his head in astonishment; though he ought to have
known that his Stine had plenty of sense behind those flat little ears of
hers.

"Does that mean that we get another lot if someone pinches them?"
he asked, with a brief pause.

"Who knows?" she answered. "There must be some sense in it, otherwise the Jews wouldn't do it. They know what they're up to."

"Yes," smiled Albert, "but so do we. We've got wise to their little dodges, and are now paying them in their own coin. Now don't you want to know how I came into this money?"

"I'm not going to persuade anyone to tell me what he oughtn't."

"That's right enough," he agreed; "though it wasn't anything I oughtn't to have done, quite the contrary in fact—the job that Comrade Footh put in my way. It was to take the place of the Hamburg excutioner in the Reeperbahn case; and I did so."

Stine sat in her chair, listened to the sound of rubbing on the shining copper, and looked into his eyes.

"You——?" she asked, after drawing two breaths in silence.

"Carried out the sentence, and sent four criminals into the next world." Stine, motionless, let the bowl drop; it fell with a metallic clang on to the concrete floor. Her lips were parted, her eyes wandered vaguely up to the ceiling, and then found their way back to his lips.

"Is it true?" she asked, in a toneless voice.

"Meister Denke was ill," he said encouragingly, "and the Führer wouldn't come to Hamburg otherwise. You know from the wireless how keen he was about the Elbe suspension bridge. So some outside help had to be got; and this time it was ours."

Stine shook her head. "I hope it won't lead to trouble," she said, under her breath.

"Yes," he agreed. "People are so silly," he went on, glad that she had taken the news so sensibly. "It had better not be talked about. But no one could have recognized me. I wore a mask over my nose, like the bullocks in old days, before the humane-killer was invented. Except that this time it wasn't the ox that wore the mask."

"And you had a tail-coat on as well," she muttered—it seemed as though her lower jaw would not lend itself to speech. He nodded. "It's a comic get-up, certainly; a swallow-tail coat with a white tie. But it's well suited to the job. Everything cut away in front. What hangs behind isn't in the way."

Stine laid her hands on her knees. She felt suddenly weak. So he had cut four heads off, had her Albert! The times seemed to turn men into strange beings. And then she was aware that she must go to her bedroom and change her linen. Her day had come. First she tried to set up father's scales on the shop counter. But the bowls had suddenly grown too heavy. "If only it doesn't lead to trouble," she repeated, tottering to the door.

"Well, you must keep your mouth shut," he rejoined good-humouredly, glad that everything had gone off so easily, "and invent a neat explanation, such as a lottery or legacy, if anyone asks questions."

As she stood in the doorway, she turned round once again. "Which axe was it?" and the syllables came with a strange heaviness from her lips.

"Grandfather's," he said cheerfully. "It had been lying so long unused in the cupboard. And in fact it looked almost exactly like an

executioner's axe, except that I had to fix a longer shaft on it.  First-rate
steel," he added, "Sheffield-made.  Everything good comes from
England."

When Stine sat down on her bed, and then quickly lay back, she was
afraid she was going to faint.  The room was spinning round her like
a merry-go-round—she could never remember anything so silly happening
to her before.  And her head was in a whirl.  Her grandmother, the
Rabbi's wife—Sunday—the Sabbath—the Sermon on the Mount beside
the Lake of Gethsemane—or was it Geneserath?  "He who sheds man's
blood, by men shall his blood be shed," she saw in the large print of her
Luther Bible.  "For I am the Lord," printed by the English Bible
Society.  Everything good came from England, Albert had said.  Didn't
he keep a bottle of kümmel in his cupboard?  She had better have
a drop and then go down to the post-office.  Fancy her lying in her
bed on a week-day like a Senator's lady!—though, indeed, she wished
she could.  But she must not so indulge herself.  She must fix her
bandage and get going.  It was lovely weather, a warm dry October
day; she could quite well put on her new brown shoes, the sports shoes
she had bought at Jew Lehman's sale.  It was really extraordinary to
have sold so flourishing a business, in such a favourable position, on
the Fischerstrasse at the corner of the Wandsbeker Chaussée.  They
wanted to emigrate, so people said.  Well, everyone to their own
taste.

As she walked through the shop, paler than before, and with dark
circles round her eyes, but neat and slim in her street coat, her reddish-
gold hair crowned with a small hat, and the handbag with the blood
money—it was odd that the phrase came into her mind!—clutched
under her arm, Albert said in a chaffing tone: "Well, there can't be many
girls as smart as Stine in all Hamburg!—You don't need to provide
anything for Sunday," he went on.  "If the weather holds, we'll go out
to Stellingen and see Hamburg's Zoo."

That was a scheme that Stine had long cherished.  Since her girlhood days she never once had been out to that model Zoo, where lions
and elephants run about almost as they do in natural life, the apes
play all their fantastic tricks, and the birds scream like real wild
birds.

"Good," she said, cheering up.  "But all the same, I think we might
have our supper hot at home, and just take a sandwich with us."

"Spoken like a frugal housewife," said he, approvingly.  "No one
knows what may turn up, and the wise woman is always prepared."

# CHAPTER TWO

### STELLINGEN

WHEN A LADY doctor intends calling on a laundry woman, and that without appointment, on the spur of the moment, so to say, she chooses a Sunday morning for the purpose; a fact which hardly needs much explanation. Both are working women, whose time during the week is taken up by the subject of their calling, whether it be dirty linen which has to be restored to a condition to withstand daily wear and tear, or the living strength of human bodies; and we will here make no distinction between these two forms of activity, though one inhabits the lowest tier of the social pyramid, and the other its peak, illumined by the pious faith of countless human beings. However this may be, on Sunday morning both of them have leisure for themselves.

On that Sunday, about half-past ten, Käte Neumeier strode in her usual energetic fashion down the long Wandsbeker Chaussée, a rather unpleasing street in the aspect of its houses and façades, which had come into existence during the years of Hamburg's expansion. It must have originally been a broad straight country highway—but nothing of that could be seen in it to-day. The whole district, thought Käte Neumeier, had, as Fontane would say, gone down in the world. In the times of Matthias Claudius, Lessing, and that stern dictator, Klopstock, it was the custom to make a country excursion here from the Alster Basin, to the City Park at Wandsbek, or vice versa, in buckled shoes, white stockings, breeches, and warm cloaks, on a fine October day like this. But in plain fact these two epochs cannot be compared. Those people not merely carried different kinds of walking-sticks, wore their hair differently and smoked different pipes, and led different dogs on leads; quite different thoughts stirred within their heads. And these were— the unity of the human race, humanitarianism, enlightenment, philanthropy, and the faith in the power of the understanding. The sun of reason shone upon their powdered locks, and in the company of Rousseau they swore by the goodness of man, who would not be disposed to cut off the heads of four of his brethren in order to earn a little more money. And if they belonged to any organizations, these were called "The Lodge of the Flaming Dawn", or "The Grand Orient", and they pledged their faith not to the world-architect, Adolf Hitler, but to the architect of Solomon's Temple, and such like imaginary figures. There were not so many uniforms to be seen in Hamburg as to-day. And as she pictured herself walking along the streets in somewhere about 1737, instead of 1937, she found herself wondering what the Hamburgers of those days would have thought had they seen an electric tram thundering along in their wake, playfully overtaking them, and hurtling down the roadway between the houses on each side. What could they have known of electricity in those days? Galvani had perhaps already succeeded in making a frog's leg quiver, Volta had invented his pillars, and Leyden

H

jars already existed. Herr Hufeland understood something of health, and Hahnemann of homœopathy, but it had not yet occurred to anyone to measure a patient's fever by putting a thermometer under his armpit, or in his mouth, or elsewhere. Would she have preferred to live in those times? Decidedly not. Despite the fact that her present problem could not have confronted her in the eighteenth century. No one would have been beheaded in those days as the result of such a case. But was that so? she asked, stopping suddenly; what about *Lettres de Cachets*, and the poet Schubert who rotted in Hohenasberg? And why did Schiller flee from Stuttgart, and what about Lessing, who called Prussia a gaol and Berlin a galley. There was a nasty penalty called 'running the gauntlet', and there were ice-cold douches for lunatics. Go easy with young horses, her father used to say, when she began to enthuse about progress and the healing art. And here was the Wagnerstrasse. She wished she knew whether it was named after Richard Wagner, or after Herr Adolf Wagner, not the Economist under whom her father had studied, but the great Adolf Wagner, *Gauleiter*, of Upper Bavaria, who had had certain S.A. Leaders' heads bashed in with quart beer-pots on suspicion of treachery, so it was whispered in Munich. . . . And here was No. 17—Albert Teetjen, Master-Butcher. Ah yes, Stine Teetjen, No. so-and-so on the card index, rather given to abortions, the last having occurred a fortnight ago.

It was three years since Käte Neumeier had made her way to the Barfey's domicile, across the courtyard and up the stairs of the side-wing, just at the time when Tom had left school. She was therefore very astonished to find in the little front room, which was entered from the roof, a short man sitting on a foot-stool, shaving himself, and possessed of a moustache which he had plainly just clipped with a pair of sewing-scissors. His withered legs tucked in beneath him, and in process of soaping his face with a shaving-brush from which the butt was missing, there sat Tom Barfey in a vest and sleeveless pullover near the opened door. His mirror was a fragment of glass a few inches square, given to him by the pretty Olga, on the occasion when a table-mirror had been broken in the Lawerenzens establishment down below. The mirror had been swept on to the floor in a violent gesture of joy by Post-inspector Lawerenz when in 1933, his Jewish chief, Post-Inspector Bandmann, had been retired on pension to make room for an Aryan, and provide him with promotion and an increase of pay.

"God bless my soul, is that you!" exclaimed Käte Neumeier, when she recognized who it was that was shaving himself with such intentness and assiduity; she was standing outside the Barfey room, on a part of the flat roof, covered with concrete and edged with a low parapet, which abutted on to the main building with its sloping tiled walls. Tom, who was using the light from the open door, let his razor drop when he recognized the visitor, and promptly overcame the flush of annoyance that any interruption produced on his mobile and expressive face, and while making his excuses, called to his mother to come and see who had done them the honour to pay them a visit. A war-widow, thought Käte Neumeier, as she entered the living-room with its sloping roof, to whom the Fatherland was duly grateful. Though, indeed, she observed that she had come from one attic to another. There was many a sloping wall in the Koldeweys' house; Hamburg roofs were mostly gabled, lit, where possible, from above.

Frau Barfey was a rather gaunt woman of forty, of middle height, with streaks of grey on her temples, and bright, observant eyes in her very wrinkled face. And yet, thought Käte to herself, astonished at the difference between doctor and laundrywoman, they must be the same sort of age. Two different beings each born under her own star, and, she added to herself, more appropriately, each in her own class. For the way in which Frau Barfey received her, sat down and waited to know the purpose of this visit, had a poise and dignity of its own. Her friend, Koldewey, would have described it as what his beloved Nietzsche called—race.

Yes, said Käte Neumeier; of course she hadn't just come round the corner on a neighbourly visit. She had a favour to ask of Frau Geesche. She had sent her not so long ago an envelope, a grey linen-paper envelope addressed in her own hand. Did she remember what had become of it? She noticed that Frau Geesche shrank back, and grew pale. The State in which they lived had introduced police inquisition into citizens' lives to an extent that had never before happened in Germany. Frau Barfey nervously rubbed the right side of her forehead, dried her eyes, already brimming with tears of fear, explained that her memory had sadly failed in the last few years, and called her Tom to her aid. The lad, she said, kept everything in his head, for her as well. "Wasn't it to a laundry over at Uhlenhorst, too far away for me, as it turned out?"

Tom Barfey trundled himself into the room, washed, combed and brushed, and with a spotless white shirt under his pullover. The little moustache lent an oddly boyish air to his face, which looked so immature above those laughing lips. But the grey eyes under the stiff cropped hair, reflected a resolute mind.

"Tom," said Frau Barfey, "what became of an envelope from the Frau Doctor? Do you remember it?"

"Addressed to Footh, the shipowner," replied the young man, without having to think for a moment.

"Right," said Käte Neumeier, "to H. P. Footh. But who could have used it? Your mother certainly didn't."

"Of course not," replied Tom. "Harvestehuder Weg is a district by itself. We don't get in there at all."

"Good," answered the Frau Doctor, full of excitement, for now the moment was at hand. "But what happened to it? It was put into the post, and reached its address."

Tom Barfey blushed, and then pointed his thumb over his shoulder. "Stine," he said. "Perhaps it was wrong, Frau Doctor. But she came along just then, bringing us some kidneys. The envelope was lying here on the table under the light. Pretty women are often inquisitive. She said Footh was a war-friend of her Albert, they had served together for more than a year in the Forest Section in Lithuania. Albert had lost his address, but he could make good use of such a connection, in his struggle against the sales of provisions by the big stores. So I gave her the envelope then and there. Perhaps I oughtn't to have done it," he added, with a rather roguish air of contrition; "but the Frau Doctor knows how pretty Stine looks when she says—please, please, with her eyes."

Käte Neumeier couldn't help laughing; she lit a cigarette, offered one to the lad, and drew a deep breath. Albert Teetjen, Master-Butcher, she silently repeated the legend over the shop. Now she recognized the end of the nose, the moustache, and the glimpse of the mouth. The man had sat in her consulting-room, and looked at her with honest eyes. Of course a man looks quite different when he accompanies his wife to the doctor, and when he cuts off men's heads, especially round the chin. Out of the stream of thoughts that dominated the next few moments, one in particular emerged: the prospective executioner had been awaiting his destiny round the corner, so short was the distance traversed by that envelope—a boomerang that was to kill four men before it returned to the thrower. Up and back to him. But she curbed her sudden impulse to get up and go away at once. It would have upset the Barfeys. In any case she heard Tom, the cripple, ask her for a second time, whether any harm had come of it.

"Harm, Tom," she answered slowly. "Well, that's difficult to say. The envelope in question put Footh the shipowner and your neighbour Teetjen into contact with each other again—two old comrades of the last war, and people who knew each other quite well, anyway. With what final result, I may perhaps tell you another time. And now I must say good-bye and have a word with Herr Teetjen himself—and see whether he is the man I'm after."

"Ha," said Tom Barfey with much relief, and his mother nodded vigorous agreement. In that case the Frau Doctor could stay quietly where she was and eat a bit of the candy-sugar that Frau Barfey kept ready for her son in case the process of copying addresses made his tongue and throat dry. "The Teetjens aren't at home to-day. They are celebrating a birthday or something of the kind with a trip to Stellingen, and they will certainly stay there till it's dark. Stine is fond of animals and Teetjen of the open air, whether field or forest, he doesn't mind. He is a great walker, is Albert, which isn't very difficult with such legs as his, or indeed with any legs at all."

Tom went on to say that he had never been to Stellingen, for him it lay as far off as the African bush, or the Polar sea, where many of its denizens came from. In earlier days he had been too small to propel himself there, and now he didn't dare to attract people's attention.

"You don't mean the people here in the house?" asked Käte Neumeier, with a sense of oppression at her heart.

"Oh no," said Frau Barfey, in defence of her fellow-lodgers. "17 Wagnerstrasse knows us, and has known Tom since he was a little boy."

"Still, I shall not put them to the test and lead them into temptation, but deliver them from the evil of my appearance—after all, they needn't come and see me."

Käte Neumeier eyed the young man's tanned, keen face, which had already proclaimed to her how strictly he had obeyed her instructions to get out in the sunshine as much as he could.

"Would you enjoy an excursion, Tom? If so, then be downstairs in the yard about twelve. A friend of mine is driving out to Stellingen and taking me with her. Wrap yourself up warm, of course; it's an open two-seater, and goes pretty fast. It's rather bumpy travelling in the back seat, Tom, by the way."

Tom emitted a shriek of ecstatic joy, seized his mother by the shoulder, and shook her. "To Stellingen!" he cried. "Think of it, Geesche. And in a car, what do you know about that!—to the Equator, and then up North to visit the polar bears, and back home again to a supper of rice and mutton-liver. This must be my lucky day, Frau Doctor—there'll be something written in the stars for me to-night!"

Käte Neumeier, as she took her leave, found herself thinking that Herr Teetjen would perhaps be of another opinion, always pre-supposing that he was the gentleman in a tail-coat and mask whom she was looking for. In any case she must go and call up Annette at once, to act both as driver and witness. She had, in fact, acted rather impulsively and on her own initiative when she invited Tom Barfey on this trip. Supposing Annette had made other arrangements for that Sunday morning, and was doing something with her father, her sisters, or Herr Footh. In that case Käte Neumeier would hire a taxi to Stellingen, and save the cost of it on something else—give Colonel Lintze's wife white asters instead of callas, and so forth. The prospect of disappointing Tom, who had set his heart on this trip, she did not even contemplate. So she asked Frau Barfey where she could telephone nearby.

"At Lehmke's public house, a couple of minutes up the street."

Annette had, of course, an engagement for that Sunday morning. "I'm not the kind of child," she said, quoting her school friend, Klara Dohmke, from the fifth-class, "that doesn't get whipped cream on my birthday," which, being interpreted, meant—minding the shop on Sunday morning, having no dates, and sitting at home with no one to invite her out. But everything else must, of course, give way to the mystery of the mask. She would drop Papa at a quarter to twelve at the *Kunsthalle*, where there was an exhibition of the works of that very advanced painter Karl Blechen, who had painted *The Semnones on the Muggelsee* when all his colleagues were painting pot-boilers; a distinguished representative of what was now known as decadent painting. They would be back again at half-past one, wouldn't they? A passenger? Certainly. Had Herr Koldewey by any chance an old warm suit? Annette would have a look. As a matter of fact men always possessed suits that ought to be taken away from them.

Käte Neumeier had been very careful at the telephone, she did not like the look in Frau Lehmke's eyes, as she watched her visitor from behind the counter. But from the words that dropped so lightly and gaily into the receiver, no one could have guessed what kind of man and mask was in question, and whether she was talking about a fancy-dress dance or merely using a figure of speech. Frau Lehmke was certainly not one of the more harmless fauna of the district. She had, if need be, claws and teeth. It might indeed be possible to rope her into the campaign of vengeance. . . . And Käte Neumeier noticed that, while she was paying for her call and hurrying to the Underground station, a plan was maturing in her mind. What it was she didn't know, nor what direction it would take—but it boded no good for the man in the mask, whoever he might be.

For Tom Barfey, as he himself said with a radiant smile, this October morning was a high-point of his life. To be able to emerge from his self-imposed seclusion, drive through the streets of Hamburg in a splendid grey, gleaming car, to sit on the low back seat so that no-one could suspect that there was anything wrong or deformed about the lower part of his body, was something like re-birth, and indeed, on a higher level of existence. The ladies had stared a bit when he first stowed away his little rolling platform into the rear seat, before swinging himself up into position: but how did they think he was going to move about the wide spaces of the Zoo? Everybody knew that cars had to be left at the entrance: the cassowaries and the ostriches would have got knots in their necks from fear or curiosity, and all the little beasts of prey would have vanished into their holes if a car had snorted past. The waistcoat and jacket which the young lady had brought with her as a present, fitted Tom admirably; they must have belonged to the leanest period of Herr Koldewey's life, when, after the creation of the Hamburg gold-mark (paper), he had brought himself this faintly-checked, bright-coloured length of English home-spun. Annette saw at once that the jacket would serve Tom Barfey for another ten years, with patching; patched with material from the trousers, which was longer than the poor wretch ever could need. This strangely deformed human entity had produced a faint sense of repulsion in Annette; she had drawn a more romantic picture in her mind—something in the manner of a folk-tale, a young lady taking a poor cripple out for a drive. However, the young man's face and the way he sat in the back of the car, made up for any unpleasantness; those undeniably fine grey eyes mirrored a very clear vision of the world.

Käte Neumeier, for her part, now began to realize that she had indeed been over-impulsive, as the little car glided westwards. How on earth had she become possessed of the idea that one could casually encounter someone at Stellingen? The park had certainly been enlarged since she knew it, and even then it had covered nearly a square mile, with its enclosures, artificial rocks, roads, and paths and copses. The search for a married couple there on a Sunday afternoon would certainly take up a good deal of time. Annette had originally proposed to set aside not more than an hour for the trip. Where had been Käte Neumeier's usual sound sense when she not merely agreed, but involved Tom in this ill-conceived expedition? The lad would get a glimpse of the lion rocks, or the stone terraces beside the large lake with their population of penguins and walruses, which would merely give him an only too well-justified yearning for time and opportunity to see the sights of this great world. She wished she knew how to make it up to him. A car was a creator of delusions. The occupant of a car can slip through a great city from end to end in an hour. The man on foot sadly miscalculates when he thinks in car-minutes.

The car had, in fact, to be left outside. There was something of a fluster among the gate-porters when Tom Barfey propelled himself through the entrances and barriers on his little wooden platform, but both ladies, who paid for him, and one of whom established her credentials by means of a Party book and her position in the Municipal Health Service, removed all difficulties by their friendly confidence. Besides, on a Sunday afternoon there were fewer of the type of visitors whose gaping astonishment would have made a sensation out of the cripple's appearance. The east wind rustled through the bare tree-tops, the lawns were strewn with yellow leaves, and a tepid midday sun shone upon the stone pavements and parapets. The flat expanse of Hagenbeck's animal park lay outstretched before the visitors, still arrayed in the pale green of grass and bushes, yew and fir. The old trees, already bereft of leaves, seemed under that October light to have been transplanted into those artificial rocky landscapes and hollows, and not to have originated and grown there. This animal park had gradually become the exemplar for all the zoological gardens in Europe. The wild animals, denizens of distant climes, were here introduced into an environment as nearly as possible resembling their own; by means of carefully concealed trenches, neatly arranged rocks, and unobtrusive parapets, the visiting human was protected from the prowling animal he had come to visit. Penguins, polar bears, and especially monkeys, confined behind steep clefts and low walls, attracted crowds of visitors in the summer. Mainly visitors from abroad. The Hamburgers themselves, accustomed to the presence of this unique establishment, only occasionally took notice of it—which is what happens everywhere on this earth. What a man has, he takes for granted. Tom Barfey was particularly struck by the apes, and they apparently by him.

"They are really human beings," he exclaimed; "the little creatures look so sensible, and their eyes seem to go right through you." And then he asked what sort of monkeys they were—baboons, or hamadryads, or shrieking apes from Brazil: but he soon suggested that they should move over to the lions, for he needed rather more time to get about than walkers did. Annette Koldewey was looking about her with an interested air; but now and again she also glanced at the watch on her wrist. Käte Neumeier felt painfully torn between the opposing impulses of her two companions. Carefully as she peered into the faces of everybody they met, or turned to look at those they overtook, none gave her any reason to suppose that they were the pair she sought. After half-an-hour's walk along the admirably laid-out winding paths and green alleys, they stopped at the ibex rock, where the chamois and antelopes from mountain lands were disporting themselves in the warm autumn sunshine, nibbling the grass, and tossing their heavy horns against a background of bright sky.

"We must go back," said Annette. "The little car is waiting for us at the other end."

A bright idea flashed into Käte Neumeier's head. "For good or ill we must bring you into the secret, Tom," she said slowly, as she bent over the downcast youth. "We are not just paying a visit to Stellingen. We are looking for Herr Teetjen, because we must find out whether it was he who beheaded those four innocent Reeperbahn men."

Tom Barfey tilted his head back and looked up into the Doctor's face, with parted lips and staring eyes. "Beheaded?" he muttered.

"At present it's no more than a suspicion. The man who got this job through Herr Footh used the envelope I gave your mother. During the performance he wore a mask, but his mouth, nose, chin and moustache were recognizable all the same."

"Albert Teetjen," gasped the cripple, tonelessly, from pallid lips.

"Suspicions are cheap," said Annette, in a calm voice to the horror-stricken youth. "Still—Albert Teetjen, Master-Butcher, there can scarcely be any more such."

"I didn't know you knew his name," said Käte Neumeier grasping her friend's arm.

"Nor I, that so much depended on your identifying the man."

"And that's how we live, side by side. Human beings are impenetrable."

"There's Stine," cried the dwarf, pointing to the lion rock beyond the path and a stretch of lawn, standing out above the bare trees.

"And the S.S. man beside her, that's Albert."

Käte Neumeier rolled up the little guide sheet that she had bought at the entrance to give to Tom, and put it to her eye. The man's head was too small, but at that moment a ray of sunlight fell across his face. In the circle of the paper tube she could see his mouth and lower face clearly enough for identification.

"Yes, it is he," she said. "The man in the mask."

Hidden behind the tall bushes beside the path from which half the leaves had fallen, Annette also looked through the paper tube. "Not a doubt," she said, "there's only one Albert Teetjen. And what now?"

"Nothing—for to-day," rejoined Käte Neumeier. "In any case you can testify that I haven't said a word I shouldn't, or betrayed anyone."

As they spoke, a strange and awful sound behind them turned their blood cold. It was Tom Barfey grinding his teeth: a sound that Annette never remembered to have heard. "Albert," he was saying to himself.

The journey home passed in silence. Hamburg, with its neatly-dressed citizens, the Party colours, the red strip flashing in the pale Sunday sunshine, and the central Swastika looking like some exotic insect—Hamburg looked attractive as they drove into it from Stellingen, rising ghostlike from its quiet park-landscape. But to Käte Neumeier it looked active, dangerous, ominous, despite or perhaps because of its superficial air of somnolence. Where was the division between beasts of prey and animate beings? Though the latter were not privileged to live inside the carefully disguised Stellingen enclosures, the apes' meditative gaze, the penguins' droll movements, the liquid eyes of the antelopes, seemed to raise them above the Albert Teetjens who frequented the walks and paths of a Sunday afternoon. She remembered the feeling with which a few weeks before she had watched Herr Lintze glide off in his car, and shook her head. In so doing she caught sight of herself in the little mirror that enables the driver to keep his eye on the world behind his back, and shivered faintly. Was she becoming an old woman already? Capricious, and incapable of self-control—and indeed sharing some characteristics with the inmates of the institution, the great buildings of which were speeding past them at the moment—the Friedrichsberg lunatic asylum? Friedel Timme and the innocent and kindly Mengers, beheaded; a butcher, Albert Teetjen, promoted executioner; an admirable person like Annette involved as an auxiliary in the affair; and Käte Neumeier had been too cowardly to do what was needed by the aid of a motor-bicycle and five hundred-mark notes.

"A dozen foreign States are standing by at Nuremberg," she read in menacing characters on the advertisement columns, as Annette had to slow down for a second or two, to let some old ladies and children cross the street, while a smaller placard of the *Fremdenblatt* proclaimed the Propaganda Minister's declaration of war against the Komintern and the plutocratic satellites of the Jews. In Käte Neumeier's mind, as the result of its enlightenment by Karl August Lintze, this could be dialec-. tically divided into the alternatives: Russia—or England and America. Or shall we perhaps fall out with all three of them at the same time? . . . Municipal Lunatic Asylum, Friedrichsberg: Diagnosis;—paranoia, of the megalomaniac variety. . . .

As they drew up in front of Käte Neumeier's house, she expressed her thanks with a kiss on Annette's cheek. "You deserve another for knowing how to keep your mouth shut," and kissed her lightly on the mouth.

"You can trust me," smiled Annette. "Gossip was invented by men. Man is inclined, my father always says, to call his neighbour to account for everything he discovers in his own soul. And that applies to talkativeness in women."

"Did he get that from Nietzsche?" asked Käte Neumeier, as she got out.

"Undoubtedly," replied Annette, turned to Tom Barfey and said brightly, "And now I'll run you round the corner. It will be quicker than with your little cart."

"Horse-power against man-power," smiled Tom in response, with a look of quite mature admiration in his eye—just like a normal young admirer, thought Annette with amusement. But Käte Neumeier, as she shook hands with Tom, drew him closer to her and said: "Forget about Teetjen for the present, Tom. Show that you can keep your mouth shut."

"For how long?"

"Until I come up to see you, or send you a postcard to say that it's all right. The S.S. are behind the man, and Preester, the Storm leader, runs the whole district."

"Forgive me, I must hurry," said Annette, and trod on the accelerator, Käte Neumeier stepped back.

"Give my regards to your efficient friend, Footh."

"Thanks: away: in Berlin."  But as the car slid past a shop window decked with flowers into the archway entrance of Wagnerstrasse 17, and Tom Barfey, lifting out his trolley, and then with many expressions of thanks, clambered out of the rear seat, both Annette and the youth eyed with the same disgust, and even horror, the innocent back-door, with an ochrous curtain hanging behind the glass upper part, and displaying a brightly polished brass plate, inscribed: A. Teetjen.  For cash down, thought both, like calves or sheep.

Yes, the Teetjens were both on their way home.  Shortly after nine that morning, Albert had got their new bicycles out of the shed, trim and shining machines fitted with resplendent Buna tyres, the small man's magic horses, to make sure they were properly pumped up: while Stine brewed some Sunday coffee of such fragrance that the divorced Frau Blohm, who lived above the Teetjen's, sniffed it greedily as she went to the kitchen window, still in her nightgown, to let in the morning air.

"Well, those Teetjens must be thriving," she said to her boy friend, Oskar Kramer, the poster artist who, among his other avocations, provided the Schneehuhn Margarine Factory with a new little advertising gadget every week.  It was only yesterday evening that he had used his influence on behalf of a packer, Agnes Timme, a very useful worker who should have been discharged when the sentence of death for high treason on her husband, Friedrich Timme, was confirmed.  Moreover, she had not turned up to work the day of the execution.  But the suggestion that the Third Reich was strong and self-confident enough not to fear the proximity of such an insect had saved Frau Timme's job.  Herr Kramer meant to make a drawing of the incident.

"You'll be suspected of being a Communist yourself," Frau Blohm had sighed yesterday, as she clasped him in her arms; and it was to this that she referred when she now called to him to get up and sniff at the window, too.

"Just you smell, you little Communist—real beans."

"A bit of fig-coffee, too," said he, to damp her enthusiasm. . . . "If you've got it, keep it long," he went on, "your plaits, for instance." And he bustled his friend and landlady back into bed.

Sunday morning.  It had rained heavily in the night.  The roads beneath their wheels were glistening and clean.  Albert and Stine beamed with satisfaction, as though she were still a maidservant, and he the son of the master-butcher, not the master-butcher himself.  When economic pressure is removed from human beings, the released sense of vitality acts like a process of rejuvenation, of which the first sign is the sense of relief that shows how heavily they have laboured under the invisible burden of existence.  Albert wearing his uniform, the full dress tunic of the *Schwarze Garde*, with the Storm markings on his sleeve, strode haughtily through the Zoo barrier, while Stine smiled at the attendants, half in apology for his brusqueness, and half enjoying it.   Moreover she was wearing her new brown shoes, and an autumn coat and skirt made of stuff that looked like home-spun; thus arrayed, she strolled with a kind of grave enjoyment along the paths and roads of that animal paradise. Her soul was uplifted and glittered from her eyes.   She, Stine, represented the very pattern and paragon of the visitor for whom this Zoo had been created.   The astonishing shape of a giraffe extracting hay with its long neck from a carefully truncated tree, stirred her to a cry of just as eager astonishment as did the little brown and white spotted lemmings swarming in their elaborate nests among the ice-floes of a polar landscape. But her quiet and discreet demeanour, as devoid of mere stolidity as it was of vulgar gush, was due to the upbringing of her mother and grandmother: from the population of the Elbe Estuary and water-front they had created that fine and sympathetic type, which, depicted on the posters of the great Shipping Companies, brought so many visitors to Northern Germany.   No, Stine was not noisy, but her delight in the young gazelles, which she longed to stroke through the fence, the monstrous moustaches of the walruses and the sea-lions, lit a fire in her eyes, and she walked as in a dream, with parted lips.   Albert, for his part, was more attracted by the polar bears, which, swaying their heads and necks, paced unweariedly back and forward in the little rocky enclosure walled with blocks of artificial lava.   When anyone threw a fish into the water at their feet, a white-pelted she-bear slid her lithe bulk into the black flood and brought it to her cub, which, rising eagerly on its hind legs, grunted frantically for her catch.   But Albert par-ticularly liked the old bear, a giant beast, heavy and silent, surveying the scene with quick glances from his little eyes, and then spread his full length along the rock, exposing his huge flanks and claws.   He would not have cared to face him armed with nothing but an axe or a lance, as the Eskimo did up yonder.   That was the ancient home of our race, of our Nordic culture, which had been always thrust out of view by the Jews and their science, and thus had never been appreciated by the foolish German Michael.   It was in conflict with such beasts that our forefathers, the Vikings and the Rune-writers, had risen to be masters of the world, as expounded on one occasion in a lecture by Comrade Vierkant.   Their ships had sailed the seas long before the Egyptians, Greeks and Romans; they had erected the stone rings, the so-called Troy-castles, and invented the Swastika as a fire-kindler, for in those days men bored for fire by means of two sorts of wood, one hard and one soft. Yes, Albert informed Stine as they went on, culture always came out of the North, and the so-called Paradise might very well have been located in Mecklenburg, as the learned Herr von Wendrin had con-jectured long ago.   At the time he was merely derided, but that was the fate of all forerunners here below.   Take the divining-rod, on which that very evening Dr. Laberdan, a doctor in Fuhlsbüttel, was to deliver a highly recommended lecture—hadn't all the men of science laughed at it, until the divining-rod and nothing else had brought us victory in the campaign in German South-West Africa against the Hereros, by indicating hitherto unsuspected watercourses?   He who could peer into the earth and uncover the secrets that she hid so jealously—that was the man for Albert. Within it lay much treasure, seams of ore, fields of coal, all manner of strange salts, oceans of oil, that would bring us victory in the conflict to come. Walruses, chamois, lions, were handsome creatures, muscled and sinewed antagonists on which a man could show his prowess. As for seals, they just existed to be killed, for their pelts and blubber. But when all was said and done, they were merely flesh and blood, some comical like monkeys, some merely grotesque like the hyenas. None of them were a match for a rifle-bullet, much less a machine-gun or a hand-grenade. No; man with his brain in his head and his deft fingers, was lord of creation, and the Nordic man—the German—was the lord of mankind. This was the message that the Führer had brought down from heaven; this was the true gospel, and the new gospel, which yesterday evening had been once more hammered into the world. It was a pity that the Party Day was always held down South, in Franconia; why wasn't Hamburg thus honoured, or Oldenburg, whither they could easily have made their way by bicycle or rail? Stine could have come too, and so got rid of all the rubbish that still stuck in her head from the days of her girlhood.

"Now, now, you must let me be, Albert," she said, taking his arm. "I am what I am, and must make the best of myself. After all we don't do so badly, do we?"

Then they strolled across to the bird rocks, where the eagles stood with beaks and throats outlined against the sky, just as on the Party standards; gigantic vultures, condors from South America, drooping their mighty wings, under a huge expanse of steel netting stretched over the lopped trees. It was a lovely October day, though the wind already carried a sniff of snow; according to the morning paper there had been a heavy fall of snow in Russia. They would soon go along to the restaurant, get the sandwiches out of their bicycle-bags, drink some hot coffee and listen to the march music on the wireless; it was getting on for one o'clock, and they still had the lions to visit, which was best done from above, on a kind of terrace protected by a disguised but needful parapet.

Albert Teetjen, as he stood upon the terrace and projected his martial gaze over the park, let it dwell for a moment on two ladies, who each held a white tubular object in their hands. He did not know them, nor did he take any further note of them, and Tom Barfey's stunted shape, which would have caught his eye, was hidden by the yellowed, now almost wintry bushes that grew very tall on each side of the path at that point. And Stine, who would have been startled and pleased to see him, was staring fixedly at the lioness's eyes, so far as she could make her out under the over-hanging rock. These were beasts of prey. They lived on blood. Blood was cheap and freely shed. She shivered —there was an October chill in the air.

# CHAPTER THREE

## DIVINING RODS

WHEN THE TEETJENS entered the hall of the National Socialist Nature-Cure Society, which would have been quite beyond the Society's aspirations before the 'Seizure of Power', they at first thought that they had mistaken the place—there were so many Army and Navy uniforms among those of the Party and its various combatant units. How in heaven did the earth's interior concern the army, thought Albert, as he managed to find two places for himself and Stine far back at the right and on the gangway, in a still empty row, so that they could slip out in case it became clear that they had come to the wrong meeting; for neither Teetjen nor his wife liked attracting attention anywhere. However, it was soon plain that there had been no mistake, and that Albert had rather misunderstood the announcement which had been published among the notices of meetings in the *Hamburg News*. The chairman, a man with a large fair beard and gold spectacles, who had previously worked hard for his living as a masseur and mesmerizer in the fashionable world, now held a Reader's position in the reconstituted Medical Department of Hamburg University. He greeted the guests, the lecturer, Dr. Laberdan, and more especially Lieut.-Col. Lintze of the Staff of the Seventy-sixth Regiment, who would say a few introductory words on the subject of the present evening. Following which there appeared at the lecturer's table an officer, with a small mouth, fair moustache and carefully brushed though rather scanty hair. He proceeded to explain that National Socialism had, as in other matters, introduced a new era in the co-operation between the science of defence, and a more unprejudiced practice of natural science. (At this point, a lady with short grey hair, in the fifth or sixth row, a doctor, who had accompanied Herr Lintze, suppressed a smile on her eagerly listening face; and she mentally substituted 'uncritical' for 'unprejudiced'. In any case she would never have imagined that so ready a talker and debater could have been rendered so hesitant and halting by the presence of a large audience; though it was true that a genuine Hamburger didn't like being looked at, or having to attitudinize in any way.) Modern war, which Adolf Hitler's genius and love of peace would avert as long as possible from his people and the civilized world—as indeed was universally known, and emphasized only yesterday at his inauguration of the Winter-Help work in the Berlin Sportpalast—modern war called for the application of every kind of force and capacity, even those that had not yet come to light; modesty had always been a characteristic of the German character. But experience in Spain and Palestine had demonstrated that next time the mine-blockade would come into great prominence both by land and sea. The men of the Navy had experimented with such devices for generations past. Now, in this grand new era, as many German men as possible must be recruited to be trained as rod-diviners, especially such as would, by their age, have been drafted into the *Landsturm* and the *Landwehr*. The divining-rod would this time not merely be used to track down water-springs—when Germany made ready to recover her colonies—it would also have to discover explosive charges under snow and sand and in soil of every sort, against occasions when our motorized regiments, caterpillars, and tanks had to move outside the road system. Germany would have to reckon with a ruthless, scientifically trained enemy, every child knew that; the nations which were incapable of producing a Frederick the Great, a Bismarck, a Ludendorff, and above all an Adolf Hitler, cherished an unrelenting envy of the German nation, and would certainly have at their disposal every kind of modern weapon and device. So when the lecturer asked for demonstrations of these magnetic forces, he hoped the audience would remember the old adage: "He gives twice who gives quickly", and also, "Cling to the beloved Fatherland—there are the roots from which you draw your strength."

Albert Teetjen felt strangely moved by these words. Here indeed would have been a better job than looking for brass shell-cases and oil-drums in those old days in the Lithuanian forests with Footh and the Russkis. The discovery of buried treasures in the earth, this was magic which one read about in fairy-tales; and now, in this handsome hall with its electric lights, comfortable rows of seats, a lecturer's desk on which stood a reading-lamp and a glass of water, here was a Staff Officer explaining that henceforward men would have to defend their country by prying into the earth, where land-mines and other explosive entities might be hidden. This was an opportunity for a fellow to show he had marrow in his bones, under enemy fire, or at night, when flares were going up all the time, with no other weapon in his hand than that comic little fork, which Dr. Laberdan was then displaying. . . . And Albert disposed himself to listen once again. One thought was still working in his brain: with such a divining-rod many more enemies of the Fatherland could be put out of action than with the axe.

Dr. Laberdan did not need to be aware of the inquisitive eyes of, for instance, his colleague Käte Neumeier upon him, in order to feel embarrassed. He was so already—Käte Neumeier with difficulty concealed a smile under bright lights of the hall when she observed in her colleague's hand a script, carefully written on quarto paper as he rose from the Committee table to mount the lecturer's desk. The gift of extempore speech is not bestowed on our countrymen. Either they must learn by heart, or entrench themselves behind paper, like the Spartacists when, in 1919 or 1920, they occupied the offices of the *Vorwärts* or the *Berliner Tageblatt*. So Laberdan fortified himself with paper. The third alternative, which is to state in plain and simple terms what a man has in his head and rises to his lips, is quite beyond our average citizen. That, in Germany, is an indication of a special gift, an inner vocation. This is one of the reasons why Hitler and Goebbels were regarded with such awe. That men should be capable, for hours together, of producing a succession of word-pictures, was surely a little uncanny. In earlier days it would have signified that God or the Devil must have had his finger in the game.  In the eighteenth century, when our Claudius was strolling under the trees of Wandsbek, Herr Klopstock singing his odes, and Lessing lashing the public into the correct dramatic path, the word genius would have been used.  It was now described as the spirit of the Nordic race, the expression of all that is most gloriously German. . . .  Yes, it was very shocking, but when anyone read from a manuscript, and dammed the emotional current that links and inspires the speaker and his public, Käte Neumeier found it impossible to listen with due attention.  Her thoughts began to wander into all sorts of surprising directions.

Had anyone predicted of Albert Teetjen that he would be all ears at Dr. Laberdan's lecture, in the literal sense, he would have been perfectly right.  A caricaturist might have depicted him as a diminutive Albert attached to a gigantic ear, which in the course of the next few minutes he enlarged by unobtrusively clasping his hand behind it so as to lessen the distance between himself and the speaker.  Modern psychology, which divides men into types in accordance with their reaction to impressions, would have described Albert Teetjen as the acoustic type, upon whom sounds, and a succession of sounds and words, made the strongest impression.  Albert had noticed this in the army without understanding it, and carried his concertina about with him everywhere, thereby producing miracles of marching, especially in his own case.  "Teetjen eats notes as fast as a horse eats hay," observed his company commander one day; "and it goes to his legs in just the same way."  The fact that Frau Stine was quite differently constructed had been rather a handicap to the Teetjen marriage.  He looked round at her; just as he expected—she was asleep.

Anyone who has been accustomed from youth upwards to listen to sermons finds it difficult to contend against the soporific spell of something read aloud.  Stine Geisow, as a girl, had learned to receive the spoken word as the direct and immediate communication of one soul with another, or with the soul of an assemblage.  If this vital force was absent, the intonations of the voice destroyed her receptive capacity, just as a dazzling light forces the eyes to close.  Something within her seemed to shrivel, her vision clouded, her breathing grew heavy, her consciousness dimmed—and she fell asleep.  Seated upright, with her hands folded in her lap, quiet and silent, she presented the appearance of an absorbed listener—and indeed it was only someone sitting near at hand who might have detected her, and speculated with the appropriate amusement or irritation on the possible causes of such a pretty woman's fatigue.  Fortunately, she was sitting too far away to offer any offence to the lecturer.

Laberdan had, of course, like a true German, begun with the Greeks.  "In the time of the ancient Greeks"—thus every schoolboy was only too glad to begin his essay.  The so-called staff of Æsculapius, symbol of the medical art, might well have been suggested by a divining-rod.  In mediæval woodcuts snakes were depicted with split tails.  The staff of Moses, which struck water from a rock, must have been a divining-rod, as could to-day be pointed out, now that the harshly rational Jewish interpretations had been displaced by a richer tolerance; this sort of thing filled up the first quarter of an hour. The fact that the divining-rod, in the hand of one who had the gift, could reveal deposits of ore, oil, and even buried treasures of coins and valuables, was established beyond cavil. He would later on take the freedom of demonstrating the working of such a rod. The friendly observations of Lieut.-Col. Lintze must surely have shaken the most sceptical among the audience. The force emanating from this rod could bend a man's hands and wrists right down and twist them round, like a powerful electric current. Whether the action of such a hazel twig—alder or beech would also serve—was to be explained by the operation of earth magnetism, he must leave to those more learned than himself, to physicists, and those familiar with atmospheric waves, of whom in Hamburg they possessed a classic representative in the person of Heinrich Hertz. His elaborate investigations proved how deeply he had been attracted by the subject. But the prospect of diagnosing disease also, by the help of the divining-rod, was—fortunately for suffering humanity—finding more and more acceptance in the ranks of the medical profession. In view of the fact that our earth, a planet among planets, is attached, as a member of the solar system—a medium-sized quite unimportant little group of stars—to the Milky Way, from the destructive emanations of which we are protected by our integument of air, it is natural to conclude that earth-rays may equally be cosmic death-rays or closely connected therewith. The earth, as an agreeable abode, and the best of all imaginable worlds, in the phrase of our worthy Leibniz, was sailing into the abyss, when our Leader Adolf Hitler overturned that disrespectable nonentity the Weimar Republic. Dr. Laberdan's close-set eyes cast a rather grimly appraising gaze over his audience. During Lieut.-Col. Lintze's address he had, as his habit was, counted the rows of seats: twenty-four, and six seats each side of the central gangway, magic figures, as was customary among these Lodge Brethren. Nearly two hundred people must have come, either out of curiosity, or from motives connected with the *Reichswehr*—for those were the days of rearmament, the re-establishment of military service, and of the honour and glory of the army. . . . Two hundred brightly illuminated faces turned towards him, their eyes upon him, seeking truth and drinking in his discourse. Two hundred people had devoted a free evening to him, and put on clean clothes for the purpose, which was the best of reasons why he should not put them off with anything less than his best. He was glad he had composed his lecture with care. Nobody could accuse him of the levity with which, in the days of the "System", so much superficial knowledge had been made to pass current.

Dr. Laberdan drew a deep breath, moistened his throat with several sips of water, and went on. Destructive forces lurked in the magnetic interior of our earth, and there was every indication that by the operation of the divining-rod a way had been found to deal with them, so as to bring the science of medicine into connection with other natural sciences, and with the political upheaval known as the National Socialist Revolu-tion. Christianity and Marxism had tried to control the demoniac savageries of our wholly mysterious existence and our imprisonment upon this globe, by the aid of theories almost pathetic in their futility. But we knew that Germany had again achieved a great spiritual victory over the scientific priestcraft of the age, as in days gone by through the efforts of Martin Luther. This new reformer, too, had arisen from the depths of the nation, a lover of music and a man dedicated to his vocation, Adolf Hitler. When Luther, in 1517, nailed his thesis to the *Schlosskirche* at Wittenberg, the cultivated world shuddered with horror at these Nordic barbarians, who understood nothing of the subtleties of the Catholic creed, and the essentials of human life. And yet this act constituted the sole step forward which the course of European history could show, and resulted in a liberation of the human spirit from which even its enemies had drawn infinite advantage. Since then, every wielder of the divining-rod knew that his activities helped to establish throughout the world the predominance of the Germanic view of life, and paid due tribute to the master-race, to the great profit and advantage of the lesser breeds that came beneath its sway. These observations filled up the second quarter of an hour. The lecturer then proclaimed a brief interval, after which he would proceed to the promised practical demonstrations; he might at this point mention that his address was— "The Infirmary, Fuhlsbüttel Prison", and that he was Chairman of the Hamburg Group of the Reich Association of Water Diviners.

Käte Neumeier felt oddly touched. Since when had her colleague Laberdan been indulging in these philosophic speculations? The idea of incarceration in an earthly prison was naturally enough inspired by Fuhlsbüttel, but the conjunction of Adolf Hitler and Martin Luther— surely that was going a little too far! And all this business about the power of the divining-rod not merely to reveal the secrets of the earth but the inward thoughts of men? She looked up at the coffered ceiling, which imparted a slightly ceremonial air to the room, and reminded her that this was really a Masonic Temple, the ceremonial hall of one of those secret societies which had been so summarily dealt with by the Third Reich. To her shame, Käte Neumeier had to confess that she knew nothing about the sort of society which held its meetings there, and what were the insignia and properties that had been removed and confiscated, and whether they had belonged to a Jewish or Atheistical Lodge, she had no notion. Scarcely anyone troubled to take note of such events, which had been quite effaced by the establishment of other privileges, and the emergence of other strata of society. This time it was a gathering of the small citizen class—shop-keepers, skilled workmen, officials, students; and the Chairman of the Association was very fairly repre- sentative of his audience. On all sides among the uniforms on the seats within her view, there were women and especially men, gazing with eager eyes upon the lecturer, and, from the expression in their faces, doing their best to master what he was saying. The Germans were an intelligent race, predisposed to all that was good, but also to all that was evil. Among them a calculating person like Herr Footh could at any time discover an instrument, a tool in fact, prepared to carry out a decision, or an order from above, and content to put money

I

in his pocket without the slightest qualm. It was difficult to say whether many people like Teetjens were to be found in the ranks of the German people. Among seventy millions, there must, on statistical principles, be thousands of varieties of human behaviour, and thousands of representatives of each. None the less it was her plain duty to ensure that this one person should be incapable of further harm. If Friedel Timme had conceived other ideas of Germany's welfare and future destiny, that was his affair, and no reason whatever for cutting his head off. And with a butcher's axe too!—used for the trimming of cutlets and marrow-bones. That was a point that might be effectively pursued. The claims of hygiene were held in high honour, and it was the duty of every man and every woman to see that they were respected. There could, alas, be no question of bringing a Party comrade into disrepute for the fulfilment of a public duty. But hygiene was after all paramount, and even if the axe had been disinfected, the soup of the neighbourhood would be likely to smell of carbolic. A laundrywoman, like Gesche Barfey, could let fall a few words to this effect here and there without being accused of speaking in disfavour of the Reich. It was essential not to arouse suspicion. The sense of disgust and loathing felt for such confederates was difficult to combat. No one could force people to supply their now modest needs at the shop of Albert Teetjen, master-butcher. In five, six, or seven minutes, by the electric tramway along the Wandsbek Chaussée, they could get to the E.H.P. Store, where sausages, ham, mutton, and beef were displayed for sale under the most unimpeachably hygienic conditions. Heaven be thanked, Hamburg was a great city, the housewife always reckoned up what she had to do, and took a little time and leisure over her shopping excursions. Moreover, in the same department, or at any rate on the same floor, she could also buy butter and cheese, radishes and tomatoes, potatoes, oat-flakes, and pot-herbs. Of course it was a serious matter to unloose the tongues of gossip and give the longed-for sign to Tom Barfey. And what about his relations with that pretty young creature, Stine Teetjen? But surely this was to look at things from too close at hand. There was no need for Käte Neumeier to think so far ahead, to involve herself in the network of causes and effects. It was essential to be capable of learning from all living beings—to behave like a dog, for instance, which shakes itself, and thereby leaves all unpleasantness behind; ah, at that moment Laberdan paused, and Käte Neumeier could look round and see whether Bert had come as he had promised. He had so much on hand, and indeed the younger generation did not find life easy in the Third Reich of the reincarnated Redeemer.

More light had been turned on, and the electric bulbs gleamed like stars in the panels of the ceiling. Käte Neumeier, stiff with sitting still, stretched and relaxed some of her muscles. Her observation of the increased lighting had coincided with a turn of her thoughts towards Dr. Koldewey. It was noteworthy how resolutely he had edged his daughter Annette out of her neutral position, which had given her access to both camps. She wished she had brought him here to make the Laberdan salad more palatable by the addition of vinegar and oil. She reflected how, when he and she met over the dinner-table, it was like husband and wife; and she wondered if in fact he had still any use for the other qualities of a wife. A clear head, an equable temperament, and as the result of several generations—why did all this appear in her mind as symbolized by the Koldewey apparatus? Crystal silver-fitted bottles, and pepper and salt in filagreed bowls. She was amused by these imaginings and let them run slowly through her mind. Were she the housewife there, she would have had the name Friedrich engraved on the salt cellar, and the name Nietzsche on the pepper-box, and thus present Heinrich Koldewey complete. Enlivened by these mental diversions, she made her way to the entrance doors, and the back rows of seats, where the late-comers had probably been accommodated.

She was looking for her nephew Bert, who had invited her here—and indeed but for his message she would probably not have decided to devote the evening to her colleague Herr Laberdan. She did, however, admit to herself that she had also gone out in order to escape the tormenting question where and how, and above all, whether, she should react to the discovery of the Fuhlsbüttel executioner. She envisaged poor Tom Barfey like a bloodhound on the trail, straining at the leash, and the moment she released him he would be after the murderer, know no mercy and no fatigue in that pursuit. A boycott. That was the answer. If Gesche Barfey, in the households where she did the washing, let fall a hint or two as she sat on a chair in the kitchen and sipped her cup of coffee, that there was an ugly story going the rounds about Teetjen the butcher—how he had cut a couple of men's heads off at Fuhlsbüttel with his own axe, and had certainly not had it consecrated or shriven after the operation in S. Peter or S. Michaelis, or even cleaned with carbolic in the Municipal disinfecting station.

Was this a hallucination? Surely, yonder under the glare of light was the face of the young man she had seen outlined against a white wall, and had called a murderer? And beside him, wasn't that his rather silly little wife's red mop of hair? Käte Neumeier clenched her teeth, just as Tom Barfey had done, narrowed her eyes and peered over the Teetjens' heads in search of Bert Boje, who very likely had not been able to come. She had to cling to the nearest chair-back, in order to control the disgust and hatred that shook her. A creature of this kind went about, slept with a woman, made trips to Stellingen, and listened to lectures on divining-rods—while Friedel Timme's proud head and keen brain had been forcibly severed from his—alas—rather coarsened body, thence to be consigned to the anatomy and dissection rooms, the refuse bins, and then scattered on the waste dumps. No, Herr Teetjen, that was not the end, my good man. Many people were going to take a hand in this business, and they would set about it in the manner of those little rodent beasts, house-mice, and field-mice. There was an old proverb that children learnt, about the mills of God, who was now rather thrust into the background. Well, there was no need to be a God; it was enough to have inherited the absurd name of Neumeier from one's forbears, and the knowledge when to stand by right and not by favour. For when public affairs stood upside down, it was doing them something of a favour to set them right side up again.

"Good evening, Aunt Käte—I'm so glad you've come," said Bert Boje, as he laid his hand on her shoulder. She turned towards him, his words cut the current of her thoughts with the abruptness of an electric shock, but before she could reply, a sort of shiver thrilled through the entire hall: a Siren! Air Raid practice! A moaning, piercing wail, combining in its cadence the notes of menace, lamentation, and imminent peril, echoed into the hall, and more insistently through the opened doors, as the audience drifted into the ante-rooms or made their way back again. Dr. Laberdan had obviously not been expecting such an incident, nor probably had Herr Lintze, although nobody had noticed him during the lecture. The lights went out. Small red emergency lights indicated the exits; from somewhere in the dimness came the voice of the chairman warning everyone to keep calm, and go down to the air-raid cellar in the basement, to which there was a broad and reasonably lighted stairway. Bert Boje held Käte Neumeier firmly by the arm, led her along the walls, and past the chairman's daïs to the staircase.

"Come along with me, Käte," said he, "up to the fireguard station."

And while the throng of people streamed in orderly and unhurried fashion down into the cellar, he guided her upstairs, whispering the word "Fireguard" into the darkness as they went, until they came to a chamber beneath the roof, from which there were only ladders leading upwards; it was filled with equipment of various kinds, tubs of sand, poles, shovels, and sacks, the sole illumination being the pocket torches of the three or four men whose turn of duty it then was. The sirens were still wailing, and through the open windows whirled a few snow-flakes, the first of the year, carried on the blast of the east wind. And Käte Neumeier reflected that she would have a slushy journey home.

"Searchlight practice," remarked a deep voice. And indeed long, bluish-white shafts of light flashed and swept through the dancing flakes; narrow and clear-cut, projected from many widely-scattered districts of the gigantic city. Through the wail of the sirens, intensified now by the deep and deeper voices from the harbour, the fog-horns of the ocean liners, came the high-pitched roar of an aeroplane engine. The white bands of light groped for its course, but could not pick it up— obviously the snow had interfered with this part of the programme.

"No good," said a voice. "No champion has yet fallen from the sky," replied another. "We don't need one," retorted a third. "And besides, hasn't Hermann promised that none will ever reach us." This produced an admiring laugh. "Fat prophets weigh double."

Käte Neumeier showed her medical card, as the electric torch flashed into her face and dazzled her; the fireguard offered his polite excuses, and they all remained in the twilight, broken at irregular intervals by the chalky glare of the searchlights.

"That's the end of Laberdan's lecture, I suppose," said Käte Neumeier in an undertone, sitting on sacks of sand, with her face turned towards her sister's son. Strange, she thought, when she was going about with Friedel Timme, this lad was no more than a child, not yet

of school age. . . . Bert laughed: Käte's unfortunate colleague would
again have to address the amateurs of the divining-rod, which, as
Chairman of that honourable Association, he would no doubt be very
willing to do.  He, Bert, would be very glad when he could get his
aunt home, and over a cup of tea talk about a small family matter,
which was now ripe for discussion.  "Let us make our way slowly downstairs; this performance won't go on much longer; current and coal are
too precious, and it hasn't exactly come off."

"But it's a grand show," said the man with the deep voice, as he
gave Käte his place by the window.

Through the blue-grey night, now awhirl with snow-flakes and pierced
by dozens of shimmering white pillars of light, especially from the
harbour district, as the liners had now joined in the display, to the
extent to which the skeleton crews could work the searchlights.  They
moved uncertainly, traversing each other, like the vast letters of a
flaming script upon the sky, groping hither and thither with pale, gigantic
fingers.  Sometimes they formed completed angles, sometimes conjoined
in an arc, but the point of inter-section never caught the aeroplane, which
was no doubt flying invisible above the blanket of cloud.  It was obvious
that the display would be called off in a few minutes; a practice in such
weather as this could only be carried out by highly-trained personnel.
As soon as the 'All clear' sounded over the roofs and streets, the trams
would start again, and very soon fill up.  It was a wonderful organization,
thought Käte Neumeier, as she drew back from the window and caught
a snow-flake on her lips—a saltless refreshing foretaste of the winter. . . .

A family affair?  Was it Annette who was concerned?  How much
better if that unaccountable girl took up with a lad like Bert, and dropped
the repellent Footh.

But when, three-quarters of an hour later, they were sitting in Käte's
pleasant study, with its green and brown striped curtains, and a thick
modern carpet in the same colours under their feet, the matter proved
to be quite different, and one of so very delicate a nature that Bert
would only speak of it when he could be sure of not being overheard.

"The S.S. to-day sent an emissary to the works to ask me if I wouldn't
now join them—he was sure I must be tired of the S.A. uniform by this
time.  The Führer's picked Corps offered every advantage; they needed
young and active men like myself, and the days of the S.A., despite its
glorious past, were ended.  Highly-paid, with the best connections, and
providing excellent social and political prospects, there could be only
one answer to this invitation.  The fellow they sent to me, Herr Sturm-
bannführer Preester from your part of the world, gave me something
to think about, Aunt Käte.  I shouldn't care to fall into that fellow's
hands, either for good or ill, and he was certainly chosen because the
Gestapo knows your past.  His comrades in my district, Barmbeck, are
a bit more presentable."

Käte Neumeier blew out some smoke.  "And what was your answer,
my dear?"

Bert Boje pulled at his pipe, and indeed the room was full of the
reek of his Dutch tobacco.  "That's why we're sitting here, Aunt Käte.

I'm not a fool, as you know, and I wasn't going to give anything away to a fellow of that sort. I don't forget June 30th, and never shall. I don't want to join the S.S. The men murdered on that day were certainly no angels; but they were bone-loyal to Hitler. They were treated like beasts, and we're expected to ignore it, Aunt Käte. Besides, a man wants to stand by the friends of the old days of struggle and success, before any of these brutes put his nose out into the wind and weather. And I won't foot any part of the S.S. account in regard to the concentration camps and so on. But that is by the way. I told him I was preparing to take up service abroad. An acquaintance of our family was Vice-Consul somewhere in the Argentine, in La Plata, if I am not mistaken, and had been keeping an eye on me. The armament industry had now so far expanded in those parts that hydraulic engineers could easily get jobs under government, the only trouble was that I would have to learn Spanish; then good-bye to my beloved Fatherland, for I'm off."

Käte Neumeier nodded, and breathed a sigh of relief. "Excellent, my dear—in case my letters are watched. There are plenty with Argentinian stamps on them."

"Yes, you must give me some," laughed Bert. "Comrade Preester revealed himself as a collector, especially of stamped envelopes. I hope you've got a few envelopes with the stamps post-marked."

"As many as you like," cried Käte delightedly. "My little collector-friends must go without this time." She bent over a drawer of her writing-table, took out a neat bundle of letters, and picked out a few envelopes.

"But they're not addressed to you, my dear; won't that matter?"

"Not a bit," said Bert calmly. "I'll say you were fixing it all, so as to spare my little mother's feelings. Only you must be kind enough to put Herr K. A. Lintze wise about it; and he must write to me directly once. And if things get uncomfortable for me here, I think I shall really disappear for six months, over to the other side. Just read what's printed in German about us outside the border. I would be better off not to meet certain people here in Hamburg. There are two people I would like to miss the sight of for a while, one extremely ugly, and one just the opposite."

Käte Neumeier looked at him affectionately: the broad short nose, the level brows above the keen eyes, the rather low but finely-curved brow, and the resolute set of the jaw.

"My dear boy," she said, "there are so many misunderstandings in life, which are more often than not cleared up all right in the end. Absence works wonders, and as for the women of our time . . ."

"Women," exclaimed Bert indignantly, as though he would sweep them all from the surface of the earth, "I could call down curses on one who, after having had friends like our Wieck and Manfred Koldewey, gets involved with a fellow like Footh . . . Käte!" And he crashed his fist on to the table, which consisted of a slab of black glass supported on steel tube legs, and nearly collapsed. "Sorry!" he ejaculated.

"All's well," said she. "Such articles are more substantial than you would think, and so are certain women. Many things will be made plain before your hair is as grey as mine. But I think you would be wise to show these envelopes to Herr Preester in his office this very day."

"That's just what I mean to do."

"And you might take a note for me for my laundry-woman—17 Wagnerstrasse. There's a cardboard box for her letters in the entry."

So saying, she tore off an unused sheet from one of the K. A. Lintze's letters, a thin sheet of strong foreign notepaper, and scribbled the following with her fountain-pen:

*"My dear Tom,*
*I have thought the matter over, and I think we ought to make known our objections, on hygienic grounds, to the use of axes for various purposes, with due caution, of course. In any case, you can tell your good mother all about everything. Perhaps the wife can be kept out of it.*
*Yours,*
*K. N."*

She folded the sheet, closed it with stamp-paper, addressed it and handed it to the young man, who stood before her in his neat brown uniform, slipped it between the buttons of his tunic, put the envelopes into his hip-pocket, and took his leave. For the moment she hesitated whether she should not let him know what, through his agency, was being set in motion. But then she thought—better not. Opening the window to let out the pipe-smoke she noticed that it had stopped snowing, but the street lamps were mirrored in a thin layer of light-brown slush.

When the Teetjen pair got home, the moon had already appeared through the lowering white clouds. Outside, an unmistakably wintry wind was blowing, but in the little apartment behind the shop it was nice to take off their outer garments, to eat a bit of lard sandwich and garlic sausage, wash, and go to bed—their double bed that, still rumpled and unmade, seemed to be waiting for the married pair.

"Well," sighed Albert, as he thrust his toes against the lower end of the bed until the wood creaked; "Well, this has been a day."

Stine sat, with her back towards him, on her side of the bed, twisting her plaits; the curves of her neck and arms, white and slim above her old-fashioned nightdress, were very expressive of her gentle, joyous nature, and would under other circumstances not have failed of their effect on Albert. But he lay there, gazing at the ceiling, from which hung a globe of elaborately marbled glass, and then closed his eyes. At once he saw a vision of the lecturer's desk, behind which Dr. . . . what was the name again?—Lange—no, Laberdan—had stood. When the lecturer had adjourned the meeting until the next time with a few concluding words, on account of the air-raid practice, he saw himself, the respectably clad *Scharfuhrer* Albert Teetjen, marching up to the Doctor, giving the Party salute, and asking to be tested to see whether he had any gift for the use of the divining-rod. Albert had noticed around him a little group of people murmuring approval and applause, the Chairman of the Association had come up to him, grasped him by the hand and looked steadily into his eyes.

"This Party comrade, if I am not wholly mistaken, seems to have very considerable astral capacities. I can feel a current in my forearm," he had observed to the Doctor, blinking his reddened eyelids behind his gold spectacles, as though he were listening to an inner voice, or was trying to discover in his own breast what was going on inside Albert Teetjen. This erstwhile mesmerist and masseur had been the subject of a few experiments in the Electrical Institute of the University during the desperate years of the Weimar Republic; the current circulating in his body had been measured, and proved to be capable of evoking currents in metal coils when he held a bare arm between them. The Doctor had told Albert about this in order to encourage him to keep the appointment they had made for the following Sunday morning in Fuhlsbüttel Infirmary.

"I seem to be having a lot to do with Fuhlsbüttel," said Albert, in an undertone. He felt the need of expressing what was making such a stir within his mind. As Stine had already slept her full measure, having earned her tribute as an attractive woman that very morning, one might indeed have expected . . . But there she was, asleep again. She lay down, switched off the light, and off she went—that was Stine all over. And indeed he had often enough envied her for it in those months when they had looked like coming to financial grief. He had got little good out of lying awake, thinking out schemes, and weighing various methods of deliverance, one of which he would put in hand the very first thing next morning, this time with absolute certainty of success. The morning had come, the day had gone, and the situation had remained unsolved. But Stine, who had always been able to sleep, had for her part insisted that he should at last write to Footh; she had dictated the letter, and so had at least put him in the way of success. The Lord bestowed his favours on his own in sleep. Well, all the better that Stine should keep to her Lord—Jesus of Nazareth, as *Sturmfuhrer* Preester called him, at the best, or—more usually—the Jew boy of Bethlehem, whom to our misfortune Herod's S.S. men had overlooked. He, Albert, was for Adolf Hitler and the new gods; she, Stine, for the old ones of the Bible and the catechism, in honour of whom those pretty chorales and cantatas were sung in the parish churches. And thus they were good friends with the powers on both sides, or at least could be, so that the course of their affairs ought never to go astray. It was a fact that the lions and Polar bears had left an unpleasant impression on him —Albert; they had seemed so sadly confined and he was conscious of so much in common with them. They, too, felt no horror of blood; they would have made excellent master-butchers, with strong nerves and muscles and sinews, and they, too, were very affectionate to their mates. How impudently that little she-monkey had tweaked her little partner in a place which a woman should not touch, Stine had blushed, but she could not help laughing—which indeed was all in order under the Third Reich, where Christian prudery had been abolished, and many a Pastor could prove in a concentration camp whether his Jesus was worth thirty lashes. And the air-raid practice—how well that had gone off. Sirens—lights out—red lights on—everybody in the cellar—fireguards on the roof—all that was lacking was the A.A. guns crashing away in good earnest. Well, if it came to the point, if the Führer did not succeed in securing Germany's place in the sun by peaceful means, if the red mobilization placards again flared from the kiosks, and the door-bells rang as the calling-up notices came round, then the great days would return, and we should show the stuff that was in us. *"Russ or Frenchy, we care not; blow for blow and shot for shot,"* as they used to sing in old days on the march along the sandy pine-forest roads, through the clearings on the edge of the ploughland—crash—shrapnel—white puffs in the sky—take cover! Sergeant Footh, where was Sergeant Footh? . . . "And the French will give in, just as they did in eighteen hundred and seventy. . . ." No; this time Albert Teetjen would be coming along, a giant with his divining-rod, a mighty figure in a fairy-tale; he would stamp his way through the pine-forest, march through the clearings, track down the veins of water and the veins of gold, and shout: "Dig a trench, blast you, and lie in it—take co-ver!" But where on earth was Sergeant Footh?

# CHAPTER FOUR

## HERR FOOTH IN ACTION

YES, WHERE WAS Herr Footh? On a business trip to Berlin, as recorded in his office, which might equally be concerned with the Äuglein ships as with the problems of the N.S.K.K.—new regulations or projects resulting from the Party Day. The fact that Fräulein Blüthe was simultaneously absent gave rise to much talk, a fleeting wink or two, and much silent speculation, between Fräulein Petersen and the Chief Clerk, Fens. Fräulein Blüthe was officially taking a holiday, which had been due to her for a long while, and which she proposed to spend in some winter-sport paradise, on the ski-ing grounds of the Saxon Erzgebirge, in the Riesengebirge, or the Alps, according to the season of the year in which Fräulein Blüthe could soonest be spared from her work. None the less Fräulein Petersen summed up her opinion on her colleague in two words, "Rotten beast," which in sporting parlance mean something quite different from what they do in middle-class life—something killed by a beast of prey and left to rot.

The Eden Hotel offers its guests the notable privilege of being awakened by the roaring of lions, while lying in a comfortable bed under a silk eiderdown. Herr Footh had been accustomed to stay at the Kaiserhof, if not in one of the great establishments on the Unter den Linden—the Adlon or the Bristol. But this time the aftermath of the Party Day still filled all the more comfortable hotels in the neighbourhood of the Chancellery, so he chose the more secluded Western district, with its luxurious international atmosphere, so well suited to the personal relations between the head of a business and his secretary. It was absurd that the decision about the Thetis Shipping Co., being a Jewish concern, should have to be sought in Berlin and not in Hamburg, but since the Reich Ministry of Marine had taken a hand in the game, Herr Footh had felt it to be essential not to play about in the foreground any longer, but to approach the very source from which these waters flowed. There were not many prizes in Germany still to be picked up. Party magnates of every description had taken every available share in the loot that fell for distribution after the victory over the Republic. Commercial combines had been established whose sole exemplar was the Stinnes Trust of the post-war period. One of the largest of these was called the Hermann Göring Works, and that wasn't merely a name. Herr Footh had been able to get into touch with the *Reichstatthalter* at Hamburg and ask for his reward for having surmounted the Fuhlsbüttel difficulty. But when important per_ons really wanted a say in any matter, he could only shrug his shoulders and express his regret that there was nothing doing.

Herr Footh's trouble lay in the fact that he never had been able to deal with an opposite number, with a person who could be got at, a man or a woman, on whom might be exercised a certain brusque charm, a plain-spoken geniality, the atmosphere of which lingers between the walls of a room like a delicate perfume when the wearer has long since gone downstairs and hurried into the street. Hans Footh's career had been conducted by means of such impressions. His smallish eyes could look sly, they could light up, they could blink confidentially, or listen with the utmost cordiality. But this time, behind writing-tables of the most various heights and sizes, sat German men, with nothing particular to distinguish one from another. Their faces were thin or round, their eyes were brown or black or blue; their foreheads arched or low, and their lips pallid or full; they looked clever or ingenuous, and they expressed themselves in the speech of Berlin or Silesia, or in High German; they were extremely polite, well-shaven, and with admirably trimmed finger-nails—but their functions were always partial only, they refused any responsibility, they always referred him for decisions to an ever higher authority, which of course sat enthroned above the clouds in the domain of the gods, whence the triumphant progress of renascent Germany was controlled, according to a definite plan and aim, and with absolute ruthlessness and craft. The German had been subjected to a compelling force that he had never known before. *Gloria in excelsis Deo.* This God must surely have a great destiny in view for the Germans or he would certainly not have sent them Adolf Hitler, the political

genius personified.    His picture, in profile, the face of a man who
speaks his mind, with parted hair, prophetic eyes, a rather bulbous ear,
and the famous clipped moustache, hung in all the public and private
offices where Herr Footh had business during those days.    In Berlin it
at once becomes clear how many things can be settled and disposed of
on the spot by a conversation, or even by a telephone call, that cannot
so much as be set in motion by a dictated letter from Hamburg.    The
Reich capital was a market, the largest one on its own part of the globe,
where the items of merchandise were influence, contracts, political
programmes, and the destinies of many men.    And the former cautious
and timorous officials had been replaced by youth, audacity, guile and
success.    From time to time perhaps it was necessary to allow or offer
the mob some entertainment, such as the night of the long knives, the
burning of the books, or *The Sturmer's* red show-cases, as a sort of comedy
of revolution.    But what went on behind this film screen was something
quite different—it was the appropriation of property, and of all key-points
in the economic and political nerve-system, by a Party which represented
the soul of the German people, within which beat the heart of German
Michael, led by the nose and exploited for so long; a Party created
and maintained by Adolf Hitler and by him led to greatness: "By
the Germans shall the ailing world be cured"; and not before it was
time either.

The affairs of the Thetis ships came within the purview of the
Transport Department, the Labour Front, the Fuel and Power Office
(Nordgau branch), the Strength through Joy organization, and the
N.S. Handelsbank, which owned a section of the Company's share
capital.

From the Western industrial sphere stretched arms equipped with
tentacles, and even from South Germany threads were moving towards
Hamburg, though for the moment they had paused at Berlin and were
seeking contact there.    All businesses were flourishing, all shares were soar-
ing, according to the quotations on the stock exchange; on every side economic interests were amalgamating, to place in the service of the Reich
what had formerly been anarchically founded or expanded in the so-called
free play of the forces of a purblind Liberalism.    An iron hand had,
of course, been necessary.    All the pay and earnings of the masses had
to be brought down to a reasonable level even if the purchasing power
of the millions was temporarily affected.    But wait a few years, gentlemen!    If Germany's present position called for guns instead of butter,
her future promised, even to the humblest member of the Party, instead
of butter—caviar, and fortunately there were plenty of speakers and
writers to make this clear to the German people.    "Wait, and you'll
soon get a house"—so ran the song in which a favourite cabaret singer
recommended patience and a sense of reality to the tenant of a furnished
room!    Of course too much light could not be allowed to filter through
from the backgrounds of German policy.    There were indeed Emigré
newspapers in Prague, Vienna and Paris which described these backgrounds as abysses.    But the world paid no attention to them, commend-
ably few of these denationalized detrimentals had been allowed into

London—the British Empire having placed the refuse-dump of Palestine at their disposal, so that no great harm was done. In all the offices, board rooms, and clubs of the capital the conviction prevailed that Europe was on the eve of great events. The dizzy tempo maintained by the Third Reich, and its dynamic force, were by now familiar to the gentry across the Rhine and the Channel; the return of the Saar to the Reich, the rearmament of the German people, the march of the *Wehrmacht* into the demilitarized Rhineland, and the creation of a powerful striking force by means of the two years' service law, the establishment of the Berlin-Rome Axis, the cancellation of the signature of the men of Weimar to the *Diktat* of Versailles, while at the same time a glorious Olympiad "united those of Grecian race in glad companionship," and last of all the State visit paid by the great Roman and Cæsar, Mussolini, to the capital of his new friend and ally—these were steps in advance, my little friend, weren't they? Seven-league boots—that was our pace. In one or two of the side streets in the Western districts of the city could still be seen some of the garlands and flags that had welcomed the new Augustus, the short, stout Duce, who had spoken German in Berlin, and was heard doing so by the multitude. Had the like ever happened under William II? Not to mention the dachshund Ebert, and the ancient Hindenburg! And yet opposition was still rife in certain hide-bound circles at Headquarters. Well, anyone who wasn't willing to learn new lessons must go his own way. Germany had never yet been poor in men of military talents, who had understood their craft from A to Z, without therefore wishing to figure as deputy-gods. And the occupation of the Rhineland had proved that the erstwhile Corporal of the world war was a few nose-lengths ahead of these desiccated aristocrats, and could see and think for himself. "Fresh blows the wind towards home" ran the words of the sailor's song when the curtain went up on the first act of *Tristan*. But Hitler's cradle had stood in Austria, and the only dispute was whether he had been born nearest to Vienna or to Prague. . . . The Styrian ore deposits, which for open cast output are unsurpassed in the world, would unquestionably acknowledge a new master, and the shipment of that precious raw material, or the valuable German consumer goods manufactured therefrom, to the Rhine–Main–Danube canal, now at last to be put into commission, would produce the effect of a goods-lift in a great store—the steelyards of the new German Hansa. . . . Always hold the inner line, as a preliminary for any expansion of the front—that was the lesson of strategy.

Herr Footh did not at first realize that his affair was making no progress, he felt so pleasantly refreshed by his many and various contacts with the centre-points of the commercial world. All the great names in Germany, in industry, trade, transport and the money market, were to be found represented in this city—and, in addition, the key-points of authority and administration, dozens of acquaintances to see, hands to shake, cigars to smoke. All this process was worth something.

It loosened his mental joints, and made him feel like a lad in a gymnasium performing on all sorts of new appliances. But all these people's friendliness did not prevent him getting a sense that he had come too late. Moreover, whereas in Hamburg he had to be content to figure as a star of the fourth or fifth magnitude, here in Berlin he had to accept an even lower position. His friend Annette could certainly have produced a quotation from Schiller or Goethe that would have lent a more encouraging aspect to his case: but all that could not gloss over the facts. Here were to be found the great names of the Rhenish, South-German, and Saxon concerns: and in his own industry, the great shipping lines, allied to them, from Lübeck, Bremen and his own beloved Hamburg, and the banking houses, on the boards of which sat the new aristocracy of the Party, beside the great ones of the Imperial régime, shoulder to shoulder, in the words of the old war communique's; pocket to pocket, as the satirists of the old days of Party struggle used to say in the broadsheets of those times. Everyone here who counted for anybody knew who Herr von Strauss was, and Otto Wolff, King Thyssen, Kaiser Kirdorf: the Hapag, the Woermannlinie, the Deutsche Levante. But H. P. Footh and his fleet of tankers, which by so happy an inspiration he named 'Äuglein' ships, and flagged them accordingly—who knew them and him? A few months ago some Basque vessels captured in the Spanish war had been put up for sale on the quiet, so that the small shipowners had been excluded from any share in the deal. It was a fair wager that these Jewish Thetis ships would go the same way. Hard was the road to Rome, harder still to Peking, but hardest of all to the Ministry of Marine, at any rate to get any business done there—lamented Herr Footh to his charming Anneliese who, arrayed in lilac pyjamas, came through the door of the adjoining room to meet him when he got home.

Anneliese was happy, a fact which she did not attempt for one moment to deny. "Hans," said she, "Hans;" and the expression of her voice and of her eyes in the discreet lighting of the room at night gave Hans Footh a thrill of delight that he had never experienced from his friend Annette. In his relations with her he always played the part of a grateful, and even almost of a bewildered, lover. Without having made any contribution of her own, her attitude was that of a great lady, a Duchess, or a Marquise, bestowing her favours on a retainer. With Anneliese he not merely lived and loved on a footing of equality; it was with the submission natural to a young woman that she lay in the arms of the stronger partner, entranced by his mastery, and his voice that echoed in his broad chest when she laid her ear upon it—such a graceful little ear, though with rather too small a lobe. He was not her first lover, but he was the first man who had really stirred her whole being to emotion, to a harmonious and absolute response; and, on the other hand, he, Hans Footh, did not need to be so careful with her as he was with Annette. On a Strength through Joy trip, through Switzerland to Lyons and the South of France, she had come across a little book by a French priest, setting forth a new doctrine on these matters, and indicating the days on which conception, in strict accordance with the precepts of Catholic marriages, might or might not, as desired, take place. The author, a scientist as well as a priest, had studied the subject in the French African territories, where the ancient knowledge of mankind had remained undisturbed by European scepticism. Anneliese, as a Catholic—

"Well, well," laughed Hans Footh, "so I've got a Catholic in bed with me——"

—believed firmly in the Abbé's instructions, as in matters of present controversy she was inclined to believe in the superiority of the great old Church and her wise dispositions regarding heretics and Jews. For the rest there was nothing religious, still less nun-like about her: her white, slim body was much more like that of a gymnast or a trapeze-artist, as Hans Footh observed with admiration.

"Twelve minutes' exercise every morning makes me fit for the whole day," replied Anneliese. "What I can't stand, is idleness. Pleasant as all this is, Hans, I should like to get away: I want to hear the sirens blowing in our harbour, sit with my back to the great window in your office, and feel the writing-table, where it all began."

Hans Footh laid his hand on her knee, as he had done on that occasion, drew her into his arms, and later on slipped a bit of chocolate into her mouth.

"Now let us go to sleep, darling. What have you been doing all day?"

Anneliese had met a friend of her father, an old acquaintance, from the same town on the lower Rhine, a place called Rheydt. He was an ex-soldier of the last war, who had at last got himself into a comfortable position, after going through a bad time during the Weimar Republic. He was now some sort of manager in the Labour Bank, where he had started as bank-messenger, one of its founders, Meyer, a Jew, having shot himself because a *Geheimrat* belonging to a Rhineland capitalist family had been put into his place. The *Geheimrat* had brought a fellow townsman with him as a minor employee, a man called Ruckstuhl, and so . . .

Hans Footh, who was nearly asleep, interposed: "Ruckstuhl?"

"Odd name, isn't it?" said the girl, as she slipped on her pyjama trousers, and stood barefooted on the carpet. Hans Footh sat up in bed, and grabbed her wrist.

"Do you think he was in the war—with us over in the East? We had a sergeant of that name at Schaulen."

"Schaulen—that's an odd name too—but it could be. He came and had a talk with my father, who by the way, has some connections with the Labour Front. I've often heard them talk about the Lithuanian Marjellanä. That's another odd word. Not everybody knows what it means."

"It's just what you are," he exclaimed, and held her tight just as she was going to her room so that he might sleep undisturbed. "Fix up a meeting with old Ruckstuhl to-morrow, darling—you may do the trick for me. Perhaps I can get a hold on the Thetis ships through you and the Labour Bank."

Anneliese stood, bent over him, her eyes shining black, their pupils overshadowing the pale iris. "Would you marry me—then?" she asked softly.

The former Sergeant Ruckstuhl beamed, when Herr Footh—Sergeant Footh in fact, of the Economic Department, Ober-Ost—stepped into his room. How long had Anneliese been working for him? he asked; he was surprised that old Blüthe had not brought them together long before. Yes, the Weimar disgrace, and the demobilization, had severed many ties, and scattered many old friends, which not even the War Graves Department could reunite, that admirable organization by means of which the astute Seeckt had re-established the old military registers and associations. Yes, now another age had opened out, other ways prevailed, and if he could do anything to assist his old comrade Footh—naturally within the confines of the law—Ruckstuhl, the Bank Manager, was entirely at the disposal of Footh the Shipowner. There was hand and foot to this sort of talk—Anneliese's hand and foot —thought Herr Footh, and promptly began to explain what had brought him to Berlin, and how he had not been able to make any progress. Herr Ruckstuhl assumed a judicial air, as he listened to the steps that Herr Footh had already taken. Of course he didn't want these ships to fall to Woermann or Hapag. He only needed to accept the obligation to reconstruct them as troop transports as well as tankers, in order to be able to take a complement of proletarian or Labour Front passengers on Strength through Joy voyages. This undertaking would have to be signed by Herr Footh at the Ministry of Marine, and his way thither would be made easier by a telephone message from the Labour Bank, which had for long co-operated on questions of this kind with Section 3B. All that would then be needed was some reason for preferring Party Comrade Footh in case his competitors in Hamburg itself made better offers, as was only to be anticipated.

"That is where the dog is buried," said Herr Footh. "I can't compete with Woermann or Wullenweber."

At that very moment a clear pleasant voice rang up on the house-telephone: it was Fräulein Blüthe, who wanted to know whether she might interrupt them for a moment, as a telegram had just come which she felt she must give to her employer at once. She entered the room, fresh and charming, as though on the wings of the autumn breeze, without either false bashfulness or confidence, and earned the benevolent, almost paternal looks of the smooth-shaven, grey-haired Herr Ruckstuhl, who successfully imitated his *Geheimrat's* jovial manner.

"Tens could perfectly well have decided for himself," muttered Footh with frowning brows. "Get through to Hamburg at once, Fräulein Blüthe, and make it an urgent call."

Herr Ruckstuhl promptly offered him a room and a telephone so that he could deal quite undisturbed on what Herr Ruckstuhl realized was the very important business of the defence services. "Your

*Reichstatthalter,*" he said, "comes from the same town as myself and Fräulein Blüthe, and so does the Minister of Propaganda. I assure you that if we can find any grounds for giving you the preference, that will turn the scale in your favour. . . ."

"Hm," said Herr Footh, gazing meditatively into Herr Ruckstuhl's penetrating hazel eyes. "There might be something that would serve."

And before Fräulein Blüthe went out to call up the Hamburg office from a room nearby, she shot a reproachful glance at her chief, to indicate that he must not be so modest and leave the Fuhlsbüttel affair unmentioned. Herr Footh made up his mind to speak. He knew very well that he was taking a risk; perhaps Herr Ruckstuhl would not care to be reminded of past events, and perhaps the story would spoil everything. But Anneliese had thrown the dice; so Herr Footh sat back comfortably in his chair, crossed his legs, pulled at his pipe, and related how, a few weeks ago, he had rescued Hamburg justice from a position of great embarrassment, by helping the Governor of Fuhlsbüttel Prison to find a deputy for Herr Denke of Oldenburg, in order to carry out four death-sentences, thus freeing four cells, and making it possible for the Führer to visit Hamburg.

"And you had this up your sleeve all the time," exclaimed Herr Ruckstuhl with enthusiasm. "Why, this is right stuff, and is bound to win the game for you with the *Reichstatthalter.* We have only to put that in to the proper quarter at the Propaganda Ministry, and you needn't be afraid of any competitor. Who was your deputy, by the way? Is he to be seen?"

"An old friend from Lithuania—Corporal Teetjen, if you remember him."

"But of course I do!" exclaimed Herr Ruckstuhl. "We travelled in the same compartment to Berlin on one occasion, when the sergeants made me sleep on the floor, and put him in the luggage rack."

He roared with laughter, and slapped his thigh, delighted that it had been possible to help Teetjen out of the unavoidable difficulties with which the small man now unfortunately had to struggle. Where could one ring him up? At Lehmke's beer-shop? Did Fräulein Blüthe know the number? It should be done. Herr Ruckstuhl rubbed his hands, and suggested to Herr Footh that he should save him trouble by undertaking the necessary negotiations at the Ministry of Marine. A loan from the Labour Bank, from the Strength through Joy account, for the purchase of the three *Thetis* ships, could not only be justified, it was offered here and now; the Bank would then put the matter right with the Ministry by telephone, and Herr Footh could return with an easy mind to his office, from which it was obvious that he could with difficulty be spared. It would merely be necessary for him to call on the *Reichstatthalter* after the interval of a day or two, and also bring Party Comrade Teetjen to see him at a time to be fixed, as soon as arrangements had been made by the Chancellery for the Führer's visit.

"And the only thing you need now bother your head about, my boy, is what you are going to call your three new tankers, so as to suit them to your list of names."

"*Ruck-eye*," said Herr Footh, "*Black-eye*—and I shall find a third all right." 'Bride-eye,' he thought to himself, as he got up.

## CHAPTER FIVE

### MAN DOES NOT LIVE BY BREAD ALONE

THE LEHMKES KNEW very well what they owed to their telephone; in a former epoch they would have called it a Temple of Fama, and brought offerings to the Goddess, which might be regarded as a more exalted form of telephone account. But what did such a monthly reckoning signify, compared on the one hand with the cash payment which had to be made for every conversation, and on the other hand with the sense of being within a network of information, even though the various conversations of the visible guests with their invisible interlocutors did not always exactly fit in. Knowledge is power—such was the old copy-book phrase; but for Frau Lehmke, as for many people of her kind, knowledge was also a pleasure, and a form of initiation, as it were, into a Masonic Lodge.

"I wonder what Albert's business is with Fuhlsbüttel—always the same number," she said, as she sat darning blue wool into one of Herr Lehmke's dilapidated grey stockings, which he had worn far too long for the hole to be re-knitted. As big as a dollar, she thought irritably.

"Yes," said Lehmke, who was reading the paper, but could none the less follow a conversation with half an ear. "The divining-rod doctor has to live there. I wouldn't be a prison doctor."

"Why not?" asked Frau Lehmke. "There's many a one in gaol now that never dreamt they would ever be there. So many businesses have been Aryanized, as they call it, and the former owners had first to be got out of the way. So all sorts of tax evasions and dirty doings were brought to light. And the folks can't help taking their illnesses to prison with them—diabetes, and appendixes and what not"—and she began to croon the word 'appendix' softly to herself. Frau Lehmke lived in constant apprehension that this superfluous part of the human system would have to be cut out of her.

"The Doctor seems to have discovered in Albert a gift for the use of the divining-rod," observed Lehmke, as he followed with a powerful, black-ringed forefinger the bit of news that he was studying at the moment. It seemed that a certain lecture in the Masonic Hall would

J

have to be repeated, having been interrupted on the first occasion
by an air-raid practice. That was the origin of the close connection
between Albert and the Doctor, who was indeed a very friendly sort
of man. "I expect they'll be coming along this old street to look for
dangerous radiations, and see whether our beds are set at the right angle,
and what happens when we're asleep."

"Albert's beds are certainly set at the right angle," observed Frau
Lehmke, speaking at apparent random.

But her husband was not to be drawn into the subject of Stine, who
seemed to have been rather too much in evidence of late. "I wonder
what we shall do if the Soviets don't voluntarily hand over the Ukraine,
the Donetz Basin, and the Black Sea ports, so that we can fetch the oil
direct from Baku."

"Rubbish," jeered Frau Lehmke. "The Russians need all that for
themselves—got a population of a hundred and fifty millions or more
to look after."

"But how they cheered when Adolf announced all that on the Party
Day. We ought to have insisted on it in the last war, when we made
the Brest-Litovsk Treaty, and Max Hoffmann banged his fist on the
table. What do you think about another world war, old lady?" he asked,
suddenly lowering his voice.

"You serious?" she retorted sharply.

"Well, Albert's business with the divining-rod isn't just a game.
A Reichswehr man was there for the performance who let out it was
an excellent way of discovering mines by sea as well as on land."

"Here you are," said Frau Lehmke, as she waved her husband's
darned socks. "The blue patches are to remind you that a man saves
his wife work, and saves the State wool, if he doesn't let his socks go so
far as this lot. Economy and love of one's neighbour should always go
together."

"Yes, indeed," said Herr Lehmke, with an apologetic grin. "That's
why they're amalgamating all these firms, though once upon a time
competition was the very trick of all business. Seems as if the Thetis
Shipping Co. is to be aryanized by Albert's friend, Herr Footh. We
must find out what's up when Editor Vierkant comes along this evening.
If Footh pulls it off, I dare say that will mean something in Albert's
pocket."

"Something more, you mean," said Frau Lehmke. "No one but a
kid like Stine would believe that story of a legacy from Heligoland.
But the Teetjens have money just now. What about that personal
trunk-call from Berlin, and brown shoes," added Frau Lehmke, "in
October."

"I see the Führer's coming here on November 9th," said Herr
Lehmke, without interest in what his wife was saying, as he held the
newspaper up to the light, "sort of compensation to Hamburg for
the Duce not having had time to honour us. In Finkenwerder Adolf
will harangue the workmen at the sites of his still unborn pet suspension
bridge. Then he's flying to Munich, you may not have noticed, for
the anniversary celebrations, of course—the Year-time, as the Jews

call it. You remember how the Samuels used to stick a taper on a cork float in a bowl of oil?"

"Yes, because they'd lost two sons in the war. That's why he's allowed to stay on in his cardboard factory, turning out caps for beer bottles."

"Two is quite a lot for the Fatherland. Can't imagine, by the way, what the Third Reich would do without aeroplanes. Wilhelm was known as the travelling Kaiser, because no sooner had he made a speech in one place, he was making one somewhere else. But compared with those who rescued us from the shame of Weimar, the performances didn't amount to a row of beans. A speech in Hamburg, a speech in Munich . . ."

"Baths on the premises," snapped Frau Lehmke quoting an advertisement-tag current in her younger days, and: "Use Luhus soap, and wash with hope," she added, rolling the socks into a ball—which was a legend that figured in large letters on the motor-buses that plied in Hamburg in the years before 1914.

Yes, Dr. Laberdan had not only accepted Albert Teetjen for a test on the occasion of his second lecture. The man with the light vague eyes, had struck him at once as possessed of the gift; and some further tests by the Chairman of the Reich Association, not merely of the local Hamburg Group, had indicated him as first-class material for training in the use of the magic rod. This was proved by leading him blindfold along a corridor in the Fuhlsbüttel Infirmary, laid with linoleum and therefore to some extent insulated, past several metal objects, grasping in his closed fist the forked rod with its ends bent outwards and shaft pointing forward, and the backs of his hands turned down. (There were already various schools of thought and controversies about the manner of walking with the rod, all relating to the carriage of the forearm.) Astonishing indeed, and especially to Albert, was the fact that on several occasions the rod turned automatically in his hands. Independently of his will, and arousing within him a thrill of satisfaction not unmixed with alarm, he felt the forward-pointing main twig turn downwards to the ground, while the ex-mesmerist and masseur led him forwards by a scarf attached to his arm. Albert had groped his way forward, helpless and devoid of will, as he had done when playing blind-man's-buff as a boy many years before. He had for some while been cursing his conceit, believing that he was being subjected to some test of nerves or muscles, and ashamed to the depths of his being that he, Albert Teetjen, *Rottenführer* in the S.S., should be lending himself to such mummery. Blue-grey linoleum had been his last impression of visible things on that Sunday forenoon. Then darkness and annoyance. When the rod quivered, and drew his fists downwards with it, he was inclined to ascribe the occurrence to accident, fatigue, or cramp. But the man beside him said in his hoarse voice: Iron. Shortly afterwards: Water; and then, after a longer pause: Gold; and took the bandage off Albert's eyes. At his feet lay, coiled like a snake, a thick gold watch-chain, bought at an official jewel sale at a valuation price. That some unknown force should have any power over Albert's mucles, filled him with bewildered amazement. So he had carried within himself for two and forty years, a magnet which operated through his entire body, engrafted into his sinews and his nerves.

"Well, we're in for some bad weather now, as you see," Dr. Laberdan had said, as the three of them sat in his study, listening to the rain rattling on to the window-panes and frames, and the lamentations of the sea wind. "I'm sorry you'll have such an unpleasant journey home." (He could not help feeling that he had met this man before, though he did not know when or how.) "So fine a gift as yours needs to be cultivated. You surely did not think to fall from Heaven as a finished master of the craft. Such things don't happen, though you read about them in books. When you are at home, put some metal objects under thin coverings, and test your reactions to the various materials. In the course of a few weeks they will become more and more definite. You have received a rare and noble favour from Nature, Herr Teetjen; see that you develop it for the benefit of our nation—I should have said in former days, for the benefit of humanity."

Thus the Chairman, who—as it seemed to Albert—possessed a slightly unctuous turn of speech. But he agreed with Dr. Laberdan on a continuation of these experiments, when this young hound had acquired a little more training—and he must take care not to waste the winter-months—so that in the spring, as soon as the weather became human again, they could practise in the open country under more or less natural conditions, and really try out Albert's talents. If a man felt his wrist turn over when he passed a watch-chain or a bowl of water, what would happen when he came upon a natural water-course or a land torpedo under his feet? That would be a grand performance, he thought proudly on his way home; and Stine would be properly impressed with him at last. Her Albert wasn't just an ordinary man; she had always said as much to him, or at any rate let him understand she thought so. But now he felt in a certain sense elevated above the ruck. During the next few days he kept on wondering how so marvellous an event, the possession of such a gift, was to be explained; but without result. He had learned too little, and what was more, he had read too little; he had not done well at school, where he had been very ill at ease; he had never been the sort of boy to sit over a book. After his marriage, Stine had taken care of that sort of thing for him; but before his marriage, no one had bothered. It couldn't be helped; there were men born to the cattle-yard and the slaughter-house, and others to books and the reading-lamp. Such as Tom Barfey, for instance. When Albert was sure he possessed the gift, he would show the boy a few experiments and ask him what was the meaning of it all. Dr. Laberdan had talked about earth-magnetism in his lecture as though everybody knew what that meant. But Albert did not know. That iron was magnetic, and that somewhere in the ocean there was a magnetic mountain which was carefully avoided by all ships because it would draw the rivets out of the wooden hulls of sailing-vessels, he had read somewhere. But how our modern iron ships coped with such a danger he simply could not imagine. Probably their powerful engines were themselves a guarantee against the attracting power of such a magic mountain. This was a point in which he could not do better than question Comrade Footh, when they next met, who would have the information first-hand from his own captains. Of course it was something connected with navigation, the magnetic needle, and the North Pole, otherwise the compass could not always point towards the North. Perhaps the divining-rod was in fact a sort of compass? A man ought to know something of the earth on which he lived, and not merely go about poking a walking-stick into moleheaps.

At home, Stine found it difficult to adapt herself to this new obsession. Brass scale-bowls had now to be put on the floor, or earthenware pots full of water, in order that Albert might practise his divining-rod; and a busy housewife inevitably tripped over such a vessel, or stepped into the scale-bowl, as she hurried between kitchen, bedroom, shop, and outhouse. And when a pot was broken, who was responsible for the damage? Certainly not Dr. Laberdan, nor the *Reichswehr* officer who, as Albert said, was interested in these experiments. And when a saucepan of beans was on the boil it was impossible to remember that a knife was hidden under the kitchen-runner, or an axe under the bedside carpet—*the* axe, grandfather's cooper's axe. Moreover, it was very easy to gash one's foot, accordingly, when wearing thin house-shoes or slippers in winter. But oddest of all was what happened to Albert's hands—how his muscles contracted and twisted. There could be here no question of earth magnetism; had it been so, ordinary folks must have had some experiences of the same kind. No; it was something different, and more mysterious, that had here gained possession of her Albert. In the old days people would have known by what name to call it. Then, when religion was still trumps, when the good God ruled men's hearts and the Devil tempted them, such a divining-rod would have been promptly recognized as witchcraft, magic, and banned as Devil's work. But these were days of enlightenment, when no one ever mentioned God in a public assemblage, and people derided the simple souls who needed to listen to a sermon on Sundays in order to be happy. The children no longer learned the glorious Chorales—'Now thank we all our God', 'How grandly shines the morning star', 'Oh Head besmirched by blood and wounds'; they no longer knew their Catechisms by heart; and the older ones were actually inured to the shedding of blood, and taken out in classes to see the slaughter of pigs and poultry, even on rainy days, which would have been much better spent in warm schoolrooms. . . . No, the Third Reich provided riddles enough, there was no need to go and look for them in depths of the earth, and ruin one's eyes reading books. Reading was, no doubt, a good thing, but telling stories was far better. Grandmother Geisow had known all sorts of stories she had picked up from shepherds, about apparitions, second-sight, and things that walked by night. Some of them in her own family. But her granddaughter, Stine, was thankful not to have inherited that gift; to her, everything was or should be simple, straight-

forward, transparent, clear as sunlight. No, Stine was impervious to any
such Devil's work; Albert might lay his axe, his accursed axe, as carefully
as he pleased under the carpet, and feel his wrists twist, as he walked
over it, and the witch-rod, the hazel-rod, twist and bend in the presence
of the axe of blood.

> *From magic, magic you must fly,*
> *In faery favours put no trust,*
> *For the witch's cat has the devil's eye,*
> *And gaudy gold turns but to dust,*
> *Unto your soul your heart endear,*
> *That it may not break in twain,*
> *To eerie whispers lend no ear,*
> *And pray to Jesus yet again.*

The verses, which came out of Grandmother's Gersow's song-book,
had stuck more firmly in her mind than she had expected. But there
was no harm in that. They were far better than the Horst Wessel song,
and all the rubbish that people sang these days, and that echoed forth
from Lehmke's windows, when she slipped over there at night sometimes, because Albert stayed out so late.

In the circle of his friends Albert was highly esteemed for having
reported and been accepted for the divining-rod service. The *Sturm*
Preester considered it an honour when he was selected for the dangerous
duty of searching for mines in the possible advent of a war with the
Russians, a man who had already done credit to the grey tunic and would
probably do so again. It had been no small matter, as the fathers of
families would often relate, to have assailed an enemy position with hand-
grenades and bayonets through a heavy barrage; and German writers
had, since the seizure of power, been remarkably eloquent on the subject
of the stress and clash of war and battle—though it was odd that their
heroic deeds were soon forgotten when the book had been returned to
the lending library. The youths who sat at the little tables in Lehmke's
back room in black tunics, with their cropped fair hair, and cold inex-
perienced eyes, had never been in any personal peril; they had only
had to deal with an unarmed and almost untrained adversary, for the
Red military associations had already been dissolved and abolished by
the Weimar Government. The S.A. did indeed come into action
sometimes, but the Party and the *Reichswehr* were always at their backs,
ready to cover them, if any of the illegal organizations dared to organize
a Sunday parade. But all that was the history, not of the 'movement'
alone, but of the whole German people; there was no longer need to
look for a chance to do great deeds. They would soon be done by the
appointed masters of the subject, of all those inferior races whose fatuous
nationalism and Socialistic creeds had undermined the whole of the
nineteenth century, opening the way for the Liberalism under which
Jews could actually be ennobled, sit in the House of Peers and assist
in the government of the country, while their agents and emissaries,
Bolshevists like Radek, Lenin, and Trotzki, stupefied the workers into

believing that the World revolution would bring them salvation. Adolf Hitler and his Paladins would decide the time and place when the final battle for the future should begin, when German Michael with uplifted sword should rush upon the hereditary foe, restoring the natural order whereby the higher elements subjugate the lower, free them from the burden of learning, and impose on them the day-labour for which alone the Poles and Slavs and Russians were created. Such was the improvised address delivered by Comrade Vierkant in honour of Albert Teetjen, who had now openly enrolled himself in the fighting front of the future. The subject of these congratulations had to stand a round of drinks, but that couldn't be helped, and had to be done with a good grace. Indeed, the thought of what Vierkant had said afterwards, would even have reconciled Stine to this expenditure.

His story was that an old schoolfellow of his and fellow-student at the Foreign Institute had come home on leave to Hamburg a week before. He had a middling sort of job in the office of the Consul-General at Cairo, but had for some time been an esteemed agent of the Party. For some years past it became the habit, to get a breath of fresh air of course, to spend Sundays in automobile trips into the desert west of the Egyptian frontier. If only they could have had with them an adept at the divining rod, like Comrade Teetjen. In desert warfare water was as essential an item as munitions, and had been since the earliest times. Well, our new friends, the Italianissimi, had undertaken—though as yet without success —to detach Egypt if possible by diplomacy, and, if not, by force of arms, from English domination. The young King would be properly grateful to those who brought him into relations with the great Duce, while, on the other side, certain holdings of Suez Canal shares would be transferred to those more properly entitled to them. Moreover, in certain contingencies German troops from the Balearics of Southern Spain could appear in Tripoli, or even in the ancient Cyrenaica, and turn the English out of Egypt, who had indeed no business there. Their overweening conceit so blinded them that they suspected no evil, even when Italian ships felt at home in all Mediter- ranean ports in Eastern waters, and the Ala Littoria secured increasing control of the air service from Aden up to Rhodes, as indeed was natural, in view of the craftsmanship and skill of Italian engineers and pilots, which the English could not pretend to rival. They had even had to relinquish to the Dutch the important route to Karachi in India. All of which was truly liberal and truly democratic on the principle of—sleep, my baby, sleep. Moreover, to Teetjen, and especially to his wife, the idea of searching for water in the desert should indeed be attractive as compared with a process of tramping the snowy wastes, where a dexterously hidden mine might at any time explode under a fellow's boots and blow his leg off. So here's to Africa, old boy, and here's to you. Albert sunned himself in all this anticipated glory and grinned. If these good folks only knew the powers he now had at his back! The reappearance of old Ruckstuhl, so opportunely promoted by his *Geheimrat*, had set his foot on very firm ground. A good time had started, there was no mistake about that. He could accept all these compliments without undue complacency; they were directed to the right address, however erroneous might be their contents. It was as if someone when asking for a dozen Vienna sausages, got some blood and liver sausage thrown in, because a bullock had just been killed.   But it was first-rate stuff, and very tasty too.

## CHAPTER SIX

### ALL ALONG THE LINE . . .

THE BUSINESS HAD picked up considerably—as Albert expressed it, the chimney was beginning to smoke.   On the one hand, with the advent of the colder months, the demand for fats and meat markedly increased, and a dictatorial system has a keen ear and a just respect for such under-currents of feeling.   The barometer of public opinion in Hamburg went up, because fat pigs were pouring in from Hungary and Rumania, and the Reich had permitted these imports in view of the fact that both these Balkan States had responded by placing larger orders for railway rolling stock, as had been announced on the wireless.   It was all a matter of policy, the listener was intended to think—and indeed that is what he did think.   Hitler's dexterous touch, by which he at the same time transformed old locomotives into young pigs, and secured himself good railway communications, in case Germany ever had to convey troop formations across the Balkans, to the aid of Turkey or Italy. . . .

Albert understood the art of sausage-making from A to Z, but Stine —in all innocence—was equally expert in that of advertisement.   The catching of customers, as Albert called it.   The Women's Organiza-tion of the Party had learned from the great publishing houses how to issue leaflets to housewives in the various districts, which contained more or less the same collection of articles, recipes, knitwork-patterns, crossword puzzles, and racial slogans, for Wandsbek, Altona, Barm-beck or Harburg, but also advertisements phrased to suit the particular quarters of the city, which was a very sensible practice in view of the differing populations and habits comprised in a great modern city. For the three Beks, as Editor Vierkant expressed it, Eilbek, Barm-beck, and Wandsbek, a weekly paper was published, in which the rhymed advertisements were a source of much amusement to its female readers, and duly lingered in their minds.

> *Sausages or mutton or whatever you may wish,*
> *Just walk around to Teetjens and they will fill your dish*

—these lines had appeared in the paper since the beginning of October, to which indeed was adjoined the address—Wagnerstrasse 17—the

tram number, and the overhead railway station. Stine had suggested
some such verse, but she had had a partner in its composition, Tom
Barfey, who had taken his fee in kind, or in such gifts from his divinity
as a pat on the head from Stine, or permission to kiss the curve of
her elbow. Albert, however, maintained that the inspiration of this
couplet had been Stine's alone, just as she had composed that letter to
Comrade Footh, which had been the fortunate beginning to the whole
story. In the Four Lands, which was the name given to a certain low-
lying part of the neighbouring countryside, after its prototype in the
Saxon forest, she had in former days been acquainted with some farmers
who supplied geese to Jewish firms; the wife of Plaut, the Chemist, who
was a brother of Dr. Plaut, the Rabbi, had dealt with them, as their
poultry was slaughtered in accordance with the strict and ancient
precepts of the Jews, eliminating the blood. Stine thought it improbable
that this sort of connection would now be permitted; so one dismal,
rainy Sunday morning she went out there with Albert, and when they
returned, soaked through but in high good humour, they had arranged
for a profitable consignment of Michaelmas geese for the second week
in November—fine fat birds, the like of which had been brought to
table on the great Reformer's birthday since the memory of man,
and as an invitation to their purchase Stine was credited with yet
another verse:

> On Michaelmas Day when the lamps are lit
> All around the table we sit;
> Steaming hot, out of the pot,
> Here comes the Michaelmas goose.
> Isn't it nice, stuffed with spice
> Somebody's been from Hamburg to Spain
> For apples and chestnuts to stuff and to flavour
> Our Michaelmas goose.

But the reputations of the Teetjens grew enormously, even in wider
circles, when the news was circulated by the Lehmkes that Albert Teetjen
was to be introduced on the 9th of November to the *Reichstatthalter* and
perhaps even to the Führer himself as a budding adept on the divining-
rod. It was a great matter to have been rung up from Berlin, by the
Managing Director of the Worker's Bank. The fact that Footh the shipowner had been the intermediary for all these attentions, and had fought
side by side with Teetjen in the World War, did honour to them both;
it proved that the Third Reich had abolished all distinctions between
class and income, and that it was human values alone that counted. In
the Wagnerstrasse there were some, indeed, who envied Teetjen his
advancement, and talked about class tyranny, which had not altered
in essentials, and should not have deluded a small tradesman like Teetjen
the butcher. Footh, of course, profited substantially from the deal—
compliments for Teetjen, cash down for Footh. However, this sort of
talk increased the number of customers: the door-bell rang more often,
and so did the bell of the cash register, as the parcels of stewing-steak,

chops or sausages, wrapped in greasepaper, or newspaper were handed across the counter, accompanied by a genial Hamburg jest from Frau Stine that added to the attraction of the Teetjen wares. Moreover, the Winter Help activities had started, bringing new passing customers into the street; many a S.A. man dropped in for a bit of garlic sausage to eat with his bread and dripping or bread and margarine, and a bunch of asters in the window produced more effect when the neighbours could see the muddy footsteps in the doorway. Good times had come to the Teetjens; they slept soundly, they walked the streets with an air of confidence, and since man does not live by bread alone, Albert actually took his Stine to the theatre on Saturday evening, where they saw a gay musical comedy called the *Hussar's Bride,* in which General Zieten and old Fritz himself appeared, and the Poles and the Russians were made properly ridiculous. And when Stine got home, weary with much laughter, she hardly knew who was undoing her hair. Anyway the hero had sung magnificently, and if only Albert could have developed a tenor voice he would have been as fascinating as the cavalry captain in the play. It had been much nicer than the divining-rod evening, and a seat in the packed pit of a great theatre, with its arc lights and rising tiers of seats, gave her the sense of belonging to a great community; indeed, as she had told Albert, no man is alone. When had that been? Not on that unlucky evening when she had had the idea to write to Footh; but how on earth had it come upon her to describe that evening, the beginning of their upward progress and their good days, as unlucky? How could the word have risen to her lips? Lucky it ought to be called, when paper and ink had begun to help them out of their mess. Poor Stine—poor little sheep! it was a good thing that Albert didn't notice anything, and would fling himself upon you in all his strength and glory, when the tiresome business of undressing was finished, and the light switched off.

Just as misfortunes seldom come unaccompanied, so good fortune brings others in its train. Herr Footh returned from Berlin, drove up to Teetjen's shop, with his arms full of winter-roses for Frau Stine— Anneliese Blüthe had insisted on sharing Herr Ruckstuhl's parting bouquet with Frau Teetjen before it faded—and in a room full of the fragrance of roses and rich with the smoke of good cigars, Herr Footh had solemnly conveyed Herr Ruckstuhl's salutations and the announcement that Albert Teetjen would be introduced not merely to the *Reichstatthalter* on November 1st, but also on November 9th to the Führer. "Make sure your boots are well polished, my boy," Herr Footh had added with a grin, and turning to Frau Stine, who had set out some coffee and pastries hurriedly fetched from Lakerde the baker's shop on the Wandsbeker Chaussée, which was noted for its cakes and supplied the Rotebaum Chaussee, where the rich Jews lived, he went on: "You must look after your young man, Frau Teetjen, and see he doesn't do anything foolish; he mustn't get drunk before the tenth, but we'll all have a celebration to make up for it *on* the tenth."

Whereat Frau Stine assured him that her Albert already took very good care of himself, and would never bring discredit on anybody, as he had already proved; and H. P. Footh, as he sat there in that homely little back room, drinking coffee and feeling very well at ease, surveyed the pair and told himself that this ought to prove a profitable connection. The purchase of the Jewish ships would be diverted by Ruckstuhl on to the taxpayer—in other words, on to the Reich treasury and the Labour Front. These two people ought certainly to be encouraged to have children: the sound and serviceable race of N.C.O.'s must be continued. The two thousand marks of working capital obviously lay in capable hands. Herr Footh had invested 7.80 marks in the transaction, and already acquired those tankers as his share—there was no manner of doubt about that. It was not everybody who could have pulled off such a job! Well, he must run to a silver cigarette-case for Albert at Christmas, and a silver handbag for Stine. But the money side of the deal, as the late beheaded Isaac would have expressed it, could scarcely be expressed in a percentage, if the transaction succeeded, and the *Reichstatthalter* didn't expect too much of a rake-off, and the *Bendler-strasse* didn't short-circuit the whole affair. But that, he thought, was not likely to happen.

"How did you conjure up this wonderful pastry, Frau Stine? You won't tell me that it grows in the Teetjen household on weekdays."

"I'm glad you like it, Herr Footh. It's a pity there isn't a Frau Footh to tell you not to eat too much of it, if you don't want to get fat."

"How do you know, Stine? There isn't now, but there may be one of these days."


On November 1st, under a tall scaffolding hung with tarpaulins to keep out the rain, the *Reichstatthalter* dug the first ceremonial spadefuls of earth from a new foundation for the Elbe suspension bridge, this time in Finkenwarder. The menacing ochrous waters of the Elbe, flecked with white foam, swept past both sides of the island, like a huge, devouring dragon plunging down upon the North Sea, three kilometres broad, rolling turbulently down from the snowy uplands of the Rübezahl Riesengebirge. It was now to be subjected to the will of the Führer, the power of the new Reich. It was true that the hydraulic engineers had only reluctantly accepted the scheme, urging that a substructure of rock was indispensable. But the embodied genius of the *Reich*, whom Providence had not in vain bestowed upon the German people, would witness the fulfilment of his desire that this island should provide a firm foundation for the bridge span which the *Reichstatthalter* would solemnly inaugurate. And so, in his Rhineland accent, the supreme official of the State of Hamburg pronounced the address composed for him by his secretary, and the only unrehearsed item was the storm which cast something of a gloom over the proceedings. Enveloped in a cloak with upturned collar, his clammy hands thrust into leather gloves, he duly performed the ceremony, after which the participants hurried under cover, or into the dry and comfortable interiors of their cars. Hence only a brief minute was bestowed upon Herr Footh, and a glance of recognition on Herr Teetjen, accompanied by the question whether he had enjoyed cutting the traitors' heads off. Albert had only time to click his heels and rap out: "Certainly, Excellency." A sound fellow, all things considered, as the great man observed approvingly later on. Albert, a little disappointed, had climbed into Herr Footh's two-seater —the rain had rather spoilt his pleasure. However, this was only the overture to the real performance, and rain was always on the cards in Hamburg. None the less, in the Wagnerstrasse Albert Teetjen was the hero of the day, and not a single one of his Michaelmas geese was likely to remain on his hands.

This time the progress of November brought colder but drier weather, which looked like favouring the Führer's visit. Hamburg presented an unfamiliar sight in its array of Swastika flags, and the huge blood-red banners gleamed in heavy splendour through the damp air of the bustling grey city. All the bells pealed when S.A. columns, S.S., and *Reichswehr* infantry marched through the main streets, and children—deputations from the schools—waited for their friend and patron with bunches of flowers in their hands. Carpets, brought out for the Reformation celebrations on the previous Sunday, still hung from the portals of the churches of St. Michaelis and St. Peter, and in many of the parishes the churches were adorned with garlands of pine-twigs, which came in useful for the great day, on this occasion at least. Astrologers, like the Chairman of the Divining-rod Association, had always been convinced that about the ninth day of November the aspect of the stars indicated upheavals in the State, as had been established by the French, Russian, and finally the German revolution. Even in the English civil war it had acquired a gloomy association as the occasion of the flight of Charles I to Scotland, but no farther; the English always did things in their own way. Salvoes of guns, squadrons of plunging aeroplanes, and a storm of cheering from the crowd, greeted the Führer as he drove from the aerodrome, first at high speed and then slowly through the crowd— to-day a wholly festal crowd. There he sat, looking, as usual, frank and kindly, bare-headed in a huge open Mercedes, accepting the applause of the multitude, and the Hamburgers greeted him as the inhabitants of any city would have greeted the advent of so mighty a lord. He was a man from among themselves, a man after their own heart, a symbol of their own strength, which had brought them from the depths up into the company of the rulers of the earth; and he had known what it was to live in squalor like the poorest of the poor. His collar had not always been as clean as it was to-day, indeed he had probably not possessed a necktie during the years he had slept in a poor house in the city of Vienna. But he had believed in himself, in his mission, and in Germany, and his example enjoined every young man to work and never to despair. There were indeed slanderous people who alleged that Adolf Hitler had done as little work then as he did to-day. He acted from the inspiration which the mob always attributed to its great men.

So the grey car glided between the serried ranks of the Seventy-sixth and Eighty-third, behind whose fixed bayonets the crouds shouted "*Heil*", cheered, and greeted him in Roman fashion; in front of the Senate House detachments of the Hamburg S.S. and the motorized Corps were drawn

up, and two men, one from each group, were summoned to escort Adolf
Hitler, while, arrayed in top-boots and riding-breeches, he mounted
the staircase to greet the chief municipal dignitaries and the officers of
the regiments representing the 10th Army Corps. They all knew that
a new tank was to be paraded that day, and hoped for honours not
inferior to the resplendent decorations of the old régime, if the model
and its performance met with the great man's approval. Ceremonial
luncheons were no longer in the order of the day, but before the speech
there was to be a brief pronouncement at a gathering of the élite on the
subject of the Adolf Hitler bridge, after which a few specially favoured
Party comrades would be introduced. Nobody in Hamburg had conceived of such a Kaiser, a man without pretension and possessed of such
all-conquering charm.

And then he vanished, not without a pleasant nod to the bystanders
together with a few privileged persons and those bidden to a special
audience behind the tall double portals of heavy brown oak which
guarded the inner chambers of the Senate house; while Footh and
Teetjen and other favoured guests sat at their ease on red upholstered
benches and chairs, and helped themselves to excellent sandwiches from a
long table spread with a white cloth, at which Senatorial footmen in
sumptuous liveries dispensed wine, porter, and hot tea, congratulated
themselves on the weather—for though it was a grey day, there had
been occasional glimpses of blue sky and white shifting cloud—and felt
extremely comfortable and important. Herr Footh, who had edged
away from Albert, and sat down in a corner with some cronies in the
Motorized Corps, drank to his friend from time to time, flung him a
meaning look over the rim of his porter glass, slapped his thigh with
the side of his hand, thumb upwards, axe-like, and then took a deep
draught of porter. Yes, thought Albert Teetjen, feeling rather embarrassed and solitary among all these fine gentlemen; Yes, Footh was
drinking to him just to show they were together, his intention being to
profit by the connection. A little while ago, while they were waiting,
being possessed of an excellent pair of ears, he had heard two men in front
of him discussing the news that the former Chairman of the Bourse, Kley,
had committed suicide because he was so disgusted with the sum for which
the three ships of the Thetis Company were taken off his hands, and that
Herr Footh had been the fortunate man who had entered upon his
inheritance.

"Where did you hear that?"

"From an excellent source. Ruckstuhl of the Labour Front Bank,
who was here about the business on Sunday. Footh has pulled off a
good thing there—he's a bright lad by the looks of him."

"And what about Madame Kley?"

"Well, well, who knows, a hostess like her always had a bit of something tasty in the larder."

"But nothing better than this ham. Man doesn't live by bread
alone: he needs something to put between the slices."

The two men were now standing at the buffet, tipping the Senatorial
brandy from great balloon glasses down their parted jaws.

At that moment the doors were flung open and the Führer dashed in, shrieking—there was no other word for it—"It's a swindle; it's open sabotage!" he yelled, in a throaty strangled voice, with Rudolf Hess, his friend and deputy, close at his heels and catching at his arm, hurried without looking to the right or left to the door of the anteroom, grey-faced, swaying as he walked, opened it, wiped the sweat from his forehead, ran down the steps and disappeared. Behind him emerged a little knot of men from the Burgomaster's office, where the discussion had just taken place, some pale, some flushed, and all excited and dumbfounded. The *Reichstatthalter*, sickly green beneath the eyes, turned to the assembled company who stood there deathly still with arms outstretched in salutation, like an array of wax puppets in their brown, black, grey-green and pale-blue uniforms, and said hoarsely, in an attempt to make light of the occurrence: "Just an attack of the artistic temperament, gentlemen—pray ignore it. The Führer's visit will proceed according to programme."

'Oh dear,' thought Albert Teetjen, 'I shan't get a word with him now, my luck's out.'

Last out of the inner door came a Colonel of the *Reichswehr*, with a narrow mouth and moustache, he too as white as chalk. He held a bundle of papers in one hand, and walked arm-in-arm with a man in ceremonial civilian dress who was also grasping a roll of papers—the head of the Municipal Engineering Department, followed by a young S.A. man carrying a large drawing-board. Albert knew none of the men, nor did he recognize Russendorf—the Public Prosecutor—who was exchanging a few hurried words with his friend Footh. But Russendorf came up to him, called him Party Comrade Teetjen, advised him not to go home, but to try to get a seat from which he could listen to the address to the Labour Front, and promised he would call the attention of the Führer's deputy to this highly meritorious Party Comrade. So he knows who I am, thought Albert Teetjen, flattered and yet rather perturbed. Well, he hoped the Public Prosecutor would keep his word. The ceremonies did indeed continue, but everything seemed to have gone awry. The Führer suddenly looked like a dull, ordinary, stocky little man, with the wild and glittering eyes of a mouse: his speech, thought Albert, might perhaps have made an impression on Lithuanian peasants, who had always been accustomed to shouts and threats from those in authority, but was scarcely adapted to intelligent dockyard workers, who stood in horseshoe array in one of the great factory yards. They were accustomed to be addressed in much more seemly fashion, with a touch of geniality and humour, a pungent jest or two, and a few pithy words of wisdom at the end. A neat allusion had more effect on them than this braying voice from the daïs and the loudspeakers in which Adolf Hitler proclaimed how drastically he would deal with agitators and traitors.

"Four ruffians belonging to this city had their heads cut off not long ago; let their Fate be a warning to you all. Anyone who sets himself up against me, whoever he may be, had better look out for himself. I'll crush him in the end, perhaps sooner than he thinks. There is no rat-hole so remote that shall save him from my vengeance. The Elbe Suspension bridge shall be built, the armament programme which we are compelled by our envious enemies to undertake, carried out; and let all the Bronsteins, Sobelsohns and Rosenfelds do their utmost, they'll soon find themselves on their flat heads instead of on their sweaty feet. Germany is moving forward irresistibly; we are a master-race and will soon show it to the world. With every blow of your hammer, with every bolt you rivet, you are forging the present and the future for yourselves and your children. What was I twenty years ago to-day? a private soldier in the trenches, and, fourteen years ago, the leader of a betrayed and defeated little band—Baldur struck down by Hoedur's random blow. And yet we kept the faith, and we believed in you, the German people, and in you, the workers of Germany. We mean to restore you your dignity, which you had lost when you were degraded into becoming slaves of Judah. That was the time of darkest night, but now the day has broken. From your harbour our ships go forth, flying the flag of the *Reich*, respected and feared throughout the whole world, and it would indeed have been a disgrace if you workers of Hamburg had left your seamen in the lurch and did not crown your work for Germany's glory. I summon you to fight the great fight on the field of toil—toil that shall bring power and achievement, and I know you will heed that summons. *Siegheil, Siegheil, Siegheil!*"

Well, we ought to be good at community shouting by this time, thought Albert Teetjen, when the crowd's response thundered across the square in a thrice-repeated *Siegheil*. Then, as the strains of *Deutschland über Alles* and the *Horst Wessel* song burst forth, he felt himself thrust forward by the little group around him to the staircase down which the Führer would have to come, and at that moment Rudolf Hess was already walking down it—a brown-haired, youngish man, not quite so corpulent as his companions—in a smart brown and black uniform. He nodded to his adjutant, who took a list out of his pocket, arranged the Party Comrades who were to be introduced in two ranks according to their places on the list. Deputy Hess, with a copy of the paper in his hand, turned to Adolf Hitler, who was refreshing himself with a glass of beer which had been placed ready to his hand in a siphon-bottle from the factory canteen, and asked him whether he would receive a few Hamburg Party Comrades specially deserving of his notice. "I must get away and lie down," he replied in a tone of exhausted irritability. However, he had so far recovered his self-control as to acknowledge the salutes of each man as Hess introduced him by name. But when Footh's and Teetjen's turn came, the Führer's strength and patience seemed really to have given out. The two men in uniform, and three others in civilian dress, were brought forward, the services which had secured them this honour rattled out just as the Führer's car drove away through the cheering crowd. But the cheering sounded flat, and—"Your Hamburgers are as cold-blooded as a catch of cod and skate," snapped Rudolf Hess in an angry whisper to the *Reichstatthalter*, before he got into his own car. The latter also had dark eyes and hair, observed Albert; he himself was the sole representative of the Nordic race, the

Viking blood. Whereat he squared his shoulders, threw his head back,
turned up the collar of his overcoat and buttoned it securely round his
neck; despite the burst of pallid sunshine, the cold had gripped him—
the shivering, damp cold of a Hamburg November. If Albert had not
kept an eye open, Comrade Footh would have left him standing in the
huge factory yard right out in dockland—for everybody was eager to
get home and to a warm stove as quickly as possible.

"Shall we be mentioned in the paper?" asked Teetjen.

"Undoubtedly," replied Footh, "though without any details, I
dare say."

"That's good enough," said Albert, with a nod of satisfaction.
"From what I can hear my axe did you a bit of good too."

Footh frowned. "Your axe?" he asked. "Oh yes, if you like to put
it so . . . a great shipping business couldn't get far without the aid of
the axe of the shipowner's butcher-friend at Wandsbek."

And Teetjen realized that he would have been better advised to
omit this allusion. So he asked where he should send his friend a
Michaelmas goose, or whether he would like to take it away with him
now, as he could do if he dropped him at the Wagnerstrasse. Herr
Footh protested, but in the end he accepted one, carefully trussed
and packed by Stine, who had indeed put the idea into Albert's
head.

"Good weather all along the line," he said, "and all the corn ripe."

"We won't eat your friend Footh's giblets," said Stine. "We'll
send them along to the Barfeys'. It would be a pity to let them go to a
bachelor household—and I kept back the wings, stomach, head, and
legs. I left only the liver inside the bird. His cook will save it for his
breakfast to-morrow. And I'll roast yours for this evening, Comrade
Teetjen. Was the Führer nice to you? What did he look like from
near-by? As fine a fellow as he does in the news-reel?"

Albert pulled off his boots, and, reflecting that he must keep his
mouth firmly shut, replied that Adolf Hitler had certainly looked a
fine fellow, but a real man too, and nothing like so varnished as the old
generals and some of the Party bosses of to-day, which makes the Party
unpopular among certain sections of the working classes.

"I shan't forget the day, Stine," he went on, "on which I was
privileged to look my Führer in the eyes, and he in mine."

"Really!" laughed Stine. "What nonsense you do talk, Albert."

"Well, well," said Albert, sinking back on to the sofa. "It's this
sort of thing one reads in the papers. And now a cup of hot coffee,
Stine, with a dash of rum in it, to prevent me catching a cold."

In the Barfeys' lodging on the top storey the light had been on since
four o'clock. Tom had undertaken a job, which might well cost him and
his employer their heads, and he was deep in his task. Frau Pastor Langhammer, of the Confessional Church at Eimsbüttel, had given him a
report to copy which her husband had smuggled out of the concentration
camp—to the effect that the Jewish artist and illustrator, Fritz Krell,

had been driven to suicide, which was a matter which no Christian could tolerate in silence. The note, which was written in a diminutive scrawl, was to be sent to forty selected addresses, as a last appeal to the conscience and intelligence of the former ruling class, among whom Paster Lang- hammer had always been respected as a man of honour who had done his part in the last war. If that effort failed, Frau Pastor Langhammer had resigned in her clean Holstein accent, then—in her husband's view—there was nothing for it but the Communists' way out. And they, too, could do nothing without the Lord's approval. Who could kick against the pricks? The tears came into her eyes, and her voice quavered—she herself was a Pastor's daughter who had lost a brother in the last war.

"Well, and would it be altogether a misfortune, if you look at it from the other side, Frau Pastor?" Tom had said, rather tactlessly his mother thought, by way of consoling their visitor. So saying, he put his work by for the day; he would make an early start next morning in daylight, and so spare his eyes as well; he moved over to the stove, and set himself to make a supper dish out of Stine's handsome present—the self-same giblets which, with the addition of a scrap of stewing-steak and some green-stuff, would provide a stew to be remembered for weeks. The vermicelli, which Stine had also sent, had to be prepared separately before being soaked in the stew. When his mother came home the potatoes must be peeled and ready—they were not very good ones, not mealy enough for Tom's taste, but not that 'pig's fodder', as he had rudely called those which Frau Barfey brought home.

Gesche had started work at the wash-tub at seven that morning, and spent the afternoon hours over the laundry in the drying loft, with only a brief break for her dinner, for Frau Rechnungsrat Pilger wanted it all finished within the day. Since Tom had taken on the cooking, and the gas company had sent a sympathetic mechanic to install a low-placed gas-fire in the Barfey establishment, she managed to get through her work without becoming exhausted, as in former years, when she could hardly have survived the day without the aid of black coffee. Under the Third Reich her earnings had greatly diminished, partly because the new housewives, who had replaced the departed Jewish families, had been accustomed to doing their own housework, including the laundry, and consequently proved much harder and more exacting employers; and partly because all wages had fallen, since guns had to be preferred to butter, and the art of providing for the household, the process of juggling with farthings and halfpennies, called for an effort after the day's work to which most people's nerves were unequal. After standing at the washing-board a woman can't wait in a queue; it was some time before the tradesmen thought to draw up a chair or an empty box for Frau Barfey to sit on, while she was provided with her supplies of herrings, petrol, methylated spirit, or margarine. But her main concern was that Tom should not be left unprotected, nor be consigned to an institution; and Gesche Barfey's quiet determination got her needs attended to without fuss or altercation. And when she got home, in need of rest after the struggle, Tom always had a pot of coffee ready for her, and three rounds of bread and jam, so that she could rightly feel that kitchen

K

and bedroom were not but merely lit and warmed from without, but also from within.

She got out the plates and knives and forks, and laid the table, which was easier for her than for Tom, after a short rest, during which she darned a pair of his socks for him, which she could do quite well while lying down. As she was arranging the table and heard what a magnificent supper they were going to have, she observed that it was an appropriate feast on Hamburg's day of celebration, when Albert had been introduced to the Führer as an adept at the divining-rod.

"November 9th," said Tom dryly. He merely contracted his eyebrows slightly, and did not reveal that he had anything special in his mind, or that he had devised a plan which he was resolved it was his duty to carry out. But his news might well have spoilt his mother's enjoyment of the choicest dish she had tasted for many a long day, so he suppressed the impulse to tell her what he had had to bottle up inside him for many days past. Frau Barfey sat down to her supper with a zest that did something to light up her prematurely ageing face. She decided that a wing, a claw, half the stomach, neck, heart, and head should be put aside for the next day, as an addition to their usual porridge. She mentioned that when Stine was in service she had learned how to make a sausage out of the skin of a goose's neck stuffed with kosher filling. But Tom objected; he did not want to save anything for the next day. He said that they should use up everything on their feast in honour of the birthday of the lamented Republic—which had perished so untimely, at the age of only fourteen years. "Well, if it had had more guts, it would be in power to-day," he said, splitting the goose's skull with a kitchen-knife and a hammer in order to extricate the brain. "But people who won't listen have to suffer. . . . And to think that Albert Teetjen to-day had the honour . . . Not many know why, Mother."

"It was for his performance with the divining-rod," returned Frau Barfey, picking a plum from the jam-dish and slipping it into her mouth.

Tom smiled. "Oh no it wasn't, Mother—it was for his performance with quite a different implement. It wasn't the hazel-twig, but his axe that did it. The man who deputized for the Oldenburg executioner at Fuhlsbüttel, Mother, was our Albert, and no other."

Frau Barfey sat up in the corner of her sofa, and eyed her son from under levelled brows; then she took the plum kernel from her mouth, laid it on the edge of her plate, and said: "I don't like that sort of joke."

"It isn't a joke, Mother—I have it from someone who saw him do it, and recognized him under his mask."

"Tom," cried Frau Barfey, "I can't believe it."

"It's as true as we're both sitting here," said her son, squatting on his haunches. "And I saw a certain lady recognize him. I won't say who it was, but I know she spoke the truth."

"Yes; but you do hate some people so, Tom. I couldn't take your word for a thing like that."

"An axe isn't used to kill a goose, Mother, so we can eat our supper without worrying. But I don't think I should get any more beef or pork or mutton from Teetjen's."

Frau Barfey sniffed, and then wiped her eyes.

"Poor Stine," she whimpered. "How will she like a thing like that?"

"I doubt if she knows," said Tom, as he threw the goose's skull into a bucket of refuse for the dogs and cats. "Anyway, we must think of it from the point of view of health. The neighbours who buy his meat really ought to know what he's been doing with his axe. If they think it doesn't matter, that's their business. We shall have done our duty to society. Some people have stout nerves."

"What has it got to do with us?" groaned Frau Barfey.

"Perhaps nothing at all, perhaps a great deal. There'll be some music on the wireless this evening, and the Petersens aren't at home. If we cared to come down, Olga said . . ."

"I won't, dear. I must go to bed after news like that. An executioner living in the house! I don't know how I'm ever going to sleep peacefully again."

"Well, Mother," said Tom Barfey, "we didn't put him up to it. You may like to know that the *Reichstatthalter* shook hands with him for doing the deed, and introduced him to Hitler. Go to bed and sleep, Mother, we didn't make the world what it is."

Frau Barfey sat in the corner of the sofa and shook her head. Then she nodded: "True enough. He who puts his faith in God, nor thinks too nearly of the morrow, he shall be strengthened and sustained, in days of bitterness and sorrow—so runs the hymn."

"Well then, that's all right," grinned Tom Barfey. "I must be up early to-morrow to finish this job for the Langhammer lady. But it's early in the evening yet, and a little music always does one good. I wonder if they thought of that, when they put Hitler on our backs?"

"Who knows what will be the end of it all," sighed Frau Barfey. "But we had better not look too far ahead."

"Let us leave it to God," smiled Tom, as he buttoned on a clean collar.

*BOOK FOUR*

# THE LATE HERR MENGERS' BOOKS

## CHAPTER ONE

### THOSE WHO BEAR THE COST

THE INHABITANTS OF Germany were at that time divided into a number of such disparate groups that they could hardly be described as a nation, or indeed as citizens of one and the same state. Under the cloak of a common speech, origin, and past, localized for many centuries on the same portion of the globe, they presented so various a social structure that it could only be adequately compared with a section of the sea bottom, or the surface of the moon—crags unblunted by the storms of ages, and vast tumbled landscapes topped by towering peaks. Up from its fissures crept or swam repellent shapes, survivors of an antediluvian mass-creation long since dispossessed, spiritual descendants of the Stone Age, wholly alien to the persons of this book, who were engaged in celebrating Christmas, 1937, and the birth of a Saviour who, in the opinion of the pious and the faithful, had assumed and atoned for the sins of the World. In the area irrigated by the river Elbe, which the ancients called Eridanus—the amber river—which flows direct from Czech territory northwards into the North Sea ideas prevailed which could not be harmonized with human life and human death, and were not even understood by those who created and exploited them. In order to prevent the settlement of certain ancient antagonisms which had already been attempted west of the Rhine and east of the Niemen, first when Goethe was young and Gauss a lad, and again in the productive years of Freud and Einstein, the ruling classes, represented by small groups of defeated generals and greedy industrials, aided by agents of the great landowners, mine-owners, manufacturers, and organizations engaged in controlling money and public opinion, had combined forces without realizing that though the wheel of history can be swung back a turn or two, it cannot be actually put into reverse. Attempts were made under various disguises to revive and glorify the stone-dead economic concepts and institutions of the Middle Ages, and by using the phraseology of a more liberal era, induce the credulous workers to believe that here was the fulfilment of the dreams for which their forbears had striven so long. As five-sixths of the earth's surface was organized on capitalist principles, which were an expression of the human soul of man, it is not a matter for surprise that the shortsighted *homo sapiens* was, in the mass, prone to accept the victory of his oppressors, and made haste to cash in on the prospects. The world lay in the birth-throes of a new age, but would not recognize the fact; and there were many horrors yet to come.

It was raining—raining in torrents. Everyone ascribed the climate to the proximity of the sea, and echoed the age-long complaints against the Goddess Hammonia's caprices in the matter of weather which had filled the pages of Hamburg's authors for centuries past. Every Hamburg baby, they maintained, should have been brought into the world complete with gumboots, oilskins, and sou'westers. The grey layers of cloud that floated over the city, and overhung it like a pall of darkness in the winter months, affected the spirits of the inhabitants and made them prone to wrath and difficult to deal with.

Herr Koldewey sat in the 'birdcage,' from which he ruled his kingdom. A letter had come with the morning's post, confirming an announcement in the newspapers which, by an ancient tradition, recorded the changes and appointments in the academic world. A fellow-student of the old days of peace, a co-worker with him on certain Nietzsche studies, Professor Walter Rohme, of Zürich, had received an appointment at Boston, to assist in the defence of European psychology—which was his subject—against American influences; and the letter added that on his journey through next spring he would be staying a week in Hamburg with his friend Pastor Langhammer, and would look forward to sitting, as before, with his wife in Koldewey's glass tower, or beside the Barlach sculpture. Professor Rohme, as a cautious and experienced experimental psychologist, had, as lecturer at Zürich during the World War, and latterly since the year '33, made a study of the manufacture of rumour and the basis of human credulity; he had published some articles in the *Neue Züricher Zeitung* on the subject, which had attracted a good deal of attention, and in the year '34 had announced a monograph on atrocity propaganda which unfortunately had never appeared. Koldewey was glad to think that he could now ask him why in fact it had not done so. For even though the majority of these atrocities had been proved true, the utilization of a fact for propaganda purposes still remained, and in the view of psychologists the doctrine that what is to produce the effect of truth, had better not be true, could be applied in more ways than one. Well, these would be delights to come. Here was the daily round of duty with which Herr Koldewey proceeded to deal. Five admissions, three releases, six transfers to hospital. He wagged his long face with its prominent eyes from side to side as he found a reference to this last point in the report which the prison doctor, Dr. Laberdan, had made on this increase in illness during December. Koldewey smiled rather quizzically as he realized that Dr. Laberdan, the eccentric idealist of the divining-rod, did not notice how the convicts exploited his enthusiasm and superstition. For his report triumphantly recorded that—as not infrequently occurred—a current of deleterious earth-magnetism must have surged up from the earth's interior, emanating very likely from the ultimate sources of the Elbe, with the result that certain cells which had hitherto been perfectly hygienic as tested by the divining-rod, were now impregnated with influences definitely dangerous to health.    Hence this sudden outbreak of rheumatoid affections.    And he recommended that, as constructional alterations to the Fuhlsbüttel prison were hardly feasible, application should be made to his colleague, Freiherr von Pogge, at Dachau, for one of his patent de-radiation installations, or better still that a de-radiation station should be established in a basement which would clear the whole prison over an area of some kilometres, from influences so injurious, and also, as he had himself observed at Dachau, keep all thunderstorms at a considerable distance away from Fuhls-büttel.    How prompt these fellows were to make every possible use of the Herr Doctor's mania or obsession.    Hospital relieved them of work, and above all from boredom, from the solitude they all so dreaded; it also involved better food, fresh faces, and a change of conversation. All this well repaid the endurance of rheumatic pains, which indeed were self-induced; for the soul of man, at least under confinement, is omnipotent.    Herr Koldewey, writing with his yellow American fountain pen, noted in the margin of the report, against Dr. Laberdan's request, that he might in the interests of science invite his former instructor to lend such a de-radiation apparatus; but that the purchase of such an item was not provided for in the prison budget.    The Doctor had been making something of a nuisance of himself latterly.    He had demanded, and obtained, the privilege of starting his divining-rod classes in the grounds of the prison, so long as the weather permitted, and their strange peram-bulations had even extended to the park surrounding the Koldewey villa.    As he had secured the support of the *Reichswehr*, in the person of Lieut.-Col. Lintze, Koldewey had had to capitulate to his insistence; in support of this new item he—Koldewey—had the support of the Finance Committee of the Senate, which would put the Doctor back within bounds again.

Koldewey had not seen Herr Lintze since the Führer's visit; but Käte Neumeier had told him soon afterwards that something must have then happened to produce a most remarkable effect on a not very impression-able army officer, such indeed that he had scarcely mentioned it in the family circle, but had had to take to his bed that very same afternoon, and that several days had passed before he had recovered his usual equanimity.    Prussian officers, Herr Koldewey reflected, had not been exposed to the artistic temperament since the death of Frederick II; and it might so be that Herr Hitler had given the uniformed gentry a dish of nuts to crack which would not have been set before them by a Bismarck or a Bülow.    All this moved in his mind as he dealt with the day's mail, made two telephone calls, answered a call from Annette, and began to long for his morning cigar, the second before noon, which, however, he only allowed himself after his second breakfast, now half-an-hour away; while the rattle of the rain on the windows enveloped him in an atmosphere of seclusion and ease.    Nothing was more potent than man, thought Herr Koldewey, as he switched on his writing-table lamp (which was really a scandalous thing to have to do at half-past nine in the morning!), whether he tamed and mastered the power of the lightning, or stimulated and found a use for the shocks of the electric eel. In each and all of us there was an exuberant young natural philosopher, whose diversions contributed more to knowledge than the half-dozen metaphysical systems through which he had ploughed his way as a young man.

A report from the bailiff that the bill for the four coffins had been queried by the Finance Committee: why had not the late Menger's books been impounded and sold to provide the funds? Only a small number of the books had been kept in the furnished room where the condemned man had lived, most of them were in the possession of his mother, the widowed Ottilie Sarah Mengers, Rothenbaum-Chaussée 79; the S.A. should take them away, sort them, get them valued by experts, and transmit the proceeds to the State treasury. The cost to the municipality of the trial and execution, as far as related to the late Mengers, could thus be covered. The prison authorities were recommended to get into touch with the appropriate S.A. command.

Herr Koldewey did not at all like the proposed economy. It was an offence against good taste to recover from a family the cost of proceedings by which it had been robbed of one of its members. But it was in fact the practice in all civilized states. The logic of the law conflicted with the humaner emotions, and tended to adopt the agelong tradition of making the whole family group responsible for the acts of one member. Not but what survivals of this kind had been gradually passing into oblivion, until they were revived as a matter of policy by the brown régime. Though it was true that this didn't apply to the item of execution costs, which had, in fact, been thus met by his predecessors. Herr Koldewey picked up the telephone receiver:

"Wiepke," he said to his secretary, "there's no help for it; get hold of the S.A. Troop that controls the Rothenbaum-Chaussée."

And, by way of effacing the uneasiness left in his mind by these instructions, he promptly rang up Käte Neumeier, and asked when she would next be free in the evening. Annette had plans for Christmas, which she also wished to discuss with her. Then came breakfast, and after it the cigar.

Yes, Annette now had plenty of free time, and had again become much attached to the home circle. Since Herr Footh had returned from Berlin, she had had tea with him only twice. The break had somehow come, and obviously to the satisfaction of both sides. Only God could see into the human heart, and the Divine vision was plainly intent upon darker matters than the emotions of the daughter of a Hamburg official. But so much was certain; a burden had been lifted from Annette since she had parted from Herr Footh. Why she had ever got involved with him, was also known only to God alone, of whom it was said in the old Arndt poem—that He caused the iron to grow, but desired no slaves.  Perhaps Frau Neumeier could help an old friend and the father of three daughters to a solution of this cosmic riddle.   Anyway, Annette Koldewey now ran up and downstairs with a song on her lips.   Herr Koldewey had actually caught the words of one of them, a cheerful catch based on an ancient traditional song which his children could only have learned from their grandmother, and began: '*Lott's dead, Lott's dead, and Jule's dying,*' then dwelling gleefully on the prospects of a legacy; except that Annette seemed to be substituting Footh for Lott, and for Jule—which astonished Herr Koldewey even more—the word Jew.   Yes, Frau Neumeier could certainly get more enlightenment on that subject than an old-fashioned papa.   She had indeed established with the whole Koldewey household such a friendship, that its warmth—as Herr Koldewey used to say in jest—could be felt rising from the stairs as she went up them.   If there had been a son in the house, this comely grey-haired lady could have admirably initiated him into her mysteries of love, in a half-material, half-passionate, and quite ideal relationship, as envisaged by the sage of Sils Maria for young men of talents, but so seldom realized.   It was a pity that he—Koldewey—had not been thus fortunate in his younger years.   He had had to wait until he was nearly thirty before encountering his Käte. . . .

It went on pouring in torrents, except that a few days later the clouds lay like the side-scenes of a theatre in sharp-edged yellowish outline against the dark-grey pall of sky.   Frau Ottilie Mengers' flat, containing several rooms, echoed with the tapping of hammers, a noise that must always be associated with the process of nailing lids on to packing cases; and it was to be heard at that time in many middle-class households—and in by far not sufficient number, as will appear later.   Frau Mengers sat, clad in black, in an antique, high-backed, winged chair, a middle class woman who, a few months ago, would have been described as a well-preserved woman of fifty.   Now she looked distinctly older, but neither young Dr. Kley nor Herr Rabbi Plaut paid any attention to her appearance.   The room was darkened by the heavy branches of a leafless tree just outside the window; it was also scarcely heated that morning and not a pleasant place in which to sit.   But these three persons sat close together, and the darkened air grew tense with highly concentrated thoughts of those involved in a common destiny.   Young Dr. Kley shook his bald head:

"God is no longer a concept we can recognize, Herr Doctor.  The Stone Age worshipped animal gods, and totems.   But we, with souls composed of electrons . . ."   His voice faltered.

Dr. Plaut, a man in his middle years, with a pointed beard and brown eyes, frowned: "You cannot hope to settle by discussion the mystery of what is eternal in humanity."

"But we hope to settle it one day by experiment."

Outside the room heavy-booted men appeared to be tramping up and down.   "All that means nothing to me, my friends.   I am just a mother, whose offspring has been killed.   Nor can I rise to the height of

Rathenau's mother, who almost asked the Court to acquit one of the culprits."

"We are poor creatures, dear Frau Mengers; all our experience dates from times that were struggling out of that very Stone Age. . . ."

"While ours is slipping back into it again," snapped the lady in reply.

Dr. Kley laid a soothing hand on the Rabbi's arm, who like himself was still wearing his overcoat.   "We have ignored *homo sapiens*, mental make-up.   You must admit that none of our religions has been able to give him the guidance needed."

"None of them could cope with his predatory instinct.   Unluckily the Bible contains an excellent account of the proceedings of a master-race."

"But Frau Mengers," exclaimed the Rabbi, somewhat scandalized, "that is not the intention of the passages in question."

"I daresay not," rejoined Dr. Kley with a nod.   "But 'living room' was a problem of those days.   Land, pasturage, and walled cities. And the earth was then less populous than now."

"Can you change man's nature and history?" exclaimed Dr. Plaut.

"You must first change his outlook, my Walter always used to say," put in Frau Mengers emphatically.   "All the wars of history were, according to Marx, class-wars.   And the ruling-classes had never shrunk from getting help wherever they could find it."

Silence fell upon the three.   Dr. Plaut listened to the movements outside the door, but the two others—the son whose father had shot himself, and the mother whose son had been killed—seemed to be searching their own minds for the harmony revealed in their two destinies.   Something of what was in their thoughts must have penetrated to Dr. Plaut as well.   "What about us Jews?" he asked in an undertone.

"My Walter used to say that they have never grasped where they stand, nor where they belong.   He wasn't speaking in the geographical sense, of course."

"You must not generalize from an objectionable minority, my dear Frau Mengers," observed Plaut.

"No—I do so from experience," rejoined Frau Mengers tartly, and Dr. Kley supported her.   "Like Newton, when he saw the apple drop. But perhaps you don't admit the instance of the apple?"

"It will be plain enough one day—and not too late, I hope."

"I can only pray that this hour of bitterness may pass," said Dr. Plaut, defensively.   But young Kley would not come to his aid, though he did not fail to catch the other's appealing look.   "My poor father," he said, in a judicial tone, "left a letter for me, in which he said that Ballin had been wrong.   His example had been really harmful, as an instance of perverted patriotism.   I hope I may be privileged to provide an example in the opposite sense, and make the world realize the cul-de-sac into which it has been forced.   My father's tankers are being taken over by a man called Footh; and he got no good from having repudiated his son Joachim, and broken with him completely when he

went to Spain to fight for the Government. He even forbade him to
use our name; Joachim reverted to our former surname Alkaley, and
must be quite out of my reach by now, though he may see a report of the
case in a Madrid newspaper."

"What disasters do come upon us ordinary people these days," sighed
Frau Mengers, with a sympathetic look at Kley. A tram rumbled past
the window and seemed to emphasize the succeeding silence.

"I didn't know you were going to leave us so soon, Frau Mengers,"
said Herr Plaut, as some particularly violent hammer-blows rang in
their ears.

Frau Mengers set her lips and shrugged her shoulders in a movement
of regret.

"I am not packing up yet," she replied; "though of course I ought
to have done. I was warned by a prophetess, which is why prophecies
have latterly been banned. But we always take the wrong decision, as
my boy used to say. Did you know, by the way, that even under the
Republic the relatives of those murdered by the State were compelled
to contribute to the cost of the proceedings?"

Young Herr Kley had heard as much. "Our brighter weekly journals
reported at the time that Frau Eugen Leviné had to pay for the cartridges
with which the White heroes shot her husband after a so-called court-
martial in Munich. The men of law have their own manners and
customs."

"My Walter would have called them class lawyers."

Rabbi Plaut was shifting uneasily on his chair. "You seem to be
talking very freely, considering what is going on next door. Who are
there?"

"Excellent fellows," replied Frau Mengers. "The S.A. from our
street. They have taken so many bribes from all sides that one can
treat them quite as friends. Bribes from the Jews, and bribes from
the bourgeoisie. In the year '33 you couldn't take any chances with
them, my Walter used to say. Poor devils;—he used to call them,
petty bourgeois bamboozled into genuine idealism, fooled all along
by their so-called Leader—leader of the blind, as Walter used to
say."

Rabbi Plaut suppressed an instinctive movement to the watch in his
waistcoat pocket. None the less it was upon his lips to excuse himself to
the 'victim's' mother, or simply take a very hurried leave. He could
see no sort of risk to himself, as the Nazis confined themselves to strictly
legal action. But Dr. Plaut was commonly described behind his back
and within his community as the frightened rabbit till the destruction
of the Synagogues and the pogroms of the year '38, whereupon he became
a 'true prophet'.

"I see, my dear Doctor," said Frau Mengers, turning to the son of
her old friend who had sought freedom by his own hand, "that you
thought it better not to annoy these licensed robbers by wearing mourning.
That is sensible, if not heroic."

The young biologist, already bald in his early thirties, smiled. "In
the first place," he announced, raising a forefinger, "my father left

directions that no fuss should be made about his case, and that as much as possible should be rescued from the Nazis, and especially from Herr Footh, which could only be achieved by an orderly liquidation. So I have already succeeded in getting our entire collection of pictures released for export—more than a dozen 'decadent' oil paintings by Paula Becker-Modersohn, which would have otherwise have been ripped to ribbons. . . ."

"They might have been sent to Switzerland in exchange for foreign currency."

This time Herr Dr. Plaut did really look at his watch.

"But I am in fact wearing mourning; in accordance with our Jewish Law, as the Herr Doctor will testify." And he pointed to a place on the lapel of his coat where the seam between the collar and the shoulder had been slit for about a centimetre, very neatly, with a safety-razor blade. "Thus we rend our garments, as the phrase goes. And I am letting my beard grow."

At this moment came a knock at the sitting-room door, and a young S.A. man entered with an opened book in his hand. "There are a few books here," he said politely, "not entered as being your son's property. Perhaps they belong to you, Frau Mengers?"

"That's very kind of you," said Frau Mengers, in an aloof tone, her brown eyes—her son's eyes—fixed upon the grey screen of rain outside the windows. "All my late son's books were stamped with his *ex libris*. Show it to your Troop-captain—Herr Boje will know what it is."

The Hamburg lad in uniform grinned. "Oh, yes—that ghastly little picture was inside the cover—Comrade Boje has explained to me already. Bolshevist art by a degenerate who has long since made tracks for Moscow."

"Quite right," said Frau Mengers; "by Heinrich Vogeler of Worp-swede."

Bert Boje appeared behind his comrade, laid a hand on his shoulder, and pushed him out of the door. "The *ex libris* is missing from about a dozen volumes, Frau Mengers. But they are on the bookshelves with the rest, among 'Memoirs and Letters'."

"Perhaps they weren't sent till afterwards," said Dr. Plaut, in attempt to anticipate any sort of incident.

But Frau Mengers, without taking her eyes off the lowering sky, replied: "In that case please take them with the rest."

"We are particularly anxious not to rob you," rejoined Bert Boje, coolly. "But duty is duty and orders are orders."

Frau Mengers nodded vaguely into the room. "Quite right, young man. That is the custom of the land."

"Quite right, 'tis how we stand," smiled Bert Boje, capping the quotation from Faust, as he departed.

From the next room now came the clatter of a typewriter in addition to the clatter of the hammer nailing the last crate. "They are making an inventory and giving me a copy," said Frau Mengers. "I am sorry that you called just at this moment."

"That young man seemed a decent sort of fellow, though," said Dr. Plaut, as he got up to take his leave.

"Yes," said Frau Mengers. "One of the victims of German idealism. Second or third series; but they will have to be removed with the rest, and I hope I shall live to see it."

"So you're not going to Palestine? That seems a pity."

"No," said Frau Mengers, also getting up. "I don't care to be mixed up in any more troubles. Walter was always against establishing yet another nationalism, and making presents to the Baldwin Empire. Thousand-pound capitalists, he called them."

Young Dr. Kley also rose, and smoothed the creases out of his overcoat. "A thousand pounds just gets you a capitalist visa," he said with a smile, "nothing more. You can't work magic in Palestine either. If my father had endowed the University of Jerusalem instead of Hamburg, I daresay there would have been excellent prospects for me there. But as things are, I prefer to remain near at hand. I would like to be out of touch of Italian fascism. . . . I shall go to Holland."

"But, my dear friend," said Frau Mengers, "the world will not provide us with any passports. It is, alas, too small for emigrants. My eldest son fortunately has a job with a Shipping Company at Queenstown in Ireland, where your father must certainly have had connections. I would make a point of putting salt water between myself and Herr Hitler, as they say on the English radio. They are nice Catholic people, the Irish. Would you ever have thought, Dr. Kley, that you would have regarded clericalism and belief in the Trinity as offering a prospect of salvation?" she asked softly, as she accompanied her visitors to the door.

"Why not, since atheism has been degraded into a Nazi creed, and Frau Foerster-Nietzsche has presented the Führer with a walking-stick that belonged to her now defenceless brother."

Frau Mengers gave her hand to the young bald-headed doctor. "There are many disadvantages in Ireland, especially the rain," she smiled; "but since my passport has been stamped with a red J, and describes me as Sarah by the grace of Goebbels . . . We Israelites would have done better, in my son's view, to have voluntarily abandoned our artificial isolation and recognized the Messiah—especially as the world looks so thoroughly redeemed. Don't you think so?"

Dr. Plaut hunched his shoulders like a man shrinking back from a blow. The door opened from without and Troop-Captain Boje stood upon the threshold, laid his hand to his cap, and said, "The job's done. Kindly countersign the inventory, Frau Mengers."

In the meantime the two men walked slowly downstairs—disgusted by the prospect of going out into the cold rain. They buttoned up their overcoats, turned up their collars, and unrolled their wet umbrellas.

"Emigration at our age is a serious matter. Who can uproot himself from the soil in which he grew?"

"Well, Frau Mengers will find a home as soon as she gets off the ship."

"But will she ever rid herself of the sense of burdening her son?" said Dr. Plaut, pursuing his thoughts. "The oriental tale of Sindbad the Sailor is a sound parable of the old on the shoulders of the young."

"Yes," nodded Dr. Kley, arranging his umbrella. "Out into the great world. When too many people get together in a congested space they come to hate each other in the end."

Dr. Plaut paused at the street door, his hand on the latch. "The Russian emigrants, you remember, found mutual warmth in each other's company. They regarded themselves as fortunate to have escaped from 'home'—the Soviet hell, they called it."

"My dear Doctor, you must excuse me," said Kley; "I have an appointment. But they longed to get back, didn't they? That's what will happen to us."

"You've said it," rejoined Dr. Plaut, opening the door. "We shall never be treated like the Russian bourgeoisie. But if bad weather does come, we have still got our umbrellas, warm overcoats, and a comfortable Hamburg home with a stove to heat it. Unless you have anything better in view, I am proposing to light the *Chanukah* candles in my home at half-past four. Year 5698 since the Creation."

Dr. Kley turned, laughed beneath his umbrella and cried: "Fortunate man! We reckon our years in millions."

# CHAPTER TWO

### GRATEFUL DEBTORS

KÄTE NEUMEIER WAS glad when Koldewey telephoned. In the course of her day's work she admitted a feeling of surprise that her relationship to that family had so wholly changed. From Annette it had strangely shifted to the father—a man who in popular belief would, to put the matter plainly, have been in a position to help the escape of prisoners whom he himself regarded as innocent of the crimes for which they were to be—and were in due course—executed; and who ignored the chance, nor could she find any fault with such an attitude. And while, during that morning, she was testing several patient's urine, and was interrupted by the postman with a registered letter from Buenos Aires which he would only deliver against her personal receipt, it came upon her that her indulgence for Herr Koldewey, her appreciation of his passivity and self-dependence, was well founded in her own nature. A prison Governor could perhaps facilitate a prisoner's escape and didn't do it. But should a prison visitor, who had really wanted that convict to escape, not have reacted quite differently to a certain proposal, which had included five hundred marks and a motor bicycle? True, she possessed neither the money nor the vehicle. Perhaps she would not have succeeded in procuring them. But to refuse that proposal so bluntly, to reject it as though it were quite out of the question, was surely an expression of Herr Koldewey's philosophical and moral fastidiousness; make no mistake about that. They were both accomplices in the achievements of the Third Reich. And they would have to answer for it when a new day dawned. For the present this new day was beyond anybody's vision; the foundations of the Third Reich were more truly laid in the German soul than those of the new Elbe suspension bridge, which, according to Bert Boje, had given rise to violent dissensions among the professional experts since the Führer's visit. Some contended that sunk concrete blocks would suffice; others were convinced that so wide a span without a base of natural rock would be mere shoddy display and would soon be shown up as such. Could an Empire based on force, forgery and lying, rely on any rock foundation in the German soul? Had the machinations of these political bagmen completely destroyed the national disposition towards truth and honest endeavour? Or had the collapse of the Hohenzollern régime and the Junker monarchy so shattered the political structure of the country, that for a long while it was only a reversion to force, as the foundation stone of authority and all it involved, that could stabilize the State? Herr Koldewey approved of these aristocratic social philosophers. She herself had in earlier days read books of quite a different kind, though unable to buy them. And now they were of course unprocurable, these books by the founders of Socialism who had thought to found society on mutual aid and reasonable contract, instead of on force. But he who had first proclaimed to his oppressed fellow citizens that they too might use force to devise a healthier, happier and more peaceable existence; and his Russian successor, the first disciple who had applied this doctrine in the liberation of a sixth of the earth's surface from the tyranny of compact groups and class—the works of these two men, Lenin and Marx, now lurked as the very imprint of evil in locked and secret bookcases of the libraries, such as survived the public and private holocausts of '33. . . . Yes, sugar in No. 1256; specks of albumen in 1257; nothing wrong with No. 58; traces of sand in No. 59—his kidneys would need to be X-rayed.

When she finally opened K. A. Lintze's letter, she found a cheque clipped to it, a cheque for a hundred marks payable at the Hamburg branch of the *Deutsche Bank*. But the text of it recalled those early, long-forgotten days of old delights. Indeed, to be frank with herself, but for her relation to the writer, she would probably never have been able so wholly to reject her former world of thought, and adapt her mind to Herr Koldewey's judgments and opinions. She took a ladleful of Irish stew, which as concocted by Marie made an excellent one-dish meal, and then another, laid the letter beside her plate, re-read it, and thought to herself that this was snow from yester-year. If Karl August had sent this cheque in September, Friedel

Timme's wild proposal might not have been so automatically repelled. She might at least have considered how she could raise the additional four hundred marks. Bert was coming in the evening, he had a bargain lot of books to offer her, though he wouldn't say any more on the telephone. Well, before her consulting hour, or after it, she would look out a few things that he might like to have for Chieftain Preester. At the moment, over a cigarette and a cup of black coffee, she felt she must at least requite so honest a debtor by trying to recall his face, and the sound of his voice. And she did try, but could not, even while she was lying with her limbs relaxed, hoping to snatch a few minutes' sleep. First she saw before her a vision of his brother, the Colonel, his neat moustache and narrow lips; and then Herr Koldewey, his long face and upper lip, and his prominent, kindly, goat-like eyes. But she heard—not Karl August's voice, which used to ring so readily in her inward ear, but Koldewey's soft and sympathetic tones, as she had just heard them on the telephone; and she found herself remembering some of his views and comments so full of kindly tolerance, by no means inspired by any affection for his fellow-men but by the fastidious need of a sensitive nature for solitude and freedom. The old song echoed in her head: "Solitary not forsaken." The girls in her form at school had found it as difficult as Annette to get the right note, and old Bomst, the music-master, had to scrape his fiddle until the class had managed to harmonize the three-part madrigal; she herself having been one of the sturdiest voices in the middle register, the mezzo-sopranos, as they were technically called. . . .

Yes, Annette Koldewey had begun to sing again. Like many people fond of music she had little control over her vocal chords; when her friend Manfred was alive, it used to be said that when she sang Annette detonated like a bomb, the verb being used in a deliberately double sense. Hence she seldom sang, not because she disliked the sound of her voice, but because those who heard it did. But she had begun to sing again, when she knew nobody was in the next room, more especially —as she confided to Käte Neumeier—since the arrival of an anonymous letter, typed on a sheet of common copying paper. Herr Footh's absence would last a long time as far as she was concerned, he having fallen into the clutches of a very predatory female whom he would probably have to marry.

"Have you any notion from whom this friendly warning may have come?" Käte had asked. Annette could not think of any likely person, nor indeed did she try. "What lay very near at hand, must be calmly viewed as fate," she said, quoting from the poet Morgenstern. Käte Neumeier looked hard into her eyes, thinking all the while of a certain Bert Boje, who had been much in her mind since that afternoon. "If that is so, how did you get involved like that?" The two friends were waiting for supper in the sitting-room, beside the wooden statue, waiting for Herr Koldeway, who was still at work, or possibly changing his clothes. By way of answer Annette sang the Rigoletto aria, that celebrates—or if you like deplores—the mutability of the feminine heart, quite inappropriately, as Frau Käte knew. "Yes, yes—but that certainly doesn't apply to you," was her rejoinder to this musical response, in which she politely ignored a certain confusion of sharps and flats.

"I just don't know how it did happen," said Annette, in order to evade any more intimate intrusion into her inner life.

Käte Neumeier nodded—women like Annette did not vouchsafe any information about their doings, never to others, and perhaps not even to themselves. Civilized citizens of the Third Reich had to maintain their balance on a very precarious basis; they were hard put to it to keep their equilibrium, especially in Dr. Koldewey's circle.

At this point the master of the house arrived, and they sat down to table; and as Käte Neumeier had a matter in hand that day, she did not further enquire into a mystery which would one day solve itself.

After dinner, while Herr Koldewey was smoking his final cigar, she came to the point. She had that day received the catalogue of a library, by a kind of accident in the person of her nephew Bert Boje, which she wanted to show to Herr Koldewey. It was in fact part of the property left behind by a former prisoner called Mengers, whom Herr Koldewey would no doubt remember; and among the books were some that were shortly to be put up to auction. These were a special collection, distinguished by an *ex libris* inscribed Heinrich Vogler, Worpswede, which threw a strange, uncanny, and prophetic shadow on the fate of the unfortunate owner. It displayed a skull, with sprays of blossom and buds emerging from eye-sockets—the skull resting on a heap of books of every size, from folios downwards. The books included volumes of fairy-tales from all over the world, collections of African folk-tales, anthologies of letters dating from the last century, Nietzscheana, with a number of memoirs and biographies. "It would be a pity," she said, "if this collection were dispersed to all the winds of chance and purchase, as one might say. They are a credit to our publishers, and to the good taste of a bookseller's assistant, whose head we permitted ourselves to cut off. Now I, alas, cannot afford to buy the whole lot; but, as luck will have it, a friend of mine in South America sent me a cheque yesterday in repayment of some money I lent him years ago. As I had long forgotten about it, I should like to use it to purchase these books. I haven't room for them of course in my flat, and my worthy Marie keeps on telling me that books collect dust and cause a great deal of trouble. Now you, my dear Herr Koldewey, could accommodate more than one new bookshelf in your attic, and if you took a share . . ."

Annette made a wry face, and clapped her hands to her ears. Herr Koldewey did not notice her, he was intent upon one of the pages of the typed inventory, while holding another between his fingers. "Good," he said, "there is much here that is new to me. *Memoirs of a Neurotic*, with an Introduction by Sigmund Freud. Have you looked into that one?"

"Not yet," replied Käte Neumeier. "And I daresay there are many others just as interesting."

"Unfortunately the prices aren't marked."

"They will be valued as second-hand books. And as the proceeds go to the State . . ."

They all smiled. "Good," said Herr Koldewey. "We will now proceed to found the Mengers' Memorial Library—if the price doesn't exceed our resources. I, Frau Käte, will have some bookshelves made in our carpenters' shop, and my house will acquire an additional attraction." He eyed Käte Neumeier, and the expression on his elongated countenance had not appeared on it in such a connection for a long time.

"Well, I'm not much excited by your discovery," said Annette in a dismal voice. "I don't think I shall be found reading in the attic."

"Who knows?" observed Herr Koldewey. Thus, he thought, an archer may shoot an arrow which the wind blows back to him again.

"I claim first turn with the neurotics," said Käte Neumeier. "The introduction sounds very promising."

"President of the Senate, Dr. Daniel Paul Schreber—who on earth is that?" asked Koldewey, but did not wait for an answer. "Well, we shall see. Freud would not write an introduction to any but an outstanding book; and it's a new impression, I see. Well, thank you for thinking of me so promptly."

"Of whom else should I think?" said Käte Neumeier, warmly. "This sort of thing would scarcely suit the S.A. Library on the Rothenbaum-chaussée; and, anyhow, young men can't afford to buy books."

"Nor can we," laughed Koldewey, still conning the inventory with a long-nailed forefinger. "And here's one that I'm sure would appeal to a friend of yours: Hans Delbrück: *History of the Art of Warfare*, Volumes I–IV. What about that for Herr Lintze? We might ask him now." And as it was not too late, barely nine o'clock, Herr Koldewey rang up the Colonel. Frau Thea answered. The Colonel had just flown to Berlin for a brief visit; he would be on duty again next day, and early on the day after he would certainly be glad to let Herr Koldewey know about the book. Though things had improved lately, they too—alas—could not afford to buy all their favourite books. But she well knew that the Delbrück would be no small temptation to her husband. "We hope that the purse may be as willing as the spirit."

"It might do for the Christmas present that's been in your mind for so long."


Käte Neumeier's nephew had brought some of the Mengers books to the house, and had been able to provide the smaller part of the sum needed from the proceeds of the cheque—which had indeed dropped on her like manna from heaven. When, in days gone by, she had lent K. A. Lintze eighty marks to pay off some lecture fees, long overdue, there had then been such a close relation between them, that *meum* and *tuum* did not enter into it. . . . And then, confronted by the deepest issues of her inner life, she had forgotten money and its value. So, no doubt, had he, though a debtor, morally speaking, should not take the same view of a loan as his creditor. However, he had for several years said nothing about the eighty marks, until a sudden rise in the Brazilian money market due to heavy German orders, from which even Consular officials could and did profit; for thanks to the use of the diplomatic cipher they got early-morning information of such orders and their amount. So K. A. had behaved handsomely and added interest to the sum repaid (at a moderate figure as between friends), and asked his kind creditor not to be offended at his doing so; she must regard it as taking the place of a packet of her favourite bitter chocolate, or a bunch of the yellow tea-roses which could only thrive in the mild climate of Germany. He would be shortly sending her, together with appropriate instructions, a few bulbs which needed only warmth and sunshine to blossom forth into the most fantastic wild forest flowers, emerging with almost magical efflorescence from their lumpish roots, like the music of Rilke's verse from the harsh lined confinement of the printed page. Such poetical extravagance on the part of Karl August made Käte Neumeier laugh. She cared no more now for Rilke, and she cared greatly for a well-spaced printed page of Roman or Gothic type—each with its own character: and she had learned from Friedel Timme to distinguish a Walbaum from a Fleischman, and an Unger from a Breitkopf. But she laughed to herself, lit a fresh cigarette and opened the book which she had picked out quite by chance, out of the list of Memoirs and Biographies, which included those of Hahnemann, the founder of homœopathy, Christ the actor, the sedate M. de Brantôme, Karl Philip Moritz the author, Quincey the Opium-eater, and Jack London, slave of the brandy-bottle. But in the course of the next few weeks, her study of the bulky volume, and the masterly seventy-page introduction, in which Sigmund Freud set forth his views and conclusions on the characteristics of mental disease as exemplified in this particular case, produced in Käte Neumeier one of those processes of inner self-enlightenment which are scarcely noticed by an absorbed reader. The book contained what purported to be a frank account by an eminent jurist, a member of the highest German court, on his conflict with the outer world, in the effort to fulfil the unique mission entrusted to him and to his sole agency by Almighty God. He had, in fact, been chosen to redeem the world. He was to achieve this end by giving birth to the Messiah, for which end he would be transformed into a woman, and so conceive—such was his statement. It was obviously within the power and purpose of the Almighty to express his love for mankind in this fashion, and select Dr. Schreber to fulfil it, and that ought to have been the general view. But a world-conspiracy had been launched against this plan of redemption, aimed at robbing Dr. Schreber of the honour thus bestowed on him, and indeed at hampering his efforts in every way possible. The dæmonic powers responsible for these malignant designs mainly belonged to the Students' Association known as the Saxonia, of which Dr. Schweber had formerly been a member. All old Saxonians were domiciled among the stars, and by attaching threads to Dr. Schreber's nerve-ends and jerking them, they

caused him excruciating pain, and prevented him from properly con-
centrating on his task of world redemption.   When he stood before the
mirror, rouged and bejewelled, and inspected his torso to see whether his
transformation into a woman was making any progress, whether his
breasts had begun to grow, these same Saxonians kept on darting between
him and his reflection.   They made malignant use of the Asylum doctor,
Dr. Flechsig, who appeared to be a careful and zealous physician, but
was in fact divisible into several superimposed Dr. Flechsigs, among
whom the lowest was possessed of a diabolic and savagely tormenting
power.   How was Dr. Schreber to redeem the world against all these
conspiracies and intrigues?   How was he to live in harmony with his
unfortunate wife?   His relatives had managed to get him into the hands
of this same Dr. Flechsig and confined in this institution, where he was
exposed to a process of vivisection and torture such as no mortal had
ever yet undergone.   But now came the surprising fact that he, Dr.
Schreber, President of the Dresden Senate, had, by the sole aid of his
native intelligence, the force and logic of his petitions and statements,
succeeded in freeing himself from internment in the Sonnenstein asylum,
and even secured the withdrawal of the verdict of legal incapacity which
had already been pronounced against him.   Admittedly, he went on,
there was something unique and unusual in his vocation, and in his
conflicts with the Saxonians; but did that justify his incarceration in an
Institution, did it make him incapable of fulfilling his civic duties, and
did his expected transformation into a woman make him in any way
dangerous to the community?   The Saxonians' conspiracy ought not
to be so powerfully supported by the State authorities, even though the
Saxonians had their homes among the stars.   Dr. Schreber's release and
his reinstatement in his position and in the control of his affairs could
not be longer delayed by the authorities, and therewith the redemption of
the lamentable race of men which ought to have made much more
progress by this time.

     This absurd farrago of mental disease, written more than fifty
years before, and now interpreted by the Vienna Professor in so masterly
a fashion, presented an obvious case of persecution-mania, technically
known as paranoia, and more exactly as *dementia paranoides*, had at
first merely aroused in Käte Neumeier a rather vague and amused
professional interest.   By what association of ideas, in the course of her
reading of the book itself, which the Professor in his introduction most
urgently recommended, its parallelism to *Mein Kampf* so suddenly and
forcibly came into her mind, she could not afterwards have explained.
When the Professor wrote his introductory essay in 1911, the man called
Adolf Hitler had been unknown outside the hostels for the Vienna
unemployed: and Käte Neumeier did not even known that these two
contemporaries were then living quite near each other in Vienna.   The
intimate details of Adolf Hitler's inner life were known to only a few,
and mentioned, if ever, in an awed and anguished whisper, as though
under the menace of a brandished whip.   But the German dictator's
abnormal relations to the female sex, his preference for highly naturalistic
paintings of the female nude, his addiction to secret exhibitions of secret

films, his prelatical and almost monastic habit of life, threw the gravest suspicion on the process by which the Disposer of the World had chosen him as the German Messiah to redeem the people from the Versailles Treaty.   Decisive, indeed, to Käte Neumeier's mind was the parallel between the vast conspiracy of the star-scattered Saxonians, and the Jewish plot, of whose existence the eloquent author of *Mein Kamp,* was just as convinced as was Daniel Paul Schreber, that his former fellow-students were in league against him, without producing any more plausible proofs of the fact.   The contention that Jewry had simultaneously launched Capitalism as well as Socialism against its fellow-men, that it sat in entrenched control of Paris and Moscow—Washington would to-day have been added, thought Frau Käte—seemed to the reader as absurd as the severance of Geheimrat Flechsig's entity into upper and lower parts.   Even before the year '33, Käte Neumeier had known that the Jews as a whole were a rather weak and uninfluential section of the population, even though a few members of the race had, in various countries, reached important positions in intellectual, economic and political life.   They did so, as in the case of the unhappy Rathenau, at the price of absolute exclusion from every Jewish connection, or, like Trotzki, inspired with an unexpressed hostility to their origin.   Only a maniacal mind like that of Dr. Schreber could transform his former fellow students into demons squatting in the star-strewn heaven, who had selected him and him alone out of the entire universe as the victim of their plots and machinations.   To Dr. Käte, the passages which she looked up in *Mein Kampf* for purposes of comparison, seemed just as crazy and absurd.   She had a copy of the seventh edition, still full of invective against the German people, for whose benefit these turgid tirades had been metamorphosed into a sort of Old and New Testament up to date.   But of course it was nothing of the kind.   It was another *Memoirs of a Neurotic,* except that his contradictions and inconsequences were often accompanied by shrewd remarks on the nature of propaganda, the effect of advertisement, characteristics of mass reactions to the grosser forms of deceit, the art of disintegrating nations and groups, and of the gradual intensification of the burden of slavery without scarifying the victims.   All this displayed that blend of madness and cunning which had carried Daniel Paul Schreber into an asylum, and then out of it again.   The German Führer was not of course an inmate of an asylum; but it might have been better if he had been consigned to one in 1923, instead of to the comfortable fortress of Landsberg, there to indite his Memoirs.

Käte Neumeier was much too much absorbed in her discovery of this new world of thought to reflect on the altered outlook which it portended.   She had first picked up *Mein Kampf* some eight or nine years ago, and in honestly trying to make something out of it, had come upon much doctrine that traversed her youthful convictions of those days, and finally accepted it, because a young creature needs some sort of creed.   When the Social Democrats of those years had in effect lowered their flag to the rearmament programme of the Hindenburg Reich, it was not merely the Party programme that collapsed, as far as Käte Neumeier was concerned, but the whole juvenescent world constructed for her by Karl Marx and his precepts.  And now the old world had re-awakened and resumed its sway with redoubled force and influence.  The qualities of the various founts of type had recalled Friedel Timme to her mind: and his notebooks recorded all the fine distinctions by which the layman could recognize them too.  It was really the dead compositor rather than herself who had resuscitated and now directed her critical ideas.  But she did not realize that fact.  More mature as she was now, and more deeply disillusioned by the course of events, she felt herself now standing, for the first time, upon her own feet, seeing with her own eyes, and reflecting with a mind now grown to fullness. These were indeed eventful weeks.  She almost forgot to record in her case-book that the old woman of ninety had caught a chill; that her patient with cancer in No. 11 Municipal Clinic must undergo an operation, and was likely to succumb to an embolism, a clot that blocked the blood-stream to the brain; and that little Fräulein Holzmuller had resumed her job as saleswoman as though nothing had happened.

The late Mengers' other books had all long since found their way to Fuhlsbüttel, a black-enamelled bookcase had been constructed in the prison carpenter's shop, to the exact measurement of the attic wall; Herr Koldewey had expressed his satisfaction with his new treasure; and even Annette had so far overcome her aversion as to admit to her bed-table, first a book about the poetress Günderode, and then the *Letters of Lieselotte von der Pfalz*.  Yes, Käte Neumeier had contrived that Bert Boje should help unpack the two crates, and had thus improved an acquaintance with Annette Koldewey that began to promise well—for him at least.  For Kate herself the situation had culminated in the week before Christmas in a conversation, rather hesitant at first and then extremely candid, with the new owner of the library. Herr Koldewey had listened intently to Käte's statement of the associations with another persecuted redeemer awakened in her mind by the lunatic Herr Schreber's book; they were such as the veriest sceptic could not put aside.  Heinrich Koldewey, like so many of his contemporaries, was unfamiliar with scientific modes of thought.  Trained in the forms and traditions of a classical education, as interpreted and adapted for that purpose under mainly philological influence, he had mastered just so much of nineteenth century thought as he had picked up from his master and teacher Nietzsche, and applied to support and elaborate that thinker's own theory of civilization.  It was not for nothing that Nietzsche had grown up in a clerical family, his father having been tutor to a Prince; his hatred of anything revolutionary, his confusion of proletarian with plebeian, his deep and genuine fastidiousness, engendered by a highly sensitive and delicate nervous system—all this had in very truth been the making of Heinrich Koldewey too; and the merciless morality and austerity of Nietzsche's thought, the enchanting music of his prose, borne of a truly humane enthusiasm for culture and the forces of the spirit, had fascinated him even as a schoolboy, when the Birth of Tragedy from the Spirit of Music had flung a flash of light upon the antique world.  How it had refreshed him after the dreary pedagogues that might well have repelled his eager soul from even Homer, Thucydides, and the almighty Plato! The pale-blue volumes of the pocket edition of Friedrich Nietzsche's works and aphorisms, never, in the exact sense of the words, left him for a day. As student, official, soldier, and again in his professional life after the world war, they fed the steady flame of intellectual independence which they themselves had kindled. The process by which the political world was becoming increasingly coarsened and dull and vulgar, he had watched with a sort of wry satisfaction, in the light of Nietzsche's criticisms of Bismarck and his work. On every ground he had decided to regard the establishment of the Third Reich, with its appeal to the mentality of the gutter, as the ultimate perversion of Bismarckian Junkerdom, after which the course of public life must again be directed upwards towards a patrician and soldierly-strict standard of national conduct envisaging Europe as a whole—but how this would be achieved he did not know. He had always told himself that the impenetrability of life, its habit of springing surprises on you, was its unique and distinguishing quality; the main thing was to stay in the offing, alert and observant, so that when the turn came there should be steady and skilful hands available to help direct the new forces in Germany and set a fresh course to European affairs. Any kind of violent opposition seemed to him vulgar, and as short-sighted as the proverbial professor. What had been achieved by all the spiritual turmoils after 1918? Neither Gustav Landauer nor Oswald Spengler had effected any permanent result, nor all the other publicists, whose flaming articles appeared in all the monthly journals to which he regularly subscribed. The revolutionary discoveries in mathematics and physics now so vehemently canvassed he did not understand, and indeed declined to understand. If Planck and Einstein were in fact the geniuses that their disciples maintained, he, Heinrich Koldewey, could wait until somebody deigned to present their lucubrations in an intelligible form. The fact that the doctrine of the Hertzian waves had revolutionized and extended the scope of physics, thanks to Marconi, now stood embodied in his own room in the shape of a wireless set, and filled his Hamburg heart with pride. After all, a man could not understand something of everything. He cultivated his garden, in Voltaire's phrase, which meant that he attended to the duties of his office, and regarded himself as having reached an age when he could no longer be expected or requested to take any active part in public life. He had heard about Freud, and had read a few articles attacking his works, but on the whole had felt no desire to study them closely. For men like Heinrich Koldewey, Friedrich Nietzsche, psychologist, sufficed for this life, and for any life that might possibly be to come.

"I never dreamt that Advent-tide would bring me such a gift," he said gratefully, when the three of them were seated in his study after a rather vehement discussion. Käte Neumeier's discovery, which she had produced with some diffidence, touched a sort of nerve in Heinrich Koldewey's mind, and indeed had dismantled the whole structure of his life. He had maintained his Hanseatic reserve towards the Third Reich for full five years, and now, on the threshold of the sixth, came a woman and destroyed the whole edifice. Could there be any sense and purpose in the suggestion that a man exhibiting such obvious pathological symptoms should have been placed at the head of the German Reich? And was the general mentality of the post-war period, though prone to all manner of eccentricities, so bereft of political intelligence as not merely to be deluded by a charlatan dominated by a mania that almost amounted to lunacy, but to let him increase in power until he was in a position to overturn an indeed rather delicately balanced Republic? No, Käte Neumeier! No community could possibly be so utterly devoid of ordinary common sense. The mentality of the group might well be slower, cruder and less acute than that of its constituent individuals. But, on the other hand, it was much more cautious, cool, and practical. Quite apart from whether this fellow Freud was right or not in his new interpretation of mental disease, the indispensable background for Käte Neumeier's comparison was surely absent. German industrials, bankers, politicians and officers looked more than twice at one in whose hands they placed the tiller of the State, to use a favourite metaphor of the last German Emperor, who had figured on many a picture postcard as a pilot, arrayed in oilskins and sou'wester, steering the ship of State over a stormy sea. Heinrich Koldewey would certainly read both the intro-duction and the book, if only because it had so impressed so valued a friend. But he would do so in an appropriately aloof and critical spirit —Käte must be under no illusion about that.

Annette was sitting cross-legged on the thick blue-grey carpet near the central-heating panel, within reach of a box of cigarettes and a Japanese bronze ash-tray made of cast-tin—she told herself as an in-sulator between herself and the others—the two grown-ups as she privately called them; she threw a searching look at her father and his friend—yes, this was a veritable Christmas present bestowed by the late Herr Mengers in recognition of the many months he had spent in her father's safe-keeping. It was as though a little anthracite stove had been lit inside her father, which radiating an ever-increasing glow had quite renewed Papa's youth—it was almost beyond belief. And Käte Neumeier too!—why, there was a sparkle in her eyes, as though a sleek grey cat were arching its back inside her head. . . . As for what was called group mentality—that could all be found analysed in the works of one Karl Marx. Existence determined consciousness. The powers of observation and judgment were subjected to the service of class interest— yes or no? This inevitably produced what Freud called repressions— as, for instance, the rejection of any idea that threatened a wish-fantasy or the maintenance of class supremacy. As for a personage of no importance, like Corporal Hitler, cautious and unbelieving men like the masters of Germany would certainly have dismissed him with derision, or clapped him in asylum to be cured or isolated for the period of his life. But Hitler, as the embodied saviour of the Class State, an instrument for the subjection of the proletariate—hail and welcome, Sir or Sire!—call them Napoleon I, Napoleon III, Otto von Bismarck, or General Boulanger—these were the men for their money.

Herr Koldewey had not read Karl Marx—which was a pity, interjected Käte Neumeier—and could not agree to the proposition that man's mentality was constituted by his economic condition. The phenomenon of Fascism, with all that had brought it into being contradicted such a contention—neither the romantic nor the sentimental attitude to life, with that they involved, could be so explained. But political mentality and mass consciousness were in fact subject to the law of group interests. It was more than a possibility that the advent of a saviour, a miracle-worker, did disintegrate the critical faculty. In the case of religions, and in the constitution of sects, no progress could be made without such aid. Man's yearning for redemption, which set him at the mercy of enthusiasts and self-deceived deceivers, obviously provided a dangerous lever, especially at a time of material distress, as Georg Büchner had argued in his tragedy, *Danton's Death*. But could Italy in 1922, and Germany in 1932, have been justly described as in material distress? Were they comparable with Russia in the years 1917 and 1918? There was some inconsistency here, as Käte Neumeier would admit.

"Wait a moment," she rejoined. Of course, there could be no comparison, and of course there was an inconsistency in the argument. When a class once possessed of unrestricted power wanted to recover its position, what then? And when the subterranean monarchial interests, headed by Hindenburg aimed at strangling a hated republic, under all the forms of strict legality, Herr President—what then? And what if a man came forward, the Hamelin rat-catcher of the petty bourgeoisie, and promised to settle the hash of this contemptible democracy by intimidation and the rigging of the suffrage? And if he were permitted to equip a private army, and play upon his magic flute, and so bemuse everybody with the song of the Tree with the Golden Leaves. When he plucked at his violin strings and sang:

> " '*Pitter-patter through the wood*
> *The old Jew goes,*
> *With a great sack upon his back*
> *And a beard right down to his toes.*
> *Then he sees the golden leaves*
> *And crams them into his sack.*
> *Pitter-patter off he goes*
> *With his great fat Jack upon his back*
> *And his beard right down to his toes.*
> *The little tree is left alone,*
> *And all its leaves are gone.*'

"What then, Mr. Governor? If this same man had with equal vehemence contended that women, or meat-eaters, or red-haired people, were responsible for Germany's misery, would he not have been laughed to scorn, and would he then have been hoisted into power? Certainly not. He would have collected no more disciples than Herr

Häuser, or the cream-cheese prophet, Weissenberg. But he had been backed by General Ludendorff, the Nationalists, the Baltic Barons and their White Guard generals, who had certainly not been ridiculed for doing so; and as, indeed, many hundred thousand Jews east of the Vistula had lost their lives in the assault on Bolshevism, with no hope of succour from anywhere in Europe—here was proof that this side of human nature, this prejudice still extant from the religious wars of a world now relapsing into the mists of mediævalism, even now provided the necessary lever, to use Herr Koldewey's own word. "Read *Mein Kampf* and substitute 'Saxonians' or 'The Lower Section of Flechsig' for every mention of Jewry and Karl Marx, and you cannot resist the view that there are intimate connections between Herr Hitler's doctrine of redemption and that expounded by the amazing and unfortunate Herr Schreber; similarities so confounding that you cannot but admit the grounds for my suspicion. Consider the matter with a critical mind, Herr Koldewey, that is all I ask of you, and then let us have another talk."

And so the sparks began to fly. Now no one had ever appealed in vain to Herr Koldewey to apply his critical faculty to a subject. Accordingly, during the Christmas holidays, he set himself to read these singular *Memoirs,* beginning with the introduction, and he at once observed that he had made the acquaintance of a great writer, and had lost much by not doing so before. The argument was set forth and developed with a sense of responsibility, a courage and clear vision, that he had encountered of late in the works of Jacob Burckhardt alone. An extremely difficult subject was here handled, not with his old friend Friedrich's dash and brilliance, but with the sober, solid conscientiousness of a scientific observer, who did not miss the minutest and most isolated detail of the case before him and, like Galileo in Pisa, knew how to relate the oscillations of the pendent lamp to general principles. It was with honest astonishment that Koldewey had to admit that the author might be as great a writer as Nietzsche, though disdaining any adventitious aids from literature, music and poetry, and confining himself to the scientific examination of the human mind: indeed he found the introduction such an admirable and convincing piece of work that he could not put it down, and when he had finished it he immediately began it again.

The days between Christmas and the New Year had been of old a time of pagan celebration, during which the dæmonic powers had had free play, or were at least allowed free intercourse with men. Annette, as she did every year, set up and decorated a large Christmas tree with garlands, gauze, coloured paper and streamers, and covered its branches with gilded nuts, little marzipan animals, and flakes of cotton-wool, to represent the snow-flakes which, in the slushy Hamburg winter, always melted where they fell. The garden round the house was a dripping desolation—where the birds took refuge, no one knew. But Annette and her sisters were more domestic than ever. The absentee was Hans Peter Footh. In his stead came a cheerful letter from the High Tatra, from Nove Smokovec or Alt-Schmecks, where he was spending his

time ski-ing, and the frozen carcass of a young roebuck, which he said
he had himself shot. "You and your dear family must not be surprised,
my dear Koldewey, if I stay away for a bit. I might go to Ploesti and
Constanza to see to my ships, which are just now loading up with oil."
And at the same time Annette was reading a letter in which he explained
that he had become engaged to a certain Fräulein Blüthe, and that they
would be married about Easter.

"Not so bad," said she, and slipped the two letters back into the single
envelope in which they had arrived. "We will celebrate the passing
of the year '37, and the beginning of the year '38, under the sign of
the roebuck, stuffed and roast, served with sour cream and Cum-
berland sauce, hot and cold. Käte Neumeier will be invited to
the feast, and she may bring her nephew with her, if he cares to
come."

But another visitor to the house during the holidays was Colonel
Lintze. He came to offer his acknowledgment for the wonderful
Christmas present which Herr Koldewey had enabled his wife to give
him. He had long wanted the *History of the Art of Warfare*, but as he
had presented himself on his birthday with the large André Atlas, on
which he still had a number of instalments to pay, this opportunity to
buy the four Delbrück volumes was a gift from Heaven. Such a book
kept him from thinking too much about the strange and difficult world
in which they now lived. Herr Koldewey, eyeing his visitor, thought
the Colonel was not looking well. His face looked more haggard
than he had ever noticed it before, and during the conversation he
kept on twitching up his eyebrows and then relaxing them, as though
in an effort to appear unconcerned. He also smoked a surprising
number of large cigarettes, which he stubbed out half-finished. Käte
Neumeier, who was drinking tea with Annette on the afternoon of
the second Christmas holiday, which happened to be Sunday, having
come to provoke Herr Koldewey into an argument—as an observant
old acquaintance, she too was surprised by Herr Lintze's nervous
condition.

"Overwork," said the Colonel, with a shrug of his shoulders. The
amalgamation of hussars and infantry into a Panzer division was a
very tricky business, on which he could not enlarge. But, in addition,
—and here he might be quite candid—army circles loyal to the Reichswehr
did not look with favour on the influences that operated, or appeared to
do so, behind the scenes. Any doubt or question elicited nothing but
evasive and suave disclaimers of responsibility, but whether in fact there
were dangerous forces at work—and on this, he repeated, he might be
quite frank—no one knew. It had suddenly proved impossible to
discover who had persuaded the Führer to order the construction of this
confounded Elbe bridge. The naval authorities would certainly not
have supported any scheme that made the lower Elbe more easily visible
from the air, nor did they want its banks, which should have been left
undisturbed for the construction of U-Boats and subterranean oil-
reservoirs, riddled with excavations for concrete blocks and emplace-
ments. The Führer's visit and his speech to the workmen had done

nothing to clear the air.  General von Fritsch had been reported to have observed in private: God preserve us from an artist in command of the Wehrmacht —a sentiment to which every true soldier would say Amen.

Heinrich Koldewey and Käte Neumeier exchanged a look: obscure as the situation still seemed to them, they wondered whether it was not their duty to take this officer into their confidence.  Or was such a step premature—would Herr Lintze understand how matters stood?  In any case, Herr Koldewey reflected, in all difficult times there had to be a general at the head of the army who was a good soldier and nothing more.  Even General Ludendorff—if a Landwehr major, a dug-out on the lines of communication, might be permitted the remark—even this gifted strategist had concerned himself far too much with politics when he had at last come into power.  General Hoffmann, whom Foch and latterly the Russians had pronounced to have been the ablest German commander, had charged the supreme genius of the world war with grievous errors in the disposition of his offensives.  They had, he wrote, deprived the German people of the fruits of their victories, and involved enormous sacrifice of life which a sounder strategist would have avoided.  What on earth would happen when a civillian was entrusted with unlimited control over the resources and manpower of Germany?

And then a strange thing happened.  Herr Lintze drew a number of photographs out of the inner pocket of his tunic—picture-postcards, he called them, taken by Adolf Hitler's Court photographer, and obtainable anywhere for one mark twenty.  "Just look at them," he said in an expressionless voice, "and tell me what you think of them.  How can a statesman allow such portraits to be published?  Ought a man to make such an exhibition of himself?  Isn't it appalling to think that there may be no cautious and competent hand at the steering-wheel when the car gets on to a risky patch of road?"

Heinrich Koldewey and Käte Neumeier exchanged the photographs, surveyed them intently, and said nothing.  On the table stood empty tea-glasses, a silver basket stacked with slices of Christmas cake, rich with raisins and lemon-peel, while the smoke from cigarettes and Herr Koldewey's cigar drifted upwards on the heated air.  From the next room came the sound of laughter, where Annette and her sisters were sitting with Thea Lintze and Paula Russendorff; the loudspeaker had been turned on, and a bewildering variety of dance music from England and America was coming through on the short wavelength.  But in the sitting-room, under the light from the ceiling globe, and from a shaded reading-lamp, three pairs of eyes were fixed upon the pictured present-ments of Adolf Hitler in the act of eloquence.  The face, the day-to-day face of a completely commonplace human being, appeared as a distorted mask with sunken eyes, gaping lips, drawn and deeply furrowed brows, and protruding teeth.  What struck them mostly were the hands, which looked quite ordinary when speech accompanied their movements, but here, as evoked by the camera, leapt from the picture like the frenzied hands of a lunatic.  Herr Koldewey laid the six photographs before him, and eyed them meditatively. Side by side they produced a film-like effect. Käte Neumeier approached and leaned over him until her cheek almost touched his ear. Under each picture were printed quotations from Adolf Hitler's speeches, but she barely noticed them. This might have been a presentment of Herr Daniel Schreber contending against the voices of his persecutors when the "lower Flechsig," or the Saxonians, were tugging at his nerve-ends, and he defied or reviled the two malignant deities, Ormuzd and Ahriman: though indeed the President of the Dresden Senate was far too fastidious to condescend to such a performance even at the height of his mania.

"Colonel," said Herr Koldewey gravely, "we must join our ladies. I should like to keep these postcards for a few days if I may. I am reading a book at the moment, which I should like to discuss with you later on. It provides a most amazing illustration of what is in your mind and, as a conservative and a soldier of the world war, I am deeply indebted to you for taking me into your confidence. Keep the first Sunday in the New Year free. Come here, or we will come to you, just as you like. I believe we may reach an understanding."

"With pleasure," said Herr Lintze, getting out of his chair and straightening his tunic. "I have a good deal more to tell you. On January 2nd, then, for afternoon coffee, and we will get together."


# CHAPTER THREE

### FEAR

HERR KOLDEWEY NEVER, during the rest of his life, forgot those days between Christmas and the New Year, when he studied the bulky volume of more than five hundred pages, which that remarkable President of the Senate, Dr. Daniel Paul Schreber, bequeathed to the world at large, and especially to the German people, in whose speech he had conceived and written it. As a prison Governor is important enough to allow himself leisure in his official hours, he wandered out of the villa and back again, with a portfolio under his arm as a schoolboy carries his lesson-books. And in the evening he got out his car to fetch Dr. Neumeier and take her home again, and worked with her like a student preparing for an examination with his tutor. The portfolio in fact contained two books only: Schreber's *Memoirs*, and Adolf Hitler's spiritual autobiography, together with the six picture postcards upon which, if the ambitions of the personage depicted were fulfilled, the future of Germany and even of the world was portrayed. Herr Koldewey had sold a valuable investment, some shares in an accumulator factory, to provide the price demanded for the Mengers library, including of course Karl August Lintze's cheque. He also unearthed reports of certain speeches which the new Apostle of the Germans had delivered on various occasions—and he was eating his way through all this material, as he put it. But in the meantime Käte Neumeier had become an indispensable member of his household, a sort of intellectual wife. Her ruddy countenance, now a little blanched by the winter climate, her kindly eyes, grey hair, and sensitive, capable hands, helped him beyond measure to endure the entire upheaval of the point of view he had adopted since January, 1933. He had, quite simply, looked the other way. His knowledge of history and his upbringing had taught him that it was unwise to be too fastidious when a new era was coming to birth; delightful as love was, it could not, as accompanied by its usual physical manifestations and results, be judged from a solely æsthetic standpoint. When new developments were in progress, especially when the act of generation was involved, there was much that was repellent in the attendant circumstances, as was known to many beside midwives. Germany's greatness was a process of gestation which would last for several years, and if from the concentration camp nearby came the sound of shrieks and beaten carpets, and not a few orders for coffins, these things were matters that did not come within Heinrich Koldewey's purview. In the same way he had accepted the death of Manfred, the youth who was to have made up to him for the lack of a son, to whose adoption Annette had affectionately and entirely given her consent. Since the seventeenth century Germany had intoxicated herself with the overrating of dilettant genius, which, in the eighteenth and nineteenth centuries, had come to fullness in the persons of many famous men. And from an early work of Nietzsche (in the definitive edition), Dr. Koldewey always kept in mind two apophthegms which supported his point of view. One from "Gay Science," and the other from "Human, all too Human". "Can a man achieve greatness without the strength and purpose to inflict pain? The endurance of pain is a common virtue, in which women and slaves may often excel. But the resolution and firmness needed to inflict pain, and not listen to its shrieks—that is a sign of true greatness." These words had been written by Nietzsche in the days when he was young and healthy, a lecturer at Basle, still unapproached by the ordeals that destiny had prepared for him in the laps of the gods. And Heinrich Koldewey had marked it for his guidance, although he was not, and never wished to be, anything but a humane man. The second of the two aphorisms was surely appropriate to those whom he had hitherto regarded as the opponents of the régime, and of Adolf Hitler's genius. "He who cannot understand that a great man must not merely be challenged, but, for the good of the community, opposed, is still a child in mind—or himself a great man." The choice of an amateur as head of the Reich was quite defensible; in crises more baffling than those that had confronted the Weimar Republic, salvation had often come from one who was not an expert, nor in any sense a professional. In such circumstances, aberrations like anti-Semitism must needs be overlooked, on which

Friedrich Nietzsche had pronounced so stinging a judgment on Richard Wagner: "He is a man of mean opinions, the meanest of them all being his anti-Semitism." There was no need to be a more ardent disciple of Nietzsche than the woman under whose tutelage he spent the last decade of that tremendous life, the sister whom Nietzsche had himself christened 'the Llama,' the animal that can bear such heavy burdens undismayed. But there was surely a distinction between an amateur and a maniac. What if the unhappy Schreber's fantasies about the world's destruction assumed practical significance in the distorted mind of Adolf Hitler? if, as was rumoured in conservative circles, he really thought nothing of sacrificing several million young Germans for the establishment of a Reich capable of accommodating two hundred and fifty millions? if he were really planning to take forcible possession of Western Russia, or at least of the Ukraine?   Manfred Koldewey had said that "the Spanish affair" was commonly regarded among the younger and abler Reichswehr officers as a dress rehearsal for total war, the political foundations for which had already been laid by Ludendorff.   "We can't help ourselves," he and his satellites would say.   "We must fight it out with the Russians, since Bismarck failed to take what should have been ours after the battle of Zorndorf."   If Herr Freud was right, as Käte Neumeier so frequently insisted, there was no distinction between the caprices of the artist and the maniac in so far as they both deliberately shut themselves within the perspectives of their abnormality, refused to equate it with the real world, nor to consider it with the eye of common-sense.   If that were so, the man thus afflicted must be removed from the real world, lest he may gamble with the ultimate destinies of Europe, viewing his fellow-men as trivial and transitory mortals, who could at need be treated with contempt.   And, in that event, the rôle of those who had allowed such a man to possess himself of power, who had let a semi-lunatic get hold of the controls of our civilization, was one which revolted the imagination.   Heinrich Koldewey, and men of like mind throughout Europe, or at any rate in Germany, would be guilty of the most shameful negligence, and of actual complicity in what might be done. . . .

Heinrich Koldewey had always loved life, though life had dealt him some heavy blows, the worst being the loss of his wife, in such sudden and senseless fashion, during the last epidemic of influenza that swept Germany after the war. If Käte Koldewey's goloshes had had no holes in them, fate might then have passed her by; but what began with wet feet ended with a coffin and three motherless children. And now here was another Käte sitting at his side radiating an aura of spiritual and truly feminine warmth. . . . There had been many a breeze between that first Käte and himself, mainly over his addiction to cigars; she could not bear the reek that those cylinders of folded leaves inevitably left about the house.   With the present Käte there could, obviously, be no such source of friction.   She and Annette were genuine friends; Thyra as well as Ingebottel had confided in her, as their doctor, the difficulties that diversified the lives of the younger generation, since it had been no longer fashionable to be anæmic.   For anæmia had vanished.   Eros and social reform had swept it off the field: the two girls were quite capable of realizing that a man over sixty might well want to marry again if he liked the lady, and she could adapt herself to his manners and customs.   Whether indeed Käte Neumeier would take him, was another matter, and beyond prediction.   However, that was for decision later on.   One thing certain was that Heinrich Koldewey would have sorely missed her, had she not turned up that evening to supper, to continue the resurrection of the dead Friedel Timme in her mind.

Adolf Hitler must go.   That emerged more and more clearly from their reflections.   He must not be in a position to realize any more of his projects.   The interests of the German people must come first.   But they scarcely dared to hint at these conclusions: they merely murmured them in form of questions, as Käte stubbed out her cigarette and Koldewey his cigar-butt in the bowl of water that formed the lower section of the ash-tray.   Someone else must put them into words, and he was near at hand.

When Heinrich Koldewey went to bed that night, lying awake as he usually did, there came into his mind a report written by a doctor on Nietzsche's collapse, during those days in Turin in 1888.  He described how the philosopher, who was in a very excited condition, had flung his arms round the neck of a little horse on a cab-stand, which was being knocked about by the driver, and burst into a flood of tears; he had been taken home and put in charge of the landlord at his lodgings, a certain David Fino or Fein, probably a Jew, and thus had the catastrophe of his life begun.   Herr Koldewey, arrayed in his green-trimmed night-shirt, the window above the hot-water pipes set carefully ajar, an ash-tray containing a rather unappetizing cigar-stump on a night-table beside his bed, lay in the dim grey light and mused.   It was easy to philosophize about the nature of greatness and the infliction of pain, while sitting in a comfortable if modest room, free to contemplate the procession of one's thoughts, undisturbed by the realities of life.   It was, of course, wrong to weep over a beaten cab-horse in a city Square; it was equally wrong to project fantasies from a mental magic lantern.   A man should take the middle course—he should take care to be neither harsh nor sentimental, but go through life like Annette who had accepted Footh in order to forget Manfred—or, more exactly, in order to reduce her loss to its proper proportions; she had indeed lost the companion of her youth, but not the only man with whom she could share a bed.   He must ask Annette's advice about marrying Käte Neumeier.   There had always been the suggestion of a taint in his hero Friedrich, even before his mind gave way.   Son of a pastor, who had been tutor to a Prince, his grandmother's name had been Erdmute Krause, a fact of which he was proud.   It was odd to think of the things that great men were proud of . . . would he ever have grandchildren who would take credit for the fact that their grandfather's name had been Heinrich Koldewey?


Strangely enough Colonel Lintze opened the subject when they sat in his study a week later, with a remark relating to his origin.

"We are the sons of Pastors, we Lintzes," he said, "and, absurd as it may seem, we cannot shed our excellent education. Self-control has been beaten into us, or injected into us somehow. I daresay we over-value it on that account."

"I don't think it can be overvalued," observed Herr Koldewey. "The contribution of Pastors' sons to the sum of German culture ought to be investigated; it might be a profitable study. Lessing was one, so was Nietzsche, and Werner Hegemann, who left Germany, and whose recent death in New York I have seen reported, and many, many others." And he looked with satisfaction at the cigar which Herr Lintze offered him, a nearly black Brazilian with a green band, which rather oddly reminded him of his night shirt.

"I had an experience a few weeks ago which upset me a good deal—on the day when the Führer favoured us with his visit. I saw how the man behaved when it was necessary to accept some unpleasant news with equanimity. I was standing by when he tore up our unfortunate Public Works Department's plan, because the facts would not square with his own pet scheme, nearly leapt at the throat of the officiating counsellor, and threw a violent fit, which appears to be a habit of his. There are plenty of stories about scenes of this sort—which really ought to be beyond belief; he is said to fling himself on the floor, and bite the carpet, so that it's now a common phrase in the Reich Chancery that the Führer 'has been eating his carpet again'. Well, gentlemen, all that didn't matter much so long as it only affected civil affairs. But now . . ."

"I'm not a man," said Käte Neumeier: "even though my hair is cut short."

They all smiled. Colonel Lintze bowed to her, and continued.

"A rumour—an almost incredible rumour—has now reached us from Berlin, which has so upset my Chief of late, that he hustled me there and back. But the rumour seems to be well-founded. It looks as though the Nazi group in the Army want to get rid of those commanders, who flatly took their stand on our ancient tradition that innovations in the Army must be limited, and subject to the consent of the Army Authorities themselves. A general reshuffle of officers would then take place, and the key positions be filled with whole-hearted satellites of our presiding genius, thus paving the way for a second coup on the lines of the Rhineland reoccupation. Herr Hitler as the supreme war-lord over army and fleet, nation and fatherland. What about that?"

Herr Koldewey opened his prominent eyes very wide indeed. "A coup, did you say, Herr Colonel? At the risk of a war?" And they watched him hold his hand with extreme care over the ashtray so as not to drop the white cone outside the bowl.

Herr Lintze's thin lips remained compressed into a faint convex curve, as he nodded.

"They'll still keep within the limits of the possible," he proceeded. "The intention is to carry out the *Anschluss*, which has been so long delayed."

Käte Neumeier found herself shaking her head as she had done before when Herr Lintze drove off in his car, after a certain conversation in Wandsbek Park, and an anecdote about four S.S. men.

"It has all been thoroughly worked out," Herr Lintze continued. "The Duce is to be induced by the promise of concessions in Spain to abandon his watch on the Brenner, and the Western Democracies are to be slowly and carefully undermined and disintegrated. Well, it's part of a soldier's duty to take risk, but there is a limit."

Frau Thea Lintze was sitting with the three protagonists, dressed in a light brown tweed frock fitting close to her slim form. "I have two boys, one thirteen and one fifteen," she observed, with apparent irrelevance, though they all understood her meaning.

"Austria;" said Käte Neumeier, and her voice quivered as she spoke. "That surely might get us into trouble."

"No—not so long as the men who launch our last venture keep their heads and their sense of responsibility. Von Fritsche, von Hammerstein, von Blomberg—such men carry weight, and the very ring of their names recalls the traditions of Düppel, Königgrätz, Sedan, and Tannenberg. No one has ever seen these men seize a sheet of plans and tear it to bits, nor are there any postcards in existence making them look maniacal apes. Well, I daresay the people in Berlin find it easy enough to forget the importance of the world beyond the salt grey waters. There's the Wannsee, of course, and the Würmsee near Munich—that sort of thing merely leads to pride. Even our Ludendorff had never seen a foreign country until he invaded it. But who can deduce a principle from such blunders? I can't. We can't. And that was why I was so struck by your suggestion. So tell me what's in your minds and trust my discretion —the discretion of a man with two sons, and a future in field-grey."

"Well, we were promised that our Führer would secure Germany's greatness without a war."

Herr Lintze nervously lit a fresh cigarette. "I hope you don't think," he said, with an angry glance at Frau Thea, "that a soldier fears a war for himself or his children. Heaven forfend, as my father would have said. A war—very well. If it can't be avoided, we have already shown how and where Germans can fight. In Flanders, the Crimea, at Gaza and Riga. But only with sane men to lead us; men who really know what responsibility means, and can take the measure of their deeds before they do them, without indulging in subsequent nervous breakdowns and hysterics. We leave that sort of thing to the ladies; and the weaker sex, so-called, have their compensations."

Käte Neumeier found herself almost openly surprised and impressed by the superiority of this firm-lipped officer as compared with the Lintze with whom she had played intellectual chess in that prehistoric age when a man called Friedel Timme was still alive. From this present Lintze of to-day something went forth which could only be called the strength of despair.

"*Si vis pacem, para bellum,*" he murmured.

"Nonsense," observed Koldewey, dryly.

Lintze eyed his guest. "I'm afraid you may be right. No one wants war, no army on earth ever did want it. Napoleon was always protesting his desire for peace.    I read in one of our military journals lately that a Rumanian professor had calculated that between 1500 B.C. and 1860 A.D., over eight thousand permanent treaties of peace had been made—average duration, two years.    In the same period there had been about three hundred years of peace upon earth, compared with three thousand years in which the Wallenstein war-fury had raged over the earth in her accustomed fashion.    Well, if that is so—I haven't verified the statement—then there's something of the kind before us now, despite the Anglo-American tendency to give way."

Herr Koldewey reached a slightly shaky hand to the bottle of cognac on the table, filled a glass and drank it off.    "You should rather say, 'because of,' than 'despite,'" he then observed in a husky voice.

Something like a shiver of fear crept round that little round table set in the bow window of an Altona flat, while the snow flurries eddied outside.    New Year's Eve had brought real winter, coating the streets with slippery ice, on which the Hamburgers fell and broke their bones. "As the armies don't want war, who the devil does?"

"That's a sort of essay question," returned Lintze.    "Armies want to maintain their vigour and their combative spirit.    Professional soldiers always have to favour sour apples.    But who the people are that pretend the apples are sweet—that's a question for philosophers."

"In earlier days, before I was so occupied by my practice, I used to read books on Political economy.    'The Satellites of Capitalism,' would have answered your question, my dear Herr Lintze.    The eternal economic crisis.    But I don't accept the answer, for some people accuse the armament industry, and the latest doctrine indicts the Jews.    What is your own opinion?"

But Herr Lintze shook his head impatiently.    "If I am not mistaken you and Herr Koldewey want to talk to me about something you have discovered during these last weeks.    The word is with Herr Koldewey."

Heinrich Koldewey first tried to retreat behind Dr. Neumeier: it was she who should be thanked for the discovery, if indeed it was one that called for thanks.    In the end, however, he undertook to explain the implications of what had occupied both their minds for some while past. As he told his story in his rather husky voice, the suggestion that Herr Hitler was a more or less exact counterpart of the crazy D. P. Schreber, had an almost terrifying effect.    Speaking very quietly and quoting his authorities, he expounded his theme to Herr Lintze.    The psychiatrists' views regarding the kinship of cleverness and madness were admirably embodied in this man.    Here was plain for all to see the dislocation of the ego from the outer world, and the frenzy to express the manias that possess the perverted mind.    Uttered by his broad cut lips, the theory—fantastic as it was and indeed sounded, became the more credible and indeed convincing; and, aided by examples from his own "trainees" he was able to explain how such a man feels impelled to display the whole gamut of his dementia—being equally and at the very same moment, capable of such sensible and lucid writing that sagacious men like the Saxon lawyers had to cancel the verdict of legal incompetence that they had pronounced against the ex-President of the Senate years before. Herr Koldewey produced a notebook in which he had recorded a few special points, together with some illuminating parallel cases. He drank a second glass of cognac, poured himself out a third, and proceeded with his exposition, as though he were under orders to state his case. Käte Neumeier heard a clock strike six melodious strokes, and thought she had never heard so excellent an exposition of the contents of a book. Then she eyed Herr Lintze in his well-cut tunic, with a row of ribbons from the last war on his left breast. He was not smoking, he said nothing, he stared at Herr Koldewey from half-closed eyes, and when the latter had finished, he too picked up the bottle, drank a glass, and cleared his throat. But he said nothing; and from the street below came the tinkle of sleigh-bells.

"Well, we all know," he said at last, in his high, courteous voice, "that the Gestapo would wring our necks if they got wind of this little gathering. There's a man who frequents your house—Herr Footh, whom I wouldn't trust with any ideas of this sort."

"He has detached himself already," nodded Herr Koldewey. "And don't forget that within my own sphere I am myself the Gestapo. If they want to lay a hand on my collar they'll have to get up earlier than they usually do."

"Good," smiled Herr Lintze; and Käte Neumeier also smiled to herself.

"So a certain Leader must be removed, if he really tries to shake off our control. The army has what it needs, as in the best of Bismarck's times, except for the absence of Bismarck. Indeed it doesn't need one; but it does need a Roon or a Moltke."

"Roon and Moltke," repeated Koldewey. "I suppose you mean Blomberg and Fritsch?"

"Or Hammerstein and Brauchitsch," added Herr Lintze. "Or Beck and Knochenhauer. The individual doesn't matter; what we want is the sort of leadership which we know won't gamble with the younger generation; which will know how to pocket an 'Olmütz insult,' and keep a good face on a poor game, like the English, now when the odds are against us."

"When you marched into the Rhineland," nodded Herr Koldewey, "all high-ranking officers had the orders for retreat in their haversacks. At least—so it was said."

"It comes off once—it comes off twice or three times," Herr Lintze observed, and again found it necessary to clear his throat. "But you can't make a system out of that sort of thing. It will go wrong some time, and then it's too late."

"And it's just a matter of luck that a few easy successes haven't lured us into a real mess up till now," put in Käte Neumeier, who had for some time been merely listening to the conversation, with her legs crossed, and her eyes fixed upon the toe of her shoe, as it throbbed rhythmically up and down. This was men's talk.

"But what can one do?" 'Five hundred-mark notes,' she heard an inner voice say, 'and a motor bicycle filled up with petrol, by the wall on the left of the entrance'. 'You shouldn't ask me to do such a thing,' she heard herself reply. 'And I can't do it'. Those were prehistoric times—and where was she now?

Colonel Lintze threw a glance at her. "How would it be to write to Karl August and ask him to send you a little dried curare when he sends you those bulbs he mentioned. You might make some experiments on guinea-pigs or mice, and evolve a serum or something of the kind."

"Curare," muttered Herr Koldewey reflectively. "I have heard that any dose is deadly, as soon as it gets into the blood-stream. It can be administered any way you like."

"In that case there's no point in experimenting with mice," observed Käte Neumeier.

"True," agreed Herr Lintze. "It might be smeared on the edge of an axe, for instance, presented as a ceremonial gift to a distinguished personage on the occasion of a state visit to Hamburg—the Elbe suspension bridge, for instance."

"When it's opened, do you mean?" exclaimed Herr Koldewey.

"No, when the foundation stone is laid," continued Herr Lintze, frigidly. "That is a favoured sort of ceremony."

"And who is to hand it to him?" asked Herr Koldewey, who rose, stretched himself to his full height, and stood in the window-recess, rocking his tall form from one foot to the other.

"Your executioner," replied Lintze; "our fellow-townsman."

Käte Neumeier drew in a mouthful of smoke and filled her cheeks before she blew it out again. "Honour to whom honour is due," she said. She had not known, she reflected, that the devil had such well-shaped lips, and such kindly deep-set eyes.

"And how," asked Herr Koldewey, "is such an exalted a personage to come by a wound? Is he to cut himself or what?"

Herr Lintze shrugged his shoulders. "By some accident," he said. "Goodness knows how—but something can be managed when the time comes. After all, an orderly does sometimes drop something on the Supreme Commander's foot. He gets into trouble for doing so, of course, poor chap. But if one man's life can save the lives of tens of thousands . . . ?"

"And how are we to get hold of the axe?" asked Herr Koldewey once more.

"No need to think too far ahead," replied Lintze.

"We possess a museum of criminological exhibits," pursued Herr Koldewey; "our guillotine is housed there. We might buy it."

"Before or afterwards?" asked Herr Lintze in his highly modulated tones.

## CHAPTER FOUR

### A PROPOSAL OF MARRIAGE

ANNETTE CAME FOR her father at half-past six. She had got three tickets for a performance of *Hamlet* to be given that evening, at the Schauspielhaus by a visiting company from Berlin. But neither Koldewey nor Käte Neumeier looked like people who were going to enjoy a play. They silently entered Annette's little Adler car. They sat in it, huddled together, as indeed they had to be, but to Annette there was a sort of frozen look about the pair. Obviously this fellow Lintze does not suit them, she thought, glad to find that the engine had not gone cold; I hope we won't be seeing much of him. Käte Neumeier, in particular felt she must get close to somebody. Never before then had she been so clearly confronted with the dilemma, of which Friedel Timme had spoken in his cell; there could be no middle course between working for the Brown Reich, or working against it. And as they drove thus through the streets, which the snow had dissolved into stark masses of light and darkness, they seemed—as there was naturally not much traffic at that hour—to be driving through a dead city. Despite the lines of lighted windows, she could not rid herself of the feeling that behind those populous houses there was nothing. Must evil take its course, did Karl Marx's catechism involve the brutal truth that capitalism inevitably led to crises and to wars? How could she face *Hamlet* that evening? What was the use of Shakespeare, or indeed of art at all? Better find a cave and creep out of the world, if it be such that a man like Lintze had to be accepted as an intimate, and an executioner's axe smeared with curare.

"I'm afraid I must disappoint you, my dear," said Herr Koldewey, slowly. "One should never commit one's mood in advance. I can't listen to any declamation to-night."

Annette bit her lower lip. Her instinct had been right. And Käte Neumeier agreed, and said she would rather stay at home.

"At my home," said Herr Koldewey, as though it were a matter of course. "We have various matters to discuss."

Annette drove cautiously over a street-crossing, and then asked what she should do. She had looked forward to that evening, and did not feel inclined to sit between two empty seats.

"What about my nephew, Annette? He is sure to know someone he would like to bring. I can ring him up, young people are always grateful for theatre tickets."

"Bert Boje?" asked Annette. "Why not? A very bright young man. And we owe him something for putting us in the way of those books. I am greatly enjoying 'Liselotte's Letters'. Let's ring him up."

So saying she drove through the gateway. Herr Koldewey got out, and gave his hand to the ladies. "There is a rug on the back seat, Papa. Even metal horses have to be protected against cold."

After dinner the two friends sat on the deep settee in the so-called study, opposite the book-shelves and the heavy writing-table; at first they smoked in silence. Herr Koldewey, since there are several levels in the mind of man and the human will can only compass one of them, found himself thinking about Shakespeare's *Hamlet*. It was foolish to have missed the performance. Something was rotten in the State of Denmark, and at the end five corpses lay prostrate on the stage, including Polonius, who had been stabbed through the tapestry. Prince Hamlet was a man of intellect and character, acutely conscious of the abominations that were sapping the structure of the State, but none-the-less, the spectre of the Weimar Republic, foully done to death by poison in its sleep, could not bestir him to buckle on his armour and act. Käte Neumeier did not know whether the Doctor was in jest or earnest, in thus arraying the ghost of Hamlet's father in a modern guise. But she had to admit that the emergence of the Third Reich had brought Shakespeare's dramatic world nearer to the man of to-day, than it had ever been to the people of the Schlegel-Tieck epoch, or the age of Bernard von Meiningen, or even the bourgeoise world of Joseph Kainz and Max Reinhardt.

"In the duel between Hamlet and Laertes, both of whom were killed because they had lost their fathers by violence, poisoned sword-blades played the decisive part. We, my good friend—you and I—have decided to get an axe smeared with curare, which is then to be manipulated just as much by chance as was the poisoned rapier which fell accidentally into Hamlet's hands, having wounded him already. Among young Mengers' books, by the way, there was an odd little collection of treatises on all the various Elizabethan noblemen to whom the authorship of Shakespeare's plays had been attributed since the Bacon theory was first formulated. I, for my part, stick to the authentic Shakespeare, and now realize how we are, for the first time, beginning to understand that age. To the man Shakespeare, the ground beneath his feet must have seemed a floor of glass, through which he could see the heaps of corpses by which that age of glory was supported. We, in the Weimar Republic, were inclined to forget our corpses. I am very much afraid they came back on us in the year '33. And now they go up and down among us, guide our movements, and have long since sealed our destiny."

He poured himself out another drink, this time Scotch whiskey, and Käte Neumeier wondered rather anxiously whether all this drink would do him any good. What had Friedel Timme said, when she reproached him with the same indulgence? When a man saw the condition of the world too clearly, he could scarcely help taking a drop of something now and again. In the Hamburg climate men plainly needed their drop of poison. In harmless doses, or in the form of curare.

The silence of the house and all around it oppressed her mind. Not a single aeroplane buzzed across the roofs. It was like a Sunday evening in a novel. They sat there, side by side, like accomplices in some dubious enterprise, or like man and wife, married for many years, and now living in a sympathy that had become physical and seldom called for speech.

"Do you really think, Doctor, that this sort of struggle for power is going on behind the scenes? Is our friend Lintze tainted with intrigue?"

"You can't imagine, Käte, how ghastly I feel about it all," replied Herr Koldewey. "We conspirators are so utterly alone in our own country. I would almost call those fortunate whom the Third Reich has already ejected, or will do so later on."

"Herr Kley committed suicide to escape that same good fortune."

"True," said Herr Koldewey; "some forms of good fortune are past human bearing. When I sold some shares the other day which I bought at 79 marks, the Bank credited me with 310 for each. Excellent; Herr Footh would ascribe it to the beneficent activities of the Third Reich."

Käte Neumeier slipped a piece of bitter chocolate between her firm white teeth, and gazed at her companion with heart-felt sympathy. She did not in any way realize that she had come so much nearer to him during the last few weeks—nearer than she could have believed possible. Koldewey was a good type, a man whose conscience would not let him rest—the best German, or rather Hamburg, stock.

"Do you really think, my friend, that this throws any light on the advent of this age of glory? Do you remember how a year ago the spectacle of a prosperous and contented Germany was presented to the world, when the last Olympiad was held in Berlin?"

"Do you think it was the last?" asked Koldewey, drawing at his cigar. "The next *was* to have been held in Tokyo, and after that Rome is going to celebrate the twentieth Jubilee of her agelong empire, of course with guests from all over the world, and games that—'unite the Greeks in amity'. Thus the next four years should be safe—if Adolf Hitler doesn't upset the apple-cart."

"You make me feel hopeful," she exclaimed, and sat up with an expression of genuine relief. "The rise in the value of your shares, the continuance of Fascism—all that can't happen without God's blessing —and that blessing comes from across the narrow seas, and the broad Atlantic also. . . . Meanwhile, something might really rid us from the spectre that haunts us now."

"There, Käte," lamented Herr Koldewey. "You are defending the survival of the Third Reich. You now believe that war would be the greater evil."

"Doctor!" cried Käte, and flung out her arms in a gesture of abhorrence. But Koldewey pulled at his cigar, nodded his long, narrow head, and continued in a low, level voice, like a speaker drawing an inexorable conclusion:

"And so we steer between Scylla and Charybdis—a monster on the left and another on the right. If we are lucky, our little craft will slip through, before the deadly rocks clash once more, crushing everything

between them.  We are companions in destiny, Käte.  Käte, that was
my first wife's name.  I am beginning to think that my second wife
must also be called Käte.  What do you think, Dr. Neumeier?"

"You are not serious," replied Käte Neumeier.

Herr Koldewey nodded his long cranium at her.  "I really feel as
if I could no longer do without you; as if it were absurd that Annette
should soon be dropping you at another house.  You needn't make
up your mind on the point either to-day or to-morrow.  Weigh the
matter, think it over, take counsel with yourself."

Käte Neumeier sat there, her hands on her knees, and her eyes
strayed from her companion to the room about her, the landscape by
Caspar David Friedrich, and the great wooden statue of the starved
Barlach.  Was it not indeed absurd that she should not be at home here,
and share the future with the man beside her?  Surely it was merely
sensible, since they must anyhow live in the same city, in the same
environment, and among the same people.  She could not help smiling,
and a most undeniable glow of pleasure spread from her heart through
her whole being.  She could not but be delighted that such a man, at
such a moment. . . .

"But what about Annette, and your two other girls?"

He eyed her for a few moments.  "Thyra and Ingebottel—yes,
there may be difficulties there.  They can be overcome.  Annette, I
think, would be quite pleased—in her new phase.  There's no need for
everything to go quite smoothly.  We are living beings, in the round,
and not merely profiles, like Egyptian wall-paintings.  But if you can
say yes, I will fight our way through.  In any event, I can see plenty of
difficulties ahead—the axe for instance.  Herr Lintze clearly thinks that
I can provide it, if needed.  But that can't be done without letting Herr
Footh into our secret, which is what we don't want."

"The axe," repeated Käte Neumeier, lighting a fresh cigarette.  "I
can manage the axe.  It is to be found in Wandsbek, my friend, barely
ten minutes away from my home.  As the crow flies, or with Annette's
car."

"Well, then—you see how fate has brought us together.  You know
just the things I don't know.  It would be nice if you could make up
your mind to-day."

"That's asking too much," rejoined Käte Neumeier, resolutely.
"Marriage is an excellent institution, but it demands reflection.  Do I
look like an engaged lady?"

"My dear Käte," said Koldewey, softly, as he took her hand and
kissed it.  "Engagements are sometimes broken."

"Not in the best families," smiled Käte, "where people are still
accustomed to think before they act."

"But they do act," persisted Herr Koldewey, as he got up, walked
round the table, and took Frau Dr. Neumeier by the shoulders.  'Was
ever woman in such manner wooed?'—a line out of another Shakespeare
play came into his mind.  It was from *Richard III*, and an utterance
by the sinister hunchbacked monarch, not at all applicable to the present
situation; indeed Heinrich Koldewey could not but smile at himself, as,

with such rhythms in his minds, he looked into the eyes of the woman who had, in these last few weeks, become indispensable to his existence.

"My dear," she exclaimed, "and what will Annette say, if she comes back here and finds us an engaged couple?"

"Philemon and Baucis," laughed Koldewey; "old friends." And then he drew her to him, lifted her chin with his long fingers, and kissed her. And he was delighted to observe that the contact gave him a most unwonted thrill.

## CHAPTER FIVE

### SOLO ADÆQUARE

IT IS USUAL for engaged couples to ring each other up early in the morning, thought Käte Neumeier, not without a touch of self-mockery, when the telephone bell rang soon after eight next morning. It was, of course, Herr Koldewey. But he had a good reason for telephoning, it was not merely to express his profound satisfaction at the experiment which, he hoped, they were about to make. "Something was forgotten yesterday," he said; "in fact it was forgotten a few days ago. Our friend, Dr. Schreber may congratulate himself on having put a Hanseatic official out of mind of his duties. You were interested in the papers left behind by the late Mengers, were you not, Käte—or has that rather slipped into the background as compared with much more important affairs?"

Käte Neumeier was taken aback. She had indeed forgotten the existence of the Mengers' papers. "So like us," she said ruefully to herself. "We take the gift and forget the giver."

"These documents must be collected and put aside," continued Herr Koldewey. "They are the property of the Court, and I must send them on without letting you see them, I'm afraid. But unless you have any suggestion to make, Käte, I will have them copied quickly this morning. I can get one of my daughters to type them out."

Käte Neumeier, by no means wholly awake yet, or perturbed by a sense of guilt, searched her memory. What was it that poor Mengers had told her, what had he been working at? Why had he applied for a second ream of paper? "The Karl Marx film, of course. I should greatly like to read it."

"The Karl Marx film?" ejaculated Koldewey in surprise, at the other end of the wire. "It couldn't be that. His notes relate to the

biography of a Berlin lawyer and Deputy, a Weimar type, of Jewish
origin."

Käte was by this time awake and in control of her recollection.
The unhappy youth had intended to write the biography—and very
pertinent it would have been—of the Communist Deputy, Dr. Paul Levi,
who had died suddenly of apoplexy, after years of rather odd vacillation
between his existence as a clever and intellectual Berlin lawyer and the
duties of a proletarian Deputy in Hindenburg's Reich. At the same
time she noticed, with astonishment and sympathy, that her friend did
not trust his own telephone. He avoided the name Levi, and so did
she. But at that moment there came before her a vision of the whole
scene: poor Mengers' high voice, his long neck, his penetrating, hazel
eyes, as he told her that he had hidden the script of the film somewhere
in Glasmoor.

"If you happen to have anything to do in town to-day, and would
give me—or rather Marie, the pleasure of lunching with me . . ."

As a fact, Herr Koldewey had some official business with the Senate
that morning. The Burgomaster needed the support of his more
experienced officers to resist the claims of the Party and the military.
The Fuhlsbüttel airport had proved too small, and was now found to
have been extended in the wrong direction. Instead of moving it
towards Niendorf, the idea was, on technical grounds connected with
the transport system, to bring it nearer to the city; and to this there were
grave though not conclusive objections.

"But wouldn't it be too much trouble? How about lunching at the
Alster Pavilion?"

Since the flower-show in the previous autumn, and a memorable
"day after," Käte Neumeier had felt a deep repulsion to that agreeable
restaurant, and indeed had never entered it again.

"We shall be more comfortable at home, my friend," she replied.
"Don't let us waste any of our lunch-hour in going anywhere."

There was time to discuss a menu with Marie, and she sent her out
to buy the meat needed in the Wandsbeker Chaussée, and not in the
Wagnerstrasse—not at Teetjen's shop. Though, indeed, she would
rather like to have sent out a reconnaissance to see whether the seed
sown by Tom Barfey had sprouted.

After lunch, as they sat in the little drawing-room with its green
and brown carpet, she produced her recollections in due order. Young
Mengers had composed that Karl Marx film during the interminable
process of months of interrogation in Glasmoor, the modern model prison,
and had there hidden it—but where, he had not revealed. They owed him
something for the service he had done to them and the good cause by the
legacy of his library, and they must search for this same manuscript.
No one could do that, except Herr Koldewey himself, if it were
really true that, in a certain sense, he represented the Gestapo in
Fuhlsbüttel.

"A betrothal trip to Glasmoor," he said; "in search of a lost manuscript, to quote from Spielhagen." Did Käte know the novel, or any
others by that author? Her mother had no doubt read them all.

"Spielhagen!" she exclaimed. " 'The Lost Manuscript' is by Gustav Freytag."

Herr Koldewey disputed this statement, but Käte Neumeier, sure of her facts, because she had read the book as a holiday task in the sixth form at school, and had had to pass an examination on it, confronted him with the reference to the book in the *Dictionary of Literature*, which she laid before him on the table.

He was surprised, but admitted that he didn't know much about popular writers of this kind. "Which is why I now have to study *Mein Kampf*. *Nostra culpa*: *Nostra maxima culpa*. We have inflated our educational world like a bubble and sent it too far above the intellectual level of the people."

"Say rather—of the masses," put in Käte Neumeier; "and we ought not to be surprised if it collapses and explodes."

"But what are we to do with this pretty flat, if our alliance is to receive the blessing of the State."

His friend eyed him in affright. "But my practice must remain here in any case—and so must my Marie; you wouldn't have me send her away?"

"Well, well, these things will settle themselves," he rejoined lightly. "We must not let such realities stand in our way. But the first thing to do is to go out to Glasmoor—to-morrow or Sunday."

"To-morrow?" said she in astonishment; "in the middle of the week?"

"Epiphany," he replied complacently. "Three holy Kings following their Star. Annette has been humming it all day—I recognized the rhythm."

She smiled; she too loved the old poem, and its setting.


Every morning three practice-suits might have been seen performing sundry evolutions in the large bedroom that comprised the whole eastern side of the upper storey, one red, one blue, and one brown. Such was the designation of a costume of thick soft woollen stuff, a pair of trousers and a blouse with a zip-fastener, which could be quickly slipped on, being secured at wrists and waist and ankles by elastic. A bare quarter of an hour sufficed for these gymnastics, and the bracing effect lasted nearly all day. The performers lay prone on the carpet and raised themselves twelve times to their feet without any help from their arms; with knees together they bent down from a standing position, touched their toes with their fingertips, revolved their arms and legs in their shoulder and hip-joints, did six knee-bends, and then rose on tip-toe, with their backs and shoulders pressed against a rug that served as a wall-covering, swung for thirty seconds on the smooth pole above their heads, and then hurried under a warm shower, of which they gradually lowered the temperature until it flowed as ice-cold as the winter air outside—not, indeed, that they ever caught cold. There had been much dissension before they could agree on a precedence in the use of the shower-bath, for Thyra and Ingebottel had to get to work carly, while Annette was not satisfied with what little hot water was left for the last user.  But they finally came to an understanding, and at early breakfast only two of the sisters appeared arrayed for the office in a tweed frock or a coat and skirt, while Annette, as she poured out the coffee, was still wearing the wadded Japanese dressing-gown which the late Footh had once given her as a birthday present.  Outside a murky sun was shining, but the rain had been replaced by an east wind and dry frost.  The branches of the trees were coated in transparent ice, or—if breakfast was extra early—in silver-grey hoar-frost.

The three sisters sat over their plates of scrambled eggs, blew into their steaming cups of coffee, cracked the warm rolls with their firm white teeth, and exchanged a few clipped and cryptic comments on Papa's crazy notion of making a sort of engagement trip to Glasmoor. To-day was Epiphany, and in days of old a choir from the orphanage used to sing the old canticles in the Hamburg streets.  During the days of rain Thyra and Ingebottel had for the first time paid a visit to the Crime Museum.  Among the curiosities that should have been displayed, they thought, was obviously the axe which had solved Papa's dilemma last autumn.  It really ought to be on exhibition, and Papa ought to get hold of it.

"If, by the way, he thinks that I can drive him on Sunday, he is sadly mistaken," smiled Annette.  "I gladly would, but the car won't. Either the plugs have rusted, or the petrol pipe is choked.  I'm having it looked over to-day, but if I know Jahnke, once he gets hold of it he won't let it out of his hands before Monday."

"Oh well," rejoined Thyra, "Käte Neumeier would just as soon go by train."

Despite her cool allusion to Käte, there was no hostility in her mind; she would be eager to welcome her as an inmate of the house, and even Ingebottel—who was rather a pert young miss—had, after her first surprise, taken a very kindly view of her father's engagement.  Her friend Riechow was to take his leave in Vienna, where quite a number of the younger officials were turning up these days, and among them Herr von Papen, who—in the popular phrase—was always sent on ahead to discover some appropriate cracks into which the Führer might subsequently insert his magical crowbar.  Events were in motion in Spain as well, that might bring surprises in the Spring.  Annette listened in silence; young Bert Boje came into her mind—he would, she hoped, stay here and, as he had promised to do, take her into a particular gallery in the *Kunsthalle*, into which she had never yet found her way, where she could see the pictures of Philipp Otto Runge, so highly esteemed by Hamburg connoisseurs.  The fact that such a fine, upstanding youth should be so enthusiastic an admirer of so romantic a painter was really quite delightful, if a little comic, but distinctly in character.  And as her father spent all the evenings with Käte immersed in books and papers, she could invite him in and look at his volumes of reproductions of the works of his favourite painters, which were so well done in Munich. The colour was lacking, of course, but otherwise the art of photographic reproduction had made marvellous progress, and they were well worth studying. Then she suddenly remembered that she had a letter for her father in her pocket—enclosing one from Käte Neumeier addressed to Buenos Aires, which he was to read before it went, so that she—Annette—could than have it registered at the Fuhlsbüttel Air-Post Office. A Zeppelin would be carrying the air-mail to-morrow across the South Atlantic; the German air service to South America was admired throughout all Europe, and everyone now used it.

" 'Morning," said the girls and departed. Annette too left the breakfast-table, and walked slowly up to her bedroom to dress. Thanks to the admirably efficient central heating, the air in the whole house, including the staircase, was already fresh and warm in the early morning, and the reek of Papa's overnight cigars had been effectively dispelled. As she eyed herself in the mirror, not without self-approval, and arrayed herself for the day, she realized with some surprise how much artistic talent, hitherto unknown to her, was to be found in Hamburg: the painter Wasmann had been born here, and he, so Herr Boje said, would really count for something in nineteenth century German art. He had indeed lived in the South Tirol, and had actually become a Catholic. Yes, she hadn't heard this sort of talk from Herr Footh, who, by the way, she hoped might be happy with his Fräulein Blüthe—the man of the Äuglein-ships. How had he come by such charming names for them all? Well, there must have been a good deal in him, or she wouldn't have carried on with him so long—a year and a half or so; and now here was this odd fellow Boje. What a singular prophecy that was he had picked up from Frau Mengers. She must repeat it to Papa. The funniest birds fly into a house and out again. Ah yes, her new mother's letter. Since a certain attractive Frau Rechtsanwalt David had migrated to England to mark her disapproval of the ridiculous April boycott, Papa had lived like a hermit so far as a daughter could judge. Which was quite natural for a man of his years. But now he wanted to marry; well—hearty congratulations, Herr Koldewey, it might have been worse.

Hans Footh . . . it was all over between them, completely over, silently and mysteriously and without a word, quite in the Hamburg manner. She had now a free half-hour, she could look out his letters and tie them up in a package, for eventual return. They were all in the deep side-drawer of her writing-table where she had thrown them. And as Annette, sitting on a small rug, strewed the contents of the drawer around her, using the polished parquet as a gigantic table-top, rummaging in the pile of papers and picking out those which by their violent copying ink at once proclaimed themselves as from Herr Footh, a strange sensation came and went in the left side of her chest—which might indeed have been just as much due to the fact that the whole weight of her body was resting on her arm, as to her uneasy reflections, her half-unconscious ideas and thoughts. Her parting from Herr Footh had really taken place at their first encounter after a certain vision through a round window, and the flower-show that followed. When they met again after that, in his rooms, or on his balcony, a sudden shiver had gone through her, which she had noticed with embarrassment, and at once suppressed or masked by an assumed nonchalance.

But although she had intended to spend the whole afternoon with him, she could not. She discovered that she was almost too late for the decisive try-on at her tailor's of her new moss-green winter suit, whose cut and colour would match so admirably with her green motor-coat, and would never be finished if she didn't go that day. On similar occasions Hans Footh had made so much fuss that he had got his way. But this time he gave in almost without resistance, except for a few formal protests, and so had the severance begun, a final severance, friendly but inexorable. . . . This went on for a few weeks, and then they both realized that there was blood between them, blood that had been shed—a strange emotion, but one that could not be evaded. Here, kneeling on the floor, with a packet of letters between her fingers, Annette sighed, both in sadness and relief. What strange beings men were! She well remembered the summer morning on Footh's balcony, when the envelope addressed in Käte Neumeier's handwriting came into both their hands, and how glad they were when they realized that something could be done for the man—or rather both men, as Hans expressed it, referring to her father. Then came the crab supper, the anxiety about the telephone call, so long awaited because Papa had forgotten to have the lines connected. Who could then have prophesied that the pleasure they had then felt would cost her her relationship with Footh, and prove a turning-point in her life. But here and now she admitted to herself that her life with Footh had been insecurely founded from the very outset. When the Spanish adventure, that marvellous rally of volunteers, had robbed her of her young lover, her cousin Manfred, something had snapped within her; a part of her existence, that branched right off from the main stem of her deep intimacy with her father, had been damaged. If she had only been able to speak to someone in those days, or weep or cry aloud. That would not have been proper, neither for a human being nor a woman, and most undesirable politically. It was not proper to mention that German airmen could be shot down in Spain by some sort of International Brigade of Bolshevist bandits. In the good society to which she of course belonged, the prescribed reaction was an attitude of silent mourning and proud heroism; a good-looking young woman had to show that she could overcome her feelings, face her fate, and accept in due time the solace and protection of a new relationship. And so she had drifted into her connection with Hans Footh, whose persistent courtship she had at last heeded and accepted. Here she was—young and full of life, in need of affection and love, and it was neither right nor pleasant to look back into the past. Who could have thought that a relation thus begun could not endure? She enjoyed her life, facing into the future, from the centre-point of the society in which her birth and destiny had placed her. And now—here was young Boje standing at the door demanding admission, and something within her said—Yes; something out of the depths of her being, something firmly rooted in her best and inmost self, though the prospect was not so splendid and attractive as that offered by Hans Footh, the owner of the Äuglein-ship fleet.

And now she held in her hand the packages of letters written in short or longer absences, in not very elegant German—for he never could shake off his usual business style.    Yes, the policy of the new Germany was to let such men make good, to promote them to the upper stratum, the new aristocracy.    These, the henchmen of the Führer, were raised by their S.S. uniform to equal rank with all those who held place and influence in the new Reich. . . .    She would look for a violet ribbon to match the ink, and wait for an opportunity to restore these letters to their sender.    If none offered, it did not matter.    She did not want to hurt anybody's feelings, nor to present herself as other than she was; she had nothing to regret, nor to excuse.    How often had papa regretted that man was the offspring of his circumstances—and she, Annette Koldewey, had been born into a definite environment.    She had not created herself; whoever was responsible it was not she.    And now she must go down and sort the laundry, which would be washed in the female part of the establishment, discuss the day's meals with Frau Brose, and see what fresh vegetables had been brought in.    She hoped there would be some brown cabbage, as there had been a touch of frost already, which so much improved it.    Botanists probably called it green cabbage, but it was called brown cabbage here in Hamburg.


Herr Koldewey sucked meditatively at his underlip as he sat over his breakfast cup of coffee and studied a letter in which Käte Neumeier asked her *ex-fiancé* to send a bit of *curare*, enough to experiment with, with the root-cuttings from the forest lianas.    He did not like one of her phrases, and it was essential that anything set forth in black and white should wear an impeccably innocent air.    The Third Reich was suspicious, and controlled an espionage service which, with German thoroughness, far surpassed its most famous predecessors.    There could hardly be a more unimpeachable writer of a letter to the German Consulate in Buenos Aires than the Director of Fuhlsbüttel prison, and a highly respectable lady doctor and member of the Party, whose correspondence with the equally respected Consular official had continued for years without so much as a question asked.    But they were not out of the wood yet. There was slippery ice about—such as that which coated the park avenues—and it was fatally easy to fall down.    Besides, Herr Koldewey knew himself to be a natural procrastinator, who gladly put off decisions, avoided sudden resolves, and was indeed a typical "Scorpion," like so many people born at the end of October.    That was the sort of thing he used to read in the Astrological Journal, to which he had subscribed for a few years after the World War, until he began to be annoyed by its folly.    Dr. Laberdan, the prison doctor, was certainly an astrologer too, a ghost hunter, a homœopath—it all hung together, and what rubbish it was !    Friend Nietzsche had somewhere dilated on the connection between astrology and morality—he must look up the passage.    The purpose for which *curare* was needed was stated to be experiments on animals, and this might cause offence.    The Third Reich combined a sentimental affection for animals with a characteristically genial intolerance of intellect and humanity: "medical experiments" would have been better. But apart from all this, the writer of this letter was the founder of a great cause. This act implied a definite adherence to the enemies of the Third Reich; a decision long deferred and assiduously evaded had now been taken. It might be that the request for a not uncommon poison-plant could only arouse suspicion in one who was aware of what had been projected in certain conversations. All these morning misgivings were doubtless directed against the plans and phantasies of the evening and the night before—a distinction that had become familiar to the author of *Mein Kampf*, though he explained it as the natural conflict between a fresh and tired mind. However, the writer of such a letter had better acquire an accomplice. Perhaps he would find Herr Lintze at home.

"Marvellous," exclaimed Herr Lintze at the other end of the wire. "This is telepathy or something like it. I had made up my mind to ring you up before lunch—and ask if you could spare me a few minutes."

"Ah well, it's holiday-time," replied Herr Koldewey gaily; "and if you drive through Wandsbek, you might bring Dr. Käte with you."

Herr Lintze came alone. What they had to talk about admitted of no witnesses. Reliable reports had reached him from Danzig that one of the highest officials there had himself heard the Führer say in so many words that he would not in the least mind sacrificing three million young Germans as the price of Germany's greatness. "General Ludendorff was satisfied with two millions, and the result was Versailles. If such a man now gambles with three millions, who knows how many may perish, and the result will be rack and ruin worse than the Thirty Years' War. And then France will be back in Metz and Alsace, foreigners in Pomerania and Bremen, and the Reich will be destroyed. Never has an Austrian meddled in our Prussian politics to any good purpose—and this man is a Catholic, into the bargain."

Herr Koldewey looked rather puzzled, leaned back in his chair and fidgeted with the butt of his extinct cigar.

"Though not, in this case, a practising one."

"They," rejoined Herr Lintze, emphatically, "are the worst kind. Such men have the clerical poison working in their blood."

"Shall I send off the letter?"

"By all means."

"But as we are sitting so comfortably together," said Herr Koldewey, "and embarking on a distinctly dangerous enterprise, we must get a clear view of our starting-point. Our foundation is obviously identical, and beyond any misunderstanding—however, we are neither of us here to give utterance to the obvious, I assume."

"We all have our part to play," agreed Herr Lintze, breathing through his thin lips on to his pince-nez.

"Permit me to ask," pursued Herr Koldewey, poising his outstretched forefinger vertically on the table top, "why these four convicted men were hounded to their death, Colonel—in the last resort?"

A gleam came into Herr Lintze's eyes at the prospect of an encounter; the intellectual sparks would soon begin to fly. "In the last resort?" he repeated. "Because they were destroying the basis of our fighting power. We saw the red poison destroying the armies of the Tsar."

"That is a reason," nodded Herr Koldewey, "but not *the* reason. Is fighting power an ultimate value? Isn't it rather the expression of a mode of thought, an attitude of mind? What do you conceive to be the highest values, my good friend, for which we are ready and glad to live and die? After all, if we could accept those of Herr Lenin, we might avoid a great deal of risk and effort. What then?"

Herr Lintze's face assumed an alert look, like that of a candidate at a viva-voce examination.

"The highest?" he repeated, and detailed them, one by one: "God, Fatherland, freedom, immortality. A man who starts out on a re-cruiting-tour must have his spiritual baggage ready to his hand."

"Within the compass of a knapsack," said Herr Koldewey, with an approving nod. "Every footslogger has 'God with us' engraved on his belt-buckle. How runs the old song—'Freedom of my dreams, that fills my heart'. Fatherland—that's no more than the authority con-trolling the soldier as well as the official, another word for modern society. But without immortality, or the belief in it, they wouldn't be inclined to venture into any ordeal in which their little earthly light might be extinguished. Walhalla, Mohammed's paradise, Manitou's hunting grounds, the Christian Hallelujah-Heaven—those are man's impelling motives."

Herr Lintze found his friend's and partner's tone almost too frivolous. "Leave us simple folk our religion," he pleaded. "It distinguishes us from the beasts."

"True," nodded Herr Koldewey, peering at him from his slanting goat-like eyes. "And that is why we hate Marxism, as it robs us of this illusion, as he describes it, too besotted in his 'liberal' astuteness to realize that this same illusion makes the history of the world—it is a power-potential that welds amorphous masses into conquering nations. But Herr Marx, bemused by a certain crazy cloud-gatherer called Hegel, grew a prophetic beard and a Samsonic mane of hair, and believed he could persuade our workers that it's more important to know what happens when a tram-ticket is taken, than when a soul passes into the beyond."

"So it is," nodded Herr Lintze, "for us. For the leaders, for the intellectual initiates. But not for the masses, the many-too-many, who fight the battles, do the work, produce the children, and don't otherwise get much to chirp about, in well-ordered communities. It was because they got on their hind legs in the Weimar Republic that we let it collapse. And what a mess they made of the powerful Russia of the Bismarck age, is obvious enough from the latest trials in that country. Well, let the People's Commissars get on with the good work. It won't be allowed to get to that point with us. True authority is not established from one day to the next. And that's the reason."

"Agreed," said Herr Koldewey, "our Heavy Industry is well content to sing '*Credo*', and let the chorus continue into '*in unum Deum*', whereby Herr Hitler may well think that he is the *Deus* in question. He also

N

conceives himself as the High Priest. But if he oversteps the limits assigned to him—those of a miracle-working image, an ikon, or at the best, a Rasputin, we shall know what we have to sing. And that will be the lines of our old friend Gerhart Hauptmann, which he wrote in the year of destiny, 1914: 'Germany must live even if we must die'. And so—here's your health."

And after a pause: "Well, that's that," observed Herr Koldewey, opened his bureau, clapped his official stamp on to the coloured ink-pad, and stamped the envelope in the top left-hand corner: "Fuhlsbüttel Prison: Governor's Office." "That will circumvent the Censor," said he, and stood up.

As he took his leave the Colonel said: "You might ring me up before you go out to Glasmoor to get the Mengers papers, as you propose. It's no joke driving on these frozen roads. Perhaps Mengers' effects have come to light long ago. You can telephone from my office this afternoon if you like. Intelligence officers have certain privileges."

"So do prison governors," smiled Herr Koldewey. "We are admirably adapted allies, Colonel. But you are quite right."

At lunch Herr Koldewey was informed that the little car would be on strike for the next few days. In that case, he insisted on going by rail.

"But the train only goes as far as Ochsenzoll," said Thyra, who knew the Harksheid country very well. "And what will the roads be like now it's freezing again after the thaw?"

"Railways are out of date," laughed Ingebottel. "The Führer is all for auto-roads, auto-buses, and the People's Car. Locomotives have had their day, and in a few years, says Herr Riechow, the railway lines will be scrapped."

Herr Koldewey wagged his head. During the last two years of the war he had been attached to the staff of the Military Railway Administration at Vilna, and had plenty to tell of the tremendous task which the Transport Section at Supreme Headquarters had been called upon to undertake.

"Our world war was the first great war to be fought with locomotives; '70 wasn't even a dress rehearsal for it. We then marched across the frontiers *per pedes apostolorum*. We have learned the lesson, and if the Leader has now lost interest in railways, that is the clearest proof of our peaceful intentions. Old Moltke needed two generations, so to say, to make the army railway-minded. So if the Reichswehr lets the great man play with auto-cars and cemented highways, you will carry your grey heads to the grave, and never endure what did indeed cost your poor mother her life."

"But, Papa," said Thyra reproachfully, "the Führer knows better than you do. Always supposing the Russians don't attack us."

"My child," laughed Ingebottel. "Just let them try it on."

The trip to Glasmoor did not take place. Herr Lintze's telephonist rang up; the papers in question had been found on the premises long before, and deposited with the editorial department of the Schwarze Korps, for what purpose no one knew. Herr Koldewey nodded, expressed his thanks, and hung up the receiver. In the evening he suggested to his fiancée that they would do better to take the fast train to Cuxhaven on Sunday if it was not raining, and enjoy the view of the North Sea from as far out as they could get along the mole; it was always a magnificent sight, especially at flood-tide. Käte Neumeier eyed her friend, she was delighted with his youthful energy; and she nearly addressed the sedate official with the familiarity of affection as he proposed the little adventure with a cheerful glitter in his eye. In years gone by she had visited the mole with Friedel Timme during the autumn storms, at the time of the Equinox. Why, Koldewey was nearly sixty!

"Yes," she said, meditatively; "that might be very nice if it isn't too cold."

Koldewey beamed at her. "I oughtn't to have to remind you," he said, only just avoiding the affectionate "Du" in his turn, "that for people like ourselves there isn't any bad weather, only the wrong sort of clothes. Warm stockings, boots, and woollen underclothes. . . ."

"And the genuine waterproof," laughed Käte Neumeier; "in which a good Hamburger is born. Do the girls come with us, or shall we go alone?"

"Let's ask them," said Herr Koldewey, pointing to the next room. His three daughters were sitting by the radio as he opened the door. A sonorous masculine voice, probably that of Herr Schlusnus, professional and yet pleasantly spontaneous, was singing Goethe's song of the Three Magi and their star. Herr Koldewey stood and watched them in affectionate silence: all three were listening, spellbound, to the lovely closing cadences of the piano accompaniment which represented with much melodic humour the masked procession vanishing slowly into the distance amid the tinkling of little bells.


That first New Year Sunday brought many men on Christmas leave from central and southern Germany back to their naval and army stations, at Harburg, Stade and Cuxhaven. None the less, the little party found an empty second-class compartment, in which there were temporarily four empty seats, the occupants of the two window-seats not having left the dining-car since Hamburg. Herr Koldewey, as host, had been delighted at the prospect of making Bert Boje's acquaintance, who, as he observed in an undertone to Käte, was soon to be more closely connected with the family. Käte Neumeier wondered what exactly he meant: had he noticed and rightly interpreted the grave, appraising look which Annette directed towards the young S.A. man? Did it mean that she was asking herself whether he was another Footh? Well, everyone must go through their own experiences—there was no dispensation from that law of life, as Heinrich Koldewey must already have learned from his old friend Nietzsche. But if Annette, who sat there, looking so charming and girlish in her tweed costume, against the grey-striped cushions of the compartment, became involved with Bert, or he with her, here surely was the beginning of something that would last. Neumeier blood ran in his veins, and it ran sound and clear. Beneath the next Christmas tree there would be a double wedding, and a long spell of prosperity under the auspices of the *Reichswehr*. What a variety of uniforms, by the way, were represented on this train. Naval artillery, naval air arm, A.B.'s, marines, Harburg pioneers, and all manner of others that Bert had identified for her and Annette's benefit. How had Herr Lintze, on the previous Saturday evening, between the three of them, expressed his amiable intentions, when they were talking about someone who should drop an axe smeared with *curare* on a certain person's foot? A butcher, and two thousand marks—that wouldn't last him long in our canteen, now that all salaries have come down, and the housewife has to work magic to make ends meet. We might catch this fellow with a fresh offer. After what he has done already he is not likely to be particular, and in this case it isn't an extensive operation. The toe belongs to the other fellow, and our master-butcher may perhaps go down to history as Marinus the Second.

His thin lips had curved into a genial smile, as he thus alluded to the unhappy Marinus van der Lubbe, and Käte Neumeier shuddered. She must soon inquire of the Barfeys how the Teetjens' affairs were getting on. It might be that her punitive expedition on behalf of Friedel Timme would produce some result that would advance their cause. It was odd, and she smiled at the thought, that they were now co-operating with the *Reichswehr* in their efforts to avenge Friedel Timme, himself a *Reichswehr* victim. The times were obviously getting more and more involved, but as Herr Lintze had mischievously observed: Germany was worth a Mass, even a Black Mass.

In the meantime the train had long since crossed the Elbe and entered a frozen expanse of snow beneath a clear blue sky overhead; and the smoke-plume from the engine was streaming westwards. And Käte Neumeier, again with a thrill of affection for her friends, observed Koldewey's long goat-like countenance eying Bert with a somewhat quizzical expression, while Annette's delicate brow wrinkled into a frown, and a look of disapproval.

"Your friend, Frau Mengers, goes a little far," said she, warmly. "Much can be forgiven her, but the suggestion that Germany will be levelled to the ground—well, really!"

Käte Neumeier knew what they were talking about. Bert had explained when he came for her that morning. He had kept one of the Mengers books for which he had long been looking—Forster's *Views of the Lower Rhine*, and as he was turning over the pages before going to sleep, a thin octavo notebook had fallen out of it, containing nothing but poems—sonnets and quatrains by Walter B. Mengers. Not at all bad—he had even copied out one of them, written in the style of the great Stefan George, and entitled *To the Leaders*. Next day he had taken the book round to the man's mother in the Rothenbaum-Chaussée, as indeed was his duty. This had so touched the good lady that when she learned that he was proposing to take a post in South America, she gripped his arm with both her hands and implored him to do so.    As far back as '36 a woman in the Reimerstwiete, whom she had visited to enquire about her son in Ireland, had foretold from the cards that Germany would be levelled to the ground and she had better leave it while she could.    She had ignored the advice and was still here, but the woman was famed for her visionary gifts; she could not mention her name, as it was no longer lawful to foretell the future from the cards or the stars—obviously because there had been too many indications of disaster.    Well, there might be an element of humbug in it, said Frau Mengers, but these people did possess some faculty, second-sight or whatever you like to call it.    The woman had told her that she would soon visit her eldest son; but her youngest son was in grave peril, and him she would never see again.    Which was not surprising—since no one can see through six feet of earth.

"Much may be forgiven to a mother, and we all know that these Delphic Sybils are visited by all sorts of people besides servant-maids. Moreover, the prohibition to which the lady alludes is really an act of public benevolence.    The very instinct for knowledge may be perverted, nor is this a recent development—as witness Eve in Paradise, to quote the *Meistersingers*."    And he hummed a couple of bars, thereby making clear that Annette had inherited her want of tonal sense from her father.

Annette nodded; Käte said she was inclined to agree, but how did this apply to Dr. Laberdan's cult of the divining-rod, and all the other perversions of science?

"Not at all," said Dr. Koldewey; and indeed in its progress to power the Third Reich had made full use of astrologers and their influence on women; especially in the years during and after the inflation, in which Theosophy, the Downfall of the West, and the Rise of the Third Reich, were strangely combined in all manner of mystical apologues.    He—Koldewey—was constantly being reminded of Ibsen's *Emperor and Galilæan*, and Maximus the Magician with his *Fifth Wheel on the Car*. After every great war and revolution, saviours and miracle-mongers were swept into prominence by the irrational elements of society.    About every thirty years, Europe indulged in this sort of pendulum-swing into darkness; after which, reason and knowledge, and the higher human faculties, revived, and banished such spectres to the middens of the past, where the remains of dead religions and superstitions await the intelligent excavator who shall discover their significance.    "The Third Reich," he repeated meditatively—"the first being that of Apollo, the second that of the Crucified Christ.    I suppose Adolf Hitler may properly figure as the embodiment of the third."

Käte Neumeier was anxious to spare her nephew any embarrassment. She pointed through the window to the level countryside, the swirling clouds of smoke and steam from the locomotive, the clumps of squat, gabled cottages, beneath the leafless trees, and asked whether it was not rather premature to dismiss the prevalent belief in the supernatural, based on natural facts not yet fully understood.    To the North, as far as Sweden, West to Finland, East to Scotland, there were tales of ordinary folk, such as fishermen, sailors, sound and sensible people in every other

way, who had actually witnessed events that had not yet happened, or were
happening far away, visible to the physical eye until they dissolved in
smoke, though they had indeed to admit that neighbours and passers-by
could see nothing at all.   The desolation of the great heath, the swathes
of mist and drifts of cloud did indeed favour such visions.   But why were
stories, nowadays, no longer about hell-hounds, and spectral horses, but
of—as in Swedenborg—about events which experience would soon
confirm.   Man's inner nature and its forces were beyond the grasp of
knowledge.   While we could decipher no more than the simplest
hieroglyphics of hypnosis, auto-suggestion, and the other emanations of
the unconscious, wasn't it better to admit that we are and always have
been inclined to close the doors on the knowable too soon?   The works
of the most translucent German genius, Goethe, contained all manner
of plausible incidents that passed beyond ordinary sense-experience; as,
for instance, when he met himself in a grey cloak, riding from Sesenheim,
or when his grandfather Textor dreamed of the future, and told his
family all sorts of things that did actually happen later on.   Of course
a man in Gothenburg can't actually see an exactly contemporaneous
event in Stockholm.   But we ought to investigate the spiritual structure
of those who possess this gift, though we do not share it.   Such phenomena
do undeniably occur; but why, and why in just those particular individuals, we do not know—not yet.   We are still novices at the process
of testing and interpreting evidence.

Herr Koldewey felt himself very much at his ease, and indeed
miraculously so for a man in a non-smoking compartment, who has had
to postpone his after-breakfast cigar, because he wanted to spare the
ladies and himself the unpleasant odour inevitably left behind by the
smoke from State tobacco in the dry and overheated air of an express
train.   What a brilliant creature she was, this new Käte of his, as she
sat there, her eloquent eyes glistening beneath her light-fitting tweed
hat, she might well have been as many years under forty as she was
over that age.   If Balzac had discovered the woman of thirty, he—
Koldewey—could propose to his old crony, the well-known author,
H. F. Punkt, *The Woman of Forty* for his next theme.   At the same
time he listened placidly to the rumble of the train, that regular, rhythmic
expression of onward motion, which denoted a permanent way well
laid and kept in good repair.   During the war the soldiers had always
embodied the rhythm of the trains in the words: "You blasted old
inspector"; now, as his nephew Manfred had once told him, with a
laugh, it stood for: "Hail, beloved Party Comrade".   Then he shifted
his thoughts to his dead nephew, and the dress rehearsal in Spain, as
Herr Lintze had recently described it, the Asturian or Basque manœuvres
and the fighting round Teruel, and the inevitable end which would be
staged in Catalonia—the victory of General Franco and his allies over
the Soviet Union and the spirit of democracy, to which the Russians
had given so much unacknowledged support.

"No, Käte," said he, "statistics will reduce the majority of these
claims to their proper proportions, by establishing how often your
prophets and Sibyls and mediums were right, and how often they were

wrong. Then you will see that the number of misses immeasurably exceeds the number of hits. I will not indeed go so far as the philosopher who maintained that if a pig rummaged long enough—and indeed that would mean a very long time—in a heap of letters he would ultimately unearth Shakespeare's *Sonnets* or both parts of *Faust*. But it is obviously a fact that among the many millions of prophecies in which men indulge daily, one or other does in fact come off—with the result that what is a mere accident gets talked about by old busy-bodies of both sexes, and provides a heaven-sent subject for coffee-table gossip. No, my dear, let us not be fobbed off with the natural science of the future. Faith in prophesies, clairvoyance, and second-sight, merely shows that the oldest religions still survive in the company of their more progressive successors, just as we still carry an appendix inside ourselves—though indeed there have been recent suggestions that it does perform important functions—in the way of preserving the inner secretion. However, I've had mine removed, and I don't feel internally desiccated yet."

And he looked so quizzically at his future wife that she tapped him gaily on the knee with her gloves, for they were sitting face to face. He snatched the slips of smooth, brown leather, drew them affectionately through his fingers, and ended this part of the little domestic argument, as he gazed meditatively out of the window.

"Of course it isn't as simple as all that. There is some foundation for a great many prophecies, especially when they relate to the destinies of nations and their rulers. Certain of the quatrains of Nostradamus are really amazing, having been in print for centuries before they were fulfilled, quite literally and in the most trivial particulars. But I won't be angered by Frau Mengers' vaticanism. '*Solo Adæquare*', the Romans called it—a phrase they used for their scorched earth policy in enemy country. It was a pure war measure, and deprived the invaded of any assistance from the country, one important item being, in Mediterranean lands, the shade from the trees. Hence the complete destruction of all timber, when the order was issued in those words. But in Frau Mengers' case the phrase is mere wishful-thinking, the visionary revenge of the men of Weimar and the Israelites, as I ventured to observe on a previous occasion. It presupposes a war conducted in Germany, and a war in which our army would be defeated—which is beyond my credence! Now I understand how right it was to ban all that sort of thing. Even nonsense must be subjected to some restraint. But now we must take some notice of our young people, and apologize for our neglect."

But Annette and Bert Boje, who were sitting next the corridor, were amusing themselves in their own way, counting the chimneys as the train passed them. Annette thought they would never get on to the mole—and indeed they ought to have consulted the coastal weather reports before they started; it was blowing harder here than they would have thought possible back in Hamburg.

"We ought to have telephoned the air-port," said Herr Koldewey penitently. "But you, my dear young prophetess, never thought to do so either."

"Do you imagine that children merely exist to play providence for Papa," said Annette in self-defence, and Herr Koldewey nodded complacently. That was the rôle for which they were destined by nature and education.

The traffic policeman by the railway-station smiled rather wryly as he confirmed his questioner's apprehensions; when the storm-cone had been hoisted, there was little chance of getting down to the water's edge. The hiss and whistle of the wind grew more insistent as they neared the harbour, until it rose into a thunderous roar that seemed to portend all the awesome strength of an element in onset, though still very far away and not yet in full career. A white sky flecked with grey, against which massed and flying clouds sped southwards to a point where the heavens were faintly tinged with yellow, cast an even bleaker, chillier gloom than usual over the Cuxhaven streets.

"It's a good sort of Sunday to come back from Christmas leave," observed Herr Koldewey to Bert Boje; "always presupposing the company of old friends, warm quarters, and no need to go out again till to-morrow morning." Well, this trip to Cuxhaven had proved a failure for which he, Koldewey must offer his excuses; whereupon Käte Neumeier vigorously protested. It was not yet evening, the weather might still change, and, after all, one must be prepared for the fact that events do sometimes express the Gods' inevitable displeasure. The next step, obviously, was to get a decent lunch somewhere. Annette should now take control. She knew all about these parts. (No one mentioned Herr Footh's name.)

But the head-waiter at the Englischer Hof provided some sound advice. He put at his guests' disposal a young lad, a handsome fair-haired youth, a member of the Hitler Youth, of course, who would guide them to a spot from which they could get an excellent view of the sea and the Elbe. Not from below, of course, that wasn't safe on a day like this; but from above, a tree-covered bastion on the former sea-wall, a favourite view-point. There they now stood, standing with linked arms, up-turned collars, and tightly buttoned coats. Before and below them stretched the harbour installations, roofs, walls, white concrete dams, a wild scurrying sky, and the air that lashed their faces was loaded with salt which they soon felt on their lips and faces and hands. But from as far as eye could reach came an onrushing surge of ochrous, greenish waters, wave upon wave, crested with foam, dashing in raving, roaring turmoil, in an onset ever renewed, against the shore and the works of man. In this savage, shrill mellay of the elements it seemed impossible for the steel-black anchored ships to ride out the storm. From the far horizon force unleashed raged onwards. The white, flashing sea-gulls whirled on the wings of the genius of destruction. Even where they were standing the dull thunder of the crashing combers made their hearts quake. The storm tore the dead boughs off the trees, snatched the very words from the lips of the speakers; down from the Icelandic mists sped the squadrons of Poseidon, myriads of grey steeds

flung in fury against the solid land.    Here was *Solo Adæquare*, thought
Herr Koldewey with a shudder, as he grasped Käte's arm and pressed
it hard, and noticed Annette had slipped behind Bert Boje, who faced
the Eastern gale laughing, with bared white teeth and glistening eyes,
and sheltered her from its violence.    Such was man, a bold, brave
animal, unwearied in his struggle with destruction, and yet himself a
destroyer.    And he took Käte by the shoulder, and Annette as well,
and—with a confidential nod to Herr Boje, they made their way back in
silence, half-deafened, down into the city, secure behind its escarpments,
into the solid streets and a welcoming fire-lit room.


# CHAPTER SIX

### THE BLACK ROSE

LATE IN THE evening of that eventful day it came about that Herr
Koldewey, for a short time, found himself regretting what had proved a
successful expedition.    Darkness had long since fallen when—as very
rarely happened to him—he fell asleep in his armchair while reading,
with a cigar between his fingers, as though the book, an admirably
written work on negro folk-lore, had failed to keep him awake.    From
the next room came wafts of fragrance from a huge bouquet of white
roses, magnificent hot-house blooms sent in during the morning upon
the order of Lieut.-Col. Lintze, with a message of regret that he could
not accompany them to Glasmoor; and two rooms away, Thyra, darkest
of his three fair-haired daughters, had picked up a New York transmission
of Brahms's second Piano Concerto, performed by an *emigré* pianist,
and an admirably conducted orchestra—the sort of music that could,
alas, no longer be heard in Germany—for the time, at any rate.    Yes,
Thyra crouching yonder in her warm evening frock of quilted rust-red
velvet with a broad, old-fashioned type of skirt, outspread on the floor
around her, and a cigarette between her firm little teeth—this Thyra of
his lived in quiet antagonism to the régime which had robbed her of the
clever young boy-friend, Wilhelm Kley, of whom the Koldewey household
had heard little since his father's rather spectacular suicide, nor indeed
for some time before that event.    She had accordingly taken to astrology,
the practice of which was forbidden under the Third Reich; and she took
particular pleasure in searching the etheric waves emitted by the western
or Slav world which still stood by the old traditions, in search of artists
and performances forbidden by the Reich Chamber of Culture.    Yes

my girl, thought Herr Koldewey, as the magic glow of the amber-
coloured cadences tossed to and fro, from piano to orchestra, compelled
his attention, and he laid his book carefully on the floor; yes—she was
quite right to keep that dark-eyed head of hers under her own control, to
think and do what seemed good to her at home, and steer her own course
—as far as practicable, of course, without any fuss or disturbance. The
Koldeweys did not indulge in revolutions, when things didn't go to their
liking; they kept still, and waited, and knew that all would come out
right in the end.   It was not in their tradition—in theirs, mark you—to
kick against the pricks.   A disagreeable sort of phrase, and occupation.
In quiet aloofness they survived the Weimar Republic, when there was
also a dominating party, which preached such doctrines as—Being
determines the consciousness of being.   As though the autonomy of the
spirit was not one of the most precious discoveries and achievements of
the European community!—as though the higher element in man was
not so precariously poised above his inward depths as barely to maintain
him against the slime in which materialism and Herr Karl Marx were
trying to engulf it.   To expel such intellectual poison every reasonable
man is ready to pay some sort of price—as, for instance, the sacrifice of
certain achievements of sound and song, expressions of the soul exultant.
And such ancient traditions, as people like themselves had preserved
within their homes, were no concern of those who walk straitly in the
streets and in the forecourts of public opinion. . . . Ah, friend Johannes,
that was nobly conceived and came from the very heart—strange to
remember the days when you were a lad in Hamburg, and played the
piano in the harbour taverns. . . . Yes, reflected Herr Koldewey, I
really ought to have behaved with greater circumspection, found refuge
within myself, and contentment in contemplation of my own activity,
like friend Johannes; in the sound of music in a still and quiet hour,
safe from the chill night air that could not enter.   Was he doing
right in taking another wife—the charming, dark-haired Käte, so
full of life and energy?   Wasn't he a fool, too, to engage himself in
dealings—not to say conspiracies, aimed at preventing one who had been
hoisted into dominance by forces now notorious, from plunging the
country into ruin.   And even if he merely offered anxious patriots like
the excellent Herr Lintze a few suggestions, a little pertinent "information," as he believed it was now called, which might start the cogs and
levers of his reasoning faculties, all indeed, based on Herr Freud's
conclusions on the case of the lunatic Herr Schreber—wasn't that going
too far?   Wasn't it quite contrary to the Koldewey, Hamburg, and Conservative tradition?   Well, a certain Edmund Burke had assailed the
spirit and activities of the French Revolution, and had finally overthrown them—speaking as a Conservative, in the name, and within the
system, of existing institutions as the embodiment of political good sense.
Was he—Koldewey—doing more than this?—Certainly not; far less.
Burke came forth and orated, overthrew Ministers and reconstituted
Cabinets.   Koldewey—alas—sat in his glass cage, as poor Manfred
used to call it, surveyed what went forward in the depths below, observed
and directed what was done, or not done, in the middle regions, and

generally speaking let himself drift with the impulse of the times—like the Reich, like Europe, and the droll planet Earth revolving uninterruptedly through the three dimensions of space, and also through a fourth, for which they had to thank Herr Einstein's genius; it was formerly known as Time, and Einstein's discoveries had again fallen into disfavour. Well, wait a bit, this new broom would have served its purpose one day and be consigned to a corner. . . . How on earth did old Brahms fall into such a mood of depression—such luxuriance of melancholy amid the autumn glory of the Wörthersee? . . . Hadn't he better try to extricate himself from all these crazy political complications, let Käte Neumeier remain as she was, and not provide a successor to Käte Koldewey the First? True it was that the one and only Friedrich was incessantly urging intellectuals and sceptics to act. But did he take his own advice? Did he plunge into the conflict, otherwise than on the printed page? After the Turin days, didn't he escape into madness; and dwell among the magical flowers of his Zarathustra world, in ravines and cloistered hollows starred with lilies and campanulas?

At this point Herr Koldewey, as he admitted to himself later, may have fallen asleep, and slumbered through nearly three movements of one of his favourite compositions. The negro book stood open on the floor, his extinct cigar smelt rather brackish through the fragrance of the roses; there was no sound, or as yet no sound, from the adjoining room—Annette had obviously not returned. His fatigue was plainly the price paid for the day's excursion, and had produced a dream which would be worth analysing later on. Herr Koldewey sat with eyes closed, humorously debating with himself whether it was fair to relight his burnt-out cigar. The radio-apparatus itself had appeared, in altered guise, in his dream. The tactful Thyra must have vanished. Little importance was now attached to dreams. The revival of that aspect of the older civilizations was best left to the various schools of psycho-analysts and therapeutists, among whom there were as many schools and as much dissension as in ancient Alexandria or Athens. And the thought that he had imagined this elegant Blue Point wireless set as capable of reviving time past, and presenting the performances of persons long since dead, made him smile. For this had been his dream:

Conductor, Robert Schumann; and on the programme which he had in his hand the soloist was recorded as—Frau Klara Schumann-Wieck; he had seen the composer seated in a box with his head between his hands, his fingers entwined in his musician's mane of hair, and his full beard spread fanwise over his stiff and bulging shirt-front. He had seen it all: the performance was taking place in the Hamburg theatre. Such an apparatus was now called television, and anyone who wanted to see as well as listen could stay comfortably at home. The concert-room was represented by a sort of opera stage, in the decorative setting of a huge black rose—like blackened masonry left standing after a vast conflagration; but these were scented walls, velvety and gigantic, rising tier by tier in overlapping curves. And on a white banner slung slantwise across the stage, the legend inscribed in jagged Gothic characters, and somehow suited to the scene: "They were killed by the scent of roses." Who? The question remained unanswered. His four boarders, perhaps. Herr Koldewey was escorted through these galleries by a certain Mengers—and he found himself recalling his youthful days of friendship with an attractive actress, when he felt quite at home behind the stage and in the dressing-rooms.

And as he, the real, the bodily awakened Koldewey, rose abruptly, went into his bedroom, undressed, and made ready for bed, he revived the dream in its full significance in the foreground of his mind and consciousness. For Herr Koldewey had a duty to fulfil, he had to give the Wandsbek axe to the ringleader, Timme. And here was Mengers, the bookseller's clerk disguised as an old-time Wandsbek messenger, in knee-breeches and a blue dress-coat—borrowed, as it appeared. "This," he explained, "is the backstage of European culture, of bourgeois civilization, and when it is ripe, it will fall."—"Fall?"—"Listen to those splendid, falling chords. So it was with the Greek rose, the Roman and the Christian and the Feudal rose. . . .    Think of Dante, Herr Geheimrat; all departed now and vanished." Herr Koldewey, splashing in the wash-basin, contorted his lengthy, faunlike countenance—as he himself described it—into a smile, with the result that he got some soap-suds into the corners of his eyes. The fact that an educated gentleman did not even in dream emerge from the framework of his book-world gave him food for mocking thoughts. . . . And now he lay, still alone, and still a bachelor, in his own bedroom, and set himself to recall and recover the curious dream that had visited him as he sat or listened, even almost when he read—burnt-out ruins in the guise of a black rose; it was the *solo adæquare* of Cuxhaven that afternoon which had produced that vision. Television; but what on earth was all this about handing over the Wandsbek axe to last year's ringleader? Herr Koldewey, the dreamer, not the object of the dream, chuckled. A high official does not handle an axe, even in a dream. At most would he issue an order for its withdrawal from wherever it might be. And even a dream cannot defy the claims of rank and station; at least, not the said official's decorous dream. All faded roses shed their leaves, didn't they? They vanish and depart; so Herr Mengers had said— who, by the way, looked exactly like Kladderadatsch in the old comic paper, with a long nose and twinkling eyes, and wearing the above-mentioned knee-breeches and dress-coat. And what then remained? Herr Koldewey had asked. 'First a leafless calyx,' came the answer: 'bleak and bristly, and a tapering red hip, encircled by small seeds.' (Yes, there were many such to be seen about the garden in October.) 'Then it is planted; and a new rose grows, once more in B Flat Major, a lovely Brahmsian rose, the everlasting return of what is everlastingly renewed, rose upon rose, *deus ex Deo*, as they sing in the Mass in B Minor; but the new one won't, let us hope, be black, smoke-black, cigar-black; it will be red with blood. Of blood there will be plenty, blood from human necks and human flesh, won't there, Herr Teetjen?' True enough, and Herr Koldewey, suddenly recalling his real self, clapped his hands angrily on his green silk coverlet. In this abominable dream—

which showed how crazy a man could be when he sends his wits to sleep
—in this dream he had been confounded with that subservient instrument
of other men's schemes, Herr Footh's protegé, Albert Teetjen the butcher.
But he, the Herr Koldewey of the dream, had not submitted to such an
outrage. "Excuse me," he had protested: "My name is Koldewey, not
Teetjen." "But, Herr Geheimrat," returned the bookseller's clerk,
bowing behind his shop counter: "A name is but a sound and a breath."
So saying, he came forth and escorted Herr Teetjewey into the last and
inmost gallery, which smelt most opulently of Brahms and fire and roses.
That was the third movement, thought the dreamer to himself; and
yonder sat, cross-legged, on a cushion of stamens, Herr Friedrich Timme,
and lifted his arm. Whereupon the leaves began to fall—the black
gigantic walls, one after the other, bare and bleak like the wings of a
deserted stage, and the old messenger laid the axe, the golden gleaming
axe, with its long blade and chiselled shaft, a genuinely American article,
like that colleague of his who laughed with such ruthless joviality; he laid
the axe—for he had it all the time, at the feet of him who sat, crowned
with a red, tapering rose-hip cap, on his mossy cushion. Then Herr
Koldewey, bemused by sleep and music, and the scent of fading roses,
stretched out a long forefinger, and said he had no sons. But the seated
figure merely nodded: "Even daughters count, in the new Reich, Excellency; and that is the fourth movement. You don't hear the sounds
of blows and shrieks in your Special Section." "You don't need to
listen anywhere," Herr Koldewey had said decisively. "Music and
cruelty go well together, and not every kind of knowledge makes for
happiness." But then the music turned to a march or dancing rhythm—
tamtara, tamtara—no, it was a tango. . . . Then he felt to be looking
at a scene from an opera, the Brown-House-catcher of Tangomeln, and if
the chiselled axe were here laid down, and vanished into the moss-
cushion, the old tom-cat would get nothing out of the plot with Hinze or
Lintze. For the whole rat-population ran after the Sun that was Adolf, at
anyrate the whole Rat-Party, brown and black and grey, and there was
nothing to be done. He oughtn't to have been admitted; he oughtn't
to have been allowed to buy the expensive silver flute, and stuff so much
moss into himself. Yonder he sat atop of it all, victim and red-cap and
high priest all in one, and the music boomed from the abyss, deep and
rich and dream-fulfilled: "Awake, the voice calls us." At which point
Herr Koldewey did awake, blinked several times, and felt a thought
slide over him, that he might have done better more seriously to favour
Herr Ebert's party, and won it a little more support. . . . Too late,
too late. Herr Koldewey would gladly have peered into the abyss from
which came the late Hans Brahms's grandiose inspiration, and the great
rose, and the cushion on which the hip-manikin sat—but he could not
do so now, not even in remembrance. But he had seen men standing
there below, with high bald foreheads, mops of wild hair, Brahmsian
beards and Nietzschean moustaches, genuine nineteenth century. And
now, lying with closed eyes upon his pillow, the vision returned. Yes,
Hamburg was a great place, and when Hammonia gave birth to a
musician, he was of no mean order. Herr Koldewey esteemed his city's

critical intelligence, and—drawing a deep breath of cool air—his mind lingered affectionately on the Hamburger's lucid conviction that two and two made four, even in the Third Reich, which claimed to have invented a new arithmetic. . . . But he would marry Käte Neumeier, and devote rather more attention to this business of the axe and Colonel Lintze than he had done hitherto. The black rose of a most solid civilization deserved an effort. A Koldewey, once Captain of *Landwehr*, must not look down upon such a task. Certainly, Herr Major! Very good Herr Colonel! . . .

# THE AXE COMES BACK

## Part II

### BOOK FIVE

## KOLDEWEY RECEIVES A SIGN

### CHAPTER ONE

#### LAUNDRY GOSSIP, TRAMCAR-RIDE

ACCORDING TO POPULAR belief it is not advisable to set up drying-lines nor to hang out washing, between Christmas and the New Year. Some-one in the family might die. Pastor Langhammer, so long as his bones were sound enough to carry him up to the Barfeys' attic, had one day explained to the intelligent young Tom how this superstition had very likely arisen. To begin with, this was the time of long nights, the darkest of the year, when in northern latitudes the sun hardly took the trouble to rise at all; obviously a suitable season for demons and the spectres of the dead to come forth and plague mankind. They enjoyed this licence until Epiphany; they could walk and appear and frequent such human company as they preferred. But phantoms were timid; like their cousins the birds, they were scared by washing hanging out to dry, and they revenged themselves by carrying off those responsible. For this reason Frau Barfey had her holiday between Christmas and Epiphany, and enjoyed it at home with Tom, who was making a number of fair copies of Pastor Langhammer's report on cases of maltreatment, martyr-dom and suicide in the Glasmoor camp, which would have baffled any handwriting expert. But before Christmas there was all the more work for Gesche Barfey, and those who employed her; landlords had to have two wash-houses at their disposal to meet the needs of all their tenants, and the house-wardens had to plan and arrange and even threaten, in order to provide for everybody's needs in time. There was washing in the house and out of it, washing at the Lawerenzens' and the Petersens', at the Dompfaffs, and the Holzhausens', at Dr. Carsten's and school-master Reitlin's, and washing for midwife Pichler, Drohm the iron-monger, and twice at the Lehmkes'—at the old Hussar. Such had been the name of the tavern before and during the previous war, after which it had fallen a victim to the general demilitarization of Germany. Herr

Lehmke had become his own patron saint. At present the Lehmkes were contemplating the resumption of something like the old name, metamorphosed to suit the times into the sign of the Tank, and had commissioned a painter, a member of the Preester Sturm of the S.S., to depict one, in weatherproof paint, on a piece of iron sheeting, such as would lend distinction to the whole street.

It was the middle of November, the eighteenth to be exact, when Gesche Barfey first let fall the secret to Frau Doligkeit, wife of a railway clerk, who could quite well have done her washing for herself in the opinion of her fellow-lodgers. But that was not Frau Doligkeit's opinion, and she was sure that her husband would agree ('he doesn't like me doing it, it coarsens my hands, and he can't stand the smell of washing in the flat'); and after all it was nobody's business but her own. She had joined Gesche Barfey at the midday meal, for she was by no means stand-offish, and indeed it was reported that in former days she had sometimes earned her living on the Reeperbahn before she had managed to catch Doligkeit. In any event, she was the first of Teetjen's customers to learn the origin of the new influx of capital that had so gladdened Albert's heart.

She paled, and had to hold on to the kitchen chair, and gasp for breath. "Frau Barfey!" said she. "In our street! An executioner! I don't believe it. It just doesn't make sense. And we all know the sort of talk that goes round the neighbourhood."

"That's only too true," agreed Gesche Barfey; "there's no end to the talk about Stine and my poor Tom. But unfortunately this comes from a good source, direct from Fuhlsbüttel, Madam, and please don't mention it."

"As if I should!" said Frau Doligkeit emphatically. "But the Public Health authorities ought to be informed."

"That would do no good, Madam. They'd say it was done in the service of the State and Party, and the man preferred the public advantage to his own. No one goes into the Devil's kitchen of his own free will."

"True," said Frau Doligkeit. "We must see what we can do on our own. But I must find out what my husband thinks. They were Communists that were executed, weren't they?"

"Yes," said Gesche Barfey; "but an axe is an axe, and blood is blood, and hygiene has got nothing to do with politics. But I'm very sorry for Stine—indeed the thought of her makes me want to cry."

"Indeed!" said Frau Doligkeit, who wanted to remain young and pretty herself, but did not much appreciate the same aspiration in others. "Frau Teetjen swanks a bit too much, vases of flowers in the shop-window—no, I shan't cry my eyes out for her sake."

When Gesche Barfey told Tom that evening, that his news had, as she put it, forced her teeth apart and slipped over her tongue, Tom nodded twice, said nothing, but shot a quick glance into the dark corner of the kitchen living-room, where the saucepans hung over the hearth. The Doligkeit woman: she was a little saucepan that could easily boil over. Her railway-clerk husband would carry the news with him into the great railway-office at Wandsbek, where he worked. In that huge building on the Gustav-Adolf Strasse, sat countless little officials, clerk-souls, as Pastor Langhammer would have called them in old days. They were kept very busy and talk was not merely forbidden, but would really have upset the office routine; in Tom's eyes the railway was an impressive institution, and its time-table represented to him the height of human achievement in the way of exactitude and organization. But during the established breaks for rest, in the passages and lavatories, especially in the canteen, and while waiting for the overhead railway, the clerks could talk, and of course did so. And if and when Doligkeit contributed his bombshell, the job was pretty well done. Tom did not know many men, but so far as he had had the opportunity of observing them, they were just as talkative as women. Munching his bread and dripping he pictured this item of news percolating through to the goods station, to the engine-drivers and guards, and thence on to the passenger trains—to the effect that somewhere in Gross-Hamburg there existed a butcher called Teetjen, who had acted as executioner of political prisoners, from a sense of civic duty, though he had also earned a fee; the story would find its way along the railway-lines into the country-side. Believed or not, disputed and discussed, praised or blamed, it would now for good and all be known. The story of the mask, my dear Albert, is now public property. A man must only stand by what he does. The slaughter of human beings at the behest of a pack of knaves and fools and blackguards in usurped authority has occurred before and will occur again, just so long as schoolboys are trained to servility and their reckless masters dignify and disguise their drunken caprices under the name of justice. But the sun brings all things to light, in the words of the poem that figured in every child's reading-book—something to do with a saucer and a reflection on the wall. A murderer simply had to reveal what he had done. As his mother had said, it forced his teeth apart and slipped over his tongue. This time an obscure little cripple who lived in an attic would make the truth known. No matter; the main thing was that masks were useless, justice was not the same as public advantage; truth and justice functioned like a coiled steel spring released. He found himself wondering when his toy-engine would arrive. Its journey would not be wholly for the satisfaction and amuse-ment of its starter—so much Tom learned from Olga Lawerenz. Since the weather had grown cold, bringing rain and snow, their meetings had to take place indoors, and it was proving rather difficult to choose times when Gesche was not there, and Olga's absence would not excite remark at home. On washing-days Olga had not a moment free—but the following day she came up to see Tom.

"Look here, Tom, you're a sensible lad," she said, as she ran her fingers through his hair. "Tell your mother to be careful about the way she talks. She told the Albert Teetjen murder-story in our place. But when I passed it on to Father, he looked pretty grim—and I know him; he was angry, but he was more afraid than angry. And he said that people who discover that sort of thing had better keep their mouths shut; the S.S. live nearly opposite, across the street, and those fellows stick together.

Albert had announced that there would be ribs of mutton to-morrow, so dad told me to go across to-morrow morning and wait in the shop a bit and show myself. Never mind about the axe, he said—but of course it wouldn't be the same one. And if it was, it would have been washed and disinfected. A man who had been introduced to the Führer should be good enough for the likes of us. As for schoolmaster Reitlin," she went on—Reitlin was Block-warden and lived in the front ground-floor flat on the other side of the large entry which divided the house into two equal parts—"he burst into a roar of laughter when Father told him the secret, slapped him on the shoulder and shouted: 'This you get in place of Teetjen, Lawerenz—*Summa cum laude*, an award with oak-leaves and swords.' " Tom, with rather a puzzled air, asked what on earth that meant. Anyway, Reitlin was crazy, everyone knew that who had seen him officiate as Block-Warden at a gathering of the inmates. She supposed it meant the same as oak-leaves and swords—prime black-sausage, as you might say. But it was no joke to get across the S.S., as Tom well knew. And if the story was proved untrue, and Albert prosecuted Tom's mother, she would find herself in gaol.

"Nonsense," said Tom. "As if Albert would prosecute anyone! Besides, if your father repeats the story he's an accessory." And that would just serve his purpose, he thought to himself. "Were the ribs of mutton good?"

"Don't, Tom," pleaded Olga. "Mother and I kept on looking at each other all the time, and Father wouldn't catch our eyes. It wasn't a pleasant Sunday dinner, I can tell you."

But Gesche Barfey, when Tom repeated Olga's warning before they went to bed, murmured, as she combed her thin grey hair: "Never mind, Tom. God will take care of all that. He who sheds man's blood, by man shall his blood be shed, says the Bible, and it is so. We must fear God more than man. When men are afraid, it does not matter; God seeks His servants among women. If men are silent, the stones will utter, says the prophet Habbakuk—or perhaps it's Zephaniah."

"And what does the New Testament say?" asked Tom, and smiled in friendly mockery, whether at the two odd names, or his mother's faith in Holy Writ. Olga, indeed, took the same line as Frau Dr. Neumeier had done at the very outset. Indeed, there was no risk in saying that a certain butcher conducted his business in an unhygienic manner. Public health was a trump card, in so far as it cost the Party nothing. Pastor Langhammer's epistle was much more dangerous matter. He hoped the Frau Pastor would soon produce the wages of sin.

New Year's Eve had been an occasion of celebration at Lehmke's. On January 1st a careful housewife puts the dirty table-cloths and the house-linen into soak, against the arrival of the laundress. She has to be well fed, for the work is heavy, Dörte had to bear a hand, and Frau Lehmke's brawny arms helped to wring out and mangle. The girl had to be despatched now and again to get some more bleaching soda or blue for another kettle. Then the two women worked alone and had a chance to gossip. Frau Lehmke needed time to shape her thoughts.

She saw farther than many of her kind; on the next day she moved about the drying-ground in silence, pondering on many things as she ironed the linen and laid it out; but for the time being she told no one what was in her mind. So that was Albert's lottery-prize, or his Oldenburg legacy. She always liked the man, and said so, but now the very thought of him gave her the creeps. On one of the following evenings, while they were counting out the contents of the till and clearing up, she chose the occasion to tell Lehmke. He sat motionless, a heavy hunched figure in his chair, peered at her sideways, and then stared into vacancy. He had trusted his friend and neighbour. The new shop-sign was still unpaid for, and Albert had earned two thousand marks and not offered a penny of it to anyone. Perhaps the Comrades had had a rake-off on the quiet; if not. . . . No one but Preester himself could say. It would be best to ask him outright. An act of service to the Fatherland; the introduction to the Führer; and now this affair of the divining-rod, which was looked upon so favourably by the new Panzer division. Lehmke was not a cantankerous man; but if Albert had put all the cash in his own pocket, that might not unfairly be called an unfriendly act. It had been nice of Barfey not to keep the affair to herself; and indeed among decent folk there should be a certain modicum of blab. To-night this aspect of the case was taken for granted; on the main point they were agreed. Common good comes before private profit; a man who minded nothing but his pocket must not complain of the consequences. Finally, friendship might be regarded as the property of the recipient, as was often stamped on postal packets.

In other circumstances Otto Lehmke could have been sure that Klaas Vierkant and Pieder Preester would be extremely astonished if Albert Teetjen had been convicted of such an outrage against the spirit of comradeship—unless Albert had prudently pre-empted the goodwill of two such important personages; and as a man who knew his petty world, he credited Albert with having duly taken the precaution. But in these last few weeks the aspect of affairs had plainly changed. Something was happening—and very much behind the scenes; but the Press, and especially that section of it devoted to the discussion of economic affairs, knew what was due to its reputation and to the Reich. The Führer had silently pointed to the south-east. General von Reichenau, one of his paladins, had been appointed to the Leipzig command, which from the days of Friedrich and Moltke controlled the invasion route to Vienna. In those times, indeed, Prague was proclaimed as the immediate aim. The future assailant of the Hofburg must first train his guns on Prague. But, since Versailles, the situation had altered, as Editor Vierkant had explained one dark afternoon over a grog with Pieder P. at Lehmke's. But had it really changed? Franz Joseph's white beard had been replaced by Masaryk's, and the elegant Herr Schuschnigg had produced a counterpart in the equally elegant Herr Benes; Prague used to mean Vienna, and now it was the other way round. But whether the egg was opened at the broad or narrow end was, according to Jonathan Swift, a matter of faith; the intention—and that was the main point, was to chip the top off and eat the egg. But as the game was risky, Adolf assembled his trumps in advance in an easily manageable sequence. Kings, Queens, and Knaves wore the uniforms of Admirals, Generals, and Air-Marshals, and the aces displayed the arms of the four great world-powers—France, Italy, England, and America.

The sofa on which Klaas Vierkant sat, was covered with black oil-cloth, decorated with an undulating design of porcelain-headed nails. Short and dark, with his keen face and double collar, he looked not unlike the famous Dr. Goebbels.

"Mark my words," said he, "nothing will happen. When the English allow Franco to put heavy batteries of German long-range guns round her rock of Gibraltar, and look on while English merchant ships, bringing powdered milk and corned beef to the Democratic government, are torpedoed by unknown pirate U-boats, everybody laughs. There are international brigades fighting in Spain. In Alfonso XIII's former kingdom bespectacled bureaucrats began to expropriate the aristocracy, the Church, and every sort of commercial and landed property. Free-masons and internationalized reptiles of that sort were aiming at the control of the Mediterranean, and the Komintern-shark had displayed its triangular fin in those waters undismayed. That was enough. No Anglo-Saxon cabinet would intervene if Germany absorbed Austria, and Mussolini seized air-bases on the Balearics in order to dominate Bizerta and Tunis. And the fact that the Duce no longer stood guard over the Brenner, but realized where his interests lay, must be well known to the French Military Intelligence and to the City of London. The astute Monsieur Barthou had fallen a victim to his encirclement policy in the year '34, both he and King Alexander, the leading spirit of the Little Entente, which was the real object of the Marseilles attack. Rumour had it that the doctors in trying blood-transfusion to save Barthou, had injected the wrong blood-group—what a tribute to French professional accuracy! But if matters were now so far advanced that the lost game of 1918 could be re-opened, and steps taken to recover Alsace-Lorraine, Eupen-Malmedy, the Upper Silesian Corridor, and the overseas colonies, some changes would have to be made in the *Reichswehr* Com-mand. Nobody must be allowed to repeat the manœuvres which had been intended to confuse the Führer's mind at the time of the march into the Rhineland, to shake his marvellous gift of intuition, and reinstate the hidebound old professionals. Never again,—had been the slogan of the besotted intellectuals in 1918. No more professional nonsense, was our cry of to-day. Anyone who refuses to march blindly forward at the orders of Adolf Hitler had better withdraw into private life, and live on his pension like a *Neese*, as the Hamburgers call a man whose folly loses him the fruits of many years' exertions. Fritsch and Blomberg had chosen the latter part, Keitel and Brauchitsch the former. Soon the call must come: All hands on deck, and clear for action. The amiable Göring had in friendly confidence given his British opposite number, Lord Londonderry, such information about the strength and striking-power of the *Luftwaffe* as had sent His Lordship back to London complacently. Germany had a thousand first-line aeroplanes, and five thousand machines in all, and technically the English craftsmanship was, of course, far superior to the German. It might be true (and unfortunate) that an English 'plane needed eleven minutes to get high enough to tackle a Heinkel. . . . And in America the isolationalists would surely prevent the warmonger Roosevelt's re-election. The pieces were on the board, and the players sat behind them, watching each other with appraising eyes. Moreover, it must not be forgotten that Stalin suffered from severe abdominal trouble and found it impossible to purge himself, to use the term of old-time doctors when they prescribed senna-pods or castor oil. . . . Albert Teetjen. . . . Who cared about Albert Teetjen now?"

Otto Lehmke made his report. He found it difficult to speak, being torn between old friendship, long years of intimacy, and his present grinding rage at Albert's greed. A man to whom he had always given credit, whom he had often defended against his wife's expressions of distrust, puts two thousand marks into his pocket, and on the strength of it buys a round of drinks and a box of discoloured and damaged cigars. The dirty dog! And what a sidelight on friendship!

But in imagining he was imparting some news to his two cronies, he was promptly undeceived. Both had known the secret for a long time, it having reached them from various sources; and indeed both of them had pricked up their ears when Albert was introduced to the Führer, and Party Comrade Footh made his offer for the Thetis ships. Pieder Preester puffed at his pipe, and looked at Comrade Lehmke with narrowed eyes.

"It's not pretty and it's not friendly—you're quite right. But there's a way to get our own back. Some of us will soon be off to Vienna, while others will stay at home. The former will inherit the property of wealthy Jews and pay rather profitable visits to ancient monasteries, while the latter will stick in Hamburg and feel rather surprised that we don't bring them any presents back. Well Otto Lehmke will be in on that party, but Albert Teetjen won't. Besides, the silly old water-diviner can be brought before a Court and charged with conduct unworthy of a Comrade—can't he, Comrade Vierkant?"

Just at that time editor Vierkant was busy fixing up a series of talks on the Hamburg radio. There were several five-year anniversaries to be celebrated in the year '38—stations on the march to victory, in the course of which the Party had seized, controlled, and exploited the State. Before the *Anschluss* became the pivot of interest, he wanted to deal with the most important events in half-hour discourses; he also wanted to be on the spot in Vienna, but not to sacrifice his substantial fee in Hamburg. He began with January 30th of course, the *Reichstag* fire would do for February, the boycott of the Jews for April, but he could not think of an event for March. The idea was that he should deliver these lectures as a sort of indication of events to come, one each week in February. Hence he had to hand in his syllabus to Norag that very day. Teetjen? All right, but no time for him now.

"Tell me, Preester, what did happen in March?"

Now Preester had the Party history at his fingers' ends, for on their way to Lehmke's that day, they had already been discussing Vierkant's difficulties.

"Wasn't the first show-down with the Stahlhelm some time in March, about the eighteenth? When the Hugenberg people first began to suspect which way the wind was blowing. And that the N.S.D.A.P. would never manage to jam themselves in between the Junkers and the Centre?"

"Right," said Vierkant, in high good humour. "That must have been in Brunswick. Thank you, Preester. It's an important point. The collapse of the Conservative hopes, and consternation of old Hindenburg, young Oskar, and his neighbour Januschauer. As for Teetjen, we'll just put him in cold storage, until he notices what's up. Then perhaps he'll begin to feel uncomfortable, and put his hand in his pocket to some purpose. Now we must get along to the train-stop—look out, the pavements are frozen. Put the drinks down to me, Lehmke, I'll settle them out of the advance fee for my talks."

When the two black-uniformed men entered the bright, warm tram-car, they did not put an end to any conversation—indeed the Hamburgers are taciturn folk, and ruminate in silence or exchange a few words in an undertone, of which no one else can catch the sense. But the conductor, who sold them their tickets, stepped through the forward door to the driver on his empty, breezy platform.

"Two chaps from the Preester Sturm," said he, and took his stand beside the driver so as to continue the conversation. At six there was a change of shift, and the news that his colleague had lately imparted to him as they passed the Wagnerstrasse, was still working in his mind and was likely to distract him for some time to come. His colleague, the driver, was familiar with the neighbourhood, being on agreeably intimate terms with the wife of a railway-clerk living thereabouts, a certain Frau Doligkeit, a pretty, tousle-headed blonde, the hue of her hair having been no doubt induced by the aid of peroxide or camomile tea. The news that Friedel Timme had been beheaded by a fellow who might at any moment board a No. I car, and demand and obtain a ticket (supposing he didn't own a season-ticket), which would be punched like anybody else's,—here was matter for reflection. The Transport Workers were highly esteemed as a union, or had been so in times past; they were the equals in reputation of the famous Hamburger Woodworkers of old days, now known as the Builders' Union, and were disposed to consider themselves superior to the Compositors and Printers, although these latter enjoyed a long-established repute in Hamburg. But in November, 1918 that was of less account, and hence the impression that Friedel Timme had left behind. On that occasion the Hamburg people had taken their affairs into their own hands, which is what is never forgotten.

The conductor went back to the bell, as his duty was, for there were passengers waiting at the Lübeckstrasse. Owing to the frost, sand had been strewn on the frozen streets, covered bins of it stood near the street corners, but anyone crossing the tram-lines might well slip, and then woe to the driver who did not pull up the car in a second. This one had a reddish grey-flecked moustache. The cold was such that he had swathed his neck in a woollen shawl, which gave him the air of a mediæval man-at-arms under his peaked cap. His name was Otto Prestow, and he had once had a sister, called Lene, who had, after her fashion, been one of the victims of the Reeperbahn case, but that was

by the way. In his mind the momentum with which his car sped along
the lines seemed a kind of driving-force accumulated against the day
when the Hamburgers began to understand how they were being fooled,
and to what abysses they had fallen in the past five years. A Germany
whose word no man could any longer take—in so far, indeed, as Germany
herself was in a position to distinguish black from white. A country
in which thousands of workers are thrashed into subservience with steel
rods for knowing what is due to them as workmen, and that their paltry
pay ought not to be squandered by half-baked students or B.M.W.
agents on luxurious villas and puffed up actresses. What was the
point of voyages to Denmark and Sweden, where a Strength-through-
Joy man could again meet a Comrade of old days before '33?

"Well," said driver Prestow, peering through the window before
him, "I used to buy a bit of liver sausage or what-not at the T's shop.
But I shan't do so any more, and no one who values my friendship will
do so either."

"O.K.," said the conductor. During a few minutes' silence this
brief dialogue acquired surprising significance, even when the car crossed
the brightly-lit square in front of the Central Railway Station, where the
great arc-lamps depended like gleaming South Sea fruits from their
tall palm-masts, and a wholly different public took possession of the
polished benches. Here the car became so full, that passengers were
standing on the forward platform—time enough for meditation and
reflection. That was an incitement to a boycott, thought his conductor, and a good thing too. A little demonstration against this
abominable régime—this Dirt-Reich as it might be called in Hamburg
speech. To think of the promises that had been made! Good Lord—
how cheap they had been bought, just because the Weimar Republic
hadn't been much of a show. But compared with the swindle that they
put across now, when they consult the so-called people or summon a
Reichstag, which does nothing but shout Yes, and *Heil*—well, we've
had about enough of it. And if Otto and he hadn't been such old friends
on the job, it would have been extremely imprudent of them to talk so,
thought the conductor. But he knew his man. And when they had all
been ten years younger, and Lene, his sister, was still a fine girl, hadn't
Otto saved my life and pulled me out of the Lower Elbe near Finkenwarder, by the Workers' bathing beach; the tide was always tricky on
the Elbe, and it was rising when I bet him I could swim across to
Nienstedten just as well as he could. And then the current caught us,
I lost my head and couldn't breathe, and was nearly done for—who
was it clutched me and soothed me as if I'd been a sick horse, and yelled
at me, and got me going again until we both lay on the opposite beach
like a couple of half-dead carp, gasping for air? And when I was on
the dole I would have had time to train for a better job, but there was no
marrow in my bones—margarine instead of butter or dripping. And
now, on our present rations, we do extra shifts—however, we aren't
young dogs any more, there's no more fun and no more swimming,
and Lene Prestow is gone, too. Thus ruminating, the conductor again
went through the forward door, and noted on his block the numbers of

tickets sold with a pencil topped with a bit of india-rubber.  Yes . . . Albert Teetjen, master-butcher.

A tramway does quite a number of kilometres in the course of a day. A considerable part of the gigantic urban area, known as Gross-Hamburg, is aligned along its course—an insect city of bricks, cement, and concrete, visible to the human eye; though the real insect-edifices, the termite mounds, by human standards and compared with the physical size of their builders, reach Matterhorn heights.  The termite builds vertically, man builds horizontally, and if Gross-Hamburg were set end-upwards, its height would in fact exceed all the mountains of the earth.  Such a tramway serves extremely well to spread a rumour among discreet citizens.  In that city a hundred thousand Nazis lived and bullied a hundred thousand convinced Anti-Nazis, and a million who accepted their leadership, as is not uncommonly the case.  And as man is not exactly happy or contented in his earthly existence, dexterous agitators with well-filled war chests find it fairly easy to impel him in any direction they may choose.

Lene Prestow had always teased and laughed at her brother Otto for his lethargic disposition.  He was accustomed to pass the end of the Wagnerstrasse many times a day, but it was not until his talk with the conductor that his thoughts about Teetjen the butcher took a more definite shape.  What would he do if no one entered his shop any more? How long would the wages of sin last him out?  What sort of running expenses were involved in such a business, as soon as the takings ceased? It was difficult to reach any conclusions on such economic matters without paper and pencil, especially for a man standing on the driver's platform of an electric tram, swinging the lever to the right and left, with his eyes on the rails and the street ahead of him, and his ears set to catch the bell, indicating that a passenger wants to get out at a Request stop, which is otherwise passed by in the interest of the Company, or, in other words, the Municipality.

To the first question Prestow could provide an answer without any difficulty: Teetjen must give up his business, leave the city, and find a job where he would be unknown.  The Party would pack him off to America, but not until he was completely ruined, and then they would use him in what had been recently called, after a catch-phrase that had come into favour in Spain—the Fifth Column.  He would be expected to work up interest for Hitler, spy on all Jews and *emigrés*, and discover cases of tax evasion, and whether the culprits were likely to slip across the frontier again in order to rescue some more of their property.  Perhaps the butcher would not be up to such work, indeed, he was probably not sufficiently astute or adaptable.  None the less, there was plenty of work to be done outside the frontiers—accidents occurred, as a result of which the enemies of the Nazis lost their lives.  And Teetjen's wife could surely get a servant's job in any great city, or go on the streets as poor Lene had done.  And even so she might be of service in various small matters to the overseas' branches of the NSDAP Foreign Organization.  Frau Teetjen looked quite pretty when she got into his car to go into town. It was Alma Doligkeit's opinion that with a little make-up she would soon develop the needful 'sex-appeal'. (Alma was fond of such English expressions—they were so 'up-to-date'.) But when he passed that corner next time, driver Prestow had made up his mind that Teetjen and wife would probably just creep away to stay with relations somewhere in the country, where everyone has a cousin or a great-uncle of sorts. Starve? Unfortunately not. But they certainly wouldn't stay in Hamburg. And if Hitler really started his war against the Soviets—but he wouldn't be so foolish. He, and his backers, knew very well that if he wanted to be carried to his grave fifty years later as a venerated and historic figure, like the late Count Posadowsky, under the title of Adolf the Great, or Adolf the Liberator, he had only to keep the peace; but that he must do. A Socialist State does not start an aggressive war. A Soviet republic does its duty to its citizens, and especially the younger of them, by utilizing all the resources of the country for purposes of defence, making the most elaborate preparations for the future. But it does not anticipate what may come. It will not start a war, for in war it is always the wrong people who are killed. So the Third Reich would be able to celebrate its fifty-year Jubilee on January 30th, 1983. For Hitler would not antagonize the Western powers. He was much too astute to be deluded by his own nonsense about the dagger-thrust of 1918. That was mere vote-catching, a demagogue's trick. The real background was quite otherwise. . . . So German Michel might sleep in peace—(why was that old bull-mastiff from the Lübeckerstrasse lumbering across the lines again so late?—he didn't pay the slightest attention to the bell!) And so, at the Golden Jubilee of the Third Reich, old Teetjen, who would then be tending pigs somewhere on a Bückeburger farm, could creep out of his stye and say to all the folks: "When I was young—believe it or not—I was presented to the Führer for my services to the State." And no one would say—And a very strange sort of State it was. Upon which the old boy would be offered a glass of schnapps, and retire once more to his stye.

And the No. 1 car disappeared into the evening haze, in which the arc lamps shimmered with an opalescent glow.

## CHAPTER TWO

### THE EARTH'S INTERIOR

AFTER THE NEW YEAR the business life of Hamburg entered on a quieter phase. Buyers had spent their money, and the tradesmen were making up their stocks, calculating their profits and losses, filling up their tax-returns, while they sent their employees, if they had any, on a holiday. Albert Teetjen left this part of his daily round to Stine, who was naturally better suited to the task. For his part, he used these days for what he had for some time described as his real profession, the more intensive study of the divining-rod. There must be books that would provide information about the earth's interior; they could be borrowed from a public library, and after reading them, he would know better where he stood. Stine, indeed, had a ticket at the nearest branch-library and could change her book every week. And he thought of Tom Barfey in his attic with all his devotion to knowledge, so ready to make good the loss of physical pleasures by spiritual meditations.

Tom laughed complacently when Stine brought him Albert's request for advice. He had, of course, no intention of giving the axe-man any genuine information about the books of popular scientists addressed to the ordinary reader. Expressions like magma, or viscous silicates, would be completely above the head of a man like Albert. And he could not even begin to understand the recent scientific discoveries about the iron kernel of the earth, the continuous increase in temperature and pressure, earth-magnetism, and the distinction between the magnetic and the physical North Pole. What business had such a moustachioed oaf within the precincts of science? But apart from his joy that Stine should be sitting at the table, praising his little cooking-stove, the delightful warmth of the attic, and his dexterity in stuffing newspapers into the cracks of the larger windows—he could, he said, suggest a book for Albert Teetjen. It was called *A Journey to the Centre of the Earth*, and was written by the Frenchman, Jules Verne—he spelt the name for her as she wrote down the title; a book that might have been written for Hamburgers, as it started in that city; a Hamburg professor was the hero, who had discovered an old volume written by an Icelander, Arne Saknussen, and he set sail with his nephew from the port of Hamburg, to Iceland, and then, following Saknussen's directions, went down into an extinct volcano, and so into the interior of the earth, where he was to meet with all manner of marvels and adventures. "It will keep Albert quiet all right, Stine," he said, stroking her hand, which lay outstretched on the table. "And when he has finished it, bring it here, I would like to look at it again. I can then give you a better answer if he wants anything explained."

Teetjen, master-butcher, had no very clear conception of what really distinguished a novel from a narrative of fact. Having attended an average sort of Hamburg elementary school, he was aware that there were such people as writers, who did not need to adhere exactly to the reality which was all-important to a book-keeper, a doctor, or a schoolmaster. A great many people told what in fact were lies, and fairy-tales consisted wholly of such material—harmless and entertaining as they were; for, after all, nobody had ever found seven little kids in the belly of a wolf. He, Albert, like most lads of his age, was never tired of such stories, and the sad thing was that mothers had so little time to tell them. But the reading of printed books on one's own account was quite a different matter. The printed word must conform to the truth, otherwise anyone could come along and deceive and delude the public, which was forbidden, and was indeed a matter that was taken up and severely dealt with by the police; there were constant reports in the papers, in the Police-Court News, about swindlers who had induced people to part with their money under false pretences, and had to spend years under lock and key for what they had done. The printed word stood in unexpressed but definite relationship with truth. And when the Republican newspapers stated that General Ludendorff had, after the war, had dealings with a man by the name of Tausend who claimed to be able to make gold, ex-servicemen in general expected that the editors would be imprisoned. But they were not, and among Lehmke's customers the conclusion was—being an occasion when Albert's father crashed his fist on the table so that the beer-glasses rang—that there was no justice in the Republic, since a man like Ludendorff must know that a man who claimed to make gold was a swindler and ought to be shown up. So when a certain Jules Verne described people climbing down into a volcano in order to reach the interior of the earth, there was no need for the story to be literally true. Some of the incidents were certainly invented to amuse the reader, as for example the absurd professor who lived in Hamburg with his housekeeper and nephew. But just as it was consonant with Nature and fact that what the wolf had swallowed should be found in its belly and not in its skull, so the account of the interior of the earth in this novel must be true. Hence no Public Prosecutor had arisen to prohibit the book *Mein Kampf*, although when it appeared the Republic was going full-steam ahead. What was there printed about the world-conspiracy of the Jews and Marxists, plutocracy and the hereditary hatred of France for Germany, was not to be disputed either, nor that International Socialism must be opposed by a National and a German brand of Socialism, in which the common good came before private profit, and the money market was stripped of its disguise. Truth, even an unpleasant truth, must be faced. And if anyone had maintained that Alma Doligkeit had shorter legs than Stine Teetjen, it would have been no use for the railway clerk to bring an action for slander. Whatever rejoinder he might have felt called upon to make, length of leg is a matter that can be established, by inspection or actual measurement. Everyone learned at school that in the beginning God made Heaven and Earth, and that the earth had been barren and desolate; that the spirit of God had brooded upon the waters, had to be presumed, for He had to be cruising about somewhere before He started to create. And a Hamburg boy could very well understand that the primeval world was a world of water, even though it was some time before he was taken down the Elbe to Cuxhaven and made the personal acquaintance of the blusterous monster known as the North Sea. (Later on, indeed, he had visited Heligoland, and been extremely sick on the voyage, but that was another story.) Latterly, however, schoolmasters had made little use of the story of the Creation, and upper forms were taught that the sun did not rise, as he was plainly seen to do, but was in fact suspended in empty space, while the earth revolved around him on its own axis, which the teacher demonstrated by means of a cleverly constructed little

apparatus consisting of a lighted candle and a number of small globes.
Each of these little globes represented a so-called planet, heavenly bodies
having broken away from the sun millions of years before, one of them
being the earth, accompanied by a much smaller cheese, the moon.  The
brighter scholars were then given a little more instruction in the science
museum about the movements of the planets, and a professor had then
explained that the knowledge of astronomy had been much extended
of late, and that the current hypothesis was that the sun with his entire
company of planets was in process of moving towards the constellation
of Hercules which was so far away that light therefrom took ten or twenty
years to reach the earth.  Nothing was now said about the fact that God
would have been hard put to it to create the whole universe in six days.
The brighter boys formed their own conclusions on the subject, and
Pastor Terspegen was fond of insisting that the biblical account was
intended to be taken symbolically; God's days each represented
uncounted millions of our earthly years.  But it was plain that there was
a catch in all this from the fact one of the aforesaid God's commandments
upon Sinai had been: Thou shall not kill.  Whereupon the people of
Israel promptly engaged in vigorous campaigns against the Canaanites,
the purpose of which was to rob them of their land.  It was true that
laws devised to meet peace conditions could not be wholly applied to
a state of war.  From which it was understandable that wars did happen,
and always would happen, because men get sick of the toils of peace,
of truckling to the law, and behaving with proper respect to authority.
After all, man was not made of paper but of flesh and blood, comparable
to his domicile the earth, which is heated by an inner fire, and vomits
up lava now and then, producing upheavals and shocks, which destroy
tens of thousands of human beings at one stroke.  From his boyhood
days, Albert had preserved the recollection of a certain Mt. Pelée on
an island that belonged to the French, in some great ocean, where there
had been an earthquake and a tidal wave which had cost the lives of
as many people as the whole population of Altona.  He had then recalled
San Francisco, too, where three Hamburgers had lost their lives.

He sat at his ease under the lamp after closing-time.  His cigar,
one of the despised discoloured batch, was drawing well, a cutting
wind would be whistling round the chimneys up above, and here and
there a star would be glittering through the flying clouds.  But all
that was out of doors.  In the room itself the atmosphere was one
of utter peace and comfort.  Stine, with her auburn mop of hair sat
opposite him, darning socks, or repairing the damage that a man's
trade inevitably inflicted on his underclothes, though the sorely-tried
housewife would always maintain that he tore them on purpose.  Under
such conditions it was with all the greater satisfaction that he read about
stormy seas, savage saurian monsters, scaly serpents as broad as tram-
lines, and men before the Flood—all preserved in the interior of the earth
and foretold by that bold Norse Viking, Arne Saknussen, a typical Aryan.

"Stine," said Albert, "now comes an exciting bit.  Listen—or if
you've finished your mending, I wish you would read it to me."

And then Stine, in her schoolgirl voice and sing-song Holstein accent, read Chapter VII, in which the Professor's expectations were considerably dashed. "They were trying to get to the interior of the earth, but so far as I can see they didn't get very far. It looks as though Jules Verne himself doesn't know much about it, and doesn't care to make it up as he goes along."

There was indeed a great deal which Albert would have liked to know. But his superiors had said nothing about these matters, and he knew nobody whom he could ask. As, for instance, how coal and petroleum came into the earth; whether the whole earth was composed of iron, because in accordance with common opinion it was magnetic, which explained the compass that had guided Columbus on his voyage to the West. How it had been proved that the earth was a globe, flattened at the Poles, though all evidence indicated the contrary. And whether it was to be believed that down below, beyond the Professor's reach, there was a core of iron or a central fire, as he had seen depicted in a popular compilation during the late war. Of course he did not for one moment believe what had been told him in those days by a Catholic friend from Fulda—that everyone knew that Hell was situated in the interior of the earth, in the shape of an enormous furnace, as big as Hamburg, and hollow like a baking-oven, in which devils carried out their duties, like the staff of a delousing station, except that souls, instead of clothes, were cleansed, and sins burnt instead of lice. "And if your religious papers are in order, you're lucky and get through quick, like when you can produce a delousing certificate from the garrison doctor. If not, you have to go on stewing until your relatives weigh in with Masses for the dead and prayers to your Patron Saint. And what I'm now telling you, only goes for Purgatory, old boy. Hell is a place you can't get out of at all."

Albert had been much amused by all these Catholic fables. The priests might persuade the Italians that a poet by the name of Dante had actually gone down into Hell, but he wasn't going to believe that. He did not believe in life after death; the next world, he thought, must be appallingly overcrowded, if all the thousand generations of his fellow-citizens sat around there clacking their teeth and chanting halle-lujahs. His Stine thought differently on these matters; well, a woman was always a woman, and needed something to satisfy her mind. It was difficult for a butcher to talk about life after death, and equally difficult for a soldier. "Live so that when you die you will be glad that you have lived," was the parting message given to him by his headmaster when he left school. How that was to be managed, was no doubt another story, but a very impressive one, dealing with obedience to father, emperor, Führer. No, he preferred the adage: "Do right and fear no man." For the rest, stand firm upon your own legs, learn your job, and let no man get in your way. No one could claim more than one life, and the domain of Heaven, the home of souls, not bodies, had never been visited by any man. No, he liked the earth, and was even attracted by the interior of that vast home establishment. As described by Jules Verne, it was certainly rather crude; he would have pictured it as much more mechanically organized, with lifts, pipes, and cables—the sort of substructure that was revealed when the Wandsbeker Chaussée was being excavated for repairs. And the fact that he really had the gift of discovering subterranean water-courses or ore deposits, seemed to him perfectly in order. Dr. Laberdan had talked about radio-active rays emanating from such accumulated elements, and said that it was a matter of proof that such centres of radiation were particularly sensitive to lightning. And the Chairman, the ex-mesmerist, had related all this to terrene electricity, though Dr. Laberdan had rather turned up his nose at this hypothesis. Well, now that business was so slack, confound it, he would have time, when the snow began to lie, to continue in Wandsbek Park the experiments with the divining-rod begun at Fuhlsbüttel.

Stine, for her part, was not inclined towards disputes on matters of faith. She had no sort of fear of Hell—Christ had suffered crucifixion to banish such a fear; Death, where is thy sting, Hell where is thy victory? Nor did she ever think about what might happen to people after death. She somehow felt that there was a sort of connection between people, and the flowers planted on their graves. Why, otherwise, should death and dying always be associated with the blossoming and withering of growing things, with wreaths and pots of flowers? And in spring, when all Nature awakened, was it not absurd to believe, as Albert did, that a created being like man could wither and pass away? When she sat at the table, glad to have Albert at home with her, she inwardly laughed at his Professor from the Laubengasse—there was no such street in Hamburg—his nephew, his Icelander, and all the rest of it. Had we not all of us one Father—as Grandmother had taught her; had not a God created us all? The rage to-day was all for Race, yesterday it was astrologers and horoscopes that were in favour, and the day before that, the Prophet Weissenberg and his white cheeses, had been the popular idol. These things were fashions, that changed like the vogue for checks or stripes, jumpers or pullovers. If she had had a child, which after all was not yet beyond hope, she would have known what to teach it, to help it to be healthy and happy upon earth. But unfortunately since the affair of the axe, there had been no indications of this kind. Well, there was nothing to be done about it. She, too, did not believe in a God, accessible to prayer; that was a female attitude, and for such people the Catholics provided their Mother of God, and a larger company of Saints, maids, women, princesses and martyrs, which would have been all right, and indeed very attractive and even seductive, if it had not been combined with all this nonsense about convents, with their monks and nuns. What could they understand about life? O man, do not forget the best thing of all—so ran the words of a fairy tale, and of course this reference was to eternal happiness. But the best of love between a man and woman was the experience that, far from becoming tired of each other, they fell more deeply in love as the years went by, which was what a hamstrung celibate could never understand. Even that forthcoming youth, Tom Barfey, knew more about it than a black Brother, vowed to poverty, chastity, and obedience. Love is eternal—those were the grandest words in the whole Bible. And though her Albert could have done better to have found another way out of his quandary than the one that had brought him to Fuhlsbüttel and to Footh . . . But stay. Was it he that had found it—surely she had been the agent? He had taken the decisive step, when the contents of the till were ebbing out, but she it was who had set their little ship upon its course and hoisted fresh sails. Albert's had been the arm, and—if you like—the heart; but hers had been the directing head and hand, and what she had done had brought her much inward satisfaction, not to mention commendation and gratitude. There he sat at the table with his head on his arm, fingering his way through the old volume that contained such very tall stories about the interior of the earth; but it was she, again, who had got it out of the library, and set in motion all the thoughts about which he now and then asked questions. Man and woman, one and indivisible they were, as the newspapers said, in flesh and in spirit. A fire in the interior of the earth—well, why not? And she was quite prepared to believe that hidden watercourses, or deposits of iron and petroleum, gave off magnetic rays. Her Albert was certainly no ordinary man—she had known that long before Dr. Laberdan or the Chairman had found it out. And in her family, at any rate in the Geisow part of it, there had been more than one instance of something like second-sight, which she hoped she had not inherited to any extent. But, for the rest, her strong points were her honesty, good conscience, and a certain amiability to everyone she met, and these sufficed. It might be that the survivors of a strange animal world still ranged the interior of the earth—she, Stine Teetjen, took no interest in such heathenish nonsense, nor in any of the disputes between German Christians and the Confessional Churches. Her Hymn book and her Testament were all she needed for the acts of life and death, and He who had brought man upon the earth, surely knew why He had done so and for what purpose. . . . It was, however, a pity that it was too cold for any windows to be opened, as some nice dance music would certainly be coming across from the Lawerenzens, and she would gladly have dislodged Albert from his book, and made him dance a foxtrot round the table.

The lull in business was not much noticed by either Albert or Stine. In January, as was the case with everyone, a tax instalment fell due, and Stine was proud to be able to send it to the Revenue Office, although the money order made a large hole in her resources. But when, at the end of the year, payments fell due to the Meat Corporation for deliveries, rent for the flat and the shop had to be paid in advance in January for the ensuing quarter, a comparison of the totals with the receipts for the last two or three months did take Stine's breath away. It was, indeed, a feeling shared by the owners of many small businesses about that time of year. The figures, tall or round, filled her with disquiet, and even with accesses of fear; especially when she found that for the last three months of the preceding year their expenditure had balanced their receipts. It was not, indeed, until the large and special January payments fell due that the lurking fear that such outgoings might not be made good by receipts became insistent. However, Albert then in-spected his supplies of mutton, pork and beef, which were maintained in prime condition during the cold months, clapped her on the shoulder, and cheerfully reminded her that they needed to buy hardly anything for the present, and that in a few days, or weeks if need be, another profitable little propaganda slogan might very likely come their way. Stine did not tell him that Tom had latterly become very pressing, and she had had very great difficulty—to use the popular phrase—in telling him where he got off. She was glad to abandon the un-pleasant subject, and turn her mind from national and municipal taxes to more agreeable matters, of which there were many in the air—such as Herr Footh's wedding.

It was not so easy for Albert to dispose of the subject which became so prominent at the outset of every year. As a conscientious Comrade and citizen he had to face the problem how and where he should enter the earnings of his axe at Fuhlsbüttel. The item must undoubtedly appear in his tax-return; but where it ought to figure under professional income, or as an incidental earning, or as exceptional item not likely to recur, was a matter which called for expert decision. As he had done the job in a mask, no enquiries need be anticipated if he omitted the payment altogether. Comrade Footh had paid him the sum in question, which he in turn had received from the judicial authorities. But, if this two thousand four hundred marks appeared in Herr Footh's return, it would surely figure as a payment possibly connected with the name of Teetjen. The revenue authorities were now extremely inquisitive, and spent as much time and trouble, as the Republican officials used to do, in analysing returns and remorselessly pursuing any such indica-tions. The name of Teetjen might well catch the eye of the gentry in the green uniforms, set them thinking and provoke a further enquiry. What was the cheapest way of dealing with this item? No man was called upon to do more than his duty, especially when he had so far exceeded it as Albert Teetjen had done in the previous autumn. He had thus sat down to his tax return in a condition of some bewilder-ment. An indication that his business had suddenly produced over two thousand marks more than in the previous year, would very likely lead to an increased assessment. On the other hand, entered as a lottery prize, it was perhaps suspiciously large, and as an incidental earning from non-professional occupation, would almost inevitably provoke investigation. With what result? It might certainly rouse a great deal of recrimination and abuse. Lawyer Cohn, who had often represented and advised his father had disappeared since the April boycott five years before; he hadn't needed another lawyer since, and didn't feel inclined to look for one now: nor did he care to bother Comrade Footh. So there was nothing for it but to ask Otto Lehmke's advice—or himself choose one of the prescribed headings, even if it might not be the one most advantageous to himself, for there was every argument against letting Lehmke know how he had come by the money. But if he deceived Lehmke, he might as well deceive the Revenue Office: indeed he would not consult Lehmke unless he could decide on no other expedient.

He left the tax return lying on the table for several days, and hung about the cattle-yard trying to find out how his fellow-butchers set about filling up their papers. He also tried to invent a story that would as far as possible connect this sort of incidental earning with the implement of his profession, but could think of nothing. And then one evening, when he had got to the end of his novel, and had accompanied the heroes on their raft out of the crater of Stromboli, he made up his mind, put on his collar and coat, and unhooked the leather jacket which he had given to himself as a Christmas present. He had presented Stine on the same sacred anniversary with a black rain-coat of the best American cloth, with nickel clasps in place of buttons, which might easily be taken for a rubber coat. They both came from the Köppler Brothers' Drapery Store, which enjoyed a certain popularity in middle-class circles as a family business, because four brothers, Siegfried, Arthur, Hugo and Louis had, by their common labours, built it up into a thriving concern —four Jews, all very much alike, large genial men, who talked in that delightful Hamburg blend of High and Low German which has been not unfairly compared to an alloy of copper and zinc. The disastrous end of three of these brothers, however, three months after Albert Teetjen met his own, was even then written in the stars.

But when Albert went across to 'The Tank' there was no one to talk to at Lehmke's. The new sign had been hoisted into place, the bar cleaned up, the woodwork new painted, the tables and chairs scrubbed, the carpets rubbed with bread, and some of the planks in the floor patched, as Dörte pointed out to her neighbour with a complacent wave of the hand. But her parents were away for a little holiday, staying with relatives on the Steinhuder Meer, a large lake in the Hanover country; and they would not be back for four or five days. Yes, Herr Teetjen had not been round for a long while, and Frau Stine had not told him the news. But business would soon begin to hum, in a way that would make Albert open his eyes. Albert looked about him in astonishment, then nodded and offered his congratulations. He would come again soon. The Lehmke's had plainly had a very good year; but he would never feel quite as much at home here as he used to do. Well, he would go back, and sit down alone to struggle with his tax return. He did not say anything about that to Dörte, but he took his decision, as he tramped home enjoying the chill night air and the stillness of the empty streets. There would certainly be a sharp frost on the Steinhuder Meer, deep snow, and probably ice thick enough to skate on. He must put down the two thousand marks as a lottery prize, or a legacy, which came cheaper. Should he ask Footh's advice first? He would consider the point.

Next morning he did ring up Footh's office on the public telephone, and received a prompt and effusive greeting from Fräulein Petersen. "Aha, Herr Teetjen, we were wanting a word with a butcher. Shall I run round, or have you got business at the harbour anyway? It's about the wedding, Herr Teetjen, a cold buffet and meat for the celebrations on the evening before. Of course we thought of you at once."

Footh's wedding did actually plug the hole in the Teetjens budget

which had been so sadly torn by rent and taxes.   In the ensuing months
to come Albert realized that this order had not really saved him, it had
indeed concealed the gravity of the position, so long as there had been
still time to buck the business up a bit.   The result was that he light
heartedly relied on something always turning up, even when things
were really almost hopeless.   A man who believed, as he did, in the
divining-rod and his own good luck, thought Stine later on, ought not
to be surprised if he found himself in queer street.

But, for the present, there was a wedding, a party, and a dance,
in Fräulein Blüthe's own old Rhenish tradition, a good deal adapted to
suit Hamburg customs.   The actual wedding, of course, had to be
solemnized in a stiff and ceremonious manner, as befitted the reputation
of the firm and the Footh family, although the said family could scarcely
be said to have existed a generation ago.   But the eve of the wedding
could provide a celebration of a very different kind, and indeed it
did.   It was a fancy-dress party, which was discussed at Harveste-
hude with lifted eyebrows and every mark of disapproval.   Shipowner Footh as a Roman Cæsar and his future wife as Messalina in
a long brocade dress (and next to nothing underneath)—the costly
gold-threaded material was said to have come from a Spanish monastery.
Governor Koldewey's three daughters, dressed alike in light blue, white
and pink, presenting at the same time figures from the old German
fairy-tale, One-Eye, Two-Eye, Three-Eye, and three of Herr Footh's
"Äuglein" ships.   Father Blüthe and Ruckstuhl, the Bank Manager, in
red hunting coats under black dominos, were celebrating their reunion
with their old comrade-in-arms, Teetjen, who had got himself up as a
miner: black uniform with long leggings, leather apron beneath the loose
jacket, a miner's lamp attached to his broad girdle, the brass clasp of
which bore the legend "Good luck!" and in his hand, not a pick but a
divining-rod.   He had emerged, said he, up from the interior of the earth,
to wish and bring good fortune and every blessing to his friend Footh and
his young wife, who was not called Blüthe for nothing.   But the real flower
of the evening—and on that there was only one opinion—was presented
by Frau Stine Teetjen, as Lorelei, with her red hair loose and a golden
comb in it.   She had in fact wanted to wear her white wedding dress.
But Albert, who had become familiar with the second-hand clothing
establishment when he had hired his tail coat, took her to the good lady
who supplied him on that occasion, and that portly dame, formerly
robe-mistress of a theatrical company, on the dissolution of which she
had acquired the costumes that formed the nucleus of her stock, had
frowned on Stine's proposal.

"Why not Lorelei—with that pretty hair?   And you'll need an
eau-de-nil silk dress, and gossamer veil.   I've got just the thing hanging
up yonder, we'll try it on at once.   And a paste diadem, or a coral-
necklace, if you prefer it.   Quite the water-nixey or sea-maiden!"

But when she had herself dressed her customer in the changing-room,
she clapped her hands at the sight of the metamorphosed tradesman's
wife—the shapely line of her shoulders above the deep square-cut yoke,
though it was a pity the hands, so coarsened by housework, were scarcely

those of a Lorelei. However, long glacé-kid gloves would meet that difficulty. When Stine saw herself in the great mirror lit by an unshaded bulb, she blushed. No woman ought to look like that. There was a lilac glitter in her eyes—and what sort of shoes could she wear with such a dress? But Frau Kaltmann could help her here as well. She would look out a quite suitable dancing-shoe, unless she preferred to buy a pair—surely a lady with her looks. . . .

But Stine shook her head and laughed; she would not need new shoes when her corpse floated down the Elbe. Hired ones would do quite well. But Albert, full of astonishment and pride at his wife's transformation, was eager to buy her a pair, and had to be decisively deterred by her from doing so. But he laid down, without a word, the price asked by Frau Kaltmann for her and his costumes, which—thought Stine—would probably absorb the whole profit on what he had supplied to Footh. Well, it didn't matter for an occasion of this kind.

Yes, Teetjen had never imagined nor experienced an evening like this. The loud-speaker discoursed music from every station on the continent. In the hall of the house on the Harvestehuder Weg more lights were burning than he had ever seen before, and Frau Stine danced —danced with men whom she had never seen, and who all introduced themselves to her—lumbering captains from Herr Footh's ships, jaunty clerks from his office, friends from the Transport Association, and a few of the women, too, insisted on a dance with her. Thyra for example, Herr Koldewey's second daughter, quite fell in love with her—she had never met, she said, so marvellous a Frisian type, and Stine was seized by a strange craving to enjoy every moment of it, she felt so full of life and delight in this dazzling environment. She could see how everyone envied Albert when he got up from the table where he was sitting with some men and came across to her, smelling rather of alcohol, for he too was having a good time. Yes, that—felt Herr Footh—was the glory of the Third *Reich*, as he rose from his gilt chair on the landing and looked down the staircase. A new society was here embodied, the butcher's wife dances with a princess from the Villa Koldewey and looks—well, just too lovely. "Heil Hitler!" he shouted with uplifted arm when, shortly before midnight, the Statthalter honoured the party with his presence.

Anneliese Blüthe, slim and golden, trod the steps of the tango as partner of the highest official in the State of Hamburg and flung a glance from her keen eyes through the throng of guests up at old Herr Ruckstuhl, who stood with her father leaning against the balustrade. Hers was the victory here, and hers alone. Yonder was the Koldewey girl dancing with H. P. Footh—a farewell dance, it might well be called. She would not share in Shipowner Footh's advancement. It was not she who had roused his ambition, and impelled him to get the Jewish ships; and it would not be she who would bear him sons and heirs. She was wearing a golden dress from Spain; but one day she would make him master of Spanish ships, which Captain Carstangen had been describing to her, and her partner must help her in this task. The battle was not yet won, neither in Spain, nor the battle in the Hamburg shipping world. But both lay straight ahead, and clearly visible on the horizon. This alluring music came from New York. . . . And she leaned yet closer on the Statthalter's arm, and murmured in the Rhenish accent, that would appeal to a fellow-Rhinelander, that anyone who couldn't see that public affairs were in the best of hands and industry never more prosperous, must be either actually or wilfully blind. She thought about such things, of course, whereas that alluring little Lorelei, Frau Teetjen, hadn't an idea in her head. She, Anneliese, resolved that the relations between the butcher and her husband should come to an end. No; she would not dance with the handsome Albert.

Dancing was not much in Albert's mind either. He sat, with a rather supercilious air, among his one-time comrades-in-arms, paying particular attention to Herr Ruckstuhl; he applied himself rather too freely to the multifarious bottles on every table, full of satisfaction at the thought that his provisions had found favour with the guests. Political affairs were being discussed at his table; it seemed that there was a political crisis in the offing, which, however, the Führer was weathering with his accustomed skill. Herr Schacht was to be replaced by a certain Herr Funk; and measures had to be taken to deal with the considerable unemployment that would result if the armament programme were reduced in the interest of more active and better business relations with the Western democracies. The *Reichswehr* rejected any such project, so the Führer had taken over the supreme command of fleet and army, new generals had been called into council; and Göring himself, master of the Hermann Göring works, the Air Force, and the Gestapo, would launch a Four Year Plan, at which certain other States, and one Eastern neighbour especially, would open their eyes very wide indeed. Such were the subjects of discussion, while Albert sat by, understanding only half of what was said, but conscious of a glow of contentment and ease. If factory chimneys smoked so profusely, and men at table talked in millions, surely he could do something to feather his own little nest, and apply himself without misgiving to his divining-rod and his Stine—the prettiest woman in the room, said Albert to himself; there she was, swinging round in a waltz with the *Reichstatthalter*, flinging a smile at him as she passed, so that he had to get up and lean against the balustrade. If the next dance were a polka or a slow foxtrot, he would give these people a little display of dancing by a young, good-looking married couple.

They had to take a cab home, and pay the driver an outrageous fare. But Stine laid her head on his shoulder, and fell asleep almost at once, and as they slid through the snowy, frosty night, Albert reflected that the evening had been worth it all, for such as these were hours of glory. A miner from the bowels of the earth, and a water-fairy—a Lorelei. . . . Footh had been dilating on Austria and Vienna, and his own efforts to reach down to the Danube, so as to bring Rumanian petrol up-river into Germany—well, he, Albert Teetjen, must see whether he couldn't get a cut out of all this. Hamburg S.S. were to be posted to the Saxon or Bavarian frontier—but at the moment his mind was rather confused. To-morrow, when he had had his sleep out, and to-morrow was fortunately Sunday, and if business looked like being as slack as ever, they

need not open at all, he could lie in bed and think a bit. How charming
Stine had looked . . . and, by the way, they must take a lunch of liver-
sausage to Frau Kaltmann when the remnants of party supper were
returned. She had a knowing eye and an air of experience.

The New Year started in strange fashion, Albert thought. People
bought neither meat nor sausage, possibly in recognition of the incessant
Government propaganda in favour of eating fish, so as to reduce superfluous imports. And it had proved painfully effective. But for the
Lawerenzens and Reitlin, the situation would have indeed looked black.
As a matter of fact, Stine noticed that people greeted her as amicably
as ever, but were reluctant to engage in any kind of talk. Teetjen began
to feel very sore at having spent more on the ball and the drive home than
the amount of two days' takings in the shop. Moreover, he had been
deeply hurt by the news, imparted to him through the Lehmkes, now
returned, that he was not to take part in the invasion of Austria, but
would remain with the nucleus formation to be left in Hamburg. Many
of the Comrades had already gone, and were now winter-sporting in the
Bavarian-Austrian borderlands from Hindelang in the Allgäu as far up
as Traunstein, plunging about on skis, while waiting for orders to
concentrate. Albert's inability to ski was a sufficient explanation of the
fact that so steady and experienced an S.S. man had to be left behind;
Chancellor Schuschnigg might plunge into a crazy and fratricidal fight if
his German brethren from the Old *Reich* came to the help of their Party
Comrades, just as in 1914. Except that on this occasion the Serbians
were not concerned; the conflict was between the nationalist Austrians
and the bigoted clericals of the Christian-Socialist *Heimwehr* Government, who, blinded by their Catholic God, dared to array themselves
against the greatest German of all history. It was reported that Adolf
Hitler had thus described himself with proud modesty in the interview
which Chancellor Schuschnigg had been ordered to attend—and indeed
how else *could* he describe himself? Albert had heard this from Comrade
Vierkant, who had returned to Hamburg to deliver the second of his
wireless talks on "Five Years of the Third *Reich*"—talks which had proved
so apposite that the Radio authorities had suggested that their number
should be increased to six, and that the subject for the month of May
should be the abolition of the Trade Unions, and the holocaust of books
which had taken place in the German University cities somewhere about
the twelfth of that month. As a subject of his sixth talk he might
perhaps choose, in connection with Austrian developments, the gradual
pacification of Europe, as accomplished in accordance with the Führer's
personal and masterly plan. The effacement of the degradation of
Versailles by the Saar plebiscite, the remilitarization of the Rhineland,
the union with Austria—so many brutal outrages inflicted on Germany
by the haughty conqueror had been at last avenged. If the brethren
of the Ostmark were now to return into the old *Reich*, thus reversing
the fate imposed on her as far back as 1740, when Frederick II, then not
yet "the Great", had been forced to appeal to the sword in the assertion

of his dynastic claims to Silesia, there could be only one problem left
before the bells could ring for final peace—Danzig and the Polish corridor.
But that question would be settled in accordance with the claims of
justice and of international order, since the ci-devant Entente now had
to deal with a resolute and self-dependent partner to a bargain. All
this had been obvious to the seeing eye since 1933; the flower had budded
and then slowly blossomed. Now for Austria—"and we may think
ourselves fortunate, Comrade Teetjen, that events are moving at such
speed."

Yes, Vierkant was a knowing and astute Party Comrade; he sat by
Albert that evening in Lehmke's bar-parlour, which, though still pervaded
with a faint odour of varnish, and looking very neat, had now resumed
a more homely air. He explained to Albert that the Austrian Fascists
were satellites both of the Church and of Capital, and had only survived
under the ægis of their great Italian brother, backed by Jewish and
democratic intrigue. When, in '34, the Marxists were overthrown,
Messrs. Dollfuss and Schuschnigg proclaimed themselves conquerors,
but they were merely snow-sweepers and street-cleaners, who prepared
a passage for the real master of the house. If Herr Schuschnigg, as he
threatened to do, held a bogus plebiscite, the wrath of the German-
Austrians would explode, guns would roar, tanks would rumble in to the
attack, and bombs rain down upon the industrial suburbs of Vienna. But
as Adolf Hitler was also a man of peace, as was now accepted by England
and France, and as Mussolini had understood and come to terms with
the great German *Reich* on the occasion of last year's visit, no Austrian
aristocrat could be so lost to decency as to shed his own brother's blood
against his own prestige. Comrade Teetjen therefore would miss
nothing if he stayed in Hamburg and stuck to his divining-rod,—on the
contrary. After Austria, only the Sudetenland and Danzig remained
on the programme, but experienced practitioners upon the divining-rod
might then perhaps be needed. . . .

In the twilight hours of those February days, Albert perambulated
Wandsbek park, rod in hand. It quivered over many places, and now
and again jerked downwards. He was obviously growing more sensitive.
God knew what lay beneath those lawns, now coated with crackling,
frozen snow. The Chairman of the Association had explained how
subterranean currents changed direction into new courses; but that the
corpses or skeletons of the dead emitted radio-active emanations to
which the divining-rod responded, not indeed in the hands of every
practitioner, but in those more highly gifted, such as Herr Teetjen.
There were many instances of people who were sensitive in this way and
could indicate, without the aid of any instrument, places where some
mystery lurked; just as horses shied at spots where the victim of a crime
lay buried. Superstitious people in old days had connected this sort of
thing with survival after death, and belief in an immortal soul; to-day
we knew that it was a matter of radiation, in regard to which much
remained to be discovered, before we could claim to understand the
invisible world, the world of rays and vibrations, which was wholly
unconnected with rewards and punishments. As Albert walked along

under the trees, conscious from time to time of a quiver in his fingers, and an unmistakable jerk of the rod, he reflected that his Stine was not such a little noodle as he had thought, but that she had merely expressed, in rather an old-fashioned and grandmotherly way, the matters with which he was now concerned.  It would indeed have been unpleasant to carry such a rod through Ohlsdorf cemetery, and possibly over certain lately-buried, headless bodies by no means yet dissolved into dust.  But a dowser might have to face just such an ordeal, and an old soldier must not shrink from challenging any ghost, and, if need be, lay about him with his rod.  If only some customers would enter his shop again! Well, the capture of Vienna might mean a fresh start.  He would now go home, and get his wife to read to him out of another book, lent by Comrade Vierkant, a little Cosmos volume on volcanoes and earthquakes; the excellent Jules Verne—Vierkant had smilingly explained—had been guilty of some exaggeration in the account of the journey from Hekla to Stromboli.  Perhaps an executioner's axe emitted radio-active rays, and people unconsciously responded to them, so that something—they knew not what—prevented them from crossing his threshold.  Against this possibility there was a certain remedy.  Suppose he wrapped it in an old indiarubber apron?  No harm in trying, after all.  There was probably an old one of his father's in the linen cupboard drawer.  He must behave as though he were scientifically minded, and an offspring of the new age.  "Endeavour and grow clever," said the old adage, which was as true to-day as it was yesterday.

## CHAPTER THREE

### THE AXE MUST GO

IN TIME TO come, Albert Teetjen realized that Comrade Footh's wedding Sunday was the last day on which the effort to conceal the facts of his existence could be maintained.  Next day, not one human soul entered the shop, and it became clear to him that something had happened.  He sat with legs outstretched behind his counter, wagged his heavy head from side to side, while a confusion of thoughts and ideas sped to and fro across his mind.  What was the explanation?  It was intolerable.  Was someone deliberately striking at his livelihood?  Could it be just chance? It never occurred to him that he was being actually boycotted.  All through that grey and rainy morning he was torn between the two conflicting explanations—that it was mere chance, or a manifestation

of jealousy on the part of those who considered him and Stine as having
got above themselves.    During this conflict of mind he sorted out the
pink and white cash-register slips for the whole of '37 by way of pre-
tending to himself and Stine that he was absorbed in his tax returns.
In the afternoon he donned his leather jacket and strolled down the
Wandsbeker Chaussée, and along many of the shopping streets in the
district.   His fellow-butchers were full of complaints, but they had all
done at least some business every day.   None of their shops indeed had
been full like the great stores, and when Albert suggested that somebody
must at last remember the unalterable Party Programme, and take care
that their profession shared in the profits of the distribution of foodstuffs,
they all agreed, some heartily, some with a touch of ill-humour or
sarcasm.   A few expressed the view that no one was better fitted than
he to start such an agitation; and one of them, Kruse the butcher in the
Kurze Reihe, thought that at the next municipal elections they must
consider whether friend Teetjen should not represent them on the
Council.   When he got home in the late afternoon or early evening he
sat down by Stine in the kitchen and asked her whether she hadn't
noticed something by now.   Of course she had.   No one came into the
shop.   Even their immediate neighbours stayed away.   Things looked
worse than they had done in the six months before Herr Footh had had
his bright idea.   What could be the matter?   She did not know, she
said.   And if she had an idea, she was careful not to mention it.   As
they barely saw their neighbours in this winter weather, she could not
tell whether anyone had started some grudge against them both.   People
who went up in the world always found their way made difficult for
them; any sort of prominence inevitably provoked jealousy, which invariably found expression first in the relation of seller and buyer.   While
she talked she was busily ironing the under-linen she had washed earlier
in the day, and gave no sign in look or voice of being perturbed or even
alarmed by the altered conditions of their lives.   Albert, indeed,
laughed that evening at the idiotic Wandsbekers, set his jaw and swore
he would find some way of coping with the crisis; he wouldn't be done
down by all this nonsense.

But, as the weeks passed, he became a prey to accesses of rage.   What
sort of government was this which made people afraid that war might be
caused by the Austrian affair, and could devise no remedy against the
public's dwindling power and inclination to buy?   But when his fellow-
butchers noticed no appreciable change—how was it that not so much as
a cat took the trouble to cross his threshold?   The Lehmkes were uncom-
municative, and blamed the weather.   Stine, however, came home one
evening with another book from the attic, and the solution of the riddle.
The rats in the alleys had multiplied lately, a fact which had attracted
attention to the unhygienic conditions in many foodshops.   It was
rumoured that not a few butcher's shops left much to be desired in the
matter of cleanliness.   It was possible that this sort of thing was being
said about them too—inspired by jealousy, malice, or mere self-importance.   It might be as well to put another advertisement in the paper,
something to the effect:

*Come along to Teetjens for your sausages and meat,*
*Where everything is spotless and neat and bright and sweet.*

But that would mean more expense, which Albert thought they could not manage. Besides, at a time when everything turned upon Vienna and high politics, who would notice such an advertisement? But the present state of affairs could not continue. They were breaking into their capital, which was a process no one could survive. He must deal forcefully of one of these brutes that slander a fellow who was trying to earn a respectable living, and knock his back teeth down his throat; then they might learn to hold their tongues. Stine objected that that would produce a discouraging effect on customers. At this, Albert was on the point of letting fly at his wife; but he controlled himself, nodded, and muttered that when she was right she was quite right.

More and more often in those days they found themselves picking up a pencil and scribbling sums on bits of paper. Once, while so doing, Albert asked whether Stine thought it possible that anyone in their neighbourhood could have had an inkling of the Fuhlsbüttel affair. If so, it must have been in some roundabout fashion, for no one had recognized him, the secret of the mask had been strictly kept, no one but friend Footh knew anything about it, and he for obvious reasons would keep his mouth shut. Stine opened her eyes wide, and flung a deep-set look at him from beneath her shock of hair.

"Since you've mentioned it at last," she said; "yes; I've thought so for a long time. How things like that get about, one just can't tell. From the very first I had a horrid feeling that the wretched business would do us no good."

Albert sucked his moustache and looked across at her. "I didn't know," said he, "that there were so many Communists hereabouts."

"One never knows," said she. "But anyway we can't be sure it's anything definite. People just fight shy of us. In ancient days we should have been said to be under a spell."

Albert shook his head. No reasonable person believed that sort of thing. It was much more likely that these Red hounds had smelt a rat, because he had had the distinction of being received by the Statthalter, and the Führer, just after the Fuhlsbüttel affair. And whether these rumours were true or false, they did not care. Such people were devoid of the national reverence for truth, and indeed it meant nothing to the Bolshevist hordes. He had heard that Timme had got his wife a job in some business house; and a woman like that would, of course, swallow and repeat any sort of nonsense.

"Can you blame her for doing so?" asked Stine softly.

Albert flung a furious look at her, and then burst out laughing.

But Albert paced the flat and the shop tormented by perplexity and wrath, reminding Stine of the polar bears at Stellingen, which he had observed so attentively on the occasion of their visit. His footsteps, as they padded over the boarded floors, sounded quite different from when he was trying out his divining-rod. The realization that people dared to spread such slanders about him—if there were such people—and he not able to take someone by the throat and throttle him for doing so, filled him with grinding fury. He kept on telling himself that no one could have recognized him; he devised wild schemes of vengeance—he would mobilize the Preester Sturm troop, ransack the district for Communist literature and thus extract the worm from the timber and uproot the enemy from the home. But his natural common sense kept him from such folly. Moreover, *he was clear that he did not* want to trouble the Party leaders with his difficulties. All this apart from the fact that from talking to Stine he understood that the position should be looked at rather differently. Who, in effect, was Party Comrade Teetjen, at a time when the Führer was fulfilling the ancient German dream, the reunion of the German race within one *Reich*? The Teetjens must accomplish their destiny as an infinitesimal unit in the great struggle for the resurrection of Germany, alone and by their own efforts. They need not starve. Their resources would last them comfortably for six months. In the meantime the tide must turn, or friend Footh, now so much richer and more influential, would devise some scheme. It was bad enough that a fellow like Albert Teetjen should be beset by these invisible pigmies. And against such foes no divining-rod was any use, nor was there any help in thought or deed.

Stine was more sorry for her husband than one could put into words. The whole affair had been clear to her mind, almost from the very day it started. Her grandmother had not said anything definite in her dreams, but alluded to it as something that needed no expression in words; "Human blood cannot be trifled with, Stine, as you very well know. It never comes out in the wash, rub as you like. And if you use kitchen soda, it merely makes holes in the clothes that you can grin through." So saying the old woman's wrinkled brown face had set into so strange a laugh that her lips and nose seemed to shrivel, and her kind old face dwindled into a fleshless skull, beneath the smooth parted hair and bonnet, though without losing the good-humour it had always worn in life. The fact that Albert was staggering forward without the faintest inkling of the real state of affairs almost made her laugh, as she stood alone in the kitchen and watched the bluish flame-jet flickering upwards from the gas-burner. Of course he had been perfectly justified in all he had said on his own behalf: he was simply a soldier, who had to kill and was allowed to kill in the service of the nation and the State, both of which wanted to get rid of the Communists. But suppose God didn't take quite that view, suppose he saw a distinction in the fact that the soldier may himself be shot dead when he confronts the enemy, so that the chances are equal, as in games on the school playground; and suppose, too, that God wasn't inclined to take advice about the side to which he should award the victory, Israelites or Amalekites, and which of the two champions He means shall fall, Goliath or David? Of course Goliath had the better chance, but with a fleck of cloud or flash of sunlight God could blind the giant to the stone hurtling towards him. So long as all went well, as long as no wrong was done by following the drift of events—well, it was all in the Book. But once temptation came and you began to kick against the pricks, as she had done when that idea entered her mind, confusion came too, and anyhow no one knew what God's purpose might be.    Everyone might indeed be sure that it was not in vain that the Lord Jesus had suffered upon the Cross, and surrendered the human soul that had been his during his sojourn upon earth.    But that Albert should be so deluded as to imagine himself hounded down by the Reds, and want to depopulate the district—all this seemed to her so painful and so pitiful, but at the same time so comic, that she could hardly trust herself to talk to him about it.    She could not tell him what she really thought, he would not have begun to understand her.    He had to be—so to speak—pounded first, like a raw beefsteak.    Ah well, there was yet time.    If God understood her Albert as well as she did, it was not for nothing that He had involved them in this horrible, guilty business: why, the Lord Jesus himself had been a convicted criminal, He had been beaten and insulted by the S.S. of those days, and finally executed with two others, Himself as innocent as a lamb.    It was probable that He would not make it easy for Albert, as a comrade of his bygone executioners.    And if he crept yet deeper into the bowels of the earth, by the aid of his divining-rod, God's finger would find him: and God knew that she would not abandon her husband, indeed before He created her He had known that.    No, Albert might rack his brains, this business would run its appointed course. . . .    Well, perhaps they might try another advertisement, for no one ought to sit with folded hands merely because he isn't setting himself against God:

> What God does is well done,
>   We bow before His will;
> And when His hand is laid on me
>   I quiet stand and still.

That evening, or rather, that same night, they were visited by a sign, in common with all the inhabitants of all Hamburg, and all Germany down to the Alps.    Albert had gone out again to stretch his legs, after sitting in Lehmke's bar wondering whether or not he should ring up Footh; he had then fallen in with Comrade Vierkant and put away several glasses of kümmel in his company.    That was the stuff to help a man through this horrible stagnation.    Vierkant had a great deal to discuss with Lehmke about the maintenance of the news-service between the Sturm troopers across the frontiers and those who had remained behind, in process of which they quietly ignored Albert Teetjen, though he had plenty of time on his hands.    The fact that Lehmke continued to deal with Albert was quite natural—it seemed so to the butcher, at any rate, who would indeed have been surprised had it been otherwise.    When they then gathered round a table and the conversation duly took a military turn, Albert learned that not merely the X Corps, Hamburg, but also the IV Dresden, and the XI Hanover, had been put on a war footing, and that General von Bock was to command a part of the newly constituted Eighth Army, instead of the Third Army Group, as his command had hitherto been called.    News of this kind did not greatly interest him, though he did not let that fact be known.    Could it be that an executioner's axe emitted rays that scared passing customers away? And was it possible that such radio-activity was not neutralized by an indiarubber apron? The sisters in the X-Ray section, so Dr. Laberdan had once told him, had to protect themselves by lead aprons and gloves against the unknown rays which had for that reason been called "X", and even so they sometimes contracted burns that penetrated deep into their systems, and ultimately made them barren. Of course the rays from the axe were not so dangerous—at least for others who were not concerned—it merely scared them away, always supposing that they were responsive to such emanations. But it was a bad business for the Teetjens—not a doubt of that. Such a diabolical object had plainly better be got out of the house at once. And as Herr Vierkant indicated to Lehmke on a map he had brought with him the line of advance into Austria, Albert strolled across to Mother Lehmke at the cash desk and got her to wrap up a bottle of kümmel and put it down to his account. He didn't want the other men to see him, thought Frau Lehmke—it was a pity that such an upstanding fellow should be so irredeemably mean; however, he was in process of paying for that defect, though he was as yet unaware of the fact. And as she smiled a little wryly and whispered that Frau Stine should not be told about this purchase, the street door was flung open, and Dörte, who had been to the cinema, dashed into the bar.

"Come out," she panted. "There's something happening in the sky." Whereupon the company broke up, grabbed their overcoats and trooped out into the street.

The night was clear after rain, and such of the stars as could outshine the glow from the great city twinkled faintly in the night sky. But at that moment it was spanned by a myriad milk-white filaments of light, floating like iridescent veils across the sky—they reminded Albert of the searchlights on the night of the air-raid practice, when his vocation as a dowser had been so suddenly revealed to him. But that far-off illumination in the heavens seemed almost unearthly, and as though it were cascading downwards from the stars.

"Whatever is it?" asked Lehmke in awestruck tones.

"Northern Lights," shrilled Dörte ecstatically, for she had found out on her way home what was happening in the sky.

Albert was stirred to his very depths. Clutching the bottle of Kümmel under his coat, he stood there, with his face upturned to the sky, his mouth half-open, gazing wide-eyed at this cosmic display. It must be significant of something. Perhaps it would be better observed from the Wandsbeker Chaussée; perhaps, too, he ought to rouse Stine so that she might not sleep through such a manifestation from Heaven. He set off down the street, walking slowly, like a man who could only spare an intermittent glance at the road before him.

"God bless my soul," said he, and again: "God bless my soul."

Despite his amazement, he was clearly aware that the others were still in his company.

"So that's the Northern Lights, is it?" asked Lehmke.

"Cosmic dust," replied Vierkant, his thin lips compressed, and plainly regarding the performance with disapproval. "Electrically charged, or under magnetic influence. How the old women will start prophesying!"

"But don't you think they mean something?" asked Albert Teetjen.

"Of course," returned Vierkant. "Sun-spots."

In the circles close to the Führer there were undoubtedly people with souls responsive to these Northern Lights, who, instead of speculating on their scientific origin, used such cosmic disturbances in the cosmic sphere as a motive power behind political decisions. The silvery radiance enveloped, like illuminated gauze, an inner structure of three or four interpenetrating arcs, like the great, shimmering bulk of the old snake of Midgard, prone athwart the heavens.

"It *is* the Midgard serpent," said Dörte. "Teacher Wiepke told us so."

That was certainly what it looked like, Albert thought. It was something quite different from cosmic dust. There were radiations and radio-activity that penetrated the whole of nature, and were only observable at night. But the axe must go. Outside No. 17 they met Stine, and from an attic window right at the top of the building a voice called down to them: "Aurora Borealis—that must mean something's going to happen."

No one seemed to notice the voice, or want to reply. But Editor Vierkant was feeling much perturbed, for since the suggestion of sun-spots as an explanation, he had been plagued by the thought that these disturbances of the sun's surface, these cosmic primeval tempests, might, as he indeed had read somewhere, exercise an influence on the world of humanity, and stir up the mass upheavals in the form of revolutions and wars, for which the appropriate causes were for the most part ready to hand. And, if so, there might be some foundation for what old women of both sexes said about these matters.

In the meantime, Stine clung fast to Albert's arm and said no word. She had climbed up to Tom's attic to get him to help her write the intended advertisement, and had been dumbfounded by the huge illuminated serpent which God had unfolded over Hamburg city, in token of his infinite mercy and goodness, so she thought. She must look at it in Albert's company, walking step for step beside him, under the silver light. If they were to be punished for Albert's deed, let it be here, in time, and not in eternity. The penalty might have to be paid. Then let them pay it here below, and in their mortal forms. Thus their eternal element would be preserved. Such were her thoughts, as she walked with her eyes upturned to the sky over which the unearthly radiance slid and swept and shimmered: like the silver walls of the heavenly Jerusalem, in the old *Chorales.*

Albert felt her warm and heavy against his arm.

"We'll get the axe out of the house as soon as possible," he whispered.


During the next few days Stine went about in a sort of trance. The magical blue-green of that night-sky, the transparent radiance from the North, had inspired her with a confidence that had been compacted into a sort of core within her mind by Albert's decision and his promise. Perhaps it would be a good move to get rid of the axe. In the general excitement over the tremendous manifestation in the sky, several old customers came back to the shop, in addition to the faithful few who had never deserted them. And the newspapers and the radio brought a sense of tension and expectancy into the foggy, slushy weather of the end of February and the beginning of March. Were their brethren in Austria to be overwhelmed by Schuschnigg and his Heimwehr? Would the Austrian Chancellor prove so shameless as to employ a plebiscite to surrender German lands to the hostile powers of Versailles? Would their Austrian brethren rise up in their hour of need even if Red Czecho-Slovakia sent their ruffianly troops and their artillery to the aid of the Vienna Marxists. Would Adolf Hitler preserve his own and his people's patience, now strained to breaking-point, merely in order to preserve the peace of Europe? Was it not time to show the world that the spirit of Germany was not to be suppressed in the Ostmark any more than in the homeland? Then came the call to march: the Ostmark returned to the Reich, Vienna fell without a shot fired, the Jews fled helter-skelter. The bells of Hamburg rang out, the ship's sirens shrieked in celebration, salutes thundered forth from the Bismarck monument in St. Pauli: German troops had occupied Vienna in order to anticipate an Marxist coup, Herr Schnuschnigg had fled and been arrested, hundreds of traitors had committed suicide to escape just punishment, but the population of Vienna and Austria were in ecstasy; they decked themselves with violets, marched up and down the Ringstrasse and the avenues, rejoicing. Home to the Reich! And no one in Europe said a word. All was well, Adolf Hitler's infallible instinct, his never-failing genius, had scored again. Germany now reached from the North Sea to the Gross Glockner, from Hamburg to Klagenfurt, as in the days of Charlemagne. First the Saar, then the Rhine, and then the Danube. And what now? Must our unredeemed brothers in Czechoslovakia turn their eyes and hearts to us in vain? Was not the Elbe a German river—and German too, all the lands watered by its tributaries, including the Moldau? Should the Slav hordes be allowed to pollute the German Vistula, insult the German city of Danzig, by setting up the wretched rival town of Gdynia and amass Polish war-equipment on the German earth of Westerplatte. The name of the German Chancellor was no longer Hermann Müller or Stresemann; it was Adolf Hitler, the unknown corporal of the world-war, and the German flag no longer looked like the Belgian black-red-mustard tricolour: here was the black-white-red of the old Imperial banner, but with added splendour and recovered youth, and displaying the badge of sovereignty, the symbol of Spring, fertility and fortune, originating in the Aryan cradle of the race though the Cross of Galilee had withheld it from the German people and driven it underground. "Heil Hitler," yelled the young folk in the street: the citizens beamed and wagged their heads, and the workers nodded approval as they made their way to their work through the Elbe tunnel in motor-buses, on bicycles, and on foot. And the consensus of opinion was that Hitler was a grand lad, and everything he did was right. And our regiments, too, had been standing-by—tanks, infantry and guns.

For the first time in five years, Albert Teetjen felt out of harmony with what was going on. The last two weeks had clearly proved that the takings of the business did not even cover the price of stock. He and Stine had to consume more of their own wares than they wanted: now and again they would present a bit of something to the Barfeys or to Reitlin for his dog. Not only were his comrades of the Preester Sturm away, the Hamburg Transport Association had diverted its whole organization and all its cars to the needs of the great war-rehearsal manœuvres. Comrade Footh was at the moment in Vienna, and Fräulein Petersen, when he rang her up, said that he could leave any message at the office or—in other words—with her. Young Frau Footh, whom Albert had held in his arms at the dance, a feather-light and golden blossom, had joined her husband by air a day or two before, and they would be just starting on their honeymoon—to the South Tyrol, North Italy, or Capri—and very nice too. But if Herr Teetjen wanted anything important forwarded—well, he was living in the same house as her uncle, and she could drop in sometime.

"Delighted, Fräulein Petersen," replied Albert, with hypocritical alacrity. "No, there's nothing particular at the moment, except that I'd like to send him my best wishes for a pleasant trip and good weather." Fräulein Petersen thanked him and said she would convey his message in just those words.

During the weeks that followed Albert was a prey to much inner torment from which he could see no prospect of relief. Wasn't this business about the axe just nonsense? Wouldn't he do much better to get Footh to put a proposal before the Municipal Council to restrain the great stores from selling meat in his district—before resorting to the Preester Sturm, and launching into some drastic action on behalf of the small tradesman, in accordance with the unalterable Party Programme. And now this confounded fellow Footh had departed with his little lady on a honeymoon, as if he hadn't been sleeping with her for months past. True, that was none of Albert's business. It was, however, confoundedly inconvenient for him, Albert; and the Preester Sturm was away too, and before they returned, his savings would have dwindled into nothing. This idleness and inaction was getting on his nerves. The slush of February and March made it impossible to practise with his divining-rod—he merely came home with mud-caked boots and no results at all. The impression made on him by the Northern Lights was probably a childish delusion. Tom Barfey had been saying that it portended war. Well—what war? Mussolini had ceased to guard the Brenner? Had the Czech artillery appeared in Vienna? And the only way out of his troubles that occurred to him—the removal of the axe—wasn't that equally absurd? An excellent, useful, valuable implement of Sheffield steel, in a new shaft of Canadian ash. That afternoon, just as he was going out to watch the throng of customers, at the big Stores from the street corner opposite, Stine had suggested that they should go down to one of the canals that evening, as it was foggy, and drop the thing quietly into the water. His sole reply to such a lunatic proposal had been a kindly shrug of his shoulders as he tapped his forehead with his forefinger. They must sell it of course. There were plenty of dealers in the old town who would know its value. And if it conjured their custom away, so much the better. Twenty years after the Kaiser's battle in the West, no new war had come, and under the lights of Hamburg city there was no magic that could wreck a man's business. If he did agree to anything of the kind, it would merely be to try the effect of getting the axe out of the house, he would not dispose of it. Why not put it in grandfather's charge— after all, he had bought it and it was really his property. The old man lay in his grave in Wandsbek Cemetery. An absurd notion, of course —still, he might try it. And Stine would be pleased.

When she reminded him of the scheme next morning, while he was slicing sausages to keep his hand in, as in old days before the slicing-machine had been invented, for he had nothing to do—he looked at her with heavy, absent eyes.

"Very well," said he, "if we don't open the damned trap this afternoon, no flies will come in. We'll put the axe on grandfather's grave under the ivy. You'd better get a bit of bacon-rind and grease it."

Stine shook her head. "I would rather you did it yourself, Albert. I should be afraid. It's a man's job, anyway."

Albert nodded. He was sitting behind the futile, vacant counter, staring into vacancy, straining his memory to recapture a dream of the night before, which had utterly vanished from his mind.

Even at midday it was so dark in the shop that the light was really needed in order to serve customers. But the Teetjens had to be economical and use as little current as they could. Hamburg was again enveloped in a pall of fog. He filled a pipe and said: "It's a funny thing to be sitting with sides of bacon all around us, and starvation staring us in the face. I believe the folks want us to cut our throats." He laughed shortly, and struck a match; his face stood out luridly in the leaping flame against the background of soupy fog that oozed down the street. Stine eyed him intently:

"I should have to rely on you for that—I don't think I could manage it myself. I should be afraid. What's that you're smoking?" she asked, with a sniff and intake of her breath.

"I'm glad you noticed it, Stine," said he, with an approving laugh. "You're a true soldier's wife, as I might say. For the last few weeks I've kept the stumps of my cigars, cut them up, washed and dried them, just as I did in 1917, and put them in my pipe; it's the very pipe I had then, and the same tobacco-pouch. There's another war on, Stine, and the enemy is quite nearby, though I can't lay hands on him. And I don't find it at all funny. But we mustn't let it get us down. We must get some support from somewhere. A visit to a dead relative can't do any harm, unless the old gentleman is angry because we've not been near him for so long."

Stine noticed that he was talking in the broad Hamburg of the harbour quarter, or the rank and file of the old Eighty-third during the last war.

In the afternoon about three o'clock, they stepped into the street which was now opaque with yellow murk. The houses opposite were no more than phantom masses pierced by the glimmering yellow squares of the lit windows. Gas was still used by a good many people, and gas-lit squares were greenish-white. The outlines of things visible seemed to waver, and the trams slid slowly onwards, their bells jingling apprehensively at crossroads, the electric arc-lamps swayed to and fro, like lumps of yellow grease. Stine was carrying her market basket, having intended to buy some sort of cabbage or carrots in the Lübeckstrasse, or whatever might be cheapest in the market. Albert carried the axe wrapped up in its old oilskin apron under his arm; it looked like a musical instrument, an elongated lute or a guitar, and excited no attention.

They made the long journey on foot. The streets lengthened out from nothing into nothing. People walked along enveloped in a sort of no-man's-land, couples clutching each other's arms, and the head-lamps of the cars flung tapering shafts of light into the gloom. Albert knew his way perfectly well, but he had to keep a sharp look-out as they went along. Stine, as she breathed, felt as though she were in a wash-house. The red traffic lights did penetrate the fog, but the green ones dissolved into an ineffective glimmer. She tried to start a discussion with Albert on whether it would have been cheaper to take a tram; instead of walking the soles off their shoes. But his replies were so curt that she soon abandoned the attempt. He had to take care they did not miss the Lutzowstrasse, where they turned off to the left. He had never thought their journey would be such a strange, laborious progress.

The cemetery gate stood open, and from near the little church came a rasping, grating sound, the creak of an ungreased wheelbarrow. Albert thought it would be easy to identify the grave, which was marked by an ash and a weeping-willow. But Master-Cooper Theodor A. Teetjen's last domicile seemed to have vanished in the mist, and they peered disconsolately at the trees and bushes over dozens of mounds as they groped their way through the cemetery. Stine held Albert's right hand so tightly that he could feel her nails. Both bumped into a bench that suddenly confronted them, and collapsed abruptly on to the seat; yonder stood an iron cross between two trees, and a few paces away, a man, half in profile, wearing an old-fashioned coat and a kind of cap that had long been obsolete. Albert stared up at him wide-eyed and dumbfounded. It was he; in true likeness of the old yellowed photograph that used to hang in his parent's bedroom.

"Stine!" Albert groaned and flung his arm around her. Her teeth were chattering audibly. At that moment the stranger turned his yellow, beardless face over his shoulder, and glared at his grandson.

"Get along home," he said in a wrathful undertone. "You oughtn't to have done the job with my cleaver, you dolt. I disown you."

He pointed with outstretched arm towards the city, stepped between the trees and the cross, and vanished. Albert and Stine sat motionless, for the time they took to breathe—once—twice—three times. Then, in the same instant, they got up.

"That was my dream," said Albert, and ran his fingers through his hair; now he remembered.

"So this isn't the right nook," whispered Stine. As they crept past the chapel wall they lifted the rusty latch of the trellised gate, which fortunately was unlocked.

"All right," said Albert. "It's after twelve o'clock." And he jerked his head towards the notice-board which proclaimed the hours of closing.

"Did you see him?"

"I should think I did!"

"And hear what he said?"

"Yes, and we weren't dreaming."

Albert transferred the axe to his right arm, and shook his left, which had gone to sleep. "What shall we do now? We're not going to get out of this as cheaply as I thought."

"You ought to have asked him."

"I didn't dare. Now let's take the tram home. A penny or two don't make any difference now."

"Oh yes it does," said Stine firmly. "We've got to get to the market."

In the face of her resolve, Albert shook himself like a dog, thrust his chin more deeply into the upturned collar of his leather jacket, and grasped her arm. Then he cast a lingering look at the little chapel, the door of which seemed to be locked.

"I wish we could get in and sit down for a few minutes in a pew."

"We can sit down just as well here," she answered, pointing to a large low bin, filled with withered leaves and fallen brushwood, which stood against the wall a few yards away. They did so; sat down with their legs dangling, and rested. Albert wedged the axe between his knees.

"I wonder who that was," he said. "One of the gardeners, perhaps—who happened to look like the old boy in this fog."

Stine shook her head, and she settled her little green hat more firmly on her head.

"Yes, but remember what he said. He called you a dolt. My grandmother was often able to see people belonging to her family after they were dead. Perhaps I've inherited the gift. And you with your little rod can discover what lies beneath the earth. How can our life really end between birth and death?"

Albert drew a heavy breath. "It was him I dreamt of. Yes, you must be a sort of magic lantern—or a film projector. You throw on to the fog the image of what I flash into your mind. Happily married people like ourselves often think each others' thoughts. Well, come along, old girl—white cabbage or green, let's see what there is."

"Green cabbage always tastes good after a frost." So saying, Stine rose, stamped her now chilled feet on the stone flags, and smoothed out her cloak.

"You're right," observed Albert, following her example. "Well, we must think what to do with it. I feel sure it sends out rays that can go through walls. Let's take a tram, and you make me a nice cup of coffee like you did when Footh came to call. A man doesn't meet his grandfather every day in the week."

And he hoisted the axe on to his right shoulder this time, took her arm, and tramped along the path into the mist.

# CHAPTER FOUR

## GERMAN EASTER, 1938

PEOPLE WHO HAVE been subjected to an impelling and unexpected experience find that they have to plunge into work in order to digest it. Life goes on, its routine must be maintained, added to which work under such circumstances is very good for any man, and those who have none to do make haste to find some. However, as a result of the 10th Corps' manœuvres, extra help was wanted in the cattle-yards as well as in the free port, and Albert, as soon as he was noticed in the streets, was called upon to bear a hand. Stine, for her part, took advantage of his absence for several days, to institute a thorough clean-up of flat and shop, for which the approaching Easter holiday offered more than one pretext. Easter fell late that year, but a housewife must not merely celebrate such anniversaries when they arrive, she must prepare for them. So Stine scrubbed the cupboards, the doors, and the inner window-frames, scoured the cockroaches and moths out of their lurking-places, but as she came and went the question never ceased to haunt her: what could that encounter with Albert's grandfather mean, what would happen next, and what would be the end of the story? What would life after death be like?—this age-long riddle harried her as she did her household tasks, under the strange guise of a ridiculous riddle game which had been popular in her schoolgirl days. They used to set each other to guess the meaning of incomprehensible phrases which had been deprived of their German sense and character by misplaced emphasis. Among many that came dimly back into her mind was one that now seemed ominously appropriate—some jingle about trees and leaf and cherish that disguised the lines of the old hymn—He who dies without belief shall forever perish. It must be an awful thing to perish forever— no mistake about that; though, indeed, the reality that lay behind the words was beyond what a simple woman could imagine. Her understanding was limited to what happened within time, and there was plenty of that. It must be averted until the very last moment—so much was clear; and that conviction was innate in everything that lived. Throw a kitten into the water and see how it struggles and clutches at the oar held out to it in sudden pity; watch it crawl out, a few inches of sodden fur, as thin as a shaven squirrel, lie down to dry itself and roll over in the sunshine, after vomiting out the water from its throat as if it were voiding its very soul. If the axe must go, then it must go. She knew her Albert. And now, how would he dispose of it? It was a blessing that he had found something to do, and could without shame bring his few marks' wages home every day. He would not let his pride be injured by any man or power in the world, and she sorely feared the day on which something of the kind might happen, as it inevitably would; she had not told him that many people who used to nod when they met them in the street, now looked away or crossed the road. They all avoided open insults, in recognition of Albert's uniform. But there were subtler arrows, and the moment a suspicion entered his mind, the moment he began to distrust fellow-men, and scented humiliations and attacks, the prospect would indeed be black. Even the Lehmkes had adopted a singular attitude. She, Frau Lehmke, had always borne a grudge against her, Stine knew that very well; but now there was hint of menace in their demeanour, that seemed to say: You wait, my girl, and see what's coming to you,—rather like a schoolmistress to a pupil discovered trying to cheat and threatened with punishment.

The trouble was that she did not know a single soul in the neighbourhood, to whom she could talk freely, and relieve her burdened heart. Her relations lived in the country, and were absorbed in their own affairs, and she had never made a friend in the district—she was well aware of the reason for that. The Barfey's were her only friends. But she couldn't possibly confide in them. Pastor Langhammer had been clapped into a camp, and wouldn't be out again for a long while; his successor was a German Christian, and they would be no use. So she remained enclosed within her own orbit, like a circus-horse running round the arena—a very unwholesome state of affairs.

Albert, too, had a secret from Stine. When he got off the elevated railway and walked home through his native city now enveloped in fog and dirt, the familiar roadways, the crossings, and the house-fronts gave him the feeling that he was in an enemy country, as it might have been Schaulen or Grodno in old days. Hamburg was a city he no longer knew, an alien city. It radiated a vague hostility which he set his teeth to resist with out-thrust jaw. If the dog gets in first, the cat won't find much left. This was no life for a man like himself. It was this sort of thing that happened in occupied territory, when the population crouched in their rooms behind closed doors and emitted wafts of hate as the conqueror marched in; all of which was quite natural. But in this city, his home since birth, here where he had gone to school, played Red Indians, served in the army, and had always felt at ease with his fellow-men—he realized with a surge of resentment, it was a new and singular sport. Helpless as a mouse in a trap, in single-handed conflict with unknown foes—this was no life for his father's son. When the boys

came back after Easter, and Lehmke's 'Tank' was once more full of
life and bustle, the old sense of warmth and confidence would come
back too, and he would resume his old relations with his fellow-men.
Herr Footh would be returning too, and provide him with the moral
support, and friends and company. Until then he must shut himself up
with Stine, though that incident with his grandfather plainly signified
more than she admitted. Some sort of unwholesome influence did
seem to emanate from the axe which, still enveloped in its india-rubber
apron, had resumed its place in the cupboard. It must go—when the
weather improved. Until then, Corporal Teetjen, Squad-leader Teetjen,
must keep his chin up. The news from Vienna sounded splendid, it
heralded the abolition of the crazy injustice of Versailles, by which
three millions of Germans had been placed in the power of the Czechs,
murderous ruffians of whose outrages the newspapers had been lately
full. Then the shop would come to life again, and he wouldn't need to
take so many little nips of kümmel unbeknown to Stine. He didn't
want to take to drink—it ran away with too much money.

When he got home Stine asked him to his surprise where they should
go for their Easter trip.

"Easter?" he asked with astonishment. It had quite gone out of
his head that Easter was now upon them. Even last year he looked
forward to the prospect a month ahead; they had bicycled out to Stine's
people, on the moor, where they sat in the low-pitched kitchen and ate
plum-cake and drank coffee. This time—well, much seemed to have
happened in the past year. He felt, indeed, so much more than six
months older since they visited Stellingen. They might go out into the
country for the last time on their new bicycles, for he saw it plainly
written on the wall that the bicycles would have to be sold, unless Comrade
Footh came to the rescue once more. Only an extreme crisis would
have induced Stine to forego the pleasure of shutting up the futile shop
for a day or two and creeping back into the family nest. But before
she could discuss it with Albert something unexpected happened. As
dusk was falling, Frau Pastor Langhammer entered the shop. Clad in
her accustomed black, but without the narrow white collar that she
usually wore, she asked for something cheap, a bit of odd ends to
make a Vienna steak, drew up one of the white, freshly-scrubbed
stools, sat down and turned a strangely altered, almost petrified face
upon Stine, and eyed her with a penetrating gaze. And while Stine
cut and weighed out her order—fortunately they had kept some oddments
nice and fresh in the refrigerator, she began to talk. Stine had no doubt
heard a rumour that the Pastor had passed away. At this news, Stine
stood wide-eyed with parted lips; no, she hadn't heard it yet—how
terrible! Yes, he had died in the camp, she knew no further details, his
coffin had arrived yesterday with instructions that it was to be buried at
once, and without any funeral service. Well, some of the local people
wanted to hold a memorial ceremony in honour of their Pastor and pro-
tector. As Easter was at hand, their intention was to arrange a gramophone performance of one of Bach's *Passions*, since no orchestra would be
authorized to play it in these times. One of their friends would lend

them a radiogram; another, an Israelite who had been a personal friend
of the Pastor, among a supply of records which he was taking with him
to Palestine, had an English recording of the Johannes' *Passion*, a real
treasure. All they now wanted was a room, preferably on the ground
floor, or rather several connecting rooms opening out of each other.
Tom Barfey had suggested that Herr Teetjen's flat and shop would be
very suitable, and was very anxious to be present. So she had now come
to Frau Stine to ask whether it could be managed. Stine had to lay
her hand on her heart, which was throbbing with emotion. They had
plenty of room, she replied, but very little to sit on, as the Frau Pastor
could see for herself. But she was very grateful, she said, for the confidence thus placed in her. She would certainly speak to her husband
about it, and perhaps they could borrow chairs from Lehmke's opposite.
There would be very little doing there on Good Friday. There could
be no harm in it, said the Frau Pastor, dabbing her eyes with her handkerchief; a commemoration of our Saviour's Passion was surely permitted.
The special occasion for it need not be mentioned. She added that she
could not believe the current rumours about Herr Teetjen. Her late
husband had always had a high opinion of Frau Stine. The Brethren-sect,
to which she had once belonged, guaranteed her sound evangelical
views, and so she had ventured to approach Frau Stine on the matter.
Seats were certainly a problem. If Lehmke's suspicions were aroused,
those who attended might find themselves in peril. They could keep in
touch through little Tom Barfey, who would let her know Herr Teetjen's
decision.

Albert, when he reached home and heard Stine's somewhat agitated
account of her visitor's errand, laughed a curt laugh of astonishment,
and shook his head. He would indeed have been glad to have a number
of people seen crossing his deserted threshold. But there could be no
question of borrowing Lehmke's chairs. The Lehmke's were too sly—
they would certainly send Dörte across and discover what was happening,
with probably unfortunate results for the assemblage of Christians.
But there must surely be an air-raid shelter in a cellar somewhere, with
plenty of seating accommodation; what about the Nasvog house?
Such an apparatus could be fixed up anywhere, and he, Albert, would be
very ready to put in a good word with the authorities, if needed. Stine
might make the suggestion to Tom.

But Tom thought the Nasvog building would be a risky place, too.
But surely one of Langhammer's flock could provide an air-raid shelter,
with plenty of seating, for Good Friday morning. It would be easy to
find such a place in the city.

On Maundy Thursday Gesche Barfey gave Stine a note inscribed
with an address and the hour of ten o'clock in the morning.

Albert went with them. Pastor Langhammer—well, well! What
had happened could well be imagined. They would soon know; the
camp to which his defiance and obstinacy had consigned him, was a
place upon the surface of the earth. But even if people did give Albert
the cold shoulder, that was no reason why he should not do something
to please Stine. The boys might indeed have taken him to Vienna.

And now here he was in a Confessional Christian congregation. It was a long way to the Niederstrasse. The city was enveloped in silence, everything was closed, not as in Catholic countries, where Good Friday was not so strictly kept. In old days he often went to church on Good Friday, out of affection for Stine—and now he was escorting her to a service in a basement. But surely the early Christians had had to worship God in cellars of this kind, under the Roman Empire. And later on the Protestants, during the Inquisition. Not actually in Hamburg, but on the Lower Rhine and in Holland. And now they were doing it again—well, it wouldn't do them any harm. He wondered whether there would be many people there.

The long whitewashed room, with benches and chairs from the offices set in rows, was in fact packed. Beside a wall-plug stood an apparatus on a small table, a wooden cabinet constructed in the Gothic style and not unlike an altar; and on a second table two large candles in black wooden candlesticks from Pastor Langhammer's church, which had for a long time been lying by in a coffer in the sacristy against a day when a storm in spring or autumn would damage the electric masts. Nearby, and next the wall, sat Frau Pastor Langhammer in a sort of tall armchair from a Company board-room. Opposite her, on a small chair, sat Herr Levysohn, the forthcoming emigrant, conveniently placed to handle the records himself. There was no conversation, the assembly—men and women in dark Sunday clothes, spoke in whispered undertones; all were invited guests and knew what the occasion signified. Most—indeed practically all—of those present were acquainted. The only strangers were a couple who had been put in the front row by the Frau Pastor, a man with a reddish-grey moustache and a baldish head, and a slim dark-haired lady, a Southern type, still almost beautiful under her crown of thick iron-grey hair—friends of the Pastor and his wife, who had been living in Switzerland, and had just accepted a call from an American university, where the professor was to occupy a chair of psychology.

Shortly after ten the Frau Pastor asked for the doors to be shut and the performance to begin. Among the crowd were Stine and Albert, seated against the wall, holding one of the programmes which had been distributed at the entrance, from a miscellaneous collection of old ones, most of them dating from several years ago. In Pastor Langhammer's parish one of the great Bach *Passions* was given every year at Easter by the church choir, trained under the Frau Pastor, who directed the performance.

When, from this strangely fashioned altar, came the peal of the organ, the tremor of the violins, and the shrill sweet notes of flutes and oboes, not a few of the women dabbed their handkerchiefs to their eyes, or looked across to the Frau Pastor where she sat erect, confronting the listeners with impassive, carven countenance. "O Lord Almighty, whose name is glorious in all lands," sang the unseen voices.

Stine and Albert sat side by side among the assembled Christians, and ancient associations revived in both their minds, except that in Stine they aroused genuine emotion, whereas Albert blinked rather

mockingly at the company around him.    Such an instigator of sedition
had very properly been gaoled and condemned, and indeed the whole
story was very much like the Reeperbahn case; the Procurator Pilate,
a military governor, bore a remarkable resemblance to Koldewey, the
Fuhlsbüttel prison-governor, and, under another aspect, to the *Reichswehr* Major or Colonel, whom he had noticed so particularly on the
occasion of the Führer's visit.    The fact that the people who clamoured
for the man's death had then been Jews, and to-day were Party Comrades,
merely served to show that the course of events, the behaviour of revolutionaries and their satellites, remained unaltered.    He himself would
not have felt at ease in the S.S. tunic of those days, but he realized that
these people too had been doing their best to maintain order, and
execution by the axe was of course much more humane than crucifixion.
But the practice in those days of allowing relations, even women, to be
present, was quite inadmissible.    The cordon should have been much
more strictly drawn.    As for Judas, whose name was so constantly
heard on the records, Judas who betrayed him—well, the man was
simply doing his duty to his Führer, known in those days as the Roman
Emperor, just as if one of his four had bought himself off by helping
to secure a speedier judgment on the rest.    His subsequent fate was
inevitable and natural; although the programme, which Albert had in
his hand, said no more about the man, he was sure that a few pages
later on the Bible recorded that this same Judas Iscariot hanged himself
on a tree.    Had the Jews boycotted him, as the Hamburgers had boycotted another servant of his Führer?    It served these idiots right that
such a fellow should let them moulder among their money-boxes by the
waters of the Elbe.    His only trouble was that he wished he could
smoke his pipe during this so-called funeral ceremony.    That Jew
Levysohn changed the records very neatly.    Unfortunately he was
partly hidden by the instrument, so that Albert could not see what was
really going on.

Stine, on the other hand, sat with closed eyes and listened raptly
to the strange and sadly diminished music, moving up to its appointed
climaxes, and indeed at the chorales, which she knew quite well, her
heart sang in a silent pæan of release.    "Beloved Jesu, what wrong has
thou done?"—"Our Father in Heaven"—"Do with me, O God, even
as Thou willst."—"Christ who makes us blessed"——

Yes, Pastor Langhammer had had many supporters in Hamburg,
as was plain enough from the sounds of weeping and sobbing that now
filled that basement, and some of the men, even, were fumbling for their
handkerchiefs, in a furtive sort of way, as befitted their sex.    But the
Frau Pastor had been wise in her contrivance.    The music of Bach was
in no sense forbidden, indeed, it was no doubt performed from time to
time in a concert hall, or transmitted on the wireless.    None the less,
this music, here, achieved another purpose without contravention of the
law, and the Frau Pastor might well sit proudly in her chair before them
all, for she had in some sense gathered the little community together in
this act of commemoration, and confirmed their faith.    Had there not
been some mention of the feast of unleavened bread?    Or was that in

the Gospel of St. Mark? What a fuss the Jews did make about it—
and she remembered those good times of her youth; the frantic efforts
of Chemist Plaut's family to make sure that no leaven remained in the
house, and how it was reported of his cousin, Rabbi Plaut, that he would
deliberately strew bread-crumbs under the sofa, so that he might find
something that could be ceremonially burnt. She remembered, too,
that for this Passover Feast, as it was now called, special crockery had
to be used, with separate dishes for milk and meat foods, which only
Jews could afford. Stine had always been accustomed, like so many
Hamburgers, to think that there were none but rich Jews in the world;
but later on she had seen plenty of poor Jews on the ships' gangways
and herded in the emigrants' pens, having fled from the old Tsarist
Russia; and had taken them baskets of food, or helped Frau Plaut to
distribute old clothes, underwear, and many a precious dollar among these
unhappy folk. There was, of course, no thought then that such a fate
would ever befall the German Jews too. Those who wished to go, those
out of sympathy with the Swastika, would not be held against their will.
They could pack up their property and take it with them if they had paid
their due taxes like every other citizen, according to what Lehmke had
told her. She wondered if the Frau Pastor would now leave Germany.
Apparently not. None of her three or four children was present. Well,
the Hitler Youth had better not get to hear about this seditious ceremony in their father's honour. . . . She wondered what was going
on in the Frau Pastor's mind. Was she, too, chanting in silence: "Deal
with me, Lord, in accordance with Thy will."

Yes, the Frau Pastor was in fact joining in that silent chant. Here
in this cellar, was an assemblage of true Christians, as in the days of
Nero and Diocletian. Here, and in this place, those whose kingdom was
of this world, and of the next world, parted company. And the future
was with this poor community who had chosen as their shepherd a man
after Jesus' own heart, a man who lived by his guidance and example
—if indeed, such words might properly be used about a fallible human
being. "Do not think of us as just a handful, Augusta," he had said,
firmly, as he was taken away. "I see the future German nation marching
in our footsteps. For the truth is and must be indivisible; and it is
written that un  ͏r one sign only shall they conquer—not the broken cross,
but the upright ( ross of Golgatha, the blessed Cross of Christ." For the
present the road t'͏ey must tread led down into the cellar—and deeper
still, into the grave. But as surely as the sun rises again every morning,
faith, and the message ͏f justice, truth and love must again shine forth.
A certain Justus Langhammer had been extinguished—but was it
really so? He had been honoured above his forbears by the crown of
martyrdom, and his testimony of blood would germinate and fructify
in his little community. And if Herod (whose name also began with
an H), robbed them of the children of their bodies, those here present
were their spiritual offspring, and would guide them in accordance with
what is written in the Bible: "Be ye as wise as serpents, and as innocent
as doves"—by such methods as were here employed, impeachable but
vitally significant. The fact that the Rohmes should have been passing

through at this very moment, sceptics as they were, who regarded the reports of what happened in the Third Reich as atrocity propaganda, also revealed the finger of God.   Professors in Zürich lived far above the *mêlée*, and those in America did not need to believe what they read merely because it had appeared in print.   But here in Germany, the Lord did not reject such doubting Thomases.   He laid their fingers in His wounds.   And they must do so, willingly or not.   No more evasion was now possible. . . .   And if the worthy Claudia still tried to blink the facts, having obviously met only the more aristocratic Nazis in Zürich, it was not for nothing that she and Rohme had studied at Göttingen many years before in the company of her beloved, brave and gloriously martyred Justus. . . .   And as the tears rolled down her cheeks, she gazed wide-eyed at her two friends, husband and wife, who represented the best and most precious tradition of academic Germany. "Go out into all the world, bear witness of what ye have seen here," so ran the Gospel.   Such was the Christian's duty, not to be evaded.

Guests and friends greeted each other with handshakes and a few whispered words, while the ministrant at the records paused for a short interval between the second and third part.

"Poor Augusta," murmured Professor Rohme, but his wife replied between pursed lips: "The whole thing is in the worst of taste."   It was surely a very ill-judged proceeding, and disrespectful to Bach's most magnificent work, and one of the most sacred Christian texts, to use it as a requiem for such a relentless adversary of his own nation and State, just as Hamsun had never forgiven the besotted Ossietzky for having refused allegiance to Adolf Hitler.   Both sides of a question must always be heard.   Pastor Langhammer's death had possibly been an accident, though very likely caused by the man's own obstinacy, which almost amounted, on occasion, to an obsession.   Who could tell? And now this catacomb ceremony, this three days' absorption in the virtues of her dead husband and Pastor—all this was in very poor taste. The Rohmes had held strictly aloof from the dubious horde of emigrants pouring across the Swiss frontier, despite their careful sifting by the Confederation authorities.   They had opposed and avoided the Popular Front manœuvres started in Spain and France against Fascism.   They did not favour Fascism, they left everyone to mind th 'r own business, but every reasonable person must admit that Hitler and Mussolini were making their countries great; whereas Stalin's policy had degraded Russia in the eyes of the civilized world, and ind d, justified the vituperations showered upon Russia at the Nuremberg Party celebrations. All these enemies of authoritarian régimes were inclined to self-advertisement, whether eminent men like Einstein or Freud, or simple souls like Augusta Langhammer.   If these people could only realize how sorry this potted music sounded in the ears of those who had for years attended Hans Lavater's performances in the Fraumünster at Zürich. And need it be so long—couldn't some of these arias and chorales be cut?

The same notion came into Stine Teetjen's mind, but with a rather more direct result.   She went to sleep.   It was lasting too long.   Moreover if the S.S. and S.A. had not been busy conquering Austria, the

Frau Pastor would have found herself in trouble. If only she had been able to get away after half an hour. When she was a young girl the Sunday Church Service could never be too long for her, such was her devotion to Jesus, and a certain young long-haired Pastor. But later on she had found Albert, and earthly joys impressed the will of God upon an increasingly receptive mind. "Be fruitful and multiply"— and if they hadn't, whose fault was it? Her dreams dwelt on clothes-lines hung with children's linen—jackets, napkins and drawers. But sheets were spread out on the grass, and Grandmother Geisow, or was it Gesche Barfey, walked up and down with a watering-can and sprayed them with an air of much benevolence. "Grow—grow," said she as she did so, and Stine could not help laughing. Spraying didn't make napkins grow.

Albert gripped her arm. "Come along," he said; "it's over. Didn't you notice that the last part was cut? The Chairman of the Church Council had a word with the Frau Pastor in the interval. It would be a grand joke to take the whole lot of them round to the nearest Storm-troop post, but I won't. Come along; just curtsey good-bye to the Frau Pastor."

And indeed at that moment all those present, both men and women, were walking past the Frau Pastor, bowing or dropping a curtsey, or shaking her by the hand. Albert, when he came to stand before the lady, had to remind himself not to stretch out his hand in the Hitler salute, and he was uncomfortably taken aback by the look she gave him from her great grey eyes. "You must put that matter right," she whispered, but her level tones rose clear above the clatter of moving chairs and boots, and struck at his heart. What did the old goat mean? He had nothing to put right, though the people in his neighbourhood certainly had. Everyone does his work in the light of his convictions, as a pastor or as a butcher. And each and all of them needs courage for his job, nor must he shirk, whatever may be the cost. But as he went out with Stine and swung himself on to his bicycle, he glanced at her and whispered: "Did you hear what she said? She's a knowing old girl."

"Yes, she takes after the Pastor," replied Stine, as she got on to the saddle.

"We'll take the thing to Ohlsdorf, there'll be a handy grave-mound, where it won't be stolen."

"When?" she asked.

"Depends on the weather," he replied.

"Let it be soon," she said, with an appealing look. "It would be so nice to go about again, and feel all decent and respected."

Albert frowned, but nodded agreement. From the myriad windows of the great office buildings, hung an array of flags, flecks of blood-red colour each displaying a black swastika on a white ground, in celebration of the revival of export trade, and thanks to the understanding with the Western Powers which condoned the Austrian achievement.

# CHAPTER FIVE

### THE ARMY-DRAGON

IN A WELL-ORGANIZED State, especially under an absolutist régime, no one can wander about a cemetery without being sooner or later stopped and questioned by the officials in charge, even though the weather comes to his aid. But friend Albert was anxious to proceed in strict accordance with the law, when he put his axe into the keeping of a dead man, and with a sly blink at Stine, he indictated what he had in mind. Why shouldn't they make use of the worthy Doctor at Fuhlsbüttel? He would cycle out there on the Saturday before Easter, enjoy a brief but heart-to-heart talk with D. Laberdan, and bring back what he wanted, viz.—a note to the Ohlsdorf cemetery authorities requesting that Herr Teetjen might receive every consideration and assistance, if needed, in the course of his practice and experiments with his divining-rod. He would forthwith take this document to the cemetery and get it stamped—an additional stamp confers a magical power on every official paper, not only in Germany. As the way was now smooth and clear for getting rid of this disturbing influence, the Teetjens could now mount their bicycles with lighter hearts and pedal across the Moorburg to Stine's sister, who was married to a boat-builder and carpenter, but grew enough vegetables in the garden of her Frisian cottage to eke out his meagre earnings. The weather continued unpleasant—drifts of fog and squalls of rain swept over the two cyclists, but Stine felt so happy at escaping from the Wagnerstrasse that she infected Albert with her own high spirits. The alders were covered with grape-like catkins, hanging in silvery clusters from the red willow branches; and if the traveller cared to make his way through soaking moss and undergrowth he would come upon a few modest violets, easily located by their fragrance, and the little lilac-coloured blooms of cuckoo-flower, which venture forth so boldly, unprotected by any leaves, in the neighbourhood of blackberry-bushes, and smell like hyacinths, plainly waiting to be picked by Stine. And so, with an armful of flowers that heralded the spring, they knocked at their sister's door, shook the clammy fog-deposit from their coats in the long, low, whitewashed hall between the bedrooms, and received the hearty welcome of expected guests, while Albert produced some gaily-coloured cigar-boxes for the children which he had put by during the preceding months. Here they spent a peaceful, uneventful Sunday and Monday in a countryside that reminded them both of their childhood. The landscape began right outside their bedroom window, a countryside of pools, rivulets running down the village street, and timbered tracks, leading to inn and Church and cemetery, with its memorial tablet to the sailors and soldiers who had died for the Fatherland in the first world war, spanned by an expanse of shining sky from dawn till dusk. How joyously the clouds sailed across the pallid arc of heaven to the west or to the north! Stine sat down sadly on a bench that her brother-in-law had brought out for her, mending a laddered brown stocking, and fell to wondering why people were so anxious to live in cities. Much better to live in the country in a place like this, much pleasanter and much less of a strain. They could cut peat, or grow potatoes and cherries in the patches of sandy ground—and a man like Albert would have done well at either job. And yet some impulse drove people to the great cities, where they lived wall to wall, in a medley of confusion, peering yard-wards from the attics or skywards from a basement. There must be something, some powerful and pitiless urge that drew and drove them into such a way of life. Not merely the cinema, the multiple stores, the tramways and the river-steamers. What it was, she did not know: and yet it had gripped her also; she did not live in a village among fields and under the open sky, but in Wandsbek, in Greater Hamburg, and in the hostile Wagnerstrasse. Well, there was nothing to be done about it, man could not be remoulded, as poor Pastor Langhammer always used to say. The story was that he had fallen down and broken his skull—so said Tom Barfey, when she had gone up to thank him for the invitation. Tom was, by the way, really getting out of hand. The spring was in his blood. He was pestering her more than he had ever done.

When they started back on the Monday, they felt fresher than they had done for a long while, though they had slept rather rough. They had done well to bring with them the last bit of pickled ribs of pork, which they would otherwise have had to finish by themselves at home, as matters then stood, and they were fortunate, too, in still possessing their bicycles. Albert called them an unwarrantable luxury, and if he did not succeed in baffling or defeating the machinations of these invisible Reds, they would have to sell their beautiful bicycles before Whitsuntide. Their joy in them had not endured for long; they would miss them sorely when they were tied to the railway again, the packed excursion compartments, and have to journey home amid brawls and crying children. People who preferred their own tobacco-smoke to other people's, ought not to come down in the world.

When the time came to say good-bye, Stine fell on her sister Else's neck, and burst into something like a fit of sobbing. She felt as though she would never see her again. Why, she did not know, but never before had she been so acutely aware of the inner bond between them, even though, as so often happened in life, they actually saw but little of each other.

"If I had any children, Else," she said, summoning up a smile, "I would leave them to no one but you. And if I am to die . . ."

"Now, now, girlie," the other said tenderly.

"—I shall leave you everything I have."

"And very nice too," said the brother-in-law, with a twinkle. "I hope it will be something worth having, Stine, my dear."

Aha!—here were a number of the boys, come back in high spirits on Easter leave. The tales they told! There was life once more in Lehmke's bar, no mistake about that. There had been all manner of doings in Vienna, Linz and Graz. The Party Comrades had revenged themselves for their long and compelled inaction; they had hunted down fugitives, searched the houses of suspects, and told Cardinal Innitzer exactly where he got off. Everyone had brought some small treasure back with him, and they all had some prizes to display such as rings and wrist-watches; they had polished off Jews by the dozen, while many others had jumped into the Danube, or swallowed pills that brought a sleep from which there was no awakening. Of course there remained a great deal to be done. The workmen's organizations had to be kept in check, and here and there a new concentration camp had to be established, guarded and administered. The Austrian Party comrades were too few for all these tasks. It had been indeed a sight to see the women hail the Führer as liberator when he at last returned to his homeland; the tanks thundered through the streets, and the aeroplanes roared over the roofs. The seasons were much more advanced there than in Germany, there were violets and lilac out, such as were hardly to be seen in Hamburg so early in the year. And the children came offering little bunches of flowers, clambered on to their new friends knees and were fed. Yes, there was much privation to be dealt with in Austria—though it was indeed a very old country. And by no means so small as it had been commonly conceived in Hamburg. The so-called Vorarlberg reached down to the Swiss frontier, Styria as far as Jugo-Slavia, since so much good German land had been surrendered to the Slavs—surrendered by the terms of the Peace of Versailles, which—in the case of Austria—was known as the Treaty of St. Germain. And as for what had been absorbed by the Hungarians, under the self-same treaty—well, better say nothing about that. Step by step—that was the Führer's method; all in good time, don't be in too much of a hurry, gentlemen!

Albert felt that it was not yet time to mention his private troubles. Storm-leader Preester had remained in Austria, and Comrade Vierkant had been given the job of getting rid of the Jews who had infested the Austrian radio-service. Moreover the new Comrades needed a great deal of help in the matter of money and currency. Their schilling was worth only half a mark, although the coins rang very convincingly when thrown down on Lehmke's bar. How was Comrade Teetjen getting on with his divining-rod? And the new permit, authorizing him to practise in the Ohlsdorf cemetery was duly inspected. Yes, and there was still a lot to be done in Spain as well, the Reds wouldn't give the game up yet. . . .

Well, he must settle on his next step alone—and why not? Man is self-sufficient, and he himself had always been so until Stine introduced him to Footh—re-introduced him, he would rather say. . . . Yes, Comrade Footh was very active in Vienna—doing big business, so the Comrades said. Possibly he wanted to get his boats on to the Danube. Strange it was that the Danube was almost as yellow as the Elbe. The beautiful blue Danube—that was all propaganda. If only we had possessed such clever writers of operettas! Well, our Elbe was pretty well-known throughout the world, wasn't it? And the new suspension bridge would be an extremely forceful dot upon the 'i'. Trust Adolf!

The fog had returned, though it was not quite so dense as on the previous occasion when the attempt was made to dispose of the axe, but denser than at Easter. After Albert had twice taken his bearings with the divining-rod on that huge expanse of open country, at a third trial he agreed with the cemetery authorities on a comparatively narrow section not yet filled by the neat graves hitherto located there, as it seemed to contain several subterranean watercourses flowing towards the great pond or lake which adorned this admirably contrived establishment, several square kilometres in size, in which the Hamburgers took much pride. This was one of the free-thinking sections, the cemetery being open to all confessions and creeds. Here lay the relatives of superior working men, or small officials. Among the rows of graves, between the juniper bushes that here replaced the more exotic cypress and were so much better adapted to the landscape, Albert had marked a grave, disposed with special care, a green mound of fir-fronds, under which his axe might find a very suitable resting-place. A white metal tablet, in place of a stone to be erected later, was inscribed with the name —Helene Prestow, and an identification for the use of visitors, who must have been numerous, to judge by the many flower pots filled with earth, but still without plants in them, which surround the tall junipers at the head of the grave, and two smaller and almost black ones on either side of it. A melancholy and still rather bleak display, which was, in fact, solely due to the solicitude of the tram-driver, Otto Prestow, and his friends.

"There must be hyacinths or tulips or some other sort of bulb in those pots, or there wouldn't be any sense in them," said Stine, as she helped Albert to clear away the green foliage—branches of pine and juniper which had probably been brought here from the heath. Then, as she investigated the pots to see if she could find any trace of green shoots sprouting through the pale, brown soil, Albert pressed the well-greased axe blade firmly into the soft earth, and then covered it carefully with fir-branches. So intent was he upon the concealment of the axe that he did not notice his watch sliding out of his waistcoat pocket under the weight of its silver chain, thanks to his bad habit of letting it dangle out of his pocket like a fob. It was late afternoon on the last day of April. Albert and Stine then had to go along to St. Pauli, to the landing-bridge, where Albert's Heligoland brother-in-law and his sister had arranged for him to meet a certain Captain, who was to take a few small matters from Hamburg for Landlord Ahlsen. Thirty-three marks Albert was to lay out on Ahlsen's account, which would be faithfully repaid when the holiday-makers brought their money to Heligoland. In the Heligoland captain's cabin, after a second grog had been ordered, Albert first noticed the absence of his watch. He must have dropped it at the grave. He did not want to go out again that evening, as the mariner had gravely assured him that this was Walpurgis-night when ghosts were abroad, and he himself had no notion of weighing anchor before to-morrow, the first of May, when he would have a word with the crew and transform the German Workers' Anniversary—here he grinned from ear to ear—into a sort of half-day of celebration. The suggestion that ghosts might be walking that night made a particular

impression on Albert as on Stine. Although the watch, notwithstanding
its protecting case, would certainly be none the better for a night in the
dew and mist, Albert decided he would not get it until the morning, and
combine the trip with some practice on the divining-rod in the Wellings-
büttler playing fields or on the Borstler Moor. They could get up
early, take some food with them, and spend the whole day out of doors—
customers would not be likely to storm the shop. He could have quite
well made the trip alone, but Stine did not want to sit at home without
him—not that day. Who could tell whether the missing axe might not
unleash all manner of trouble in the house? Ghosts at sea, and ghosts
on land, and Pastor Langhammer had died of a fractured skull; he
had been, so it was reported, interred in the Fuhlsbüttel camp, having
fallen down a stone staircase—not a very high one. But neither Albert
nor Stine wanted anything more to do with Fuhlsbüttel. The name
was associated with a crisis in their lives, which was uncommonly
suggestive of witches' or devils' gold; the solid dollars, or blue notese
received on pay-day and put away in the cupboard, changed in a tricn
into pine cones or withered leaves. It wasn't quite as bad as that in
their case. But there had been clearly no beneficence nor blessing in an
enterprise that seemed at the time to promise them salvation.

They were both up early, ate a hasty breakfast, put some food in
their pockets, and glided on their bicycles through the still sleeping city,
lying under a greyish light that seemed to be shed from a greyish sky;
and they slid into an equally noiseless and colourless world, except that
in certain quarters of the city, flags still hung like blood-red patches on
the walls. From far away came the sound of drums and fifes—it might
be the Hitler Youth or the reveille bugle. They entereu the Ohlsdorf
cemetery by one of the eastern gates, and cycled along the broad paths of
the vast enclosure; they only dismounted and left them chained together
when they believed themselves to be near where the watch had been
lost. The juniper bushes, hedges, grass and shrubs, with their drab
or blackish leaves and foliage, emerged rather hesitantly from the
brooding mist of dawn and seemed to recede before the intruders.

"It must be somewhere about here," said Albert. "There's the
juniper bush, with the . . ." then the words stuck in his throat, so
suddenly did Stine grip his arm, just as he was going to say—"pots of
bulbs round it." Instead of which he gripped his divining-rod as though
it had been a weapon.

"Don't you hear—don't you see?" asked Stine tonelessly. "There
was a white woman glided past . . ."

Albert laid the hand holding the rod above his eyes, and peered
between the graves.

"She sighed," quavered Stine. "She won't have the axe on her
mound."

"Nonsense!" exclaimed Albert, "I'll go alone." But she would
not let him, and he too now believed he could see a figure gliding among
the graves, in a white garment, with fair hair, a face distorted by grief,
and a hand pressed against her side.

"She shouldn't take on so," rasped Albert between clenched teeth.

"We all have our troubles." There lay the grave containing the axe; and there lay the watch. But when he looked up again, there were no longer five juniper bushes standing round them in a rough half circle, about four or five yards away, but the tall black forms of five decapitated men, standing round the axe, holding their heads by the ears at the level of their waists, their grinning faces gazing down at the axe, or the grave, beside which Albert and Stine stood clutching each other's arms.

"They're nothing but juniper bushes, dear," hissed Albert, but his teeth were chattering.

"No—no," wailed Stine, now crouching on an adjacent mound. "They've come to take us away—it's all up."

"Keep off," yelled Albert, and slashed with his rod at the grey swathes of fog; then he unbottoned Stine's coat and dress, rubbed her forehead and temples, and begged her to be sensible and control herself. They would go away at once, he promised her, and it was already getting lighter. When he stood up again and looked about him, the wind—a light breeze from the west—was clearing the haze from a pallid morning sun, which hung just above the horizon, rayless as a moon, backed by the white expanse.

"Have they gone?" asked Stine.

"There's nothing here but juniper bushes," he said in a reassuring tone. "They've marched away with the drums and fifes over yonder."

"And who was the fifth?" asked Stine, her arms still quivering, and her eyes closed.

"That was the fellow old Ruckstuhl beheaded," he blurted out. "A nasty, grinning Jew."

"Has he gone, too?"

"Now you must be brave," he said: "and get up; they're marching down the main avenue to the lake, which looks more like the bank of the Niemen, than the Ohlsdorf lake, I'm damned if it doesn't."

She rose to her feet; it was true that here were the juniper bushes, but yonder ahead of them five black figures were drifting into the distance, much taller than men—they had grown taller in their graves, she thought. And what was that on the move behind them, while from far away came the rattle of drums and the whistle of fifes?

"Soldiers," he exclaimed in astonishment. "Can they be holding the spring manœuvres on May the first?"

Down the long avenue came a column of infantry, in full campaigning equipment, with rifles shouldered, close to their steel helmets, field-grey, dark-grey, and smeared with camouflage colours. At intervals huge tanks, in their multi-coloured war-garb, rumbled past; to the right and left of the marching columns chugged the motor-cyclists, while the officers stood in their cars with arms outstretched towards the lake; at that moment aeroplanes from Fuhlsbüttel roared out of the mist, drowning the rattle of the guns, as the field artillery appeared, gunners squatting on the limbers and the black muzzles of their pieces dipped towards the ground. But all the time, and above the din of all the engines, from far away came the imperious command of the drums and fifes: "Forward."

R

"Come away, for God's sake," pleaded Stine. "This means war."

"Nonsense," he laughed. "It's a May day parade."

"In Ohlsdorf!" she exclaimed. "But where are they going? Into the lake?"

So it seemed. Before they reached the bank, the mist had enveloped them, but they moved on, rank upon rank—more in number than the whole garrison of Greater Hamburg—now stationed in Austria. He rubbed his eyes as the mist descended on to the road, and peered after the departing multitude.

"Well," said he, "let's get along." And he bent down to pick up the axe. "But what shall we do with this?"

"Take it to Fuhlsbüttel," she replied decisively. "That's where it belongs. Leave it outside your Doctor's door—we won't have it in the house again."

He picked it up, wiped the soil from the blade, wrapped it up again in its oilskin cover, rearranged the fir-branches on the grave; then they tramped back with stiffened limbs and clenched teeth by the way they had come, to their waiting bicycles. But they could not swing themselves into the saddles; they wheeled them stiffly and unsteadily to the outer wall, and thence into the open country. They kept their eyes fixed on the tyres, and when they looked up again there was not a sign of the marching column.

"Let's sit down by the road, and have a bit to eat and drink. We shan't get far on empty stomachs."

The clatter of motor-bicycles still reached their ears, but they might well be Hamburgers, out for a trip into the country, on this First of May.

# CHAPTER SIX

## LIGHT IN FUHLSBÜTTEL

FROM AN OUTSIDE view no one could have said whether the lights behind the curtained windows of the Koldewey official residence had been turned on again, or had not yet been turned out. The latter was what had happened. On the last day of April, those two university graduates, Doctors Koldewey and Neumeier, had gone through the civil betrothal ceremony before the Hamburg Municipal authorities. The witness for the bride was a tanned, upstanding S.A. man, her nephew Bert Boje, and for the bridegroom in place of Lieut.-Colonel Lintze, a figure not

unknown in learned circles—Professor Walter Rohme, who was staying
in the city on his way to take up a post at Harvard University. And as
everything connected with this wedding was unusual, it was this same
witness, and his wife Claudia, *née* Eggeling, who would be proceeding
on a honeymoon trip; the Koldeweys, for their part, could not and would
not think of one until the summer holidays. As the widower now to
be married already possessed a well-supplied establishment, the Hamburg
purveyors were called upon only to provide what was appropriate to such
a wedding feast—lobsters, a turkey stuffed with chestnuts, asparagus,
a bowl of game-keeper punch, compounded of rich old Zeltinger and
fresh May herbs, topped by a Burgundy so deeply crimson as to be
almost black; the whole meal, which had begun late, being rounded off
by a magnum of champagne and a cheerful drinking of healths. The
other dishes and dainties laid before the guests had been Annette's
concern, the eldest of Koldewey's three daughters, with the assistance
of Bert Boje, the two younger daughters having gone out, claiming the
privilege of youth to enjoy their own dance at the Asgard Club. The
prospect that these middle-aged academics would spend an entire night
in learned conversation seemed to them absurd, especially as they had
found suitable partners, Papa having done so rather late in the day.
Annette must sacrifice herself—and serve her right; she had had her day.
So they departed and were driven off; Annette and Boje listened to a
symphony concert from New York conducted by the banned and exiled
Toscanini, interspersed by reports from the central Moscow radio
station about the May Day review on the Red Square, and the two
married couples, one so 'experienced' and the other so untried, became
absorbed in a discussion of what was really involved in the Third Reich,
the former trying to connect it with eternal Germany and the teachings
of her writers and philosophers, and even to equate it with what
Germany once was; the other two, who must stay put and at their
posts, being in the difficult position of not wanting to abjure their
share and responsibility in what had happened. What puzzled the
Koldeweys about the two Rohmes was their unconcealed dislike of the
*emigré* intellectuals, the whole non-Jewish and Jewish upper stratum
of public life, as it might be described. One of their newspapers had
had the hardihood to maintain that the whole of literary Germany,
in so far as it was of any importance, was now to be found outside
the Brown Reich; which was the starting-point of the night's conversation. This had been summarily refuted in the *Neue Zürcher Zeitung*,
many respected and honourable names had been adduced on the other
side, and the controversy still continued. Yes, there were plenty of
authors in Germany, and philosophers as well, and an immense amount
of scientific and psychological research was being carried on by numbers
of first-class men and women, even though it was true that the Nobel
prize-winners were not among them. It was not a characteristic of
the Germans, said Professor Rohme, pulling at his reddish-grey
moustache, to advertise themselves. They had always left that sort of
thing to the scientists, whose achievements seldom survived more than
twenty years.

Frau Koldewey, in a grey silk evening frock, a cigarette between her lips, and her grey eyes opened wide, asked whether this was meant to include Einstein and Freud; the latter hadn't got the prize, and judging from one of his utterances, was not likely to. As for Hindenburg and Ludendorff, and *tutti quanti*, it wasn't a case of self-advertisement, but demand for idolatry by their fellow-countrymen. But Frau Claudia deftly diverted the conversation; what she had said applied mainly to a particular Nobel prize-winner, who appeared to neglect his own sphere of literature, to devote himself to writing pamphlets and delivering radio talks on matters outside his concern. What had really happened in the case of Justus Langhammer, the Rohmes were very anxious to know, as atrocity stories were sooner or later to be expected. The Communists were openly sending out feelers from Western Europe, to Prague, Amsterdam, and Paris, during the confusion and bewilderment caused in Eastern Europe by these mystifying Moscow trials. Frau Dr. Käte Koldewey, meditatively contemplating a new ring on her finger, interjected: "We don't know anything either. The Third Reich operates in a special area of German space confined by barbed wire, though Germany, thanks to the efforts of the Third Reich, now extends to Hungary and Jugoslavia. And as all the nerve-threads, sinews, and muscular tissues centred in that compact domain of power, we are all controlled from thence, and indeed have lost the power of autonomous movement."

"Surely," exclaimed Claudia Rohme, "the German people must now stand or fall with Adolf Hitler and his genius?"

"The nation has now no other choice," smiled Frau Käte.

"On which point I would offer two comments," nodded the bridegroom, who was regarding the strife between the queens, as he described it to himself, with genial amusement. "In the first place, the nation is always responsible for what is done through its agency and in its name. Whether morally or not, we do not know; France of 1871 got no practical advantage from turning on Napoleon III; 'I catch and I hang,' laughed Bismarck, as he pocketed Alsace, and presented a bill for five milliards of gold francs, which, as we all know, were paid off in a few weeks. But the Loire peasant, the Besançon schoolmaster, or Cassis wine-grower —what had they to do with the beautiful Hortense Beauharnais's son? Just muck and all, as the young people of to-day would say. But they were all in it, and had to stand by the fate Eugenie's ambitious husband had brought upon them. No historian has ever suggested otherwise."

"Because the possibility never entered their heads," laughed the new Frau Koldewey, who had been taking this wedding conversation far too seriously. "Our friend Karl Marx would have had something to say on the point, I fancy—indeed perhaps he has had, only we haven't come across it. He would perhaps have said that the bourgois mentality— or the Junker mentality, since we are talking about Bismarck—always shelters behind the nation, when that class, which in fact cuts across all frontiers, gets into difficulties. The peasants and the workers of the world live as the more or less inarticulate core and filling of a globe, the polished outer surface of which is represented by good society—all over the world. This same good society, to which we, too, belong, controls its own activities, and all the contents within the globe. In many countries these human contents are consulted; in others, as in ours, their mere formal agreement is sought from time to time. But this game is played with human beings all the world over by the members of the surface caste, into which new-comers are continually rising from within the globe. In our time, here and now, we see many thousands of them arrayed in uniforms. But, my dear Rohme, would you have been what you are if, as a student, you had lived in a barrack and not in academic freedom? Would you have found Claudia if you had had to choose her in accordance with racial laws. Don't you think that a military cap, or anything of that kind, impedes the free working of the brain? We belong to the old Germany, and have no notion what surprises the new Germany has in store for us—whether heroic deeds or horrors."

"Heroic deeds, of course," Claudia exclaimed. "I got to know so many fine young men and girls in Zurich, and observed so many dubious and eccentric *emigrés*, that I entirely approve the process of selection as now established in our native land. But as regards Justus Langhammer——"

At that moment, from the vestibule below, came the chimes of a clock striking the hour—either four or five. Immediately afterwards, the door opened, and a young man appeared in evening-dress, and just behind his shoulder Annette's smiling face. With arms outstretched he carried a bluish-green glass bowl about the size of a small table-top, rather like an antique shield with a ribbed hollow in place of the boss. On it lay the tangled stems and blooms of a forest liana, like a fantastic gold and green bunch of grapes, each fruit an open blossom with a cluster of red and ivory stamens; a gift from fairyland on a glittering glass salver.

"Just arrived from Buenos Aires," said the young man with a bow, as he set the great bowl on a round footstool opposite the bride—a flower-piece more lovely than any decorative artist could have devised. Its sharp sweet fragrance blended with the smell of wine and tobacco that pervaded the room.

"Marvellous," said Käte Neumeier, bending over it and breathing the rich exotic odours of its distant home.

"My instructions were not to present this denizen of the primeval forest before the first of May. You, Aunt Käte, have been so absorbed and occupied by other matters during these past few weeks, our little surprise came off. But I am not responsible for the vase. The donor sent us the money, but the taste that chose it was—well, whose?"

Käte turned to Annette, took her in her arms and kissed her.

"Did anything come with it?" asked Herr Koldewey briskly.

"Yes," said the smiling emissary, took a little stoppered and sealed aluminium tube out of his waistcoat-pocket, which must once have contained tablets of some drug, and laid it on the broad rim of the glass bowl, among the leaves and blossoms.

"Aha," exclaimed the bride, "he didn't forget. Old affection makes faithful friends."

"May I keep it?" asked Herr Koldewey, "until the signal to open it is given?"

Frau Käte nodded, still entranced by the play of colour against the bluish-green glass, the rich moss, the green and golden blossoms. So Karl August still remembered the First of May as an anniversary in their lives—perhaps it had been for that reason that she had half-unconsciously proposed the previous morning for their betrothal. . . . They used to dance round the maypole in those days, and sing the old country songs, ecstatic with the joy of youth, and the glory of spring. . . . And here they sat confronted with the presence, an autumn of ripe fruits, strange tasks, and ominous possibilities. . . . With keen, affectionate eyes she watched Herr Koldewey as he silently locked the arrow-poison in his writing-table, while the Rohmes praised the artistic genius of the Third Reich which could create such a bowl.

"Not at all," said Annette, "that belongs to the Republic, and even so it's a reproduction of an original in Holland or Paris."

"Weren't you asking what had happened to Pastor Langhammer, just as I was bringing in the masterpiece?" As he spoke, Bert Boje turned from the sullen, melancholy visage of the Barlach peasant woman and met the unknown lady's vivid, sparkling gaze. "He rather injudiciously intervened between a S.S. man with a truncheon and a prisoner, who, as a Christian, ought to have kissed the hand about to strike. And as the incident occurred at the top of a stone stair-case, Pastor Langhammer unfortunately . . . fell down the ten or twelve steps—or at any rate enough of them to break his neck. This report is authentic, it comes from my S.A. Club."

So saying, Bert Boje pointed to his button-hole, which displayed the badge of a middle-ranking S.A. officer which, since the purge of four years ago, was now cleared from any suspicion of disloyalty to Hitler. The Rohmes exchanged a glance; the jealousies between the original and the more lately founded Party defence-forces had been a subject of frequent discussion and regret. Here was an obvious example.

"Bert!" cried a feminine voice from the next room, and the young man, with an answering cry of "Coming!", vanished as suddenly as he had appeared.

"A polished outer surface in which our materialist bourgeois society is only too clearly mirrored—I dare say that's what we are," said Herr Koldewey, thus dispelling the painful impression that the words of the new relative might have made upon his guests.

"Let us hope it will recognize its own reflection, though a bowl-shaped bottle would be more use as a mirror in a conjuror's cabinet."

"—or to shave in," interposed Frau Koldewey gaily, "and don't let us take this Austrian escapade too seriously."

"As long as it doesn't start a war, there's no harm in it. That's why all these malignant refugees from Germany are just waiting for the moment to brew their poison and smear their arrows with it, like the pygmies in the primeval forest. It's fortunate that they are so entirely negligible, no one pays them the slightest attention—at least decent people don't. That's why nothing comes of all these conferences, with the result that the Jewish Professor Weizmann could observe sardonically that the League of Nations would probably have to apply to the Palestine Government for certificates, as this was the only country that would accept immigrants."

"Only a handful want to go to Palestine," said Professor Rohme meditatively. "They let themselves be scared by the Hebrew language. And yet everyone knows that the Levantine coasts absorbed foreigners, even adopting their speech and customs; just as this Frisian coast of ours has done. There won't be any war, there won't be another 1914, everything will work out all right, and on Adolf Hitler's seventieth birthday the emigrés in Washington, Shanghai, and Tel-Aviv will have a celebration and send him a congratulatory telegram."

"No, there won't be a war," agreed their hostess, as she drained her cup of coffee. "Only the wrong people are killed in a war, as one of our writers observed after the last one. But generals and the diplomats come out of it safe and sound."

Through the window came a sudden burst of drums and fifes, and a rhythmic thud of marching feet outside the garden wall—and the Koldeweys jumped up to see what was happening. But Annette, feeling rather heated and flushed, had already drawn the curtains in the next room, and gone out on to the miniature balcony over the front doorway.

"Hitler Youth," she cried over her shoulder, "out for a May Day parade."

"Good heavens, what sort of time can it be?" said Walter Rohme, in a voice of humorous horror. "We've been sitting here all through a spring night and never heard a single clock strike."

Slim youths, with bulging haversacks, belts and shoulder-straps and dirks, marching sturdily up to the aerodrome, eighty or ninety of them, between the ages of thirteen and fifteen.

"Grand lads," said Frau Claudia Rohme admiringly. "The German breed has certainly much improved."

"Physically, I agree," said Frau Käte Koldewey. "But will they stand up to the battle of life and make good against a competing world?"

"I'm told they may now attend the parachute manœuvres and even take part in them, like the young Russians," said Annette, as the sound of the band grew fainter, and the posse of small marching figures swung into the haze and vanished.

"If the Weimar Republic had understood youthful mentality, which finds honour in the field rather than in the class-room, it would be alive to-day," observed Professor Rohme.

Heinrich Koldewey laughed and shook his head, but contented himself with saying: "Well, what about breakfast? Here's someone coming upstairs."

Someone was indeed coming upstairs; several persons, in fact, by the sound of the footsteps, and the door opened to admit a woman in an American cloth overcoat, and a man in a leather jacket, headed by Ingebottel, with Thyra bringing up the rear, both brandishing willow and alder switches. Annette, as her sisters marched in radiant with glee at their little performance, laid her fists to her lips with a flourish and trumpeted in high falsetto the Wagnerian fanfare for the procession of the singers into the Wartburg. In the meantime Stine, bashful and nervous, and yet at the same time amused and ready to play a part, surveyed the jubilant little company, and then found herself looking with eager eyes at the sea-green flower-bowl. Her colour! Albert, with the gesture of one making a presentation, stood proffering a long-shafted object with a blade wrapped in oil-cloth, of which he was so anxious to get rid. The fact was that the young ladies, escorted home by their cavaliers in their respective cars, had found Stine and Albert sitting disconsolate on the stone parapet on either side of the villa entrance; and having discovered, after a brief and rather hilarious dialogue, what he was holding on his knees, they clapped their hands and begged him to join in a little joke in which the axe should play the leading part; the idea was to present it to their father, Prison-governor Koldewey, upon the occasion of his wedding, to be housed in the municipal museum, and they persuaded him to come up with them forthwith for that purpose. But Party Comrade Albert must first confirm that this was the axe with which the four men of Fuhlsbüttel had been beheaded the year before, otherwise there would be no point in the gift. And when Stine, suppressing an exclamation of surprise, promptly assured them that it was, that this was the Wandsbek axe, Albert, quickly grasping that the ladies would certainly be prepared to spend a few talers on their little joke, curtly asked for 12 marks 50 as personal expenses, and was solemnly assured that he should receive that sum, as soon as two poor typists got their wages next morning.

"But I dare say Annette may put it in with the wedding expenses, and pay it out of the housekeeping money. Then I shan't need to owe it you," said Thyra, who seemed to Albert the more reliable of the pair, concluding this part of the conversation; she asked Stine's and Albert's names, and invited them in to breakfast. Thus it came about that the Teetjens visited Herr and Frau Dr. Koldewey to offer their congratulations, and grinned or laughed as Ingebottel, speaking as the Spirit of the City or the Genius Loci, asked the Herr Doctor to accept this symbol of justice from the youth of the Third Reich, as a wedding present and a gift of honour, and to present it to the museum. Ingebottel, a slightly cruder version of Annette, with more pronounced Slav cheekbones and fairer hair, played her part admirably, and no one understood why Herr Koldewey seemed to pay very little attention to his charming daughter, but fumbled in his pocket for a writing-table key, and eyed it absent-mindedly; it was not until Frau Käte laid a reassuring hand upon his that he became abruptly conscious of the company, the occasion, and his duties as a host. But soon afterwards, when the visitors were led out to breakfast by Annette, Herr Koldewey took the opportunity to exchange a few words with Frau Käte, who alone could understand.

"If I were superstitious, I should describe this as an omen. First curare—then the axe."

"And all three by the agency of your children," said Frau Käte, with a mocking twinkle in her eye. "Exceptional times demand exceptional measures, says your friend Nietzsche somewhere—and, any way, I shouldn't have said—all three; I should have said—both."

It was a gay and genial little party that sat round the breakfast-table, laid for the occasion in the dining-room with high-backed chairs, and indeed all the events of that day fell quite beyond the routine of such occasions. Herr Koldewey, in a short speech immediately after they sat down, had thanked his daughters and the Teetjens for their highly appropriate gift, and promised that he would duly perpetuate the donor's name on a small metal plaque—"if indeed in this precarious world one can speak of perpetuating anything." Whereupon Professor Rohme prophesied that the Third Reich would last at least ten times as long as the Weimar Republic. After Moscow had been taken, which would happen in the next year or two.

"Yes, my dear Rohme," laughed Herr Koldewey; "you may safely prophesy war. During the last one you were lecturing at Zürich, and now you are off to America, where, as you know, life is much more satisfactory."

"Yes, no ruined castles, no traditions, and complete isolation from European affairs. The general opinion at Geneva, except among those impervious to reason, is that there will never be another Woodrow Wilson at Washington, after the experience of the first. These latter really believe that they can detect the finger of your Gestapo behind the 'timber-felling' in the Red Army, as they describe the removal of the most capable Russian generals. We merely laugh, because revolutions always devour their own children. But you can pursue your policy of recovery without needing to regard the Russians as serious enemies— the very sparrows that twitter on the Zürich roofs could tell you that. It is highly interesting," concluded the professor, respectfully sipping Annette's delicious coffee, "for a scientific observer to witness the rise of so forceful a genius from the lowest stratum of society, and working his way up to a height where he can find no equal, no one qualified to share his task of reshaping the history of the world. If a Platonic idea was ever embodied in a single man, it was the idea of the German nation in the person of the once-despised Adolf Hitler."

Annette and Bert, who were facing each other in the centre of the table, listened while Rohme went on to assure the company that nothing more than a military demonstration would be needed if Germany now proceeded to clear up the Czecho-Slovak problem, in other words, the position of the German minority in that artificially inflated State. Then they turned to the young people's corner, as Annette called it, where the talk was also about the prospects of war. Thyra, darkest of the three sisters, looked to and fro from Stine to Teetjen with rather a puzzled expression in her brown eyes; for Ingebottel, her mouth full of bread and butter, had explained that her sister must be treated with respect, since she could read the stars and hear the grass grow. Whereupon Herr Teetjen had asked whether she could provide an explanation for the strange apparition of a column of soldiers which had been seen marching past or through the Ohlsdorf cemetery, or whether manœuvres on such a scale so early in the day were likely to have started yet. Certain people, replied Thyra, with a drooping, meditative air, and more of them than was generally supposed, possessed certain gifts. The Third Reich had helped to bring them into prominence. She would come and visit the Teetjens one of these days, and hoped they would tell her more about what they had seen, if the two Party comrades would not mind. And while Stine set her lips, and a look of apprehension came over her face—she hated to have the subject mentioned—Albert swallowed his second or third cognac, and said he would be delighted. Their new mother knew the house and the street. So saying, Albert felt two eyes fixed upon him, looked round, and encountering Frau Dr. Neumeier's contemplative gaze, raised his glass and drank her health. He must never come down in the world again, said he to himself, as he drank; he would always be someone like these people sitting round the table. Never again would he do any man's bidding—not he!

Yes, Käte Neumeier was gravely eyeing the man, Albert Teetjen, and his poor little wife, the kindly Stine. What a strange coincidence that these two people should have appeared in that farcical fashion at her actual wedding-feast, which had ended another epoch—the second or the third, perhaps, and had begun a new one, the fourth and last, if everything went according to plan. If Karl August Lintze had in a manner chosen Bert as his deputy, in this man Teetjen she could discern the lineaments of the erstwhile Friedel Timme, with his axe and his forebodings, which none but Koldewey could interpret. Herr Koldewey, her Heinrich, whom she must now address as 'Du', and indeed already did so, and with whom sooner or later, though not perhaps that actual day, she would be asked to share the bond of physical experience. No one was better qualified than Friedel Timme, if he had been still alive, to understand and sympathize with her growing pity for Teetjen. True it was that property and power, influence and rank are mighty driving forces, and those who as members of a class possess them, defend them with teeth and claws, and by them are inexorably impelled, such being the law of expanding energy. If entire nations allowed themselves to be transformed into instruments of such power-groups, as in contemporary Spain, how could she condemn a mean little tradesman like butcher Teetjen, the man of the axe, who had indeed been started on his course by her envelope, her instinct for service and goodwill, until he was now gathering speed like a launched ship down a slipway. Perhaps she had sent this man and his wife plunging down the greased ramp into the water where they would drown. But what would thereby be achieved? Who would be benefited, and who avenged? She had—foolishly enough—been trying to deal with one abscess only, and taken an old-fashioned knife to that indeed repellent eruption, instead of getting at the root of the trouble, the poison that pervaded and corrupted the entire system; but this needed a fundamentally different treatment—powerful doses of a drug that, like the lately discovered Dagenan, had laid hidden for decades past in the laboratory of world history, until first brought into use by men of another race, under the leadership of a dapper little man called Lenin. Her error she had committed, her miscalculation, yonder it sat embodied in human form at the breakfast-table, raising a glass and drinking her health. Very well, Teetjen, my man—you look like a good fighter, let the wind blow brisk about your ears, for the time will come when your services will once more be required. You will be chosen to co-operate in the process of recovery, to help expel the poison from our people, but first you must be pounded into compliance, by an inexorable process from which there will be no respite. The first time you came forward of your own free will; this time you must do the deed whether you will or not; and if Thyra can discover that in your horoscope I will sacrifice a chicken or a rabbit to Astrologia, or whatever victim may be appropriate to that goddess and her creed. And Käte Neumeier, now Frau Dr. Koldewey, raised her cup of coffee, and answered Albert's toast with a quizzical smile. Again the clock struck, and this time they all heard it—seven o'clock.

That morning the Koldewey house was enveloped in a yellowish spring haze, all its windows open wide, and nearly all its rooms in the disorder in which they usually remain after the celebrations of civilized life, until servants emerge from the nether-world and clear it up. On the 1st May, Labour Day in Germany, they might well have left such an exceptional mess until later in the day, but they did their work gladly and without fuss, though they did turn on the wireless to hearten their labours. Herr Koldewey and his wife withdrew to what had been hitherto the Governor's bedroom, the two younger women were already fast asleep, and Fräulein Annette, amiable as ever, had offered to drive the Rohmes back to the Atlantic Hotel, which was easier said than done, as the whole centre of the city was swarming with marching men, making their way to the Park and the Holy Ghost Field. However, they got there at last. Bert Boje, who had accompanied them in the back seat, as a certain Tom Barfey had once done on a journey to Stellingen, got into the seat next the driver, and as he did so, exchanged a lingering look with that lady, the meaning of which was: Well?—what is going to happen to us now? And the same thought, rather less defined, slipped through the lady's mind as well. The last few months had established between Bert and Annette a relation of friendship, and almost of familiarity, arising from a hundred contacts, all of them connected with Käte Neumeier's wedding. But two young people cannot take part in an older person's marriage without some effect upon themselves. . . . Bert gazed in silence at Annette's face, and the Slav or South Sea contours in the high cheek-bones. Both were plainly disinclined to go back to the villa, where they would be merely in the way, although the Mengers attic, as the yellow-washed upper room with the round window was now called, had long held a spare bed for Herr Boje. He clapped a hand to his forehead with an air of mock decision. "They say the Lord speaks to the faithful in their sleep, don't they? Well, there's nothing like a car-drive for bringing something back into one's mind. I promised my new friend, Storm-Leader Preester, to bring him the Argentine stamps from the parcel containing the bulbs and the curare. Drive me to Käte's place."

Annette concealed a smile, in recognition of the abrupt familiarity of his address. "In that case we ought to have brought the Teetjens along," said she, and accelerated. She was still wearing her gaily flowered evening-dress, with a tweed cloak over it, the upturned collar buttoned up to her chin, and in her anxiety to keep her silk skirt from touching the oil-stained petrol-switch, she pressed her knees together and pulled the silk dress up to them.

"Can I help?" asked Bert Boje, laying a hand on the skirt, or rather on the knees, for the driver needs both hands to manage the wheel. The excellent Marie was on holiday, she had taken a tearful leave of the Frau Doctor on the previous evening, for her daily routine would now be a good deal changed; Marie could now take a job as maid in the mornings or the afternoons, it was only during consulting-hours that she would be helping the Doctor as before. By good fortune Bert had Käte Neumeier's key in the pocket of his overcoat, the presentation of the bowl of flowers having been conceived and prepared in the Wandsbeker Chaussée. When they reached No. 2, he jumped out and held the car door open.

"No," she said firmly, and remained in her seat.

"Please," he begged, "how else shall I find the stamps?"

For a few moments she looked at him, his clear, level eyes, his fine brows now arched in doubt, then she lifted one leather-gloved hand from the wheel, took out the ignition-key with the other, alighted, locked the car, and with Bert's hand lightly on her arm to guide her, followed him up the polished stairs to Käte Neumeier's now deserted dwelling. No sooner had they reached the landing than he took her in his arms. She shook her head. Then she opened her cloak and let it hang about her, he clasped her slim form beneath the heavy tweed, and set his lips on hers.

"Where is Herr Footh now?" he asked.

"Drowned," she answered. "He never existed."

Once inside she maintained a half-hearted resistance.

"No, please," she pleaded. "I'm much too tired. After such a day and such a night I shall be no good to you."

"Oh, yes you will," he muttered.

The brilliant silk frock hung in disorder over Käte Neumeier's little table, his evening clothes beside it.

"When I was a little girl, after Mamma died, I used to creep into Papa's bed and cry myself to sleep on his shoulder. Now he has a wife, and I'm not wanted."

"And I, as a boy, used to take refuge with my youth-leader," he replied quietly. "We had to go a long way round before we met. Life as it really is, can't be learnt from school-books. Will you wait for me if I go to B.A., as they call Buenos Aires?"

"I'll go with you," she smiled, with a tear in each corner of her eyes, and went to sleep.

Clasping her slim hips he lay upon his back, gazing up at the yellow-washed ceiling above him, infinitely content, and confident of the future. He would let her sleep for twenty minutes, then they would search for the stamps, leave them at Lehmke's, and drive out into the country. He did not think they would be allowed to park their car in the street for long.

All through those hectic early-morning hours, Herr Koldewey had been hard put to it to force two words into the background of his consciousness, and the two words were: an omen. Really, all this was enough to make a man superstitious. This wedding, that seemed to solve all problems, had brought the man with the axe into the house, together with the flowers and the poison. Enough to upset any man of rather unbalanced mind. Well, he, Heinrich Koldewey, with his clear goat-like eyes, was very well balanced. His best man, Herr Lintze, had not been able to come, having been involved in the war-game, and was now in Leipzig or Dresden, or even in Vienna. The omen had to come —and here it was. It was not an accident, or any sort of association-mania. And yet—and yet. . . . "To-day, was a day of celebration, let us go to bed. You must get used to going up these stairs, Käte, and I hope you will grow fond of them. Instead of a knight's cloak, I lay this wish before your strong and shapely feet."

So saying, Herr Koldewey led his wife into their bedroom, where the yellow-curtained windows stood wide open to a pale sky, now faintly blue behind the haze.

"Ripe apples like ourselves needn't be in a hurry, Käte," said he.

"Indeed, no," she agreed. "One of these days . . . we needn't mind the calendar. Where is the bathroom; I'll undress there."

He undressed in front of his wardrobe, found his night-shirt in his bed, as usual, except that this time it was one adorned with blue cross-stitch; realizing that he must no longer smoke in his bedroom, neither now nor ever again, lay down, excited and fatigued. A singular being, this mammal called Man, he thought, with all his rites and customs and usages. He lay in the half-light, waiting for a woman, about whom he knew so little and so much; he could look back upon his past, he could see almost nothing of the future, and yet he behaved as though he knew what it would be like. . . . Men of his type had lived through a great deal. What a gulf had opened between Walter Rohme and himself. What was one of the last things he said?—that he had invested Claudia's money in Spanish stock, Rio Tinto's. In that case he had better pray for Franco's victory. But where was his newly-acquired Käte?

She entered, looking a little perturbed, in her lilac-coloured bath-gown.

"I wish I knew where Annette had put my night-dress," said she.

Koldewey sat up, and laid his fingers to his chin.

"Annette is an orderly person, so I expect it's here."

He pulled back the coverlet of the bed beside him, and there indeed it lay: a delicate garment patterned in pale-brown and pale-blue.

"How stupid of me," laughed Käte, and without thinking, threw off her bath-wrap. And Heinrich Koldewey saw that a well-grown woman of between forty and fifty can still look very desirable.

"Käte!" he cried.

# BOOK SIX

# THE SOUL OF MAN ROOTS THROUGH

## CHAPTER ONE

### A LEAK

THE LOWER ELBE, like every mighty river near its estuary, is regarded as difficult to navigate. This is especially obvious to the sailing-boats and dinghies that toss about on it even when the weather conditions are favourable—as at this moment, the beginning of July. Unless you have had long experience of the river and its ways, you will discover too late that the current on which you have been gliding so pleasantly along, can be almost maliciously deceptive, and your frail vessel may well be inexorably swept into the North Sea, if you are caught by the change of tide, and the ebb sets in. Then you will suddenly realize that an irresistible force had seized upon you, when you ventured upon the smooth and yellow back of the huge Elbe serpent, which had been latterly described by the schoolmasters of the Third Reich, as a German river from source to mouth. And you can count it for luck if someone comes to your help and saves you from being carried out into the open sea, which would soon smash your boat to matchwood and toss you about like a football. . . . You may begin to suspect, too late, that you misunderstood the buoys you passed as you slipped so gaily over the cool and sparkling waters. But then comes an anchored barrel, or a great steel globe, and your companion asks you in sudden apprehension what they can mean, and whether it wouldn't be better to put in to the shore. Too late—and if you blame him with not having indicated the fairway sooner, you will merely be commiserated by the experts. Bend to your oars, my friends, and pull—pull for very life, if you mean to deprive the fish of a treat, especially the eels and catfish, who will otherwise feast upon your carcase.

. Although Albert was keeping his eyes open for various prospects, and had cut down all superfluous expenditure, he did not grasp the real peril of his position until, at the beginning of the half-year, the tax-assessment came in, in response to the return he had so carefully drawn up several months before. It appeared in an officially folded form, and demanded not merely a further payment of 8 per cent in respect of the supplementary earnings, they being a childless couple, but also an increased instalment of the year's taxes. The formula—'Children: None'—had been, as though inadvertently, marked with a blue pencilled cross, and a printed note had been slipped into the tax-demand indicating in general terms the advantages of a family in a State with properly balanced taxation and emphasizing the special obligations which the National-Socialist commonwealth imposed upon its citizens, both men and women, in the highest interests of so creative a people, and in fulfilment of the destinies of Germany. It was a silly document, and Albert crumbled it in a rage, but Stine smoothed it out, sat down at the table, and said gloomily:

"As if it was our fault."

"Those fools don't understand a thing," growled Albert. "A hundred and twenty marks more—it just can't be done, you must go along and explain."

"Not I," said Stine, paling.

"Perhaps I'd better go?" rejoined Albert sharply; "I expect they'll advise me to divorce you."

Stine gazed at him wide-eyed. "They wouldn't dare. That would be too much."

"Well, you know all the regulations they have made to keep the race pure. If the word goes out again that the Kaiser needs soldiers——"

"I shan't go to the tax office," said Stine with decision, and Albert eyed her grimly.

"There's no point in it anyway. Perhaps the best thing would be to see Footh's lawyer, but that would mean more expense. And we know what the final answer would be: taxes support the Reich. Five years ago Adolf issued an announcement that he was giving his services gratis, that his earnings as an author were enough for his needs—one could not expect more than that." After a pause, during which he inspected his now idle fists, he added: "We don't hear much about that now. Ships, bombers, tanks, oil, auto-roads, and aerodromes—that's what we're up to these days. One doesn't say anything, and I suppose we ought to be proud of it all. But the small man mustn't be crushed in this process."

Stine, who had nervously taken her account-book out of the drawer, and jotted down some figures with a forefinger firmly pressed against the reddish-brown pencil, looked up again, her face now quite pale.

"If we have to hand over a hundred and twenty marks to the Finance Ministry, we shall be finished in three months—utterly."

Albert took the book from her, although he did not doubt her verdict, stared at the brief columns of figures, without comment. Meantime, Stine recovered the blue-columned book, checked the items one by one, and muttered:

"Yes, up to September, inclusive. So that business got us through exactly a year."

Albert got up, shuffled across to the cupboard, and produced the bottle of kümmel—he was now going very slow with it—poured out a small glassful, and drank it off.

"We've still plenty of time," he growled. "Something must happen. Footh will help."

"Need we apply to him again?" sighed Stine, but to avoid suppressing the remains of confidence that she saw glimmering in his face, she stifled her doubts—she who a year ago had so pressed him to renew his connection with the rich shipowner.

"Fräulein Petersen has left a parcel for you," she said, in sudden recollection. "She came to see her relations here last evening."

"Cigar-ends," said Albert, "she collects them for me. People in offices often throw away half a cigar."

"You might ask her to coffee," went on Stine, "and get her to tell you whether there are any prospects for us there; whether Footh is back, and if not who does his job."

"Who?" said Albert. "Who does my job when I'm away? That's what a man marries for."

"I will create one that shall help him and be with him," nodded Stine, quoting the Bible.

"But I don't know whether young Frau Footh is likely to be as friendly to us as Fräulein Koldewey. Did you notice how pretty she looked out in Fuhlsbüttel. Who would ever have thought that Frau Dr. Neumeier would marry at this time of day?"

"Well," said Albert decisively, "there's no harm in ringing up Footh and asking when he'll be there. His fleet is now doubled, and we are importing oil from Mexico."

"I'm glad you feel so cheerful, Albert. Otherwise we shall have to return the shop-fittings, the refrigerator, and the whole business. Then I shall take a job as a maid, and you'll have to get one in the slaughter-house, or in an armament factory."

"You can't be serious," protested Albert.

"What else can we do?" she asked, gently but firmly. "We must think ourselves lucky if we can keep the bedroom stuff, crawl under the feathers, and keep each other warm. We are born into a hard world, as Pastor Langhammer said in his last sermon."

"That's a long while ago."

"Some two thousand years ago," she answered, in the opening words of the old fairy-tale. "Now go and telephone, and pay the tax-cheque into the post-office at once, there's no trifling with the State."

Albert strolled along to the post office, but not to telephone. As far as Stine was concerned, he would have the excuse that Footh was still detained in the Ostmark on business, or on service with his car. The spring was now in its glory, the trees on the streets, the grass in the front-gardens, and all the shrubs and plants so freshly green under their veil of city dust, as befitted the time of year, but he, Albert, no longer felt in a mood to match the season. His troubles—as he had hitherto described the destiny in which he had become involved, and which was partly his own fault, and partly wasn't, so to say, had begun to get on his nerves. He felt exhausted in the daytime, and at night he lay awake for hours listening to the chimes of the church clock nearby, or the music on the radio across the yard. The corner shop on the street was a positive headquarters of gossip and slander. Frau Krusen's green-grocery establishment, where all kinds of vegetables were displayed, together with the flowers of the season in earthenware pots or glass vases, also provided a clearing-house for all the ill-will and malignant talk of the Wagnerstrasse, and the adjacent section of the Wandsbeker Chaussée. The needs of the men in this respect were met by the barber's shop across the road, where Albert regularly had his hair and moustache cut —though he always shaved himself, being an expert at keeping blades sharp. When he had gone to get himself tidied up a few days before Easter, the conversation had suddenly died away as he entered. Both the long-nosed Herr Blecher and his bald-headed assistant seemed suddenly non-plussed—the former bent down over a customer's lathered face, while the latter manipulated the electrically-driven hair-cutter; though after a pause they hailed Albert in the usual manner,—"Please take a seat, Herr Teetjen," assuring him that he would only have a minute or two to wait. Albert swore under his breath, and buried himself in some illustrated papers, which depicted the Führer's triumphal entry in Rome, the new Adolf Hitler Avenue there, battle pictures from the Spanish war, and a collection of athletic young winter-sportsmen who had won prizes that winter in Switzerland. And as he sat, Albert wondered whether he was right in surmising that he and his "troubles" had been the subject of the conversation, or whether he was already seeing ghosts, beset as he was with suspicions that he had never previously known. What sort of strange happenings were these. He had then decided to go to another hairdresser and to cut Herr Blecher, much as he had enjoyed sitting in those comfortable chairs and inhaling the pleasant odours which accompanied the barber's profession, unlike the butcher's. Well, here he was on the way to pay out money, to fill up the postal cheque, which he could just as well have done at home. He must keep Comrade Footh as a last resource, when every other expedient had failed. . . . But when his eyes fell upon the brightly painted post-office, which was not much frequented at that hour of the day, the open door of the telephone box tempted him inside. He rang up Footh's office, asked for Fräulein Petersen, and enquired when he, Teetjen, could have a word with Party-Comrade Footh. At the beginning of July, said Fräulein Petersen; Herr Footh would certainly not be back in Hamburg before then. Should she put him through to Frau Footh? "No," replied Albert, "it isn't a matter for ladies. Please send him our best regards, I'll ring up again at the beginning of July."

In accordance with the English usage, Frau Footh continued as Fräulein Blüthe in the office. She worked in the morning only. She kept her hours with strict punctuality, and she took special care not to allow her contacts with the other members of the staff to be in any way disturbed. But, as Herr Peiffer observed confidentially to Fräulein Petersen, she had, for quite a time, been "the soul of the butter business", as the captains, who knew how to handle women, promptly discovered.

"My dear Lotte," she said that morning before she drove home to Harvestehuder Weg 3, "do keep that fellow Teetjen off us. Herr Footh has so many difficult decisions to make, as you know—the opening up of the Danube route is a very big affair, and a canal may be built connecting the Danube and the Moldau, as Herr Vierkant has suggested, which would provide a life-line for Hamburg, as the Moldau flows into the Elbe."

"I know," smiled Fräulein Petersen. "As soon as Klaas Vierkant gets back, he can act as a sort of buffer against our worthy Teetjen, who can't have anything very urgent to say."

Klaas Vierkant had got on friendly terms with Herr Footh in Vienna, which would never have happened in Hamburg; this had led to his appointment as private secretary for the morning hours, and the scheme for the waterways and the Moldau-Danube canal between Budweis and Linz had been his. In the Third Reich, and over the supply of oil to Hamburg, the question whether the upper waters of a river were navigable hardly mattered—it was promptly rendered navigable.

"So keep Herr Teetjen at a distance for the time being," with which words Fräulein Blüthe took her leave, and was transformed into Frau Footh. Poor devil, thought Fräulein Petersen; however, he should continue to get his cigar-ends.


Albert strolled home full of thought; the ice-floe on which they now existed had appreciably diminished. The fact that Stine had got some sewing work to do, and was knitting children's garments when he wasn't there, he was not supposed to know. He himself still possessed his father's gold watch-chain, a fairly substantial article, but of rather reddish gold, which would not fetch very much—he had had it valued last year. Then Stine had thought of Footh, Gesche Barfey had provided the envelope, and there had been no need to get rid of it. He had meditatively put it in his pocket when he went out, and here he was standing in meditation outside Lutjens, the jeweller's, window, where he had taken the chain a year ago. Who would have imagined that he would have got to the same point in the space of just one year? Perhaps the price of gold had risen in the meantime? Perhaps it hadn't. The purchasing power of the public had dwindled, and anyone who did not belong to the great combines was in for a rough time. Was it for this that they had withdrawn their allegiance to the Hindenburg Republic as far back as '30—he and many hundred thousand others like him, and thrown in their lot, once and for all, with Adolf Hitler's army? He and his followers had then announced an Irrevocable Party Programme— absurd as it seemed now. The watch-chain weighed 42 grammes, and he had but to turn the handle of the shop-door, lay it on the counter, and receive its equivalent in marks and pfennigs, good banknotes imprinted by Herr Schacht, who had now been succeeded by a certain Herr Funk, Albert did not know why. Well, Comrade Vierkant would be sure to know, and he might be expected home at Whitsuntide. Albert lingered outside the shop, looked at the clock-pendulums swaying to and fro in the window, all indicating the hour of a quarter to twelve, Herr

Lutjens being a man of exactitude, inspected the watches, the modern silver cutlery, the table decoration in the form of a well-head several storeys high, and said to himself: No—not yet. These countless swastikas to whom might they bring luck? He would keep the bit of gold in his pocket, the last memento of his father. This afternoon he would go down to the cattle-yards, the harbour and the Wandsbeker goods station, and look for work; he would hire out his strong limbs. After Whitsun the Comrades would be back again—Klaas Vierkant and Peter Preester. It was true that an incident had occurred at Lehmke's which had taken Albert considerably aback—indeed it had left an extremely disagreeable flavour in his mouth. When several of the Comrades came home on Easter leave, and exhibited the loot they had picked up as occasion offered—rings, jewellery, watch-chains, Albert had for days afterwards complained on his own account to his friends and neighbours that those left at home had come off empty-handed. Upon which Lehmke had retorted that none of these articles were worth two thousand marks; and there was many a Hamburg man might ask why nobody had been offered a share when he pulled off such a very big job. This remark had taken Albert's breath away—after all there was a bit of a difference in that case, wasn't there? These fellows were engaged in a very agreeable sort of war, and got their pickings without any strenuous effort of their own; what Lehmke alluded to had been no mean task, which he had undertaken for very sound reasons, in order to extricate himself from a quandary that hung like a noose round two people's necks. Fortunately the wireless was blaring out news from Vienna, and the men listened in silence, though Dame Lehmke sat behind her desk alert and ready to speak her word. Albert didn't want any more talk just then. A friend had put a spoke between his wheels and that had done the trick. Lehmke was an excellent thermometer. Perhaps it would have been wiser to hand over a proportion of his earnings to the benevolent fund— say three per cent., or five. It would have paid him good dividends now. But when a man of business raises new capital it does not commonly occur to him to set part of it aside as a kind of insurance. Generosity was not a prevalent virtue in the Third Reich, foresight was regarded as the mother of the proverbial porcelain goddess, and if foresight were often short-sighted, there was nothing to be done but take the consequences. Preester was unfortunately still in charge of the concentration camp at Graz; Albert could have come to terms with him even as late as this. There was an infernally small sum now standing to his name in the Post Office Bank . . . at that moment he heard the boys telling how they had got a man in Graz who, after the Dollfuss affair, voluntarily executed two National-Socialists condemned to death by the Schuschnigg régime—hanged them on a gallows according to Austrian custom. They had finished him off at Graz by making him run the gauntlet round the camp until he dropped. In a few days he was dead—he was a fat man and his heart gave way . . . Stine had said that no one was alone. One needn't be prouder than Mussolini, who was now accepting the help of the Third Reich in Spain. It was true comradeship to pull a man out of a mess. So—eyes front; attention;

Section!—forward march. May had come, the trees were bursting into leaf. All changes in nature, so he had learned on the wireless yesterday, were produced in a series of something like jerks. That was how every bud opened, and every blossom came to life. This was to be exemplified in the person of Storm-trooper Teetjen, as he strode across the street with his eyes fixed upon his own corner. It was indeed, but not quite in the sense that Albert had in mind as he neared his home.

# CHAPTER TWO

## COMRADESHIP

TEETJEN, MASTER-BUTCHER, stood arrayed in a spotlessly white apron on the threshold of his open shop-door, hands in his pockets. A cloudless blue sky spanned the Wagnerstrasse, it was a hot day at the beginning of July—and the proper thing to do on a day like this was to take a trip out to Finkenwärder, swim in the Elbe, or better still lie in shallow water basking in the sunshine. Teetjen did none of these things, for the Finkenwärder bathing beach had been completely spoilt by the Elbe suspension bridge—sensible people no longer went there. But Albert Teetjen smiled to himself as the thought came into his mind, for this of course was not the reason that kept him at home. He stood in his doorway, looking enquiringly out into the street, much as a soldier, with a hand on the grenade in his pocket, watches the enemy creep towards him. He would show them, whoever they might be, known or unknown, that he was not afraid. Moreover he did not want to miss any customer who might turn into his shop in ignorance of the situation, for the road repair works had already restarted, the municipal cement-mixing machines were grinding noisily in the Wandsbeker Chaussée, and piles of gravel, sand and cement were beginning to accumulate where certain street crossings were to be laid with rough asphalte in place of the existing rubble surface—it was probable that the pick-men and mixers had not heard that one shouldn't buy from Teetjen because his shop was not kept properly clean, that cats or children found their way into his sausage-machine, or that as like as not they would be paying high prices for the carcases of drain-rats. Such, surely, were the stories that must have got about, for it was not every day of the week that Communists were beheaded in Hamburg. . . .

Albert Teetjen gazed up at the sky, where some aeroplanes were speeding overhead. The *Reichswehr* must have opened a new aero-drome somewhere, for these were war-planes, so-called Messerschmitts.

And the heavy machine which they were escorting was a Heinkel, a Heinkel-bomber. A Heinkel 54, if Albert was not mistaken; and indeed he was not. What was he awaiting, here on the threshold of his shop? Yesterday the holidays had begun, to-day was the first full holiday, and now the trouble with the children would begin again, who, as it used to seem, deliberately chose the pavement outside his shop for their play-ground. It had been so in his father's time. The game they favoured was the hopping-game in which a pebble is propelled in accordance with a set of rules from square to square within a certain area outlined in chalk, the whole game being called for some unfathomable reason— Heaven and Hell. The little brats hopped about on their spindly shanks, propelling the pebble with the tips of their toes, until they came to Stop in "Heaven"; in a word, the whole performance was the most effective means of interfering with the public outside a shop-entrance. Year after year Albert had called down curses upon it, and it had been only Stine's prudence that had prevented him dashing out upon the little players in a fury. But she had been right, a shop-keeper must not frighten the children if he wanted to keep their parents' custom.

So that morning Albert waited anxiously to see whether these infernal frolics were going to start again. During the Whitsuntide holidays there had been no trouble, it had poured with rain as usual, and indeed other matters had been happening just then. . . . But Stine had assured him that the playground had been shifted a good way back, beyond Lehmke's shop in fact, Lehmke having presented the children with a stick of chalk, so that the new ground should not be located just outside his door. Yes, the axe could cast no more spells. It was hanging or lying somewhere in the Criminal Museum, and yet . . . and yet . . . Albert laid his hand above his eyes. Yes, yonder they went, hopping already, the little group was gathering, and the game had begun —there was no help for it. Stine—he thought—Stine, we must go.

As a matter of fact, thought Albert, he could be well satisfied with himself. For a man whose backbone had been broken by his treacherous comrades, he held himself pretty stiff and straight. His grandfather had indeed called him a dolt, but he wished he had put down in writing what he had reason to expect from Storm-Leader Preester's return and from the Storm's support in his struggle against the elusive Reds. Five days before Whitsun he had sold the bicycles to provide the instalment due on the shop-equipment, without touching the last hundred. They had fetched little enough—indeed Stine had first thought they were really pawning them, and had for that reason agreed to the low sum offered. But it was then heard that Pieter Preester would certainly get Whitsun leave, and Albert was exultant: now he would soon be getting his own back on that slanderous gang.

It was on the Tuesday after Whitsun—Albert would never forget that day. He went across to Lehmke's, where ten or twelve men were already gathered, Pieter Preester at their head. Dame Lehmke had shot a sharp flash at him from her little eyes, though she smiled at him as sweetly as ever, while Lehmke himself leaned with a bulldog air against the back of the Storm-leader's chair. His lower jaw slightly out-thrust, and—as it seemed to Albert—a drawn and savage look upon his face. The redecoration of the bar had to be paid for, and the newly-painted sign, which displayed a tank smashing into a birch tree—while the economic life of the community, in the words of a recent newspaper article, showed a tendency to contract.

"You have a request to make to us, Comrade Teetjen? But there's a little matter to be cleared up first. What about a nice round sum you picked up on behalf of the Party, without making any contribution to the Party funds, Comrade Teetjen?"

Albert was confronted by twelve pairs of angry eyes, twelve faces—red and brown and pale, twelve heads with cropped or parted hair—but all equally merciless and greedy. They were all short of money, and here they saw a chance, twelve against one, and surely their claim was a matter of plain justice.

On behalf of the Party? A contribution to the Party funds? Albert felt like a hunted hedgehog, and put up all his prickles. But as it was a case of twelve against one, he had to keep himself well in hand, and keep quite calm. So he took a meditative draught of Lehmke's sparkling Hamburg ale, wiped his moustache, and said good-humouredly:

"Not too fast, friends. As you seem to know everything, oughtn't you to have cut some workers' heads off before you can make such a claim against the Party funds? I've always said you should be grateful to me—on behalf of the Party—now that the Reds are at my heels, and I'm on the point of going under."

In the meantime Klaas Vierkant had come in, and, promptly discovering what was going forward, laughed and waited with a kind of sporting interest to see how Teetjen would extricate himself; he was obviously in the wrong, apart from the fact that he was in the weaker position, and one against twelve must surely be in the wrong.

"Want to deny," shouted Preester, "that it was the Party, in the person of Party Comrade Footh, that put this chance in your way? Two thousand marks for four strokes with the axe—shame on you not coming across with the cash of your own free will. And here's a fellow who is always cursing the big Stores, though they have long since been Arianized, and forgets that the common good comes first. No, my lad—you pay up twenty-five per cent of the amount, and then we'll see."

Albert felt himself grow pale and then flush. The room felt as though it were revolving round the chair which he was clutching with both hands. The last few months had plainly left their mark upon his nerves. His hand gripped the handle of the heavy mug in front of him, itching to crash it down upon the skull of the man opposite, which was how—so it was said—Gauführer Adolf Wagner had dealt with the mutinous S.A. leaders in the Munich Brown House.

"Twenty-five per cent.?" he asked, in steady tones. "Of the whole sum, or of what is left of it?"

At this point Klaas Vierkant intervened, remembering the connection between Teetjen and his future employer, Footh the shipowner. A quarter of the whole amount, he said, would under present conditions be excessive, although it would have been a right and reasonable contribution at the time.   And there was no means of discovering how much of the amount was left.   So he suggested as a compromise—ten per cent. to the Benevolent Fund, and the matter to be regarded as closed.

Albert Teetjen turned a heavy gaze on the rather personable young man, to whose talk he had always listened with so much pleasure.   The last occasion was the night of the comet—or was it the Northern Lights? If he now had to pay two hundred marks out of the miserable few hundred marks that still stood to his credit, in order to satisfy these greedy brutes, he would indeed be sunk.   He looked despairingly about him—perhaps a gush of cold black water would pour through the windows and doors as he had once seen in a film somewhere; then, when the corpulent Preester continued in a very hostile tone that he seemed to need a long time to express his gratitude for such a lenient proposal, which offered him the means of recovering his reputation as an honourable S.S. man, he could only shrug his shoulders, nod, agree that it was so, and express his hearty thanks.   What more could he say?   Could he proclaim to these people here that it was for them, for the Third Reich, that he had risked his whole existence, and struck at a venture?   Since then, everything had gone wrong with him, and even though his affairs looked very bright on the surface they brought him nothing but honour.   Should he tell these people the tale of the debts that had then beset him, and explain that but for the pressure of dept and the prospect of disaster, he would never have deigned to act as executioner?   What were the words that then passed through his head?   Hard it was for a man to march to his downfall and behave as though it was a matter of no moment. There were his comrades—these were the men upon whose support he had relied.   If his Stine had not been waiting for him at home, he would have picked up the nearest oak chair and smashed it down on to these brutes' heads, especially Lehmke, that blackguardly neighbour of his—well knowing that a knife in his own back, or a bullet through his doorway, would lay him out and end his troubles.   As a young man, that is, he would certainly have countered such a treacherous attack, but now it was different.

"All right," said he, "nothing else to be done.   You might have known I did it because I was broke then.   However, if you insist . . ."

They did indeed insist, on the whole amount, cash down.   It did not work out at more than twenty marks each, anyway.   Well, he must discuss the matter with Lehmke, replied Albert, as he got up and went into the public bar, where Frau Lehmke sat behind her desk, and received reports from her husband of what was going on—with an ominous eagerness, Albert thought.   Then followed a brief colloquy as between friends, in the course of which Frau Lehmke suggested that Albert should pledge his bedroom walnut or mahogany or whatever it was, including the bed linen, to the Lehmkes, to become their property, in case he were not in a position to pay back, within three months, the requisite loan of two hundred marks, together with ten marks interest, which was surely reasonable. Frau Lehmke accordingly scribbled a memorandum in these terms, which Albert with set teeth, gripping the wooden penholder firmly in his powerful fingers, duly signed.

"Won't you go to Spain, anyway?" said Lehmke, in a consolatory tone, before he vanished into his bedroom, to return with the ten banknotes; "and Stine goes to her sister at Nienhagen—isn't that where she comes from?—and so all will be settled nicely. Wasn't fair how you treated us over that job of yours. Now, you have righted yourself and you are welcome again. Wasn't kind, to leave us out, see?"

Albert admitted his error. He would have admitted more than this on that evening, nauseated as he was by what had passed. Was this the real character of the Third Reich, on which the Führer flashed his lightning glance from an enlarged photograph, now encircled with a wreath of oak-leaves? In that case it hung not inappropriately above the till where dame Lehmke was accustomed to keep her large person warm on a thick cushion in a knitted cover. Well, all he wanted now was to get home and lie down, and not so much as mention the miserable affair to Stine, otherwise she would begin to quote her grandmother and the New Testament and lecture him about the sin of shedding human blood.

"Much obliged," said he, as he signed the receipt for two hundred and ten marks, repayable on 7th September, and re-entered the back room, now known as the saloon. There, during the conversation in the interval, there had been mention of Parson Langhammer's latter end, and of the ceremony which his old cow of a wife had had the impertinence to hold in his honour. But Pieter Preester, his sharp eyes fixed on Albert, and highly satisfied with the course events had taken in that quarter, burst out laughing, banged his fist on the table, and inspired by words in which the affair had been described, struck up the song of the Pastor's Cow; "which might be regarded as their tribute to Pastor Langhammer's memory."

*The good rich soup from the kidney-fat of the good old Pastor's cow.*

And the company took up the refrain:

*Here's how, here's how—to the good old Pastor's cow.*

"And so good-bye to the late Pastor Langhammer," exclaimed the Storm-leader, as Teetjen and Lehmke appeared behind his chair.

"Fixed it up?"

Albert then realized that this demonstration took the place of a reckoning with Frau Pastor Langhammer, handed Party Comrade Preester the little packet of twenty-mark notes, forced himself to express his thanks to the company for this truly friendly settlement of this unfortunate affair and soon afterwards went home, after making all those present, including the Lehmkes, promise not to mention the matter to his wife, who had better not know of it, at any rate for the present. She was attached to her bedroom, and was, besides, too sensitive to be able to use it with any peace of mind, if it no longer belonged to her. Well, perhaps another miracle would come to Teetjen's aid, a real lottery prize, a genuine legacy, or possibly the good God, with whom Stine kept on terms, would bring the Wandsbekers back to reason.

"Good-night, Albert," said the Lehmkes, as he closed the door behind him. The bedroom furniture was still worth five hundred marks, even though Jewish furniture was being sold off cheap.

"There's ox-tongues a-plenty in Schleswig now, from the good old Pastor's good old cow," roared the singers within; then the closed doors swallowed up the jubilations of the victorious legionaries. And Albert really felt, as he walked heavily and slowly down the street, that he had not been dealing with Germans of to-day, but with Pilate's mercenaries, to whom he had delivered up a man, as it might be Pastor Langhammer, or the Jew whom Ruckstuhl had beheaded, or one of his own four victims. How oddly they had thrust their heads out over their stomachs, yonder in Ohlsdorf. Indeed he could not now have distinguished between them—which was Merzenich and which was Timme. They had played no part at all in his life, until he had conceived the idea of cutting their heads off to help himself out of his difficulties. It was not to benefit such men as these he had made that pact with Footh in the Uhlenhorst roadhouse. Now he would again have a secret from Stine —for how long, who could tell? However, the affair was now at all events cut and dried. On 7th September, everything must come out, one way or another. He wished he had drunk more beer so that he could have got to sleep quickly. He felt completely shattered, his bones, and especially his spine, seemed on the point of giving way. These were his friends—the support and comfort of his life. With their aid he had hoped to smash the Reds, visible or invisible. He might as well have implored the stars in Heaven for assistance. If he slipped in very quietly by the back way, Stine might not hear him. He had indeed aged by several years since the New Year. But he had never yet felt as he did now, so desolate and desperate. It was a pity that there wasn't a hole in the Wagnerstrasse roadway leading into the interior of the earth, as described by Arne Saknussen to his Professor. A man could not creep into a deep enough refuge after such an experience. . . .

Next morning, when he had not been long awake, though he had slept late into the day, he washed and made up his mind what he would do. Now on to Footh. There was no sense or use in hesitation. Well, he had slept pretty soundly in a bedroom not his own. He wondered what sort of tale he should tell Stine, and when. He gazed with a sort of savage pride at the shining wood of the beds and the tall wardrobe, on which dame Lehmke had long since had her eye. It was warm in the house, Stine was busy in the kitchen, she did not use gas any more as the gas-bill had to be kept as low as possible. Old planks, chopped up by Albert, with a little coal refuse, served to cook the midday meal, which to-day consisted of beans with a few bits of rancid bacon. When they went out they always chose the streets where the householders were beginning to get their winter stock of coal for the central-heating furnaces. Then he would put a small sack in his pocket, and when dusk fell, collect the fragments scattered round the pavement plates through which the precious substance was tipped into the cellars. He had long since given up smoking cigars. In certain public-houses, where his name was not known, he had an arrangement with the waiters whereby he was allowed to buy the cigar and cigarette-ends which would otherwise have been thrown away. During the war years men had learned how to crush and wash them, eliminate the nicotine, dry the resulting tobacco in the sun, which could then be quite well smoked in a pipe. It only cost a few pence a month and tasted quite tolerable. Stine, for her part, saved on stockings. She now wore short socks all day, and, when at home, slippers on her bare feet. She looked quite respectable when out of doors; and fortunately people were so intent upon our great successes, and on the removal of the injustices of the Versailles Treaty, in the Sudetanland, in Czecho-slovakia, that they scarcely paid any attention to individuals. Unfortunately the Heligolander brother-in-law could not for the moment repay the loan of ten talers; there would be no more holiday seasons, Heligoland had become a naval port again, and the fleet came first.

It was not so very difficult for the Teetjens to tighten their belts further, as the phrase goes. But under no circumstances must anyone observe that it had become necessary to do so. No one must be in a position to look down upon Albert and Stine, whether in sympathy or curiosity, in kindness or contempt. No; that must never be. In business life there were always ups and downs. But a Teetjen, and one born a Geisow, did not let anyone look into their cards. Were they well off, or on the verge of starvation—that was their affair. It in no way concerned their neighbours, the kindly inhabitants of the vicinity, that miniature town which forms the centre of every man's acquaintance in the great cities. More was at stake than the maintenance of the outer surface of the façade. For it was like the skin of the human face, the nexus of the most delicate nerves, so that a blow is felt, not upon the skin, but on the soul or heart. Even when people evade you, look past you, decline to greet you, avoid your shop—never mind. You must fight, you must never yield, and above all you must never lose your self-command. And you must never deal a trump to your adversary. No one may here sit in judgment upon any other. The outer door, above which was inscribed the name of Teetjen, divided the domain of the public from that of home and all it stood for, which was nobody's concern.

Albert and Stine were possessed of sound and average powers of thought, though indeed but little used. Their ability to take account of their own position did not extend very far; like all their kind they were more disposed to look into the distance, and not to take much thought for the events of their daily life. In the conception they had evolved of this affair, this strange and even insulting boycott, they had until the last few days distinguished two elements, one personal that concerned themselves alone, and one which ought to have attracted more general attention and, indeed, have come to the notice of the Party, the ruling power, which in 1933 had taken over the German Reich, and behind and high above it, of Adolf Hitler himself.

"They're jealous of us, Stine," said Albert, trying to put the matter into words, while the Whitsuntide rain pattered down outside; "as we well know, because there's never any upsets in this house, no sounds of quarrelling as in the Blohms' place, when the old man was alive, and we don't slam doors like the Lawerenzens. Because you are still my pretty girl after all these years, and because I'm somebody and look it when we go out together."

"I say you do," said she with a radiant smile.

"Well, that's what they can't bear," said he meditatively, with his head on his hands and his elbows on his knees. "Odd, isn't it? And as we haven't any children, and no one can come along and complain that our brat has thrown a stone through their ground-floor windows, or dropped a horse-apple down little Edith's neck—that makes it worse."

And Stine, who had been very near to tears on account of having had to sell the bicycles, began to titter, for that was the trick that Drohm, the ironmonger's son, had played upon little Edith's Doligkeit, and had entertained the Wagnerstrasse during the entire Michaelmas holiday.

"And you think that they really loathed us all the time, and that all their friendliness, and even when they used to call me darling Stine, and pretty little Stine, was all put on?"

"I don't know," said Albert, contemplating the blue and white tiles on the shop-floor, kept so spotless by Stine, and in winter so cold to the feet, that wooden slats had to be put down before and behind the counter. "I don't like to believe it; we weren't doing anyone any harm, and it's not a German habit to be treacherous, like the Polacks and the Czechs. Did you see the article in Reitlin's *Fremdenblatt* the day before yesterday?"—the Teetjens had given up taking in a daily paper several weeks ago, and had made an arrangement with the House-Warden whereby they were allowed to look through his paper a few days late.

"No," Albert continued, "they liked us well enough. That's why I always thought that the axe scared them away from the shop. But perhaps it was the little bit of honour and glory that came our way lately."

"It came to you," she interposed. "Yes, they don't like that. People must walk the streets as they do, and not dash by on bicycles. If we appealed to them for sympathy, you would see how they would come back. But they'll wait a long time for that. They're not likely to see the Teetjens doing anything of that kind, are they?"

And Stine dried her eyes, thrust out her pretty underlip, and exchanged a look of complete understanding with Albert.

The other side of the affair, its general and political aspect, had often been discussed between them and they viewed it in the same light.

"I used to think," Albert would say over and over again, "that the

Republic was dead and buried, that the Reds had gone out of business because everyone realized what a blessing the Third Reich was to the country. We were again respected and feared, and in the words of the old song: Yonder stands the German flag, in honour and respect. And the little Doctor and our great Führer are never tired of hammering into people that such progress demands sacrifices from every one. But—no. You can see from the behaviour of our so-called Comrades that it pours into one ear and comes out at the other, it never gets into their heads at all. Public advantage before private gain—that's what they never understand. Every man of them is wild because he or his old woman has to go without something that they need: if they can't sit in the back seats at the cinema; if they have to go on wearing an old pair of gloves, which have been darned so you couldn't notice it; or the Carsten woman has to have her husband's overcoat invisibly mended, where it caught on some barbed wire or a nail when they last took a trip into the country. In other days, she thinks, they would have got a new one. And now they've got a chance to express what they feel."

"Yes—on us," said Stine with a sob.

"Well, and why not?" asked Albert heavily. "There's no risk in it, that sort of slanderous talk can't be brought home to anybody."

Stine realized that this was what most infuriated a man of his violent temperament, as he continued: "If I only knew who had started the story that our shop wasn't hygienically run, I'd knock his teeth down his throat."

The use of this rather pompous word he could not pronounce properly did not alter the impression that his threat made on Stine. He would not let himself be downed, she was sure of that.

Such had been the sense of their talks before the longed-for event occurred and Pieter Preester came home on leave. On the Wednesday after Whitsun, while she was watching the large, coarse beans to see they did not burn, and Albert was sitting over his breakfast at the kitchen table, pouring out a cup of substitute coffee, Stine noticed with surprise that he who had been in such a hopeful mood the day before, now sat in silence, his shoulders hunched, spreading plum jam on his bread and not inclined to say anything to anybody. Stine had proved during the early stages of this miserable affair that she could refrain from asking questions. No good had come of that: she must not make the same mistake twice.

She pushed the asbestos plate under the beans, pulled up a kitchen chair, sat down opposite Albert, propped both her elbows on the table, and clasped her face between her hands—an attitude that had been forbidden to her at home, and had been called 'The Arms of Mecklenburg'—from the ox's head on that device. But she knew that it rather pleased Albert, for reasons unknown, perhaps because it showed off her pretty arms; and so, her face framed in her hollowed hands and her reddish hair hanging loose on either side of it, her shining eyes fixed searchingly upon him, she asked the decisive question:

"Out with it, Albert, what happened yesterday?" And as he said nothing, but merely muttered as he chewed, she went on: "The likes of us mustn't try to be too clever. If I had asked you what you were up to at the time when you were training, who knows whether I might have had the strength to persuade you not to do that job. Now, when all we've suffered during these last months has pretty well taken the heart out of us, I'm not going to make the same mistake again."

Albert, staring heavy-eyed at her face, her arms, her hair, softly whistled a tune from an operetta, the words of which ran: 'Such a very little woman.' And his expression meant: Would you be able to face it? He had meant to keep his mouth shut.

"Yes, Stine," said he. "They put the screw on me yesterday. Pieter Preester, and the fellows left behind. They wanted their share—ten per cent—for the Benevolent Fund; the help being directed to themselves, of course. And what I hadn't on me in cash, Lehmke lent me; nice of him, wasn't it? I merely had to pledge the bedroom furniture as security. If I pay him back the two hundred marks on the ninth of September, your bedroom will be ours again."

Stine said nothing for a little while. Albert watched her eyes blacken, as the pupils gradually expanded. The rain was still thudding down outside.

"My bedroom," she then replied softly. "Our refuge. So when I polish it now, I'm keeping the Lehmke female's property in order."

"Not quite," he answered, "but nearly so. Blessings on the small man."

She took her hands from her face, and began to count on her fingers. "June—six, July—seven, August—eight, until the ninth of September it still belongs to us."

"Quite a few days," he agreed. "A lot may happen in that time."

"Thank heaven," she said, standing up. "At least we know how long it can last."

"Otto wants our linen-cupboard, too, but for that he's to produce an extra note or two. If Adolf knew the sort of ramps that go on. And when it rains like that, I can't go out with my rod, or get a job unloading in the cattle-yard. I'll get something done."

"Had a good breakfast?" she said. "Well, give me a kiss. And if you can't fix anything, we'll go off together."

"To Spain?" he asked.

"And farther still," she replied. "He who sheds men's blood, by men shall his blood be shed. 'Shall' or 'must'—that was the argument many a Friday evening at Plaut the chemist's house, when the tapers burned in the silver candlesticks, and the Herr Rabbi came to supper. You have seen, Albert, those beheaded men are leading us into war— your four, and Comrade Ruckstuhl's tall Jew, Ruckstuhl the Bank Director of nowadays. Whether you are blown up by a mine and a 'plane bomb hits me here, who knows where that's written. Better then, we settle it together. Have still time until the ninth of September, nobody is going to look into our cards, we must keep ourselves smart and clean, even go to the cinema now and again—and then end it: how, remains to be seen."

"You don't mean you want me to shoot you, Stine?" Albert's

throat was dry and constricted as he spoke the last words. "Won't happen, girlie; besides, I know whom I mean to plug a hole in first." And he went across into the living-room, and took from the cupboard the black holster containing the automatic pistol which was part of his equipment. He might as well take it to pieces, and clean and oil it.

As a matter of fact he did not know against whom he would like to use that weapon. Yesterday he had still believed in his Führer, but to-day something seemed to have gone wrong with the Party, some indefinite and impalpable evil presence had slipped between him and his fellows, between him and his people. Had Adolf not again announced in thunderous tones to the Reichstag that his sole will prevailed, that nothing could be done but by his knowledge and direction; but what about yesterday evening's outrage? Blackmail, blatant and unashamed. While he took his pistol to pieces with a screw-driver, he glanced from time to time up at the photograph of Hitler, which he had bought a number of years ago, depicting him in profile wearing the simple collar and tie of the S.A. jacket, without any badges, such as had been in circulation long before the seizure of power. Behind that glass, in that self-same frame, had hung his grandfather's yellowed photograph, from the identical nail and in this same room, which was really an enlarged passage between shop and bedroom. The old man's photograph was probably now lying in the bottom drawer of the cupboard, wrapped in newspaper, put away with other such old oddments. Perhaps the day was not far distant when the two pictures would again change places.

Then the weather cleared again, the rain stopped, the ground dried, and Albert applied himself to practising with his divining-rod. It was fortunate that he possessed this resource. Without it, the bleak idleness of his existence would have gone to his head and might easily have driven him into one of the frantic outbursts that he had inherited from his father. It was true his membership of the S.S. had schooled him in self-control, which was all well and good, but it wasn't decent that a healthy man, full of enterprise and energy, should have to walk about like one of that herd of unemployed whom the Weimar Republic had apparently been unable to help, whereas our Adolf had promptly restored to them their self-respect and the chance of earning a modest living. However, he could reckon on a measure of progress from week to week. The parade-ground behind the Wandsbek barracks had been turned into a sort of practice-ground where, under the direction of Lieutenant-Colonel Lintze, metal objects were hidden at various depths and places, only known to the military authorities. As all ranks fit for active service had been moved into Austria, the inmates of the orderly-room and any other elements that had remained behind, had both time and inclination to be present at the trials. Here were dud shells from the world war, bombs with the pins removed, long sabre-blades; a careful record was kept of the itineraries, and the number of successful finds, entered, like the hits in a shooting-book. At Dr. Laberdan's suggestion, Pinnow, the regimental clerk, also made a note of the weather,

as indicated on the selected days by the level of the barometer and the
cloud conditions, not forgetting the temperature. And Albert held his
Dowser's Record, as he called it, in high honour. A French seventy-five
under a couple of feet of sand would, after all, be detected by a Stellingen
rhinoceros when he was on top of it. But the location of a hussar sabre
eighteen inches below ground, and the direction in which it pointed,
was much less simple, and so were shrapnel bullets scattered near the
surface. Albert himself could only discover them under favourable
circumstances. Lieutenant-Colonel Lintze would be delighted when he
got back. He wondered if there would be anything doing in Spain.
There was one particular circumstance which both Albert and Stine
noticed, each on their own account. They had not said a word about the
Ohlsdorf Cemetery nor the Fuhlsbüttel wedding breakfast, until Pieter
Preester and Otto Lehmke forced them into utterance. They had both
been brimful of that uncanny experience as they sat on the stone
balustrade at the Fuhlsbüttel gate—incapable of stirring from the spot,
and eager to talk of what they had seen, to unburden themselves of it,
and digest it, and indeed they often reminded each other of what their
feelings had been; how glad they were when the two girls in their flowered
dance-frocks had taken them into the house and asked them to sit down
at the wedding-table. Yes; but then they found they could not utter.
Dr. Koldewey and his guests were not the sort of people who could be
told about such apparitions of smoke and air, even after several glasses
of the cognac which was so hospitably displayed on the table. And
indeed Stine sometimes quivered all over when she remembered how
the five juniper-men had stood by the grave, holding their heads by
the ears with the noses scornfully tilted, until they finally drifted to the
van of the long column of marching men and headed their disappearance
into the Ohlsdorf lake. People to whom that sort of thing happened
did well to conceal it. Whether it was an appearance of the supernatural in the world of every day, or whether it was a figment of the
individual mind, a dream of waking hours, made no real difference to
the embarrassing nature of the occurrence. People who saw things like
that were outside the ordinary run—and not altogether what they should
be. Everyone must keep quiet about such strange matters; not only in
Hamburg, but especially here.

And so Albert managed to brace himself against the blow that had
descended upon him in those days of Whitsuntide—on him and Stine,
but more especially on him. To all outward appearance, at any rate.
But when the rainy days continued, after he had finished cleaning his
pistol, he set himself to clear out the shed with its melancholy empty
rack in which the two bicycles had once stood, which Stine could no
longer bring herself to mention. Two hundred marks, and ten marks
interest for three months—that was what he had to find. While Albert
was carrying out an old ironing-board, which he meant to chop up into
firewood, he tried to work out in his head the rate of interest which
friend Lehmke was extracting from him. But he could reach no result,
until he discovered a bit of chalk, and using the back of the board as a
slate, arrived at the figure—twenty per cent. And how did it square

with what was said in the twenty-five points of the one and only Programme about income not arising from work or effort? He stood in
the windowless, echoing room and laughed. Adolf Hitler—hail and
victory; but ruin and destruction upon those who used him for their
evil ends. And therewith he pulled out the ancient tricycle, which had
been replaced by the handsome bicycles for so short a time, alas! It
had a sort of carrier between its back wheels, and sorely needed a fresh
coat of paint, if it were to be pedalled in daylight through the streets of
Hamburg. There must be a pot of the needful paint left, and he could
surely rout out a brush from somewhere. He must not spend anything
on it, but it was essential to smarten up the contraption which Albert's
father had always called the trolley—even if he wanted to pawn or sell
it. Perhaps Stine would consent to curl herself into the cube-shaped
carrier, and ride round the neighbourhood with him, as in better days.
It was quite possible to endure it for half an hour, with legs drawn up
and leaning against the rear-board. Of course the inside must be
thoroughly cleaned out with lysol and water, and set to stand for a few
days in the open air, with the lid off. Well, Albert had time enough.
He dragged out two trestles, laid the ironing-board across them, and
skilfully dismantled the machine until nobody but a professional
mechanic from the Wanderer Works could have put it together again
without a mistake. An old preserve tin filled with petrol, three worn-out
tooth-brushes, the oil-can belonging to the bicycles, a pile of cotton-wool
and old rags—and Albert fixed up a workshop for himself in an angle of
the yard under Frau Blohm's window, where, with rolled up shirt-sleeves
and in his mouth a short pipe filled with his own home-made mixture,
he got down to it with a vigour that it was a pleasure to watch.

So, at least, Frau Blohm felt as she dished up dinner for her friend,
Herr Kramer, when he came back from work in the late afternoon.

"Just look at Teetjen—there's a stout lad, who knows how to set
about a job of work."

"Yes," said Herr Kramer, as he stepped back from the window—
they were eating in the kitchen—and sat down again, and smoothed the
napkin out across his knees. "I must talk to you about that. Agnes
Timme is going off in the middle of July, on a Strength through Joy trip
to Norway—but she isn't coming back again. From there she can get
across into Russia. Her two sons will be waiting for her on the frontier.
Now I've been thinking that you could do the job just as well as she can,
with her artificial hand—her left hand got crushed years ago in the
service of the firm. You're neat with your fingers, and far from being
a fool, but you must get a bit of practice at the work now. She'll be
quite willing to help. I've been doing what I can for her, and she
hasn't found it easy, I can tell you. That's why I know all about it—
Oslo and Leningrad and the children. As we aren't married, we don't
come under the class of Double-Earners, if you yourself bring a wage
envelope back home every Saturday. And I fancy we shall make pretty
good use of it, shan't we?"

"If it's clean work," said Frau Blohm, thinking aloud, "we could
lunch at the canteen and have a warm meal in the evening.

T

Everything is getting so dear nowadays. Do you think I can manage it, Oscar?"

"Of course you can. But you'll have to get her to put you in the way of the job, Otti."

"I don't mind, and I can pay her back by telling her who took care of her husband last summer. She might be glad to take her children a picture of the handsome Albert, or to take a fond farewell of him and his Stine."

In the meantime, Oskar Kramer had put away a very satisfactory dinner of bacon and peas and a pudding to follow. What a devil there was inside this little woman of his—it was an aspect of her that sometimes came out just like that. He lit a cigarette, went to his window once more, watched Albert wheeling his machine back into the shed, and observed, shaking his head, and quite involuntarily:

"You could snap him from here."

The deep blue sky of a July morning spanned the Borstel heath. Over the tops of the birches and alders white summer clouds drove inland from the sea, rose, and scattered into haze. In the tall grass, yellowed by the summer heats, stood the old three-wheeler in which Albert had driven his Stine out from Hamburg—trundled her out, as they called it. Fortunately Hamburg is as flat as a table, and Albert was still a stout fellow in the early hours of the day; but he had begun to tire quickly, though not as the lover of his pretty young wife. And yet it must be said that, in this relation too, since Whitsuntide something of an estrangement had come upon him and upon her also. Something had turned off the current that usually sprang into such light and lively play between them; now it was only at moments when their feelings were in some way stimulated that they remembered they were not a couple already staled by familiarity, but that the sight of Stine's shoulders and back, the glint in her eyes, the smile on her lips, even the red fluff of hair under her arms, could fire Albert's senses. It had been so that morning when they awakened in the beds that still were theirs, and again when Stine, as she climbed out of the box-like carrier, and set her long and shapely legs upon the ground, while her dress caught for a moment on a projection in the machine, offered such an alluring spectacle. Fortunately no one was near, it was not until later in the morning that the holiday children would be prowling through the heather, looking for butterflies, wild raspberries, and stag-beetles, leaving sandwich papers behind despite the stern police notices posted up everywhere. Albert had his divining-rod with him—he knew this precise neighbourhood very well, its subterranean water-courses with all their twists and turns and new outlets, had revealed him many a secret. But to-day he lay on his back on the grass beside Stine, and she, too, made no move to unpack the bundle of children's clothes she had brought with her. They had no need to go hungry, they could still buy potatoes, and cut a few slices off a side of bacon. They still got their days' old newspaper from schoolmaster Reitlin, and Albert had constructed a little petroleum lamp out of an old tobacco-box in which a spark could be kept burning to save matches when he smoked his pipe of home-made tobacco. In the first days of July the gas-man, having observed the very trifling use they made of the gas supply, suggested that they might allow him to remove the installation, as gas meters were very scarce, and the manu-facture of new ones was strictly limited by the needs of the armament industry. Upon which Albert had wondered whether he would not do best to get rid of his shop equipment, and put his premises at the disposal of the landlord once more; together with the workshop and the shed. He only refrained because the shop and the flat were both covered by his tenancy agreement. Besides, he would, at need, be allowed to fall into several months' arrears of rent for premises which his father had occupied; but if he moved elsewhere he would have to pay money down, not only on the conclusion of the agreement, but first instalment of rent immediately afterwards. All this passed through his mind as he watched the clouds floating over his head, and savoured the pleasure that Stine had given him once more.

"Do you really want to go on paring and scraping like this any longer, girlie?"

She shot him an almost violet-dark look out of the corners of her eyes, a slanting, sideways look, as he was lying close to her.

"Just so long as you, and not a minute longer."

To the left of him, red and black beetles were crawling through the grass, about the size of peas and quite flat, commonly known as grave-diggers. Albert knew them quite well, both as a boy and as an old soldier he had often followed and watched them for hours, as they buried a dead bird or frog, in order to deposit their eggs upon it in comfort and security. He called Stine's attention to them, they both sat up, leaned their backs against their tree, and watched the little gaily coloured creatures darting about all round them.

"You do know, Stine," said Albert after a pause, "that I don't wish to go on struggling like this much longer. Do you remember what you said to me a month ago?"

"One thing and another," said she. "What are you thinking of?"

"It was after what you said that I cleaned my pistol."

"Ah yes," she replied calmly. "You swore you would never lend a hand to put me off the earth."

"Right," he said with emphasis. "And I stick by that. I've often thought it over between-times when we were unloading frozen mutton from the Australian ships, or driving Rumanian cattle out of the ships' holds. But to do that for a lifetime—— No! I'd sooner the Devil came to fetch me, and he can be a hearty sort of fellow, as we know. It's grand to be alive, but only as a free man and in fine weather. But when its drizzling and you have to grind at a job for nine mortal hours each day, without letting up for a moment, or the fellow behind will be battering at you to get on with it, and quite right too—well, I'm just not made for that sort of thing. But I wouldn't do you in first—don't you think it."

As he spoke he let himself slide backwards into the grass, clasped his hands under his head, and looked up at the tree, an aspen, the leaves of which danced and fluttered in the breeze, and formed a green arch above him. Stine, who was still seated, let her gaze rest upon him, his home-clipped moustache, his smooth cheeks—his fine sharp razor had indeed fulfilled its destiny that morning. Fulfilled—strange how the word had drifted into her mind, one of the last words uttered in Golgatha, and she pondered on the implications which gradually took shape before her inward vision. She remembered that she had dreamt of her grandmother, her kind, brown, wrinkled face with its merry eyes—grandmother Geisow, who had warned her that a good woman ought often to go ahead of her husband and spare him the burden of unpleasant decisions. There were many ways that led out of life. Albert had allowed the gas to be disconnected, but a razor would do the job quite as well, it would sever the main artery in an instant, if it was thought best not to use a butcher's knife. She had also dreamed of Judas Iscariot. It must have been on a tree like this, but with a strong stripped bough, on which he had hanged himself. They had made such a good life of it together, Albert and she. They would leave no children behind them, and they wanted to stay together whatever happened, in life as in death. Ahead of them they heard the tapping of a woodpecker—that must be the decaying poplar beyond the bridle-path. It was still early in the day, the riders had not yet begun to canter past, scattering the scared birds from the trees each side of it.

"No," said Albert, beginning again. "I won't think of any such thing. While there's any sense in doing so, I'll go on with my job, you can rely on that. Footh must come back sometime—at the beginning of July, Fräulein Petersen said; in the last resort I'll get a job on one of his tankers bound for Spain, and you can get a passage as stewardess, there's a passenger-steamer to Spain every week, and in a few weeks we'll be together again, German house-servants are wanted every-where . . ."

"But you know I couldn't learn a word of a foreign language," said Stine, bringing him back to reality, "nor could you."

She watched him smile, as he thought of the three or four Russian phrases which he had picked up in the war: *pascholl* meant forward, *na levo*—to the left, *Stakan Tschajy*—a glass of tea.

"Very well," he admitted, "then you'd better creep along to your sister's place and wait till I come back."

She did not reply, but when he looked up he saw her shake her mop of silky reddish hair, and smile to herself in silence. The smile meant that she was not made to creep into a nest, a place from which she had quietly and resolutely departed as soon as she could.

"All right," he said as he got up. "Then we'll have a go at friend Footh. These last few weeks I've been wondering whether it was wrong of me to take on that job last autumn."

So saying, he stretched out a hand, she gripped it with both hers, set her feet firmly against his, and let herself be pulled up—he did it with one arm. "I don't get to sleep as easily as I used to do. And I must say that if Adolf Hitler was right to alter the laws as they used to be.

Albert Teetjen was right to carry them out—in all due modesty. Did the people not help him into power? Didn't they cheer him when he came to Hamburg? Didn't they make him master over death and life? Yes. So he bears the responsibility, and I am free to act as I choose. All's in order."

"But supposing it is not God's will?" asked Stine, who was engaged in esconcing herself in the carrier, which still smelt rather disagreeably, though they had scrubbed it out and fumigated it with elderberries.

## CHAPTER THREE

### THE LAW OF THE JUNGLE

ON AN AFTERNOON of one of the following days, a delivery-tricycle, with a white-enamelled carrier fixed between its two back axles, stopped in one of the quiet side streets leading off the tree-shaded Harvestehuder Weg. A tall fair-haired man had for some while been patrolling the quarter where the elegant Villa Footh lay in its hedged garden. He walked past the tradesmen's entrance, and also the front entrance, having first rung the bell at the former and received the answer that Herr and Frau Footh had ordered nothing and could not be disturbed. The man cursed himself for not having gone to the front door, it was beneath him to be so diffident. But as he did not like to go home without achieving his purpose, and wasting time was the sole luxury in which he could indulge, he prowled round Footh the shipowner's home, three times, four times, like a lover round his lady's bower.

Madame Footh, Herr H. P. Footh, and the private secretary, Herr Klaas Vierkant, were in the meantime sitting at tea on the terrace outside the Footh bedroom. In contrast to the previous summer a grey and blue striped tarpaulin had been stretched across the terrace to the balustrade, affording a view from beneath it, especially at two extremities, but preventing any observation from without. The reason for this was that young Frau Footh was anxious that the golden-brown of her slim person should not be marred by any patches of white skin. To-day she had asked Herr Vierkant to tea, in order that he might lay before her husband and his chief, the ideas that he himself had explained to her in confidence during the past few weeks—ideas that might well dazzle the imagination of a former sergeant, which H. P. Footh had once been, and a man who had hitherto been living in a backwater. His face had grown more lined, and fleshy during the preceding months, and he had put on weight —the result, no doubt, of the rich Viennese cuisine. But there was a more penetrating and resolute look in his eyes, as of a man burdened with with problems and ambitions. And this was the decision that now had to be faced: was it to be Göring or Goebbels?

"The German Reich," observed Herr Vierkant, who was wearing white tennis clothes, and held a cigarette between his slim fingers, "our home, has touched a stage of development upon which other countries entered long ago, before Heaven deigned to send us Adolf Hitler. It is known as the concentration of capital, two ugly but indispensable foreign words, and it stands for the massing of the national resources into the hands and under the responsibility of smaller and ever smaller groups of leading industrialists. The inevitability of such a process is best indicated by the foundation of the Hermann Göring works, which was conceived as a concern established under the auspices of the Reich, to operate, for purposes of rearmament, certain mines which had not proved profitable under private ownership, the capital of which has expanded with amazing rapidity from five million to four hundred millions of marks. What we discussed in Vienna is to form part of this new and gigantic industrial entity: it will absorb anything of value in Austria, in the name and in the furtherance of the programme of rearmament. If we propose to take a share in the navigation of the Danube, we can only do so within this framework. If, in the forthcoming war, we mean to free ourselves from British control of the sea, and import oil on our inner lines from Rumania, that also cannot be done without the Hermann Göring Works. That was the standpoint on which we parted a few weeks ago when you, Herr Footh, were detained by what followed on the partition of Czechoslovakia, while I was again breathing the air of our native city, which, as we all know, makes us wise."

Herr Footh sat there, by no means so comfortably clad as he used to be when he spent most of his time on that terrace, listening now and again to the tread of a military boot below. His affairs had indeed prospered—though it was not until now that he had really grasped the obligations undertaken by a prominent industrialist of his stamp, if he were to keep on forging ahead. A man could not succeed and rest content, one success drove him forward to another—this was a conception for which he had in the first instance to thank his little friend Anneliese Blüthe, who had now indeed provided herself with an ally in the person of this keen, energetic, rather military man of the pen, who described what Herr Footh had naïvely conceived to be the making of money, as the acquisition of power and influence, and elevated it into a theory, which had, however, the misfortune of piloting him, Footh, away from his familiar fairway, away from Hermann Göring, a splendid fellow and an example to every German, in the direction of the rather crooked little hero of the intellect, Dr. Goebbels from the Rhineland. However, he might as well send someone down to that extraordinary person, Teetjen, and ask him what he was here for and what on earth was the matter.

"I wish you would tell me why you think the moment has now come for me to give up my independence. You surely remember, darling, when I first asked you whether I should go in for amalgamation or not."

Frau Anneliese smiled; of course she remembered. She took from a chair a copy of one of the lavishly printed and illustrated publications, of a kind that had already appeared in the times of the late Dr. Stresemann—a sort of German Vogue. She meditatively turned over the admirably reproduced photographs of the Spanish Civil War, depicting the ruins of the little town of Guernica, which had been reduced to rubble by German aeroplanes under the orders of German generals, on behalf of the Caudillo or Führer, the victorious and increasingly important General Franco. Why the Basques had not yielded of their own free will, she could not understand; but their wrecked streets and burnt-out ruins should now convince them that it was foolish to withstand the stronger side, and that folly had to be paid for. Could not the Basques have realized in time that God was always on the side of the stronger battalions, the faster bombers, and would always be so?

"Then," she replied, as she poured out for Herr Vierkant another cup of amber-coloured tea, "then it was much too soon. But now—please go on, Herr Vierkant."

Klaas Vierkant threw a sympathetic glance at the little lady in the white silk frock, whose Rhenish accent had not been wholly effaced by her sojourn in Hamburg, which, in his mind, brought her nearer to that bright and brilliant denizen of the Rhineland, and also indeed to the *Reichstatthalter*, who had carved out so bold a career for himself, after his enemies in the Party had done their best to drive him into the desert.

"Well," he said, beginning to develop his views, "the sole distinction is between an ancient concern and a new one—the power that has already got its start, or the power that has yet to acquire it, or to catch up in the race, if you prefer to put it so. When we were together in Vienna, the Göring concern seemed to offer the best prospects for your 'Äuglein' ships, Herr Footh; and at that time I advised you to write and make a tentative proposal. But in the meantime a genuine giant has shown an inclination to absorb us, the oldest German concern, which in the war of 1870 was already supplying both sides with cast-steel guns. So I should withdraw your proposal and go in with Krupp."

"There's more cash down to be got from the Göring works," said Herr Footh meditatively. "The Krupp people tend to pay in shares. After all, I could approach Göring personally, as man to man, as one soldier to another. But Krupps—the men behind them are dignitaries and Excellencies of the old type, just the sort that I can't get on with at all."

"You ought to visit the Rhineland first, Hans—it's a forest of chimneys, square miles of factories, foundries, ovens, Bessemer plants, miles of railways, thousands of switch-points, and all the rest of it. A gigantic concern, and indestructible—especially as you are so susceptible to a personal impression. What could bring a greater sense of pride than membership of Krupps—the function representing their foreign trade, the connecting threads that they send out across the seas."

This, thought Herr Vierkant, is a clever little lady; and he said, coming to her assistance, "I don't believe, Herr Footh, that you would have to sacrifice much of your personal freedom. You know how many things are connected with the Krupp concern here in Hamburg. Multiplicity in unity, it would have been called in the old æsthetic text-books, or unity in multiplicity. If you join the strong, it's best to join the strongest. The absorption of the small in favour of the greater and the greatest— that is the law of life. After all, the Ruhr represents the strongest concentration of German forces that there is—probably the strongest on the Continent. To-day, they have a chance; Krupps are acquiring a tanker fleet, which will be permanently maintained in their own docks, and kept in constant service on the high seas. The Hermann Göring Works must first prove what they are, and what they can do—but Krupps were and are and always will be. Germany is now putting her back into it, mark my words. We live in memorable times. You will see the old democracies make room for us, when we shout Hullo!—and tell them we are there. I'm prepared to bet that our way to world-power will be littered with small existences, middling people and middling states. It is only thus that great trees can grow and overshadow many centuries. We are beginning late and have much to overtake, much to contend with, and the way to our living-space will not be opened to us without payment made. We shall have to destroy a great deal of human happiness, our victims will cry robbery and murder, the moralists will fall into paroxyms of indignation, and, if they see a chance, shed tears. But life is not a Choral Society. He who would get the most of it, must have his purpose clear, for not otherwise shall he succeed. And surely we are put into the world to make the most of life. And the achievement, Herr Footh, is worth all manner of sacrifice, it will stand firm for generations, too—and that is to speak cautiously and prepare the way for generations more. And every married man must be one of these pioneers if he wants to transmit his strong blood into the future. And he who can't adapt himself, must go under. I need not tell you that."

Hans P. Footh shook his ponderous cranium. "I shall have to go to Essen, if that's what you think—personally I don't feel altogether happy about it."

"You'll find yourself agreeably disappointed," exclaimed Frau Anneliese jubilantly; "and mind you make haste. Otherwise the division of the spoils will have started before you have made up your mind, and then we shall have got up early to no purpose." And she burst into a laugh of relief, in which there was a quiver of hysteria, and threw herself back into a gaily coloured deck-chair, as slim and elastic as a steel spring. Klaas Vierkant looked over her husband's shoulder at the lovely and alluring creature and drew a deep breath; he would contrive to meet her alone sometime later on. Here, perhaps, was the inspiration that would carry him to the heights of the Third Reich that was to endure for a thousand years, to use for once the boastful phrase of common talk; in the distinguished company of the wizened little Arian with the club foot and the flashing brain.

Herr Footh, who had approached the corner of the balustrade, and stood peering through the gap between the two tarpaulins, looked back over his shoulder and observed: "There goes a lost existence."—"Beyond the reach of help," rejoined Klaas Vierkant: "These middling people must acquiesce in their own abolition. There's no room now for little one-man businesses. Organization, gentlemen—we must all subordinate ourselves accordingly."

"But don't let him go down altogether, if I have to be away—twenty marks or so now and again won't break me. He is my old friend Corporal Teetjen, with whom I floated down the Niemen on a raft in days gone by."

"Wait a moment, please," said Frau Footh. "Let me put a word in here. There's a lady in the case whom I don't at all appreciate."

"Poor Stine," smiled Herr Vierkant.

"Yes—Stine; the Lorelei of the back-streets. She must go back to the country, where she belongs. If you want to please me, wait till then. After that, she's welcome to an allowance of twenty marks a month."

"And who wouldn't want to please you, Frau Footh?" exclaimed Klaas Vierkant with genuine enthusiasm. In the meantime her husband had turned towards his two younger companions, and walked towards them with the rolling gait he had picked up from his captains, and back to his chair.

"There he goes, my wielder of the axe. He came in daylight into this neighbourhood on a delivery-tricycle. What outrageous vulgarity!"

"Hard necessity, I fancy," smiled Vierkant, lighting a fat cigarette of Austrian origin. Frau Anneliese looked up at a white cloud dissolving above her into globes of bluish vapour.

"I think there's going to be a tremendous storm," she said to herself. "The flies are dancing like mad." And she drew up her legs in their long white silk trousers on to the chair, and flung a thin gauze wrap over her feet.

"These middling people," she went on dreamily, "there was a time when they were needed."

"Yes—to make their way upwards, or downwards," agreed Klaas Vierkant. "Without them, in the twentieth century, our Party could never have come to life, any more than literature in the nineteenth century, music in the eighteenth, choral singing and religion in the seventeenth. But now!—on the threshold of a new epoch—a new Æon, as Stephan George puts it. Haven't you noticed how these small folk represent our future aristocracy; Teetjen and his kind will find their destiny in ruling the inferior races. Nobility in embryo, just as our Jews stand for aristocracies in decadence—or did."

"Why—did, Herr Vierkant?" asked Anneliese, who was listening with high satisfaction—how clever the man was!

"Yes—decadent and finished. These fine fellows are no longer needed, as they still were in the nineteenth century—we don't want Rothschild or Marx, any more than we want Heine or Börne. We do all this for ourselves now; in Aryan fashion and far better—that is, more thoroughly."

"Ah, that is why so many are now leaving the country," said Herr Footh, sipping his brandy and soda. He wished he could go down to the harbour with Anneliese, where *Blühäuglein* lay at anchor, and there while pacing the deck consider the decision that the other two had tried to extort from him. Klaas Vierkant, his lean, fastidious face turned first to Herr Footh and then to his mistress, as he called her to himself, this sleek, clawed creature, realized that his cue was now to go. He would have liked to sit down by the radio downstairs, and listen to the short-wave reception from Burgos, New York and London.

"Good God, the Jews," he said, as he got up, "imagine they are at home in Europe, and do not know, stupid as they always have been, that they provide us with funds, payment, and targets for the popular indignation. As we have to disappoint our populace, like our predecessors the Roman Emperors, we can at least, as they did, provide them with *panem et circenses*, bread and games, in the persons of our Israelites; and as we must continue to disappoint them by an ever closer concentration of power, capital and freedom in ever fewer hands. Well, thank Heaven, there are eighteen million Jews in the world, half of them within our grasp."

"You should include Palestine," said Herr Footh, as he remembered Captain Carstangen and his tale of the shop-counter covered with butchers' knives.

"Why not?" replied Herr Vierkant; "anything accessible by railway, or on the way to Mosul oil and the Baghdad line; and, in saying good-bye, might I ask the favour of being allowed to listen to your wireless downstairs for a quarter of an hour? Ankara will be coming on in a few minutes, and I should like to hear what our Herr Papen has been up to lately."

"News of trouble," said Frau Anneliese with a nod.

# CHAPTER FOUR

### FRAU TIMME TAKES HER LEAVE

WHILE ALBERT WAS anxiously pondering the question whether he, as a former wedding-guest and companion in arms of the owner of the house, should again try his luck at the handsome glass door, inscribed—For Visitors Only, Stine was sitting in her shop embroidering stars on blue and green baby garments, and looking wistfully out into the summer street, where the children no longer played outside the shop. When the almost forgotten shop-bell tinkled, a strange woman entered, and took her stand before the counter, Stine was almost frightened; a customer! No fresh meat, no mince, no chops? Thank the Lord she asked for *salami*?—Yes, there were still three in the shop, two small and a long one, which could easily be cut up—very tasty.

"A little *salami* sausage?" she enquired. "Excellent for sandwiches."

"I want them," smiled the woman, "as a present for two little Hamburgers, who asked their mother for some."

The two women exchanged looks and liked each other. Such a mutual inclination often springs to life in a few moments, and it is with regret that the sales-woman watches her customer go, for it is not professional to admit any personal feeling into such relations, with the result that the customer often departs for ever from the vision of one who would gladly have become closer acquainted; but often, too, the attraction is mutual, and changes human destinies. Such seemed to be the case here. In any event, the tall and rather haggard woman with the greying hair under her small, dark straw hat, eyed Stine sympathetically as she weighed out the sausage and wrapped it up—with eyes that were larger and greyer than Stine ever remembered to have seen before, even in a film where they were artificially produced. But these, in the gaunt face, pallid from want of fresh air, had the effect of two signalling lamps or the headlights of a car—indeed they would have been alarming, had they not also expressed a diffident but friendly interest. Such a look from a man would have been normal enough, but it was strange as coming from this woman. She looked, thought Stine, as though she had just come back from a long journey and was surprised to find me like this; however, she laid the little parcel down on the counter, named the price, which was not cheap, and watched the woman, who obviously had a paralysed left hand on which she wore a knitted glove, feel for the money in her purse, which, however, she was quite able to hold in the damaged hand. Her dark brown coat with its small cape was unashamedly old-fashioned, especially the row of buttons from the collar down to the hem, and gave her rather the air of a foreign visitor from a faraway island, where the fashions were out of date.

Against the wall stood a small table with two chairs, varnished white, dating from the times when people used to come in for fresh sandwiches and a pennyworth of garlic sausage for their breakfast, which they ate standing. The woman now drew up one of these chairs, and asked if she might rest for a moment, as she had been about a good deal in Hamburg that day.

"Saying good-bye," she said, with a piercing look and narrowed lips.

"We shan't be here much longer either," rejoined Stine, involuntarily, as her eyes wandered round the bare shop and up to the discoloured greyish ceiling. So she had heard, said her visitor; she really wanted to speak to Herr Teetjen. Stine replied that her husband was unfortunately out, he was very busy at the moment—could she give him a message? That might do, said the woman, as she could not call again, being on her way to board a ship for Norway. A longing and dreamy look came into Stine's eyes.

"Ah yes—the Fjords," she said. "Strength Through Joy."

"Only partly," said the woman; she wasn't coming back to the Reich, her name was Agnes Timme—Timme, she repeated, of the Reeperbahn case. She was the wife of Friedel Timme, on whom Herr Teetjen had carried out the sentence of the court.

Stine sank down on to the little bench behind the counter, on which lay a blue embroidered baby's dress, and held it tight. There she sat with parted lips.

"You are . . ." she began, her horrified stare fixed on her visitor's pale eyes.

"I am the man's wife," explained Frau Timme once again. It had taken her about a year to overcome the past, she continued, to get the necessary permits and papers so that she could visit her children who were being brought up in Leningrad, under the S.U.—the Soviet Union, she repeated, observing that the abbreviation meant nothing to Frau Teetjen. And now, before she went, she wanted to set eyes just once on Comrade Teetjen, so that she could tell her two young people what he looked like. But if Frau Stine and her husband were well matched, she—Frau Timme—would think again—and anyhow what was the point in poisoning children's imaginations? It might be as well to let them think that the instigator of the *Reichstag* fire, Göring, had beheaded their dear father with his own hands.

Stine still sat clutching the bench. She felt as though she and the whole shop were sitting in a car on one of those gigantic wheels that are erected for the annual fair at St. Pauli or on the Holy Ghost Square, and always made Stine so dizzy.

The silence that followed was broken by the howling of a child, probably one of ironmonger Drohm's family.

"How did you find us?" she then asked weakly, with something like a gasp.

Frau Timme wagged her head. "Through your worthy neighbours," she rejoined. "How could your husband imagine that anything of the kind could be kept secret nowadays? It was very naïve of him. He should hang himself for betraying his own champions, men of his own kind, for thirty pieces of silver. Hang himself, as Judas Iscariot did," she went on, "poor devil. What did you think about it?" she turned, and fixed her eyes on Stine's with an almost aggressive air.

"We had to do something to get ourselves straight," pleaded Stine.

"Protect yourself against the great stores—by means of an axe, eh? Against the trustification of the foodstuff industry, and the combines—with your two fists?"

"My husband trusted the Führer and the Unalterable Programme."

"Everyone, according to his capacity," nodded Frau Timme, "must strike and not just think—cut off a head or two, even of his own representatives, men of his own class and destiny."

Stine searched her brains in the effort to understand what the woman meant. She even rubbed her temples, like a schoolgirl trying to concentrate her attention. Then she thought she understood.

"But we are not workers," she said eagerly.

"No," nodded Frau Timme. "And you poor little bourgeois haven't noticed it yet."

There was no ill-feeling in the woman's words, thought Stine, but was she a Christian? These people were Reds—Communists. "We do notice it now," she blurted out; "but now it's too late."

Agnes Timme shook her head, clenched her small gloved hands. "Never too late," she exclaimed. "Learn to know your position, your enemies and yourselves," she went on, raising her voice. "The situation of the classes—that's the word you want to understand."

At this, Stine shook her head. All that could be said about the word was to be found in St. John. "The word was with God," said she, like a schoolgirl, but she felt it too with all the fervour of a child. "And God was the word, and the word became flesh and lived in our midst."

Agnes Timme smiled, and a melancholy look came into her eyes, as though to say:—Poor Stine. "But the darkness understood it not— isn't that how it goes on? You haven't a notion how sorry we are for you."

Stine did not understand what she meant. The Gospel words rang in her ears like a threat: 'He that sheds man's blood . . .' "It wasn't long before I told my husband that we must ask your pardon."

Agnes Timme produced a handkerchief and dried her eyes. Then with levelled brows she answered: "There was no need, it wasn't meant personally."

"But anyway . . ." said Stine, on the point of reaching out a hand, but she did not venture.

"My husband and his friends," said Frau Timme, getting up, "will rise again. We are, as a class, marching forward, but not merely to attack. We most of us have children, which stand for eternal life in this world, and mine are in the U.S.S.R. And in this world one can get about a bit," she said in conclusion, with a flash of humour, as she tucked the white parcel of sausage under her cape. But this touched a raw nerve in Stine's mind. "He who stakes on this world," she cried, "has lost his game. Ours is the true eternal life which we shall enter, like Pastor Langhammer, through the narrow gates of fear."

But the visitor pulled her hat down, and shook her head. "And all for profit," said she with resignation, "so that the smoke may pour out of the chimneys on the Ruhr, and the generals, as the masters of the house, may have all that men can need, these days. Poor deluded people," she sighed, as she sorted out the contents of her black leather hand-bag; "Poor unfortunate Germans."

Stine felt that the woman was about to take her leave, and wanted to say something friendly before she went.

"Well, it will be nice if you've got someone to care about you over there."

"Someone—yes, the second Five Year Plan, a hundred and seventy millions, controlling almost a sixth of the earth's surface."

"Our earth is here," replied Stine, and as she spoke she thought of Albert's divining-rod, and the subterranean water-currents so constantly shifting their courses. "Our way leads elsewhere. But the blessing of God go with you, Frau Timme."

"And with you, Frau Teetjen," replied Frau Timme, approaching the counter. "If your God can forgive those who have brought all this upon our unhappy people: the Third and last Reich."

It was a pity, thought both women, that they had not made each other's acquaintance before, and a pity that each was so sorely beset. Then Frau Timme turned towards the door, but a pair of broad shoulders obscured a section of the glass panel, and a man came in. Stine recoiled in alarm: she was glad as she always was when her husband returned, but she did not know whether she ought to be glad this time.

"This is my husband," she said, introducing him; "and this is Frau Agnes Timme, who has come to pay us a farewell visit."

Agnes Timme surveyed the man who had offered himself as an instrument to kill her Friedel; and Mengers—such a clever fellow; and Merzenich and Schröder. A very average sort of man, she thought, and was conscious of a sudden pain in the region of her heart, and a sort of indignant urge to take him by the ears and give him a good shaking.

Albert's hand was rising mechanically in the Hitler greeting—but he let it drop, and attempted an awkward bow.

"I must get along to the ship," she said, "and see to my luggage, supper is at half-past six, and I've seen—what I came to see. I wanted to describe you to my children, if they come to Hamburg later on to visit their father's grave. That is if Hitler doesn't start his war first, and the whole place is laid flat by Russian bombers."

"Nonsense——" said Albert Teetjen, but then controlled himself, and smiled into his visitor's grim grey eyes. "We shan't be here then," he said. "We are going to Spain."

"To Spain," exclaimed Agnes Timme, raising her clenched hand in salutation. It was the Red Front salute. "You have something to atone for, Herr Teetjen," she cried, "but you have also learnt something. And with your present experience behind you, you'll be all right."

Albert began to think the old creature was crazy, but he nodded good-humouredly, and replied: "A Teetjen knows his way about."

"Well," added Agnes Timme as she turned towards the door. "You have a great deal to make good, Herr Teetjen, and you must bear to be told so. The wrong you did was committed against all workers, against an entire class. An entire class has its eye upon you. Yes, go to Spain, and you will find that I have rightly understood you. Here, take your photo back. I can't say I wanted to take my children a likeness of their father's executioner—though he really hangs over there." And she pointed to the presentment of a bland and handsome Adolf Hitler, with a large and slightly bulbous ear and hair close cropped on the flat back of his head. "The grave already gapes for him too."

Stine reached out for the photograph which represented Albert as he was when dismantling the tricycle, and in the act of blowing out his cheeks—not a flattering, but an amusing likeness.

Albert bent over it. "Where did you get this?"

"From certain friendly neighbours," cried Frau Timme. "It's No. 1

tram to the station, isn't it? The Red Front, Comrade Teetjen—you join it."

She closed the door behind her, and disappeared in the direction of the tram-stop. Albert watched her go, sat down in the chair, and wagged his head, holding the photograph in his hollowed hand.

"Red Front," he repeated. "Comrade Teetjen. They'll drive a fellow crazy with all this nonsense. But Spain's the place for us—we shall do better there. Footh hasn't made any sign—the only man in whom I still believed. I don't know, Stine, whether the world has gone mad, or whether we have."

That this Timme woman could be so mad as to imagine that he, Albert Teetjen, would fight on the side of the so-called Republicans, the Spanish Bolsheviks, gave rise to much merriment in the course of the next few days. What sort of calves' brains did these people carry in their heads! Dolts—the whole pack of them! Who, after all, had put him in his present quandary if not the secret revolutionaries themselves, the partisans of Red Spain. The old woman would naturally suppose that anyone who went to Spain would as a matter of course be against the bringer of order, peace and work, General Franco! It must by now be a matter of common talk among these people that he, Albert Teetjen, had been the man in the mask. He would sit down, just where he had been standing, on his sofa, on the kitchen chair, the edge of the bed, his head resting on his hands, and staring at the floor, as though the answer might be written there. Was it so? Did they perhaps possess some sort of subterranean organization? If so, sooner or later, on a suitable dark night a knife might slip into his, Albert's, back, especially as the Party had now left him in the lurch. Comradeship was only to be had for cash down. Hadn't someone said at Lehmke's that one of the chief witnesses for the prosecution had mysteriously fallen from a harbour derrick during an air-raid practice, and broken his skull. He would not mention such possibilities to Stine, but if he went out in the dark it had better be in her company.

And now Footh had left him in the lurch, comradeship no longer counted. As he slouched around all day dressed in undervest and trousers, with his slippers on his bare feet, in his melancholy, desolate rooms, much too large and much too empty, so futile for two solitary people, he began to feel uncomfortable in his skin for the first time in his life. He would have slipped it off, like a mechanic's overall, had he only known how another skin could be manufactured which would fit him better, a lucky skin, a golden skin. Often of an evening, when he undressed, and surveyed himself in the tall upright mirror, he noted with an expert eye where the cuts should be made to detach a skin that had now become too tight. Not for nothing had he skinned all manner of animals in his early days. The best place to start would probably be under the left armpit, carry the cut down the side of the body to the ankle, and open the inner surfaces of the legs, but on the right outer-side to bring the cut only so far as the hip, so that the whole bulk would hang together down the side. The hide so obtained must remain service-able, so that it could be tanned and sold as leather. Yes, then he would be able to walk and breathe more freely. Life in his present skin had certainly become very irksome. No comrades, no work, no earnings, and no friends—that was too little for a man; Stine would be sewing in the living-room, but he, Albert, often felt exhausted and lay down hoping to get a quarter of an hour's sleep, and then lay awake till twelve, grinding his thoughts round in his head, like beef or pork in a mincing-machine. Surely his Stine was losing weight, her breasts were beginning to sag? Had they been lacking in attention to Footh? Should he ring up again—at the office, and ask for Fräulein Petersen? And above all what had happened to the Unalterable Party Programme? Had the big businesses been Aryanized according to plan, and the Jews turned out, merely for the old game to continue as before, and worse than ever, owing to the rearmament drive. Were all those grand words no more than words, in which the leader and creator of the Party had adjured his countrymen to allow themselves no rest nor respite, and at need to sacrifice health and life, so that all Germans might enter upon the enjoyment of their home; to this end the hyenas of finance, the usurers, and profiteers, would be swept away, the ruthless enrichment of the individual at the cost and to the damage of the community would be punished by death. For five years, Comrade Vierkant had thus bellowed on the radio, for five times three hundred and sixty-five days the Party now possessed unlimited power, and could treat the German nation as freely as the marionette-man in the Lammerstraat could treat his puppets. Indeed they had actually imprisoned Count Westarp for life, a man who had led the Conservatives during the World War, and had in his time been called the most powerful man in Germany. And what was the result? "All housewives should buy their sausages at Teetjen's." But they didn't: and Teetjen's had for the moment ceased to exist. Nobody would miss them if they went to Spain—even though Spain lay somewhere else, not on the earth, but under it—beneath the waters of the Elbe. No, that wouldn't do; they were too expert swimmers. It was for that reason that sailors did not learn to swim, so as not to prolong their agony in the water. He and his Stine had had their good times in the days of the Republic, what with public sports and free baths and bathing beaches. All this would have remained at the disposal of such as he without National Socialism, and more of it too. True, there had been unemployed in those days, and a great many of them, and he had lost their custom. But now at a time of full employment, overtime, and all-day shifts, all his customers had dropped away from him—none but unemployed were left, including himself. Had he after all been such an ass as to do what was indicated in the line the Socialists used as an election slogan: "It's a very silly calf that votes for its own butcher." That's what he had done; he had voted for the N.S.D.A.P. list, he had joined the S.S., the Führer's elite troops, which had been so happy when Thyssen at one stroke threw a million and a half workers on to the streets, and contributed several million votes to the Hitler party for these men had wives and parents. He began to be possessed by the idea that the N.S.D.A.P. had been merely catching votes by means of their pamphlets and placards and speeches, and that, at a most charitable view, the Führer himself, as soon as his back was turned, was promptly ignored by the bosses, patricians, and great property-owners, by the very people in fact who sat on their packets of shares, kept down wages, and blocked the sources of supply to the middle-class, the little man, who was to be the special care of the new State.  Had he been rather premature in removing his grandfather's faded photograph from its handsome carved frame, and substituting that of Adolf Hitler? It was now lying in a drawer together with the old placard "Back in Ten Minutes," on which the children of the Wagnerstrasse had scrawled such impertinent remarks.  (Now they scrawled no more. . . .)  He might again change photographs, and put Grandfather back in his own place.  Yes, the old man had been right.  It was not the axe that had scared people away, as he—poor fool—had thought.  This had been effected by men, people of flesh and blood, who knew the use of speech. There was no radio-activity behind this affair.  And it had been very cleverly arranged by hints that his shop was unhygienic. . . .

Suddenly an idea flashed into his mind, and he sat up in bed—for a long while now they slept with only sheets and a woollen blanket—a clue at last!  Frau Timme had left a photograph of him behind her, that must have been snapped here in the yard, and not so long ago: she had said nothing about unhygienic conditions, she had come on behalf of her husband, whose head Albert had cut off.  The snapshot must have been taken from one of the windows looking out on the yard, and a print given to the Communist lady.  This must be investigated.  He would wheel the delivery-car into the place where he had cleaned it, and check the view from all the windows with the photograph in his hand.  Men from the Preester Troop had to be let in, even when they didn't appear at 4.0 a.m.  But here Albert lay down again, and tossed his head back and forward on the pillow.  These swine, who had taken two hundred marks off him, and appointed the ninth of September as the fatal day when his handsome bedroom furniture would be removed, and his existence ended.  What did they expect to gain, what could he use to lure them into such an expedition?  For a man who had to be sparing of matches—and, anyway, private smash and grab raids were strictly forbidden.

It was awful to lie awake and toss from side to side.  Stine must have gone to bed just now, while he was still snoring in his first doze; the room was dark and hot.  But she was asleep.  Under the cupboard in the right-hand corner, a mouse was scratching; the cupboard had stood in its place since his father's day; and the boards had very likely been gnawed through by this time, he must shove it aside and have a look. For whose benefit?  For what successor?  If the mouse had any sense, it would slip out, avoiding the doorway.  Comrade Vierkant, who in the meantime was said to have become Footh's private secretary, had once told how after the war his father had got out a suitcase full of books and notes from a small railway cloakroom where it had laid for several months.  When he unpacked it, he found among the packets of printed matter a nest of six young mice, little pink corpses, dead of starvation because not even mice could live on paper.  Well, a good many lived,

U

and lived extremely well on the paper of the Party programme, and what they themselves had printed on the subject. Should he perhaps make use of Vierkant to get at the now exalted Footh? Or would he prove a barrier rather than an approach?

First he would shoot Stine and then himself. It was quite a simple thought. But would it prove as simple an act? Indeed, would he do it at all? He yawned from time to time and yet he could not sleep. How loudly the clock on the night-table ticked! Perhaps he ought not to have cut off those four heads. But probably he should have begun this self-questioning at an earlier stage. Perhaps he ought not to have set such store on being something better than these workers, these Socialists and proletarians. Perhaps he ought to have paid more attention to the phrases with which they adorned their announcements, about those who laboured with head or hand; but he had been proud of his independence from the very beginning, he had looked up to his superiors, glad to be among them, to make himself agreeable to them, and to devote himself to their service.

And so his way now led—to Spain. What enormous eyes that Frau Timme had. Something between cow's and cat's eyes. Fancy imagining that Albert would fight for the Republicans, the so-called Government, which seized and expropriated estates and properties! But what did it matter? To-morrow Stine must go to Dr. Neumeier, and to Plaut the chemist's, for some sort of tablets that would help her husband to sleep. And then she must induce Lehmke to part with another bottle of kümmel —after all, the old brute was going to do pretty well out of his bargain.

## CHAPTER FIVE

### NO POISON

FRAU DR. NEUMEIER, during those July and August weeks, found herself in a very cheerful mood, such as she had scarcely known since her parting with K. A. Lintze. She radiated happiness and contentment, and a general sense of warmth, ripeness, and sympathy. She had never believed that life could again have become so delightful, and she had forgotten the scale or standard by which to measure such a condition. "We Borsdorf apples," she would say to Heinrich Koldewey, "ought to smell good; we were suitably stored, and ripened slowly." And Dr. Koldewey also produced a general effect of youth and warmth, renewed and refreshed.

On that morning Annette had driven her 'mother' to her work, and looking straight ahead down the road in front of her, announced herself as a patient. She was unmistakably in her third month, and something must be done. Käte Neumeier had promptly overcome her first suprise, and suggested that she should duly have the baby. That could be managed without difficulty out at the villa, and if she grew very large, she could go to the seaside for the last few months; the child could then be born at Fuhlsbüttel and brought up as Heinrich and Käte Koldewey's baby, and perhaps even adopted as such.

"By the time I grow very large," Annette had replied, "it will be a howling winter by the seaside, you can't deny that."

And it was not before they had crossed the Lübeckerstrasse and stopped outside Käte's consulting-room, that they conceived the best idea: why shouldn't Bert marry before he went off to the Argentine? And she join him later, with baby or without? That, indeed, was Columbus's egg. Annette would be as willing as Bert. The main point was to hurry up so that the young bride should not differ too much in shape from the bridesmaids, her sisters. And while they were being welcomed by the faithful Marie, and the Doctor was washing her hands and putting on her professional overall, they began reflecting with much amusement on what relationship the future Boje child would stand to Käte Koldewey. On the father's side great-niece or great-nephew, but on the mother's, grandchild-by-marriage.

"Great-nephew," cried Annette, as she shut the door behind her.

Stine Teetjen had already been sitting in the waiting-room for half an hour, having arrived first. She looked ill, the doctor thought, pale and emaciated, and plainly depressed in mind. She at once almost nervously protested that she had not come on her own account. It would be the last straw for her to fall ill, when they simply did not know how they were going to pay the fee for this visit, in case the doctor charged it to her. She only needed some sort of sleeping draught for her husband, who always awoke soon after the light was switched off, and then lay awake for hours in torment of mind. And she, too, of course. But he had to hold his head up, and so, because she did not know what to ask for at the chemist's, she had made a point of coming before the other patients arrived, and wouldn't keep the doctor for more than a moment. She had once been in service at Plaut the Chemist's, and he or his wife would let her have a few tablets gratis, if she knew what to ask for.

Käte Koldewey had in her cupboard dozens of 'doctor's samples', presented by the Chemical industry as advertisements; neat little packets with highly technical labels, and among them half a dozen sleep-inducing specifics. Her first impulse was to slip one of these little packets into the poor little woman's hand, but then she reflected that scarcely any of her patients had such an access to a chemist, and that the sick fund authorities were more and more reluctant to supply such drugs, when it was not a matter of life and death. She therefore picked up her prescription block, jotted down three suitable drugs one under the other, adding at the bottom: 'or smg smr' (or something similar), and told Stine not to fail to come back if her chemist could not produce what was required. Then she thought it necessary to ask Frau Teetjen why her husband could not sleep.

"It's worry," answered Stine, and resisting her desire to tell her troubles, she went on: "How did it happen, Frau Doctor, that people found it out so soon?"

"Found out what?"

"Well, about the axe we gave the Governor for a wedding present, when the two young ladies found us on the morning after Walpurgis night, wasn't it?"

Käte Koldewey, betraying no emotion, merely said: "Oh, that! My dear Frau Teetjen, the ways of Heaven are wonderful. Haven't you ever noticed"—she found herself involuntarily saying—"that seen through a round window"—adding, to impart some sense to words that must otherwise sound meaningless—"filled with red and blue panes, instead of plain glass, the world looks quite different. So it is with rumours."

"Well, but tell me, Frau Doctor—tell me what you think about death. It is talked about a great deal just now—and I hear it said that we shall die and not live."

"There is nothing much I can say on that subject; we doctors are here to deal with life, to make births easier, and dying less painful."

"And what comes after it?"

"You must ask a Pastor."

"But there must be something after this life. We can't just come to an end."

"Yes," said Käte Neumeier or Koldewey, overcome by this urgent expression of fervour and faith. "Change is the principle of Nature. And it must surely be so with humanity. Ill-matched elements will part, whereas those well-matched will be more closely united. Solitude in an ice-cold universe—that is the modern hell."

"Well," said Stine, with a sigh of relief, "we are taken care of somehow. Love never ends."

"You should make your poor man some valerian tea of an evening," said Käte Koldewey, by way of concluding the interview. "It is quite harmless, and only costs a penny or two." And she wondered at the sly expression in Stine's eyes, as she looked up from her prescription: Were none of these poisonous? she asked.

"No," said Käte Koldewey, laying a hand in farewell on her visitor's shoulder. "None of them contain any veronal, you could swallow a whole packet of any of them."

"Veronal," repeated Stine, as she thanked the doctor, and almost curtsyed. And while Käte Koldewey looked meditatively after her, reflecting that she had called Friedel Timme's executioner a 'poor man'; while Stine, as she walked downstairs, repeated the word 'veronal' until it was firmly fixed in her memory. She had often made valerian tea for Albert; the purpose of her visit lay in the question that she had asked last, she wanted some genuine poison in the house, something that would get them round the corner, as the phrase went, without causing

them much pain. She did not want to be put out by her husband—
and, anyway, whatever he might say, he would not have the heart to
do it. Nor did she want to mix rat-poison into their food, apart from
the fact that it was not to be had without a poison order. It used not
to be so; her mother had told her about a friend who had taken her life
by means of a packet of Schweinfurth green. Her mother had indeed
spared no pains to describe what a horrible death poor Lene had died.

It was a long way to the Grindel Allee, and Stine was wearing her
green, white-spotted summer dress; she must go home first and fetch her
raincoat, in case of a shower. She wondered whether she should get
Albert to take her there in the delivery car. It was uncomfortable to
get in and out of, especially when someone was looking on; but the
fare both ways was thirty pfennigs, and for people who were reduced to
next to nothing, the avoidance of any sort of expenditure was the only
possible policy. They would not be much helped if the sleeping draught
was to cost them several pence for tickets on the elevated railway.

When Albert heard why she had come back, he said decisively:
"Grindel Allee—excellent. I'll apply for a job on the cattle-yards,
behind the Sternschanze. As they're calling out reservists already,
I'll have a bit of luck—if it isn't unprofessional."

Of course, as an independent shop-keeper, he could not apply for
workers' relief, without coming badly up against the existing trade
regulations. But perhaps, now that there was a process of mobilization
going on, the Butchers' Association might not be too rigid. He could
not possibly beg for a job; no Teetjen had ever done such a thing. And
what seemed the simplest thing in the world to widow Timme's perverted
mind—namely, to go over to the proletarians,—that was outside the
bounds of sense and reason. So he would convey Stine to the Grindel
Allee, and they must arrange where to meet afterwards. As they passed
the university, they would fix on a bench where they would wait for
each other, like a pair of lovers, boy and girl students, who had nothing
better to do than flirt. But for the journey there and back they would
choose the quieter side-streets. Not the Steindamm and the Central
Station, but the Mundsburger Damm, beside the Alster, and across the
Lombard bridge, where indeed they would have to contend with cars
and trams. However, that couldn't be helped, and the police kept the
traffic reasonably in hand.

"How long will it be before we starve?" asked Albert, while he dabbed
a little oil in the axles of the tricycle.

And with a distraught expression on her face, Stine answered:
"Yes, that's what I'm wondering."

"We still have the big sausage," he replied, "and a hundred and
seventy marks in the Savings Bank, deducting the rent for the last quarter,
which Reitlin has already asked for. But if we reckon in the rent for the
shop equipment for the current quarter, we're really broke already."

"Yes, we must take that off too," said Stine firmly, with fear in her
eyes, as she climbed into the square carrier.

"It's a hard world," he growled. "Those people have made plenty
out of us. When we modernized the shop, I ought to have had more

cash in hand and bought the stuff.    Then it would have been ours
long ago, we could easily have paid the instalments, and if we had to
close down, we could have got a good bit of our money back, instead
of its costing us money every month.    The poor man always lives the
most expensive sort of life.''

So saying, he closed the lid or door, in front of which he sat, gave a
vigorous thrust of his foot at the wall of the passage-way leading into
the street, and set forth, glancing at his closed shop door, on which hung
the announcement that he would be back in ten minutes—at the present
juncture the rude remarks scrawled on it in red pencil by the children
of the district were now well founded.

As they rattled past the 'Tank', dame Lehmke happened to be
standing at the door of the bar, and looked after him.    "I'd like to know
what Albert is carrying in that contraption of his,'' she observed to her
husband, as she turned back into the bar, where he was examining his
billiard cues.

"He's got something in the carrier, you could tell that by the way he
was pedalling.    I expect he's doing someone a favour by moving their
goods—he hasn't got any of his own.''

"True,'' rejoined his wife, "but there's the linen.    And that's ours.
Well, I'll say no more now, but we mustn't let ourselves be cheated.
I'll manage to get a look into Stine's cupboard one of these days.''

"Let them be for the moment, old lady,'' said Lehmke, in his shirt-
sleeves, making a casual shot on the green cloth.    "A clothes-cupboard
is a point of honour for you women, and I won't have the girl
annoyed.''


Starvation—thought Albert, as he pedalled vigorously along on the
right-hand side of the street, taking due note of the traffic lights—that
would be the last straw.    It wouldn't be the worst thing that could happen,
when it could be borne in company.    But to be quite alone, boycotted,
and without the support of human company, deprived of reputation—
and then have to endure starvation; that was too much.    Not a friend
left, except his little wife in the carrier behind him; Footh, too, had
abandoned him.    And, by the way, he found an announcement in
schoolmaster Reitlin's old *Fremdenblatt*, under the name of Footh, which
would not normally have caught his eye—to the effect that the almighty
Krupp had considerably extended his interests in the Hamburg shipping
world by forming a connection with the Footh Aüglein Shipping Co.,
and that Gauleiter Kauffmann had been active in concluding the
negotiations.    That was food for thought, surely; but not at present,
now only pedalling, waiting, pedalling.    But for Reitlin's red pencil
mark—for Reitlin knew of his connection with Footh—he wouldn't
have spotted the paragraph.    Why, the business must be in the million
class by this time!    First the Thetis ships, and now Krupps.    And he,
Albert, was trundling his Stine to the Grindel Allee because he wanted
to get to the cattle-yards, and the journey both ways for the two of them
would have cost sixty pfennigs. . . .

The familiar approach to Plaut's abode remained unchanged. Still the same dark, badly-lit entrance-hall of a building that must have been standing for fifty years when the neighbourhood round the Synagogue was accounted one of Hamburg's best residential quarters. As Stine, from old habit, chose the tradesmen's entrance, she came straight into the kitchen. There sat Frau Plaut with reddened eyes and tear-stained face, and the old cook, who had been with them ever since Stine's departure, was trying to persuade her to eat a little breakfast—a roll and butter and another cup of coffee. At that moment Frau Rabbi Plaut, her sister-in-law, trotted in from the long corridor that led from the living-room into the said kitchen. Tax-Inspector Federsen wanted to go now and leave the packing to the ladies themselves—he would come again in the afternoon before the crates were nailed down. Whereupon the two ladies hurried to the front of the establishment, and Stine, sitting down on the vacated chair, learned that Herr Plaut, the chemist, had been compelled to sell his business into Aryan hands, as Line, the cook, announced with mocking emphasis, and that the Plauts were off to Palestine, because they didn't seem likely to make a decent living anywhere else.

"Frau Teetjen," pursued the cook with an air of mystery. "There's a wise woman in the Reimerstwiete, who tells fortunes from the cards. She didn't find very much for our family—only a journey to a country where the people wore turbans, and there would be shooting. But the things she told Frau Mengers from the Rothenbaum-chaussée. That she could see the Synagogues smoking, that the Jews had only three months left, that the Scorpion, which controls November, would this time sting them to their very marrow, and I don't know what else. So Madam wrote to Egon and little Ruth in Denmark, where they're staying on a farm training for work in Palestine, that they should be ready for the beginning of August. And now she got Knudsen the Forwarding Agents to provide a six-yard crate—the packing is being supervised by the customs authorities so that everything will be in order. Yes, Stine hadn't been there for some while, but it was now clear enough from the Nuremberg Laws and all, what was fair and right in the eyes of the State. She, Line, wasn't at all pleased to have to find a new place; she had felt she was settled for life with the Plauts. She wouldn't at all mind going with them among the wild Arabs—except that the Arabs threw bombs about, tore up railway lines, and fired at tram-cars.

The living-room looked changed and bleak, the summer light shone harshly through the uncurtained windows, the open cupboards displayed their empty shelves, the nursery was being used as a packing-room, as was visible through the half-open door, packing-cases were lying about, rolled-up carpets stood propped against the walls, and a large unfaded square brown patch on the wallpaper revealed where the large copy of the Ruysdael painting of the Jewish cemetery picture used to hang.

"Sit down, Stine," said Frau Plaut, still a plump little woman with brown eyes and a brown wig. "Tell me what has brought you here, and let me have a look at you,—well, you haven't got any younger, my dear. To tell the truth, we should have gone away without seeing you again. Sorry I am to say so, but I dare say I should have sent you a postcard later on, of the Church of the Nativity or St. Joseph's carpenter's shop. They're all there, and that's where we're going because we must. . . ." And she dabbed her eyes once more. "But we belong to Hamburg, and shan't feel at home anywhere else. Such misery as has come upon our people. . . ."

At this point Stine felt like bursting into tears. These were true words. Who was it had brought misery upon her Albert and herself, who were not Jews at all, but respectable members of the butchers' fraternity, now, as before, in process of being robbed of their customers by the great stores? But she controlled herself; her good lady might be allowed to betray her feelings, but it wouldn't be proper for her to do likewise, so she said she would be delighted to receive some pictures of the Holy Land as it now was, and if the people of Israel returned to the land of their fathers, then Christ's second coming might be at hand, and the rebirth of life in the spirit and in joy, as Madam would, she hoped, see for herself. But before the Messiah must come Antichrist, as was prophesied in the Revelation of St. John, with war, pestilence, famine and death, floods and dreadful beasts with wings, which perhaps signified the bombers in Spain and China. But the land of Israel would have peace, and Jerusalem would not be touched by Gog and Magog. The good lady might rely on that, and the two little ones as well, Egon and Ruthie.

"Ruth is still called Ruth," whimpered Frau Plaut with moistened eyelashes; "but Egon has taken the name of his grandfather, Ephraim. It's a name that is really used in Palestine. And what brings you here, Stine, what can I do for you?"

At this point Stine's self-control did nearly break down,—the companionship in suffering with this woman, in whose house she had been able to keep the Sabbath, and in whose care she had been placed by her mother and grandmother, first brought to her consciousness how lonely she had felt throughout her struggle, and how she longed for a motherly shoulder on which she could lay her head and weep. She said that things were not going well with her and Albert, he could not sleep for worry, and that she had here a prescription from Frau Dr. Neumeier, and had come to ask for a few tablets, out of old friendship, as a sort of parting gift.

Frau Plaut took the prescription and studied it reflectively. She had in her private possession several tubes of veronal, for purposes that no longer came into question, and might well hand one over to Stine— the drug, though a poison, would certainly do no harm to a man with her husband's powerful nerves. On the other hand, it was an offence to supply an Aryan with drugs, even such mild and harmless ones as were there indicated. Moreover, it was important for Plaut to take with him as many medical supplies as he could, since it was only in this way that he could get any of his property, which he had acquired by so much toil and self-denial, out of the hands of the Nazis—transfer it, was the word now used.

"Is your husband still kind to you, Stine?" she asked, as she rose and went over to her little cupboard—which she had used for the last twenty years—and to which Stine had so often gone for headache tablets, or medicine for the children in the seasons of early cherries and unripe plums.

"Oh, Frau Plaut," she cried, with wide and happy eyes. "My Albert."

"Well, that's a good thing at any rate," sighed Frau Plaut. "Wasn't he in the S.A.?"

"The S.S.," replied Stine.

"Here you are, then. If it's for yourself, a half one is enough. If for him, a whole one. But don't tell anyone where you got them." And in pursuit of a subconscious connection of thought, she added, as though in farewell, that Plaut had always said emigration was a kind of death, and they should know something about that by now.

Stine, who in the meantime had deciphered on the tube the word that she had impressed on her memory while going down Dr. Neumeier's stairs, was startled by the finger of God, for she had forgotten to mention it, bewildered as she had been by all her impressions, old and new. Veronal! Poison! And without any effort on her own part. She wondered what death might be like, she said, slipping the tube into her handbag, since death had been swallowed up in victory, as was recorded in the Scriptures. So it couldn't be so dreadful after all. It was the fear of death that caused all the trouble.

Frau Plaut observed that she was used to the sight of death. The washing of corpses was a religious duty. It was strange that they all wore an expression of something like deliverance. Kley, the broker, had never smiled so genially in all his life as when he was found with the pistol bullet in his heart. And Frau Mengers, who had hanged herself three weeks before, because she could not manage to get her visa for Ireland—Frau Mengers had looked almost like a young girl. Of course the rope had already been taken off her neck, but she had soaped it well, and death must have come to her in a flash. Stine looked meditatively up at the ceiling. The name Mengers reminded her of something that had happened recently, but she could not recall what it was. Her head was really getting weak. . . .

"I wish we could all get a real rest, madam," said she, as she took her leave.

"Yes, we shan't find rest anywhere else," nodded Frau Plaut, as she set about rolling up her table-silver in linen covers. But Stine turned back down the long dark corridor—first the children's terror and then their playground—to the kitchen, and asked Line for a couple of slices of bread-and-butter, for she must sit on a bench in Edmund Siemers Allee to wait for her husband, who could not tell when he would be able to get away from the cattle-yards.

It was pleasant to sit on that bench, under the shade of the trees, looking down on to a green lawn scattered with daisies, like a country churchyard. Hamburg was such a fine, neat city, with its bright grey and red houses, its bicyclists and cars, and the men and girl students streaming out of the university building when midday struck from St. John's church.  It was long since Stine had sat in the open air in such a mood of peace and contentment, eating some excellent goosemeat sandwiches—all she longed for was a glass of milk, though guiltily conscious that it was wrong to mix milky and meaty substances.  Here on this green lawn it still made a difference whether a person was a Jew or a Christian, and the Nazis were really playing the Devil's game, if worthy people like the Plauts, who did not want to go, had to leave the country.  But beneath the grass, in the presence of the eternal Judge, the difference would be nil, as Reitlin always said, when he moaned: 'as good as none'.  Yes, she took many things for granted, did Stine Teetjen, but she was also of an independent turn of mind.  She never let anybody peer into her bedroom, and if Albert didn't succeed in getting it out of the hands of the Lehmke pair. . . . At this point she went off to sleep, placidly sitting on her bench, in the fresh breeze, amid a cloud of flies intent upon the grease-paper lying on her lap. Why—yonder was grandmother Geisow coming out of St. John's Church, with her prayer-book in her hand, and her grey hair stiffly parted—it was naturally grey, and turned white later on—and the countless wrinkles round her keen bright eyes; morning sunshine bleaches the linen, and tans the skin, she always used to say.  No need to be afraid of the rope, Stine, she laughed—what the rustic doesn't know, he doesn't eat—and when women start hanging themselves from window-bars. . . . Stine gazed at the green grass and the graves, neat little mounds topped with shining, white marble crosses.  Judas Iscariot really ought to do it himself, grandmother continued, but if he thinks himself too grand, and indeed it *is* rather beneath his dignity, his wife might well do the job.  The mystery of vicarious sacrifice, Pastor Langhammer called it, and he ought to know.  Then grandmother stamped on the grass, and a stairway opened, leading downwards, like the long corridor in the Plauts' house, not much gloomier than the Elbe tunnel, but steeper, and there stood Albert in his miner's overalls, lamp in hand and lighting up a notice-board on which, beneath a red arrow, was inscribed: 'To the Centre of the Earth.'  Yes, said Stine, if we are to go below, we at least know where we are going; she opened her eyes abruptly, and there stood Albert in person, in his everyday working clothes.  He had, he said, been just considering whether he should awaken her, or sit down quietly beside her and eat up the remains of the sandwiches.

"Ah, well," she sighed.  "How did you get on at the cattle-yards? Any luck?"

He told her he had been well received, as a man who did honour to the profession, and that he had been allowed to work, because they had just received a flock of sheep and were in fact short-handed—but that he had done the job on the basis of a master-butcher who was doing them a favour, and that they had laughingly pressed one mark twenty (after all due deductions made) into his hand, and presented him with half a sheep; but that he could not think of asking for more work there without becoming an object of talk and ridicule. That solution was barred, if indeed it had ever been possible. And yet it would have been pleasant, and would have amused him to get back into his old job again, as though nothing had happened. . . . Stine looked about her with wide eyes. She was really looking for grandmother, the hole in the grass, and the stairway leading downwards; and wondering whether Albert knew anything about the mystery of vicarious sacrifice, and a rope round one's neck. At the same time she grasped what he was telling her, said that that was all right, she would buy some rice, and go on ahead by the elevated railway and get the dinner ready—perhaps someone in the house would like to buy a joint of leg or ribs.

"Good," said he. "I've skinned the head, and packed it separate, so you might make us some brains soup, with the sheep's head to follow. Someday I'll go along to Footh's and, if he isn't there, I'll ask to see Fräulein Petersen; I'm sure he'll help us out with a couple of hundred marks, and buy us out of Lehmke's clutches. You can have my stick here to make the fire."

And he handed her a short cudgel, which he had put between the wheels to serve as anchor, as he said, and snapped in two across his powerful knee.

"You get along to the elevated," he said. "We'll see who's home first."

And he swung himself into the saddle.

When she stood before their door half an hour later, there was a post card in the letter-box, stamped: 'From the Military Authorities.' Corporal Teetjen of the Landwehr was required to present himself within the next few days at the orderly room of the Wandsbek Hussars (the old forms were still being used), in order to receive an important communication. What could that be? thought Stine, with a shrug of her shoulders. The way to the centre of the earth was to be otherwise achieved, with no aid from the divining-rod. And she threw a brief, appraising glance at the hook screwed into the ceiling above the table, from which hung the pendant lamp. Then she quickly slipped on a kitchen-apron, lit a fire, and put a saucepan on. She could change her clothes while the water was boiling.

The events of that day produced a strangely exhilarating effect on Albert as on Stine, so much so that they spent that evening like a pair of lovers once again, and needed no sleeping draught. Stine, indeed, no longer felt, with the tube in her hand, like a trapped rabbit waiting to be hit behind the ears and killed. Now once more mistress of her fate, it was with complete composure that she looked for a suitable rope among those lying in the outhouse, in case she could not overcome her bucolic mistrust of "rat poison". As far as Albert was concerned his appearance as a respected master of his trade had re-stiffened his backbone—even though one more outlet into the future had thereby been blocked. But after the brief interval of consideration and respect he had enjoyed that morning, it seemed to him more dignified to go down with flag flying rather than to save himself in some despicable fashion. On the way home he became more clearly aware of the mistake he had committed when he went to Footh's house, by going to the back entrance intended for servants and tradesmen.    Surely it was through him and none other that Footh had been put in the position to do a service to the Gauleiter and the Senate, and indeed to the Ministry of Justice and the Führer clique.    Who but Teetjen had lifted him out of the ruck of small Hamburg business men?    A man who behaved like a small man, was one; he who wanted to be considered, must impress himself on people.    Erect on the saddle of his not very elegant tricycle, as though he were himself Footh the shipowner, Teetjen pedalled down the Wagnerstrasse.    He stopped outside Lehmke's, put his head into the kitchen, and asked whether they could do with a leg of mutton, demanded a bottle of kümmel, to be put down to his account, and presented himself to Stine with a bunch of cheap roses he had bought at the greengrocer's opposite.    At that season of the year, and if they did not look quite fresh, five blooms could be had for ten pfennigs.

Alert and vigorous after a good night's rest, carefully shaved and neatly dressed, he presented himself next day at the orderly room, with what he called his Dowser's Record in his pocket.    Yes.    Colonel Lintze had returned, but would have to dash off again immediately to South Germany, where Excellency Knochenhauer had remained, but he would gladly take the book with him and make it known in expert circles; during the autumn manœuvres there would certainly be an opportunity for demonstrations and tests, so that Herr Teetjen could reckon on being promoted to the rank of a supernumerary non-commissioned officer, with an appropriate rank, if he were prepared voluntarily to place his services at the disposal of the Wehrmacht. And if—here the Sergeant-Major expressed himself with elaborate caution—if no international complications arose from the Sudeten-German problem, the unit should be so far ready for service by the middle of October that it could be put into action on the field of manœuvres.

"The middle of October," repeated Teetjen, with an impenetrable expression on his face, which equally concealed his hope and his contempt; in any case he would continue his exercises in sandy soil, and enter the results in his Nazi calendar instead of his Record.    "The Colonel has my address, but you had better make a note of it again—Teetjen, Wagnerstrasse 17."

Here are some more people, he reflected on the way home, who don't ask how a man lives.    Perhaps it never occurs to them that people like us don't enjoy settled incomes as they do.    All from the tribe of Take,— White Jews, the whole pack of them, as Pan Preester would say.    Well, it looks as though Stine would have to dip her pen in the ink again, this time for Herr Lintze's benefit.    These gentlemen will have to fork out some money, if not only my Record, but I myself, are to be produced to the experts in the middle of October.    In any case, I now have a reason for stirring up friend Footh.    He must keep me above water until the authorities of the military district realize that it is their affair.

And he decided to telephone from the Wandsbeker Strasse post office, first to Fräulein Petersen, but then to ask for the great man himself, and thus to stamp some fresh cement into the pavement of his existence, like the municipal workmen over yonder who were repairing the Burgersteig footway, while the passers-by had to keep close to the houses, or use the roadway.

Klaas Vierkant had turned a little three-cornered store-room in the Footh Shipping office into a workroom for himself, and shown his talent by the fact that he had redeemed the little room from its humbler functions without making any undue claims on the other office premises. "Fräulein Blüthe" admired his good sense and enterprise, and had the little cabinet furnished with a small writing-table, two easy chairs and a telephone, and freed the entrance-door from the passage, which had been blocked by a cupboard full of files; she also had an enamelled plaque bearing the legend "Private Secretary" affixed to this door, and arranged that anyone who asked for Herr Footh personally should be put through to Herr Vierkant first.   She dealt as before with all the correspondence in the typists' room, where she retained her old table, but only, as she admitted to herself, because she had lacked Herr Vierkant's enterprise. She liked the young man, and she knew that she had made a strong impression on him, but that he had only one thing in his mind, and that was to get' on, under the auspices of Dr. Goebbels, and that to achieve this end he would sweep aside whatever stood in his way . . . and she was glad it was so.   Such ambition could be profitably used to get her good-natured, easy-going and beloved Footh into the right fairway, and keep him there.   H.P.F. needed a lot of polishing, and a man like Vierkant should prove an excellent agent for that purpose.

Klaas Vierkant, for his part, was quite captivated by "Fräulein Blüthe," and hoped one day, that should not be too far distant, when her passion for Herr Footh had begun to fade, to enter into possession of her person and take advantage of her abilities, including all the assistance which she could provide to a gifted young author and political economist.   She reminded him of a decorative and charming character in one of Gottfried Keller's works, and it was a pity that the Swiss Democrat so distinguished for his work on behalf of the Jews should now be in bad odour.   It would have been an agreeable means of getting on to more familiar terms with Frau Footh, by applying to her a private nickname out of the *Landvogt of Greifensee* or *Green Henry*, and be able to tease her accordingly.   For the present he must win her approval in more ordinary fashion, and Teetjen came in very appropriately for the purpose.

Albert Teetjen sat in a very wrathful mood before the little table in the three-cornered room, which he did not regard as a proper room at all.   It seemed to him that only unimportant persons like himself would be received in such a room; and why was he refused an interview with both Herr and Frau Footh?   Why was he fobbed off with Comrade Vierkant, one of the bandits who had got him into this tight corner?   Didn't they know with whom they had to deal?   Herr Footh was important, certainly, but the Reichswehr was much more so.   The

Dowser's Record might serve as a recommendation, a Hamburg shipowner might indeed find it useful when, in connection with his N.S.K.K.
duties, he had to deal with land mines, which could only be discovered
by the agency of the divining-rod. But he wouldn't reveal that to
the bandits of Lehmke's bar.

"It's very strange that Herr Footh should be unable to see me. When
it was a question of doing him and the Party a service, he was not always
out of town."

"My dear fellow," returned Vierkant, smoothly; "mundane affairs
are under constant readjustment. What was once a favourable conjunction of circumstances, like a conjunction of the stars, never, or very
rarely, recurs."

Albert Teetjen clenched his fists as they lay on his thighs underneath
the table edge.

"Then I must ask Herr Footh to lend me the two hundred marks
advanced to me by Lehmke; I can't have my bedroom furniture
auctioned off."

Herr Vierkant looked meditatively at the door, behind which "Fräulein
Blüthe" sat; she was probably typing letters, which he had drafted, and
which should advance Herr Footh's interest with the mighty firm of
Krupps. "My wife is attached to our bedroom furniture, and if it
was sold, or removed by the Lehmkes . . ."

"She wouldn't survive it, as the phrase goes in a *Courts-Mahler* book.
And who she is I'll explain to you later on."

Albert Teetjen eyed the man who spoke so lightly of his Stine
with the appraising gaze of a boxer considering just at what point on
his adversary's jaw he shall land his next blow. And as Vierkant quite
liked Comrade Teetjen, though he got rather sick of the constant refer-
ences to the Unalterable Party Programme, he resolved to do what he
could to placate the man.

"In the centre of the earth," he began sententiously, "all things are
equally heavy, the scientists tell us, and so are the more essential laws of
Adolf Hitler's state organization, which, as you know, is constructed on a
long view. On a short view, surveyed from the earth's surface and the
conditions of daily life, their weights are different. For that reason it may
well be that a business house may not be in a position, without the usual
security—which you cannot offer—to make an advance of two hundred
marks. You should make up your mind to sell your bedroom furniture,
break up your business, and disappear for a time into the country with
your Stine. In the meantime new conditions will arise here, and there
may very likely be an opening for you in due course, but naturally only if
you make no difficulties on your side, and all goes well. You can understand what decisions will now be made, if the Führer really comes to an
agreement at Münich with Chamberlain and Daladier, thereby cutting
out the Russians, supposing the City of London drops Dr. Benes, and there
is a wholly new regroupment of forces in Europe. When such matters
hang in the balance, as the English say, you cannot expect any particular
attention to be paid to the fortunes of an individual, as though they were
of importance to the Third Reich, and the present and future destinies

of our people. Let me tell you, Comrade Teetjen, that you and your Stine have a good friend in this house. But you must not make difficulties for us. You must not show yourself exigent during the approaching phase." (It did occur to Herr Vierkant that Comrade Teetjen would not be likely to understand these foreign words, but they seemed somehow to slip on to his tongue that day.) "You have relations somewhere in the country,—everyone has. In the meantime twenty marks a month pocket money shall be put at your disposal, as a guarantee, so to speak, that you will not be lost sight of. Go along to Fräulein Petersen and draw the first instalment—or she can bring it to you here; I must go along at once to the broadcasting station—and regard the whole thing as a necessary sacrifice imposed upon you by the community. On you and on her. The tide is rising, my dear Teetjen, and we must take it at the flood; when it ebbs we shall be well out on the high sea, the proud flag of the Footh Shipping Line flying side by side with a much prouder flag. You will get the August instalment now, the September one in a month from to-day, the October one shall be sent to you at Oevelgonne, Nien-hagen, or wherever it may be that you come to anchor. I'll gladly have a word with Lehmke, but I haven't the faintest hope. And now stay where you are, Fräulein Petersen will be here in a moment. Heil Hitler," he concluded, though the Roman salute was rather too grandiose for the little three-cornered apartment, and vanished through the inner door, to report his success to "Fräulein Blüthe."

Albert Teetjen did in fact remain in his seat, like a man paralysed or turned to stone. He was scarcely conscious of all that had poured into his mind while the young man was talking all this nonsense. So that was what they called comradeship; that was the intention of the Programme. In the centre of the earth all things were equally heavy, but here,—curse the fellow! He, Teetjen, understood more about the centre of the earth than this young nincompoop, but ought he to let all this rubbish get past him without a word? Shouldn't he come back with an axe and smash up this ape-house, if possible with Comrade Vierkant inside it. What did they intend? To buy him off with a tip of twenty marks? Him and Stine? Get him out of Hamburg, out of his shop, his independence, his honourable trade and calling? Yes, he was an ape indeed to go on sitting there. He would get out at once.

But at that moment Fräulein Petersen came in, with a folder in one hand and a filled paper bag in the other. When Albert saw the kind and motherly expression on her face, he breathed more calmly. It was not until then that he realized—indeed, he was quite out of control—how profoundly he had been roused by the impact of Comrade Vierkant's personality, which he had once found so agreeable. Fräulein Petersen put the bag in front of him; "Here are quite a lot of cigarette stumps this time; we had a visitor who only smoked half his cigarettes, then stubbed them out and threw them in the ash-tray. It's all wrong, isn't it? It's a waste of raw material and adds to the trade balance against us. We can't afford that sort of thing, can we, Herr Teetjen? Good National-Socialists blend their tobacco themselves and back up the Four Year Plan."

What a lot of nonsense the girl talked, thought Albert, half annoyed and half amused. But his expression relaxed a little when he thanked Fräulein Petersen for her kindly thought and help in the present rather difficult circumstances.

"And here," she continued, opening the folder, "is a little receipt that needs to be signed," and she carefully detached the twenty-mark note from the bit of paper to which it was affixed with an office needle, handed Albert a copying pencil, and pointed to the place where he was to sign:—Hamburg, 27th July, 1938. But Albert did not sign. He eyed the paper, the pencil, the banknote, and Fräulein Petersen's brown and friendly face.

"What's the good of that when a man has reckoned on two hundred marks—and needs them too, Fräulein Petersen?"

"Yes," said Fräulein Petersen, sympathizing with his distress. "There are people who need it, and people who have it. And you've got to start early to get it, and keep hold of it when you have got it. Please sign, Herr Teetjen, I must get back to my letters."

Teetjen shook his head.

"For your dear wife's sake," she urged.

"Too much to starve on, too little to live on," said he slowly, while he signed—Albert Teetjen, master-butcher.

"Just to save you unpleasantness, Fräulein Petersen," and he got up, slipped the note into a pocket, and picked up his cap from where it lay on Herr Vierkant's typewriter.

"Ah," said Fräulein Petersen. "I would gladly help you out if I could. But how can one lay hands on two hundred marks?"

A bell buzzed. Fräulein Petersen thrust the bag of cigarette stumps into Albert's hand, snatched up the folder, nodded to him, opened the outer door and shut it behind him. "Private Office" he read, shook his head, and looked for the lift. The shaft was lit by electricity, and ventilated through a slanting aperture in the compressed glass roof. On the elevated railway, while Hamburg sped past the windows—the opulent city with its harbours, docks, bright sky, smoking chimneys, in all its summer glory—two thoughts revolved in Albert Teetjen's head. One was—how on earth had Vierkant managed to establish himself as Footh's private secretary; the other, greeted with a nod and squarely faced, confronted him with the fact that he was now never admitted to his old friend Footh's presence. Vierkant acted as an insulator, he thought bitterly. His sound human understanding told him that this was probably the work of the young Frau Footh, who was detaching her husband from his former cronies. Did she know what she was thereby inflicting on the Teetjens? Definitely not. She had been so charming at the wedding, a slim, fragile little figure in the gold dress. Stine must go to her, and explain everything. It could not be their serious intention to uproot him, Albert, from his native earth. For twenty marks a month.

At home Stine was awaiting him, with a postcard from brother-in-law Ahlsen in her hand. He had had to give up his inn, he wrote, and would pay off his debts in quarterly instalments, out of his wages as cook on a Spanish-going steamer, this being the job he had managed to get. He would be coming to Hamburg in a month's time, which was the home port of the ship in question, the *Eleanora Kröger*. He suggested that his brother-in-law might come and see him on the ship, he would send a post card later on with more exact instructions.

"Spain again," thought Albert, as he took off his uniform, and put on some old house-clothes.

"Your friend Footh doesn't seem to have produced anything this time," said Stine, after a glance at his expression.

"Yes—a bit," replied Albert, and smoothed out the twenty-mark note that lay before him on the table.

"Is that all!" she exclaimed, wide-eyed with anxiety.

"It is," he growled, and the recollection of his interview rose up within him like a wave of hatred. "Get out of Hamburg, into the country somewhere, Footh the great shipowner will send you a note like this every month. Don't be too overcome with astonishment. And later on, when he has become a really great man, he will find a modest job for us in one of his warehouses. What do you think of that?"

Stine stared into vacancy. Grandmother had indicated the right way —down into the innermost places of the earth. "The Fooths don't want to be reminded of the past," she observed. "Since he married, she has taken over. And she will make something out of him—you shall see." Or not—she added in her own mind.

"I thought you might have a go at her?"

"I can't do that," she said decisively. "Perhaps because Footh used to look at me rather too affectionately. And in any case—past days are done with."

Albert in loose cotton trousers and a faded grey-blue shirt was buckling his belt. "I dare say you're right, my dear," he said complacently. "Well then, we must give notice to terminate our agreement for the flat and shop and all the outfit, on the first of next month. The Epa Stores is planning to put up a huge buffet near the Central Station, with every sort of modern improvement. Our company will be quite pleased, they can get Epa to take over all our stuff. Then we shan't need to pay any more rent as from 1st September. But we can fix it so that we don't move out until the 15th. The whole place will have to be done up. The floor-boards have worn right through under the cupboard."

"Have we got enough in the bank?" asked Stine anxiously.

"Enough for that," he reassured her. "You can check it in the bank-book."

"How long have we been here?"

"I came straight back here after the war. I don't exactly know how long father had had the place."

"The Plauts had been in the Grindel Allee for about thirty years, and now they've got to go. The madam gave me some good sleeping tablets."

"Don't call her a madam. They're only Jews."

v

"Yes," said Stine, "and what about us? Because we've got to go, too."

"True," exclaimed Albert, rather taken aback, crossed the room and stood in front of the Hitler picture. "Were you having us on, or were you yourself fooled?" said he to the profile with the slightly bulbous ear and the vertical cranium. "In any case, we'll make a little change here. We'll put the previous owner back into his frame." He rose on the tips of his toes, unhooked the picture, which was covered with glass, and laid it on the table. "Grandfather used to be in that frame, and he shall now go back there; for our last four weeks."

"And what then?" asked Stine.

Albert raised his eyebrows, and wagged his head from side to side. "If it won't hold Grandfather, because the Führer has loosened the tacks, I'll stick him on to the 'Back in Ten Minutes' notice,"—and he pointed to the card on the glass door.

"And I'll have a talk to Ahlsen about our affairs. If he can get a job, there must be one for us on an *Eleanora Kröger* or *Fiete Karsten* or *St. Louis*. We must get out of the Wagnerstrasse *and* out of Hamburg. . . ."

"I know where Spain is," said Stine, without further explanation, and went into the kitchen to make sure nothing was burning.

When Grandfather was again in his place on the wall, and his countenance, with its mobile lips and quizzical expression, appeared to be eyeing his grandson rather doubtfully, the latter was shaking the contents of Fräulein Petersen's bag on to an old newspaper; then he spread a piece of old packing-paper beside it, and began to prepare his tobacco. The cigarette-ends and cigar-stumps were equally charred and carried a good deal of ash; he split the former with the point of a knife, and peeled off the paper, the latter he cut into circular slices with the large old-fashioned shears, then he mixed it all together and tipped it into an old earthenware dish in which, with the addition of a little water, it was soon reduced to a brownish pulp. Stumps, thought Albert, as he gazed up at Grandfather—why, we're stumps ourselves now, old boy. The proper place for the Teetjens is the sausage machine. Footh—once a very small foot—was expanding into a giant, and it was for people like this that the Weimar Republic had been abolished. 'But there is a little difference,' he continued in his own mind, as he strained the dark-brown brew through a bit of lace curtain, squeezed out the lumps of tobacco, and again spread them out on the packing paper to dry; 'I make good use of this stump-tobacco, but no one is going to make any good use of me. I'm not going to be cut up, and mixed among the workmen, and stuffed into a munition-factory pipe. Stine and I—we'll go side by side; we so often used to shout "Germany, awake", now we can blow the call for Lights Out—don't you think so, Grandfather?' Then he carried the powdered tobacco to the window-sill on which a shaft of warm sunshine lingered longest before the sun disappeared behind the roof opposite, put a broad-bladed knife on top of it to prevent it blowing away, and lay down, as he thought, for a short rest, before the carrots and potatoes he had brought home with him were ready. But he went to sleep, and dreamed a dream that Sergeant Ruckstuhl and Sergeant Footh, of his old Orderly Room, had been attacked and murdered. When Stine came to look for him when the dinner had long since been ready, he sat straight up in bed, rubbed his eyes, chewed his moustache, stood barefoot on the warm floorboards, decided to pour some water over his head, and as he did so asked Stine whether anyone could tell him why he was taking all this lying down, without throttling one of these fellows, Vierkant or Preester. Stine, when they had sat down to table, confessed that she was afraid of the Lehmkes only.

"Let them just crook a finger," said Albert, as he cut off a slice of the large smoked sausage. "And they'll get what's coming to them."

"Ah, Albert," said Stine, as she slowly took her share of the sausage, picking it off the dish with a fork. "I don't want to get mixed up with the police at the very end. We've kept our record so clean that they don't even know us at the police-station."

"That's my affair," he replied. "We've been fools—and fools we always should be. I ought to have handed that Timme woman over to the police when she talked all that rubbish about changing fronts and going over to the Republicans."

"Well, never mind now," she said in a soothing tone. "She wasn't the worst."


In the afternoon, when Albert went over to the parade-ground on his delivery-car, to practise with his divining-rod and at the same time to find out how he could write to Lieut.-Col. Lintze—he wanted to ask him whether he and his wife could not draw rations from the soldiers' kitchen, if their situation grew desperate—on that same afternoon Stine slipped a faded blue boiler-suit over her underclothes, and made her way up to Tom Barfey's garret. The said overall belonged to a former apprentice, and she put it on because there was a strong draught that blew up the well of the central staircase, which was liable to flutter a skirt when the wearer was climbing up the ladder and her hands were thus engaged. Besides, having regard to what Tom Barfey was like, it was wiser to go dressed as a boy so as to be able to defend herself better. She only wanted to ask him for some paper in order to rough out a letter to her sister, of which she would then make a fair copy, and give it to Tom to send to Else, in case anything unexpected happened to her, Stine. Tom's bright, bold eyes devoured the slim youth who stood before him as he propelled himself to the trap-door on his trolley.

"Stine!" he exclaimed. "I didn't know whether you were still here or not."

Then they sat in the warm midday breeze on two sacks filled with old newspapers to serve as mattresses, and told each other all that had happened since they last met. Frau Pastor Langhammer had been refused a permit to deliver lectures in America and England on the condition of religion in Germany; the Teetjens were boycotted by all the people in the quarter, so that not even the Wagnerstrasse children now played outside their door, which had been a source of such annoyance in the past; that they would have to clear out sooner or later, they had no notion who had been behind all this. Albert, of course, thought Tom viciously, but was promptly caught by a genuine gust of grief at the thought of losing Stine. He had, in fact, struck a blow into his own flesh.

"Stine," he cried in a low voice, and tried to catch hold of her ankle, which she at once drew out of his reach. "Stine, you must stay within reach. You can't go away from here, you really can't. The Drohm woman will get you as much work as you want." (Drohm, the iron-monger's wife, had, before the ban on double earnings, conducted a much-frequented and thriving employment agency for domestic workers, and still did so under the surface.)

"At the Lehmke's, I suppose," said she, with a sneer; "who are going to take my bedroom furniture off me for a debt of two hundred marks, if Albert can't raise the money."

Tears came into Tom's eyes, which he brushed away with his fists; without a word he rolled back into the living-room and returned with Albert's concertina. "Do take it," he said eagerly, "and get what you can for it—it's yours, anyway."

"I'm afraid that wouldn't do us much good," sighed Stine. "Keep it till we ask for it."

Stine knew how much this so-called sailor's piano meant to her impulsive young friend; and she felt a surge of warm emotion such as she had not known for a long while. "Will you do what I came to ask?" she asked him affectionately.

"Anything you like," he said solemnly, with two fingers in the air. And Stine realized that this was no exaggeration. If only Tom had had money!

Then, on her return, she sat down at the dinner table, and with a forefinger firmly pressed against the pencil, she wrote the letter to her sister that she had long meditated. She explained that she had had to pledge to the Lehmkes, whom Else had heard of, her bedroom furniture and bed-linen, but nothing further, and that everything else, in case anything should happen to her, was to come, with Albert's consent, to her—Else; that she had entrusted this letter to a trustworthy friend in the house, and that accordingly, if it reached Else, that would be an indication that she should come at once, and see to her little property. She and Albert might possibly take service on a Spanish-going steamer, in which their brother-in-law Ahlsen at present had a job as a cook. The latter still owed the Teetjens thirty-three marks—perhaps a little less if he began to pay the instalments in the meantime, but that this money, too, was to come to Else, so that she could allow herself to spend a little money, and not leave the Lehmkes more than was their due. Then came an expression of friendly greetings and good wishes, and a promise to send picture-postcards from wherever they might be. A postscript referred to a list of her possessions, which she would not be taking with her; this she would add later, as she needed time to consider it—for she still had some; time enough for hue and hurry, as Albert often used to say. Yes, Tom Barfey did sincerely love her. It was odd, and yet really rather touching. She wouldn't trust the Lehmke woman and the Dörte girl across the street. The green dress with the white spots, the almost new brown shoes, the two pairs of unmended stockings, the raincoat—all for Else. Tom would see to that. All that Heaven owed her now was a suitable rope, one with which neither calves nor sheep were led to the slaughter bench. It was the last tribute she owed to her self-respect.

## CHAPTER SIX

### "GIVE IT UP . . ."

THE CIRCUMSTANCES IN which Albert Teetjen reached the point where he gave up the unequal contest, let his hands fall, and accepted his fate, were never cleared up. It is established that on the morning of the day in question he put his father's gold watch-chain in his pocket, slung his handsome new leather jacket over his arm, and still holding himself fairly straight, had marched out of the house and under the entrance doorway; but that he had returned in the early afternoon, said little, undressed, laid himself down on the bed, and showed small inclination to get up again, though he had awakened about six o'clock. All that Stine could get out of him as she sat in the stuffy bedroom on the edge of the bed, was that he had got for the watch-chain and the jacket together as much as the garment had cost by itself, six or seven—or was it nine? —months ago, when their future looked so rosy. And, moreover, the postcard, on which brother-in-law Ahlsen had fixed a meeting that morning on the landing-pier—Stine nodded eagerly—had brought him in three marks in cash and a snack in a St. Pauli restaurant, over which the said brother-in-law had so enlarged on the difficulties in the way of emigration or signing on a ship, that he, Albert, had reached the conclusion that he had better go to sleep and let matters come upon him without making any further effort.

"Including the 7th September?" asked Stine; Albert made no reply, he pulled the sheet up to his mouth and turned his back on her. The time comes when a beetle which has fallen into a dry glass ceases to dash against its sides in its struggle for the air to which the organs at the lips of its antennae are so acutely sensitive. The great black ships, their bows, their white decks, their rows of lifeboats, appeared before his inner vision with a strange allurement. Never before had he so longed

to get out into another world, and leave all these complications behind
him. Well, if he wasn't allowed to emigrate under lawful conditions,
surely more than one good fellow had been smuggled out of Hamburg
on the sly. . . .

When Albert finally got up and in search of coolness crossed over with
Stine to the central park, now growing dim in the falling darkness, he
confessed to her that he had thought it would be easier to dispose of the
Lehmke debt. The northern rim of the sky was still glowing with a
turquoise radiance from the distant midnight sun which would continue
to shine on Polar lands for a few more weeks. As they were leaving
the house, a yearning cadence from Tom Barfey's concertina floated
down to them from the roof—the song of the linden-tree by the well
outside the gate. And Stine, clasping Albert's arm, had told him how
nice Tom had been to her, in response to which Albert had grunted,
pipe in mouth: "He'd better keep the thing. It wouldn't fetch much.
Though we certainly oughtn't to afford such generosity."

They they sat on a bench under a tall dark tree, from which a pair
of lovers had just got up to go home.

"They're going off to sleep together," said Albert in a whisper.
"When shall we go?"

But Stine realized that he meant something quite different, leaned
against his shoulders and whispered: "Not yet—there must be something
else we could try." And she felt him, instead of answering, shrug his
shoulders.

"Take refuge with your people?" he asked, after a few minutes'
silence. "That would be only possible for a week or so."

"At most," replied Stine. But she looked up through the thickly
laced branches and foliage of the walnut tree under which they were
sitting, to the faint stars suspended in the darkness, as though she expected
one of them to fall, as an omen of good fortune to come. But they
remained firmly fixed above and declined to transform themselves into
shooting-stars. Out of the distant glow the noises of the city and its
traffic were borne on the night-wind over the roofs. Grandmother had
indeed shown them the way below, the passage to the interior of the
earth. It was permitted to many people to do the things that Albert
had done last autumn, and to prosper: to others, not. And they had to
atone for such errors here on earth. But in recompense their immortal
part would be saved, and the heavenly Jerusalem would accept them in
the end.

"But you must promise me, Albert," she whispered, after a long
pause, "not to take me by surprise. Not suddenly and from behind, or
anything like that. I shall tell you when I feel ready."

Albert held his breath for a moment, so clear had been the vision of
his pistol in the cupboard, the brown handle which contained the magazine full of cartridges, and the sight that tipped the blue steel barrel.

"It is only the beginning of August," he said, as he laid a reassuring
hand on hers and on her knee. The clock in the tower struck the half-
hour—half-past nine, half-past ten, half-past eleven—he did not know.
If he sold his silver watch as well as the chain on which he wore it, he

could certainly raise another five marks.  But it hadn't come to that yet.  The tricycle, as he had now reconstructed it, would certainly bring in twenty; indeed, he knew a fellow butcher who would gladly take it off his hands.  People out for a walk strolled by, one of them sat down beside them, smoked a cigarette, and then wandered on, possibly in order not to disturb the pair.  It was this very bench on which, more than a year ago, Lieut.-Col. Lintze had had his talk with Käte Neumeier.

"I wish I knew," said Albert after a while, "why it hasn't occurred to me to polish off those fellows over yonder with the pistol"—he pronounced the word 'pixtol' in order to emphasize the joking character of his remark.  "I might go across to the 'Tank' and start a friendly conversation among friends, the result of which would be that a couple of those gentlemen, *and* a lady, would have to be carried out, and then me."

"Because you aren't a murderer," exclaimed Stine softly, but with an undertone of horror in her voice.

"I daresay you're right," he replied; "but then, why did I use my axe last year?"

"Because it was your Führer's will," she rejoined with conviction.

He nodded, lit his pipe, glancing as he did so at her agonized face, wide-eyed in the darkness.  "But why do the likes of us need a Führer?"

"Because they all shouted for one"—and Stine reached for his right hand, "and because you learnt to follow him."

"Yes," he nodded, and sighed, "that's God's truth.  Always someone to follow.  First my father, and then Grandfather, eh?—and the schoolmaster and the Pastor, and the lads in my class at school.  Then the Sergeant, the Company-Commander, the battalion, and the regiment.  And then the speakers at the Party meetings.  One after the other."

"You were always a fine fellow, Albert," said she, to rouse him from the mood of self-reproach which she detected in his words.

"Ah," he rejoined, "and what's the use of being a fine fellow when it leads us into a sandpit or a pile of cement from which there is no way out.  Why did the Timmes grow up to quite a different way of life?"

"But didn't it lead them into a sandpit, as you call it?"

"I did that, with this hand," answered Albert gloomily.

"If it hadn't been you it would have been someone else," insisted Stine, stroking the indicted hand.  "If the man from Oldenburg hadn't been ill. . . ."

"My hand or another," repeated Albert meditatively.  "But suppose it hadn't been possible to find one?  And there were people who took care of Frau Timme.  She managed to get on all right, and now she is waiting in Norway and may be going on to Russia, didn't you say?  Who is there behind us?"  And he turned his head to peer behind the tree as though there might be someone standing there who muttered to him: "Give it up."

"Almighty God," whispered Stine, "our Lord Jesus."  She clutched his knees, put her arms round his neck, and drew him to her.  "He will not desert us."

If it comforted her to think so, well and good, he thought.  After a lengthy pause, during which they got up: "I would sooner," he said, "get a free passage to some place in the interior of the earth, than up into the draughty sky." And he thought with longing of the *Eleonora Kröger*. First, he must get away; then write and send for Stine later on.

If they had waited for a little while longer, they would have witnessed a solitary but very bright shooting star clear in the now black sky. But it was observed by Klaas Vierkant alone, as he left Lehmke's bar, in a mood of high good humour. He had, in the meantime, arranged several matters to his advantage; above all, he had established still friendlier relations with Frau Footh, which appealed to the lady even more agreeably, because he did not address her as a woman, but as a contemporary and an intellectual equal, without remaining impervious to her personal charm. Klaas Vierkant professed high respect for the wife of his chief, but he wanted to get a footing in such an admirably conducted business, and was honest enough not to conceal this fact from Annaliese.

"What is a poor writer but a straw in the wind. Independent ideas and projects need the basis of a well-filled pocket-book on which to thrive. No man can display character who has not provided for his next six months' subsistence. And not even emigrants with empty pockets are well qualified to play Don Quixote."

Annaliese Footh was entranced by this sort of talk—she had been long enough in a dependent position, she said, not to take it in bad part. If the amalgamation with Krupp came off, it would be largely thanks to Klaas Vierkant's services, and it was but right that he should profit by it. She would sound her husband on the subject. But she was also ready to consult Bank-Director Ruckstuhl, who would obviously be greatly concerned in the success of these negotiations. Vierkant meant to express his gratitude by ensuring that the Teetjen affair was duly liquidated, in the phrase now fashionable, which oddly enough had been adopted from the Russian. That evening, accordingly, he had transferred himself to Lehmke's bar for his daily hour of listening to news from abroad, taking the opportunity of dealing with a few matters affecting the Preester Troop. In a pause between the London medium wave and the Moscow long wave, he referred casually to Comrade Teetjen's affairs and said that something must and would be done to get the chap on his legs again. But there was no hardship in giving up an untenable shop, clearing out of his home, and disappearing for a longish interval into the country, was there? Anyone who prevented him from making a nuisance of himself to Standard-leader Footh was doing him a service, though he might not realize the fact till later on. He would be borne in mind, for special service, and he would be extricated when the time came from what looked like disaster. But many such people needed to be plainly shown where they stood, so Lehmke must abate nothing of his claim, and on no account allow it to drop or be deferred. In response to which Frau Lehmke had beamed, and her husband blown out his cheeks with satisfaction—Madame Teetjen, the glass-beaded Lorelei, would cross Frau Footh's path no more. But this had been a small matter to Klaas Vierkant, which he had disposed of by the way. His main occupation had been to sit, with a sharpened pencil in his hand, listening to foreign views on current

affairs, and especially from France and England, about the striking
power of the Reichswehr, whether there was likely to be war over
Czechoslovakia now ripe for absorption into the Reich, and what sort
of fantasies were being broadcast about conflicts between the army and
the Party.   In the more intimate circles of the Information Service it
had in the meantime become known that in the year 1933 Herr Pilsudski,
and in the year 1936 the Sarraut Government, had been ready to intervene in Germany: first, when Adolf Hitler overthrew his enemies at
home; then when he dared to march into the Rhineland with the intention
of refortifying it.   On both occasions the generals, a pack of rabbits in
resplendent uniforms, had done their best to hamper policy.   He had
had to use his utmost nervous force in order to secure his end.   Before
the swoop upon Vienna he had prepared the way with more elaboration.
But now, confronted with the besotted Czechs, the diplomatic field began
to look like a highly complicated game of chess.   The Bolsheviks had
been outmanœuvred and reduced to stone-cold impotence; this was a
fundamental fact.   Czechoslovakia would not be attacked as such, but
as a Russian outpost, and as the penultimate injustice of the Versailles
treaty—second fact.   Only if Germany attacked her in the military
sense would the war-trump have been played, as far as France was
concerned.   If Adolf Hitler secured the essential readjustments of
frontier, and the cession of the Sudeten territories, France and Germany
would not need to march, and peace would be maintained—peace,
the smiling boy with his flute and the garland in his hair, so dear to
Mr. Chamberlain and his heavenly hosts of lords and gentlemen.
England, England, with her back to the wall, who is now the glory of
them all?—the Führer, triumphant genius, might well ask.   He had
already reduced old Count Westarp to impotence by clapping him into
gaol, to the indignation of certain epauletted dignitaries.   If this stroke
succeeded, then the last one—the removal of that final blot upon the
face of Europe, the Polish corridor, must also succeed.   All without war,
but not without the risk of war.   There was still an older generation
in Germany, mostly with Junker connections, and without understanding
of the young Reich, which did indeed embody strength enough to
maintain the hegemony of Europe for a thousand years.   People with
exalted names and offices, who could not get the year 1918 out of their
bones—what Bismarck had called the nightmare of coalitions.   It was
only to be expected, as was rumoured from Berlin, that they should be
sweating with fear, and indeed were in active conspiracy to block any
policy involving risk, and that at such a time Herr Count Westarp
had necessarily been disposed of.   He who, on the 30th June, only
four short years ago, sacrificed his most faithful followers, would not
stumble over trifles.   These people did not understand that democracies
are not in a position to wage war twice in a generation—not a real war:
a life or death struggle; and that a nation must be armed to the teeth
and prepared to risk her destiny in order to secure it.   In any event,
the war with Russia for the Ukraine and its approaches would be hard
enough.   But Germany's constellation would then stand at the zenith
of Europe for an astronomical period, her creative force would establish

her as the political champion of the world, and between the Anglo-Saxons of the West and the Russians, now thrust back into the East, Germany victorious would spread wings. Germany as the dispenser of justice and civilization to Europe, as proclaimed in verse by the great Stefan George. He had indeed died in Switzerland, having turned his back on his disciple Goebbels. Well, many a man was unequal to his great ideas. Everything now depended on how the world-wheel turned in these very days, perhaps, even, in these hours. He, Klaas Vierkant, now walking down the Wagnerstrasse and on the point of turning into the Wandsbeker Chaussée to catch a No. 1 tram, knew that everything would prosper. The wheel would turn in Adolf Hitler's favour. And he himself would rise; with Annaliese Blüthe's help. All that was needed was a sign to indicate whether all was going well; whether we should enter Prague without a war. Then he could sell his paltry Brazilian coffee shares, and take prompt steps to put all he had into the Äuglein Shipping Co., even to borrowing another thousand marks from the bank. If Krupp absorbed Footh, the debt would be wiped out at a stroke. But if war came, Brazilian holdings would naturally stand very high in the share quotations. He decided to go along to the Central Station, get a cup of coffee in the waiting-room, write a letter to the bank, then drive down to Gebrüder Lahusen and personally drop the letter into the box. The dice would then be thrown, and the game set for all or nothing. There he stood, a slim fair-haired young man, with a graceful head, narrow lips, and a slightly crooked nose, grasping the lamp-post at the tram-halt, and gazing up at the stars. And behold—the heavens vouchsafed a sign. Suddenly, leaving a long and dazzling trail of light behind it, a shooting-star flashed through the atmosphere from left to right; surely a very auspicious omen.

"Central Station," said Klaas Vierkant to the conductor, counting out the needful pennies.


Thus, for the Teetjens, passed the first hours of the nights; to get through the later ones they had from time to time to resort to Frau Plaut's white pills, lest sleep—Death's brother, who keeps men alive—should never come to them at all. If the Teetjens had really consulted Frau Dr. Neumeier on the subject, she would have eyed them with a smile and said: "That is how you have to pay for your elegant summer tan, my young friends." For during the day, the pair led a sort of holiday existence, or—as Albert remarked bitterly—the life of luxury adapted to their income. By the aid of an india-rubber sucker they affixed to shop-window an unobtrusive placard bearing the legend: 'Closed during Removal.' They could not visit Finkenwärder, their favourite bathing-beach, since the engineers engaged on the Elbe bridge had covered the island with bore-holes, trenches, pits, and timber-fences. So during those weeks they went out several times a week to Blankenese, either by the local railway, or on one of the little green paddle-steamers from the pier. They then lay on the sand in the sunshine and bathed their exhausted limbs at certain points on the Elbe beach, where no deposit of oil or greasy foam tainted its tawny waters. The return fare, more than a mark for both of them, was provided out of Stine's earnings as a seamstress; moreover, they used the delivery-car to the Dammtor Station and back. The place itself, with its villas and gardens, they avoided, and as they passed the many little restaurants which catered for the most modest purses, they quickened step. Outside it, near the beach-road, among clumps of osiers and in the shelter of a wooden breakwater, they pitched their tent, drank the unsweetened malt-coffee they brought with them in soda-water bottles, ate cold potatoes, bread and dripping, and a slab of the perennial sausage, and talked of days gone by, when to slake their craving for sunlight, they had gone out into the country, to Finkenwärder as it was then, where many thousands of their fellow-citizens, young and old, were doing likewise, and the air and the beach thrilled with the bustle of a holiday crowd. Now, as they realized, such a throng would have been too much for their nerves. But they used to enjoy it in the old days—particularly Stine, in a green bathing-dress, with her lovely white skin that tanned so slowly, and her red-gold hair knotted under her oilskin cap. That was when Hermann Teetjen was still alive and carried the business on his sturdy shoulders; before the war, and just after, when Albert and Stine were just beginning to become intimate. Such hordes of young people, such an array of tanned arms and legs, shoulders and backs, so soon to be swept into the conflict, and then broken, pierced, and torn in the turmoil of war. In his father's time they often drank coffee at Blankenese. The business was then prospering, though the old man always used to grumble at the burden of his work; as soon as Albert was ready to replace him, he would take a rest. As a matter of fact he died in harness, as the phrase goes, without any apparent illness, of a heart-attack. He had opened the shop one morning, but feeling ill had gone to bed again; then he began to talk rather confusedly, saying that the chops hadn't been cut yet, and exhibiting much anxiety about the oxtail; but when Dr. Samson, who had been summoned much too late, gave him a camphor injection, Meister Teetjen, with his shrewd little eyes, grizzled beard, and shaven lips, was already beyond assistance. A powerful and a good man, as Albert realized after the event, and was quite ready to admit. But during his lifetime there had been no overt affection between father and son—for no particular reason. It was the fault of neither, or of both; it was a rough life in those days, and any regard or appreciation remained a matter for surmise. . . . The sand behind the breakwater was scattered with shells, green outside and white within. After all, a father and son often had nothing in common.

And yet such was not the fact in this case. Now, when Albert was giving up the business, and there was business to clear off, he began to envisage his father for the first time as a real person. He looked through the old ledgers, on whose fly-leaves his father had inscribed the words 'With God', encircled by a wreath of intertwined flourishes. He inspected the tenancy agreements for the flat, shop and outhouse, dating as far back as 1905, when Wilhelm II of the tip-tilted moustachioes, still adorned the throne, but Hamburg still boasted her own autocratic Burgermeister, who would suffer no dictation from Prussia—*i.e.* Altona. His father's handwriting and signature made all this ancient history seem strangely vivid; and now Albert was to see it all collapse, under Adolf Hitler, who had come forth as a Messiah, to make the small man great, to free him from his harassing, sordid cares, and set him on a broad course towards a life of ease and prosperity. Hermann Teetjen, master-butcher, had presided over the self-same shop from which Albert Teetjen, master-butcher, was soon to be uprooted. When all dues were paid, the savings bank account could be closed, for it would contain no more than two marks fifty. But an honourable tradesman would be departing from the Wagnerstrasse, leaving no debts behind, and having injured no man. It was good to dwell upon this thought, which indeed had rather a paralysing effect; he found himself gazing at the zinc counter of the tavern, longing for that glass of ale he could not now afford. Hermann Teetjen would not have looked at the job which his son had had to take; he would indeed have gasped at the very notion, and cursed and swore that anything of the kind should be conceivable in his Germany, his Hamburg—that an honest butcher should stoop to such a deed, in order to keep himself and his wife above water—and even so without success! The blood money—for it could hardly be otherwise. described—had lasted for just a year, and now it was dragging its recipients into the abyss as sure as three times three made nine. Three times three is nine, for you and yours and me and mine, hummed Albert Teetjen, as he rubbed the sand off his legs. Yes, in his father's time, there had been no Hermann surnamed Göring, only one Hermann, whose other name was Teetjen. The bland Herr von Bülow was in charge of political affairs, while the fleet was controlled by Tirpitz of the forked beard, and General Keim, Chairman of the Navy League. How this mob had enthused over Count Zeppelin in those days and his flying cigar, his lovely silver airship. It had been wrecked near Echterdingen, but the whole nation had subscribed the sum of five millions to replace it; the Navy League for Wandsbek had headed the local list with a subscription of ten marks, and what had been his name?—Hermann Teetjen. Such an example was infectious, as Albert now realized. Patriotism was the Teetjens' strong card, and why on earth it had brought him to ruin in Adolf Hitler's Reich, he was not likely to understand in this life. True—Stine offered him another and a longer life in her Christian heaven. In that case, during the intervals between the Hallelujahs, there should be time at the Teetjen family table, where grandfather and father, sat over a glass of celestial ale in judgment upon the earthly destinies of their son and grandson, to get a clearer view of all these matters, and grasp their significance; the world below would no doubt look like air photographs of the shattered streets of Canton, Barcelona, and Madrid.

Reitlin, the schoolmaster, had, like so many teachers of a previous generation, adopted his profession in order to revenge himself on the children he had so hated as a boy; and with his gaunt cheeks and inquisitive nose, his perky, pointed beard and bristly hair, he was the happiest mortal in the entire district.

"When I think," he used to say, "that I am privileged to see these days, that we Germans now have our own Christ"—in his own mind he always wrote the word Christus with a K—"and that we can again walk forth in steel-shod boots . . . !"

The sinking of the German fleet by its own crews in Scapa Flow, so he would say among his familiars, had saved him from suicide, having restored to him the measure of self-respect without which a man can scarcely survive. Now at last the Germans had the religion they needed; the whole nation sat in a class-room and looked up to its divinely appointed teacher, Adolf Hitler, repeating his utterances in chorus, learning his ideas by heart and respectfully approving all his acts. Insubordinate pupils had been ejected from the class-room, by one means or another. The slogan: one Reich, one nation, one Führer, found an infallible echo in the heart of Christian Reitlin, who lauded everything the Führer did, regarded all his allocutions as sacrosanct, and (in imagination) would have recoiled from nothing to fulfil his will upon earth.

In Block-Warden Reitlin, Albert found the readiest understanding and every eagerness to help. Party-Comrade Teetjen was a genuine man after Reitlin's heart, he was profoundly convinced that the Communists were seeking Teetjen's life, and that they did in fact represent a vast dæmonic organization operating beneath the surface of German life. The fact that this was difficult to reconcile with his faith in the omnipotence of Adolf Hitler and the Hitler Reich, did not in any way disconcert the ingenuous and loyal Block-Warden. The element of evil represented by Catholics and Jews in earlier times, and in Catholic countries by Freemasons and Jesuits, was now embodied in the Reds.

"Yes, yes," he groaned; "the rabble scented the accursed gold, and fell upon it like an insect horde—says the poet, and we know very well to whom he refers." Comrade Teetjen's plan to go to Spain in the service of the Wehrmacht, though no official mention could be made of the fact that he proposed to turn the machinations of enemies to their own destruction, was well understood and heartily approved by Christian Reitlin. It was only right and proper that every effort should be made to help a man like this. He was not proposing to renew his lease? Very regrettable, but the fact would be noted. The building was in very bad repair—the Teetjen family had rented it for thirty-three years, hadn't they? It was disgraceful of the former owners and agents not to have provided two fellow-citizens with a more comfortable and healthy domicile. The repair work would start on the shop and kitchen, the living-room and bedroom would be taken in hand last. Party-Comrade Teetjen could certainly continue to occupy the latter while the workmen were in the front premises. Rent? Well, he would be moving out officially on September 1st, but not in fact until the 15th; his belongings could remain where they were until he could arrange to shift them gradually to their new abode. In him the neighbourhood would be losing one of its best-known inhabitants; the children would boast later on that they had been allowed to play outside the shop of one who patted them on the head and always regarded them with benevolence.

"Ah, yes—the children," said Albert heavily, as he put his leases back into his pocket. "They have left our corner, and now they hop around in the stuffy yards between the houses." He nodded gloomily, whereupon Herr Reitlin briskly reminded him of the Latin proverb to the effect that children were children, and behaved in childish fashion. He quoted the apophthegm with special emphasis, for this was the beginning of important activities on his part—changes all along the line, and dispositions that would have done honour to a Napoleon. He must consider how the vacated rooms should be assigned to the best possible advantage; and wasn't this a chance for getting the Barfeys out of their domicile, which plainly contravened all the air-raid instructions? A shop, a kitchen, two living-rooms, an outhouse—and Herr Reitlin began to sketch out a rough ground-plan of the premises, indicating the doors, windows, and water-installations, the position of the closet being one of the most important points—in short he was in for a grand time. He would, as soon as he could manage it, measure the habitable surface of the premises with an architect's ruler. So many rents must be made up, including the few marks paid by Barfey the laundress, that the attic storey could be left out of the reckoning. The Barfeys need not move before the middle of September, when their scanty belongings would be safe from damage by sudden storms, which, indeed, there was a risk of even in August. Thunderstorms, accompanied by torrential rain and hail—the North Sea was capable of all sorts of vagaries, and schoolmaster Reitlin was observed every morning from all the windows of the Wagnerstrasse standing in the centre of the roadway, and looking apprehensively up at the sky and its cloud formations, trying to guess what they portended: cumulus, stratocumulus, altocumulus, or cumulonimbus, the last of which indicated lightning. . . .

However, on one of the days that followed, while Herr Reitlin was inspecting the Teetjen shop, pacing out the space from back to front, a magnificent idea came into his mind. At the National-Socialist Freethinkers' Union, Herr Johannes Wohlgast, also Chairman of the Rod-diviners' Association, the erstwhile masseur with the gold spectacles, had proposed and was now arranging the formation of a new branch of the National-Socialist People's Burial Association. The proposal would be put into force as soon as a suitable office, organization, and staff could be procured. The new branch was to include the districts of Eilbeck and Hamm—but why not also Wandsbek? Surely the Wagnerstrasse was very suitably situated for the purpose, and the Association would enrol plenty of members in the neighbourhood. And the window of the shop adjoining the living-room was obviously and admirably adapted for the display of the equipment necessary to the humblest as well as the most magnificent funeral. Even Frau Stine's flower-vases could remain, duly adorned with black and silver stripes. Immersed in contemplation of the vacant shop-window, Herr Reitlin tapped his forehead; there could hardly be found a more efficient and cheaper manager of the branch than Gesche Barfey's lad. He was said to write an excellent hand; he was alert and intelligent, and for this job his physical disability would not be any handicap. Reitlin would have the satisfaction of introducing him to his duties, and making the most of the importance of his new post. In that case the vacant flat would reckon as part of Barfey's wages, the problem of the closet was solved, the rent would cover the loss of the attic-storey—in short, the whole arrangement was admirable, without any new tenants who might cause trouble and difficulties. Yes, he must make a success of the scheme; and he resolved to go immediately to the office of the N.S. Free-thinker organization, where Party-Comrade Wohlgast could be seen any day between eleven and one o'clock. In that case, indeed, it would perhaps not be necessary to redecorate the premises throughout—a little cleaning, and a coat of whitewash and distemper, would suffice.

Herr Reitlin was not one of those people who talk about schemes when they are only in the preliminary stage. So Stine learned nothing of his plans. In those days she was busy drawing up an inventory of her possessions, however trivial; she did not, incidentally, forget the tiny ear-rings that she had worn since childhood, little greenish-blue forget-me-nots on thread-like rings, which she had inherited from her grandmother. Indeed, she was immersed in the past, as she walked to and fro from a chest of drawers or a cupboard to the table, entering on her list: 3 fruit-knives (horn handles), 3 fruit plates (vine-leaf), 1 kitchen fork (silvered), etc. How all this had happened, what sort of changes had taken place, and what she carried in her mind, Stine Teetjen, née Geisow, simply did not know. This realization came most clearly to her consciousness when she was dealing with the linen-cupboard. Some incident occurred to her as she turned over each and every towel and napkin and sheet, something that happened when she bought it, washed it, mangled it, or mended it. And her mother-in-law appeared most clearly before her inner vision, Albert's mother, née Posthorn, from Holstein, from whom her husband had inherited his eyes and handsome mouth. She had withdrawn into the background with such promptness and good grace when, after Albert's father's death, she had shared the flat with the young married couple, her bed having occupied the place where the sofa now stood. It was an arrangement that would not have worked had any grandchildren announced themselves, which she none the less so longed for, though without in the least reproaching her daughter-in-law, or the good God, for their absence. How she had treasured her linen, how she had caressed it; and many an excellent piece of it still survived, pure linen, home-made from flax grown on the little Posthorn farm, dried, split, spun, and woven at home. So infinitely cooler to lie in than anything bought later on—cotton trash, as mother-in-law contemptuously called it. Stine laughed to herself as she laid the sheets neatly back in the drawer—the old lady had always regarded cotton as an inferior substance, a sort of waste product, while Stine, from familiarity with the harbour and documentary films that she had seen, realized its significance for territories overseas the shipping industry, the trade of Hamburg, and the German manufactures.

"It's soaked in the sweat of slaves," Anna Teetjen used to say. "I won't touch it." She had often stood, intent upon her linen, between the two opened doors of the cupboard, as though in a little private room; and Stine had often wished she were a little girl again and could sit on the open bottom drawer and deal out the ironed linen, white and fragrant, and as solid as the homely citizen life of those days. When she was buried in the Wandsbek cemetery, nearby grandfather, all Wandsbek was present, and young Pastor Langhammer had preached on the text: 'Let not your hearts be troubled, believe in God and believe also in me. In my Father's house are many mansions.' It had been a lovely summer day, as blue as to-day, and just as hot. Albert had behaved with dignity, though the tears had come into his eyes from time to time, but she—Stine—had wept bitterly when the brown coffin sank into the yellow sand.

And now the Lehmke woman was to get it. No; she shouldn't get it—never. The lovely bedroom, Stine's home and refuge; the wardrobe with its shining, brown doors; the wash-stand, its basin and ewer decorated with water-lilies; and the linen. No, and no, and three times no. Not while Stine lived. It was shameless blackmail—flat robbery and theft. Had it been possible without setting the house on fire, she would have soaked the furniture in petrol on 6th September, and set it ablaze, rather than hand it over to that abominable woman, merely because the lads of the Troop had got their claws into Albert and demanded a tithe of the wages of sin, as though they were priests in the Temple, or ministers of Baal. It was as though Judas Iscariot's men-at-arms had claimed their tenth share before he went out and hanged himself, which they did not do. They contented themselves with the seamless vest and cloak, for which they threw dice. Anna Posthorn's homespun linen reminded Stine of this seamless vest, which must obviously have been a kind of pullover, probably of linen too, for wool would have been too heavy for the climate of the Holy Land. The outset of the affair still remained a mystery to Stine. Who had betrayed whom, and how her Albert had become involved, she could not understand, and never would, as she herself admitted. For her, the story started with the wages of sin, and the fact that she had herself led the easy-going Albert into the deeds that he had done, without the slightest inkling of possible results and consequences; but she, none the less, had been the author of the scheme. The Third Reich was a dangerous country nowadays. The Reich Propaganda Minister proudly proclaimed the fact on the wireless, as they could hear blared forth from the Lawerenzens' flat overhead, and since the year '33 the official loudspeaker at the post-office had preached the dangerous life in no uncertain terms to the whole Wandsbeker Chaussée.

Stine Teetjen sat between the cupboard doors on the opened right-hand drawer. She propped her elbows on both her knees, clasped her ears, gazed up at the white, scrubbed shelves, and pondered. Frau Timme had left something implanted in her mind, she did not quite

know what.  In our Father's house were many mansions—surely for
people who had shed innocent blood, though it had been innocently
shed.  Not quite innocently, perhaps, but nearly so.  And when the
culprit had admitted that modicum of guilt, taken the rope and slung
it over the walnut-tree bough above the bench; when the doer of the
deed—whether man or woman—had confessed and made atonement,
Jesus would call it quits, and reunite Albert and Stine in a modest little
chamber of his palace, which would have to be under the staircase, for she
knew that Albert would be frenzied with grief and misery without her, and
would follow her as quickly as he could.  He had been, as it were, the
ship lying between derricks in the harbour on a carefully oiled and greased
runway; she had merely cut the retaining rope.  Bind and loose, said the
Evangelist.  She had written the inventory and a letter to Else, she
must surely leave a few lines for Albert, some words of greeting, to bid
him come and awaken to a new life with her in the heavenly Jerusalem;
and beg him to provide her with an undiscoverable grave so that she
could not be found and maltreated when she was no longer there to
defend herself. . . .  This overall of hers was very cool and comfortable
in summer weather like this.  Their flat had been very pleasant to live
in of late, fresh and airy until far into August, and the shower in the
bathroom was a great boon.  But those days were past, the whole house
was sweating, and up in Tom Barfey's attic the heat must be unendurable.
Still, there was probably a breeze up there at nights.

As Stine went through all the drawers, which she had not troubled
to do for a long while, a number of strange objects came to light—oddments of all kinds from the backwash of her past.  A number of booklets
known as tracts, intended either to confirm her own faith, or convert her
Israelitish employers to the Saviour, the Preacher of the Lake of Gene-
zareth.  With no result, of course; and her own life, too, had been spent
in dealing with other and more tangible tasks.  Here were hymns from
the Herrenhut hymnbook, which could now arouse nothing but a smile.
Near the tracts lay a packet of banknotes—sheets of paper elegantly
designed and printed, once significant, but now, alas, worthless; marks,
not Reichsmarks.  They were handsome and impressive notes, adorned
with men-at-arms and arabesques, and bearing the figures—10,000,
20,000, and even 50,000 marks.  They dated from the inflation era.
She could well remember how the price of a loaf had soon risen to hundreds
of thousands, millions, milliards of marks.  But none of these latter
notes had been preserved; the Hamburg Senate had issued a stabilized
currency long before the Reich had done so, and no doubt the milliard
notes had been changed by Teetjen Senior into solid pfennigs.  Yes,
this was the stuff with which Albert should have settled the claims and
stopped the mouths of the bandits in the "Tank" bar.  Well, it was now
too late, this paper fortune could be handed over to Tom Barfey, who
might use it to make streamers, or scatter it from the housetops.

But among all this truck she came upon a length of cord, an odd bit
of woven hemp, no thicker than her little finger, with a metal cap at
each end, like a giant shoelace.  At first she did not realize what it was;
nor how it had got into the cupboard, since its proper place was obviously

w

the shop or the outhouse. Then as she held and eyed the cord, so neatly rolled and looped, she remembered. It belonged to the time of Albert's military service, and was what was used for cleaning a rifle-barrel, being known as a pull-through. She could no longer recall all the details of its use—whether it was enough to open the lock, whether it had to be taken right out, to get the cord through the barrel. She had become a poor sort of soldier's wife during these intervening years, though the story went that among the Reds in Spain and Russia, the girls learned to handle weapons just as well as the men. Well, there was just one thing that Stine did still understand. And she *had* become a housewife, and a frugal one, as required by the Reich. Where was the bit of soft soap she had found in the lid of a tin? That would make the cord smoother and more flexible. And hardly conscious of what she was doing, or why, she fixed one end of the cord under the window frame, pulled it taut—it was rather over a yard long—and carefully anointed it with the remains of the soap, till it became as smooth and soft as silk. Then she carefully rolled it up, looped the ends round it, and put her discovery away in the top drawer of the cupboard beside the inventory and the letter to Else, both of which still had to be copied out fair. Later on, in the cool of the evening, she would take the letter up to Tom, dressed as a boy, of course, in her faded blue overall. It was a pity that she could not be there to see what became of Tom Barfey; such a fine, good-looking lad—with such pitiful, misshapen extremities to take the place of legs. If he grew up and had children, would their limbs be more or less normal? The Nazis thought not, but what did *they* know?

She now had time for Tom. Every day Albert came home at more irregular hours, which was natural in a man out of a job, who did not wish to be accounted unemployed. In that vast harbour with its dozens of cranes, hundreds of landing-bridges and quay-installations, there was always a chance to lend a hand and earn a bit. If a man belonged to the Party, and produced a card or a badge under his coat, he could not be curtly told to go away. But it was not possible to make a job of such work, and he could only go back when actually needed. The struggle to earn a few pence had become a hard one, so Albert reported, and there was little chance of work for those not duly enrolled as "skilled workers". Fortunately appeals for emergency labour were now to be found posted all over the harbour. Probably Bremen would absorb a good deal of the Spanish and African business. But Hamburg would not be squeezed against the wall.

Stine did not mention the bit of cord to Albert, or the inflation notes. She knew why. He returned home every day in a more and more nervous condition, touchy and ready to bang his fist on the table and abuse her on the least provocation. She knew quite well why he was so enraged by any sort of contradiction, and any trifle caused what Anna Teetjen used to call the Teetjen saucepan (far too small, she always said) to boil over. It was a man's job to earn money, keep his wife and his good name. But he must be able to unload his troubles and his wrath on somebody. That was where the wife came in. She must know how to hold her tongue and suffer in silence, with what Frau Pastor Lang-

hammer used to call the most exalted kind of patience. Well, Stine
had done a good deal in that line. An empty store-room, an equally
empty coal-cellar, a shop-bell that no longer rang, a purse that never
contained more than a windfull mark or two to meet the day's needs—
all this wore a woman out and got on her nerves. And when Albert
lost his temper because she had again forgotten to cut up the old newspapers into toilet paper, she had to keep a tight hold on herself in order
not to retaliate, and now and again her self-control nearly gave out.
Was he so very busy that he could not pick up his butcher's knife, and
make himself so far useful on that job? It was nonsense to suggest that
scissors were meant for cutting paper, and he wasn't going to spoil his
knife. They had been on very short rations for a long while; some
coal-dust, a handful of swedes, the fag-end of a sausage, a few hoarded
apples—how on earth was all this going to be made to last until the end
of August? They must at least avoid rows.

One day Albert returned looking very mysterious, and after he had
washed and changed, he produced four resplendent and quite valid
ten-mark notes from his pocket-book. What had happened? He had
sold the tricycle-car to his fellow-butcher, Schmidchen of Altona, near
the landing-pier on the Wittnerstrasse. He had really only meant to
offer him an option on it; but they had agreed on a deal whereby Albert
retained the right to keep and use the vehicle until 7th September inclusive.
And the worthy Schmidchen had thrown a fine smoked sausage into the
purchase price. He had, incidentally, made some enquiries at the
harbour; the *Eleonora Kröger* was due to sail during the next few days.
And—as a final bit of news—the Lehmke woman, who had been standing
in her doorway as usual, watching the children at play, had looked
very queerly at Albert when he pedalled off on the tricycle that
afternoon. If she didn't suspect that the Teetjens were conveying their
house-linen into safety, Stine could hang her Albert from the lamp-
bracket.

"I daresay she just wanted to get a breath of air," said Stine, quietly.


It was true; Frau Lehmke was much concerned and anxious. Why
should that fellow, Teetjen, have grinned at her so insolently as he
trundled past on his old machine? "Closed for Removal," said the
notice now hanging in the shop window. Yes, Party-Comrade Reitlin
had triumphantly announced yesterday that he had a scheme in hand
for No. 17 which would bring credit on the entire street. If it came
off, if the projected tenants liked the accommodation, if too much was
not demanded in the way of redecoration—in short if an agreement
could be reached, he would bring a new and important customer
across to the "Tank", who would be doing his telephoning from there
to begin with, before he got a telephone of his own. In other circumstances, his air of voluble mystery would have certainly made an impression on Frau Lehmke; but as things were, she listened vaguely, and
silently cursed the new customer as a probable nuisance. That stuck-up
creature, Stine, might well have induced her silly husband—all handsome

men were weak in the head and in other parts too very likely—to get
the stuff out of the way before dark, which meant before she, Marthe
Lehmke, could get hold of the house-linen.    Two hundred and ten
marks!—at a time when rates and taxes took a man's glass of beer
from before his very nose: when only great folk could profiteer; while
the whole loot from the Jews was kept in the upper and exclusive
circles of the Party, the Aryanized businesses thrived and grew, and
the little man had to sweat blood and water to keep going.    They
had had the Teetjen case right under their noses, and he had handled his
affairs like the veriest fool.    But when she, Martha Lehmke, went shopping
in the market, she heard that so-and-so, once an independent small
tradesman, had now got a grand job at Blohm and Voss, Vulkan, or the
Hansa Electricity Works, at which he would have to work just twice
as hard as before, but he could earn his living, by the good grace of the
Führer and the government.    At the beginning of September, this
would be Teetjen's position; the Lehmkes had invested two hundred
marks in him, almost their total net profit for the last quarter, and in
settlement of that loan they meant to get their due—all of it and more.
Dörte had often been with Stine when she was hanging out the washing,
and indeed helped her to do so; and she had told her parents all about
the embroidered pillow-cases, open-hemmed coverlets and sheets
belonging to the grand old days—so heavy that when wet, Frau Barfey
and Stine had as much as they could do to wring them out.    There
were towels, too, and napkins, just what was always needed in the
Lehmkes' establishment.    A complete outfit for a restaurant, in fact.
And though the Lehmkes would scarcely be strictly justified in extending
the word linen in the agreement to cover all these items—they would
try it on, and (she believed) not without success.    The Teetjens knew
this, and would accordingly do their best to dodge the claim.    But if
they went too far, Martha Lehmke would step in and call a halt; indeed
she would do her own police work.    When Dörte, who was now in the
German Girls' Association, got back to-morrow or the next day afternoon
from helping with the harvest on the *Vierlanden*, they must take the
matter in hand.    A friendly call—why not?—and a glance at the contents
of the linen cupboard.    No one could take offence at that.    And if
Stine so clung to her bedroom and its contents, and Albert couldn't
earn any more money, or at all events didn't bring it home, there were
parts of Hamburg where a pretty woman—and Stine still regarded
herself as such—could earn a little extra, if she understood how to go
about the job, and wasn't too fastidious to take a chance.    If Herr Footh
declined to have any more dealings with Albert—he had been anxious
enough at one time to have some with Stine, and probably still was.    If
she wanted to play the butcher's wife and stay at home, then she must
pay the penalty and pack up.    If only the rain would come.    The
stagnant air and heat between the houses was becoming almost unendurable.

One afternoon the uneasy tension caused by the weather reached such
a point that the temperature was recorded at the meteorological station
with real misgiving.    This was Hamburg in the veritable dog-days, on

the edge of the North German plain, Europe versus the Atlantic. "In Basra," said Captain Carstanjen, "that"—and he pointed a thumb at the slightly ochrous blue sky—"would not surprise me. Nor in Alexandria. We should expect a sand-storm and clamp down the portholes. But here in old Hamburg . . ." His voice almost quavered with astonishment. Perhaps on the spire of St. Michael's Church something could be seen of the oncoming conflict of the cyclops or cyclones of the air, but below on the ships' bridges and the house-roofs all that could be observed were gusts and squalls veering from the North round to the South, while the afternoon light deepened into yellow, as though the sun were going to set at six instead of eight. And all the time the seagulls screamed and swooped over the roofs of the old town.

# BOOK SEVEN

# FLOTSAM

## CHAPTER ONE

### STORM IN THE HARBOUR

IT MAY BE that some of those now living remember the flashing and foaming tidal wave that in those days carried certain leading cliques, backed by peoples schooled and organized for blind obedience, into predominance and power. Japanese generals, their armies and their fleets, had carved great Empires out of China's living body, and not one single nation, except the Soviet Union, made any effective protest. The Roman Cæsar was allowed to construct an Empire which embraced East Africa, threatened Aden, turned the Eastern Mediterranean and the Red Sea, too, into a *mare nostrum*, and cast envious eyes upon Egypt, the Arab States, Palestine and Persia. The Spanish Government and Spanish people were strangled by the closure of their land and sea frontiers; and the German dictator, at his pleasure, dismembered the living land of Czechoslovakia, a truly democratic state, which only failed to look and reach towards the East when the Western democracies, after certain amazing excursions by aeroplane and the consequent discussions, impressed the names of three German towns, Berchtesgaden, Godesberg and Munich, upon the public mind, no longer as holiday and health resorts, but as places where the destinies of nations were decided. No one reflected that such a wave must break, and carry the audacious swimmer or oarsman at least as far down into the depths, if it did not actually engulf him beneath the weight and mass of waters. But they who lived through those days, especially the Germans, delighted in the sense of being swept onto the wave's crest, the impetus and exhilaration of the tossing dazzling foam, the roar of the wind, and the glittering vision of triumph uprising from the waters. They had to swim, keep their balance and their breath, or drop behind. The fact that such a way of life must needs intensify the struggle for existence might well have caused the little man to pause and think; but incessant celebrations and successes were designed to stop him doing so. "Peace in our time," exclaimed an elderly gentleman, standing on an aerodrome, brandishing a piece of paper and an umbrella—his photograph went round the world. . . . Forwards, upwards, go on!

"I say," said Albert Teetjen, pointing to the round port-hole window, in its heavy brass frame above the brown wooden counter of the little bar, now blurred by the lashing rain and hail. "What sort of weather is this?"

The ship was quivering and rocking at the anchor-chain and cables that secured it to the Africa quay. The lightning must have struck something that time, but the heavy chairs were screwed to the floor and provided a steady seat, while the iced brandy which they had been drinking pretty freely, deprived the scene of much of its reality. A stiff bit of weather, certainly, for the old home town; likely enough the spire of St. Michael's had been struck, but it was duly protected—not by Almighty God, but by an effective lightning conductor, maintained in proper order by the Senate and the Party. No serious damage could be done.

Albert Teetjen had gone to see his brother-in-law during the lunch hour, eaten a meal with him in the galley, taken five marks off him —not much of a sum, certainly, but accompanied by some advice and information, as a result of which, at Ahlsen's instance, he was now sitting in the brown-tiled bar with the blue linoleum floor and easy chairs.

"Look here, Albert," Ahlsen had said. "I got into conversation with a passenger yesterday, a certain Dr. Kley, son of old Kley the broker, who had to give up the Thetis ships. He spent three week-ends with me in Heligoland when we still had the hotel there, and our Adolf hadn't yet slipped the naval treaty on to the Englishers. We shan't keep it— Chamberlain can count on that on his ten fingers. Ahlsen, says he, what are you doing aboard the *Eleonora Kröger?* Just exactly what you are, Herr Doctor, I answered; I'd like to see a bit of the world, though I didn't exactly want to go to sea, but we don't get any holiday visitors now. He laughed, and said he was sorry he had come aboard too early. Now I already knew that he had served in the Eighty-third, in '17 they shoved quite young fellows into the army. So he's an old regimental comrade of yours, and I told him you would be around to-day, Corporal Teetjen of the 7th Company, 2nd Battalion. Teetjen?—he said, I ought to know him. Why, of course I do. He used to keep a concertina hung over his palliasse, and he cheered up many a march with it. He was shifted to Ober-Ost, didn't he have some dealings with one Footh?"

"Yes, Kley was the bright lad of the battalion orderly room," said Albert meditatively. "We never met again, nor heard of each other after demobilization, but that's how things happened. The regiment was disbanded, and the men scattered, and after a few weeks we had all forgotten each other."

"Well, I'm sure the Doctor would be delighted if you would keep him company. He doesn't like going ashore now, being a Jew. And" —Ahlsen went on, as an idea struck him; "he's full of money. And emigrants are only allowed to take cash out of the country—just pocket-money. If you get the right side of him, I don't see why he shouldn't let you have two hundred marks out of his blocked account. There's nothing much he can do with it when he's out of the country. It will get into the hands of the Party, somehow—the State, I should say. I'll watch out for when he's had his nap, and send a boy along to the saloon where he'll be drinking coffee. You'll see, he'll come below, and then it's up to you."

Albert listened to his brother-in-law open-eyed. He, like most Germans, had not realized that *emigré* Jews were allowed to take only a small proportion of their property out of the country, and even so, subject to certain conditions and arrangements that would benefit foreign trade; it had never entered his head to try to extricate himself from his difficulties in this sort of way. Nor did he much care about the scheme of the former Heligoland inn-keeper, now a ship's cook. However, it was certainly an idea; if that was really the position, and little Kley was still an amenable sort of fellow, he might venture on a word in season, from one old soldier to another; he might do himself a bit of good,—take cover underneath the best bed you can find, they used to say in the army.

The contact was quickly made, or rather renewed. Dr. Kley was quite sure he would have recognized his former comrade in the street, so little had he changed in general appearance. He himself had been a weedy youth in those old days, with all his hair intact, allowing for a small bald patch, over which he carefully combed his hair every morning. Yes, said Albert, and had to stop himself from taking his old patronizing tone. "Yes, men went bald from working in store, because they hadn't been used to wearing a cap or a helmet when they were lads."

"In store," laughed Herr Kley, pausing at the top of the oiled and polished companion-way that led down to the passenger accommodation and the bars. "It's a long time since I heard that word."

The store was the place where military clothing and equipment, as distinct from weapons, were housed and distributed; the soldier got everything "out of store".

"So your affairs aren't going too well, Comrade Teetjen, I understand from Ahlsen."

"No," replied Albert. "All isn't cheese that stinks."

He drew a deep breath, and steadied himself to face a furious gust of wind that caught them on the promenade deck as they emerged from the shelter of the various superstructures and made their way across the thirty yards of deck to the bar.

"God bless me," exclaimed Dr. Kley, clinging to the bulwarks, "what's all this?"

"Spring-tide," said a deck-officer in a blue jacket, as he sped past, propelled by the wind behind, to help in certain operations astern beyond the holds. The hatches were already closed, and the crew were busy constructing a tarpaulin swimming-bath on top of them, now almost ripped from its moorings by the lashing wind.

"Spring-tide," repeated Dr. Kley, as he opened the bar door, and motioned him through it. "Just at the right time. Old Hamburg is giving me a farewell performance."

The North wind was driving the tide up into the Elbe estuary. Its cold, damp blast swept in from the sea, swooping low over the harbour in its whirling onslaught. It whistled and hissed against the iron flanks of the cranes and gangways, hurtled round the stretched hawsers, and the posts and piles on the quayside. The *Eleonora Kröger*, an eight-thousand tonner, had been manœuvred round to face the wind, the city telephone had been hurriedly disconnected, and the cables mooring her amidships groaned and creaked against the bollards. The great city lay enveloped in a sickly glow. On a distant quay the blast was whirling a bundle of newspapers, with their blatant, bellicose headlines, out of the grasp of a struggling newsvendor. From the sailing-ship harbour, beyond the warehouses, came a clamour of shouts and whistles as the sailors hurried aloft to lower the sails or make them doubly fast. The black or leaden-grey, a heaving expanse of waters, rancid with the stench of depths upheaved, slowly rose. Black—palely black and edged with yellow, stabbed by harsh gleams of sunlight, came eddies of hail and rain, beneath the towering skycastles of the gods so soon to clash in storm; and the lightning flickered all the while from cloud to cloud.

The ship was a scene of bustle, enlivened by a sort of controlled excitement. Most of the passengers had gone ashore, while the others had not yet arrived. But they were all to be aboard for dinner. The ship was to cast off at nine o'clock; but if the present state of affairs continued, there must be some untoward incidents. The spring-tide would pour into the streets, the canals would overflow and fill the cellars, so that cars would find it difficult if not impossible to approach the gangways, and the motor-boats and small green passenger steamers could not fail to be delayed. The storm might burst at any moment, and God alone knew how long it would last. The women's summer frocks and the men's light suits would be soaked. Everyone would stay under cover as long as possible, mistrustful of their umbrellas, which were likely to be blown inside out or torn out of their grasp. If only this damned weather had held over until the *Eleonora Kröger* had safely passed Cuxhaven.

The ventilator was humming in the bar—for no one's benefit. The heat of many a long day's sunshine had long since been expelled by the stream of cold air. A bottle of brandy and two glasses were produced, and Dr. Kley proposed his favourite toast, Martje Flor's toast in Detlev von Liliencron's ballad: "May all be well with us in our old days."

Old days, thought Albert Teetjen gloomily. Let's get beyond Cuxhaven, and 7th September. Then they fell to talking of all the troubles in which Hamburg was involved by its situation and climate; they were inevitable, and very serious they could be, for they meant an annual loss of many people, sheep and houses. But what the ordinary Reich German never could understand was that Hamburgers liked to think of themselves as neighbours to the ocean. "And so—Prosit, and long live Hamburg."

An aeroplane sped through the lowering clouds and a flash of lightning threw a momentary, ochrous glare on to the Bismarck memorial. Dr. Kley would have liked to talk a little about Liliencron's poems, which he had once read in the company of Thyra Koldewey, but as they would be a book with seven seals to his companion, and remembering that Ahlsen had told him some strange story in which this same Teetjen had been concerned, he said: "So you would like to come along with us,

Comrade Teetjen? But you are a member of the S.S. Where exactly does the shoe pinch?"

Albert was not used to drinking in the middle of the day, and he was enjoying his brandy, especially as it cost him nothing. Moreover, the Doctor offered him a cigar the like of which he had never had between his fingers in his life, with a band embossed in red and gold, on which were inscribed in gilt lettering a couple of mysterious words that looked like Romeo and Juliet. Not only did the Doctor ask to hear his story, he did so with a really friendly air. He looked rather distraught, and Albert remembered that his father had shot himself on being forced to give up the Thetis ships that were now Footh's property. And hadn't he told Ahlsen that the entire Footh concern had now been absorbed by Krupps? The man was a more genuine Hamburger than many that so described themselves. And yet he was a Jew. However, if there was a chance, however faint, of saving the bedroom for little Stine, and keeping Lehmke's thievish hands off it—well, Albert had nothing more to lose. He would stand in the open market and confess himself a fool for having allowed himself to be lured into such a besotted act under pressure of his needs.

"Yes, Dr. Kley," he said. "It's an odd sort of story. I hope you don't mind, but you are sitting at table with an executioner."

"And you with a Jew," grinned Dr. Kley. "I am in fact a biologist, and accustomed to handling carcases. So fire away."

Wilhelm Kley clipped his companion's cigar, listened to the intonation of his voice, his words, his aim and drift of what he was saying, through a magical haze of brandy. The thunder crashed and rolled, like gigantic boulders hurtling through the air; the howling of the wind, the swooping sea-gulls, the yellow glow through the porthole, the huddled roofs peering through wreaths of mist, and then blotted out by the lashing, hurtling rain—all this sounded like a musical accompaniment to this man's story, the story of a Hamburg veteran, and his strange experiences and adventures. Here was an instance of the sort of dung-heap into which these people had transformed our beloved Germany, thought he. Corporal Teetjen of Hamburg cut off my friend Mengers' head, and here am I hobnobbing with him in a ship's smoking-room instead of throwing him overboard. Hadn't the late Timme been a champion of the working-class? And did the events of 1918 express what we all felt when, at the end of November, those conquering heroes, Ludendorff and Papa Hindenburg, went down? And in 1933, when Papen, Schacht, Kirdorff, and Thyssen moved all Acheron, brown gutter-wash flooded the streets, my brother flitted to the Balearics, and adopted the old family name of Alkaley—in those days citizen Teetjen brandished a banner and fixed his eyes raptly upon Adolf, leader of the blind, as poor Frau Mengers used to call him, and descried Valhalla on the horizon, eager for the moment when it should descend upon the centre-point of earth, Munich. In other circumstances we should, in the words of Handel's chorale, have invited the daughters of Zion to rejoice, and Jerusalem to exult aloud. But as matters stood, these two localities were unlikely to indulge in any such demonstrations; they were absorbing a horde of thousand-pound immigrants, while Noble Lords were saving their faces and working for an alliance with the Party-Comrades of the latest brand. In the year '18 Comrade Lenin showed how the resources of a nation could be socialized. And, by way of counter-stroke, the money interests were studying the process by which Benito Adolfo was nationalizing socialism. Everything in its own time, observed the potentate, who once governed the mandated territory, and indeed in his eyes all was vanity. Here was the fellow who beheaded Walter Mengers, in need of two hundred and ten marks—well (so his thoughts rambled on), what with legacy-duty, emigration-tax, share-control, transfer-laws, he would have to leave twenty times that sum in his current account, and God (who had indeed deserted His people) alone knew how much of it he could manœuvre out of Germany in the form of goods exported to his order. It was ludicrous that an elderly English gentleman should be sending a letter of birthday congratulation to the murderer of 30th June, while Friedel Timme's executioner lay gasping like a stranded fish on the beach, an old comrade of '17, and a most undeniable fool, whom he was apparently expected to set afloat once more. He—Kley, a Hamburger ejected from his native city, with a J on his passport, saw through the wholly sickening business, taking shelter from the storm, and adding one to the total of German Jews in Erez Israel—would now produce his cheque-book and throw fish Teetjen back into the water. The fairy-tale of the fisherman and his wife came into his mind. For if his banker had obeyed instructions, he had bought Pilsen Brewery shares in Amsterdam, or would do so at the right moment, when they were to be had for next to nothing. But in Germany they would increase and multiply, for there wouldn't be a war, Montagu Norman wouldn't provide the money for it, as Madame Rothschild was said to have refused to do a century ago. And Prague would revert to the Reich to which it never had belonged. Why, Heaven was providing the illumination by which he wrote this truly magical cheque.

With a hiss and a roar the lightning struck; according to Dr. Laberdan, at the junction-point of subterranean, negatively-electric water-courses. It flickered like a network of blue and yellow nerve-strands or interlaced veins, over the great plain and the outspread roofs of Hamburg. It flung its glare on to the tide breaking in yellow foam at the gates of the Africa basin, and surging up the main water-way to the city. It was mirrored in Stine's glazing eyes, and on Albert Teetjen's mask-like face, as he sat leaning across the table-edge, his cigar between his teeth, his gleaming eyes wide open, gazing at the incredible spectacle; not Hamburg in the grip of a tornado, but Dr. Kley, a gentleman about to emigrate, a man with pale-blue eyes and a bald head, writing out a cheque for two hundred and ten marks, as though it were a matter of course, a sight beyond imagination and yet quite real, as though Adolf Hitler had never revealed the true nature of a Jew. He, Albert Teetjen, had accepted it, in the way an average man accepts what one is told. . . .

For nearly eight months he had been struggling to extricate Stine and himself out of a trap. The water had risen to their necks, and to their chins—now he need not escape as a stowaway, help had come, the worst was over. The cheque was on the Hansa Export Bank—H.E.B.— known all over the world, and the signature now drying in his tremulous hand, Dr. Wilhelm Kley, was good for ten—twenty times—the amount, as Ahlsen had told him.

"Comrade," said Teetjen hoarsely. "I'll never forget this. And the day will come when I will do the same for you."

He wiped the back of his left hand across his eyes, and reached out his right to Dr. Kley across the table, which was fortunately screwed to the floor—for at that moment the engines started up with a jerk to counteract the impetus of the tide. Wilhelm Kley hesitated for the fraction of a second, then he laughed and laid his slim hand in the powerful hairy fist which had cut off his friend Mengers' head. Blood is cheap, he thought to himself, and blood will be poured out upon the earth.

From this moment Albert had to be forcibly prevented from leaving the *Eleonora Kröger*. "I must get away," he kept on saying; "back to Stine. My God, how glad she'll be."

But it was not until the thunder had rumbled into the distance, the rattle of the hail had ceased, blue drifts of sky and red streamers from the setting sun appeared beneath the edges of the clouds, that the first batches of passengers in motor-boats and green steamers were discharged on to the *Eleonora Kröger's* companion-way. Albert boarded one of the first to return, with his cheque in an envelope inscribed with his new friend's temporary address at Amsterdam. He would take a taxi on the quay; to-day was one of celebration.

## CHAPTER TWO

### "THY KINGDOM COME"

IN THE MEANTIME our friend Stine stood, a lithe and graceful figure, in the paved yard, gazing up the walled well-shaft at the sky, and shook her head anxiously; a lovely head, crowned with luxuriant hair, and poised on a slim and fragile neck. She had indeed urged Albert not to let his brother-in-law Ahlsen sail without appealing to his conscience.

"You'll see, he won't turn up, he'll send us a postcard from Bremen or Rotterdam to say how sorry he is, and when he gets back . . . and all the rest of it."

And Albert had agreed; perhaps he knew, when he borrowed the thirty-three marks, that he would not be able to pay that money back;

it was the sort of thing that happened now, even among ordinarily decent people. To-day, as she looked up at that ominous sky, she regretted having sent him out into that maze of waterways, walled quays, streets, paved and timbered islands and landing-piers, which the Hamburgers call their harbour, one of the largest in Europe. The *Eleonora Kröger* was no doubt lying far out beyond the new Elbe bridge, in the South-Western basin, at the Africa quay, somewhere behind the sailing-ship harbour, where probably they got the first inkling of the storm. The atmosphere was becoming beyond bearing here on the ground floor, and she had in any event intended to show Tom the letter and the inventory for Else. Although on a day like this she scarcely needed to fear an upstair breeze, she slipped on her overall, the faded blue-grey garment once the property of Willi the apprentice, locked the door outside, as Albert had his own key with him, and trotted up the staircase. Even at the foot of the attic ladder she heard the hollow roar and whistle of the wind-gusts sweeping over the roofs.

Tom Barfey gave her an exultant welcome. He swept aside the sheets of gummed paper on which he was writing, in his neatest classic script, hundreds of addresses from old members' lists—appeals for enrolment in the Nat. Soc. Popular Welfare Burial Association, which were to be circulated to the former members of the Free-Thinkers' Burial Association, on envelopes actually belonging to this erstwhile Social-Democratic Association, whose property and funds had been confiscated by the N.S.D.A.P. five years before. The somewhat surprising idea of appealing to those then despoiled to subscribe once more for the same purpose, had been conceived by Herr Johannes Wohlgast and his friend Reitlin.

"Stine!" cried Tom, "listen. What a splendid show!"

He trundled his trolley out of the hot and stuffy attic room on to the front leads, after stacking his papers under a bit of bent iron rod and two large shells bestowed on him by Olga, tiger-shells from the South Seas, flecked with brown and milky spots. Stine winced. Up here the storm raged and hurled malignantly, and the streamers of grey cloud sped past so low that it seemed as though an outstretched arm could have caught them overhead.

"And I sent Albert down to the harbour," she groaned, as she sat down on the heated metal with her back against the sloping tiled face of the rear gable. She was glad not to be alone, but in the company of this good-humoured loyal lad with his shining stone-grey eyes, and tell him all that was gnawing at her mind. But first she handed him the letter with a groschen for the stamp. It might well be that Albert would bring back such good news from the *Eleonora Kröger* that they might be able to clear out in two or three days, or even to-day or to-morrow, leaving everything as it stood. So Gesche would perhaps be kind enough to knock at the Teetjens' door the first thing every morning, before she went to work, and if she got no answer, post the letter. In that case Albert and she would slip their keys through Reitlin's letter-box—

he already knew that the Teetjens might be leaving at a moment's notice.

"Oh dear," Tom lamented: "I can't bear the idea of your going away. When shall we see each other again?"—and he laid a hand on her ankle, which this time she did not withdraw.

"Up there, anyway," she replied with a smile, and pointed to the rumbling yellow citadel of Heaven, riven by the howling storm.

"That's no good," said he. "I want you here, my lovely star, I want to love you; a woman like you could make something out of a bit of drift wreckage such as me."

And as their shoulders rested level against the roof, he flung his arm round her, clasped her to him, and pressed his hot lips against hers. Stine was surprised that she allowed him, but made no resistance, possessed by the comforting thought that he had very strong arms, and that here was a lover with a quite different moustache from Albert's, with which she was so familiar. Then she pushed him away, shook her head at herself, and said severely: "Be sensible, Tom."

"I'm not sensible," he cried. "I adore you. I have held a star embraced. You can't deprive me of that."

"I would sooner you gave me a little advice," she said, fending him off. "I simply can't let the Lehmke's get my bedroom furniture. I'd sooner burn it. But I might set the house on fire if I poured petrol over the furniture. It would burn like matchwood, the beams are very old, and so is the floor. I wanted to ask you how I could prevent a fire from spreading."

He looked at her open-eyed, with a smile of something like happiness. "I always thought you were much too patient, and would stand for anything; thank God you're a human being after all. Now I'll read you my poem; my last, written a few days ago. Goebbels believed on the wireless that his Führer was now bringing the Sudeten Germans back into the Reich—as though we hadn't learned the Reich frontiers at school. You wait, they'll get Prague as well, and that will mean the end. For the Soviets won't let our Adolf enter Warsaw, everybody knows that."

Stine lifted her eyebrows. What had she to do with Warsaw? Where was it, anyway? Albert had told her about it—things that had happened there in the war. But Tom had trundled off and was now back again triumphantly brandishing a sheet of paper, which looked rather yellow, though it was certainly white, like the rest of the paper on which he had been writing. He took his stand before her, with a set expression on his face, and read in a loud voice that echoed down into his chest, to drown the roaring of the wind:

> *With Heil and Hoch and raucous roar,*
> *Germany moves on,*
> *Hyena Goebbels at the fore*
> *Thirty silver pieces have an old familiar ring,*
> *These are thy guerdon, so—*
> *Sing, Germania, sing.*

"Oh dear," cried Stine. "Are you mad?" But Tom continued:
"Second verse":

> *The war has opened up the pit,*
> *The Leader of the blind*
> *Has brought you to the edge of it.*
> *To seek and not to find,*
> *Hear Ley's lies and Göring's boasts,*
> *Take the silver pieces that you may not keep—*
> *Leap, Germania, leap.*

"Now for the last:"

> *With Heil and Hoch and raucous roar,*
> *Germany moves on—and crashes;*
> *Her bull-throat broken, she will rise*
> *And see amid the flashes*
> *The doom she brought upon the world,*
> *The corpses hurled*
> *Into that abyss*
> *Take my courage and thine own,*
> *Germania, and with other eyes*
> *Strive upwards, now alone.*

A lightning-flash hissed across the sky, but he scarcely noticed it, he was looking anxiously into Stine's face, and her eyes, which had never seemed to him so green. "Do you like it?" he asked. "Honestly?"

She shook her head. "It's insulting," and she wondered that she did not get up and go. It was, in fact, high treason, which would have been the term for it in former days. "And how do you know about the war?" He was not there, she reflected, when the five beheaded men led the marching column into the Ohlsdorf lake.

"Everybody does," said he, irritably. "That's why the moneyed interests and the generals have made a sort of myth of Adolf, so that he can't be deceived or ridiculed. There'll be war, and then a crash."

Stine recoiled, for the heavens seemed to say Amen to this wild youth's outburst; a crack of thunder split the ochrous heavens.

"I wrote it," said Tom, radiantly. "But you're responsible. You're making something of me, Stine. Later on I shall put your name to it—'Dedicated to Frau Stine Teetjen'. Then I'll circulate it, but not of course before all this beastly Nazi mess has been cleared up. How many strong young lives will it cost, do you think? However, I shan't be called up, and what I think will stay between my ears till the time comes. Then they'll all be gone—the Timmes and the Mengers, the Schröders and Merzenichs, there'll be no one left but people like Tom Barfey steering themselves around. However, our people won't have deserved any better fate, even if Heaven shies bricks for Hitler three times over." And he shook his fist at the yellowish grey firmament, from which came a succession of ominous flashes and detonations. (It was one of them that set the *Eleonora Kröger's* deck-officers in motion.)

Stine told herself that she must not go on sitting here. Tom had become horribly Red.

"Tom," said she, pulling herself together. "I must go now, or I shall get as soaked as if I were in a bathing dress."

"I wish you were," he cried.

"But you haven't yet told me how to manage, so that I can burn the furniture without setting fire to the house."

"You must sprinkle the whole place, roof and floor and all, with water from the hose, and then smear methylated spirit, not petrol, on the furniture, pour benzine on the mattresses; leave the windows open or shut, according to whether you want it seen at once or later on. You only want to damage the furniture, and the enamel and varnish and paint will be ruined in ten minutes."

"Thank you," she exclaimed, flung her arms round his neck, kissed him, and fled; before he could recover himself, her reddish hair had vanished through the trap-door.

Stine chased down the stairs. When she reached the yard she heaved a deep sigh, reflecting that this was perhaps a farewell. She felt a good deal more cheerful, and certainly relieved. She shivered to think of the risk the lad took in writing down such rhymes. He had described Dr. Goebbels as a hyena. As she opened the street door Stine remembered one she had seen at Stellingen, a crooked, black-striped creature, like, and yet quite unlike, a dog. And how had he, who never left his attic, got the idea that war was inevitable? If Albert had thought so, it would have been understandable. But Tom?—no. How oddly comforting it was to feel herself in her own home once more, her little nest and refuge. She would not allow any ghosts inside it, nor any of Tom's nonsense. It was beginning to grow dark on the ground floor—she would have liked to switch on the light, had it not been for the electricity bill, which someone would have to pay sometime. She cleaned herself up a bit, looked into the top drawer of the wardrobe where she had put the rough draft of her letter to Albert, of which she had never yet made a fair copy, explaining what she wanted done in case anything happened to her. And she had just decided to change her clothes, and revert to a woman again, when the bell rang. "Come in," she cried; but the door had already opened and Frau Lehmke and Dörte, arrayed in rain-cloaks with hoods, stepped into the room.

"I hope you won't mind, Stine," began the landlady of the "Tank"; "We're in rather a hurry—what an awful storm, I hope your Albert isn't out in it. . . ."

"No," said Stine.

"Someone has just been to our house with some house-linen for sale, so I thought I had better come along and see what we are going to take over from you."

Stine grew pale, and almost ceased to breathe. This—in her own house, her own home! She felt herself hounded out of her last refuge, like a frightened animal that merely wants to creep into safety and lie low, a badger in its burrow, or a cat chased by a dog on to a post or tree.

"There's plenty of time yet," she said heavily, her eyes fixed upon the enemy, whom she now so thought of for the first time.

"Time or not," rejoined Frau Lehmke. "We want to be able to make our arrangements."

Stine stopped between the sofa and the oval table, like someone suddenly stricken with paralysis; the door to the bedroom stood open, the lightning flashed, and its azure glare flooded the little room. Dörte, an impertinent little creature, whom Stine had always allowed to make herself quite at home in the Teetjen house, slipped into the bedroom, and cried to her mother:

"Quick, mamma, we have to get along home at once." Then came the sound of the key turning in the linen cupboard.

"Yes, we must settle this little matter," said Frau Lehmke, following her daughter.

"It's all there," cried the girl, in a voice that combined anxiety and impudence. "Six sets of everything, coverlets, sheets and pillow-cases."

Stine at last found her speech, of which the robbers' incursion had deprived her, and the sleek little cat prepared to defend herself.

"Frau Lehmke," she exclaimed, with claws in her voice, "whose house is this, I should like to know?"

"Why, bless me!" snapped Frau Lehmke, but with an echo of satisfaction in her tone. "There's a packet of money at stake."

At last Stine recovered her power of movement. She stepped forward, though she had to hold on to the table, she was trembling so violently that she had to clutch it.

"Get out," she cried, pointing imperiously towards the door. "This is too much."

She looked like a slim boy compared with Frau Lehmke's massive bulk, who had just emerged from the bedroom and was backing towards the door.

"Come along, Ma," gasped Dörte, as the lightning flashed again.

"You beasts," shrieked Stine. "You pack of thieves"—she raised her fist in menace. Then came a crash of thunder, and a savage yellow lightning flash. Frau Lehmke stood there for an instant, her eyes phosphorescent in the enveloping sulphurous glare, and what she shouted in reply was drowned by the rumble of the thunder. She slammed the door so violently that the frosted glass panes rattled. Stine ran after her, turned the key in the lock, pulled it out, and flung it into the opened drawer. Why hadn't she thrown the creature out of the house? But her first impulse to retaliate promptly turned to loathing and self-contempt. She snatched the coil of cord out of the drawer, and untied the knots with flying hands. The Lehmke woman was an embodiment of the Party of the evil spirit, the witch, that boiled men in a cauldron, first cutting their heads off with the sharp edge of an apple-bin. Not with an axe, nor with Albert's hands either. Only Tom had denounced her for what she was—Albert never had. She had stood in this same room with her brat beside her, and laid her greedy hands on his Stine's bed and board—the old beast with phosphorescent eyes and poison in her voice. Well, that should never happen any more. She climbed on to the sofa,

X

propping herself against the wall, and then on to the table, giddily reached up to the hook and detached the hanging lamp, which she dropped on to the sofa. While her hands were busy with all this, her eyes were wet with tears of pity for herself, her teeth and lips and tongue shaped the words of the Lord's Prayer, which she had not uttered since Anna Teetjen's funeral. Her soul was now divided, one part of it in agony, the other accomplishing her own destruction, as she stood knotting a noose. Too often and too long had she listened to her grandmother's enticements, pointing the way within, the escape into death, the suppression of the individual ego, the desperate plunge for freedom through the integuments of the soul, now weaned from life by the slow subjection of many days and many nights. "Our Father, which art in Heaven . . ." The cord slid round her neck and hung taut from the hook. At the words—"Thy Kingdom come, Thy will be done, and forgive us our trespasses," she dropped on her knees and in so doing overturned the centre-table, the round top of which rested on a single shaft split into three curved legs. The murderous terror, the inexorable strangulation, the sudden failure of breath, the rush of blood against the skull—all this lasted only a few seconds, but their concentrated horrors outweighed the whole content of a life.

Fortunately, Stine's slender neck cracked at once under her body's weight. Whether she was aware of the flash that fell from heaven at that moment, no one will ever know. Through the terror that possessed her, a face appeared, encircled in a yellow glow; and the face was that of Albert, romanticized and glorified, and of the Lord Jesus, benign and smiling, the Jesus of the children's picture-books, as conceived by the sculptor, Thorwaldsen, a century before. Her limbs still beat the air, her feet twitched convulsively; then—a slim youth in a blue-grey overall swung from the ceiling just above the table, oblivious of the rain that pelted down into the yard. In the house above her head a door slammed, and windows were abruptly closed.

# CHAPTER THREE

### A MAN COMES HOME

THE COMMON VIEW that a shock sobers a man, and restores a drunken man to reality, can seldom have been so exactly exemplified as in the case of Albert Teetjen that evening. He sped through the soaking windswept streets of Hamburg in a taxi, aglow with the joy of anticipation. While he waited, he had made brother-in-law Ahlsen explain how a cheque can be transferred to a third person who can pay it into his account. He was singing a snatch from the Hohenfriedberger march as he opened the door, but as it was now nine o'clock and Stine usually went to bed when there was a thunderstorm, he paused for a moment before calling softly: "Stine." Then he switched on the light, which to his surprise flashed forth in a lamp that was lying on the sofa; Stine must have taken it down to clean and then been called away. But there was surely an odd smell in the room, all the windows were shut—and what was that hanging from the ceiling? The bulb with its circular shade was facing him and dazzled his vision—but . . . the table was lying sideways on the floor, and what on earth was that depending from the ceiling, an overall—a doll?

He laid a hand upon it: "Stine!" he cried. It was unquestionably a human being; and it was Stine. Almost unrecognizable, with upturned eyes, her tongue protruding from her soft, curved lips, her hair dishevelled, and her small head tilted onto her shoulder. "You must come down, my dear," he said softly in the silence of the room. He set the table on its legs, stepped up on to the sofa, and lifted her off the hook. How heavily she lay across his arm. Darling Stine—no longer warm, but not yet stiff; she must have destroyed herself while he sat drinking with his new acquaintance, Kley.

He set her in the corner of the sofa with her legs still bent, drew her eyelids over her eyes, pushed her tongue back between her teeth, and closed her mouth. He was accustomed to dealing with corpses. Then he threw his handkerchief over the electric light bulb, took off some of his clothes and washed his face and head. He shut the still open linen-cupboard doors in the bedroom, then he crept back to the table—it was the only way to describe the unnaturally slow movements which were all that he could now manage—and sat down in the opposite corner of the sofa, facing Stine. What on earth had happened? How could the resolve have come to fulness in that poor little head without his knowing anything about it? So many futilities had lately been invented, such as radios and loud speakers, which were then bellowing overhead about the war with Czechoslovakia, so dexterously averted. But there was no hint of any invention that would help in the discovery of someone else's thoughts, or what might be happening inside a woman's head. He must be mad; or dreaming. He was lying drunk, and a stowaway, on the *Eleonora Kröger*, which would be soon putting out to sea, and dreaming the ghastliest dreams that had ever beset a distracted brain. When he opened his eyes, the phantom would depart.

But his eyes were open, and the phantom was still there, huddled in the corner of the sofa, just as it hung from the ceiling. Stine in an overall. What was this between his fingers? His old pull-through, carefully greased. He had duly stowed it away after the war, and in the end it had been used for strangling all that was left to him on earth. How had she found it?—it had been in one of the lower drawers among all sorts of rubbish. The house was strangely quiet. A drip . . . drip . . . drip of water reached his ears. He jumped up and tightened the

main tap. One of the drawers in the wardrobe stood open, and in it
lay a pencilled note:

> *Dr. A.*
>
> *Don't be angry, and come soon.   Make sure they don't disturb us when
> we aren't there to see.   You couldn't have done it for me.   There are plenty
> of large grave-holes at Finkenwärder.   Till we meet again, wherever you like.*
>
> *Your St.*

When he had deciphered this message by the harsh light of the
unshaded bulb the tears came into his eyes at last.   He flung himself
with his arms across the table, laid his eyes against his elbows, and wept
convulsively, moaning through his clenched teeth.   Where, now, was
the use of that heartening slip of paper in his pocket?   If he took and
held it under her eyes, waved it to and fro before her face, she could
not see.   She could not hear him tell her that her bedroom was now hers
once more, that it had been saved from the Lehmkes.   How rash
people were, especially women.   Couldn't she have waited until the
6th September?   Only another week.   There she sat, her legs bent and
stiff, and absolutely silent; still he felt bemused.   He found himself
wondering whereabouts her soul was—somewhere near, no doubt.   If
she could do as she liked, it could not be far away.   It would cling to
her husband, her Albert.   And if the four men from Fuhlsbüttel, and
Lene Prestow, proved that the soul was a reality, a sort of emanation, or
radio-activity, and if the divining-rod could, as Dr. Laberdan maintained,
actually indicate disease, there was some element in man that did survive
death.   In most cases, however, it departed when its integument was
duly deposited in the earth to which it belonged.   But at first it lingered
nearby; how otherwise explain the occasional stories in the newspapers
about the restoration to life after apparent death?

Well, if Stine wanted to lie at Finkenwärder, he had some jobs of
work to do.   He must eat, write out various messages, stick the new
owner's name and address on the tricycle, put the cheque in an envelope
addressed to Herr Otto Lehmke, and inscribe on the back of it—Albert
Teetjen, Butcher, and the date, 29.8.38.   Stine had told him that she
would send word to her sister through Gesche Barfey, if they left at short
notice, and the key was to be dropped in Reitlin's letter-box.   But he
was much too tired to do anything just yet.   Why shouldn't he sleep
in one corner of the sofa, and Stine in the other?   She would fit admirably
into his tricycle-carrier in her present attitude.   It did not matter now
—indeed, nothing mattered any more.   Grandfather's photograph looked
well on the wall again—there he was, pacing the room with his hands
behind his back; and his grave was in this room, under the ash and
weeping-willow.   He and Stine were sitting on a bench in the fog.

Albert awoke in the middle of the night.   The waning moon stood
just above the roof, shining into the yard-shaft, and shedding a dim

radiance into the room. Albert promptly grasped the situation—indeed he had never made up his mind with greater clearness and decision. He took a sheet out of the linen-cupboard, and spread it over his poor little wife, washed, went into the kitchen, put some remnants of food on the freshly scrubbed table, a bit of baked plaice, some cold potatoes, and sour milk, and ate the kind of supper that a man needs, when he has a job of work before him and a long way to go. As he sat munching and swallowing, many thoughts drifted through his head, mostly connected with what might have been. She had never trusted Ahlsen; the result being that she had expected nothing from this visit, and that had been the real blunder. For her, there had never been any man called Kley. Rightly regarded, the money now on its way into the Lehmke's pockets came in a certain sense from Footh and from the Party, for it was they who made Dr. Kley an heir, and then turned him out. Well, so Stine and he would set out for Spain, they would make their way into the innermost parts of the earth, like the miner, and the adept of the divining-rod. All was well; destiny had spoken. The Last Post of his life would be duly sounded with due ceremony by an expert bugler, not by an amateur from the Hitler Youth.

It was half-past twelve when he took out his watch for the last time, slipped it out of his waistcoat, and put it in the cupboard, with a note for Tom Barfey, as a memento. There was still some life in the battery of his pocket-torch, so he wheeled the tricycle out of the shed to his own entrance-door, opened the carrier, stepped softly up to the sofa, and picked up the white, shrouded form, with the words so often used in wartime by leave-men or new recruits trying to get off with a girl: "Come on, darling, just once before we die."

"You won't have any flowers, darling," said he, and the tears came into his eyes again. "No cross, and no stone. Well, it doesn't make much odds." So saying he closed the flap of the carrier, put on his tunic, buckled his pistol to his belt, donned his cap, metamorphosing himself into an S.S. man on duty, so that no one should stop him, or ask what he was carrying through Hamburg by night. He stepped once more into the doorway of the bedroom, cast a lingering look of farewell at all the things that Stine had so loved, the background to so many years of human life—two, perhaps three generations; then shut all the doors, wrapped up the key in an old rag, and slipped it under Reitlin's door on the ground floor. By way of a grim joke he previously hung "Back in Ten Minutes" placard in the window. And on a bit of cardboard, in which he had bored a hole and put in his pocket, together with a piece of string, he had inscribed in large clear characters the name of the new owner of the vehicle: Friedrich Schmidchen, Butcher, Altona, Wittnerstrasse 5.

Hamburg lay breathing the cool air, fanned by a light breeze under the late-risen moon. Here and there a cat with tail erect prowled through the darkness. Albert pedalled on and on. Scarcely anyone was about, though the now freshened air was an inducement to a stroll. He avoided the populous districts round the harbour, where the fire brigade and pioneers were carrying out the necessary salvage work, by the aid of electric lamps and the full street lighting. In the meantime the *Eleonora*

*Kröger* must have moved down the river at the slow pace imposed on sea-going ships by the vulnerability of the banks, and there was a vacant berth where he had met with what might have been a turning-point in his life, if poor Stine had not behaved like a sheep or a rabbit, and if. . . . The "if" gnawed at Albert's heart, while he pedalled mechanically along the Elbe bank. She had done it with his own rifle cord, while he had experienced a miraculous piece of luck—a sort of recompense for not having pretended to any remorse or penitence for his deed. What he had done, he had done, and would do again, except that he would make himself more secure against hidden enemies and so-called friends. Strange, thought he, as he glided past the neat front-gardens; when a fellow boasts of what he's going to do for the Fatherland, and make Germany great, I shout *Heil* and *Hurrah*, and applaud him; but when a fellow says he means to help the workers get their rights, I say—Down with him,—and cut his head off. And yet I'm a worker myself. I was trained as one, I understood my job, and now in this box behind my saddle I'm carrying to the grave all that I loved on earth, and my business and my life has gone to smash. And yet I wouldn't have cared much what I did to save myself. Strange; when a man struggles against ill luck, he's sure to be done down. He stopped to refresh himself with a draught of kümmel, and, as he did so, noticed a clump of tall roses close by the fence. He could not reach them from his saddle; so he dismounted, and finding the gate open, he walked, clasp-knife in hand, across a short stretch of lawn. Suddenly and without a sound, a powerful boxer with bared fangs dashed upon him from the shadow of the bushes; a stocky dark-striped dog which, without barking, immediately attacked the intruder. But Albert was one too many for him; he thrust his knife under the dog's left shoulder, snapped off some roses, put the great mass of creamy blooms at Stine's feet in the carrier, swung himself into the saddle, and pedalled off. As he slid past the houses that lined the road, silent and ghostlike under the waning moon, smiling grimly, he pictured the surprise that awaited the owner of the villa next morning—no, early that morning; burglar kills boxer, nothing taken but a few roses. Yes, it isn't every day that such a cur meets so alert an adversary, and the rich may well contribute something to Stine's funeral.

There was no doubt in his mind about the way; since his youthful days he had bicycled along that road, often with Stine beside him or behind him—rather differently from now. On their last few trips before Whitsuntide they had laughingly agreed that this Elbe bridge would also be much welcomed by cyclists; the Pioneers had bridged the Kohlfleet, and laid down a number of wooden tracks in order to connect the various building sites and trial shafts. By one of them, where much work had been done, they had dismounted, leaned over the parapet and looked down. It was square, covering a good deal of space, on each of its four walls a ladder led down into the depths; it was partially covered by crane-like timber structures, and was to be used for sinking trial shafts for artificial foundations where no rock could be found. The excavation reached to ground-water level, and even a good distance beneath it, and it was already filling up with a slimy mush of sand and water, which could never provide a basis for a block of concrete, which must be set upon fixed emplacement, as two ancient workmen had observed that Sunday morning with true professional gloom. 'Ah, Stine darling,' he said to her with a nod, as he got off his tricycle by the fence, 'you little thought you were visiting the site of your own grave, when you suggested we should go and see what Finkenwärder looked like now.' Overhead the bright eyes of night and the level moon gleamed with an almost genial radiance. The tall masts, gigantic pine-trunks, tilted inwards, supporting a sort of platform congested with scaffolding, hooks and tackle. More watchmen ought to have been on patrol, there was so much about that could be stolen. But it was nearly three in the morning, the worst hour of sentry-go, when the mainland cocks had already uttered a few hesitant crows. Another great success had just been achieved, some sort of *coup* against the French and Czechoslovakia, as he had understood aboard the ship, which called for celebration. How long ago it seemed— that pleasant talk on board the *Eleonora Kröger*. Go back to Wagner-strasse 17, and look at the watch ticking in the wardrobe drawer. The black velvet heaven still glittered with a myriad stars.

Now came the most horrible part of the affair, but it had to be faced. Several deep draughts of kümmel, which emptied the bottle, provided Albert with a final respite; for a smoker like himself it would have been natural to fill and light a last pipe, but he felt no inclination to do so. He opened the wooden gate into the enclosure, which was not locked. A narrow gallery ran round the inside of the shaft above the four ladders, one in the centre of each wall. He lifted Stine out of the carrier—his girlie had never weighed so heavy, often as he had held her in his arms. He placed her carefully on one of the ladders, laid the roses against the sheet where it bulged above her knees, and in so doing remembered that the tricycle was no longer his, and that a decent citizen must be careful of other people's property. So he went out once more, hung the written label on the handlebars, and wheeled the tricycle half a minute or so away from the place where Stine was awaiting him. There was no need to leave a too obvious track. 'Yes, girlie,' he said to himself, 'now the time has come, you must go down into the mud. Arne Saknussen had a better start for his journey to the centre of the earth, but we must take the way we find. I've got my rod with me, anyway, stuck in the leg of my boot. My Dowser's Record is not worth much without me—the Lieut.-Col. will find out for himself.' He then closed the gate behind him, and now had finally to face what remained for him to do. So awful was it that he could scarcely get his limbs to move. The storm had raised the level of the water by a good deal, and the stars were now mirrored in the surface below, yonder was the Great Bear poised in the sky right above Albert's head. How was he to get Stine down to the water? He wanted to lower her in such a way that there should be no impact, that she shouldn't be shocked or hurt by a sudden plunge; but she was so heavy that he could not clamber down while holding her in his arms. Perhaps the sheet would bear her weight. It was one of his mother's, and made of the finest flax. Should he take a last look at her face and lovely hair? No, that would be folly. Adolf had flung

him into the gutter—why him, of all people? No answer. Pah!—
what matter. Down into the soup, Madam. He swathed the sheet
tightly round the sitting figure, twisted it above her head into a kind of
rope, and let her slide gently into the water, with the roses at her knees.
There was only a faint splash, then the waters closed above her, and the
placid surface once more mirrored the Great Bear, and the array of stars.

Then the last deed, hardest of all, and indeed, without the aid of
schnapps he might not have faced it.   As he climbed down the ladder,
rung by rung, until he stood thigh-deep in the chilly ooze, gripped the
ladder with his left hand, pulled out his pistol with his right, and put a
bullet through his temples, he saw, in a momentary flash, not the ladder
on the shaft wall, but the four beheaded men, blacker and more gigantic
than in Ohlsdorf cemetery.   They carried their heads once more upon
their shoulders, and the expression in their faces said: It shall suffice.
Like a bright-coloured dove Lene Prestow—or was it Stine?—seemed to
flutter between them—and dart upwards to the stars.   All this in the
less-than-second while a body, shot through the head, can fall off a
ladder sideways into the water.   Above him, too, closed the mirror of
the waters—no one had heard the detonation.   From the handlebar of
the tricycle, where it stood on a gangway, a cardboard label inscribed:
Friedrich Schmidschen, Altona, Wittnerstrasse 5, danced and fluttered
in the morning breeze.

*ENVOI*

# THE AXE COMES HOME

"ALBERICH AND HIS Nibelungs awake!" Fresh from Berlin, Lieut.-Col. Lintze thus expressed a slightly sardonic appreciation of the effects produced by the combined decorative efforts of Reitlin, the schoolmaster, and Herr Johannes Wohlgast. "There have been some strange doings here," said Käte Neumeier, with equal astonishment. So saying, and with a shake of her head, she alighted at Wagnerstrasse 17, behind the officer and in front of her husband, from the army car which, newly painted and reconditioned, betrayed nothing of the vicissitudes to which it had probably been subjected.

Entering the car, Herr Koldewey had scrutinized his fellow-conspirator, before asking him whether he had got hold of himself somewhat and Lintze nodded. But his hair, the thinning fair hair at his temples, seemed to Herr Koldewey interwoven with grey and his eyes still showed signs of that fluttering disturbed look of a few days ago. Directly after his return from Berlin, Lintze had come to visit him in his bird-cage on top of the prison.

On that day also Herr Koldewey had read his morning-paper with anxiety. He had walked a short way through the early autumnal, the yellowish park. The newspaper published a short *communiqué*, obviously officially inspired, according to which the garrison of Hamburg and the entire Wehrkreis 10 had to wear mourning for a week. Its commandant, the highly meritorious General of the cavalry, Knochenhauer, had fallen victim to an accident on the artillery shooting grounds at Jüterbog, as happens from time to time in the practice of sharp-shooting. The Führer had honoured him with a State funeral, which had taken place the day before yesterday. Herr Koldewey, the cigar in the corner of his mouth or between his fingers, had watched a drinking bumble-bee on his black-red dahlias, felt his heart beat quietly again, and inhaled the wet morning breeze that came through the bared tree-tops. He had asked himself: Why could not this really be an accident? Most probably the artillery-men had been experimenting with the craziest devils-devices for the new armour-battles and it could have happened that a gun had blown up or a piece of shrapnel had penetrated the commander's brain. A State funeral—that of course was suspicious. And General Knochenhauer, it could not be denied, belonged to the half-dozen senior officers who knew what was really happening.

When Herr Lintze then sat opposite him in his governor's room, greyish and faded-looking, with blinking eyes and a small mouth,

377

that he contracted, so that his lower jaw would not tremble, dread had seized him. Was it accident or chance? In any case this death was very opportune for certain cliques, who wanted to make the ingenious Führer the sole master of Germany's destiny and also War Lord in an aggressive war for broader Lebensraum.

"I'll bring the axe back one of these days, my dear Koldewey. Nothing doing for the time being, and, I fear, we shall not extricate ourselves cheaply."

"But now tell me, for the so-called heaven's sake, how could the half-boiled ideas, existing in five or six heads, have become known? Magic does not occur and thought-reading isn't even in the power of my most astute colleagues from the Berlin Gestapo centre."

"Yes," retorted Lintze, and now his lower jaw actually trembled, "you won't take it amiss, dear Koldewey, that in the first moment of panic, I even doubted you for a time."

Herr Koldewey smiled indulgently, waving his long cranium. "Nothing must be thought impossible," he uttered sententiously, "by those who choose the dangerous roads of providence, I could also say, those of 'Ananke'."

"But then I got on the trail," continued Lintze. And with an accusing nod he said that his general had dined, about ten days ago, with the Hungarian Ambassador, in a small intimate circle, drinking those delicious Tokayer wines. The gentleman, a military attaché at the embassy, before he became ambassador, often entertained senior Reichswehr officers, who were critically disposed towards the Nazi régime. He was thought one of the most able opponents of the Führer cult and its ambitions—those extremist plans which would endanger above all, the State he was representing, and where, since 1919, the power was in the hands of the conservative aristocracy. But to be sure, this gentleman, what was his name, had belonged to the trusted circle of the unhappy Herr von Schleicher, and many voices had hinted, after the happenings of the year '34, that this Herr Dombas, was quite possibly in the pay of our Gestapo.

There Herr Koldewey had contracted his brows and his goat-eyes sharply pointing to his *vis-à-vis*: "I'll find that out, my friend, and if I have to travel specially to Berlin; but I shall not move now. Know how to wait, that is one of the chief virtues we have to learn from our hunting owls. Had your general heard about me?"

"But no," reassured him the other.

"Well and good," nodded Koldewey, and drew a line with his bony hand through the air. "That's finished. Then you really may bring back the axe. Now it is ripe for the museum, or for its former owner, especially as we have not heard from this Herr Teetjen for weeks, to whose domicile my wife will guide us. She, by the way, needn't know about this épisode Knochenhauer."

"Of course," Herr Lintze had agreed, rising from his seat, stiff-limbed at the time, without push or strength. "And when shall we bring the bankrupt-tool to its waiting-place?"

"To-morrow, the day after to-morrow, always at your service."

"Popular Welfare Burial Association, N.S.D.A.P.—we must look into this. By the way, is it polite to let your wife go first into an establishment of this kind?"

Herr Lintze smiled his thin-lipped smile, whereupon Governor Koldewey rejoined that the uncertain situation in Europe made it all the more essential to maintain the conventions, even in the face of death. A longish parcel, tied up with string, lay on the seat beside Ehlers, the driver.

In the shop-window on a low catafalque stood an imposing black coffin, with a palm-branch and a Christian cross on its elaborately bevelled lid; it was adorned with silvered feet and handles, having once been the show-piece of the firm of Julius Israel Hauser, Undertakers, Altona. In what had once been the shop, now painted black and white in stripes, a huge silver swastika, encircled by rays and clouds, figured on the wall near the door where the refrigerator used to stand, and over it the legend: "Solemn Tombs in Nordic Earth." The small table and the chairs, once white and now violet, still stood against the same wall, and on the table there was a vase of violet asters, as in old days. But the counter had been replaced by a stepped daïs and a writing-desk, behind which sat Tom Barfey, supported by stacks of papers, lists, writing materials, and a brand-new telephone, not to mention the complete Hamburg Telephone Directory. A couple of spreading palms in large square boxes completed the impression of solemnity.

"Tom," cried Käte Neumeier, whose astonishment, as well as her familiarity with the house, indicated her as the best person to conduct the conversation. "What are you doing here, and what on earth has been going on?" In the meantime her husband had recognized the suit the young man was wearing, and was rather baffled by the penetrating, searching look in the bright eyes beneath the low, broad forehead and the stiff, cropped hair.

"Our Block-warden, Herr Reitlin, was so kind as to offer me the post when the Teetjens disappeared, and he installed the 'Popular Welfare' here. He is also responsible for fixing up the place as a sort of chapel." And his gaze rested on the inscriptions on the main and back wall. The fact that he had suggested the inscription and got it accepted, and that the initial letters composed the word Stine, he kept to himself; nor did he mention that Herr Reitlin had refused to agree to the simpler version; "Quiet Funerals in Nordic Earth."

"Colonel Lintze wanted to see Herr Teetjen on Service affairs, about the divining-rod trials," pursued Käte. "Doesn't anyone know where the Teetjens went?"

"They may be inspected in the mortuary," said the rasping voice of a new arrival, with a short, curled beard, grey hair parted in the middle, who emerged from the further living-room, bowed, introduced himself as Herr Reitlin, ready to provide all available information.

He had believed the story of the sudden departure for Spain, until he discovered the watch in the wardrobe drawer, labelled—For Tom Barfey. A man starting on a journey would take two watches if he had them, he certainly wouldn't leave one behind. This looked like a farewell gift, a last will and testament. The cheque for Herr Lehmke, which had incidentally been duly honoured, completed the picture of a conscientious German citizen hounded to death by the red rabble of underground Hamburg. The fact that the delivery car, which Teetjen had sold, had turned up at Finkenwärder, guided Herr Reitlin's suspicions in the right direction. Unfortunately the usual official procrastination had delayed the investigations he had at once suggested, and it was not until yesterday that the bodies of the pair had been recovered, and he and the other legatees had been summoned to identify the remains. It was not known when they would be released for burial. The presumption was that Herr Teetjen had first shot his wife, and then himself; further details might be revealed by the post-mortem, but these would be points for experts. The Popular Welfare organization would provide a double grave in their own section of the Ohlsdorf cemetery near the round-point with the tall junipers, and the Preester Troop would convey their "fallen comrade", and his faithful helpmate with full military honours to their last resting-place. Comrade Vierkant would lay a wreath on the grave in the name of Group-Leader Footh and deliver a short address on the text; Judge not that ye be not judged. He, Reitlin, had chosen this theme, when objections had been raised on the ground this looked like a case of murder and suicide; it was a profitable pronouncement, although certain colleagues from the Ostmark had maintained in an educational journal that the "not" would be overlooked by the young and uneducated sections of the public, and the text would be read as an endorsement of trials, punishments and executions. These fellows from Vienna, he concluded with a laugh, are just a little too free with their good advice.

"Yes, they're rather absurd," said Herr Lintze; he thanked Reitlin, and tapped the lid of the ceremonial coffin. So we shall have to take our parcel back with us, he thought, nodded to Tom, and in the company of Herr and Frau Koldewey left the shop, obsequiously escorted to the car by Herr Reitlin.

"One moment," cried Frau Koldewey. "My gloves!" and hurried back.

"Tom!" cried she as she picked up the gloves she had purposely left behind. "That was not intended! How on earth did all this happen?"

"They've been hounded down ever since that day at Stellingen, Frau Doctor," replied the young man, with a look of grim intensity—indeed he was grinding his teeth as he had done on that very day. The jungle methods of a capitalist society, he thought, and the loathing in his eyes was also directed against her, and against himself.

"I'll look in again," exclaimed Käte, hurriedly. "We must have a talk about this. Poor Stine."

"We're living down on the ground floor now," observed Tom, refraining from any further comment. But Frau Koldewey felt, as she shut the door behind her, how very unwise it would be to make this youth into an enemy.

As the car drove off round the still beflagged corner on the way to Fuhlsbüttel, Herr Koldewey threw a sidelong glance from his yellowish, goat-like eyes at his wife, who was sitting beside him on the deep-cushioned back-seat of the car. She was staring into vacancy, tapping her gloves against the leather seat, and seemed to him unduly perturbed by what had passed. He must help her to get her impressions into order, and view these occurrences in a proper light. What a populous neighbour-hood she had chosen for her dealings in birth and death. "In our times, when people only raise their eyes when sections of the population are or soon will be on the move—as, for example, in Russia of to-day—the destinies of individuals are losing significance. In the U.S.A., so I read a few days ago, 40,000 people were killed (or killed and injured —I forget which) as the result of motor-car accidents. Take a daily average of 110, and as our total population is only half that of the U.S.A., our figure would be 55 per diem. Traffic accidents; and these Teetjens were two of them."

Käte guessed his meaning, threw him a grateful look, and then replied: "Yes, but for those near to them, each accident contains an element of fate—as well as for the principals themselves."

"I've got his Dowser's Record," said Herr Lintze, complacently surveying the glittering panorama of Hamburg, with its green squares and stretching quays. "But it's no good now."

Herr Koldewey, however, thought something could be made of it— Dr. Laberdan would certainly be glad to have it, and Herr Lintze was ready to hand it over—without the author it would be of no value to the army.

"Well," he interjected, "the war has again been averted. Germany's luck has held, and the divinely-appointed arbiter of our destinies has again won the game." He leaned over one of the centre-seats, picked up the parcel containing the axe, laid it across his knees, and tapped the blade.

"We'll deposit it in the museum," said Herr Koldewey, "it shall there await its hour. *Habeant sua fata*—not only *libelli*, but also *fasces*."

"If you are not in a hurry, come in and have a drink," said Frau Käte, speaking in broad Hamburg, with a smile of invitation.

"Alas," said Lintze, with a shake of his head. "You've got just as much younger as we've got older during the last six months. I would like to, but I can't to-day. People like ourselves have learnt from practical experience and must now adjust our theories.—Well, I'll come in for ten minutes."

The garden was basking in the rich September sunshine, flooding through the red-berried rowans into the open windows, and the clock in the hall struck twelve; time for lunch, and three sat down, not for the first time together, to a glass of the old brandy which Frau Käte had produced with true Hamburg hospitality.

"We shall miss a fellow like Teetjen when the time comes," observed Herr Lintze, as he lifted the balloon glass. "It came off this time—the war-game, I mean—though how it did, God knows; we can't be said to have deserved such luck. Our generals say they won't play, but they all do in the end. Like the fisherman and his wife in the fairy-tale,

when he keeps on saying it's no good going out to fish, but he lets his
wife persuade him and has another try for a fish.    Well, it's all right
as long as it *is* all right.    Then comes a real bad day, and we're in the
pigstye again—with respect I say it—for my wife Ilsebill doesn't see
things like I will: Well, General von Fritsch knows, and my chief
Knochenhauer knew, and until the foundation stone of the Elbe suspension bridge is laid, so to say it, we'll look around for another axeman—
what was the fellow's name?    Albert Teetjen, Master-Butcher."    And
he turned over the leaves of the Dowser's Record, and laid it down
again on the writing-table.

Herr Koldewey remembered, as he pledged his guest, that he, too,
had once used a simile from this same fairy-tale.    But that was all a
very long time ago, and life was now embodied in Käte and the future;
the cares of State and its affairs were no more than the snows of yester-
year.    Let them pass, the coachman laughed, settled himself firmly on
the car of destiny, and whipped up the horses of Eternal Recurrence.
Forward—yet once more!

Then he got up and escorted his guest to the door.

### EPODE.    ASTROLOGY

Next Sunday Dr. Koldewey's house, the red roofs and turrets of his
official residence, were enveloped in the same golden glow.    Lithe and
slim as a chimney sweeper's lad, Ingebottel, his youngest daughter, stood
in her gym-dress on the ridge of the roof, clinging to a chimney, and
examining the aerial with a professional eye.    As she used to say in a
voice of lamentation to the resident doctor, when an inflammation of the
ear was coming on: "There's a sort of crackle in my ear"; so yesterday
evening when they were all listening to the latest report from Munich
on the Führer's glorious victory over the Western Democracies, she had
in the same sort of voice cried: "It's the aerial," when the rasping,
crackling interruptions transformed the act of listening from a pleasure
into an unpleasant and sometimes infuriating nuisance.    Koldewey's
daughters were much too impatient to wait until the defect could be
dealt with by the slow-moving official machinery.

Thyra Koldewey, darkest of the three fair-haired sisters, sat on the
window-sill in the Mengers attic, as it was now called, from the books
it contained, wearing a long gaily-coloured morning dress of the newest
pattern, carrying a design of red sea-dragons—Viking ships, with a pale
green moon behind of them, riding on indigo waves against a cream-
coloured background.    She leaned out rather venturesomely to see what
her sister was up to, but soon retreated.    The table provided by Annette
for books was now decked with astrological signs, and sheets of paper
covered with certain calculations which she had put aside for the moment.
A volume of *Friedrich Nietzsche's Letters* lay nearby; she had been vainly
trying to find the passage in which the philosopher expounded his views
on apocalyptic visions to the musician Köselitz—the composer Peter
Gast Köselitz, of whom he thought so highly, but whom the historians
of music omitted to mention.

From time to time she looked out and upwards at the delicate blue autumnal sky, veined with soft clouds, then she plunged once more into the world of figures and equations—two horoscopes she was comparing: her own and her sister Inge's. Born on different days in different years, their life-histories displayed an ever-increasing resemblance, and their ends were exactly similar. This stuck her as uncanny, and she was trying to discover the probable error.

A huge bomber droned over the rooftops, flying very low, from Riga or Copenhagen to the Fuhlsbüttel airport. Then came a slithering sound along the roof, and a minute later Ingebottel stepped through the door, washed her hands under the tap, and flung herself on the spare bed to get her breath.

"Have you found out what's wrong with yours?" asked Thyra, her level brows set in a worried frown above her slanting eyes. "As to mine, I can't."

"Yours is all rubbish, anyway. It was nothing much," said Ingebottel cheerfully. "A big bit of insulating tape stuck into the metal clip on the chimney. Let's go down now and turn it on. I should like to hear if it's still crackling."

Thyra noticed with disapproval that her sister spoke in a faintly South German accent; surely occasional nights spent with a South German was no excuse for imitating his speech. She was very fond of her sister—her gay and forceful character so strongly contrasted with her own rather dark intensity,—were their destinies to march in equal rhythm to the end? She slipped her pencil behind her ear through the mop of shingled dark blonde hair, as it was then worn.

"It seems that we shan't live to be old—either of us."

"I don't want to," said her younger sister, emphatically; "I can't imagine myself old. Do you see me walking around like an old schoolmarm, or the mother of a family with half a dozen brats on my back? Not on your life," she cried, flinging her arms wide. "The thing is to begin to live as soon as possible, and that we have done; to take a good deep bite into the juicy apple, and go out, when we must, before the dew is off the grass. . . . When I see Hamburg from our roof, I do so wish I were a painter. The spires and shop-windows in the old city, sparkling in the sunshine, the red and black steamers in the harbour, and the waters, so delicately blue and still in the clear September light. And the white walls make such marvellous ground tones. . . . I must get out my old water-colour box."

Ah well, thought Thyra rather sadly, Inge's boy-friend would help her to express all these emotions. People so full of life never concerned themselves about death. She closed the volume of Nietzsche, replaced it on its shelf, rolled up her papers, and smoothed out her gown.

"Wilhelm Kley has just left in one of those same steamers. He was the only man I could have had anything to do with—he didn't merely want to take and hold, he had something to give. He liked to tell you what was in his mind."

"Let him go," rejoined Ingebottle. "It would have been a racial crime, and must have turned out badly."

Thyra nodded, but her close-set eyes avoided her sister's.

"Papa and his Käte wouldn't have objected."

"Papa!" ejaculated Ingebottel with a sort of indignant affection. "What do you think he said to me not long ago when I tried to draw him on the subject of his beloved Nietzsche. I asked him what he would do if Nietzsche's doctrines were realized, and the blonde beast started waging totalitarian war against the West or East. He explained that the realities of thought were purely intellectual. They were only valid within that sphere, and did not apply to the crude world of every day— and then he went on about a Cave and Plato, and I didn't even try to remember what he said. These old gentlemen will be surprised when the younger generation, with the Führer at their head, put them all out of business."

"Did you happen to see Dr. Laberdan pass while you were up on the roof?" She followed her sister on to the landing and closed the attic door. Then they went downstairs. Ingebottel shook her head under its coronal of plaits.

"I wouldn't be likely to," she replied. "He's mourning for his old friend Teetjen, and training new pupils to use the divining-rod out in the country somewhere."

"Yes, Teetjen and his Stine. Do you remember how we brought them in to the wedding breakfast playing the march from *Tannhäuser?*"

They both smiled at that comic recollection.

"It's a pity I didn't work out their horoscope," said Thyra meditatively. "They gave me the impression of being so vividly alive. Besides, we should now know if there really is anything in all this, or whether I am just wasting my time over ours."

"You do take yourself so seriously," said Ingebottel, bluntly. "You and your Jew would have been well-suited, if you don't mind my saying so."

She knelt down by the wireless cabinet, turned the dial to a short wave, and caught an American station, proclaiming that the Senate approved and supported the Munich decisions and the developments in Europe; the share market had reacted most satisfactorily, and that the Isolationist—Senator Miller—had received the congratulations of his friends.

"What rubbish," said Ingebottel. "Let's have some music;" after a few attempts, the room was filled with marching, dancing rhythms; Ingebottel jumped up, took her sister in her arms, and as they slipped into the opening steps of a rumba, she said gaily: "The crackle has quite gone. Reception perfect."

The great clock in the hall began to strike twelve.

# EPILOGUE

### RESURRECTION

ONCE AGAIN, AFTER exactly seven years—and what years of menace, destruction and triumph they had been, burying themselves in the nerves and hearts of all who had lived through them—two of our friends met at Haifa, a place already spoken of. It was in the autumn of 1945, under curious circumstances. As they recognized each other, in the garden of the Officers' Mess of a British Convalescent Camp on Mount Carmel in Palestine, they burst out laughing and then shook hands.

"If it isn't Plaut," called out the younger and more sunburnt of the two, who was similarly dressed in khaki.

"Reunion of two chaps from Hamburg! The *Wandsbek Herald* in a new and improved edition!"

"But translated into English, don't forget." Lieutenant Wilhelm Kley seemed delighted to cap Captain Plaut's little joke. (Plaut was a padre in the Jewish Battalion of the Buffs.) Both men did in fact look younger in their brief wide shorts, with their bare knees and light strong shoes, their bare necks and forearms. With their city clothes they had also shed their stiff Hamburg ways. They slapped each other on the back, stood each other a whisky-and-soda, and agreed to go for a stroll to exchange their experiences and reminiscences instead of staying in the mess-garden, which was overcrowded with their comrades.

Pleasant shade lay under lofty old pines through which a stretch of the fabulously blue Haifa bay and of the delicate sky seemed to beckon them. They could also see that tract of land covered with oil-tanks which Dr. Goebbels' news-service had more than once laid in ruins. On the borders of the plain, through which the Kischon river wound, it sparkled up, quite undamaged, dominated by the Pharaonic towers of the oil-refinery, built after the American model.

Nobody would have noticed that the two men spoke German to each other, for all the varieties of the world-dominating English tongue could be heard around them—from Indian, Scottish and South African lips, speaking in the London Cockney which you can learn in Australia, or the King's English which comes from Oxford and Cambridge; but the two 'volunteers' still preferred to take the long military highway, frequently winding at first, which finally ran level and straight, past grey-green encampments, guard-posts, barbed wire, the steel filigree-work of the radar-station, the covered rows of lorries painted brown and yellow, to reach the summit of Cape Carmel. There, monastery gardens and a lighthouse softened the warlike appearance of this chalk promontory, covered with new houses and gardens, and with gorse, and turned it peaceful again.  Small tank-squadrons and great ack-ack guns still remained concealed even from them in the olive groves.  And at last, directly beneath them, lay the glassy bay and the harbour of Haifa. And while they sat on a low wall and let their legs dangle as they had not done since their schooldays, their thoughts and words were shot through with memories of another harbour, of a northern city which also began with an H, and which until the spring was being steadily, demolished by Flying Fortresses and heavy bombers of the American and British air forces.

While they spoke it still stood in ancient splendour, too much for the eye to take in at a glance with its landing-stages, its harbour-basins, its stone embankments and its shrub-covered escarpments.  And their feelings could hardly have been put into words: the mixture of grief, satisfaction and loathing with which they dwelt on that departed glory.

"By the time you went away, Kley, on the *Eleonora Krüger*—September 1938, wasn't it?—we had seen scarcely anything of what was going on—there were only the reports of the concentration camps which we didn't believe, looking on them as so many Communist atrocity stories.  But by November we were compelled to believe them: windows were being smashed, furniture was flung into the streets; synagogues were burning and Jewish citizens disappeared in the canals; S.A. re-inforcements marched into Hamburg, for the Hamburg fellows weren't quite reliable.

And from that time we all began to get a move on with our emigrating. And as I happened to have some affairs in the Customs the following spring—in what used to be *our* harbour—I was witness of how the four men executed after the Reeperbahn trial came back, risen from the dead in an entirely new and totally unexpected way."  (Among the people after whom Lieut. Kley had enquired was a certain Teetjen—Albert Teetjen—a butcher, of whom, however, Captain Plaut had never heard as far as he remembered.  But this man was the association which called up that particular story and so Captain Plaut's news was to the point.  Wilhelm Kley had put off mentioning the name of Koldewey to a later occasion.)

"A message must have been received from Cuxhaven over the telephone, for suddenly the place was full of uniforms drifting about brown and black, S.A. and S.S.  And then with a lot of tooting and blowing four freighters arrived in our basin, brand new ships, each of three thousand tons under the Soviet ensign, with Hammer and Sickle. It wouldn't have been anything unusual—in our harbour ships of every seafaring nation could be seen with their flags hoisted, and the Third Reich had trade-relations with them all.  But after borrowing Customs-Inspector Lawerenz's telescope in order to read for myself what the people were shouting about to each other, I understood the excitement stirred up by these four broad-built freighters with their sparkling new red and white paint.

" 'What a nerve!' I exclaimed, 'real Russian brass! They'll something they remember.'

"For there were names on the ship, painted white in fresh lettering—on the port side very suitably—which read

> " *F. Timme*
> *W. B. Mengers*
> *F. Merzenich*
> *K. Schröder* "

"Good Lord," muttered Wilhelm Kley, staring across the bay to the white cliffs of Ras-en-Nakura. "What a cheek!" And he sucked at his pipe. "Go on, Rabbi."

"I only heard later what happened next. Inspector Lawerenz told me when we met again on duty. The Russians had hardly reached the landing-stages and lowered their gangways, before our types in uniform streamed round them in ferry-boats and filled the first of the ships with an armed horde."

" 'These names must be removed at once!' demanded the S.S. man in charge, Herr Klaus Vierkant, who was private secretary to the ship-owner Vooht and was later hanged by the Russians at the Charkow trial for atrocities. At that time he still had quite a civil and polished manner and didn't expect any serious trouble—he just made an indicative gesture with his hand, to his own people, and seemed to expect that his words would work wonders. And so they did, but in a rather different way than he had thought. The Russian captain—the scene took place in his cabin—struck a bell and blew a sharp blast on a whistle—he was a young man, not older than Herr Vierkant, smaller and stockier, and clean-shaven, and he spoke perfect German with a Baltic accent. As soon as he whistled, the gangways right and left were filled with his men, all with tommy-guns, while the stokers came aloft with their crow-bars and tongs.

" 'You've quite forgotten, gentlemen,' said the captain with perfect calm—and I can well imagine how his eyes must have twinkled— 'You've quite forgotten that at the moment you're on Russian territory. I give you just thirty seconds to leave my ship. One, two, three . . .'

"You see, the Russians were prepared. They had certainly expected that something of the sort would happen. And by the time he reached twenty, the captain could see nothing but the backs of their heads as they shoved their way out of the cabin, and heard their boots and shoes clatter across the iron deck over his head and down the gangway. Our Nazi heroes had never folded up so fast since the rising of Hitler's star. And the four ships, with the spirits of the four executed men at the prow, unloaded their cargoes and took good German wares aboard, and steamed away, the Hammer and Sickle fluttering in the sea-breeze or for that matter in the rain, I can't remember which now.

"Anyway, as you can see, somehow or other that event warmed my heart—and my heart was remarkably heavy, for I had to leave my homeland, knowing that she was driving on unchecked towards a torrent which would bring down the whole earth with it in a tumult of destruction. Two of my colleagues remained in Hamburg with the rest of the community—and you certainly know how blamelessly they behaved—and went with them to Lithuania and Esthonia, and then disappeared. I often wonder whether we must share the blame for all the horror which we call the Third Reich and whether, if we had resisted the Hitler-régime, things might have turned out differently. But still we German Jews were a mere half million."

Lieutenant Kley knocked out his pipe and unscrewed the stem to blow out the nicotine. "Our original mistake, of course, was much earlier, after the last war, when the Junkers started to perk up again, and our bankers and steel magnates, by the magic of their gold, turned our war-guilt and war-debts into smoke, and blew it away in clamour against the Versailles Treaty. At that time we ought all to have sided with Timme and the wise Herr Mengers. But we had to build up our existence again from the start and so did the whole of Germany, and the result was Reichspresident Hindenburg and finally Reichschancellor Adolf Hitler. I've often though it over when I was fighting malaria here or in the Sudan, with my microscope and test-tube—it gave us plenty to do. West-African and Indian blood crossing with New Zealand and Australian in the stomach and viscera of the Egyptian anopheles— you can call that another wonder of the Third Reich—thanks to Dr. Goebbels."

"But, after all, do you really understand why, apart from a few feeble attempts at resistance, Germany's ruling classes—who weren't entirely powerless—followed the Braunau ratcatcher and his flute Goebbels into the unfathomable abyss?" asked Dr. Plaut uneasily.

"'Nothing succeeds like success,' says the American, and they weren't lacking in success at first, any more than in 1914. Only this time, fortunately, they flung us out first."

"And so we've not only survived it all but thriven and profited by it—typical, irrepressible Hamburg folk that we are. For isn't it fine here in the Holy Land, in the shade of the olives and the fig-trees!" concluded Captain Plaut, his brown eyes resting mournfully on all the brilliant scene: the little wells far below at the foot of the cliff and the greyish-yellow stripes of dried up vegetation on the slopes of the wadis.

Wilhelm Kley understood how he felt; and so for the time being he refrained from mentioning the names which were on the tip of his tongue or from asking whether Herr Plaut had heard anything of the beautiful Thyra Koldewey, or of her father and sisters. Perhaps they were lying buried under the ruins of a red-brick villa in Fuhlsbüttel—or perhaps they still lived among the ruins. At any rate, when the time came, he was to learn through the Press and the radio that Ingeborg Koldewey, known as Ingebottel, would be condemned to hanging by an English War Crimes court.

While acting as the no less fiendish assistant of scientific fiends, in some hideous fashion she had turned a women's Labour Camp on the Lüneburg Heath into a veritable hell. It somewhat eased him that Herr Heinrich Koldewey was among those who had been hanged for trying to exterminate the Madman of Berchtesgaden at the last moment.

The beautiful Thyra, however, never appeared again; and while he was working later under the English in the Hamburg service he often looked out of his office-window in the direction of the air-field, with a heaviness in his heart which related not only to this one vanished German girl, but also to the soul of a whole people, which she had so finely incarnated. It had never been willing, this people, to listen to those voices warning it from the path along which, guilty and innocent together, it followed its leaders, the path to the abyss.

THE END

# ACKNOWLEDGMENT

THIS NOVEL HAD its vicissitudes before it came into the hands of its readers. It was inspired by a report which the author found in 1938 in the *Deutsche Volkszeitung*, at that time published in Prague or Paris, and was worked out and brought to completion during the following years. By spring 1943 it was finally committed to paper, so that its translation into Hebrew could appear in the *Sifrioth Hapoalim* of that year.

Meanwhile, all the difficulties of war-time conspired with the author's ill-health against the production of legible copy. The ordinary despatch of manuscripts was already meeting with obstacles, while the question of translation into English, in a London devastated by flying bombs and rockets, seemed insoluble. Moreover, through severe concussion and failing eyesight, the author was in no condition to prepare a manuscript which would be fit for translation. Apart from the unwearying co-operation of his wife, he owes the fact that all this was overcome to the devoted friendship and active help of the authors Robert Neumann, in England, and Lion Feuchtwanger and Berthold Brecht in California.

The comradeship of these men proves that the most destructive world-war cannot hurt relations born in decades of common struggle. This unity, maintained notwithstanding their own great personal output, seems to be a good omen for the vitality and the creative power which the widely-scattered children of the German exodus embody; and which, in spite of all the mischances and the horrors of the Hitler régime, remain immovably active.

I hope that the readers of this book will readily join me in my gratitude to these friends.

A. Z.


HAIFA,
    Easter 1947.